The Will

KRISTEN ASHLEY

Copyright © 2014 by Kristen Ashley

First ebook edition: April 2014

First print edition: May 2014

ISBN: 0692208879

ISBN 13: 9780692208878

Discover other titles by Kristen Ashley at:
www.kristenashley.net

Commune with Kristen at:
www.facebook.com/kristenashleybooks
Twitter: KristenAshley68

THE SAFEST PLACE I COULD BE

"Ashes to ashes, dust to dust."

My mouth filled with saliva when I heard these words, my eyes—shaded by both sunglasses and a big black hat—moving from the shining casket covered in a massive spray of deep red roses to the preacher standing at its side.

I wanted to rise up from my chair, snatch the words from the air and shove them down his throat.

This was an unusual reaction for me. I wasn't like that.

But he was talking about Gran.

Gran, *my* Gran, the Gran whose body was in that casket.

She wasn't exactly young, this was true. I knew it was coming, seeing as she was ninety-three.

That didn't mean I wanted her to be gone. I never wanted her to be gone.

Outside of Henry, she was the only person I had. The only person in this whole world.

Ashes to ashes, dust to dust.

Gran wasn't dust.

My Gran was everything.

On this thought, I felt them coming and I couldn't stop them. Fortunately, when they spilled over, they were silent. Then again, they always were. The last time I let loose that kind of emotion was decades ago.

I never let it happen again.

I felt the wet crawling down my cheeks from under my sunglasses as I moved my eyes back to the casket. I felt them drip off my jaw but I didn't lift a hand. I wanted no one to notice the tears so I wouldn't give them any reason to do so, not even movement.

On that thought, I felt something else—a strange prickling sensation of awareness gliding over my skin. My eyes behind my sunglasses lifted and slid through the crowd standing around the casket.

They stopped when my sunglasses hit his.

And when they did, my breath also stopped.

This was because in all my life, and I'd had a long one, and in all my wandering, and I'd wandered far, I'd never seen a man like him.

Not once.

He was wearing a dark blue suit, monochromatic shirt and monochromatic tie. His clothes fit him well and suited him even better. I knew this from experience not just liking clothes but also being on the fringe of the fashion world for the last twenty-two years.

With a practiced eye, I saw his suit was Hugo Boss, which was a little surprising. The small town where Gran lived had some money in it and apparently that man was one of the people who had it.

The surprising part was the rest of him didn't look Hugo Boss. It definitely didn't look moneyed.

His black hair had a hint of silvery-gray in it. It was thick and clipped well but in a way that was not a nod to style, instead it was apparent he didn't want to spend time on it so his style was wash and go.

Even so, it looked good on him.

He also had lines on his forehead and around his hard mouth, that even hard still had lips that were so full, they were almost puffy, especially the lower one. His sunglasses, I was certain, hid lines around his eyes.

These told me he was not a stranger to sun.

They also told me he wasn't a stranger to emotion.

He was tall, broad and very big. I'd been around a variety of men and women who had commanding presences, Henry being one of them, but this man's wasn't that. It wasn't commanding.

It was *demanding*.

Strange, but true and also somewhat startling.

This was because, not only was his frame big but his features on the whole were aggressive. I'd never seen the like. His brow broad and strong. His jaw hard and sculpted. His neck and throat muscled and corded. His cheekbones cut a line from his square chin to his dark sideburn. His nose had clearly once been straight but it had been broken and not set well, he'd gone with that and it was not a bad choice by any stretch of the imagination. And he had a scar across his left cheekbone that stood stark against his formidable features, taking rugged to extremes.

He was not close to me, he was also not far, the day was sunny but from his distance with his sunglasses on, I couldn't imagine he could see my tears.

Yet I knew without doubt the way his shades were locked to me, he was watching me cry, his face impassive, his gaze unwavering.

I found this strange, his attention and the fact that even if he couldn't miss I was looking at him, he didn't look away.

Strange and again somewhat startling.

In order to breathe, with some effort, I tore my eyes from him and saw at his side a young man, perhaps twenty years old, wearing a dark gray suit, a light blue shirt and a rather attractive tie. Although not the spitting image of the man next to him, with his thick black hair, his height, his frame and his features, he could not be anything but the man's son.

I pulled my eyes from the young man and looked the other direction only to see a young woman, maybe fifteen, sixteen, long red hair and delicate features set firmly at bored. She was standing slightly away from the man, arms crossed. I didn't know why I knew, she looked not a thing like him, but I still knew she was also his.

Down my gaze went and I saw standing in front of the man was a boy, maybe eight, nine years old. Again, the dark hair, the frame that would grow to be tall and strong, it was impossible not to see he was another offspring of that man. It helped that he was leaning against the man's legs and the man had his fingers curled around the boy's shoulder.

The boy seemed uncomfortable and—I peered closer without giving away I was doing it—his face was red. Either he was crying or he had been.

He knew Gran.

Obviously, they all did, being at Gran's funeral, but that boy, at least, knew her well.

Gran and I talked regularly, several times a week, and she'd told me (in some detail) about a variety of people in her town. I'd also lived there for a time when I was young and visited her frequently over the years, so I knew many of them personally.

She'd never told me about that family.

I would remember that family.

I looked no further, turning my eyes back to the casket. I didn't want to see the woman that was undoubtedly somewhere at that family's side.

I didn't need to see her to know her.

I knew she'd likely be a redhead. That was the only "likely" thing I knew. The rest of what she would be was certain.

She'd be unnaturally slim or attractively curvy, depending on what that man's preferences were. What she would not be was a woman who looked like she'd borne him three children over twenty years and had let her body or herself go in any way. Not that, never that. If she did, she'd lose him. For certain. His eye would wander and she'd be replaced. Therefore, she'd do all she could do to make certain that didn't happen.

She'd also look younger than her years. She'd go to pains to do this. Most definitely.

And, considering his suit and how well their children were turned out, she'd be stylish, her clothes and shoes expensive, as would be her hairstyle (and she would have *no* gray), her manicure, pedicure, everything.

He would accept nothing less, that man. He would have what he wanted and if he didn't get it, he'd throw what he had away and he'd find it.

I put him out of my mind as the preacher thanked people for coming, on behalf of himself *and* me.

His speaking for me might annoy me if I didn't know that Gran liked him so much, not to mention went to church regularly. And when that became hard for her, I knew that Reverend Fletcher had arranged for someone to pick her up, take her to services, take her out to breakfast and then take her home. Sometimes, when no one was to be found or just because she liked doing it, this someone was Reverend Fletcher's wife.

It was a nice thing to do. Gran needed to get out. She was social. But she was also independent, stubborn and didn't like to ask for help. That didn't mean she wouldn't accept it if offered. And she accepted it from the Fletchers.

Reverend Fletcher nodded to me and I stood, feeling the tears drying rough on my face, making the skin scratchy. I still didn't touch it. I could do that later, when I was alone. Now, I had my hat and my sunglasses to hide behind. And I would use them.

I felt people milling about as I made my way to Reverend Fletcher. When I got close, I offered my hand. Just my hand, I kept the rest of my body distant to make a point.

I was not a hugger, not touchy, not affectionate.

Not with anyone but Gran.

He got my point. He took only my hand, closing his around mine firm and warm, and he murmured, "Lydia will be missed, Josephine."

He was correct.

She would be.

I swallowed and nodded once. "She will. It was a lovely service, Reverend. Thank you."

"You're welcome, my dear." His hand squeezed mine. "And please, if you're staying in town a while, come over to Ruth and my house. We'd enjoy having you for dinner."

"That's a lovely offer, Reverend. I'll think about it and let you know," I replied quietly as I put pressure on my hand for him to release it, knowing as I said it that I would most definitely not be having dinner with him and his wife.

Gran was social.

I was not.

He let my hand go.

I gave him a small smile and turned away. I wanted to get to my car and get back to Lavender House. Fortunately, Gran had instructed that she didn't want a maudlin get-together after her funeral and this meant that I could get away from that place and these people and not have to endure munching on hors d'oeuvres and listening to people tell me what I already knew.

How great Gran was and how sad it was she was gone.

This desire of Gran's was probably for me. She knew her two sons wouldn't show. My dad and uncle had long since disappeared from her life and mine. And if they did show (which, thankfully, they didn't), the idea of them socializing, even at a post-funeral get-together, would be alarming. Neither of them was young and I'd not seen them in decades but I knew without a doubt that if they were still alive, they had not changed.

They never would.

They were apples that fell right to the root of the tree. Not Gran's tree. My grandfather's. And he was mean as a snake, selfish, controlling and all of these to the point where it wasn't in question he was mentally unstable.

And luckily, he was also long since dead.

So there was no reason to socialize, no one left of Gran's blood to stand around hearing how wonderful she was and thus what a loss it was now that she'd been laid in the ground.

As expected, it took some time for me to get to my car, what with the amount of people there, the amount of love Gran had built in this town, therefore the amount of people who wished to share with me they were sorry for my loss.

I was glad Gran had that.

This didn't mean I enjoyed the journey to the car. As lovely as it felt to know she had this kind of esteem, I already knew it. I didn't need to be reminded of it.

I told myself it made them feel better to say the words, make the eye contact, think their sentiments in some small way made *me* feel better. And Gran would want me to give them that.

So I did.

I managed to negotiate this obstacle course to my car only having to endure two hugs and I didn't trip or even falter. Not once. Henry would be proud. Gran would be disappointed.

Gran thought my frequent stumbles were hilarious but whenever she threw her chuckle my way after she'd witnessed one, I knew she was laughing with me, not at me. She'd long since tried to teach me that we should embrace who we were, even, or maybe especially, what she called the "special things, buttercup, the things no one else has, but you."

For me, this was being awkward. There were times when I could forget, but if there was something to trip over or something to set crashing to the ground, I would find it.

Gran thought it was cute.

When I did these things, I'd more than once seen Henry's lips twitch too.

Try as I might to take Gran's advice, I found it annoying.

However, I didn't manage this journey without the heels of my Manolos sinking into the turf, which I found irritating.

Finally, I made it to my rental car. The lanes winding through the cemetery were packed with cars, many of them now purring, cars doors slamming, wheels pulling out.

Amongst this, I heard a girl's annoyed, whiny, "Dad!" piercing the solemn air of the graveyard.

This tone was so inappropriate I stopped in the open door of my car and looked down the road.

Some three or four cars up on the opposite side from where my vehicle was parked, there was a big burgundy truck. It seemed relatively new. It was one of those that had four doors in the cab making it a tall, long sedan with flatbed. It wasn't flashy but somehow it was. Maybe because it sparkled in the sun like it had just been washed and waxed.

All the doors were open and climbing in them was the man who'd been watching me earlier and his three offspring. His eldest son was pulling himself into the front passenger seat of the truck. His youngest was already in the back. And the man was standing in the open driver's side door facing his girl, who was standing in the street, hands on her hips.

No wife.

Surprising.

I heard an indistinct rumble then the girl leaned slightly forward, her face screwing up in an unattractive way and she yelled, "I don't care!"

This was also surprising because, considering the place we were in and what had just happened in it, it was beyond rude.

I glanced around and saw some of the other attendees were obviously, but studiously, avoiding this exchange.

Since the man had his back to me and the girl had her attention on her father, I didn't bother avoiding it. They were in the throes of a squabble. They wouldn't notice me.

I heard another rumble then the girl shouted, "I said, I don't care!"

To this, there was no rumble.

There was a roar.

"Jesus Christ! Get in the goddamned truck, Amber!"

Her face twisted and I saw her body do a physical *humph!* She then moved and climbed into the backseat of the truck.

The man slammed her door and turned to his.

I instantly moved to get in mine thinking anyone who had the means and good taste to own a Hugo Boss suit should not be so ill-mannered as to shout obscenities at his daughter in a cemetery after a funeral service for a ninety-three year old dead woman.

However, in saying that, Gran would probably laugh herself sick at what just happened. That and wander over to the quarrel and wade right in.

As with my awkwardness, she found the foibles of others amusing and got away with this because she had the uncanny ability of pointing them out to people and guiding them into finding *themselves* amusing. Gran didn't take anything too seriously and she was quite adept at helping others see the world her way.

She'd had enough serious to last a lifetime with the man she married and the sons he gave her, and when she got out of that, she put it behind her.

The only serious she let leak in was me. How I was raised. What it did to me. What it made me become.

And Gran let me be me. The only one to do that, except Henry.

By the time I'd started the car, got it in gear and checked my mirrors, the big burgundy truck was driving by. I didn't get the chance to look into the cab. I also didn't think much of the fact that the man, nor his kids, approached me to tell me they were sorry for my loss.

That was probably good, seeing as I knew the kind of man he was and if his and his daughter's behavior was anything to go by, I never wanted to meet them.

And with them gone, I found myself strangely relieved that I knew I likely never would.

———◆———

"I SHOULD HAVE come with you," Henry muttered in my ear through the phone and I drew in a deep breath as I stared out the window at the sea.

"I'm all right, Henry," I assured him.

"There's no way you should be there alone."

"I'm *all right,* Henry," I repeated. "You have to be there. You do this shoot for *Tisimo* every year."

"Yeah, which means I need a fucking break from it."

I sighed, sat in the window seat and kept my eyes out to sea.

The sun setting had washed the sky in peachy pink with slashes of butter yellow and tufts of lavender.

I missed those sunsets over the sea.

I just wished Gran was right there, sitting with me.

"I get done with this, I'll fly out there," Henry said into my silence.

"You get done with that shoot, Henry, you need to be in Rome."

"I need to be with you."

I closed my eyes, blocking out the sunset, having wished so many times in my twenty-three years as personal assistant to Henry Gagnon, renowned fashion photographer, video director and handsome, dashing, reckless, adventurous, audacious, daring international lady's man, that he meant it in a different way when he said words like those to me.

Not that he valued me as his personal assistant.

Not that he liked me just because he did.

Not because we had over two decades of history and no one knew him better than me and the same was true for him with me (though, he didn't know me quite as much but that was part of me being me).

No.

For other reasons.

Now it was too late.

Not that there even was a time when that would be a possibility. He had models and actresses on his arm (and in his bed). And I'd lost count how many times I'd seen him smile his lazy smile at unbelievably gorgeous waitresses, tourists or the like and fifteen minutes later, I'd be finishing my coffee alone or heading to a park with a free few hours because Henry was away to our hotel to enjoy those hours a different way.

There was no way Henry Gagnon would turn his beautiful eyes to me. Not then.

Definitely not now, with me forty-five, way past my prime. Even if Henry was forty-nine.

Then again, Henry's last two lovers had been thirty-nine and forty-two respectively.

In fact, thinking on this, it occurred to me his lovers had aged as he had. He hadn't had a twenty-something since, well…he *was* twenty-something (or, at latest, he was early thirty-something).

"Josephine?"

I blinked myself out of my reverie and came back to the conversation.

"I'll meet you in Rome. Or in Paris," I told him. "I just have to go to the reading of the will tomorrow and see to things here once I know what's what. It shouldn't take long."

Why I said this, I had no idea except it was my job to make Henry's life aggravation-free and I'd lived and breathed that for so long, I didn't know how to do anything else.

The truth of the matter was Gran had a home and it was packed to the gills. I had no idea what I was going to do with it all.

However, I could easily hire an estate agency to deal with an auction and I didn't need to be present for that. Nor did I need to be present for a sale of the property.

I felt acute pain in my midsection at these thoughts so I put them aside and returned to Henry.

"A week, at most two," I said.

"If it's over a week, I'm there," he replied.

"Henry—"

"Josephine, no. Not sure you could miss the fact that you've been taking care of me for twenty-three years. I figure this once, once in twenty-three years, I can do whatever I need to do to look after you."

"That's very kind," I said softly.

There was a brief pause before he returned, just as softly, "That's me looking after my Josephine."

This was one of the reasons I stood by Henry all these years.

And it was one of many.

First, it wasn't that difficult to do my job. Henry was not a male diva, even if his talent meant he could be. He was pretty no-nonsense. I wasn't rushing around picking up dry cleaning (well, not all the time) and trying to find a coffee shop that made lattes with unpasteurized milk.

Second, he paid me well. Very well. Actually *extremely* well. Not to mention he gave bonuses. And presents (one of these being the Manolos I wore to the funeral, another being the diamond tennis bracelet I had on my wrist at that moment).

Third, we traveled widely and he didn't make me sit in coach when he was up in first class. No, I sat next to him. Always. Further, it wasn't hard being the places we'd go. It was true I didn't exactly enjoy that time in Venezuela (nor the one Cambodia, the one in Haiti or the other one in Kosovo) but only because he wasn't doing a fashion spread but instead taking other kinds of pictures and thus we weren't exactly staying at the Ritz.

Henry liked adventure. Me, that was a different story. But I was always at Henry's side.

Always.

Except now.

And last, and maybe most important, he could be very sweet and he was this way often.

"I want you calling every day," he demanded. "Check in. Let me know you're okay."

"You're too busy for me to call you every day," I told him something I should know, since, even though *Tisimo* magazine had given him a young man named Daniel to take my place temporarily, I still knew his schedule like the back of my hand.

"How about you let me decide what I'm too busy for, sweetheart. But I would hope you know by now, one of those things is not and never will be you."

Oh my.

Yes.

So very sweet.

"Henry—" I started on a whisper.

"Now, do something good. Like go out, buy a great bottle of wine, and drink it watching some ridiculous TV show you would normally hate so you can tell me all the reasons you hate it. Do not sit around, drinking your tea and doing something worthy. Like emailing Daniel to make certain he's on his game or trying to read *War and Peace* for the seven millionth time."

"I'm going to finish that book someday," I vowed on a mutter.

"Let's not make today that day," he replied and I smiled.

"All right. Reality TV and a good bottle of wine it is," I murmured.

"Good girl," he murmured back and I could hear the smile in his voice. "Tomorrow, I want to know all the ways the housewives of wherever get on your nerves."

I smiled again before I asked, "Would you like me to take notes?"

"Seeing as they'll probably get on your nerves in so many ways even you'll forget a lot of them, yeah."

"Then consider it done."

"Right." I could still hear the smile in his voice. "Now go. Wine. TV. And while you're at it, buy something good to eat. And I don't mean an excellent wedge of brie. I mean something like a bucket of chicken."

I made a face that he hopefully could not hear in my voice when I lied, "Consider that done too."

"Liar," he muttered and I smiled again.

Then I said, "I should let you go."

"For now, sweetheart. I'll talk to you tomorrow."

"Tomorrow, Henry."

"Be bad," he said quietly.

"I'll try," I replied and both of us knew that was a lie too.

There was another pause before he whispered, "Chin up, Josephine. Always."

"It's up, Henry. Always."

"Okay, sweetheart. Talk to you tomorrow."

"'Bye, Henry."

"Later, honey."

I disconnected and threw my phone on the cushion in front of me.

Then I looked out to the sea.

There was no buttery yellow in the sky, the peachy pink was fading and the lavender was taking over.

It was stunning and it made me wish that Henry was, indeed, here with me. He'd take a fabulous picture of it.

I was in the light room at Lavender House, the house Gran inherited from her mom and dad when they died which was thankfully after she'd divorced her husband.

The house that had this room, five stories up a spiral staircase. A circular room that was curved windows all around so you could see everything. The sea. The outcroppings of rock and beaches along Magdalene Cove. The centuries old, tiny town of Magdalene. And the landscape beyond.

This room with the window seats all around. The big desk in the middle where I knew Gran always wrote her letters to me. Where she sometimes took and made her phone calls to me. Where she paid bills. Where she wrote out recipes. Where she opened my letters to her and she probably read them right here too.

The room that had the half-circle couch she found and bought because it was, "just too perfect to pass up, buttercup."

And it was. That couch was perfect. It had taken seven men, a pulley and who knew how much money to get it up there through a window. But Gran had seen it done.

She loved it up here.

I loved it up here.

And I sat in this very spot years ago after I became well enough to move around a bit after she saved me from my father. I also sat in this very spot after I called her and told her I had to get away, I just *had* to *get away*, and she flew me here.

Here. Home.

Here was where I put my father behind me.

Here was where I put my world behind me.

Here was where I got the call from a girlfriend who had moved to New York to do something in the fashion world (anything, she didn't care, and she succeeded and was then working as a minion for flash-in-the-pan diva designer who thought he was everything who had recently been fired from his job designing clothes for discount department stores).

A girlfriend who told me Henry Gagnon was looking for an assistant and she knew I loved clothes, I was an admirer of his photos and she could talk to someone who could talk to someone who could maybe get me a meeting with him.

And here was where I took the next call when I learned she got me a meeting with him.

Here was where my life ended…twice, even as it started again…twice.

It still smelled like Gran here even though it had been years since she could get up to this room.

She was everywhere in Lavender House.

But mostly she was here.

And now she was gone.

And on that thought, it happened.

I knew it would happen. I was just glad it didn't happen at her graveside, in front of people.

It happened there, the safest place I could be, the safest place I ever had, with Gran all around me.

The first time in over two decades when I let emotion overwhelm me and I wept loud, abhorrent tears that wracked my body and caused deep, abiding pain to every inch of me rather than releasing any.

I didn't go out and buy a bottle of wine.

I certainly didn't get a bucket of chicken (not that I was going to anyway).

And I didn't watch the real housewives of anywhere on TV.

I fell asleep on that window seat with tears still wet on my face and with Gran all around me.

The safest place I could be.

MY MOST PRECIOUS POSSESSION

"Ah, Josephine Malone. I'm Terry Baginski."

I stood from my chair in the waiting room and took Terry Baginski's outstretched hand, noting her hair was pulled severely back from her face and secured in the back in a girlish ponytail.

I noted this thinking that there were many women in the world with strong or delicate enough features to be able to wear that hairstyle at any age.

She just wasn't one of them.

This thought wasn't kind. However, it was true and I caught myself wishing I could explain this to her as well as share that she may wish to use a less heavy hand with makeup and perhaps buy a suit that didn't scream *power!* but instead implied femininity, which, if done right, was much more powerful.

Then I didn't think anything at all except wishing she'd release my hand for when she took it, she squeezed it so hard my hand was forced to curl unnaturally into itself and this caused pain.

Fortunately, she released my hand only an instant after she grasped it in that absurdly firm grip.

She kept talking and what she said confused me.

"Mr. Spear is late, which isn't a surprise. But I'll show you to my office and we'll have someone get you a coffee."

She then turned and walked away without giving me a chance to utter a word.

I had no choice but to follow her.

As I did, I asked her back, "Where is Mr. Weaver?"

Arnold Weaver was my grandmother's attorney. I knew him. He was a nice man. His wife was a nice woman. On the occasion I was there for Christmas, we always went to their Christmas party. This meant I'd been to a goodly number of Weaver Christmas parties and therefore I knew Arnie and Eliza Weaver were nice people, my grandmother liked them a great deal and I thought they were lovely.

"Oh, sorry," she threw over her shoulder as she turned into an open door and I followed her. "Arnie is on a leave of absence," she stated, stopped and turned to me. "His wife is ill. Cancer. It's not looking good."

I let the shock of learning the sweet, kind Elizabeth Weaver had cancer and it was "not looking good" score through me, the feeling intensely unpleasant, but Ms. Baginski didn't notice.

She waved a hand to a chair in front of a colossal desk that was part of an arrangement of furniture that was far too big and too grand for the smallish office. She also kept speaking.

"I'll send someone in to get you some coffee. But as Mr. Spear is late, and I'm quite busy, if you don't mind, I'll take this opportunity to speak to a few colleagues about some important issues that need to be discussed."

I did mind.

Our meeting was at eight thirty. I'd arrived at eight twenty-five. She'd come to meet me in reception at eight thirty-nine. She was already late and that had nothing to do with the unknown Mr. Spear. Now she was leaving me alone and I had not one thing to do for the unknown period of time she'd be gone.

And last, I still did not know who Mr. Spear was.

"I'm sorry, I'm confused," I shared as she was walking to the door. She stopped, looked at me and lifted her brows, unsuccessfully attempting to hide her impatience. "Who is Mr. Spear?"

Her head cocked to the side sharply and she replied, "He's the other person mentioned in your grandmother's will."

I stared at her, knowing I was showing I was nonplussed mostly because I made no attempt to hide it.

"I'll be back," she said to me, giving me no information to clear my confusion, and she disappeared out the door.

Therefore, I stood there staring at the door.

And doing so, I thought on the meager information she imparted on me.

What I thought was that my grandmother was well-known and well loved. I would not have been surprised if there were a dozen or more people at the reading of her will. I wouldn't even be surprised if she willed parcels of money and trinkets to half the town.

What surprised me was that the only other person that was supposed to be there was a person whose name I'd never heard in my life.

Without anyone to ask further questions, I moved to the chair she'd indicated, took my handbag off my shoulder and tucked it at my side.

A few minutes later, a young woman came and asked me my coffee preference. I gave it to her. When she left, I emailed Daniel on my phone to remind him to charge Henry's iPod before they got on the plane for Rome the next day. He'd need to do this since Henry liked to listen to music all the time but especially on long haul flights and LA to Rome was definitely long haul. The young woman brought my coffee. By the time Ms. Baginski returned, I was half finished with it, it was nine o'clock, I'd sat there for twenty minutes with nothing to do and I was fuming.

"He's not here yet?" she asked without greeting, entering the office while surveying it with unconcealed annoyance.

"Ms. Baginski—" I started just as the young woman who brought my coffee appeared in the door.

"Terry, Mr. Spear phoned. He said he's been held up but he's five minutes from the offices," she announced.

"That means he's twenty minutes away," Terry Baginski murmured strangely as well as irately and reached out to the phone. "Thanks, Michelle," she called and her eyes moved through me. "As I have a bit more time, I hope you don't mind if I make a phone call."

Actually, I again *did* mind and I opened my mouth to tell her that but she hit one button and a quick succession of tones filled the air. Before I could make a sound, she grabbed the handset, put it to her ear and swiveled her large, pretentious chair slightly away so I had her side.

I felt my mouth get tight, turned my eyes to my foot and started tapping my toe.

I felt slightly mollified looking at my shoes.

They were beautiful shoes.

Indeed, all I had were beautiful shoes. I didn't own a pair of sneakers or flip-flops and I hoped to God I never would.

Handbags and shoes were my passion.

Actually, apparel on the whole was my passion.

But I couldn't take comfort in viewing my garments as I couldn't see my outfit though I was again wearing black. I'd donned my outfit because I felt it was apropos for the occasion. A black pencil skirt that fit like a glove all the way down to my knees. The hem fell further, to mid-calf and it fit so snug to my hips and legs, the only reason I could walk was that there was a slit that went up to the top of the backs of my knees.

My blouse was also black, and it was silk. It looked from the front like a simple blouse (though, with a fabulous high collar that hugged my jaw and had an equally fabulous wide strip of matching cloth that I tied in a big bow at my throat). The back, however, had a cutout that exposed skin from the base of the neck, and from shoulder blade to shoulder blade, the rest of my back was covered.

It, too, fit me perfectly.

The outfit (outside the extraordinary fit, simplicity, excellent quality fabrics and that cutout) was quite unremarkable. Elegant (I thought), but unremarkable.

My shoes, however, were *very* remarkable

Dove gray patent leather slingbacks with a pencil-slim four-inch stiletto heel and a pointed toe. The toe was black patent leather. The heel and sole, however, were bright fuchsia.

They were *divine.*

My hair, as it always was, was pulled loosely back in an elegant chignon. This one I'd teased a hint to give it volume but it sat smooth and full along the length of the base of my skull.

My makeup, as ever, was superb.

And I usually didn't give way to these thoughts as Gran had taught me there were pointless (not to mention unkind). But in that moment, staring at Terry Baginski's profile, taking in her arrogant, dismissive demeanor along with her hair, her harsh makeup and her clothing that had been bought off the rack, which wasn't bad except for the fact it was the *wrong* rack, I allowed myself to feel smug.

Gran would be disappointed but I couldn't help but admit these thoughts made me feel better.

She murmured into the phone.

I leaned forward and took another sip of coffee.

I was replacing the cup in its saucer on Ms. Baginski's desk when, from behind me, I heard, "Mr. Spear has arrived."

Apparently, as Ms. Baginski alluded, he had not lied. It wasn't twenty minutes. It was five.

I looked around my chair to see the young woman standing there.

One second later, my back shot straight in shock when the man who had been staring at me at the funeral strode into the room.

Today, he was wearing a superbly cut black blazer, a tailored black shirt, blue jeans and black boots.

It was far less formal attire than his suit of the day before but, oddly, it suited him far better.

Far better.

His eyes hit me.

My lips (expertly lined, filled and glossed, though some of that was now on my coffee cup) parted and my stomach twisted in a knot.

"I have something happening," Ms. Baginski said into the phone. "It won't take long. I'll call you back later."

She said this and I ignored it for I was watching with rapt attention as that man walked into the office. Thus, I was also watching when he came to a stop several feet from the back of the chairs. And thus, I could feel the full force of the fact that the office wasn't big but we could be in an amphitheater and his overwhelmingly male presence would fill the space.

"Finally, we can get started," Ms. Baginski stated. "Ms. Malone, do you know Jake Spear?"

I slowly rose from my chair, turned to him and started to move around the chair, lifting my hand, doing all this finding myself in his overpowering presence unable to speak.

I saw him lift one of his mighty paws as I walked toward him thinking I was not petite but his hand would engulf mine when he took hold of it.

Something about that made my skin feel funny, like I wasn't comfortable in it or it needed soothing attention.

And it was on this thought the point of the toe on my shoe caught on the thick pile of the overlarge rug that covered the office carpet (for some odd reason) and I stumbled.

This happened frequently. I found it annoying and, regardless of how cute Gran found it or how amusing Henry did, I detested it.

I detested it more that I'd done it in front of that man.

I couldn't think on that, however. As I flew forward, I felt my hand caught in a firm grip even as I brought up the other one to brace me wherever I was to land.

Fortunately, or perhaps unfortunately, Mr. Spear moved quickly at the same time he jerked the hand he held. Therefore, instead of landing on the floor or staggering across the rug, I hit him.

As in *hit him*.

My temple collided with his collarbone, my forehead banged against his jaw and my shoulder crashed into his arm.

His hand holding mine lifted both of our hands up his chest, gripping tighter as I felt his other arm round me at my waist, pulling me against him so we were fit snug together, my forehead in his neck.

Up close, I saw his neck was more muscled, his throat more corded than either looked from afar.

Dazedly, I tipped my head back and saw he was tipping his down.

Yesterday, he was clean-shaven.

This morning, he had not shaved and he had a dark shadow of black and silver stubble on his jaw.

This also suited him.

Greatly.

My eyes caught his and I noted three things instantly.

One was the fact that he had unusual gray eyes. I couldn't quite put my finger on what was unusual about them except for the fact that they were alarmingly attractive.

He also smelled good. I'd inhaled the scent of a variety of men's colognes but not one was that alluring. It was, as was everything about him, aggressively masculine, assaulting my senses, making it hard for me to breathe.

And last, his body was far bigger and more imposing than it was from a distance.

And it was *very hard*.

"You all right?" his deep voice rumbled. I heard it and felt it, and I blinked.

It was then I remembered to be mortified *and* to keep my distance.

So I pulled at his hold and I felt his arm around me and his hand in mine strangely tighten for a brief moment before he let me loose at the waist. I moved away half a foot but not further as he kept hold of my hand.

"Steady?" he asked.

"Yes," I said quietly. "My apologies," I went on to murmur, putting pressure on my hand as an indication he should let it go.

He didn't let it go.

"Not a problem," he muttered, his lips quirking with amusement. "Obviously, you're Josie."

My back went straight because no one called me Josie.

No one but Gran.

"Yes, *Josephine* Malone." I put significant stress on my proper name. "Lydia's granddaughter."

This got me another lip quirk and a, "Know that. Heard a lot about you, Josie."

I was not certain this was good.

"Now that you're here, maybe we can get started. I have a full day and this delay has put me off my schedule by half an hour," Terry Baginski butted into our exchange, her voice terse, like Mr. Spear and my taking a moment to greet each other was exhausting her patience.

Of course, he had been late, though he had also called (albeit tardily) to explain he would be. But he was the reason we were delayed.

Therefore, I wasn't certain what came over me when that woman spoke those words.

Perhaps I was feeling embarrassment at tumbling into this man. Perhaps it was the fact that I'd laid my beloved grandmother in the ground the day before and that hadn't exactly been fun. Perhaps it was because I didn't sleep very well after sobbing myself into that state the night before.

Or perhaps it was because this woman had not been polite at all since my arrival at her office. An arrival for a meeting to hear my beloved grandmother's will read. Something I didn't want to do as it was another in a barrage of constant reminders Gran was no longer of this world, I was going to miss her, I was facing a lifetime of missing her, and Ms. Baginski should have a mind to that.

But, for whatever reason, it came over me.

Therefore, I pulled at my hand and Mr. Spear released me as I turned to Ms. Baginski and stated, "I've no idea how you can be behind seeing as you were delayed in meeting me in reception. Not to mention, since that time you've not let Mr. Spear's late arrival deter you from continuing with your work even though a long time client's granddaughter was waiting and she wasn't even offered a magazine to occupy her time."

I moved carefully to the chair, bending to grasp my trim, patent leather fuchsia handbag that I'd tucked into the side. Primly seating myself, I continued to speak.

"As this occasion is not a happy one, I won't speak for Mr. Spear as I don't know him." I crossed my legs and looked to her. "But I, for one, would like to see this unfortunate business concluded. So, yes, please. If we could finally get to the matter at hand, I would be grateful."

Her mouth got tight. It didn't look good on her but then again, nothing really did and this had very little to do with the fact she didn't know how to arrange her hair or do her makeup and everything to do with the fact she was a genuinely unpleasant woman.

I didn't look at Mr. Spear.

I tucked my handbag in my lap and waited.

I felt Mr. Spear take the chair beside mine as Ms. Baginski moved behind the desk, stating, "Then we'll delay no further."

"As I've been here over half an hour, I would find that agreeable," I replied.

She cast a baleful glare in my direction.

I returned it coolly.

I heard Mr. Spear emit a strange (though not unattractive, alarmingly) grunt that sounded partly amused and partly surprised.

I ignored him and held Terry Baginski's glare.

She looked away first and started fiddling with some papers on her desk, saying, "Let's proceed."

I decided I'd made my point so I let that one go.

She upended some papers, tapping them on her desk and her gaze moved from me to Mr. Spear to the papers.

"Mrs. Malone has a legal and binding document outlining her wishes as to what is to become of her property and possessions upon her death. However, she's written a letter that she explained she'd like read instead of that document during these proceedings," Ms. Baginski began. "It outlines these wishes in a more succinct way."

I said nothing.

Neither did Mr. Spear.

"Therefore, as Mrs. Malone bid, I shall read her words," she went on.

I took in a deep breath in order to prepare to hear Gran's words.

Without delay, Ms. Baginski started to read.

"I, Lydia Josephine Malone, being of very sound mind and annoyingly questionable body, due hereby bequeath all my worldly possessions to my granddaughter, Josephine Diana Malone. This includes Lavender House, its outbuildings, the entirety of their contents and the land on which they sit. This also includes the funds in my checking and savings accounts as well as the certified deposits held at Magdalene Bank and Trust. It further includes the contents of safe deposit box six-three-three, also at Magdalene Bank and Trust, the key to which can be found in my desk in the light room at Lavender House. And last, it includes the funds in the investment accounts managed for me by the advisors at Magdalene Bank and Trust."

I listened thinking that Lavender House and the two acres on which it sat, right on a cliff, right on the coast, its vast contents, its sheer size and its location made all of it undoubtedly worth some money. That said, Gran had not lived frugally but she was also not a spendthrift.

We'd never discussed money, she never seemed to need it, she never overspent it, so there was no need. Therefore, my assumption was, when I spoke with the employees at Magdalene Bank and Trust, I would find Gran's holdings not meager but also not extravagant.

I didn't care either way.

Whatever was at that bank, none of it was Gran.

I additionally listened wondering, if she bequeathed all this to me, why was Mr. Spear there.

"That is," Ms. Baginski went on, "I bequeath everything but one hundred and fifty thousand dollars. This will be provided to Mr. James Markham Spear in order that he put it in trust, fifty thousand dollars each for Connor Markham Spear, Amber Joelynn Spear and Ethan James Spear."

Well, that explained that.

And that also shared that Gran's holdings might be more extravagant than I thought.

"Jesus Christ," Mr. Spear muttered into my thoughts and my eyes slid to him.

He was staring at the papers in Ms. Baginski's hands and I could tell he was equally surprised at Gran's holdings, not to mention her largesse.

Surprised and moved. His expression was clearly startled.

It was also soft.

And last, it was very attractive, that softening of his hard features.

At this thought, I pulled in another breath.

"Jake," Ms. Baginski continued and I looked back to her, wondering why she said this name. "I'll leave it to you to invest wisely, as I know you will. However, the kids shouldn't see this money until they're twenty-one. That is if they remain in university until that time. If they don't go to school, I'd rather they not have it until they're twenty-five. We both know this would be prudent, especially considering how enamored Amber is with purchasing her cosmetics and those platform shoes."

It sounded like I might have something in common with the unknown Amber.

Also, apparently, the man beside me was known familiarly to Gran as "Jake."

But listening to this, and hearing the amount Gran bestowed on who I knew were the three young people I'd seen with Mr. Spear yesterday at the funeral, I again found it strange, as well as disturbing, that I had not heard of Mr. James Markham Spear or any of his children.

"And last," Ms. Baginski carried on. "My most precious possession, the thing I treasure above anything else in this world, that being my granddaughter, Josephine Diana Malone, I hereby bequeath to James Markham Spear."

After these words were read, unprepared for them and even if I had been, I would still be unprepared for them mostly because they were just plain *mad*, I gasped.

James Markham Spear muttered a rumbling, amused, "What the fuck?"

Terry Baginski didn't even look up. She kept reading.

"Jake, my Josie is quite awkward and I don't mean simply that she's a complete klutz, though she is that as well. I find it adorable and I hope you do too. She's also aggravatingly tidy, so I do hope you'll teach her how fun it is to be a slob once in a while. Further, she doesn't know how to enjoy herself, and I'm *sure*," Ms. Baginski put a strange emphasis on this word before she went on, "you'll be able to teach her how to do that and do it well. But under all that, she has the kindest soul you'll know, the lightest touch you'll feel, and, if you find your way to coax it out of her, she gives off the sweetest light that will ever shine on you. I'm trusting you, my Jake, in my absence, to take good care of her. But even saying that, I know you will."

I was blinking rapidly.

Ms. Baginski was finishing up.

"Those are my wishes and I will them to be done. And just a warning, if they're not, I'll know and it'll make me very upset. I know neither of you want that. Now, be blissfully happy my Josie and my Jake. That is my final, most important wish. Please do what you can to give that to me."

Terry Baginski quit reading and looked at us.

"Did Lydie give me *you* in her will?"

This came from my side and it was no less rumbling or amused. In fact, it was far *more* rumbling and amused, and slowly, my breath coming in fits and starts, my head turned his way.

Yes, he was amused. I knew this because he was smiling a large smile, his even, strong white teeth stark against his dark stubble.

My stomach again twisted in knots.

"Obviously, the bequeathal of a human being isn't binding," Ms. Baginski put in and I thankfully tore my gaze from Mr. Spear and looked to her. "This bestowal, however," she continued, "is also in the legal document. Regardless if it isn't binding, the rest of it is."

She picked up a legal-sized manila folder and plopped it across the desk my way.

"Copies of Mrs. Malone's official last will and testament," she carried on, pointing at the folder. "The letter I've just read, and information about deeds and the like are in that folder. Should you not desire to join us here in Magdalene, there's also contact information for Stone Incorporated, a firm that has approached Mrs. Malone in the past to share they're interested in purchasing Lavender House."

What did she say?

Someone had approached Gran to buy Lavender House?

Gran hadn't told me that either!

"That folder is yours to take," she announced, her eyes on me, and she stood but did it leaning forward, hands on her desk. "Now, if there aren't any questions…" she rudely uttered a thinly veiled prompt for us to stop wasting her time.

I had a million questions, of course, none of which I spoke because I didn't act fast enough.

"Paper isn't legally binding but blood is," Mr. Spear declared and I looked his way to see he was addressing Terry Baginski.

"I'm sorry?" Ms. Baginski asked.

"Words on paper might not be legally binding." His gaze came to me and his voice deepened as he concluded, "But blood is."

I found my chest rising and falling rapidly as he held my eyes and the meaning of his words assaulted my ears.

"You can hardly think you can own a woman, Jake," Ms. Baginski snapped dismissively.

"Own her, no," Mr. Spear stated, his eyes still holding mine captive. "Do *precisely* what Lydie wanted me to do with her, yes."

Oh my God.

The way he said those words sounded suggestive.

Very suggestive.

My breathing grew even more rapid and additionally it became erratic. I decided to ignore the suggestive part of his words and focus on something else.

"Gran was...she was..." I searched for a word and found it. "*Protective* of me."

"I'm gettin' that seein' as she left me *you* in her will in order to keep that shit goin' on," he replied and my back again went straight.

"I'm quite capable of seeing to that myself," I informed him.

Something shifted through his features so swiftly I couldn't catch the meaning of it before he whispered, "Not from what I hear."

At *that*, I felt my eyes get big.

"What has Gran told you?" I inquired sharply.

"With respect, could I ask that perhaps you two continue this conversation elsewhere?" Ms. Baginski requested. "I actually *do* have other business to see to today."

I thought that was an excellent idea. Not continuing the conversation. I was quite done with this conversation. Instead, I wanted to get myself elsewhere.

Therefore, I jumped to my feet and sensed Mr. Spear rising to his. But I didn't sense his hand coming my way as if to spot me should I tumble.

I saw it.

When I did, my eyes slashed his way. "I'm adept at rising from a chair, Mr. Spear," I snapped.

"Just bein' careful," he muttered, studying me and doing it grinning.

Albeit attractive—his voice *and* his grin—I found both annoying.

I didn't share that.

I looked from him to Ms. Baginski. "Is there something I need to do in order to get the funds my grandmother wished to be put in trust for Mr. Spear's children *to* Mr. Spear?" I asked, hoping there wasn't as I intended to leave that office and Mr. Spear behind and never see either again.

Terry Baginski shook her head. "No. Mrs. Malone has already made those arrangements. This office will take care of that money transfer." Her eyes went to Mr. Spear and she warned, "And Jake, you'll need to report this gift to the IRS."

"No shit?" he asked and it occurred to me in a vague way that they seemed to know each other and not get along.

Or, at least, Ms. Baginski didn't like Mr. Spear all that much.

This didn't concern me.

Escape concerned me. That as well as dealing with Gran's estate and getting to Rome (or Paris) as soon as I could.

In order to see to these things without delay, I secured my handbag on my shoulder, reached out and took the manila folder, saying, "If that's in order, I'll thank you for your time and be on my way." I looked up to Mr. Spear. "Although Gran didn't mention you, it's clear she held a high regard for you and your children."

He didn't let me finish. He butted in to say (still grinning, I might add, and the way he said it sounded almost teasing), "Yeah, Josie. She held us in high regard."

"Well then, that being so, it was a pleasure to meet you." I took my eyes from him, sliced them through Ms. Baginski and finished, "Now, I'll leave you both to your business. Good day."

After delivering that, carefully putting one foot in front of the other but doing it quickly, I exited the room.

I did this with Mr. Spear calling, "Hang on, Josie."

I most certainly didn't "hang on." I kept going. Swiftly.

His voice was much closer to my back when I was in the hall and he said, "Whoa, woman. Hang on a second."

I kept going but spoke to the reception area I'd just entered. "I don't mean to be rude but I have business to see to and quickly as it's important I get to Rome."

"Rome?" he asked when I had my hand on the front door.

I tipped my eyes up to him. "Rome," I stated, pushed open the door and exited it, moving speedily toward my rental car.

He did not call to me again but I knew I hadn't lost him and this became glaringly apparent when he caught me by my upper arm right when I'd made it to my car.

He pulled me around to face him.

"Josie, give me a second," he said quietly.

I looked up to him again. "Of course, Mr. Spear, but not to be rude, I have only a second."

"Jake," he replied.

"Pardon?" I asked.

"Name's Jake," he said.

"Fine," I returned then prompted, "You wanted a second?"

He didn't take his hand off me as his eyes moved over my face in a way that it felt like he was studying me.

And that was when I saw what was unusual about those eyes.

Because in the office, they were a clear light gray.

Out in the sun, they were a clear ice blue.

Extraordinary, intriguing *and* striking.

Blast!

"Mr. Spear…" I prompted yet again and felt his fingers curl deeper into my arm even as he pulled me a half an inch closer.

"Jake," he murmured.

"Are you detaining me because you want me to address you by your Christian name?" I queried.

His extraordinary, intriguing and striking eyes focused on mine. "Do you talk like that all the time?" he queried in return.

"Like what?"

"Nothin'," he muttered, his lips quirking again. Then he jerked his head toward the building we just left and reminded me, "Somethin' big happened in there."

"Indeed," I agreed then went on and did so being purposefully obtuse. "And if you're concerned I'll take issue with the gifts my grandmother bestowed on your children, please don't be. I know Gran was of very sound mind to the end of her days so if she wished your children to have that money, then that wish will be done."

"That was a beautiful thing Lydie did," he replied. "But I'm not talkin' about that. I'm talkin' about the *other* gift she bestowed on me."

"And that would be?" I asked, still being obtuse.

"Josie." My name shook with his amusement and it was annoying because the way it did sounded lovely. "She gave me you."

I ignored that and the way it made my stomach twist and my breath come uneven and informed him, "No one calls me Josie."

"Lydie did," he contradicted.

Oh yes.

Gran definitely talked to him about me.

I did not like that.

"All right, then no one calls me Josie but Gran," I shared.

"And now me."

I drew in a breath, this reminded me his hand was on me so I requested, "Will you unhand me?"

His lips twisted in an unsuccessful endeavor at hiding his humor before he replied, "I will *unhand* you, but only if you promise not to take off."

"I can promise that," I told him.

"Right," he murmured and let me go but he didn't step away.

I decided not to do so either as it might communicate the wrong things and I felt it imperative to communicate quite clearly with James Markham Spear in the very short time I would be communicating anything to him.

"Tonight, we need to go to dinner," he declared.

I looked to my handbag, maneuvering it open to find my sunglasses, because any woman knew, she shouldn't be out in the sun without two things. One, a very good SPF moisturizer under her makeup. And two, an excellent pair of sunglasses so she didn't get lines from squinting her eyes.

I secured my glasses while talking. "I'm afraid dinner is out of the question."

"Why?"

I slid my sunglasses on my nose and looked again to him. "Why?"

"Josie, I see you're tryin' to pretend that shit in there didn't happen but, just sayin', that shit in there happened."

I sighed and agreed, "Yes, it did."

"Right, then tonight, we're goin' out to dinner."

"No, we aren't."

His head cocked to the side and he opened his mouth to speak but I got there before him.

"Listen, Mr. Spear—"

"Jake," he cut in, his deep voice lowering with impatience.

"Of course," I hurried on. "As I explained in Ms. Baginski's office, Gran was very protective of me. We were also very close. I loved her deeply and she felt the same about me. But with relationships like ours, the person in Gran's place can often get stuck in a time when they're needed and they might not realize they're not needed in that way any longer. From what she wrote in that letter, it's clear that's what occurred with Gran."

His face had returned to hard, with the addition of cold, when he stated, "So you're sayin' you didn't need Lydie."

"No," I whispered, at his words a different kind of twist happening in my stomach, one that felt far worse. This feeling was reflected in my voice and the cold left his face at my tone. Alert warmth replaced it. It was no less arresting than everything else about him, but I kept talking. "I needed my grandmother. I *still* need my grandmother. Just not that way."

"She disagreed," he replied quietly, his voice now reflecting the warmth in his face.

"She would be wrong."

"Josie—"

"*Josephine*," I cut him off to stress.

"Whatever," he returned impatiently. "I've known Lydie for seven years. This means that letter we just heard was written sometime in the last seven years. My guess, recently. This means she felt the way she felt about you in order to include that in her last wishes and she felt that way recently. Are you honestly gonna ignore that?"

"Yes," I answered immediately and his face changed again, his eyes changed, everything about him changed.

I just couldn't put my finger on *how* he changed.

Until he whispered, "Don't."

My entire body froze solid.

"Don't do that, Josie," he went on. "She wanted me for you."

He couldn't be serious.

"Are you saying—?" I began to force out through stiff lips.

"No." He shook his head. "What I'm sayin' is, the least we could do is get to know each other. Give her a little of what she wanted. We both owe her that respect and, I don't know you outside of what she told me about you and the last twenty minutes I've been with you, but I'm gettin' that you know we do."

A little of what she wanted.

What, exactly, *did* she want?

Gran had known this man for seven years. She'd given his children large amounts of money. And she'd given *me* to *him*.

And yet, she did not mention him once.

I didn't understand this.

What I was coming to understand as my bizarre morning trundled on, was that it didn't feel very nice.

"Dinner," he encouraged softly. "Just dinner. You think I'm a dick, that's it. Sayin' that, I'm not gonna be a dick to Lydie's girl because that woman meant a lot to me, to my kids, and that's just not gonna happen. You feel that from me anyway, we're done. But give it dinner."

I could give it dinner.

In actuality, I could tell him I could give it dinner because it was clear he wasn't going to give up until I did so.

Then I would not go to dinner. The town was not big but Lavender House wasn't exactly on Main Street. In the brief time I was there, I could avoid him.

Then I'd be gone.

Therefore, I decided to do just that.

"Fine. Dinner," I lied.

His lips curled up. "Great."

"Where shall I meet you?" I asked and his lips turned down but his brows inched up.

"Meet me?" he asked.

"Meet you."

"Josie, a man takes a woman to dinner, he picks her up at her door and he returns her there," he decreed and I found this decree troubling.

I found it troubling because, although I didn't date, had never really dated, that didn't mean I didn't frequently spend time around a goodly number of females who *did* date. And these days, men and women more often than not met places for said dates.

I disliked this. If I were to date, I would not abide a man who told me he'd meet me somewhere. A man who couldn't act with gallantry, in other words, make the effort to come collect me and see me safely home, wasn't worth my time.

And it was troubling that James Markham Spear agreed with me.

"I'm uncertain what my day will bring," I told him and this was the truth. "I have some things to do for my employer." This wasn't the truth. "Not to mention a variety of things having to do with Gran's passing." And with that I was back on the truth. "I'd rather be free to take care of all that without having to worry about meeting you at Lavender House since I'll likely be in town anyway, we'll be coming back to town to have dinner, so I can just meet you where we're to eat."

He looked at me again like he was studying me.

"So, when and where shall I meet you?" I asked when this went on for some time and he said not a word.

This lasted longer and I was about to say something again when he finally spoke.

"The Lobster Market, six thirty."

Six thirty.

I didn't like this. I never ate dinner until after seven thirty. I was a night owl. I usually didn't get to bed until after midnight.

Eating this early meant I'd be needing a snack before bedtime which would be annoying since I wouldn't have one and not because there was very little food in Gran's house but because I never snacked.

Ever.

The fortunate thing was, I wasn't actually meeting him so this wouldn't be a problem.

"I'll see you there," I stated. "Six thirty."

"Great."

"Fine."

He didn't move.

I was about to open my mouth to tell him I wished for him to do so when he finally did.

He stepped back half a foot and stopped, locking his now-blue eyes with my sunglasses.

And it was then he said quietly, "It's real good to finally meet you, Josie."

And when he said it, he meant it.

And him meaning it, the tone in his voice, the intent look in his eyes, it gave me that feeling on my skin again. All over. A feeling that felt like an urge for me to do something, say something. I just didn't know what.

I also didn't know what to say.

So I inclined my head.

"The Market, see you there," he murmured.

"Yes," I replied.

"Later, Josie."

"Good-bye."

He lifted a hand in a low wave and walked away.

I watched him thinking it was quite remarkable how he moved that big body of his without it looking like it took any effort.

But in the back of my head, it occurred to me that this was so fascinating I could watch him move for a long time. Minutes. Hours.

An eternity.

On this utterly unhinged thought, my stomach twisted yet again and before I went off my lunch, I hit the button on the key fob to open the car so I could get in and get to the bank in order to begin my business that would conclude my time in Magdalene.

Forever.

Thus taking me to what I dreaded the most.

My final farewell to Gran.

Three

THE FOURTH MRS. JAKE SPEAR

I sat sipping Chambord on the veranda of Breeze Point, an excellent restaurant one town over from Magdalene. It, like Lavender House, sat on a cliff and its views were stunning, by day and, as it was now, by night.

In the clear, inky, star-filled night, I could see the lighthouse jutting out from Magdalene beaming its rotating beam.

If I'd left all the lights in the light room burning at Lavender House, I would have been able to see that too.

I knew this because Gran and I had been to Breeze Point often. We'd experimented once and found this to be true.

Breeze Point was an oft-visited destination for me and Gran. From when I would visit her as a little girl to when I took her there the summer before, we would dress up and come here to eat their superb lobster bisque, sublime crab cakes and their elegant take on whoopee pies.

All of which I'd eaten that night, remembering Gran and maybe not enjoying it as much as when she'd partaken of the same with me, but still enjoying it.

I was also there because it was not close to the Lobster Market where James Spear would be. I deduced I had probably at least a week of avoiding him and I did not delay in putting that in motion.

I drew in a deep breath as I drew the soft shawl closer around me to keep the evening chill of an early Maine September at bay.

I did this thinking that the day started out with a variety of surprises and it continued in this vein.

This being, I had gone to Magdalene Bank and Trust, spoken with the manager and found that I was in error about Gran's assets.

She had fourteen thousand some odd dollars in her checking account.

She had twenty-seven thousand some odd dollars in certified deposits.

But she also had over five hundred thousand dollars in her savings account. And if that wasn't enough of a surprise, she had over five million dollars in investments.

Further, the bank manager shared that a recent appraisal of Lavender House put it at over seven million dollars.

Seven.

Million.

Dollars!

The house had a great location, five bedrooms and was fabulous, but seven million dollars?

I had not stopped at Lavender House to pick up the key to her safe deposit box and I was glad of it. Knowing Gran was worth nearly thirteen million dollars was enough to take in for one day.

As promised, when I got back from the bank, I'd phoned Henry to check in. I'd told him of the rude Terry Baginski. I'd further told him of the money I'd found in Gran's accounts and the appraisal of Lavender House (to which he'd whistled low in shock).

I had not, of course, told him my grandmother left me to an unknown, extremely masculine, quite attractive (okay…exceptionally attractive) man who had three children. Nor did I tell him of Gran's gifts to his children.

I'd wait until later, when we were together in Rome (I hoped) or Paris (I vowed) and all of this was behind me.

"My Josephine is loaded," Henry had remarked when I was done sharing my surprising day with him and he was not wrong.

I was. Between Gran's money, as well as mine, I was loaded.

This was because I was paid well and I traveled so frequently and was so busy with Henry's life, I'd never had a home of my own so I'd also never had that expense. When we settled for the brief periods of time that we did, I stayed in the pool house at Henry's home in Los Angeles. And Henry paid for everything when we traveled. Therefore, with very few expenses of my own, I'd saved a great deal over the last twenty-three years.

A *great* deal.

So much, many could retire on what I had in my own accounts.

Add the money in Gran's, I could be a lady of leisure.

Of course, this would bore me out of my skull so the thought entered my mind and left it precisely one second later.

That didn't mean I wasn't taken aback by what I'd learned that day about Gran's finances.

She'd divorced my grandfather before I was born and he'd died before I was old enough to know him.

She had shared about him, of course, when I was much older and could take the stories she had to tell, stories she told in order to try to explain my father's behavior and why I, too, seemed to make poor choices when it came to men.

Not excuse it. Explain, "for understanding a soul, buttercup, can settle a soul."

It hadn't settled mine but I'd hoped it settled hers.

It was, however, my understanding that in order to be done with him, Gran had left my grandfather and done it taking nothing with her.

She'd also worked, doing so until she was seventy-eight years old. She was the receptionist for a doctor's office. She'd loved it. They'd loved her. And she'd been so sharp and sprightly, she had no problems working well past retirement age and only quit so she'd have more time to cook, knit, play bridge with her cronies and meddle in everyone's affairs.

But apparently her parents, who had a fabulous home on the water, also had a goodly amount of money to bestow on their daughter for there was no way she made that kind of money as a receptionist at a medical practice.

And as I stared into the dark night, I found all this disquieting.

It wasn't that my grandmother was wealthy and I didn't know it. I was glad she was comfortable but I knew that. She'd never given me any indication not to think precisely that.

That said, the fact remained that there seemed to be a good amount about my grandmother I didn't know and I thought I knew her very well.

But that wasn't all it was.

I just couldn't put my finger on exactly *what* it was.

"May I join you?"

I turned my head, looked up at the man standing beside me and recognized him from inside the restaurant. Prior to retiring to the veranda with my liqueur, I'd eaten alone inside. He, wearing a quite nice suit, had eaten with three other men in what was clearly a business dinner.

He was not unattractive. However, unfortunately for him, I worked for Henry Gagnon, who was extremely attractive, and I'd that day met James Spear, who was extortionately attractive, so this man most definitely didn't compare.

But that wasn't the reason I didn't want him to join me.

On the whole, I preferred my own company and had since I was a little girl. I had friends, all of them were good friends, but they were few.

Truly, the only two people in my life who I spent any amount of time with and shared anything deep with were Henry and Gran.

I also wasn't in the mood for company. I had a variety of things on my mind. I wanted my mind to be on those, not on trying to pull up meaningless conversation with a stranger to pass the time.

And lastly, I was in no mood for sex and it was clear he was approaching because he was interested in me.

If the need arose, I'd take a lover and I'd do this no nonsense, finding a man who I was attracted to, who suited me and then I'd take him to my bed. On occasion, this activity would be repeated or I'd exchange contact information and when I was again in his locale, I'd seek him out.

Mostly, however, I took care of myself. I found this more efficient and, in most cases, more enjoyable.

This was because intimacy wasn't easy for me and although the act of copulation was often quite pleasant, it was rare a man was very good at it and when he was, by the time I would return to where he was, he'd be taken.

This man, I could tell by just looking at him, wasn't very good at it. Although he was confident enough to make an approach, there was something about his manner that reminded me of Terry Baginski. An arrogance, which meant he'd undoubtedly be selfish in bed and that was never enjoyable.

The problem with this was, his arrogance was such that I'd learned a man like him was not easily put off, certain he could talk me around to his way of thinking.

And after the last several days, I simply didn't have it in me to talk him out of what he was certain he was going to get.

This was why I lied.

"I wouldn't mind you joining me, however, I've a man in my life who would."

"Ah," he replied on an easy smile. "And would this man be averse to me buying you another liqueur?"

I studied him through the dim, romantic lights strung around the edges of the veranda, wondering how he could ask such a question since I'd already told him the answer.

"Indeed, I believe he would," I shared, pretending to sound like I was disappointed and doing a poor job of it on purpose.

It wasn't poor enough for whatever he heard in my voice made him pull up an Adirondack chair next to me and sit in it.

"If I were that man, I probably would be the same," he told me after he was seated.

I decided to say nothing.

He didn't return the favor and his voice lowered when he went on.

"Then again, if I were that man, I would be more averse to allowing you to dine alone."

He'd seen me in the restaurant. This did not surprise me since I'd seen him there as well.

"He's busy this evening and I had a taste for lobster bisque," I replied.

This was a mistake and I knew it when I said the word "taste" and his eyes dropped to my lips. His gaze returned to mine and he declared, "If I were that man, if you had any taste, I would see to you getting it."

I fought rolling my eyes or curling my lip and edged away from him in my seat.

"Actually, Jake knows I'm quite capable of seeing to getting what I want on my own."

"Jake?"

"Jake Spear."

This was another mistake and I knew it even before he sat back in his own chair and his eyes got wide right before his lips curved into a sneer.

I knew it because we might be one town over from Magdalene but Magdalene was tiny and anyone would need to go further afield for a variety of things. Therefore, anyone who had lived in that area for very long could be known further afield.

However, I'd had an unusual day that wasn't entirely pleasant. This encounter was most definitely not pleasant. The day before was the most unpleasant of my life, save the day two days before that when I'd learned Gran had passed away. I wasn't my normal self.

But his reaction was strange.

"You're seeing Jake Spear?" he asked.

I didn't answer. Instead, I took that opportunity to mentally kick myself for being foolish.

"You?" he pressed.

I continued to be silent.

He stared at me before he asked, "Did you used to dance for him?"

What an odd thing to ask.

Odd and disturbing.

Also offensive.

Therefore, I snapped, "Of course not."

He continued to stare at me as he crassly remarked, "Class piece, Jake's finally learned to trade up."

That wasn't odd even if it was disturbing and *highly* offensive.

Therefore, when I spoke, it was again in a snap. "I beg your pardon?"

"Sweetheart, you're aiming to be the fourth Mrs. Jake Spear, let me just tell you, he might make a fortune from that strip club so that'll keep you in lobster bisque for a while. But in case no one else has warned you, I will. He goes through women like water and you'll be out before it's time for him to trade up his truck, something he does every other year."

The *fourth* Mrs. Jake Spear?

Good God.

And *strip club?*

My goodness!

Regardless of how shocking I found this information, this man was loath-some and therefore I retorted, "You seem to know a good deal about Jake."

"Lived in this county all my life and doing that, it's hard not to know pretty much everything about *the truck*."

He said his last two very confusing words with not a small amount of derision then he stood.

"Do me a favor and don't let *Jake* know I tried to buy you a drink. Seeing as you're how you are, he might actually like you and want to keep you and I don't want to know how *the truck* would react if he knew I'd offered."

Yes.

Most loathsome.

"Please, then, before you leave, share your name so we can see," I returned.

He continued to stare at me for a moment before he shook his head and sauntered back into the restaurant.

I watched him go, not pleased in the slightest that that encounter made me feel even more uneasy.

However, just in case he remained at the restaurant to hit on another woman, instead of doing what I wished to do, get up and go straight to Lavender House, in order to communicate how little I thought of our disagreeable encounter, I simply looked back to the view and sipped my Chambord like it didn't happen.

Unfortunately, it did happen.

Therefore, my eyes were to the view and my lips often tasted the deep headiness of the liqueur.

But my mind was on three previous Mrs. Jake Spears, a strip club and wondering what on earth was "the truck."

<hr />

I BECAME AWARE of the sunlight hitting my eyelids moments before I opened them and rolled in the big iron bed with its high comfortable mat-tresses, flowery sheets, vast array of downy pillows and fluffy duvet.

My eyes went to the view of sparkling sea and bright sky out the big diamond-paned window across the room.

Then they went to the alarm clock by the bed.

Seven thirty.

Early for me but then again, I was still on LA time.

As ever, no matter what time it was when I woke up, I needed coffee.

I threw back the covers and then threw my legs over the side of the bed, gaining my feet.

When I did, my dusty pink nightie fell over my bottom.

The nightie had a hem that covered my lower hips and upper thighs that was a four-inch swathe of dusty pink pleats edged top and bottom in a trim of cream lace. The straps were thin and the bodice ran straight, exposing very little cleavage, but it had another one-inch wide section of trimmed pleats.

It was girlie, but alluring, and not obvious, thus not vulgar, and this was the reason I bought it.

It was also quite comfortable.

A plus.

I walked to the overstuffed chintz chair in the corner and grabbed my cream satin robe. I didn't bother cinching the belt. I was alone in the house so there was no need. However, even alone, it was unseemly to wander around wearing nothing but a thin, short nightie.

I grabbed a ponytail holder before I padded out of the room and secured my hair in a messy knot at the back of my head as I moved down the hall and two flights of stairs.

I did this not taking anything in.

Usually, when I was at Lavender House, I consumed every inch, recommitting every vision, every smell, even the feel to memory to hold close until I returned.

This time, I didn't do that and it wasn't because I was still half-asleep.

I made it to the kitchen and I especially didn't take any of that in.

This was because, outside the light room, the kitchen was where Gran spent most of her time. It was a fabulous kitchen and she was a fabulous cook. I couldn't count the number of mouth-watering smells I'd smelled in that kitchen or the number of delightful tastes I'd experienced with what Gran created in that room.

Gran had cooked for me in that kitchen.

She'd also taught me to cook in that kitchen.

And like every memory with her in it, those I knew even before she passed would be some of the ones I would hold most dear.

Therefore, I moved directly through to the coffeepot, which I'd prepared for brewing the night before and I did it still not taking anything in.

I lifted a finger to hit the on button and saw it already lit.

I stared at the pot.

It was programmable but I didn't program it because I didn't know how, and to learn, I'd have to find the instructions which meant looking around, something I wasn't going to do. In fact, the little button with its little light that would light up if it was programmed was not lit.

Instead of hitting the on button, I moved my hand close to the stainless steel carafe.

It was warm.

"What on—?" I started to say but ended this in a stifled scream while whirling when a deep voice came at me from behind.

"Not a big fan of gettin' stood up."

After my whirl, I went completely still as I stared at James Spear sitting in the sun pouring in the multi-paned glass that surrounded the nook where Gran had her beaten wood kitchen table.

He had a cup of coffee on the table in front of him.

"Wha-wha-what are you doing here?" I stammered.

He didn't move, except his mouth. But when he moved that mouth, he didn't answer my question.

"Pain in my ass, gettin' Amber to look after her brother. First, she charges a shitload, fuckin' twenty dollars an hour. And since she had plans with some of her friends last night and I needed her to change them, she upped that shit. Drove a hard bargain. That bein' her gettin' an hour added to her curfew on Saturday night and fuck knows, Amber and an hour on a Saturday night could mean anything. A visit to a bondsman or a different kind of visit in a few months to Babies 'R' Us."

It was clear he was there because he was angry I didn't join him for dinner so I didn't need to repeat my question, thus I asked another one.

"How did you get in here?"

He shoved his hand in his jeans pocket and lifted it. I saw a key dangling from a thin ring looped on his long forefinger before he dropped his hand, shoving it back in his pocket then he pulled it out to rest it again on the table.

"Looked after Lydie and sometimes Lydie looked after Ethan after school. Me and all the kids got keys."

"I, uh…well, I'll have to ask for all those to be returned," I told him.

"Are you fuckin' serious?" he asked, his dark brows rising.

"Well, yes," I answered and I saw his dark brows snap together.

"Jesus Christ, Josie, you stood me up."

"I can obviously see that you'd see it that way but since I didn't actually wish to go to dinner with you in the first place, I don't see it the same way."

"Fuckin' hell," he murmured.

"And really," I foolishly went on, "your language is quite—"

"Do not fuckin' tell me what my language is," he cut me off to bite out. "And do not stand across Lydie's fuckin' kitchen and give me your bullshit," he ordered and I blinked.

Then my back snapped straight. "Pardon me?"

"You're standin' in Lydie's kitchen knowin' what she wanted for you, and what that was is *me*."

He jerked his thumb to himself on his last word but he wasn't done speaking.

"You jacked me around last night, made my daughter change her plans and she was lookin' forward to that shit. Made me sit in a restaurant by my-fuckin'-self for forty-five fuckin' minutes waitin' on your ass, when not a lot of people have forty-five minutes of their lives to piss away and I'm one of them. You're a no show and you give me this bullshit?"

Unfortunately, this made me uncomfortable. This was because he was right. His daughter changed her plans (though I couldn't know that was needed, but that didn't mean it wasn't). And he'd had to bargain with her to do that. Not to mention, he'd settled on a bargain he wasn't comfortable with and, by the sounds of it, it was indeed an uncomfortable bargain. And while I was enjoying lobster bisque (well, some time before, but still), he'd been sitting alone at a restaurant waiting for me to arrive and I didn't.

If that had happened to me, I would have found it supremely annoying. And I'd done it to him.

I stared across the kitchen into his angry eyes and I did what I had to do. I apologized.

"That was rude," I said quietly. "I have no excuse. I should have explained more firmly how I felt about the dinner without wasting your time or involving your family."

"Damn straight," he returned.

"Well, I apologize."

"And you should," he shot back.

I closed my mouth.

He didn't.

"So, babe, where do we go from here?"

Babe?

I'd never been called "babe" and the angry way he did it, I didn't like very much.

I ignored that and stayed focused.

"Where we go from here, Mr. Spear, is—"

I stopped speaking because he'd been sitting and mostly not moving but when I called him Mr. Spear, he stood.

And when he stood, the force of him invaded the entirety of the kitchen and this was no small feat. Gran's kitchen was enormous.

"My name, Josie," he started slowly, "is *Jake.*"

"All right," I whispered.

"And I shouldn't have asked you about where we're goin' from here because I don't give a fuck about where you think we're goin'."

I said nothing to that.

He didn't need me to. He kept speaking.

"You know her. You know that bullshit you pulled last night would piss her off."

I detested this because he was right. It was clear Gran cared deeply for this man and if she knew I'd done what I'd done, she'd be angry.

Therefore, I admitted, "Yes."

45

"And like I said, you know her. She said it straight up in that letter yesterday. The woman had a lot of love to give and she gave it freely. But the one person on this fuckin' planet who had the most of that love, who she treasured above anyone, is you. And there is no way in fuck Lydie would feel that way about you and steer you wrong about me."

It was then, I was again foolish.

And I was foolish by asking, "Did she know you own a strip club?"

The force of his presence expanded and heated to the point I felt it press against my flesh and burn in my lungs.

I retreated a step but it was only a step because I hit counter.

His voice was vibrating with anger when he shared, "Yeah, Josie, she did seein' as she loaned me the money to buy it."

I blinked. "She did?"

"Yeah, she fuckin' did. I paid her back but she put it up so I could keep my gym and keep my kids in clothes and food and for once have the cake to give them a decent life."

My voice had risen when I asked, "By owning a strip club?"

His eyes narrowed on me. "Fuckin' hell, you ever show Lydie how far that stick was shoved up your ass?"

Well!

I never!

"Mr. Spear," I threw out my hands and snapped, "You *own a strip club.*"

The instant I was done snapping, he leaned toward me and roared, "*Jake!*"

His behavior and this scene first thing in the morning so incensed me, *very* unusually (as in, I wasn't certain it had ever happened before), I lost my control, leaned toward him too and shouted a word I'd never used in my life in that manner, "*Whatever!*" I leaned back and kept at him. "Your business is to subjugate women."

"What the fuck?" he bit out.

"Subjugate. Oppress. Use women who are in dire straits to do something demeaning for money."

"Babe, I need a dancer, I put an ad in the paper. I don't go out on the street, kidnap them, jack them up with junk and force their asses on the stage."

"You know what I mean," I hissed.

"Yeah?" he asked, leaning back and throwing out his arms. "I do? Well fuck me. I'm an asshole and I never would have thought it seein' as the least talented of my girls makes five hundred dollars on a slow night. Must suck for my girls, walkin' to their Corvettes after work wearin' seven hundred dollar shoes."

Five hundred dollars?

On a slow night?

I was stunned. That was quite a bit of money.

He kept speaking.

"My girls aren't stupid. A guy thinks with his dick, using his money to do it, all they gotta do is dance around and take it from him. They feed their kids, got good furniture in their houses, nice cars to drive and live in good neighborhoods, depositing cash in their 401Ks and taking their vacations in the Bahamas. Not sure that's oppression but figure they don't think of it that way. But you wanna think narrow, not my job to stop you."

I opened my mouth to say something but he wasn't quite finished.

"And a woman's body is beautiful, standin', sittin', lyin' down, definitely dancin'. They know that, they use it, there's not one fuckin' thing wrong with it. Though, says a fuck of a lot about you that you look down your nose at it."

I truly wished I didn't have to admit it but he was not wrong. A woman's body was beautiful.

And I'd never thought of exotic dancing like that.

I decided at that juncture not to admit that out loud and instead move us to a different subject.

Therefore, I asked, "Has it struck you as strange that you know me but I know nothing about you?"

"No."

"Why not?" I queried.

"I don't know," he answered sarcastically. "Maybe it has somethin' to do with you bein' a judgmental, stick up your ass bitch who'd react just the way you reacted about a minute ago if she told you about me."

I glared at him, not altogether thrilled with his words and especially not his sarcasm. "Yes, perhaps you're correct, as I might be a wee bit judgmental and react if she told me she was loaning a man money to buy a strip club, a man who's been married three times."

His arms crossed on his chest and his face got hard. "You been askin' around about me?"

"No. A not-so-gentlemanly gentleman hit on me last night at Breeze Point and I've had a difficult few days, was not up to dealing with him, and unwisely used you as my pretend lover to get him to leave me alone. He then shared a good deal about you in a scathing way. The good news about this was, my ploy worked. He went away. The bad news was, he shared a good deal about you before he did."

More pressure hit the room, making me press back into the counter before he asked, "Some dick hit on you last night?"

"That isn't the point," I informed him.

"And what is the point, Josie?" he asked and didn't allow me to answer. "With this shit, you sayin' you know me when you don't. You got my ticket when you have no fuckin' clue. You want me to piss off when your grand-mother wanted me in your life. Is that what the point is?"

"I don't know the point," I returned. "I might know it if you didn't break in and start berating me practically the moment I awoke and definitely before I had my first cup of coffee."

"Berating?" he clipped.

"Rebuking," I explained. His face got even harder and I correctly took that as a sign he didn't understand that either so I snapped, "Scolding."

"You know, babe, it's cute, normally. And it's *real* cute, you in that nightie," he stated, throwing out a hand and sweeping it up to indicate what I was wearing.

It was also something I forgot I was wearing and doing it without closing my robe, which was something I immediately rectified, my hands going to the edges of my robe and wrapping it around me.

"The uppity shit you got goin' on," he continued, explaining what was "cute." "What isn't cute is you hiding behind that shit in order to shield your-self from living your life."

I felt my eyes get big as my heart started shriveling.

"You don't know me. You can't say something like that," I whispered.

And he didn't.

Except for what Gran had told him about me.

Was that was Gran thought about me?

"Babe, I don't have to know you to know your fucked up gig. But, just sayin', I *do* know you. It's *you* who's totally clueless about you."

And on that, he turned toward the door, prowled to it and used it.

I lost sight of him and within moments heard the front door slam.

I stared at where I last saw him for some time before my feet moved.

And they moved to the family room where I could find them on the mantel over the fireplace.

Dozens of frames of all different sizes.

My eyes scanned them and I saw what I already knew was there.

Photos of my father and uncle when they were babies and young boys, nothing later than when they were nine years of age because, as Gran explained, "That's when they turned, buttercup, and I don't need a reminder of that."

Photos of me from growing up to grown up.

Photos of my great-grandparents and my Aunt Julia who'd died in town, hit by a car when she was eleven.

I moved out of the family room and into the formal living room at the front of the house.

Two long, thin tables behind the two facing couches. More frames on both, all silver. Most of the photos black and white and old. My grandmother. Aunt Julia. My great-grandparents. Their siblings and children. And even older photos of long since gone family who'd lived in Lavender House.

And me.

The largest photo of them all, taken by Henry at a Dolce and Gabbana show years earlier. I was sitting beside the runway, my elbows to my knees, my chin held in my palms, my eyes turned up, my expression rapt. It was in profile.

I loved that picture. Henry had given it to Gran the Christmas after it was taken. And Gran had put it there and never moved it so when you walked into the house, if you turned your head left, that was what you'd see.

Me.

My heart was beating faster as I moved out of the living room, into the foyer then deeper into the house. What was there tried to force itself on my consciousness but I fought it back, my feet dragging but taking me there anyway.

The den.

Gran had had her bedroom set up there when it became difficult for her to negotiate stairs.

I hadn't been in that room since I'd been home

I didn't want to go there now.

But I went there, opening the door and feeling her loss burn through me just like it was fresh when I saw all that was her all around, smelled her perfume.

I swallowed and moved to the bed.

It was unmade. The nurse who came in and made sure she was up, bathed, dressed and fed had found her there. They'd taken her from there.

Gone.

No one had made the bed since.

She'd died in that bed, in those sheets, that was the last place she'd been breathing.

Then she'd slipped away.

I turned my eyes from the bed to the nightstand.

Another silver framed photo. Me and Gran. Taken that summer when I left my life behind and came to her. We were outside the house amongst the lavender. It was in color. She was sitting in one of her wicker chairs and I was bent to her, arms around her, my cheek to her cheek, both of us looking in the camera one of her friends held. Both of us smiling.

I closed my eyes and turned away, taking in a deep breath, feeling it fill my lungs.

I opened my eyes and looked to the other nightstand.

There it was.

Slowly, I moved there, wrapped my hand around the side of the big frame and lifted the picture up to take a closer look.

Jake Spear surrounded by his kids, all of them surrounded by lavender, and, behind them, the sea.

It had been taken outside the house.

His daughter was at his side, her front pressed into it, her arms around his middle, her cheek to his chest, her eyes to the camera, her lips smiling.

His eldest son was at his other side, Jake's arm was around his shoulders too, and I could tell the young man had an arm around his father's waist as they were standing tucked close. The young man was also smiling.

And standing in front of the girl was Jake's youngest son. He was leaning back against her body.

He, too, was smiling at the camera.

As was Jake.

I turned and sat on the bed, staring at the photo.

They were all younger. Not by much, years maybe, but with children, much changes as years pass.

And she had them close. By her bed.

Yet she never told me about them. I'd even been in this room more than once in the last seven years and had not seen this picture.

But it was there and she kept them close.

Close until the day she died.

They all had keys to her home.

She'd given them large sums of money.

She'd given *me* to that man.

"Why didn't you tell me about him, Gran?" I whispered to the photo then looked up.

I aimed my eyes across the room to the window seeing lavender grown high and beyond that, sea.

"What did you tell him about me?" I asked the window.

The sun glinted on the sea and the lavender swayed gently in the breeze.

I shook my head.

"What did you want him to do with me?"

The lavender, the sea, the room, all of them had no answers for me.

Four

ONLY THERE

I parked in the curving lane at the front of Lavender House, opened the door and got out, slamming the door behind me and moving to the trunk where I'd stowed the groceries.

I wouldn't be in Magdalene for very long but I would be there for a while. I also had a life where I ate most of my meals in restaurants or at parties and rarely had the chance to cook.

After Jake Spear left and I got no answers to questions that were hounding me, I decided that since I was there, I'd take advantage of being there.

Meaning I would give myself a treat and cook.

Thus, I prepared for the day and went to the market in town.

I had filled brown paper bags in each arm when the SUV drove up the lane.

I looked through my shades to the shiny black Escalade and primarily the man who sat behind the wheel.

I'd never seen him before.

I watched him approach deciding I did not need this.

I had a number of things to do, the priority at that moment was getting the groceries in the house, but it was never a priority to deal with an unannounced visitor seeing as it was most rude to show up unannounced.

He could be someone who simply wished to give his condolences. However, he could call, like dozens of other people had done since Gran had died. He didn't need to come to the house.

Especially since I had no idea who he was.

His sunglassed eyes never leaving me, he got out of his vehicle and I saw he was tall, lean and well-dressed, in well-fitting, excellent quality dark blue trousers and an equally well-fitting, tailored light blue shirt.

No tie.

His dark brown hair was cut well.

And at a glance, I knew his sunglasses cost five hundred dollars.

"Can I help you with those?" he called when he was about ten feet away.

"Not to be rude," I replied. "But I don't know you so I'm afraid I'll need to refuse."

He nodded his head, stopped four feet away and suggested, "Let's remedy that. I'm Boston Stone."

My face must have betrayed my response to his absurd name because he smiled and it was not an unattractive smile.

"My mother said she was under the influence of drugs post-birth," he explained his name in a manner where I knew he'd done it frequently in his life. Then again, with that name, he would have to.

I nodded and asked, "How can I help you, Mr. Stone?"

His head tipped slightly to the side before he answered and part of his answer included him strangely repeating himself, "I'm Boston Stone. CEO of Stone Incorporated."

I said nothing.

"I believe Terry told you about me?" he queried.

"Terry?" I queried back.

"Terry Baginski. The associate at Weaver and Schuller who read your grandmother's will yesterday."

I felt my body lock as an unexpected and unpleasant pulse thumped through it.

Stone Incorporated. In all that had happened, I'd forgotten.

The other thing Gran never told me. This man wanted to buy Lavender House.

"Yes," I stated. "Ms. Baginski told me about you."

"As you're busy," he replied, tipping his head to the bags in my arms, "I'll not keep you except to ask if you'd like to have lunch with me tomorrow to discuss your plans for Lavender House."

That pulse thumped through me again and it was far more unpleasant.

Boston Stone of Stone Incorporated.

A man behind a company.

Not a family with children, the wife cutting lavender to put in the family room and on the kitchen table, the kids playing Frisbee in the back yard around the arbor with petals of wisteria blowing through the air around them, the husband knowing how to fix the sink and keeping the house in tiptop shape with loving care…forever.

I tasted something sour in my mouth and forced through it, "Mr. Stone, I don't wish to be rude, but as you can see, I'm busy. And as you know, my grandmother died only five days ago. There are a variety of things on my mind and one of them is not having lunch with someone to discuss my plans for Lavender House."

This wasn't strictly true. I'd given vague thought to it.

It was just that it was vague.

Now, with this man standing in front of me, it was not vague in the slightest and I didn't like how that felt.

"Of course, my apologies. It's too soon," he murmured.

"It is," I agreed.

"Then I'll repeat my offer of lunch but I'll do it in order to give you a lovely meal and, perhaps, take your mind off your recent loss."

I studied him as I processed his words.

And then I processed his words.

Good God, I'd just met the man in my grandmother's driveway and he was asking me out.

Although he was quite handsome and it was done smoothly, in a kind tone, and with respect, I couldn't believe it.

"Mr. Stone—"

"Ms. Malone, just lunch, no business, getting you away from memories and taking your mind off things. I know a place that does wonderful things with mussels. If you like seafood, I'd enjoy introducing you to it."

He was quite nice, not to mention I loved mussels and all seafood.

I just had no desire to have lunch with him.

"That offer is kind, Mr. Stone," I said quietly. "But I'm afraid your endeavors wouldn't succeed. I have much to think about and even more to do."

He nodded and lifted then immediately dropped a hand. "Of course. But if you change your mind, the information Terry gave you includes a direct line to me. Just phone and we'll make plans."

"If I change my mind"—highly unlikely—"I'll do that."

His smooth voice dipped lower and even smoother when he said, "I'm sorry for your loss, Josephine. Lydia was much loved and there were many reasons for that. So please know, I understand this loss is grave."

I felt my throat close so I just nodded.

"I hope you call," he finished, still talking lower and smoother.

"I'll think about it. Have a nice day, Mr. Stone."

His sunglasses held my sunglasses before he dipped his chin, turned and moved to his SUV.

I watched him get in and slam the door. After he did that, I moved to the house.

When I'd entered, I kicked the door shut behind me with my pump and stopped dead.

I did this because it hit me.

All of it.

Everything I was seeing.

Everything I was experiencing.

But most of all, everything I was *feeling*.

The shafts of light piercing the shadows, dust motes drifting making the air itself seem almost magical.

The abundance of furniture stuffed in the large rooms opening off the foyer. All of it old, all of it plush, all of it comfortable.

And then there was the profusion of knickknacks, some of them likely worthless, some of them perhaps priceless, but all of them precious. The gleaming wood of the antique tables. The framed prints on the walls that had hung there for decades, maybe some of them for over a century.

My mind's eye conjured an image of the land around the house. The rough gray stone of the coastline. The rocky beach with its deep pier. The massive bushes of lavender that hugged the sprawling tall house all around. The green clipped lawns. The arbor covered in wisteria with the white wicker furniture under it pointed at the sea. The rectangular greenhouse leading to the mosaic-tiled patio, also pointed at the sea. The small garden surrounded by the low, white fence.

My family had lived in that house for over one hundred and fifty years. My grandmother had grown up there. She'd lost her sister there. She'd escaped there after her husband used and abused her. She'd helped me escape there after her son used and abused me.

I'd only ever been truly happy there.

Only there.

Only there.

On this thought, I numbly moved through the house to the kitchen and, once there, dropped the bags on the butcher block, shoved my sunglasses back on my head and took in the huge expanse.

The Aga stove that stayed warm all the time and produced sublime food. The slate floors. The deep-bowled farm sink. The plethora of cream-painted glass-fronted cabinets. The grooved doors of the cupboards below. The greenhouse leading off it where herbs grew in pots on shelves in the windows. The massive butcher block that ran the length of the middle of the room, worn, cut and warped.

I shrugged my purse from my shoulder and set it beside the bags. I then moved back out to my rental car, getting the last bag, slamming the trunk and taking it into the house.

I put the groceries away and I did it not feeling numb anymore.

Not even close.

My brain felt heated, even fevered.

I no longer felt uneasy.

I felt unwell.

Something wasn't right.

No, *everything* wasn't right.

Then again, there was no right to a world without Lydia Josephine Malone in it.

And I only knew one way to make it right.

I folded the bags and tucked them in the pantry then moved directly to the phone.

Gran kept her address book there.

I opened it and flipped through the pages, finding the M's. There were sheets of M's and sheets of names written amongst the pages.

But I wasn't there.

I moved back to J.

My brain cooled when I saw it in her looping script.

Josie.

She didn't write in the lines. She scrawled all over the page however she wanted to do it and I felt my lips tip up slightly even as I felt the backs of my eyes tingle.

On the page was my mobile number, several before it crossed out when I'd changed them over the decades. Henry's mobile number(s). Henry's address in LA with a big looped *Pool House* scribbled beside it—this meager information taking up the entire page.

I drew in a calming breath and closed my eyes.

I opened them and flipped close to the back of the book. I found the number and grabbed the old phone from its cradle on the wall. So old, it had long twirly cord. A cord, I knew, that was long enough that you could talk on it and get to the sink, the butcher block, but not the stove. I knew this because I'd seen Gran talking on it as she moved about the room.

I punched in the number from Gran's book in the keypad and put it to my ear.

It rang three times before I heard a man answer, "Hello?"

"Mr. Weaver?"

"Yes."

"It's Josephine Malone."

A pause then, "Josephine. My dear. How lovely it is to hear from you."

I swallowed and said softly, "And it's lovely to speak to you, Mr. Weaver. But, just to say, I'm calling because Ms. Baginski shared about Mrs. Weaver."

Another pause before, "Of course. Yes, I should have called and explained. That was why we weren't at the funeral."

"That's entirely understandable," I murmured then went on to say, "But I'm phoning to share I was distressed to hear this news."

"Yes, dear, it's distressing," he agreed in a kindly way, pointing out the obvious without making me feel foolish that I'd done the same.

Even mucking this up, I still carried on.

"Is Mrs. Weaver well enough to receive visitors?" I asked quietly.

This was met with yet another pause before, softly, "I think she'd like that, Josephine. She always enjoyed seeing you. She's best in the mornings, however. Could you come by tomorrow, say about ten?"

I didn't want to go by the Weavers tomorrow at about ten. I didn't want to visit a kind woman in the throes of a grave illness or spend time with a kind man who was in the throes of possibly watching his wife die.

But Gran would go.

And I would detest knowing what I knew about Eliza Weaver and not taking the time to visit at about ten tomorrow to find some way to communicate that I thought she was kind and she'd touched my life in a way I appreciated.

"I would…yes. I could. Absolutely," I accepted.

"She can't have flowers or—"

"I'll just bring me," I assured him.

"Eliza will look forward to that, as will I."

"Lovely," I replied. "I'll see you both tomorrow."

"See you then, Josephine."

"Take care, Mr. Weaver."

"You as well, my dear. Good-bye."

I gave him my farewell and put the phone back in its receiver. Then I moved back to Gran's book and flipped the pages until I found it. I grabbed the phone and punched in the digits.

There were five rings before I heard, "You've reached the Fletcher residence. We're unable to get to the phone right now, but please leave a message."

I waited for the beep then said, "Reverend Fletcher? This is Josephine Malone. It seems I'll be in Magdalene for some time and…well, you mentioned dinner. And I would enjoy having dinner with you and Mrs. Fletcher. Or you can come to Lavender House and I can cook for you to express my gratitude for all the thoughtful things you did for Gran. Whenever you have time, I'd be happy to hear from you. You can call me at the house or use my mobile."

I gave him my number, said my good-byes and I hung up.

Once I did, I took in another, deeper breath and flipped to the S's.

There was no listing and I found that unsurprising.

Then it occurred to me and I flipped back to the J's.

One page from mine, there it was. *Jake* and a number.

I stared at the number for some time before I made my decision.

I moved to the butcher block to get my phone from my purse. I went back to the address book and programmed his number into my phone.

But I didn't use it.

What had to be said, and done, needed to be face-to-face.

Therefore, I moved to the drawer where Gran kept the phonebook.

I flipped through the pages at the back that were printed on thin yellow paper, not knowing what I was looking for.

Then I found what I was looking for.

One listing with the bold heading *Exotic Dancers*.

It had a phone number and address.

I ripped the page out of the book, replaced the book in the drawer, folded the page and tucked it in the back pocket of my jeans.

That done, I moved to the spiral staircase to go to the light room so I could find Gran's safety deposit box key.

I SAT IN the dark parking lot staring at the building.

There were no windows in the building. However, the parking lot was well-lit.

And almost completely full.

The sign out front said the establishment was called "The Circus." This sign was surprisingly quite tasteful, black with blue scrolled letters. No flashing lights or neon and there was only one on the front of the building, not even one on a big stand protruding out into the street.

The building was a lone building in the middle of nowhere, the parking lot large. But there were no weeds growing through cracks. The black paint with gray trim of the building was clean, looking fresh, and expertly done. No graffiti or markings.

The door to enter was padded with buttoned black leather. There was a large man standing beside it wearing a blue windbreaker and black trousers. And there were a goodly number of cameras mounted under the eaves. Those, as well as the lighting, making the outside feel safe.

I got out of my car, closed the door and hit the button on the key fob, hearing the beep. I did this wondering if I should have changed clothes.

I'd never been to a strip club. I had no idea what to wear.

I'd decided not to change from what I'd worn that day to the market, and while stripping Gran's bed, doing Gran's laundry, unpacking my suitcase and emailing Daniel on my phone a variety of reminders of how to take care of Henry.

I was wearing my dark blue bootcut jeans, my well-fashioned eggplant-colored top that had an intricately draping neckline, and my navy blue patent leather Manolo Blahnik pumps. Before leaving, I'd simply refreshed my makeup and perfume, pulled on a well-tailored black Italian leather jacket, and made my way to the address on the phone listing.

At that point, it would have to do.

I walked through the lot and approached the door. When I got close, I noted the man beside it had a twisted wire leading up to his ear.

As I approached, he dipped his chin, murmured, "Ma'am," and moved, opening the door for me.

He gave no sign he was surprised a woman was entering such a club and I found this interesting, as I found his good manners the same.

I gave him a small smile, walked in and stopped.

This was partly to allow my eyes to adjust to the dark. It was also partly to allow my ears to adjust to the music. But mostly it was in shock.

Like the outside, the inside was clean and well maintained, but more.

There was a large circular stage in the middle on which there were five women dancing. There were shiny silver poles that were not smooth but had spirals formed in them. Off the stage, there were two runways that led back to a wall and across the length of it, these with more poles and dancers.

It was not a surprise that they were not clothed. They had on G-strings and nothing else.

What was a surprise was that they were all very attractive with lovely, toned bodies, a variety of interesting and not-unfashionable (but all very high-heeled) shoes and sandals and all but one had very becoming hair (the one who didn't had her hair dyed a rather brash red that did nothing for her coloring).

What also was a surprise was that, surrounding the stages, there were rather attractive black padded, semi-circular booths with small round tables in front of them to hold drinks. Further, there were stylish tables and chairs filling the rest of the space with larger booths upholstered in dark blue leather and having larger tables in the middle of them set against the walls not taken up with stage or bar.

And the bar was also very tasteful, fully mirrored at the back but it had cleverly positioned lights shining blue on the bottles and variety of clean, some of them rather chic, glasses on glass shelves. Around the bar were tall, backed, comfortable-looking stools covered in dark blue leather.

And the last surprise was that there were a great number of people there. The club was situated between Magdalene and the town to the north, which was fifteen miles away. As there was only one listing in the phonebook, obviously, if you were looking for this kind of entertainment, this was the only place close you'd find it. Therefore, this perhaps should not have been a surprise.

But it was and it was because it didn't appear that the place was filled with foul, ill-kempt, lascivious men wearing big coats with their hands in their pockets.

In fact, quite a number of the patrons weren't paying attention to the dancers but appeared to be there simply to enjoy a drink.

And three of the booths lining the stage were filled with women, all of them wearing varying tiaras with one woman who was strangely sporting a hot pink boa of questionable quality. She was also wearing a tiara but unlike the others, hers had feathers protruding from it and words formed in that proclaimed her proudly as the "Bachelorette."

How odd.

I moved to the bar and took one of the stools available at the side close to the wall. I put my purse on the bar and waited for the midnight-blue-shirted, black-trouser-wearing, young and quite attractive bartender to make his way to me.

He smiled an easy white smile when he did and asked, "What'll it be?"

"A Shirley Temple," I ordered. He blinked. I ignored that and went on, "And I'd like for someone to tell Mr. Spear I'm here, if that's possible. You can tell him it's Josephine Malone."

He stared at me for a moment then asked, "You want a Shirley Temple?"

"Yes, please," I confirmed. "And for Mr. Spear to be told I'm here, if you don't mind."

He studied me another moment before he nodded and moved away. I saw him grab a glass and do things with ice, bottles and the soda gun. I also saw him catch the eye of a large man in the crowd wearing another blue shirt and black trousers.

That man went to the bar. The bartender leaned into him, said something and jerked his head to me. The large man outside the bar glanced at me, nodded and moved away, his hand going to his back pocket to pull out a phone.

The man served me my drink. I paid for it after expressing gratitude and he moved away to an area cordoned off from the rest of the bar by two high, curved silver poles.

It was then I saw the waitress who was waiting there and noted that she, too, was dressed tastefully. I couldn't see her bottom half but I did see her off-the-shoulder black top that was form-fitting and showed a hint of cleavage but it was far from risqué. She had a black velvet ribbon tied around her neck, her makeup was excellently done from what I could tell with the dim light and she had quite lovely hair.

I sipped my drink and looked through the crowd to see the other waitresses dressed the same. Off-the-shoulder top, velvet ribbon at the throat and this was paired with a slim-fitting, quite short but not vulgar dark blue skirt. Sheer black hose. Very attractive black platform pumps.

I surveyed the waitresses and the dancers and even the multiple men in blue shirts and black trousers. None of them were thin, pale, sunken-cheeked, glassy-eyed or appeared woebegone in any way.

They all seemed simply to be at work and the waitresses quite often smiled what looked to be genuine smiles at their customers while they moved amongst the tables and booths.

Yes. Glancing around Jake Spear's establishment, I realized I had done precisely what he said I'd done.

I'd been judgmental.

That sour taste came back to my mouth.

I washed it away with a sip of my drink.

Five minutes later, the large man who the bartender spoke to walked through the club to me.

He stopped close, leaned in and said, "Mr. Spear is unavailable, Ms. Malone. Can I give him a message?"

I was not surprised he was unavailable. If someone had treated me as I had treated him, I would be unavailable too.

I shook my head but elevated my voice to be heard over the music in order to say, "No, but thank you."

He nodded and moved away.

I sipped at my drink, watched the goings-on at a tasteful strip club and did so considering my dilemma.

I needed to apologize (again).

And I needed answers.

I sighed, knowing I had no choice because Jake Spear wasn't giving me one and I didn't blame him. I wouldn't give me one either.

I reached into my purse on the bar, pulled out my phone, found his number and hit the screen to connect.

I put a finger in my other ear and listened as it rang five times before I heard his rumbling voice command, "Spear. Leave a message."

I got the beep and said into my phone, "Mr. Spear...uh, Jake, this is Josephine Malone. I'm calling because I'd very much like the opportunity to apologize for my behavior and the things I said to you this morning. Also, I'd like the opportunity to discuss, well...other, erm...*things.* You've every right to be angry at me for I've behaved very badly. But I'd be most grateful if you gave me the chance to, um...rectify matters." I paused, not knowing how to end it then I decided on, "I hope to hear from you. Do take care."

I disconnected, put the phone back in my purse and again took up my glass. I sipped at my drink until I finished it, thinking I really wished I'd have the opportunity to talk to the redhead about her choice in hair color. If she was dead set on red, a deep auburn would suit her much better.

There was also a blonde who would benefit from a keratin treatment. Her hair was lovely but there was a good deal of it, it was quite long and it was clear she did her own blowout. This was not clear because it was done poorly, just that it wasn't as sleek as she was likely going for. With that amount of hair, it had to take her ages to do it. And the way she used it with her dancing, straightened and softened, it would make quite a splash and perhaps up her—from what I could tell protruding from her G-string—still rather plentiful tips.

She might drive a Corvette and it was clear she was far from the least talented dancer but everyone enjoyed having more money.

With a sigh, I put my finished glass to the bar, waited until I caught the bartender's eyes and gave him a grateful smile.

He returned it, tipping up his chin. I dug in my purse, got my wallet and slid a five-dollar bill under my glass then slid from my stool and made my way out of the club.

Once outside, the man by the door invited me to "have a good evening."

I returned the sentiment then promptly tripped over my pumps when I saw Jake Spear resting lean jeans-clad hips against my driver's side door, his black leather jacket covered arms crossed on the wide wall of his white shirt covered chest.

When I tripped, he looked to his feet and I lost his face in the shadows. Luckily, by that time, I'd righted myself without hitting the pavement but I did this mentally cursing my infernal clumsiness.

I moved to him with no further incident (thankfully) and stopped three feet away.

When he lifted his impassive eyes to me, I greeted, "Hello, Jake."

"She finally uses my name," he muttered in return.

I pressed my lips tight, uncertain what to make of this.

"Got your message, babe," he said.

Well, that didn't take long.

"Good," I replied quietly.

"Hauled your ass to a titty bar to see me," he noted.

"Uh…yes," I agreed to the obvious seeing as we were both standing outside said *titty bar.*

"Classed up the joint in there, Josie," he went on to remark and I blinked.

"You saw me?"

"Got cameras everywhere, inside and out," he stated, jerking his head toward the building.

"Of course. Yes. I noticed the ones outside. It's quite good you have an eye to the security and safety for your establishment."

His lips twitched before he returned, "Yeah, good for my *establishment* when drunk, horny assholes wanna do shit that makes them even bigger assholes, someone sees it, it stops before it starts."

I found his comment intriguing and thus observed, "You seem not to have a great deal of respect for your clientele."

"Most of them pay for their drinks, give the girls bills to pay for their show, got no problem with them. It's the drunk, horny assholes who suck."

I would imagine this was true.

"Of course," I murmured.

He said nothing, just held my eyes.

I found this uncomfortable and didn't know how to begin to say all the things I needed to say.

Therefore, unfortunately, I decided to stall.

"Well, Jake, I don't know if you have advisors that see to this kind of thing, I would guess you do as your club is quite refined, but I'd have a word with them, whoever they are. The redhead is very attractive but with her skin tone, a darker auburn would suit her far better. That said, she'd make a striking brunette."

He stopped holding my eyes and started staring at me. There was a nuance of difference but I could sense that difference. Most definitely.

"And," I sallied forth when he made no reply, "the blonde could use a keratin treatment. Her hair is remarkable but she'd find it much more manageable on a day to day basis and with her, well...*moves*, I believe she'd also find it quite beneficial with her...um, *work*."

He again said nothing, simply kept staring at me.

I, for some unhinged reason, kept chattering.

"It was well-chosen, the platform pumps for your waitresses. Platforms elongate the legs beautifully but they're also very comfortable. Further, they're attractive."

When I finished this inane statement, he burst out laughing, the deep richness of it ringing through the cool night air.

I decided again to press my lips together as this would stop me from speaking.

When he'd stopped laughing but was still smiling, he caught my eyes again and whispered, "Lydie was right. Adorable."

"Pardon?"

"Nothin', babe," he murmured but his voice was stronger when he said, "You got something to say?"

Well, here it was. I could delay no more and not only couldn't I, I shouldn't as I was making a fool of myself.

"This morning I behaved badly—"

"Yeah," he interrupted me, his voice gentle. "You mentioned that shit on the phone, Josie. Heard it. Got it. We can move on from that."

That was very kind.

I nodded while taking in a deep breath.

Then I said, "I'd like for you to come to Lavender House for dinner tomorrow night."

His head tipped to the side and he asked, "Yeah?"

"Yes, I think..." I hesitated then admitted, "Actually, I don't know what I think except for the fact that you're correct. Gran clearly very much wanted us to get to know each other and, well...we should do that."

"Yeah," he said again and it was gentle again. "We should."

Now was the hard part.

"I, well...I'm just uncertain *how* she wanted us to get to know each other and we should probably discuss that. But I...well, that is to say I believe—"

"Babe," he yet again interrupted and it was still gentle, but this time more so, "This is not that. You're pretty, really fuckin' pretty, and you got a lot goin' on and all of it's real good. But you're not my thing."

I was confused.

"Your thing?"

"My type," he explained. "I get off on big hair and big..." he hesitated, his lips again quirking before he continued, "other stuff and don't mind my women showin' skin. You're a seriously good thing. You're just not my thing."

I understood what he meant and three seconds ago, if I was told I'd be given this knowledge, I would have guessed that I would find it a relief.

Having it, I didn't feel relief. I felt a number of things but none of those things were relief. They were far from it. They included my brain again feeling fevered and my skin again prickling, all over, like jolts of electricity were dancing across the entirety of it. I wanted to claw at it, rip it off and this made all of it worse because I didn't know *why*.

To hide this reaction, I turned my head away and looked down at the pavement at my side.

When I did, I felt him move, felt his body come close to mine and heard his voice whisper, "Shit, babe." A pause then, "Fuckin' shit."

After he said that, I felt his big, warm hand curl at the side of my neck and I looked up at him.

When I did, he said softly, "I didn't think I'd be your thing either."

I told the truth. "You're not." After I did that, I lied (or it felt like I lied, but I actually didn't know what I was thinking), "I think you've mistaken my reaction to your pronouncement."

His lips yet again quirked and his fingers at my neck squeezed and he asked, "And what's your reaction to my pronouncement?"

"I don't understand what Gran wanted for you and me."

"Maybe she wanted us to be friends?" he inquired, but even doing it, it was an answer. "Maybe she wanted to know you got someone who cares, who'll look out for you, listen to you, take your back when you need it and give a shit not just when you need it but all the time?"

There it was.

The answer to my questions.

But I still didn't understand.

"Yes," I whispered. "She'd want that for me." My eyes strayed to his shoulder and I murmured, "But that makes no sense. She knows I have Henry."

"A boss is a boss," he declared, giving me a hint of what Gran had shared with him and that was that he knew precisely who Henry was. I looked back to him when he kept talking. "Always, Josie. He can give a shit but bottom line, it comes down to it, whatever that it might be or even if it never happens, he's just a boss."

I, of course, knew Henry was my employer. There were times when knowing this was all he'd ever really be was painful.

But after two decades and then some together, that had grown.

Hadn't it?

"Henry is—" I started.

"Not here," he interrupted me to say. "He gave a shit, Josie, no way in fuck, don't give a shit what excuses you might have for the guy, would he be anywhere but sittin' at your side while you cried behind your shades, starin' at your grandmother's casket."

Well, there was the answer to that.

He saw me crying at the funeral.

Jake wasn't done.

"And, he was here, no way you'd have dinner alone last night, open to some fuckwad to make a pass and upset you. That's the bottom line, babe. Think about it."

I stared into his eyes and thought about it.

Henry wanted to come, declared he was going to come, but I told him that he had to do the shoot. He was contracted. It was set up. And a location shoot for a magazine wasn't something you walked away from. A number of people were involved and quite a bit of money.

Further, Henry never did things like that. Even when he had the flu that one time when we were in Alaska, shooting a bathing suit spread in the snow, he'd zipped up his parka and done the shoot. He had a reputation for not only his immense talent but his dependability, his easy-going ways and his bent toward no muss, no fuss.

But Jake was correct. The bottom line was, when I told him not to come with me and do the job, he'd agreed.

"Josie," Jake called and I focused on him again. When I did, his fingers gave me another squeeze and he asked, "You have dinner tonight?"

"I'm not hungry."

"Honey, you gotta eat."

It took me a moment to respond. This was because four people in my life called me honey. My father, when he was in a good mood or he'd done something horrible and was trying to make amends. Gran. Henry.

And now Jake.

And Jake's, like Gran's and Henry's, felt nice.

I let myself feel that before I assured him, "I went to the grocery store today. I'll have some fruit and cheese when I get home."

"Right. And tomorrow night"—he grinned—"you promise you aren't gonna disappear, I'll show. But I gotta say, Ethan's gonna be with me. Not givin' Amber another hour to do fucked up shit with her moron of a boyfriend and not givin' her another wad of cake to blow on mascara."

This was not good news.

Not that he'd agreed to come. I was actually looking forward to that in a strange way I didn't quite comprehend.

No. Because I didn't like children. I found them loud and attention-seeking. They interrupted and, these days, parents didn't admonish them for this rudeness. They broke things. They spilled things. They whined. They refused to eat food they hadn't even tried, declaring erroneously they didn't like it when they could have no idea if they did or didn't.

And when they ate, they often did it with their mouths open, which was repulsive.

Obviously, I shared none of this with Jake Spear.

"Is there anything he, or you, don't like to eat?" I asked instead.

"Ethan helped Lydie cook a bunch a' shit in that kitchen. She taught him to dig his food however that comes. I already learned that so whatever you make, we'll eat."

I highly doubted that, at least about Ethan.

I didn't share that either.

"All right," I replied.

"We'll be there at six."

Six.

Very early.

Wonderful.

Well, I'd have to work with that seeing as his son probably had to be at school early the next day or do homework or take care of the class gerbil or something so they couldn't be out late.

"Fine," I agreed.

"Okay," he murmured, again grinning.

Then he said nothing.

I didn't either.

When this stretched for some time, and the fact that his warm hand was still wrapped around my neck became uncomfortable mostly because it didn't feel uncomfortable in the slightest, I broke our silence.

"Are we done?"

"Not by a long shot," he answered. I drew in a deep breath at his reply and he finished, "But we are for now."

"Well then…goodnight, Jake."

"Right," he muttered and I watched, my eyes widening in surprise as he leaned in and whispered against the skin of my forehead, "'Night, Josie."

I felt his lips brush there and that was also not uncomfortable. Not in the slightest. In fact, it felt so *not* uncomfortable as to make my skin again prickle but this time in a different way.

He pulled back, gave me a squeeze at the neck and a smile before he slid away.

I watched him move for a second before I forced myself to stop watching him move.

I did this by getting in my car, starting it up and not looking back as I drove away.

Five

GOOD NIGHT

The bell rang at six-oh-four the next evening and I moved quickly to the front door, feeling the strange anticipation I'd been experiencing all day heightening significantly to the point I was finding it difficult to breathe.

I stopped at the carved, polished wood door and my mind for some reason took flight.

And where it landed was that I decided I should polish the door, as I had many times at Gran's behest and as I'd seen her do many times as well.

I then turned my attention to my attire.

I'd gone for casual seeing as it was a home-cooked family dinner. Jeans that were expertly faded and again boot cut. Nude, patent leather platform pumps with peekaboo toes. And a blush colored cashmere sweater with a high neckline that was a slash from shoulder to shoulder. It had deep batwings but the wings ended just below my elbows and the knit was tight along my forearms.

Subtle makeup that was a hint dewy.

And my hair was pulled back in soft twists on either side that led to a plethora of slightly teased, full curls I'd arranged in a supremely feminine chignon at the back of my head.

The hairstyle was more suited to an evening gown but I liked its complex elegance juxtaposed with my casual garments, so I'd gone with it.

I realized I was thinking about my clothes while Jake and his son were standing outside waiting for me to open the door. Therefore, I stopped thinking about my clothes and opened the door.

When I did, I froze solid.

This was not because Jake Spear was standing there exuding his demanding masculinity wearing a dark blue turtleneck, faded jeans and brown boots (or, not only because of that).

This was also not because his young son was standing in front of him wearing a sweatshirt that declared his devotion to some sports team, his black hair was in disarray and he was staring up at me for some strange reason with his mouth wide open.

No, it was because, standing removed at her father's side, was Jake Spear's daughter wearing a surly expression, way too much makeup, having her hair teased out in a style that even Jake's exotic dancers eschewed and sporting a short knit skirt that I knew, when she moved, would ride up in ways that would be quite alarming.

She was not supposed to be there.

I could, maybe, handle one child. But a child and a surly teenaged girl who dressed like her heart's desire for a future profession was to dance at her father's club?

No.

"Yo, babe," Jake greeted and my eyes shot to him. "Woulda called but seein' as Amber was grounded about two minutes before we left the house, it wouldn't have helped anyway. So, as you can see, Amber's here. If you don't have enough food for her, I'll order a pizza or something."

I forced my lips to move in order to assure him, "I have enough food."

"Great," he replied.

I stood there.

They stood there too.

Then I realized I was standing there and that was rude so I turned my eyes to Amber.

"Hello, Amber. I'm Josephine. It's lovely to meet you."

She glared at me and muttered, "Whatever."

"Babe," Jake clipped at his daughter in a clear warning.

Her baleful eyes cut to him then back to me whereupon she mumbled, "'Lo."

I decided to leave it at that and looked down to the boy.

"Hello, Ethan."

He stared up at me for two seconds then bizarrely surged forward, threw himself bodily at me and wrapped his arms around my waist, pressing close.

I'd never had a child hug me. I'd never even had a child touch me. Therefore I didn't know what to do and thus stood there with my hands slightly raised, staring down at his dark head hoping I wasn't doing it in horror.

He didn't seem to mind that I didn't return his embrace. As quickly as he came forward, he released me, jumped back and looked up at me.

"Lydie talked about you all the time," he announced.

That felt lovely, *very* lovely, but even so, I wished I could say the same.

However, I didn't get to the chance to say anything because he kept speaking.

"You're way prettier than she said *and* all your pictures."

At least that was nice.

I decided a return compliment was in order so I gave him one.

"And you're quite handsome."

He grinned a grin I had to admit was rather adorable.

"Yeah. I know. Look like Dad and he's the hottest dude in town," he declared.

This was likely not in error.

"He is not," Amber put in at this point, shoving forward and doing it grabbing her brother and taking him with her as they pushed past me. "Mickey's way hotter than Dad. And Coert might be even hotter."

"Are not," Ethan returned as they moved into the house.

"Are so," she retorted. "And everyone knows Boston Stone is Magdalene's most eligible bachelor."

To that, I would disagree. Mr. Stone might be wealthy but money was not everything.

"Boston Stone may be loaded, Amber, but he's not all that. And anyway, his name is retarded," Ethan shot back.

I would use a less offensive adjective but it seemed Ethan and I were of like minds.

"Josie." I heard murmured from close.

I started and looked up just in time to see that Jake *was* close. *Very* close. Close enough to curve his fingers around my hip, lean in and brush his lips against my cheek.

Oh my.

Again, he smelled very nice, his scent assaulting my senses in a way that was far from unpleasant.

He pulled back and as he did so, I attempted to pull myself together. However, this was difficult seeing as, in the dim light of the foyer, his eyes had again changed color. They appeared now to be an inky blue.

With effort, I took my thoughts from his mercurial eye color and greeted, "Hello, Jake."

He grinned.

Then he used his hand on my hip to shove me gently in the house before he let me go to close the door.

When I just stood there staring up at him, he tipped his head toward the house as an indication we should enter it and I decided to stop making an idiot of myself and get moving.

This I did, hurrying down the hall toward the kitchen.

The instant I hit the room, Ethan turned his eyes to me and exclaimed, "It smells boss!"

"Jesus Christ, it does, Josie," Jake agreed, coming to a stop beside me. "Wasn't hungry, smell that smell, now I'm starved."

I had no idea why but their comments made me feel suddenly very warm.

"It smells like meat," Amber oddly declared and I looked to her.

"It smells like a lotta shit, Amber, but not meat," Jake replied.

She ignored her father, looked to me and announced. "I'm a vegetarian."

"Yeah, she decided that this morning," Jake noted at my side.

"Killing animals for human consumption is disgusting," she informed her father.

"Wonder what killing daughters for bein' pains in the ass is," Jake muttered in a voice that could likely only be heard by me and I found his remark so amusing I had to swallow down a laugh.

"Holy crap!" Ethan cried and my eyes shot to him to see he was now standing in the open refrigerator. He slowly turned, pointing inside the fridge, and asked with open wonder, "*What* is *that?*"

I looked into the refrigerator then back at Ethan. "It's a pavlova."

"It's a what?" he queried.

"A pavlova. Meringue, cream and strawberries. We're having it for dessert," I replied then turned my gaze to Amber. "In your vegetarianism, do you eat eggs?"

"Yes," Jake answered for his daughter.

"No," Amber answered for herself at the same time.

"This is unfortunate as meringues are made of egg whites," I shared with her.

"It doesn't matter anyway," she returned. "I don't eat dessert. My ass is already fat enough."

I looked down to her *ass* and saw she was very wrong.

I didn't address this mistaken impression of her body, although I had a strange and overwhelming desire to do so. This was partly because I didn't know what to say. It was mostly because Ethan had taken a blue beverage from the refrigerator that I'd noticed prior and wondered about (thus wondering no longer) and Amber had turned her attention to her brother.

"Get me one of those, runt," she demanded.

"You want one, don't call me a runt," he rejoined.

She gave him a face.

He returned it.

"Grab me a beer, will you, bud?" Jake called, moving deeper into the room.

I moved into it too, stating, "Dinner is almost ready. We'll be eating shortly as I didn't want to delay you should you need to get home early in order to take care of the class gerbil or do homework or something."

"Their homework's out in the truck, Josie," Jake told my back.

"And we got a hamster in class, not a gerbil. But I never get to watch him seein' as I killed the last one when it was my turn to take him home for the weekend," Ethan also shared this relatively dire information with my back.

I turned to him and the room to see father and son had drinks and Amber's head was in the fridge.

They seemed comfortable here and I knew they were because they'd been in that kitchen time and time again.

It was still strange.

And it was also strangely welcome.

"Dad said it was his time," Ethan shared. "Not because I dropped him on his head."

I blinked.

"He was squirrely. He didn't want me to hold him and he got his way," Ethan further explained.

I said nothing.

"Don't worry, honey, we bought the class another hamster," Jake assured me.

Before I could reply, Ethan dashed to me and asked, "Can I help with something?"

"Well, you could but most everything is done. I just have to mash the potatoes," I told him.

"I can *so* mash potatoes. Lydie taught me how," he declared.

She'd taught me how too. And knowing she taught him how made me feel even warmer.

I didn't share this.

"All right then." I moved to the stove. "Let's get these drained and get you started."

"Amber, babe, put another place setting on the table." I heard Jake order quietly as Ethan shadowed me carrying my pan of boiled potatoes from Aga to sink.

Thus commenced the final preparations for dinner where not only Ethan but everyone got in on the act.

I found in supervising him that Ethan was expert at mashing potatoes.

I also found that Amber knew where everything was and put another place setting on the kitchen table that I'd already prepared (I felt a family dinner should be consumed in the kitchen, not made formal in the dining room, so that was where we were to eat).

Even Jake helped and he did this by ordering Amber to assist with putting the peas, carrots and corn in bowls and working alongside her, putting the warmed rolls in a basket.

When I approached the table with the main dish, all was on it. Jake had even put my wineglass and the bottle of wine I'd opened earlier and began consuming while preparing dinner by my seat at the end.

"Shit, babe, you made *meatloaf?*"

My alarmed eyes cut to Jake to see him staring at the dish I was arrested in the endeavor of putting it on the table.

He was also smiling which was contradictory to his tone and thus confusing.

"Rosemary meatloaf with a tomato-based sauce," I told him.

"It...smells...*awesome!*" Ethan announced, his big eyes on the meatloaf.

"Rosemary meatloaf with a tomato-based sauce," Jake strangely repeated after me, his gaze moving from the dish to my face.

"Don't you like meatloaf?" I asked, finally setting the dish on a scrolled-iron hot plate.

"I do," he replied. "Though, a pretty woman who wears five hundred dollar shoes and two hundred dollar sweaters serving meatloaf is shocking as shit. I thought we'd have to force down coq au vin or something."

I decided not to inform him that my shoes were *six* hundred dollars and my sweater *four*. I also made a mental note, should they come over for dinner again, that I shouldn't make my coq au vin, which I thought was excellent and was one of my signature dishes, but clearly it would not be well-received.

Then again, I had no chance to inform him of anything as he continued speaking.

"Though, rosemary meatloaf in a tomato-based sauce is less of a surprise. Not sure I've ever had rosemary in meatloaf, but by the look and smell of it, I'm lookin' forward to it."

I tossed the oven mitts I was wearing to the butcher block and sat, murmuring, "Well, I hope it satisfies."

"I'm just glad there's lots of veggies and rolls," Amber mumbled into our exchange.

Jake sighed.

"Can we dig in?" Ethan asked.

"Please do," I invited.

Without delay, they did.

It was after bowls were passed around and plates were passed to me so I could cut and serve the meatloaf and everyone was eating, all of this done in silence (and rather swiftly), when I decided conversation was in order.

"And what's your eldest son doing this evening? Um…Conner," I asked Jake.

"Probably a threesome," Amber muttered.

Ethan chuckled.

I stared at her with wide eyes.

Jake bit out, "Amber."

She looked down to her plate.

Jake looked to me. "He's got a job in town, Josie. He works at Wayfarer's. He's on tonight."

"Ah," I murmured.

With nothing else to add to that, we all resumed eating.

After I buttered my roll (purchased, incidentally, at Wayfarer's Grocers, the only market in town—it had a variety of the usual sundries but mostly it was a gourmet market with a superb butcher's counter, fresh organic vegetables, an extraordinary seafood selection, a large plethora of cheeses, and a fabulous bakery that made excellent breads, rolls and also pastries), I asked, "And how old is everybody?"

"I'm eight," Ethan shared immediately, mouth full.

Amber said nothing so Jake told me, "Amber's sixteen. Conner is seventeen, nearly eighteen. She's a junior, he's a senior."

"Ah," I repeated my murmur, surprised at Conner's age. He'd appeared older.

We again lapsed into silence as we continued to consume the meal.

"This is really good, babe," Jake eventually said.

I looked to him and smiled, again feeling warm inside. "Thank you."

He winked at me and turned his attention back at his plate.

But when he winked at me, my stomach did something strange. It felt like it dropped and when it did, tingles shot across my skin, and neither were disagreeable sensations.

They were, however, confusing ones. But it wasn't the time to process them so I looked to Amber to see her eyeing the meatloaf.

I felt my lips curl up slightly.

She was no vegetarian and although she loaded her plate with veggies and potatoes, I knew she wanted to try the meatloaf that her father and brother were gratifyingly devouring.

I didn't bring attention to this. I picked up the basket with the rolls and offered it to her.

"Would you like another?"

She looked to me then back to her plate. "I'm good."

I studied her as I put down the basket.

She was very becoming and thus I wasn't surprised she had a boyfriend. She probably could have several if she chose.

And more if she didn't look like a teenaged lady of the evening.

Studying her, I made a decision and put it into action.

"Amber," I called and she looked at me. "I don't know if my grand-mother told you, but I work in fashion."

"Yeah, she said," she muttered, looking back to her almost empty plate. It seemed that was mostly all she could do: mutter, mumble and murmur.

She also had a lovely voice so this was unfortunate.

Now was not the time to get into that, however.

Priorities.

"Then, I hope you don't mind that I share, you're exceptionally pretty."

Her eyes darted back to me and they held some surprise.

And this surprised me. Surely, she'd looked in the mirror.

Then again, the way she applied cosmetics, perhaps not.

I kept speaking.

"However, you've a heavy hand with cosmetics. Your eyeliner is quite thick and eyebrow pencils are meant to fill in what's already there, not draw something new."

The air in the room changed as Amber's face changed. It went slack then started twisting.

Nevertheless, no mention had been made of these children's mother, Jake was clearly no longer with any of his wives and someone had to tell her.

It was imperative.

So I kept talking.

"Jean-Michel DuChamp taught me how to do makeup," I declared, her face stopped twisting, her eyes got huge and her lips parted. "If you'd like,

I'd be happy to show you some of the things he showed me. You've clearly got an eye to what shades suit you best, you simply use too much of them."

"You know Jean-Michel DuChamp?" she breathed.

"Of course," I replied.

She blinked rapidly for a long moment before she told me, "I've got both his books. The one where he did all those supermodels up in crazy ways, like making that chick look like a baby doll and doing Acadie up in that badass futuristic look. I also have the other one where he did awesome stuff with all those Hollywood movie stars."

I knew the model Acadie. She was very beautiful as well as very sweet. I also knew of those books mostly because Henry had worked on one.

"Henry shot that one with the models," I told her.

"Ohmigod," she whispered. "How didn't I know that? Lydie told us you worked for Henry Gagnon. I should have known that."

I shrugged. "I've no idea how you didn't know, though that book was about Jean-Michel's vision, not Henry's photos. He's often like that. Sometimes, it's about the pictures. Sometimes it's about what's *in* the pictures. And when it's the latter, he doesn't like overshadowing that. He was credited in the book, of course, but with that book, he wished for it to be about Jean-Michel so, if memory of his contract serves, his credit was unobtrusive."

"Cool." She was still whispering.

I threw out a hand and offered, "If you like, I can take a photo of you. I'll send it to Jean-Michel and ask him to share some pointers. He does this for me often. I'll take a picture of an outfit I'm wearing and tell him where I'm wearing it and he'll email me rather detailed instructions on how to make up my face. I'm sure he'd be happy to do something of that ilk for you."

Her eyes were now very large and very bright and she was still whispering when she said, "Are you freaking *serious?*"

"Of course," I replied.

"Ohmigod, oh my *freaking* God," she breathed and then looked to her father. "Dad, you *so* have to lift the ban on my cell. I *have to* tell Taylor and Taylor about this!"

Jake opened his mouth but I was able to ask before he said anything, "Taylor and Taylor?"

"Her best friends," Ethan answered. "Taylor is a girl. The other Taylor is a boy and he's gay."

"He wants to be a makeup artist just like Jean-Michel," Amber shared. "And Taylor wants to be a model."

"You can tell them at school tomorrow," Jake put in at this point and Amber's eyes shot back to her father.

"Dad! Please! Seriously, we're talking *Jean-Michel DuChamp!*" she cried. "They *have* to know, like *now.*"

"Babe, you'd cut the shit you been pullin', they'd know, like *now*. But you didn't cut the shit you been pullin' so they're gonna know, like *tomorrow,*" Jake stated and finished on a, "Yeah?"

"That's totally unfair and totally crazy," she returned. "It's like…like… Jimmy Choo strolled in and offered to fit me with shoes and you won't let me tell my friends about a dream come true."

Surprisingly, it appeared I shared some things in common with Amber as well.

"Tomorrow, Amber," Jake declared.

"God!" Amber snapped and slouched back in her chair.

"This is, alas, a rather difficult lesson," I noted and felt all eyes come to me but I was looking at Amber. "I don't know what…*shit* you've been pulling but it clearly upsets your father. You can, of course, choose to act dramatically and feel misunderstood. But in truth, the easiest route to getting what you want is behaving as your father wishes. Then, your freedoms would be granted and you'd not feel like you're feeling right now. And thus, you would be able to share this with your friends."

"Right. Do what he wishes when Dad's totally unreasonable," she hissed.

"And how is that?" I asked.

"He doesn't like Noah," she answered.

"And who is Noah?" I queried.

"My boyfriend and he's totally righteous," she replied.

"I'm uncertain I understand," I admitted. "Your father is being unreasonable because he does not share your opinion that this Noah is"—I paused—"*righteous?*"

"No," she said. "He's being unreasonable because Noah wants to take me to a concert in Boston and Dad refuses to let me go when *everyone's* going.

It's just one state over, it's not like it's in Miami or anything. And I guess Dad didn't like it all that much when I told him *exactly* how I felt about him being *totally* unreasonable."

"She used the f-word," Ethan shared. "Like, a *bazillion* times."

Good God.

The f-word?

It was clear someone needed to take this girl in hand and having her at my grandmother's table with my grandmother not there to do it, I decided it would be me.

"First," I began, "A lady shouldn't curse. It's crass. There are times when foul words have their uses but they are rare. Second, the idea of a sixteen year old girl going to another state with her boyfriend to see a concert is utterly preposterous."

She stared at me, again blinking rapidly, and I heard a grunt come from Jake but I was not done.

"Amber, I'm certain I don't need to point out your father is a man—" I began but she lost her astonishment and interrupted me.

"No, you don't need to point that out," she snapped.

"As I was saying," I went on unperturbed when she'd stopped snapping. "Your father is a man which means he was once a young man much like your Noah. You're an exceptionally pretty young woman. I'm certain this fact is also not lost on your father. It would be my guess that your father knows much more about young men, seeing as he used to be one, than you do. So, if he dislikes this Noah, if you look at it from this perspective, he probably knows what he's talking about."

I heard another grunt, this one swallowed and amused from Jake. I also heard a not-swallowed giggle from Ethan but I kept going even as Amber glared at me.

"Regardless, Noah could be a paragon of virtue but if your father loves you, it's his duty as a father not to like him. If he didn't care you were spending time with a boy, *that's* when you should be upset. The fact that he cares about anything, Amber, says a great deal and you should take a moment and hear him because he does."

When I was finished speaking, Amber was no longer glaring, there was no humor coming from the two male Spears and the air in the room felt heavy.

I knew why.

It was because they knew about me. About Gran. About my grandfather and my father. And about how my father didn't care about me.

Not in any way.

No way at all.

My mind was torn from this alarming understanding when Amber spoke and she did it quietly.

"That's what Lydie would say. She wouldn't say it like that, using words like 'paragon of virtue,' but that's probably what she'd say."

"As my grandmother was the wisest person I know," I replied, "then perhaps you should listen. Now, do you want some meatloaf?" I asked and finished, "Or, is Noah a vegetarian and you fear you'll appear unattractive in some way if you are not as he is?"

"I heard it's a good way to lose weight," she shared.

"Well, it isn't," I returned. "It's a practice that people who do it have a belief in. Although that does not factor, if your belief is to do it just to lose weight considering there's no need for you to concern yourself with losing weight. You have a fabulous figure. I can't imagine why you'd try to change it."

"That's what I said," Ethan piped in.

"You're *eight* and my *brother*," Amber returned, eyes narrowed on her brother.

"Well, I'm not eight or your brother and I've worked in haute couture for twenty-three years," I reminded her and her gaze came to me. "And trust me, you have a fabulous figure. You've made two mentions of losing weight and you've barely been here an hour. Cease doing that. It's ridiculous. And if someone tells you differently, simply inform them of that ridiculousness."

She again blinked at me.

Ethan burst out laughing.

"Now," I spoke through his laughter, "after dinner, are we taking your photo for Jean-Michel or are we not?"

"Totally," she whispered, not in wonder this time. I didn't know what made her whisper and it mattered not to me.

"Excellent. You'll need to wash your face," I instructed. "He'll need a clean palette."

"I can do that," she agreed.

"Fine," I returned and then looked to the table and asked, "Is anyone wishing seconds?"

"Meatloaf!" Ethan said, doing this for some reason over-loudly.

And I found that coming from Ethan, who was a very amusing and sweet boy, it was not annoying in the slightest.

"Give me your plate," I ordered.

He handed me his plate.

I gave him meatloaf.

Then I returned my attention to my plate but after partaking of some carrots, I felt something unusual so I lifted my eyes.

And my stomach dipped in that way again when I saw Jake watching me. His face was soft and his eyes, now gray in the lights of the kitchen, held something in them I couldn't decipher.

Before I could put my finger on it, his mouth slowly, lazily lifted in a devastating smile that did devastating things to my breathing pattern before he turned to his daughter and said, "Pass the rolls, babe."

I found that I really wished to know what was behind that look. What he was thinking and maybe more, what he was feeling.

And I found that it caused an inexplicable pain that I would never know because I would never ask and it was likely he'd never tell me.

In order to get past the pain, I decided to finish eating so I could serve dessert because the meatloaf (a recipe I looked up on the Internet seeing as I'd never made a meal for a family that included young children so I'd branched out) was quite good.

But my pavlovas were *divine*.

IT WAS AFTER meatloaf and after pavlova.

The children were at the kitchen table doing homework and I was doing the dishes with Jake.

I found it intriguing that Jake did dishes. I also found it felt nice doing dishes with Jake. Then again, when I'd cook for Henry, he also helped me do the dishes and I liked that too.

"Meal was superb, babe. That thing at the end, fuckin' hell," Jake murmured while drying a plate.

"I'm pleased you enjoyed it," I replied, feeling exactly as I told him, pleased (*very*) and I handed him another wet plate when he set the one he'd finished on the stack he was making.

"Told Lydie, will tell you, need a dishwasher," he declared.

"Gran always said she had two. Her hands."

"Yeah, that's what she always said," he replied quietly, his deep voice amused but I could hear the melancholy.

I decided not to reply because his tone made me feel the same, *sans* the amused part.

"You have an okay day?" he asked.

I had not.

"No," I answered.

"No?" he asked on a prompt and I handed him another plate as I looked at him.

"I visited Eliza Weaver this morning."

"Who?"

"Eliza Weaver, Arnold Weaver's wife."

"The attorney?"

I nodded and his brows drew together.

"Somethin' wrong with the will?"

I shook my head and turned my attention to the silverware at the bottom of the sink. "The Weavers are family friends. Eliza's ill." I paused, thinking of her in the hospital bed Mr. Weaver had set up in their dining room, and finished. "Gravely ill."

"Jesus, babe, sorry," he whispered.

"I…" I looked at him and handed him some rinsed forks. "It was unpleasant seeing her that way. She used to be quite vivacious." I looked back down to the sink and searched for more cutlery. "And Mr. Weaver adores her. He always has. He's quite obvious about it, which I always thought was charming. He's suffering."

"Sucks, Josie," Jake murmured.

"Yes," I agreed and handed him more clean silverware without looking at him. "I spoke with Mr. Weaver. He's taken a leave of absence from work but he's a partner and this is difficult too. I talked him into allowing me to come over in the mornings for a few hours while I'm in Magdalene. He says Mrs. Weaver is tired of most of her company being nurses and her friends have to work during the day, and while I'm here, I don't. So I'm going to go sit with her while he spends a few hours in the office."

Jake said nothing.

Jake also didn't take the dripping silverware I was offering him so I looked up to my side to find him staring down at me, unmoving.

"Is something the matter?" I asked.

He gave his head a slight shake and took the silverware, saying, "Nice thing for you to do, honey."

I shrugged and turned my attention back to the sudsy water. "They liked Gran."

"They also obviously like you."

They did and I liked that. I just didn't like it that they were suffering this way.

I didn't reply.

"So, how long you gonna be in Magdalene?" he asked.

"I don't know," I answered.

And I didn't.

I had not called one auction house. I had not called a real estate agent. I had not started sorting through Gran's things.

What I'd done that day, after deciding the menu, going into town, getting the food and visiting the Weavers was tug on my least nice top and Gran's wellies and go work in her garden to prepare it to be at rest for the winter. I didn't know who planted it, as Gran couldn't actually work out there anymore, and there was far less in it than when she tended it in earnest, but it had been worked that summer.

I'd also made a note that I needed to go to the mall in order to acquire clothing that would be more suitable to tasks such as these.

And then I'd been troubled that I made that mental note because making it made no sense.

I wasn't going to be gardening in my future.

So why would I buy clothes to do such a thing?

"How are you leaning?" Jake asked as I unplugged the sink in order to set the pans to soaking.

"I need to be in Rome," I told him.

"When?"

When indeed?

Henry had flown there today so tomorrow would be the best-case scenario.

However, that was impossible.

And strangely, the idea of packing and boarding yet another plane, spending hours imprisoned on it, getting out and heading to yet another hotel, even if that hotel was in the fabulousness of all that was Rome, wasn't all that appealing.

"I need to be in Paris," I went on, speaking to myself and not realizing I wasn't making any sense.

"What?" Jake asked.

"Or, I'm thinking, I should join Henry in Sydney."

The job in Sydney wasn't for a month.

But I wasn't thinking about Sydney, even though I *adored* Sydney.

No, I was thinking more that I should join him when he was back in LA for a break.

And that break was three months away.

"Josie…*what?*"

I turned fully to him and looked up into his eyes.

"Boston Stone came here yesterday," I announced.

His presence did that swelling and heating thing again even as his eyes narrowed and he whispered in a peculiar (but somewhat alarming) sinister tone, "He did what?"

"He wishes to purchase Lavender House," I shared.

"Yeah." I heard Ethan call from the table. "He wishes it but Lydie told him to go jump in the Atlantic."

"She didn't say that," Amber contradicted with big sister superiority. "She told him over her dead body."

I felt my stomach twist as the air again went heavy and Ethan's eyes sliced to his sister.

"Jeez, Amber, be more stupid, why don't you?" he snapped, but his voice held a small tremble.

He didn't need to tell her she was stupid. She was looking at me and her face was pale.

"I'm sorry, Josie," she said softly.

Wonderful.

Now the children were calling me Josie.

"It's quite all right," I said stiffly and turned back to the pots and pans.

I turned on the tap to fill the potato pan with hot water but Jake's hand came out right after mine and turned it off.

I looked up at him again.

"What did you say to Stone?" he asked.

"I told him I wasn't prepared to discuss it with him, seeing as he showed up unannounced five days after I lost my grandmother."

"And are you gonna get prepared to discuss it with him?" he asked and I shook my head.

"No."

I said it and I was surprised when I did because I hadn't made that decision until right then.

Even so, I meant it.

"So you're keeping the house?" Jake asked.

"Heck yeah," Ethan answered for me and I looked over my shoulder at him. "Lydie said the only person who loves Lavender House more than her is Josie and she'd never let it out of the family."

At his words, I put a wet hand to the edge of the sink and drew in breath, my mind blanking.

"Babe?" I heard Jake call but I said nothing. Then I felt a hand warm on the side of my neck and saw Jake's chest in my vision as I heard, "Josie? You okay?"

I tipped my eyes up to him.

"The only person who loves Lavender House more than Gran is me and I'd never let it out of the family," I whispered. "So yes, to answer your question, I'm keeping the house."

This was, again, a decision I made right then.

And it was another decision I meant to keep.

I just had no idea how.

Or why.

Lavender House did not fit my life. I couldn't leave a huge house unattended while I traveled the globe.

I also couldn't let it go.

Not ever.

Not ever.

Once I died, it would understandably go "out of the family" seeing as I had no children and at my age, never would.

But it would remain in the family until that happened.

"Cool!" Ethan cried and I started, focusing again on Jake who was staring down at me intently, his hand still on my neck. "Totally knew it," Ethan went on. "This means we get to keep comin' over but now Josie'll cook for us."

"Yeah," Amber replied with less enthusiasm, then again, it would be difficult to have more than Ethan.

"Babe," Jake called and since I was already looking at him, I nodded to indicate I was focused on him. "You okay?" he asked quietly.

"No," I for some reason shared.

He studied me.

Then he said, very quietly this time, "We'll talk. Tomorrow. Without the kids."

Again, for reasons unknown to me, I nodded my agreement.

His hand gave me a squeeze. "Go pour yourself more wine and relax. I'll finish the pans."

"I can finish the pans."

"Babe." Another squeeze, this one deeper as his face dipped close and his voice dipped low and serious. "What did I say?"

I found this surprising. It was inappropriately overbearing and dictatorial.

It was more surprising when I found myself nodding, slipping out from in front of him and doing what he inappropriately dictatorially told me to do.

This meant I spent the next fifteen minutes before we all retired to the family room to watch TV sipping wine at the kitchen table. But only after I went to go get my phone so I could check Ethan's answers to his multiplication homework (I was hopeless at math) on the calculator.

He got one wrong out of thirty.

Which meant he was also bright as well as amusing and quite sweet.

And I felt this to be the utter truth even when I asked him to do the incorrect problem again and he counted it out on his fingers with his lips moving.

And I felt this because, I decided, that was adorable too.

IT WAS THE end of the evening. We were standing outside close to Jake's truck and I was addressing Amber.

"I'll inform your father when Jean-Michel gets back to me," I told her as she'd cleaned her face with my face wash and I'd taken her photo. Though I wouldn't text it to Jean-Michel until the next day as it was late, he was in New York and that would be rude.

"Right," she mumbled.

"It was lovely meeting you," I went on.

"Same," she muttered, lifted a hand in an awkward wave and moved to the truck.

She barely started her short journey before Ethan darted forward and gave my waist another hug.

This time, I dropped a hand to his shoulder and gave it a squeeze before he pulled away.

"Super cool to meet you and the food was fah-ree-king *awesome!*" he declared.

"I'm glad you thought so and it was lovely to meet you as well," I replied.

He gave me a big smile, a wide wave and hastened to the truck.

Jake filled his place and when he did, he declared, "It was a good night."

It actually was and it appeared it was so for all of us.

I nodded.

"Tomorrow, nine o'clock. Meet me at The Shack."

I stared at him, aghast.

I was aghast because The Shack was, well…a *shack*. It was on the wharf and although I'd heard of it and knew Gran had been there on occasion, I'd also seen it and it was, well…*ghastly*.

"The Shack?" I asked and he smiled.

"The Shack, slick," he stated strangely for I couldn't comprehend why he added the world "slick." "Nine," he finished.

"I, uh…perhaps I can make you breakfast," I suggested.

"You could, but if you did then I wouldn't get to introduce you to their seafood omelets that are so good they'll knock you on your ass. And I want you focused on tellin' me all the shit that's goin' on behind those pretty blues and not on cookin' breakfast."

Pretty blues?

Was he referring to my eyes?

Just the thought made my stomach again pitch.

"So nine. The Shack," he ordered.

I sighed before I agreed, "All right."

He gave me another smile, leaned in and gave me another brush of his lips on my cheek and then he moved back nary an inch before he whispered, "Thanks for a good night."

"You're most welcome."

Even in Lavender House's dim outside lights, I could see his eyes light with amusement before he shook his head and moved away, saying, "Later, babe."

"Uh…erm…later," I called.

I watched him swing up into his truck.

I waved back when Ethan waved at me from the backseat.

I only moved to the house when the truck started growling along the drive.

Once inside, the door closed and locked behind me, it wasn't until I hit the kitchen to turn off the lights that I felt it.

The house felt strange.

As in, strangely empty.

It had never felt that way. It always felt the opposite, even with only Gran and me.

Vibrant.

Alive.

Now it felt quiet.

Lonely.

"Or maybe that's just how you feel, buttercup."

The words were said by me and not only the fact that I'd utter them, but the words I uttered were so startling, and troubling, I instantly shoved them out of my head and moved to the light switch.

But I reversed directions and instead of turning out the lights, I went to the stoppered bottle of wine and poured myself the last of it.

Carrying it with me, only then did I turn out the lights.

And I headed to the light room.

Six

FIERCE

The house mostly dark and totally quiet, a bottle of beer in one hand, Jake reached his other hand into the drawer he'd unlocked in his desk.

He pulled out the tall stack of envelopes tied in a blue satin ribbon the color of Josie's eyes.

He drew in breath, set the stack on the desk and tugged on the end of the ribbon until it slid apart. Then he ran the tip of his index finger down the stack until he found it.

His favorite one even if it was the saddest.

The envelope was pink.

Setting the beer aside, he turned the stack on top of the pink envelope over and nabbed it.

Then he shifted up the stack and slid out the blue one.

He grabbed his beer and moved to his chair at the window. The standing lamp was already on so he sat in the chair, put the beer on the table beside him and pulled out the often handled letters, carefully opening them.

He grabbed his beer again, sat back and lifted the letters, the blue one on top, his eyes moving over the small, tidy, yet somehow delicate and definitely feminine writing.

Dearest Gran,

We just got off the phone and I'm concerned about you. I know that sounds strange since our phone call was about how you were concerned about me.

Please don't be. Please?

I'm happy, Gran. I truly am. Honestly.

When we were talking earlier, I wanted to say this but I didn't know how to say it. Perhaps I couldn't get my mouth to say the words because I didn't want to admit it out loud or say it to you and upset you more.

But you should know—I'm fine with being alone. I want it to be that way. Honestly, I do.

You know I'm not alone most of the time regardless. But I do think you know what I mean.

My first memory is him and her in the kitchen, she was on the floor, you know how it was. I told you. And there were more memories after that that were even less pleasant. You know of those too.

And yes, the truth is, this affected me. Yes, it made me shy away from connections. And I know you don't think this is healthy, but truly, it's fine.

There are people who need people, sometimes a great many people. And I understand that what happened made me not that kind of person. But it means the connections I make are actually meaningful, not a collection of souls in order not to feel lonely. I don't need that for I never feel lonely.

If I were to have a man, he would need to be very gentle and understanding, patient and kind, thoughtful, softhearted, and yes, maybe dashing and refined, definitely intelligent and successful.

All of these things and the last mostly because I would wish him to have his own diversions for I wouldn't wish him to need to spend too much time with me. This is because I like being alone. I like my own company.

This isn't to say I didn't sometimes long for a gentle touch, a man's eyes falling on me appreciatively, building a shared history where we might one day simply gaze at each other, understand and smile.

But I long ago gave up these yearnings. I meet many men and this man, this man that I would need to share my life with, he doesn't exist, Gran. I've come to understand that and it's settled in me. I've built a life I enjoy, one that keeps me busy, and I'm happy with that.

Truly.

I find it remarkable, after all that you endured, that you'd still believe in love. In romance. In all that heady possibility. And I adore it that you want that for me.

What I wish you to understand in your heart is that, although it feels lovely you wish for me to have all kinds of beauty, I'm perfectly happy without it.

I have your love and that's all I need.

And you have my love too.

Forever and completely.

Yours,

Josie

Jake took a sip from his beer, set it aside and brought the pink paper to the front.

He tagged his beer and tipped his eyes down to the untidy, scrolled girlish letters.

Granny!

Oh my goodness! You would not believe!

Alicia heard it from Tiffany so she told me and I didn't believe her and then he came up to me at lunch!

Andy Collins!

It was amazing. He sat and talked with me all during lunch. And he said he'd see me there tomorrow!

Now, you know, I'm not going to settle for anything but <u>the best</u>. My man is going to be strong and tall and handsome and smart and protective and <u>fierce</u>, so very <u>FIERCE</u>, and <u>wonderful</u> and he's going to <u>adore</u> me. Then he's going to let him talk him into moving to Maine and living at Lavender House and having three babies (two girls, one boy, the boy the oldest, of course, so he can look after his sisters) and I'm going to garden and tend the lavender and cook at the Aga and he's going to be, I don't know, a fisherman or whatever.

I'm not sure Andy's up to all that, although he's strong and tall (he's on the football team!) and <u>very</u> cute.

I wish I could show you his picture.

Of course, Dad says I can't date until I'm seventeen which is <u>bizarre</u> and <u>mean</u> because most of my friends started dating at fifteen (just not car dates) and

95

I'm already sixteen (and have my own driver's license, for goodness sakes!) and I've already had to say no to two boys! It was a disaster! I hated it! And everyone thinks I'm a big priss, which is terrible!

But neither of them were Andy, the cutest boy in school!

I'll write again tomorrow and let you know if he sits with me at lunch.

I wish you were talking to Dad. Maybe you could talk him into not only letting me come to Lavender House this summer but also allowing me to go out on a date with Andy (if he asks and just in case you didn't get it, I hope he asks!!!!!!!!!).

OK. Well, I should go. I have homework to do (Algebra. Blech. Mr. Powell is such a bore!). I just wanted you to know that. Now, I have to go steal a couple of stamps from Dad's desk. One for this and one for the letter I hope to write you tomorrow that tells you Andy sat with me again.

I love you. I hope you're doing good. I miss you.

Start to talk to Dad again. Please? I missed Lavender House last summer.

But mostly, I missed you.

All my love, forever and completely,

Josie

Jake set the letters aside and looked out the window at the sea knowing that Andy sat with her again the next day.

And he knew Andy did more.

He beat her, lamb.

He closed his eyes as Lydie's words hit his brain but that didn't stop them from coming.

She wanted to go out with that boy so badly, she snuck out. She did it for over a year. When she got home one night, he'd found out and he beat her, lamb. Her father beat her so badly, she was in the hospital for a week.

Jake opened his eyes and took another drag from the bottle.

He beat her, lamb.

He drew in breath.

Beat her so badly, she was in the hospital for a week.

He stared out the window, not seeing anything.

My man is going to be strong and tall and handsome and smart and protective and fierce, so very FIERCE, and wonderful and he's going to adore me.

That he could do.

He would need to be very gentle and understanding, patient and kind, thoughtful, softhearted, and yes, maybe dashing and refined, definitely intelligent and successful.

That he couldn't.

Jake took another pull from his beer.

He beat her, lamb.

He felt his jaw get tight even as his fingers gripped the beer hard to stop himself from throwing it. If he did, he'd have to clean that shit up and it might wake the kids.

Instead, he put the letters back in their envelopes, got up and took his beer with him as he moved back to the desk. He put Josie's letters that Lydie had given him back together and tied them with the ribbon.

Then he opened the drawer and was about to toss the pile in when he saw it at the bottom.

He set the letters on top of the desk, reached into the drawer and pulled out the frame.

It was of Josie.

She was on a beach. Her skin was tan. The breeze blowing so much at her long blonde hair, she had her hand lifted in it, pulling it away and holding it at her crown, but tendrils were captured by the lens arrested in flying around her face. Her other hand was resting on her hip. She was standing, smiling into the distance, a scarf blowing back from her neck, sunglasses on her eyes, her sundress plastered against her tall, slim but curvy body.

That shit for brains photographer boss of hers took that picture, gave it to Lydie and Lydie had given it to Jake.

It looked like a shot from the '50's of some Italian bombshell. Italian because Josie looked sophisticated. Exotic. Glamorous. Classy. So much of all those, she couldn't be American but something foreign, unknown, unobtainable.

Impossible.

So I'm going to go sit with her while he spends a few hours in the office.

Jake didn't take his eyes from the picture even as he belted back more beer.

And trust me, you have a fabulous figure. You've made two mentions of losing weight and you've barely been here an hour. Cease doing that. It's ridiculous. And if someone tells you differently, simply inform them of that ridiculousness.

He smiled at the picture.

He beat her, lamb.

His smile died.

Fuck, that shit for brains photographer boss of hers had all that for fucking years.

Years.

And she still sat beside her grandmother's casket alone.

So yes, to answer your question, I'm keeping the house.

She was keeping the house.

That meant they might get to keep her.

Jake just needed to see to making that happen.

He put the picture back in the drawer and returned the letters there. He closed it. He locked it. He slugged back the last of his beer, turned out the lights, went to his bedroom, undressed and hit the sack.

It was late and he needed some sleep.

Because tomorrow morning, for breakfast, he was meeting Josie.

Seven

WINDED

My high-heeled boots thudded on the boardwalk as the heavy breeze blew my Alexander McQueen scarf behind me.

I spied Jake at the window to The Shack through my sunglasses that I was wearing even though the day was cold, gray and threatening rain.

I was lamenting my choice of the McQueen scarf. It was cream with hot pink skulls on it (one that was of his signature design) but it wasn't exactly warm.

Still, it was fabulous and fabulous required sacrifice. I knew that from years of practicing fabulous.

Or trying to.

As if he sensed my approach, Jake turned, his non-sunglassed eyes did an obvious head to toe and his unfortunately attractive lips spread into a wide smile that exposed equally unfortunately attractive teeth.

He moved my way as I got close and I heard him call to the window, "Just yell when they're done, Tom."

"You got it!" was called back by the invisible Tom.

I stopped where Jake stopped, at the end of The Shack where there was a tall table with a variety of things on it.

"Good morning, Jake," I greeted.

"Mornin', Slick," he greeted back, still smiling big.

But I blinked.

Slick.

I finally understood his use of the word "slick."

Good God.

He'd given me a nickname.

And it was Slick!

I opened my mouth to protest this but he stuck a hand toward me and I saw he had two white paper cups.

"Coffee," he pointed out the obvious.

Forced by politeness to express gratitude rather than express aversion to my nickname, I took it and said, "Thank you."

"Shit's here to put in it," he motioned to the table. He then put his coffee on it and pulled off the white lid.

I eyed my selections and noted with no small amount of horror that they had powered creamer and no sweetener.

"Thought Fellini was dead," Jake noted bizarrely, pouring a long stream of sugar from a silver-topped glass container into his coffee.

"I beg your pardon?" I asked.

He kept pouring for a bit then put the sugar down and turned to me. "Babe, you look like you're walkin' on the set of a Fellini movie."

I blinked at him again before I asked, "You've seen a Fellini film?"

And he smiled big again. "No, but that doesn't mean you don't look like a broad from one of those old art house movies where the babes are all sex kitten bombshells dressed real good, wearing sunglasses with scarves flyin' all over the place."

I stared at him thinking this might be a compliment.

A very nice one.

Or, a very nice one Jake Spear style.

"Scarves, I'll add, that don't do shit when it's fifty degrees but the wind chill makes it feel like forty," he went on.

I kept staring at him.

"Josie? You awake?" he asked when this went on for some time.

"You use too much sugar in your coffee," I blurted.

"Yeah," he said, going back to his coffee that he was now stirring. "You're not the first woman to tell me that."

I found that interesting.

He looked at me, down to the table then at me again and asked, "You gonna set up your coffee?"

I hid my distaste as I looked at what was on offer to "set up my coffee" then I looked back at him and shook my head.

I usually took a splash of skim milk and a sweetener.

That morning, I'd drink it black.

"Right, let's sit down," Jake said and tossed his stirrer in the (filthy and encrusted with a variety of things, not all of them coffee) little white bin provided on the table.

He then started moving to the mélange of unappealing white plastic chairs with their equally unappealing white steel (liberally dusted with rust) tables that likely saw cleaning only through the salty air and sea breeze.

"Sit down?" I asked Jake's back, following him. "Outside?"

He selected a table (there was a wide selection seeing as no one was there) and turned to me. "You got a problem with outside?"

"Not normally. Al fresco dining is usually quite lovely. But not when the wind chill factor is forty."

"Al fresco dining," he repeated.

"Dining outside," I explained and this got another smile.

"Know what it is, Slick," he stated. I opened my mouth to share how I felt about this nickname but he returned to his earlier subject before I could say a word. "You need a decent scarf."

"This *is* a decent scarf," I retorted. "It's Alexander McQueen."

"Maybe so but I'm not sure Alexander whoever's been to Maine."

I wasn't either. Alas, he nor his genius was with us any longer so if he hadn't, that would now be impossible.

This conversation was ridiculous and he wasn't moving so I decided to seat myself. As I did, I longed for some antiseptic wipes (about a hundred of them, for the chair *and* the table). Since I didn't have any, I settled in a chair and sipped the coffee.

After I did that, I stared at the cup mostly because I was surprised that it was robust and flavorful.

"Tom doesn't fuck around with coffee," Jake murmured and I turned my eyes to him.

"It appears this is so."

He smiled at me again.

I gingerly set my coffee on the table and equally gingerly shrugged my handbag off my shoulder to join it.

"Your mornin' been good?" he asked quietly.

I picked up my coffee and looked at him. "Thus far."

"When do you go to your friends' place?"

"After this," I said before taking a sip.

His head cocked slightly to the side. "You sure you're up for that? That's a lot, what with all you're already dealin' with."

He was right.

Even so.

"Mr. Weaver needs a break."

"He may need one, Josie, but I think he'd get it if you weren't up to giving it to him."

"I offered," I pointed out. "I can't renege now."

He said nothing but watched me even as he took a sip from his coffee.

When our silence lasted for some time, I shared, "I like your children."

"Yeah, they liked you too."

I felt my brows rise for I found this surprising.

Ethan liked me, I knew. I couldn't miss that, what with the hugs and the like.

Amber, I wasn't certain.

So I asked, "Even Amber?"

"Amber likes boys, makeup, shoes, clothes and boys is worth a repeat since she likes them so much. You're all about three of those so I figure she'll put up with you. What she doesn't like is schoolwork, her dad, her mom, helpin' out around the house and pumping gas into her car. I know that last one since I've had to go get her five times when she's run out of gas and she's had her license for two months."

"Oh dear," I murmured.

"That's about it," he agreed.

Wishing to make him feel better, I asked, "Isn't it normal for a girl her age not to like those things, including her parents?"

"Maybe," he replied then continued, "But she doesn't like me because I'm precisely what you said I am. A dad, a protective one and one who knows what that Noah kid has on his mind when he asks her to a concert in Boston which would mean they gotta spend the night in Boston. And I'm strict about that shit and her gettin' decent grades because my girl's smart as fuck and she could do something with her brain, so she should. And she doesn't like her mother because she's about gettin' laid, the more often the better, the younger the guy she lets in there the better. The bitch hit mid-life crisis early, shot right to cougar and Amber's not big on her mom bein' competition for boyfriends."

I gasped loudly at this shocking news.

Jake repeated, "That's about it," when I did.

"Is she, well...Ethan's—?"

He shook his head. "Conner and Amber have the same mom. Married a woman in between, thankfully didn't get her knocked up seein' as that lasted three months. Ethan's got a different mom. That lasted three years. She lives in Raleigh now with her new man and she's all about shovin' her nose up his ass and that means treatin' his kids like gold and forgettin' she made one of her own."

"Oh no," I whispered, not liking the sound of that at all.

He muttered, "Yep. I can pick 'em," and took another sip of coffee.

I took one too thinking, poor Ethan.

And poor Amber.

"Yo! Jake! Food's up!" I heard yelled through the wind and I looked back at The Shack to see two Styrofoam containers sitting on the ledge outside the window but Tom was still hidden in the murky shadows of the diminutive ramshackle structure.

"Be back," Jake said, got up and went to get our food.

He came back and set mine in front of me. This included a see-through plastic wrapped parcel that held a napkin and plastic cutlery.

"Crab, cream cheese and green onion omelet," Jake declared.

I couldn't believe it but that actually sounded delicious.

Tentatively, I opened the container.

It looked delicious too and the aroma wafting up smelled *divine.*

I set my coffee aside, grabbed my plastic wrapped parcel and asked, "How long were you together with Conner and Amber's mom?"

"Seven years," he answered. "She lives local and I wish she'd move to Raleigh too." He paused then finished on a mutter, "Or maybe Bangladesh."

I turned my eyes to him and smiled at his joke.

Then I looked back down to my omelet and thus missed his eyes changing before they dropped to my mouth.

"You, um…said that Amber charges money to look after Ethan and that Gran would watch him after school." I forked into my omelet and brought it to my mouth as I looked back at him. "While I'm in Magdalene, I can help out if you need someone to watch him."

"Brings us full circle, Slick," he stated and before I could get into the "Slick" business, he continued, "You thought more on your plans?"

Actually, I had, over a glass of wine consumed staring at the dark sea from the window seat of the light room last night.

Therefore, I shared them with him.

"I think I've decided to stay for a bit. Take a kind of sabbatical. I can do a lot of what I do for Henry from here, given a phone and Internet, the second Gran doesn't have but it's easy enough to get access. So I won't get bored. But after losing Gran, I'd like to feel"—I searched for a word and found it—"settled for a while."

I took my bite and he was right. It didn't knock me on my behind but it was shockingly delicious. It wasn't just crab, cream cheese and green onion. There was a subtle hint of garlic as well, the pepper was clearly freshly ground and the crab was succulent.

Superb.

"That's a good idea, Josie." I heard Jake say and I lifted my eyes to him to see him studying me intently. "Slow down a bit. Deal with Lydie passin'." He grinned. "Hang with us, people who loved her like you did."

After years of a jet-set lifestyle that was interesting and fulfilling, that still sounded marvelous.

That said, there were things to discuss, things to know.

And I set about doing that.

I dug back into my omelet and said before taking another bite, "I'd like to understand that better, Jake."

"Understand what better?"

I chewed, swallowed and looked to him again. "How you came to know Gran so well."

"We don't got the time to get into that before you gotta be at the Weavers."

That sounded like a stall tactic and I opened my mouth but he lifted a hand.

"Tell you it all, honey. All of it. But seriously, it might not be a long story but it might bring up questions and I'd like to have the time and focus to answer them."

That was thoughtful, nice and I had a feeling he was right. I would have a lot of questions and I'd like him to have the time and focus to answer them. So I nodded and took another bite.

"Owe you dinner, take you out, give it all to you." I heard him say as I munched.

I swallowed and looked to him. "That sounds doable."

He grinned.

My phone in my purse rang.

I let it and continued eating.

It kept ringing.

"You gonna get that?"

I looked back to Jake and answered, "No. It's rude to answer the phone during a meal or in someone's company."

He grinned again and said, "Babe, don't mind and we're not at a meal. We're at The Shack."

I wasn't certain about the distinction but our conversation turned moot when my phone stopped ringing.

I took another bite of omelet.

My phone started ringing again.

I felt my brows draw together.

"Babe, get it. Like I said, don't mind and someone obviously wants you," Jake urged.

I nodded, set aside my cutlery that was so light I was worried the breeze would sweep it away (so I tucked it as best I could under what remained of my omelet) and reached to my purse.

I got my phone and the display informed me the caller was Henry.

I looked to Jake and said, "My apologies, Jake. It's Henry. Something might be wrong."

His face changed minutely, going slightly blank but more noncommittal and he jerked up his chin in what I was deducing was his telling me I should take the call.

I took it and put the phone to my ear, greeting, "Henry."

"What the fuck?"

I blinked at the table because Henry had never said this to me, nor had he ever spoken in that tone. Or at least, with the last, not to me.

"I…pardon?" I asked.

"What the fuck, Josephine?"

What on earth?

"I-I'm sorry," I stammered. "Is something wrong?"

"Yes, something's wrong. You haven't called in two days."

Oh dear. I actually hadn't.

"Henry—"

"Worried about you Josephine. Told you to keep in touch, check in, let me know you're all right."

"You were traveling to Rome yesterday," I reminded him.

"Yes, and that flight's long but it doesn't take a year. And you know my schedule, Josephine. You know when I left, you know when I landed, and you know when I turn my phone off and on for a flight."

I did. He waited until the last second to turn it off and he turned it on the instant he could when we'd land.

"I'm sorry, Henry. Things have been somewhat…strange here."

"Strange how?" he asked immediately.

I sat back and trained my eyes to my lap. "Strange in a variety of ways. None of which I can get into right now because I'm at breakfast with Jake and then I have to go over to the Weavers. But I'll call you later and explain."

"Jake?"

"Yes. Jake."

"Who's Jake?"

"A friend of Gran's."

"Have I met him?"

Henry had been to Magdalene with me frequently and met a number of Gran's friends and acquaintances.

But I was relatively certain he had not met Jake.

"I don't think so," I answered.

"He one of her bridge cronies?"

The thought of Jake playing bridge with Gran's cronies, none of whom was under seventy years of age, made me smile at my lap.

"No."

"Then who is he, Josephine?"

I vaguely wondered why he was so determined to know.

I didn't ask that.

I said, "It's a long story, Henry, and I'm sorry, but I don't have time to tell it to you right now. I'm sitting outside on the wharf and my omelet is getting cold. It's delicious and I'd like to enjoy it while it's warm. Not to mention, Jake's sitting right here and it's rude to chat on the phone when I'm in company."

This was met with silence and this lasted quite some time.

"Henry? Have I lost you?" I called into the silence.

"No, you haven't lost me," he answered. "You're on the wharf eating an omelet?"

"A rather delicious one," I shared.

He said nothing.

"Henry?" I called.

"Phone me when you get a chance," he ordered oddly tersely. "I don't care how late it is here. Just call. I'm concerned. You're coping with a great deal and you're on your own."

That was proof Jake was wrong. Henry was irate because he was concerned about me. Yes, he was my employer, but he also cared.

However, Henry was wrong too. I wasn't on my own.

Jake was with me.

This caused that warmth to return even if all around me was cold but I ignored that and assured Henry, "I'll phone."

"And I'm telling Daniel to cancel Paris."

I blinked at my lap then looked up to the boats bobbing along the wharf. "You can't do that."

"I can, Josephine, and I'm going to."

"But, it's a video shoot that took months to set up," I reminded him.

"They'll have to find another director," he told me.

"Dee-Amond only works with you," I continued recounting things he knew.

And Dee-Amond *did* only work with Henry and had only worked with Henry for the last seventeen years.

He was a renowned hip-hop artist who'd started his own fashion line, which was remarkable and thus quite successful. Henry did all his work on Amond's music videos *and* his fashion shoots.

Amond was also a very handsome, though somewhat frightening black man, who had, in his early days, beat a number of what he called "raps," the charges being rather violent.

He'd since settled and he could be very charming. This was why I spent a particularly enjoyable night with him after a party that we attended after the VMAs seven years prior. After that, he'd asked me to join his "posse" but I'd refused, with some hesitation (this was because he was *very* charming, and as I'd mentioned, also very handsome and our night had been just that enjoyable).

But I could never leave Henry.

Then again, there was also the small fact I was not a woman who would be comfortable as a member of a "posse."

Henry never knew, of course. I was always, without fail, discreet and fortunately Amond was too.

"Then he'll have to reschedule when we can both do it," Henry replied.

"Henry, I hardly need to be—"

He interrupted me. "Are you going to meet me in Paris?"

I hesitated, looked back to my lap and whispered, "Things are such that that's unlikely."

"Then I'm canceling."

I sighed before I asked, "Can we discuss this later?"

"Right. Your omelet and Jake."

His tone was unusual and vaguely disturbing.

I pressed my lips together.

"I'll speak with you soon," he said.

"Of course," I murmured.

"Until then, Josephine."

"Until then, Henry. Good-bye."

He didn't say good-bye. He simply disconnected.

He'd never done that before either.

I stared at my phone for a moment before putting it back in my bag and regaining my cutlery, saying distractedly to Jake, my eyes on my food, "I apologize. That lasted too long."

"And it didn't sound like it went real good."

At Jake's comment, I turned my eyes to him. "He's canceling work to come to Magdalene."

I watched as his mouth got tight for some strange reason and I watched as, seconds later, it relaxed as if he'd willed it to do so to hide his reaction, which was even stranger.

"It'll be good, you have your people around you."

"He shouldn't cancel. It's a video shoot. That's even more involved than a photo shoot. They're shooting on location, so they need to get permission, permits. There's a good deal of money tied up in it, not to mention all the personnel."

"You're worth fucking all that."

I stared at him as that warmth swept through me again but I replied, "It's foolish."

"You're worth bein' that too."

His words were making me feel such that I decided to return my attention to my probably now chiller-cabinet-cold omelet. So I did.

After I took a bite and found it was, indeed, now chiller-cabinet-cold, Jake asked, "When's he coming?"

I looked back to him. "The job in Rome lasts just over a week. If he cancels Paris, he'll be free to fly here next Saturday."

"Right."

I took a sip from my coffee cup and returned my attention to my omelet.

"Your offer, I'm gonna take you up on it," Jake declared and my eyes went back to him.

"My offer?"

"Lookin' after Ethan," he said. "He, Con and Amber would go over to your place a lot after school. I got shit on, it falls to Con and Amber to step up, look after their little brother, take him places, shit like that. Lydie wasn't real young, but the kids loved her. It wasn't really her lookin' out for them so much as all of them havin' each other and my kids havin' someone to go to when school was done. Like my kids havin' good in their lives and Lydie was the best."

He was not wrong about that.

He was also not done speaking.

"And Amber needed a good, decent woman in her life. Lydie was that too."

She was indeed.

He went on.

"Part of Amber bein' a pain in the ass is she doesn't know what to do with the hurt she's feelin' with Lydie gone. Ethan lets shit hang out, too young to bury it or really know how to deal with it. Con was tight with Lydie too but he's not a kid anymore and thinks he's gotta hide emotion to be a man. With that all around Amber, she doesn't know which way to go. And Lydie gave her a lot which means she lost a lot." His voice dipped lower when he finished, "I figure you know all about that."

I very much did.

I didn't agree verbally. I nodded.

"It'll be good they got a bit of Lydie to fill that hole. That being you."

I was not a mother but I could see a father would think this true.

And this felt oddly nice, filling that hole, and that hole being the one Gran left, not to mention him thinking I could fill it as any hole Gran left, I knew too well, was enormous.

I nodded again.

"That said, Amber's grounded for a week so her ass is tied to Ethan or the house or Lavender House, you take them on. After that, you're around a while, it'd be cool you give her a break. She's sixteen years old. That's too damn early to be a mom to an eight year old kid but with all the shit I gotta do with the club and the gym, I had to lean on her."

"I can give her a break," I said quietly.

"That'd be appreciated."

"I...should I start today?"

"No. You keep settlin' in. Tomorrow's Saturday. Amber's not goin' on her date because of the shit that came out of her mouth yesterday. They're covered. But if you could start next week, I'd be grateful."

I nodded yet again.

"Since Amber's on enforced babysitting duties, I'll take you out to dinner tomorrow night. Fill you in."

Dinner with Jake.

Alone.

Again, that strange anticipation I'd experienced all the day before hit me and I knew in that moment that it was because I enjoyed being around this man. What I didn't know was why I'd anticipate seeing him, that feeling coming on strong, when he was sitting right next to me.

"Dress up, I'm takin' you to a decent place," he ordered.

That anticipation spiked in a way I felt it in my nipples.

My *nipples*.

Oh dear.

"I...uh...all right," I replied.

"Be at your house at seven," he said.

Finally, a decent hour for dinner.

"I'll be ready."

"You done with that?" he asked, tipping his head to my omelet.

I nodded.

"Then let's get you to the Weavers."

By this, he meant he would collect all of our refuse, leaving me only to grab my coffee cup. This he did, depositing it in the big barrel with its black plastic liner that served as a rubbish bin for, perhaps, the entirety of the wharf and not just The Shack.

He called, "Later, Tom," and got back a, "Later, Jake."

I looked and still, no Tom could be seen in The Shack.

"Your omelets are lovely." I decided to yell because they were and he probably knew that but it always felt nice getting a compliment.

"Thanks, darlin'!" I heard called back but still could see no Tom.

I completely forgot about Tom when Jake grabbed my hand and started us up the boardwalk.

I also completely forgot to breathe and my heart completely forgot to beat.

We walked, Jake guiding us to my car, and as we did, although I couldn't breathe and mostly couldn't think, what I *could* think was that walking with me holding my hand seemed altogether natural to Jake.

Then again, he'd had three wives, he had a daughter and in our brief acquaintance, he'd shown he could be affectionate and it was doubtful he was only this way with me.

For me, I had never, not once, not since high school, walked holding a man's hand.

And doing it, that...*that* knocked me right on my ass.

In a nice way that felt splendid.

"Thank you for breakfast," I forced myself to say when I'd forced myself to breathe again.

"No worries," he muttered.

I turned my head and looked up at him. "You were right, it was delicious."

He dipped his chin and looked down at me. "Told you it'd knock you on your ass."

Staring in his eyes, now a stormy gray that seemed to reflect the skies above, I knew I was.

I was getting knocked on my ass.

But not by an omelet.

By something altogether different.

And this feeling would continue when he stopped me at the driver's side door to my car and leaned in. He brushed his lips against my cheek, which gave me another waft of his attractive cologne as well as an altogether too appealing scrape of his stubble (he had again not shaved that morning).

He pulled back and, smiling, murmured, "Later, babe."

"Yes. See you tomorrow night."

He winked, squeezed my hand, let it go and I watched him walk to his truck.

I forced myself to get in my car and drive to the Weavers'.

But I did it feeling a peculiar feeling.

That being knocked on my ass.

Thus winded.

And not minding at all.

———◦•••◦———

I DIDN'T KNOW why I did it; it was as if my eyes were drawn there by unseen forces.

But as I was driving back to Lavender House from the Weavers, my mind consumed with Eliza, her frailty, the pain etched around her mouth, the effort she still was making to pretend everything was all right and chitchat when her eyes were drooping, I turned my head and saw it.

Magdalene was not large and had long since had a town council that was rabidly determined to keep the old Maine coastal town feel about the place. Thus, the commercial areas of town were mostly untouched and had been for well over a century and things like fast food restaurants were firmly placed at the outskirts of town so you couldn't even see them unless you were on the road driving that way.

That didn't mean that off Cross Street (the main street in town), there weren't other business that had sprung up over the decades.

And this included a large store that once was a hardware store but now, as I turned my head to look down Haver Way, it had a sign in the window that did not promote hardware.

I hadn't taken in that building for years.

But after I drove by it, I found my opening to circle back, turned left on Haver Way and parked in the large-ish parking lot outside the building.

The gold painting edged in black on the window said "Truck's Gym."

And inside, through the now misting rain, I saw it was, indeed, a gym. A specific kind of gym. And I spent no time at all in gyms but even so, I knew exactly what kind of gym this was seeing as from what I could take in from my vantage point, there were two boxing rings set up in the vast open space.

They were down one side. Down the other side, there was weight equipment and I could see those bags suspended that were always in boxing gyms in movies, the little ball-like ones and the large tubular ones.

There were men punching things, lifting things and jumping rope inside. Several of them, which I found surprising seeing as it was early afternoon on a workday.

I could also see, standing outside the ring closest to the window, Jake. He was not wearing jeans, boots and a sweater as he had been that morning when he bought me an omelet. He was now wearing a pair of dark track pants with three white stripes down the side and a white, long sleeved t-shirt. There were boxers in the ring and Jake was calling out to them.

He'd mentioned his gym more than once.

This must be it.

And the name was "Truck's." That odious man at Breeze Point had referred to "the truck" and I didn't think this was a coincidence.

More to learn about Jake.

I had a feeling there was much to learn about Jake. Three wives, one he had only three months. He clearly had at least partial custody of all of his children. Even though he mentioned one of his ex-wives was local, he didn't mention her children staying with her, and Conner and Amber were both hers. He owned a boxing gym and a strip club, which were vastly different enterprises. He was well-known, if that man from Breeze Point was to be believed, not to mention, the bad-mannered Terry Baginski knew him as well.

Yes, I thought, watching him watch the boxers in the ring, there was much to learn about Jake Spear.

And I found myself already fascinated not even knowing what it was.

I reversed out of my spot, pointed the car back to Haver Way, then Cross Street and I drove out of town and to Lavender House.

I waited until I was out of my jacket and had a cup of tea in hand before I got my phone, went to the overstuffed chair by the window in the family room and called Henry. The time difference was such that it would be late in Italy but Henry was like me. A night owl. He'd be awake.

"Josephine," he answered.

"Hello, Henry," I replied.

Then I didn't know what to say and clearly, Henry didn't either because he also remained silent.

It was me who broke it.

"I'm sorry I didn't call," I said softly. "It's just that something happened the day before yesterday. A man came to the house. He'd approached Gran about buying it and he approached me too. And I had a very strong reaction to it."

"Someone's trying to buy Lavender House?" Henry asked.

"Yes, and Gran didn't share that with me." Amongst other things and I again didn't tell Henry about these things for reasons unknown to me that I decided in that particular moment to process later.

"And he just showed up at the house?"

"Yes."

"What an ass," Henry murmured. "You just lost your grandmother."

"Indeed," I replied.

"And what was this strong reaction you had?" Henry queried.

"I…" I paused, drew in breath and lowered my voice when I shared, "I don't want to let it go."

"Of course you don't."

I blinked at his quick acceptance of that fact.

"Fuck him, sweetheart," Henry continued. "Tell him to leave you alone. If he doesn't, I'll tell him when I get there."

"I—" I began but he kept talking so I didn't get any more out.

"I've been thinking and we need a break, both of us. So we'll take it at Lavender House. And you'll need to do things that are unpleasant, like go through Lydia's belongings and you should have help when you do that. But we have a problem."

I wasn't exactly keeping up with him but I still managed to ask, "We do?"

"Yes. I told Daniel to cancel Paris and he looked into it but Amond got wind and got hold of Cecile. Reminded her of my contractual obligations. There's an out in the contract but if Amond pushes it, which he inferred he would do, it could get unpleasant. She's advised I don't cancel but she's looking into cancelling Sydney. As there's more time for them to get another photographer, she thinks that can be accomplished as well as clearing my schedule after that. But that means I won't be able to get to Magdalene for a few weeks."

Cecile was Henry's agent and had been with him for years. If she said Sydney was cancellable, it would be.

This made me feel better.

"That sounds like a better plan, Henry," I told him.

"I'm not pleased it'll be weeks until I can get there," he disagreed.

"I'll be all right," I assured him.

"I know you will, sweetheart. I'm still not pleased."

I said nothing mostly because I was relieved he was sounding like Henry again.

Then he stopped sounding like Henry when he went on, asking, "Right. Now, who's Jake?"

I opened my mouth, shut it, opened it again and when I did, I reminded myself this was Henry.

So words finally came out.

"Jake and his children are close to Gran. My guess is he's around our age, he has three kids, two teenagers, one young son and they spent a lot of time with Gran here at Lavender House. The kids, and I think Jake too, are missing her quite a bit and they, well…we're establishing a connection because we all feel the same way." I again lowered my voice when I finished, "And it feels nice, Henry. It feels very nice to be around people who cared so much about Gran."

It seemed he only heard part of what I said because he asked, "And the connection you're establishing with Jake?"

"What do you mean?"

"You had breakfast with him this morning," he reminded me and I thought I understood what he was saying.

So I explained, "It isn't like that. I'm not his, well… *thing*. He likes big hair and big"—I paused—"other stuff. And he's really not my thing either."

That last, I was beginning to fear, was a lie.

Still, I carried on.

"He owns the local strip club and boxing gym."

Henry's voice was no longer interrogatory but trembling with humor when he asked, "He owns what?"

I repeated myself.

He whistled before I heard him burst out laughing.

Still chuckling, he inquired, "Lydie spent time with the owner of the local gentlemen's club?"

Something about the way he said this made the hairs on the back of my neck stand on end.

"He's rough, Henry," I said quietly. "But he's very nice, he's a good father and he loved Gran a great deal."

Henry was silent.

I wasn't.

"He's treating me with care and kindness and I…well, his daughter is somewhat of a mess but his young son is quite adorable." I drew in breath and concluded, "It's nice to have them around."

"Then I'm glad you've got them, honey. And you'll have me too, as soon as I can get there."

I nodded even though he couldn't see me and said softly, "I'll look forward to you getting here."

"Now I'm going to let you go but I want you to remember to phone in."

"I will, Henry."

"Good, sweetheart. You take care and if you need me, don't worry about the time difference. Call."

Yes, Jake was wrong about Henry.

He cared and not just in an employer/employee way.

This was why I was smiling when I replied, "I will."

"All right, Josephine, speak to you soon."

"Yes, Henry, goodnight."

"Good-bye, sweetheart."

We rang off and I took a sip of my tea, my eyes moving out the window to see the mist was still shrouding the view, when the house phone rang.

I took the call, it was from Ruth Fletcher, the reverend's wife, and after some (slightly annoying but she was trying to be polite) back and forth, we agreed they would come to Lavender House on Sunday night after evening services and I would cook for them (rather than the other way around).

I was heading back to my chair by the window, and my tea, when my mobile on the table beside the chair rang.

I looked at the screen and took the call.

"Amond," I greeted.

"Beautiful, what the hell?"

Oh dear.

"Amond, please listen. Henry is just—"

"Don't give a fuck about Henry. Know what he's just. Anyone could do my shit as good as him, I'd let him do what he's just gotta do seein' as it's for you. What I'm askin' what the hell about is that you lost your Granny and you didn't phone me?"

I blinked at the window as I asked, "Pardon?"

"Josephine, you're my girl, you know you're my girl even though you decided not to officially *be* my girl. You still know I give a shit, a massive shit when it comes to you. Cecile said this was your only livin' relative, you're tight, you lose her, you haul your sweet white ass to fuckin' Maine and don't tell your boy you lost your Granny?"

"I...uh—"

"And Henry lets it swing out there, you alone in fuckin' Maine?"

"Henry had jobs," I explained.

"I know, I'm one of 'em. That's still bullshit."

My back went straight. "Amond, I'll remind you, *you* just today wouldn't let him out of one of those jobs."

"That job wasn't scheduled when your Granny just died either."

This, I found with deep, somewhat annoying surprise, seemed to be a theme with the men in my life. Men, I'd add, that I didn't even know *were* in my life.

"You need company?" he asked into my thoughts.

"I'm fine," I assured him.

He wasn't assured.

I knew this when he queried, "You sure?"

I softened my voice and said, "Yes, Amond. I'm sure. Gran had a lot of friends and they're taking care of me. I'm not alone very often. It's all fine. I promise."

He hesitated a moment before he said, "Okay, girl."

I took in another breath, let it go and told him, "It feels lovely that you care."

"Josephine, every time I hit a red carpet, still think, whatever bitch I got on my arm, she's not you. Class, straight up. Outside, ice cold. Shit-hot ice cold, but still ice cold. Inside, so fuckin' warm…beautiful. You don't give me that, I dig. That's not in you. Don't mean I still don't wish I had it. It also don't mean I can't give you what I can give back. So you need anything, you call. I'm there. You hear me?"

And yet again, I was knocked on my ass.

Winded.

Because this was very nice, very sweet and very unexpected.

I knew he liked me. I knew he was attracted to me (that, during our night and even before, and if I was honest, also after, was absolutely not in question).

I just didn't know how deep it ran.

Even winded, I replied, "I'm with you, Amond."

"Right, your ass is back in LA, it's also at my house. I'm cookin' for you and listenin' to you talk about your Granny."

I smiled. "We'll plan that."

"Right, beautiful. Now lettin' you go."

"Thank you for calling, Amond."

"You got it. Later, Josephine."

I said my farewell and we disconnected.

I again felt warm.

I also felt strange. It wasn't a bad strange. It also wasn't a good one. It was like I was missing something, was supposed to remember something, but I couldn't call it up.

I attempted to call it up, staring at the gray sea and sipping tea when the house phone rang again.

I sighed, put my tea down and went to get the phone.

"Lavender House," I greeted.

"Josephine?"

"Yes."

"It's Boston."

I closed my eyes in frustration.

I opened them and started, "Mr. Stone—"

He interrupted me. "I'm not calling about Lavender House. I would assume, after the things your grandmother shared with me about how she felt about the house, and that you shared those sentiments, that you'll not be selling the property. I'm calling to ask you out for dinner."

Good God, what was happening?

Luckily, I had a truthful reply that was also a negative one. "I'm sorry, Mr. Stone. I have plans."

"Please call me Boston."

I said nothing, unsure I could address a man by such a name.

"The night after," he went on.

"I'm having dinner with Reverend Fletcher and his wife."

"Monday night, then."

I sighed.

"Josephine?" he called when I said nothing after my sigh.

"Mr. Sto…erm, *Boston,* I mean no offense, but at this time, I'm not looking for romantic entanglements."

"That's understandable," he said gently, his smooth voice going suave. "However, I'll take this opportunity to remind you that at times like these, any entanglements are more enjoyable than those likely occupying your mind."

This was true.

Even so, I didn't want to be entangled with him.

But before I could utter a word, he unfortunately continued.

"And you're an exceptionally beautiful woman. So much so that it's prompted me to act outside good manners to take *my* opportunity to make certain you understand I'd like to get to know you."

"That's very flattering, um…Boston. But—"

He interrupted me again with, "A drink."

I wasn't following.

"I'm sorry?"

"Not dinner. A drink. I'd offer to collect you but I feel you'd be more comfortable meeting me so we'll do that. At the Club. I'll give them your name at the gatehouse. Monday night. Seven o'clock."

I sighed.

The Club was the Magdalene Club, an exclusive club that had once simply been a gathering place for the haves of Magdalene where they could go and commune with other haves while not having to mingle with the have-nots. Over the decades, they'd added a dining room to their bar and I'd never been there but Gran (and others) had told me it was quite excellent fare and had a lovely view of the sea.

I also had a lovely view of the sea from a variety of windows in my own home but I had the feeling that Boston Stone was not to be put off. Not Magdalene's most eligible bachelor.

Unless I put him off face to face.

Which I would do over a drink.

"Fine. Monday. Seven o'clock."

There was a smile in his voice when he replied, "I'll look forward to that, Josephine."

I didn't share this sentiment so I made no reply.

"See you then," he said.

"Yes," I agreed.

"Try to have a good rest of your day."

"I will, Boston. You too."

"I will. Good-bye, Josephine."

I gave my farewell, disconnected and decided not to answer the phone again that day.

I also decided not to think of a drink with Boston Stone, going to have it solely for the purpose of telling him I was not interested, as this would irritate me and I wasn't in the mood to be irritated.

But I did this remembering why I didn't get tangled up with men. They could be extremely irksome.

I turned my mind from that to my chair and my tea and in sipping it, my mind turned to something Henry said.

And in doing so, my body moved out of the chair and I set the tea aside again.

Slowly, I moved through the house to the den and entered Gran's room.

I had not remade the bed. This was because I had a mind to returning that room to its rightful state as a den and, being in it, that was what I decided to do as soon as humanly possible.

I didn't want a reminder that Gran got to the point she couldn't enjoy all of Lavender House to its fullest, something she did even being there for decades all on her own.

But more, I didn't need a reminder that was where she ended her days.

I then moved to the wardrobe she'd had put in there.

I opened the doors and saw her clothes.

I took one look, closed the doors and exited the room. My throat had closed. My eyes got blurry. My mind had blanked. And in this state, I made my way back to my chair in the family room.

And my phone.

Without even thinking, I picked it up, found the number and dialed.

I got five rings before I heard, "Spear. Leave a message."

"Jake?" I said after the beep. "Josephine. I…would you, well…when you have a moment, could you call?"

I didn't say good-bye before I disconnected.

Then I stared at the phone wondering why I connected in the first place.

Not having the answer to that, or perhaps not wanting an answer to it, I moved to the kitchen to refresh my tea.

By the time I was moving back to my chair, trying to think of what else to do that day, anything to keep my mind off a variety of things that I didn't want to think about, coming up with nothing but sitting in that chair and staring at the bleak landscape thinking about those variety of things, my mobile rang.

I snatched it up immediately and hit the screen to connect.

I did this thoughtlessly and inexplicably.

But I did it because the screen declared Jake was calling.

"Jake?"

"Josie, you okay?"

"I…" God! What was I doing? "I…Gran's clothes," I stated stupidly and said no more.

"What, honey?"

"I went into the den," I explained. "Gran's clothes. I…there's no reason to keep them. Someone can use them. And I-I-I need the den to be a den again. I can't think of her…I don't want to remember what happened…" I swallowed and concluded, "I wish it to be a den again."

Not even a second passed before he replied, "Don't think about the clothes. Don't even look at the clothes. I'll deal with the clothes. And I'll talk to some guys. Get them over there. We'll deal with the den."

At his words, warmth swept through me so immense I had to sit down in the chair.

"Thank you," I whispered into the phone.

"Not a problem, baby."

I closed my eyes as more warmth swept through me at his deep, sweet, soft voice.

"I…uh, I won't keep you," I said.

"You're good. Anytime you need to call, do it."

And more warmth.

"All right."

"You okay now?" he asked.

"Yes."

"I gotta work but you need me to swing around tonight? Have a beer? Talk?"

It was then I knew.

I *knew.*

This was what Gran wanted for me and this was what Gran gave to me in giving me to Jake Spear.

I just couldn't understand why she kept it from me before.

"I'm fine, Jake. That's very kind but really, I'm okay. I just had"—I hesitated then admitted—"A moment."

"You have any more of those I'm a phone call away."

Yes.

This was what Gran wanted for me.

"Thank you, Jake," I whispered.

"Any time, honey," he whispered back. "You okay for me to let you go?"

"Yes."

"Right. See you tomorrow."

"See you then."

"Later, Slick."

That nickname sent a jolt through me, taking me out of the moment. I opened my mouth to say something about it but got out not a sound.

He'd disconnected.

THE COURAGE TO TRY HIS HAND

Thirty seconds after Jake rang the bell to Lavender House, Josie opened the door.

And when she did, Jake froze.

"Hello, Jake," she said. "I'll just get my coat."

Jake didn't move.

This was because the vision of her was burning itself on his brain and he was enjoying the feeling.

Then she turned and he got her back.

And Jake didn't move again.

This was because the vision of her back was making his cock get hard and he was fighting the feeling.

She was in a dress that was an unusual shade of yellowish-green satin, like the color of an apple. Thin straps, a diagonal neckline that had a flap of material falling down her front. The top fit her snug, accentuating every line and curve. The skirt caught at her hips, somehow turning into panels that ended in a spiked hemline, the spikes brushing her knees.

But the back…

Fuck.

There *was* no back.

It bared her from shoulders to the top of her ass.

Jesus.

Her hair was up again, this time in curls arranged in a bun at the side of her neck. All Josie, it was elegant. But, unlike Josie, it also was almost playful.

And fucking hot.

Even as much as he liked her hair, he'd prefer to see it as it was in that picture he had of her.

Down.

But not blowing in the breeze.

Spread on his pillow.

And he liked that dress a fuckuva lot but he'd like it more on the floor by his bed.

From top to toe, she was the shit. Maybe especially her toes seeing as their nails were painted fuck-me red and they were exposed in shoes that were a mess of very thin, dark silver straps. So many straps, the fuckers had to be zipped up the back.

And the heel was tall and lethal.

He had no fucking clue how she could walk on those things.

But she did, gracefully this time, no tripping. He watched her do it and he watched her grab her coat from a chair in the hall. This finally spurred him to move.

Which he did, right to her, taking the coat from her.

"Got this, Slick," he muttered, shaking it out and rounding her to hold it up for her to put on.

Her face appeared startled when she looked over her bared shoulder at him but he looked away from her face, and her bare shoulder, then he couldn't find anywhere to look because all of it was too good.

Finally, she stuck her arm through the hole, he got her other one in and he settled the shiny silver coat on her shoulders, covering her.

Thank fuck.

He had no idea how he was going to have dinner with her wearing that dress without dragging her to his truck then taking her back to Lavender House and probably fucking her on the floor of the foyer.

Then again, when she'd walked on her classy high-heeled boots, wearing her classy shades, that scarf blowing in the wind yesterday, he'd thought the same thing and he'd managed it.

He'd do it again.

Somehow.

She grabbed her purse and turned to him.

"Ready," she said softly, her sweet voice as it always was, from the very beginning, cultured but melodic.

"Right," he muttered and grabbed her hand, moving them to the door. "House locked down?" he asked.

"Yes," she answered.

"Great." He was still muttering as he moved her out the door.

He stopped her, released her hand, dug in his pocket for the keys and used his own to lock the door behind them.

Then he grabbed her hand again and walked her to the truck.

"You look nice," she noted.

"Thanks," he replied, distracted, thinking about her ass in his truck. More to the point, thinking about reclining his seat and dragging her ass over to his side and what he'd do with it when he got her there.

On this thought, a thought that wasn't helping him keep his cock from getting hard, he opened her door for her as she asked, "Where are we going?"

"The Eaves," he answered, pulling gently at her to maneuver her in his truck.

But she'd stopped dead so he looked at her.

"That's very expensive, Jake," she whispered.

"Babe, you're you," he replied. "And you're you in that dress. Where the fuck else would I take you?"

He saw her draw in a soft breath, and that was sexy as fuck too, making him wonder how he could make her do that with his hands, or his mouth, before she luckily took him from this train of thought and pointed out, "You took me to The Shack yesterday morning."

"And gave you the best omelet in the county."

"This is probably correct," she murmured as if to herself, her doing this reminding him she could be cute, which finally made him grin.

"It's definitely correct. Now get your ass in the truck."

She looked into the truck and hesitated a second before she put her fucking fantastic shoe on the running board and he put his hands to her waist to heft her up.

He got her ass in the seat and she looked at him. "Thank you. I wasn't sure I could get up on my own."

"Well, you're there, Slick," he noted.

She opened her mouth to say something but he stepped out of the door, ordering, "Buckle up," before he slammed it.

He moved around the hood, hauled his ass in at the other side, buckled in and started her up.

He sent them down the lane and did it deciding to get the tough stuff done first.

"I'll be over tomorrow, first just me to box up Lydie's stuff, and then some guys are comin' over. I'll be around about ten. They'll be around at eleven. You gotta know what you want done with the den by then, babe. I've got a place to store Lydie's furniture. You want it sold, I'll get Con on putting it on Craig's List. You got a use for it and decide you want it back, just let me know."

"All right, Jake," she whispered.

"That's done," he replied. "But just sayin', the boys are over hauling furniture around, you're gonna have to feed them. You don't have to go whole hog. Pizza is good."

"All right," she said, louder this time. "And thank you. I don't know what to say about all you're—"

He gentled his voice when he cut her off with, "You don't have to say anything, Josie."

He heard her sigh and pointed the truck toward town.

"If you like, the kids can come over," she offered. "The Fletchers are coming for dinner tomorrow night but I can make enough for all of you."

"Not sure Reverend Fletcher wants to break bread with the owner of the local strip club," he replied.

"Oh," she whispered, then again louder, "I hadn't thought of that."

"We'll come over Monday night. Con's off work and Ethan's been talkin' your meatloaf up. Con's feelin' left out."

"I would enjoy meeting your eldest child but I can't do Monday night. Maybe we can do Tuesday?"

"Can't do Tuesday. Con's workin'," he told her. "What do you have on Monday night?"

"I'm having a drink with Boston Stone at the Club."

His chest seized and his hand tightened on the steering wheel as his lips forced out, "Come again?"

"I know," she stated even though he didn't know until she gave it to him, "It's irritating."

He looked her way and saw she also looked irritated. Then again, as polished as she was, Josie still tended to let it all hang out.

He looked back to the road and asked, "He on you about selling the house?"

"He's told me he's given up on the house," she shared. "He wants to"—a pause then, with frustrated emphasis—"*get to know me.*"

Jesus. Shit.

"He's makin' a play when your Gran just died?"

"Yes, and he isn't easy to put off. So I'll put him off face to face."

No, she wouldn't.

Jake would put him off.

Therefore, he declared, "I'll deal with it."

He felt her eyes on him. "Pardon?"

"I'll deal with it," he repeated.

"How?"

"Don't worry about how. Just know it'll be done and me and the kids'll be over Monday night."

"I…" Another pause then, "Maybe I should phone him and be clearer about how I feel about not wishing to get to know him."

"Babe, what'd I say?"

"What did you say?"

"Yes, what'd I say?"

"I don't—"

"I'll deal with it."

She fell silent.

He simmered.

Boston Stone, fucking dick.

Jake barely knew him but from this shit, he knew he was a fucking dick.

That said, the man was perfect for her. All his money, his class, his power. It wasn't surprising Josie caught his eye. He had the money to get the best of everything and he was the kind of guy who had it in him to know exactly what the best was. And he didn't have to know the guy to know he frequently indulged in both, what with the asshole lording his shit all over town.

She decided to change the subject and he knew this when she asked, "What are the children doing tonight?"

"Amber, pouting because she had a date with Noah that she had to break because she's grounded. She also has no access to the phone so that means she can't call his ass and talk with him in her bedroom for hours like she normally does. Ethan's probably eating a shitload of crap so he'll have a stomachache that'll wake him up at about two in the morning, which means my ass will be up at two o'clock in the morning. And Con's always got his old man's back. In order to look after Ethan and make sure Amber doesn't do anything that'll get her into more trouble, one of his girls is comin' over rather than him takin' her out."

"*One* of his girls?" she asked.

"He's got five. Steady."

There was a heavy pause before, "How can he have five *steady* girls?"

"No clue how the kid manages it, Slick, just know he does. That doesn't mean those five get along and like sharin'. Just know they put up with it whatever Con does to make 'em do it."

"I do not see good things in the future about this, Jake," she declared. "Women don't like to share. This détente may last for a while but it won't last forever."

"He's got his hand in the candy bowl and he's keepin' it there, he's gotta deal with the pain when someone bitchslaps him to pull it out."

"A difficult lesson to learn," she murmured.

"Conner's like his dad. He learns by doin' or, in some cases, by fuckin' up and tryin' to be smart enough not to fuck up the same way again."

He knew he had her eyes again when she protested, "But people are involved, in this case girls *and* their hearts, and they might get hurt."

He looked her way to see she was looking at him and he gave her a shake of his head before looking back to the road. "That's the difficult part, Josie.

A man's any man at all, the first woman he hurts, he learns not to do that shit again. Good he learns at seventeen rather than twenty-five when shit might count."

She said nothing to that for some time and Jake had pulled off Cross Street and onto the coastal road when she spoke again.

"When did you learn that?"

"How do you think I got married three times?" he answered.

He sensed he again had her eyes when she asked, "Pardon?"

"Learned early. Not at seventeen but saw a girl, had a girl on the side my sophomore year in college. They found out about that shit, it did not go down very well. I felt like a total fuckin' asshole mostly 'cause I was. The look on my girl's face. Fuck." He shook his head at the road. "Never forget that look, honey."

"And how did this lead you to getting married three times?"

"Didn't want to see that look again, got no clue how to get shot of a woman so I find I got her ring on my finger instead of seeing her in my rearview."

"You…" she paused and her voice was higher pitched when she went on, "*married* women instead of ending things with them?"

He grinned at the road. "Never claimed to be Einstein."

"Indeed you haven't," she murmured.

"How real do you want it?" he asked.

"How"—another pause—"*real?*"

"Honest. Straight up. How much of that can you take?"

"You've been astoundingly open already, Jake."

He glanced at her again before looking back to the road and asking, "We gettin' to know each other?"

"Yes."

"Are you mine?"

A shocked, "*Pardon me?*"

"Did Lydie give you to me, babe," he explained.

"Well…yes."

Fuck yes.

There it was.

She was his.

"Then you're mine," he stated. "And that means you're my kids'. And that means we gotta dig in there and give each other shit. So we shouldn't hide and anyway, I got nothin' to hide. I did what I did, made stupid decisions, fucked up, I'm still standing, my kids are healthy and happy. Not countin' Amber pouting and being an occasional pain in the ass, Con serial dating and Ethan mourning the only grandmother he'll really ever know."

There was another pause before, quietly, she began, "His other grandmothers—"

"My ma's dead, babe. So's my dad," Jake told her. "His mom's dad is also gone and her mom lives up in Bridgewater. Sweet lady but a little whacked. She's a hoarder, doesn't leave her house and I don't want my kid in a house like that. Plus, it isn't exactly close. They talk on the phone. That's all he's got."

"I'm sorry to hear of this, including about your parents, Jake," she said, voice still soft.

"We deal, Josie," he replied in the same tone.

He didn't ask about her parents.

This was because he knew her father was dead. He'd asked his cop buddy, Coert, to look into it because Lydie asked him to and Coert found that shit out. He also knew her uncle was alive. And he knew her mother was off the grid, probably buried so deep under whatever identity she took when she escaped Josie's assclown of a father, if she was alive, she'd never surface, even though her motherfucker of a husband was long gone.

Bitch should have taken her daughter.

But the bitch left her daughter to a monster.

"Would you like to, well…share about how you lost your parents?" she asked carefully.

He didn't hesitate before he gave it to her.

"Dad, aneurysm. Right at work. Sixty-four. A few months from retirement it hits him, he's down. Gone. Ethan was born three months later."

"Jake," she whispered but said no more.

Jake did.

"Ma died when Eath was nearly two. He doesn't remember her. She had an infection, didn't catch it, thought it was just bein' tired 'cause she was sad she lost Dad. By the time she looked into that shit, it had done a number on her heart. Too much damage to repair. Few months later, she just slipped away. Amber was tight with her, though. Like with Lydie, she took it hard."

To this, he got nothing.

When he continued to get nothing, he turned his head and saw she was looking out the side window.

He looked back to the road.

Fuck, he was a dick.

"Josie," he said gently. "I'm sorry, baby. I shouldn't have gotten into that shit."

"Life happens, Jake," she replied quietly. "And you're just being"—she hesitated— "*real*."

Too real.

"We'll stop talking about that."

She said nothing.

He drove on.

Finally, she broke the silence. "So, being, erm...*real*. Your wives?"

Terrific.

Now he got to give her not him being a dick but instead being an idiot.

"Donna, the first one, loved her. Probably shouldn't have divorced her. She wanted it, I didn't get it, but I gave it to her."

"That sounds odd," she noted when he said no more.

"It was," he agreed. "To this day, I still don't get it but what I get pisses me off so I try not to think about it."

"You don't have to share," she offered.

That made him grin.

"Babe, laid myself out already. Too late for that."

"Indeed," she murmured but he heard a smile in her voice too and he looked at her to catch it.

He got a glimpse before returning his eyes to the road and he was glad he took that shot.

She was pretty normally. When she smiled though...

Jesus.

"Though, I don't want you to get angry," she went on.

"Too much time has passed, not worth it to get angry anymore," he told her.

"All right," she replied and he went for it.

"We fought, not all the time, but that shit happens," he told her. "And honest to Christ, don't know what was up her ass but something was. She got her teeth in it and wouldn't let it go then wouldn't let anything go then wanted to let me go. How I remember it starting was she wanted a new car. I couldn't afford a new one so I bought her a used one. It was better than the one she had so I thought she was good. She didn't. Told me I never listened to her. I told her I did but we couldn't afford a brand new car. She got shitty, kept bein' shitty, kicked my ass out. Lost her man but got herself a new car."

"That's ridiculous," she snapped, suddenly pissed and he fought back the grin. But he had to admit he liked it that she gave him that emotion.

"That shit happened. She tried reconciliation. What we had was good, so I tried with her but seein' as that shit kept comin' up for me and pissing me off, it didn't work. She threw away a marriage, a family, for a new car. Not down with that."

"I heartily agree," she declared and at that, he didn't fight the grin.

He gave into it.

"Still, life led me to eventually gettin' Ethan outta it, wouldn't have had him with Donna so I guess shit works out the way it should."

"Yes," she agreed.

This was breathy and he didn't know why. But he liked the way it sounded.

"Mandy, number two, was the shit," he kept going. "Loved her too. She was all over me, all over bein' stepmom to my kids. Put a ring on her finger, she wanted me, realized, 24/7, she couldn't hack kids. She took off. Just one day came home and she was gone. Got the divorce papers in the mail. Haven't seen her since. Good news was, I didn't have her ticket, but the kids did so it rocked my world but they were glad she was gone."

"That, well…rocking of your world sounds unpleasant."

Jake shook his head at her words and the way she said them.

Fuck, half the time with her and the way she talked, he didn't know whether to laugh or kiss her.

Unfortunately, he couldn't do the last and didn't think she'd appreciate him doing the first so he did neither.

"It wasn't, honey, but don't worry. Got over it quick, her hauling ass like that. Not cool. Figured, in the end, she was like that, I got off clean and did it fast, so I did all right."

"And the last?" she prompted when he stopped talking.

"Sloane, Ethan's mom."

"Yes."

"And you're down with real?"

A pause then, "Yes, Jake, I'm *down* with real."

He grinned again at the way she said that then stated, "She was fuckin' fantastic in bed."

When he said no more she asked, "That's it?"

"No," he answered. "She was *unbelievably* fuckin' fantastic in bed."

"I, um…well, that is to say…it doesn't sound like you wanted to end things with any of these women."

"You open your eyes, you see signs. You keep 'em closed, you don't see dick. Lookin' back, every one of them gave me reason to throw in the towel before things got legal. I didn't see it because I wasn't man enough to look for it."

Again, he got silence for a long time before she said, "I don't know much about these matters, Jake, but I would think it would make a man less of a man if he was in love and he didn't have the courage to try his hand."

The courage to try his hand.

Fucking hell.

She kept going.

"Therefore, outside of Ethan's mother, who you didn't claim to love, you just followed your heart and I find that very manly."

Followed your heart.

Fucking *hell*.

"Jake?" she called when he was silent.

"Yeah, baby," he answered quietly.

"I…" Another pause and then, "Are you all right?"

"Laid it out, it was ugly, you went gentle," he replied, reaching out and finding her hand. He gave it a squeeze and finished, "Appreciate that, honey."

"Well, you're welcome," she murmured and it took her a second but she squeezed his hand back.

He kept hold of it, resting the back of his on the sleek silk over her soft thigh and her hand again squeezed his, reflexively this time. He figured he knew what this meant but he didn't let her go even as they hit The Eaves and he turned into the parking lot. He only let her go when he stopped the truck outside the front door.

He put it in neutral, opened his door and jumped down. Rounding the hood, he pulled open her door.

"I'll let you out here. Place is always packed. I find a spot far away, don't want you walkin'," he explained.

"That's kind, Jake. Thank you," she replied and undid her seatbelt.

When she turned to the door and cautiously put one of her shit-hot shoes to the running board, he put his hands to her waist. She put hers to his shoulders and he pulled her down, setting her on her feet.

He let her go, she dropped her hands but he grabbed one and walked her to the front door and through it.

Once he had her out of the cold, he lifted his other hand and squeezed the side of her neck as he squeezed her hand in his, bent close and said, "Be back."

Her blue eyes held his and she murmured, "All right."

He grinned at her and took off.

He was assaulted with the vision of her in that dress when he returned. Obviously, they'd taken her coat.

He was still dealing with her and her dress when she turned her eyes to him near on the second he came through the door, her lips tipped up, her eyes for some reason bright, and she said, "I inquired. Our table is ready."

Then she held out her hand to him.

Christ.

It hit him in that moment in a way he knew he'd never forget that he could take that hand and she could lead him anywhere. Just tip up her lips, turn those eyes to him and hold out her hand and he'd go straight to hell with her and do it smiling.

He knew the idea was fucked.

He also knew no one grieved like she did for Lydie without feeling deep. He knew she wasn't giving up the house, something that would break Lydie's heart—and his children's. He knew she was looking after a dying woman she barely knew so her husband could have a break. He knew she was the only person who seemed to pierce even an inch through the web of teenaged girl drama Amber had woven around herself. He further knew that his daughter was a vegetarian for a day and then she gave that stupid shit up, definitely because of Josie. He knew she helped his son with his homework. He knew he gave her all his fucked up shit with women and she made it sound like he was a knight in armor on a white horse. And, last, he knew she knew she'd fucked up with him and she didn't even leave it for a day before she hauled her ass to him and apologized.

She was wrong. With Donna and Mandy, he'd been blind.

Now he had his eyes open and he liked a fuckuva lot what he was seeing.

He strode forward and took the hand she was offering. Then he pulled it up and tucked it to the side of his chest, his eyes going to the hostess.

"As the lady said. Spear," he said to the hostess.

She nodded, grabbing some menus. "Of course. Please follow me."

He held Josie close as they walked to their table. It was not lost on Jake that never, not once in his life with the women he'd had in it—and some of them had been good ones, all of them had been good-looking—had he ever felt the pride he felt walking through that restaurant with Josie at his side.

When they made it to their table, one he liked, which was in the middle of the restaurant so everyone could see him and the woman on his arm, he let her go only to pull out her chair.

He settled her into it and watched as the hostess flicked out Josie's napkin and Josie sat back with practiced ease to allow it to be placed on her lap.

Jake grabbed his own, not about to have the hostess do the same with him.

They were handed their menus, told that their server would explain the evening's specials and the hostess slid away while a busboy came in and filled their water glasses.

Josie looked up at the kid and murmured, "Thank you."

It was then she turned even brighter, totally shining eyes to him.

When she did, Jake felt his chest seize for the second time that night, but this time it was an altogether different kind of feeling.

The busboy left and Josie leaned into the table immediately.

"Gran and I have been here three times," she announced.

Fuck.

He watched her closely, wondering if he misinterpreted those bright eyes and it was about tears, not happiness.

"I love it here," she went on. "We came twice for my birthday, once for hers. It's one of my favorite restaurants anywhere."

Well, that was good.

She smiled a big smile, a smile that lit up her face and exposed her pretty white teeth.

His gut clenched.

He'd seen her smile. But never like that.

It was phenomenal.

"I went to Breeze Point and Gran and I would go there too, more often as it's not as expensive. And I went by myself. It wasn't a terrible experience but it made me melancholy and not simply because that odious man approached me," she shared, still smiling.

It was then she gave it to him.

"But now I'm in a lovely frock, you look very handsome in your suit, you're very gallant which is most charming, and we're at a fabulous restaurant where I'm certain we'll partake of an excellent meal. And it doesn't make me feel melancholy because I know Gran would be happy we're here enjoying this…together."

She reached out, grabbed her water glass, took a sip from it and put it back, returning her eyes to Jake. All through this, Jake, still dealing with her smile and her words, couldn't think of fuck all to say.

"Now *we* get to make a lovely memory here. Isn't that marvelous?" she asked.

"Yeah, babe," he forced himself to answer.

She kept dazzling him with a smile a moment before she continued rocking his world.

"Thank you for giving this to me. It means a great deal."

"You're welcome, honey," he whispered.

And that was when something else hit him.

Since he'd first seen her, she was covered in a cloak of grief. She carried on day to day, but it was still smothering her.

Now, she was happy.

And he gave her that.

Shit, fuck, but that felt good.

He watched her tip her head to her menu and murmur, "I wonder what their specials are. They always have something quite splendid on offer with their specials."

"Live it up, Slick, whatever you want," he murmured back and she tipped her head again, gave him her shining eyes and another dazzling smile.

He grinned at her then he grinned down at his menu.

He'd not made his choice when a waiter arrived at their table and Jake watched with confusion as the guy put a glass of champagne in front of Josie.

"Good evening," he said as Jake looked from the glass, to Josie studying it, to the waiter. "That's from the gentleman at the bar," he explained, smiling and tipping his head toward the bar.

The waiter went on, asking Jake's drink order but Jake looked beyond Josie, who was looking over her shoulder toward the bar, and he saw him.

Fucking Boston Stone.

And the fucker had the balls to send a drink to the woman sitting at Jake's table.

"Sir?" the waiter prompted and he cut his eyes to him.

"Bud. Bottle if you got it," he ordered curtly.

"Of course," the waiter replied. "Would you like to hear the specials?"

Jake looked to Josie to see her now glaring at the glass of champagne.

"Come back," he said.

"Of course," the waiter murmured then slid away.

The instant he did, Jake knew how irritated Josie was because she didn't hesitate telling him.

"This is beyond the pale," she hissed. "Utterly *tactless*. I'm at a meal with a gentleman and he sends a glass of champagne only *to me?* That is *not done.* It's exceptionally *rude* not to mention *arrogant.* Does he honestly think this will impress me? If he does he's very *wrong.*"

After she delivered that, Jake rose from his chair, tossed his napkin on the table, reached across it and nabbed her glass of champagne.

He rounded the table, his eyes on his target, his blood hot in his veins, and only stopped when he felt her hand curl around his.

He looked down at her to see she'd paled and was now looking concerned.

"Jake—" she started in a whisper.

"It'll be okay, baby," he assured her. "Stay here. I'll be right back."

Then he pulled his hand from hers after giving hers a squeeze and prowled to Stone.

He put the glass on the bar beside Stone and growled, "Outside."

He didn't wait to see if Stone followed him. He might not know Boston Stone but he knew the kind of man he was. Even though he knew Jake could take him, and not just because Jake had two inches and thirty pounds on him, he wouldn't take the hit to his manhood that would be keeping his seat when he was called out.

Jake wasn't wrong. When he got outside, Stone was there. The asshole rounded him and they faced off, Jake going first.

"You got stones," Jake clipped.

To that, the motherfucker grinned. "Is that a pun?"

"I'm not bein' funny, asshole," Jake bit out. "Seriously? Sendin' a drink to the woman sittin' across from *me* at *my* table?"

"I bought the entire bottle but I'll drink the rest. I'm relatively certain Dom Perignon would be lost on you," Stone replied, his voice smooth, his words snide.

Jake let that slide. What Boston Stone thought of him did not factor. Not now and it never would.

What factored was Josie having a good night, smiling bright and then a minute later being pissed because of this jackass.

"Josie's got too much class to lay it out for you," Jake returned. "But on the way here, she told me about the drink she's supposed to have with you. She also told me she didn't want that drink. We talked about it and decided I'd lay it out for you. And now that I got that opportunity, here it is. She's not into you, man. Let it go. And heads up, a woman like that with class like that, the shit you just pulled doesn't do anything for her except piss her off."

"We'll see Monday night if Josephine is *into me*."

Jesus. Was this guy deaf?

"You didn't hear me," Jake returned. "You won't be seein' shit 'cause, if you show at the Club, she won't be there seein' as she'll be makin' dinner for me and my family."

Annoyance chased across Stone's face before he hid it and lifted his chin. "It appears she's in the mood to go slumming but a woman like that always comes around when that particular thrill is gone."

What was with this guy?

"She's just lost her grandmother, asshole," Jake reminded him.

"And in times of sorrow, it's good to turn your mind to other more pleasurable things and, when she gives me the opportunity, I'll enjoy turning her mind to just those things."

"Christ, honestly?" Jake asked. "I told you she's not into you. Do you seriously think your dick is that big?"

"I've never been a man to compare. We don't have that in common. We don't have anything in common, Spear. Except for the fact that both of us know precisely how fuckable Josephine Malone is. And I wouldn't have believed it possible but tonight, seeing her in that dress, proved she's even *more* fuckable. If *you* have the stones, my suggestion, get in there and do it fast. Tonight. Before your charms wear off. But please, not against the wall of the foyer of Lavender House. That's where I'll be taking her our first time."

Jake's vision went red but he didn't have the chance to say a fucking word.

This was because she came at him from behind. And he was so pissed and focused he didn't hear her heels on the pavers. He just felt her shoulder as it hit his arm then she slid in front of him and he watched Josie pull back a hand and slap Stone hard across the face.

Stone's head jerked to the side and Jake moved. Wrapping his fingers around her wrist, he pulled it down and around her belly, yanking her back to his front then stepping them both back as he wrapped his other arm around her chest.

But now, *she* was focused.

"You *cad*," she snapped and Jake lost his fury instantly and had to clench his teeth to stop himself laughing at her ridiculous insult that, even ridiculous, was fucking cute because it was pure Josie. "How *dare* you!" she kept at him. "You're...you're...*unspeakable*," she finished on a hiss.

Stone's face changed entirely, his eyes on her, his lips murmuring, "Josephine—"

"Do not utter another word," she warned angrily. "I'm afraid I must inform you that with your behavior tonight and the things I just heard you say, I'll not be meeting you for a drink Monday. Indeed, I'd rather not see you again *in my life*. Have I made myself clear?"

"It's unfortunate you heard that, Josephine, but allow me to—" Stone started.

"Actually, I find it quite fortunate," she cut him off to declare. "I simply thought you were arrogant and insensitive. Now I know you're much more and none of it is good. Alas, what's *unfortunate* is that Jake and I were having a lovely evening. The first lovely evening I've had since my grandmother died, and you cast a pall on that. However, with the likes of you, it's easily forgettable so we can put the unpleasantness that is you behind us, return to the restaurant and continue enjoying our evening."

Listening to this, Jake was making a mental note not to piss Josie off when she pulled from his arms but caught his hand.

"Come, Jake. Your beer has arrived and I've just discovered I'm in dire need of a martini."

She tugged on his hand.

He grinned at her then grinned at a frowning Stone who was giving Josie a dark look Jake didn't like all that much. Then again, the asshole could do nothing. She was lost to him even more than she was before. It didn't matter he was loaded and could send a glass of Dom Perignon to her table. He'd ceased to exist for Josie.

On that thought, Jake kept grinning as he let her start to pull him toward the restaurant.

But when she turned, she wobbled on her high heel so he jerked on her hand to send her flying his way. He let it go but caught her tight to his side with an arm around her back as he swallowed down a bark of laughter when she muttered an infuriated, "Drat!"

"Just keep on keepin' on, baby," he whispered. "You leveled him. And it wouldn't matter what you do in those shoes. You're gonna look good doin' it, he's got no chance, so it's all good."

He negotiated her up the steps and reached out to open the door for her when she declared, "That man is a toad."

"That man is in your rearview mirror and what's down the road is a martini and a fuckin' good meal."

He heard her draw in a breath as he pulled her through the door, then she said, "Indeed."

He gave her a squeeze and felt her arm slide around his back as he headed her to their table.

They only let each other go when he held her chair for her. She sat in it. Jake tucked her under the table and resumed his seat.

He was putting his napkin back on his lap when she again spoke.

"I was correct. You're very gallant."

He looked at her to see her eyes direct on him. "What?"

"I found what you just did to be both honorable and brave. I've never seen a man behave like that. You acting when I was annoyed to handle that matter without delay was quite gratifying."

He grinned at her and noted, "So, you're giving me a compliment."

She nodded once. "Indeed. No wonder Gran liked you. She always said that chivalry was fading alongside nobility and she thought that was a shame. She said those kinds of men are now very rare. She found one in you. I'm seeing more and more clearly why she'd give me you for, her knowing this, she'd want me to have it."

Jake said nothing. This was because he was again frozen in order that he could fully experience her words searing through him.

"What I don't understand is why she kept you from me," she stated, her eyes sliding away and she began talking to the carpet. "However, that encounter was vexing." She looked back to him. "So can I ask that we dispense with discussing anything that may be distressing and just sally forth enjoying the evening?"

Jesus, she was too much.

And too fucking cute being it.

Jake again grinned at her. "We can sally forth however you want, Slick."

Her eyes flashed when he quit talking then he watched something move through her expressive face, settle in it, warming the entirety of her features, and finally she smiled.

He let that smile sear through him too then he saw their waiter out of the corner of his eye. He caught the man's attention and jerked up his chin.

The guy hustled to their table.

"The lady wants a martini," Jake told him.

"Vodka, with olives," Josie put in.

"I'll see to that right away," the waiter replied.

"Then we'll want the specials," Jake added.

"Of course," the guy nodded, bowing slightly. "I'll return shortly."

"Now," Josie started when the guy moved away. "I'll need to know if there's anything Conner won't eat so I can plan Monday's menu."

He reached for his beer, ignoring the chilled glass they'd provided, answering, "Con's allergic to vegetables."

He took a tug from the bottle and smothered another grin when he saw her big blue eyes get wide.

"That's horrible," she declared. "Allergic to vegetables? *All* vegetables?"

He put his beer back to the table and leaned into her. "Baby, it's a turn of phrase. He's not allergic to them. He just hates 'em."

"Oh," she mumbled. Then her gaze grew sharp. "He should get past this. It's not healthy not to have vegetables in your diet."

"I'll let you share that with him on Monday."

She straightened her shoulders and stated, "I'll do that without delay. It's my understanding that young men continue to grow into their twenties. He's far from small but if his diet was more robust, who knows what could happen."

Fucking hell, she was the shit.

"Yeah, Josie. Who knows," Jake muttered.

"Now, I've got the taste for steak," she changed the subject. "What do you have the taste for?"

Straight up, he had the taste for cute, klutzy, classy pussy, eating her and listening to her moan.

He didn't tell her that.

He said, "Waitin' for the specials."

She nodded and smiled.

He took her smile and gave her one back.

Then her martini arrived.

———◆·•◆·•◆———

JAKE SAT IN the window seat of the light room, legs stretched out up on the seat, ankles crossed, a glass of Lydie's Scotch in his hand, his eyes to the moonlight on the sea.

Josie was down from him, curled up with her legs under her, body twisted, torso pressed to the seat back, facing the windows.

She'd given him a treat and taken off her shoes, making it the first time she was even slightly casual in front of him. She hadn't let down her hair and after that night, he was thinking he *really* needed to see her with her hair down.

But this would come.

She was drinking some purple liquid from a snifter that came from a fancy-ass bottle and smelled like cough syrup when she'd handed him her glass after he asked what it was. He didn't taste it. A sniff was enough to put him off and his expression must have told her that because she immediately took the glass from him but did it on a cute little giggle.

After asking him in for an after dinner drink, getting his Scotch, getting her drink and taking off her shoes, she'd led him up to his favorite room in the house.

It had been a good night and he knew this because he'd quit counting the times she smiled because she was doing it so often, he couldn't keep track. She'd even laughed, mostly quiet and sweet, but once her shoulders shook with it.

What made her smile and laugh was his stories about the kids or the guys at the gym or how his dancers and bouncers were always dating, breaking up, acting out and trying and failing to hide that shit seeing as he had a no fraternization policy.

She'd also made him smile, relaxing more and more as the dinner went on and sharing about places she'd gone, things she'd done and the people she knew and worked with. Some of the names of recording artists he definitely knew. He even knew some of designers' names.

The one thing that made him uneasy about this was the way she talked about it. She clearly enjoyed her work, liked and/or admired the people she worked with and it was obvious she loved what she did and the people she did it around.

In her globetrotting lifestyle with the fashion and music elite, he could see it would be difficult to settle in a small town on coastal Maine no matter how pretty the town was or how phenomenal her house was in that town.

She took him from his thoughts when she said softly, "Before it became too hard for her to negotiate stairs, Gran and I used to sit up here all the time."

His eyes went to her to see she still had hers to the view and she kept talking.

"When I was young, I used to make up stories and tell them to her. I think she knew they were my daydreams but she never said anything. When I was older, we wouldn't have to say anything at all. She'd sip her Drambuie, me my Chambord and we'd just sit here, staring at the sea, and we'd just *be* but in being we did it together."

Jake said nothing, reading her mood and deciding she didn't need a grief counselor or a conversationalist.

She needed a listening ear.

So he was going to give it to her.

However, he was wrong.

He knew this when she turned his way and caught his eyes in the dim light.

"Can you just tell me how you met?" she requested quietly.

"I'll tell you anything you want, baby," he replied quietly.

She nodded and Jake gave her what she needed.

"My gym was goin' down," he shared.

She tipped her head to the side and he kept going.

"To make a real go of that place, I need to offer boot camps, spin classes, aerobics and shit. In a town this size, a boxing gym is not gonna make a man a shitload of money. And it didn't. Problem was, I had three kids to take care of and a wife at that time and I needed to make money. A friend of mine is a reporter for the county paper and when it looked like the gym was gonna go down, she made a big deal of it, hoping to get me more members. The Truck losin' his gym. The kids losin' their league."

"The kids losing their league?" she asked.

He nodded. "Got a junior boxing league runs outta the gym. They train three afternoons a week after school and have matches on the weekends.

There isn't a shitload of kids in it but we always got around twenty or thirty. Makes no money, dues they pay barely cover equipment and it eats up gym time. Still, it keeps kids from doin' fucked up shit and it teaches them discipline, gives them confidence, shows them it's important to take care of their bodies, and gives them the means to stick up for themselves."

"You never mentioned that," she noted.

"Haven't known you that long, honey," he replied.

She nodded then said, "I've heard this 'truck' business and your gym is named that. What does that mean?"

"I'm The Truck."

"Pardon?"

He grinned at her. "I'm The Truck, Josie. Used to box. That's what they called me."

She straightened in her seat. "You're a pugilist?"

His grin got bigger. "Uh…yeah, I'm a pugilist. Used to be a pretty good one. That's how I could make the paper, even if it was just the town paper. Started boxing early, just for a workout. Wasn't into team sports and my dad wasn't into havin' a kid layin' around watchin' TV. Found it suited me. Liked bein' in my head, havin' it be about what my body could do but more, while my body was being challenged, I had to keep my head. You get trained, you learn your opponent, you have people drilling strategy in you, but when you're in the ring, there are only two of you and the goal is pretty extreme. You gotta beat the shit outta the other guy so he doesn't do it to you."

When he stopped talking, she asked, "And you were a pretty good one?"

"Yeah."

"How good?"

"Had a couple pay-per-view fights in Vegas. That good."

She sounded adorably confused when she asked, "Is that good?"

He smiled at her again. "Yeah, Josie. That's good. Boxed in college, had a trainer-manager approach me, ditched school my junior year, went all in. It worked. Got some big fights. Made decent money. Did some traveling and saw some nice places. It was good, exciting, I liked it and I loved to box. But you gotta do it smart and you gotta get out when it's time to get out. Your body can't take that forever. I got out, came home to Maine, used my earnings and opened the gym."

"I still don't understand why they call you The Truck," she said.

"I'm called The Truck 'cause I knocked out a kid in college three minutes into the first round. When the college paper asked him what happened, he said my right hook was like getting hit in the face with a Mack truck. It stuck."

"I'm taking it that's complimentary," she guessed and that got another smile out of him.

"Yeah, babe. *Very,*" he confirmed.

He saw her teeth flash before she prompted him to get back to the story, "So, you were going to lose your gym…"

"Yeah. And Lydie saw the article," he told her. "She came to see me. Not sure she wanted The Truck to keep his gym. It was probably more about the kids having their boxing league. But whatever it was, she came to offer me money to help bail me out."

"Ah…" she murmured.

"Lydie's Lydie, way she was, she got me to talkin' and she got the whole story. Dad was dead. Mom was draggin' and we'd find out not too long later she was dyin'. My gym was in the red and to put food on the table, I was a bouncer working nights at The Circus. We were livin' in a two-bedroom apartment close to the wharf and that place wasn't good normally, but it smelled like dead fish depending on which way the wind was blowin'. Donna was beginning to embrace her inner cougar so she was more interested in getting laid than having her kids during her custody times. This meant Sloane was up in my shit, not happy to have two kids most of the time 'cause Donna was out carousing and a baby in that small pad."

"Is this why she left you?" Josie asked.

"She didn't leave me, babe, kicked her ass out."

Her voice held surprise when she asked, "You ended things with her?"

He leaned her way. "With Sloane, finally learned how to do it. Life sometimes sucks and right then, it was suckin' *huge* for me. I knew that apartment was shit. I didn't like my family to be there either. Tight with my dad, loved my mom, not doin' good with him gone and her goin'. I was not hangin' on to the gym. I knew it had to go. It killed me. I love that gym. But my family was more important. I was workin' two jobs, I'd drag my ass home at three in the mornin', get up to open the gym at seven, crashin' whenever I could.

I didn't want that and was tryin' to find a way out. She wasn't tryin' to find anything but ways to ride my ass. When shit gets heavy, you stand by your man. You don't drag him down when he's already circling the toilet."

There was a pause before she whispered, "This is very true."

"I know it is."

She kept whispering when she said, "I'm sorry she was that way with you, Jake."

So fucking sweet.

"I was too at the time, honey," he replied. "But the way she turned her back on me, but mostly on Ethan when she got her new man and set up her new life, not upset I'm shot of her."

She held his eyes a long moment before she asked, "So is this when Gran offered you money to buy The Circus?"

"Yeah." He nodded. "Place was a shithole. And Dave, the guy who owned it, was a dick. Paid the girls nothin', sayin' they made their money on tips. Had two bouncers on each night. Just two. For a club like that, that's inviting trouble. Had girls behind the bar who couldn't do shit should somethin' go down. He still made money. A load of it. And when he was looking to get out, I knew, if I could buy it, I could turn it around, make a shitload more."

"Therefore you told Gran this and she believed in your vision."

Jake smiled again. "Yeah. She believed in my vision, Slick. Told me, I leverage the gym, she'd give me the rest of the money and, I could make a go of The Circus, pay her back along the way. Obviously I said no."

She straightened and leaned toward him, sounding surprised when she asked, "You said no?"

"I said no," he confirmed. "Taking pity money from an eighty-six year old lady?" He shook his head.

"But you eventually took the money," she noted.

Jake nodded.

"I took the money. I said no about a hundred times first. The good part about this was, she was interested in me, she liked me, I liked her, and she kept at me. In this time, she met the kids, got involved in our lives, we liked her there, we kept her and she kept us. Eventually, she wore me down. I took the money, got a loan on the gym seein' as I owned the building outright. I closed The Circus down for two months, me and some buddies fixed it up, reopened, paid Lydie back within a year. Paid off the loan on the gym within three. Got myself a four-bedroom house where my kids all have their own rooms. Life changed. Quit sucking. Got good. And Lydie was the catalyst for all that."

"And that's how you met," she said softly.

"That's how we met," he replied just as softly.

She was still talking soft when she said, "I'm glad she was there for you, Jake."

"I am too, honey."

He watched her turn her head to the view before she said to it, "I just don't understand how she could be so involved in your life, your children's lives, and she never introduced any of you to me."

This was the sticky part.

And it was a fucked up move, he knew it, but she was suffering so Jake waded into the mire.

He would deal with the blowback when, but hopefully only if it happened.

"Babe, she was all about you when you'd come to visit," Jake told her and she looked back to him.

"Pardon?"

"She talked about you all the time. Thought the world of you. And when you'd come for a visit, she'd get real excited. She couldn't wait. Not hard to see she missed you when you were gone and she missed you bad. So, my guess, when she had you, she didn't want to share you."

"We went to parties and I saw her other friends all the time," she returned.

"Yeah, but I'm not exactly in her age group and my family isn't exactly in her social set. We're not invited to play bridge and we don't go to church socials."

"This is true," she murmured.

"And I know from what she told me after you were gone that she did not live her life on the go, socializing rabidly like she always did until she couldn't do it anymore. When you were here, she took a break. She gave her time to you and sucked all of yours in that she could get."

This brought on silence until she broke it, saying quietly, "We consumed each other."

"Come again?" he asked.

She looked again to the window. "When we were together, we consumed each other. I thought it was just me missing Gran. When I was with her, I took every moment I could get with her and in this house. Committing it to memory. I did that even before..." She trailed off then began again. "I did it even when I was a little girl. I loved being with her and I loved being with her in this house."

"So maybe that's why we didn't meet."

She looked back at him. "You and your children are not bridge cronies, Jake, but you meant the world to her too. I know this to be true. She has your picture on her nightstand."

Jake had no reply to that.

Strike that.

He had one. He just couldn't give it to her.

Not now.

"I could see, in the beginning maybe. But seven years?" she asked.

He bent a knee, leaned deep and stretched a hand out, catching hers. "I have no answers for you, baby," he told her gently, none of these words sitting well because they meant he'd lied to her gently. "And, it sucks but she's gone. This is clearly fuckin' with your head but you gotta let it go because with her gone, you're never gonna get those answers. Just settle in that it was whatever it was and she made it so we have each other now."

"We have each other now," she whispered.

"Yeah."

Her hand turned in his so she could curl her fingers around and she held tight.

And when she did, she held his eyes and kept whispering. "I'm glad, Jake."

He held her back just as tight. "Me too, honey."

She gave him a small smile.

And on that, Jake decided it was time to go. Her in this mood made him want to find creative ways to guide her out of it and he knew which way that creativity would go.

He was not Boston Stone.

In the beginning, the minute he saw her in her big black hat and big black shades at the funeral, he'd felt the urge, definitely. A woman like that, few men wouldn't.

Then again, he'd felt the urge long before that seeing her pictures, reading her letters, listening to Lydie talk about her.

He didn't know about the will at the funeral but he knew where Lydie was leaning, what she wanted. She never said it flat out but that didn't mean she didn't make the message abundantly clear and she did this repeatedly.

But Jake didn't figure Josie would want anything to do with a guy like him.

He knew differently in the parking lot at the club when he let her off the hook, telling her his tastes for women leaned elsewhere.

He didn't lie. He liked big hair. He liked big tits. And he didn't mind his women showing skin.

That said, he also liked ass and legs and curves in all the right places and high heels and melodic voices and thick blonde hair and big blue eyes and pretty much everything that made up her package.

She'd surprised him by exposing she'd go there.

She said he wasn't her thing but he knew she lied.

But now was not the time for her to make those decisions. She lost the only person she was close to on this earth—he knew not only a grandmother but a savior. And he sensed she was at a crossroads. He'd be a dick to make a play while the first was fresh and the last was uncertain.

He'd wait.

She'd told him at dinner her shit for brains boss was not likely to show for at least three weeks, maybe longer.

So he had three weeks to get in there and during that time, he'd go gently.

So fucking her on the window seat in the room where she told stories to her recently deceased grandmother when she was a kid was not the way to go.

"I got furniture to move tomorrow, honey, so I best be hittin' the road so I can hit the sack."

Her hand flexed in his like she didn't want to let him go and he liked that.

But she said, "All right, Jake."

He downed the rest of his Scotch then got up, pulling her out of the seat.

She made it without taking a tumble. Then again, her feet were bare.

He held her hand down the spiral staircase, thanking fuck the thing was wide so he could do it, and he held her hand all the way to the front door.

He kept hold of it as he put his glass on a table at the side of the door, took hers and set it beside his. He also kept hold of it even as he slid his other one from the side of her neck to the back and pulled her forward, leaning in.

Then he kissed her forehead and moved back an inch to catch her eyes.

"Another good night, Slick."

"Yes," she agreed breathily, her eyes holding his and hers were not hiding the fact she didn't want him to walk out the door.

Yeah.

He was her thing.

He wouldn't have guessed it. Wouldn't even think it was possible. Spent years not thinking it was possible.

But yesterday, she let him in. Calling him when a new wave of grief poured over her and he knew she did that shit the instant it happened with the way her voice sounded on her message and even later, when he called her back.

He just had to glide the rest of the way in, slow and easy. For her. For him. For his kids.

Like Lydie wanted.

Precisely like Lydie wanted.

"Sleep tight, baby," he murmured.

"You too, Jake."

He grinned at her and squeezed her with both hands.

Then he let her go, opened the door and walked out, ordering, "Lock this behind me."

"Of course," she replied to his back. Then she called, "Goodnight."

He turned at the door of his truck and gave her a low wave and a smile. She waved back.

Then she stepped back, closed the door and she was gone.

———

JAKE HEARD THE TV when he came into the kitchen from the garage.

He threw his keys on the counter and was shrugging off his suit jacket when Conner came in.

His eyes went to his boy.

"What's her curfew?"

"It's Saturday, Dad. We got until midnight."

He bunched his jacket in a fist, walking further into the room and asked, "How many sundaes did Ethan eat?"

Conner grinned. "Three."

"Terrific," Jake muttered.

Conner leaned against the island and his grin died. "Just sayin', Amber was a total bitch all night to everybody."

Time to get her ass back to Josie. She might not have been sunshine and light after the last time she was with Josie, but at least that bought them having her quiet and reflective for a day or two.

"I'll have a word."

"Have twelve," Conner replied. "Ellie got fed up with it. Told me she wanted me to take her home. Took a lot to talk her out of it."

Jake wished he hadn't. That would mean they'd make out and whatever the fuck they were doing in Conner's car, not on Jake's couch.

"Said I'll have a word, Con," he reminded him.

Conner nodded then grinned again. "How was dinner?"

"Josie's the shit," Jake replied, tossing his jacket on the island and moving to the fridge.

"You into her?" Conner asked and Jake came out of the fridge with a bottle of water and gave his eyes to his son.

"We havin' a heart to heart while your girl is in there watchin' TV?"

Conner's grin got bigger. "Just askin', seein' as Ethan said she's mega pretty."

"You'll see for yourself Monday night. We're goin' over there for dinner. And, heads up, she's concerned you don't eat vegetables. She's a class act but she's also Lydie's granddaughter. Lydie's been riding your ass for years about eating your greens. Josie laid it out for Amber within half an hour of meeting her. She won't hesitate over vegetables."

His son's grin didn't waver. "I'll brace."

Jake shook his head, moved to his boy and grabbed him around the back of the neck for a squeeze.

Then he let him go and muttered, "Get back to your girl."

Conner lifted his chin.

Jake moved to the door to the hall but stopped, turned back and called his son's name.

Conner turned to him too. "Yeah?"

"Pick one," Jake said quietly. "Think about it, think long and hard and pick right. But cut the others loose. You've had your fun. Now it's time to make a choice and cut the strings so you aren't draggin' them all with you only to eventually drag them down. You with me?"

Conner had no smile when he started, "But, Dad—"

Jake cut him off. "Trust your old man. A woman's heart is fragile and it's precious. Don't be that asshole who kicks it around."

He watched his son swallow.

"Now, you with me?" Jake prompted.

He hesitated, but only a couple seconds before Conner replied, "Yeah, Dad."

Jake nodded. "Good. 'Night, Con."

"'Night, Dad."

On that, Jake went up to his room.

Nine

ALAS

The next day, I drove up the lane to see only Jake's truck in the drive, Jake in the back of the bed arranging boxes.

Boxes of Gran's clothes.

I swallowed as I brought my car to a halt behind his truck.

That morning, Jake had called me and suggested that it might be less traumatic for me if I wasn't around when he and the guys were working.

This was a kind suggestion (as Jake, I'd learned, was very kind) and thus I'd agreed. I then phoned Mr. Weaver to ask if he wanted to spend some time in the office, even though it was a Sunday, and I could come over and sit with Mrs. Weaver.

He'd taken me up on the offer, so as Jake suggested, I was out of the house by the time he came. Before I'd left, I'd taken the time to write out detailed notes and tape them to pieces of furniture, lamps and knick-knacks that I remembered used to make up the den but had been disbursed throughout the house so Jake's "boys" could put them where they were supposed to be.

I'd also left money so Jake could order pizza.

Now, it was after one in the afternoon and he was the only one left.

I watched as he jumped down from the bed of his truck as I got out of my rental car, slammed the door and moved to him. I did this thinking that he could even jump down from a truck in a way I found attractive. I also did it thinking that everything about Jake Spear was attractive, most especially the entirety of his gallant and candid behavior the night before, not to mention his being amusing and thoughtful.

"What's shakin', Slick?" he called on a grin, making his way to me.

At his words, I stopped thinking of Gran's clothes in those boxes, grinned back and stopped close to him. "I'm uncertain how to answer that since nothing's shaking, Jake."

His grin spread into an attractive, white smile.

Then he did it. Reaching up a hand, he slid it along the side of my neck to the back, pulling me gently forward so he could move in and kiss my forehead.

I would vastly prefer he kiss me somewhere else, felt this desire sweep through me with almost the strength it had the night before when he performed the same maneuver, and felt it equally difficult to quash the impulse to tip my head back to give him a different target.

I managed it, but when he pulled away, he did something different than he had last night.

He slid his hand from the back of my neck to cup my jaw and kept his face close.

"It's all done," he said quietly.

I nodded.

"You wanna see?"

I nodded again.

He let my jaw go (alas), but caught my hand and pulled me to the house.

We made it to the door of the den and I felt something different sweep through me when I looked in to see that it appeared much like it had for the years prior to Gran making it her bedroom. There were a few things put in the wrong places and there was some adjusting of the furniture that needed to be done.

But mostly, it was as it should be.

And in seeing it, I felt relief.

Therefore, staring at it, I whispered, "Thank you, Jake."

He turned my way with a tug of my hand indicating he wanted my attention so I turned to him as well.

He kept hold of my hand and my eyes when he informed me gently, "Got a couple boxes of stuff that wasn't clothes. Put them in her bedroom upstairs. What I got in the truck is just her clothes, like you asked. I'll take it to Goodwill. That's done. You take your time with the rest of her stuff, but you need me around when you do it, just call."

I was wrong.

Jake wasn't kind.

He was generous, selfless and tenderhearted. He loved Gran too. This couldn't be easy for him.

"I don't know how—" I began but he interrupted me not only with a squeeze of my hand but also with words.

"Think we established you don't need to say or do shit. Like I said, this is done. Move on, honey."

I pressed my lips together and nodded.

He kept speaking.

"Now, boys had pizza and I cleaned up the boxes, the paper plates. Your trash was overflowing so I took it out."

Generous.

Selfless.

Tenderhearted.

Jake.

"Would you like to stay for a beer or something?" I offered, trying not to sound hopeful and luckily succeeding.

He shook his head, giving my hand another squeeze.

"I'd love to hang but Amber's lookin' after Ethan while Con's at work so I need to get home so she can continue to sulk in her room by herself and not bug Eath with that shit."

I nodded.

He continued speaking.

"We'll be over tomorrow night at six. Cool?"

"Yes, Jake, erm…cool," I agreed.

He again grinned on another squeeze of my hand. He then leaned in and gave me another kiss on the forehead.

He moved back this time without touching me further (alas), kept grinning at me for a moment before he said, "Later, babe."

"Um…yes. Later."

He winked, my stomach dipped then he let me go and he was gone. Alas.

TWENTY-FIVE MINUTES AFTER the Fletchers left after dinner that evening, my mobile rang.

I moved quickly to it and even more quickly took the call when I saw on the display who was calling.

"Jake," I greeted.

"Yo, Slick," he replied. "How'd dinner go with the Reverend and his missus?"

At his words, I went still.

Good God, he was calling simply to talk.

That felt nice.

Very nice.

It felt so nice I smiled at the phone and moved to the kitchen to put the kettle on to make a cup of tea. "It was quite enjoyable. He's a very interesting man and she's delightful. They both cared a good deal for Gran. It felt lovely having them here."

"That's good, babe."

I put the kettle on the burner and asked, "How's Amber?"

"No clue seein' as she's only come out of her room once since I got home and that was to grab a plate of dinner and disappear in it again."

"Oh dear," I murmured.

"Usually," he went on, "I'd get on her ass about shit like that but we eat in front of the TV so it isn't like she's missin' a big family dinner. She's also never been a big fan of football, she's dedicated to her moping so if she's there, the boys and I can enjoy the game."

He enjoyed football. This shouldn't have been a surprise considering he'd been an athlete in his past. However, it caused me some concern although I didn't know why. I didn't enjoy sport, none of it, and spent no time on it. Not since having to do so when I lived with my father. And furthermore, Jake and I would be nothing but friends so it wouldn't matter that I didn't share his enjoyment of a certain pastime.

It still caused me concern.

I thought this.

I said out loud, "Of course."

"I'll give her today. Tomorrow, she's gonna have to pull her head out of her ass."

"I don't envy you having to manage that situation," I told him.

"Yeah," he replied, his voice on that one syllable shaking with what sounded like humor. "I don't envy me either."

This made no sense. Of course he wouldn't envy him.

I didn't point that out.

I shared, "Jean-Michel has replied to my email about Amber so perhaps tomorrow evening when I share his reply with her, it might brighten her up a bit."

"I'm guessin' from her reaction last time, that'll do the trick."

I smiled again, pleased I could do something that would please Amber.

"Okay, babe, gonna let you go. Con just came in with Ro-Tel dip so it's time to eat until we're sick and watch the second half of the game."

At his words, I felt my brows draw together.

"Ro-Tel dip?"

"Ro-Tel dip," he repeated then explained. "Dump a can of Ro-Tel on a cake of Velveeta, nuke it, stir it, nuke it more until it's smooth and then eat the fuck outta that shit usin' corn chips."

I had no idea what Ro-Tel was but the very mention of Velveeta turned my stomach. Velveeta assumed the guise of cheese but I knew cheese and I enjoyed nearly all varieties of cheese and Velveeta wasn't that. It made me squeamish even to look at it.

That said, this made me think seeing as I'd never actually tasted it. And thinking this, it occurred to me that I was making a judgment without knowing of which I spoke.

This made me just like those youngsters who refused to eat food they couldn't know they didn't like. And thus I decided to buy some Velveeta and make a proper assessment.

On that thought, it occurred to me that it was after eight thirty. I would assume the children would need to go to bed at a decent hour since they had to go to school the next day. And it made sleep difficult to eat before it. What were they doing eating again?

I said nothing of any of this.

Instead, I said, "Then I should allow you to get back to the game."

"Next Sunday, you should come over."

My entire body went warm, not with enthusiasm of watching football and definitely not the possibility that I'd face this Ro-Tel dip, but being with Jake and his boys doing, well…anything.

"I'd enjoy that," I replied.

"It's a date," he declared. "See you tomorrow, Slick."

And there it was again.

Slick.

This being something I decided the night before that I not only liked but very possibly loved. There was a familiarity in it, also humor, definitely (for, I could see, in his eyes I was indeed "slick"), and there was an intimacy.

The former two, I liked.

It was the last I very possibly loved.

Of course, I didn't share that either.

I said, "See you tomorrow, Jake."

"See you tomorrow, Josie!" I heard shouted in a distant way through Jake's phone but it wasn't Jake shouting it, it was Ethan.

And again, my body warmed.

"Please tell Ethan I look forward to seeing him again," I requested to Jake.

"I'll tell him, babe. Tomorrow."

"Tomorrow, Jake."

"Bye, Josie."

"Good-bye."

Then he disconnected and thus was gone.

Alas.

THE DOORBELL RANG and I hurried down the hall.

It was six oh two.

Jake and the children were there.

I'd made an effort with my appearance not only because I normally made an effort with my appearance but because I would be meeting Conner, something I anticipated all day (as with anticipating seeing Ethan and Amber again, but mostly Jake), but also something that made me vaguely nervous.

I didn't understand precisely why but, reflecting on it, it occurred to me that a son could be very like his father. And as Jake was thoughtful, generous, selfless and tenderhearted, his son may be the same. And being thus, he could be protective of his family, of my Gran, and I reflected on Gran and was spending time with his family.

What a seventeen-year-old boy thought of me was not something I would ever imagine would cause me concern. I hadn't felt the same way about Ethan and Amber.

Then again, I didn't know Jake as well then. Now I knew Ethan and Amber liked me. And I most certainly knew I liked Jake.

Therefore, I felt it necessary to win Conner.

This meant I was in casual clothing again but my brand of casual. Jeans. A blousy thistle-colored sweater that fell off my shoulder, narrowed in at my waist in ribs and hugged me there down to mid-hip. And finishing this ensemble were simple smoky-gray suede pumps with graceful, four-inch stiletto heels.

I took a breath, smiled and opened the door.

The instant I did, I was accosted by the exact vision I'd had some days before…almost.

Jake looking handsome (this time in a v-neck sweater and I could see the collar of his t-shirt under it at his neckline). Ethan wearing a hoodie this time, but it also declared his devotion to some sports team. Amber, her makeup a bit less heavy, but her outfit no less inappropriate, looking sullen and standing removed.

Then there was Conner, far more handsome up close, wearing nearly the same garments as his father except his sweater was crewneck. And last, he was surveying me closely.

I swallowed.

"Josie!" Ethan cried, dashed forward and gave my waist a hug.

I put a hand to his shoulder and looked down at the top of his head, which was all I got in before he jumped back and looked up at me.

"Hey!" he greeted.

But he allowed me to say not a word as he dashed by me and into the house.

"Babe," Jake murmured as he came close and then he came closer.

Putting a hand to my hip, his fingers squeezed as he bent in and I got no kiss on the forehead this time. I was assaulted by his alluring cologne and the onslaught didn't stop there. He slid his stubbled cheek down mine and brushed his lips right in front of my ear.

With a grave amount of effort, I controlled the shiver that was threatening to shake through me at his touch and simply smiled at him, whispering, "Jake," when he moved back.

He returned my smile before he shuffled me in.

Amber and Conner came with him and after he closed the door, he again touched my hip with his hand and introduced, "Josie, meet my boy, Conner."

I looked up at Conner, smiled and offered my hand. "Conner, I've heard such good things about you. It's a pleasure."

"Seriously?" he asked oddly in return and I blinked.

"Well, um…of course I'm serious," I answered.

His face spread into a very attractive smile before he moved in and wrapped me in a tight hug.

I stood there, frozen, arms down at my side, not knowing what to do with myself but unable to do anything because he was quite strong, his body cool from the out of doors but still it warmed me and his hug felt more than nice.

Like his younger brother, he showed his affection easily but it was brief.

Thus, he moved back and looked down at me. "Heard a lot about you from Lydie and then Ethan. Really cool to meet you."

"I…well, yes. Good," I stammered then drew in breath to pull myself together and I looked at Amber.

"Hello, Amber," I greeted.

Her shoulders slumped, her eyes moved beyond me and she muttered, "'Lo."

I continued to look pointedly at her and stated, "If you'll promise not to mutter, mumble or murmur another word this evening, I'll show you what

Jean-Michel sent me. And, before you decide whether or not to agree to this arrangement, I'll share that Jean-Michel was rather taken with your image and he went well beyond dashing off a few recommendations."

Her eyes had cut to me as I spoke.

So I held them and finished, "*Well* beyond"

"He did?" she whispered.

"Indeed," I replied.

"He was taken with my image?" She was still whispering.

"How this could be a surprise, I have no idea since I've already told you that you're very attractive."

She also held my eyes before hers darted to where her father was standing next to me then they darted back to me.

"I guess I can make that deal," she agreed.

"Excellent," I replied and started moving toward the kitchen, feeling the eldest members of the Spear family following me. "I'm eager to show you what he's done," I went on and entered the kitchen.

"Beer, Dad!" Ethan for some reason shouted even though he was at our side of the butcher block and thus his father was no further than five feet away.

"Thanks, bud," Jake replied.

"Ethan, after Amber and I go over a few things, I'll be making hollandaise sauce from scratch. I'd appreciate your assistance," I said to him and his face lit up.

"I don't know what hollandaise sauce is but…*cool!*" he replied.

"Hollandaise sauce is delicious, but it's also tricky," I shared. "It'll need constant vigilance."

"I don't know what vigilance is either but I'm up for whatever that is too," he told me.

"It means you gotta keep an eye on it, Eath," Jake explained, moving further into the room.

"I can do that," Ethan told his father.

I looked to Conner and announced, "This will be poured over asparagus. I would find it most gratifying if you'd at least try it."

His lips quirked for some reason and he replied, "Sure."

I nodded then moved to the kitchen table, calling, "Amber. Come."

I felt her following but when I stopped at the table, Amber stopping beside me, I looked to Jake who was drinking from his bottle of beer and standing beside Ethan at the butcher block. I was not surprised to see that Conner had his head in the fridge.

I addressed Jake when he'd finished drinking. "Today, I went to the electronics store and purchased a printer and desktop. I also set it up."

A slow grin spread on his lips, that grin spreading on me as it did, and I fought the feeling that gave me with great difficulty when Jake teased, "Congratulations, Slick."

I felt my lips curl up as I shook my head once and continued.

"I also called the cable company. Gran has cable but no internet access. They can switch that on but need access to the house to install outlets."

"Right," he prompted, still grinning at me and I was still fighting my reaction when I sallied forth.

"These errands reminded me that I'm paying for a rental car and I decided I should see to that. I'll need transport while I'm here and I don't need to pay the exorbitant costs of a rental to have it. I inspected Gran's car and not only does it not start, it's not my style. I'll need to trade it in when I purchase another vehicle but I can't do that if I can't get it started."

Something shifted in his face at my words and I didn't fully understand it except for the fact that it was good.

"Con and I'll go out and have a look at the Buick while you and Ethan make hollandaise sauce," Jake offered.

"I'd appreciate that," I accepted. "But I must ask another favor as I've only once purchased a car and it was an unpleasant experience. It's my understanding that car salesmen take men more seriously than women and as you're rather large and known locally as a pugilist, if you would accompany me, I would assume they would not take advantage. I know it's a good deal to ask, but—"

Jake didn't let me finish.

"Whenever you're ready, let me know. I'm there."

He was there.

It seemed he was always there in ways that mattered.

And I liked that.

"Thank you," I said quietly.

"Whatever you need, Josie," he replied just as quietly.

I felt my eyes get soft. I also felt something else and thus I looked through the kitchen to see Ethan smiling up at his dad, Conner's gaze moving between his father and me, his face speculative, and when I finally got to her, Amber was also looking at her father and her face was a mirror of her older brother's.

This prompted me to turn my attention to her.

"Amber," I called and she looked to me. "Let's go over what Jean-Michel did for you."

She nodded. "Okay."

I turned to the table and opened the folder where I'd placed what I'd printed out that Jean-Michel had sent me. I'd had to connect my phone to the computer to get the images on paper and this was what sent me to the electronics store.

But when I opened the folder, I heard Amber gasp.

And it was with delight.

I liked that sound so much more warmth swept through me as I reached out, grabbed her hand and tugged carefully to pull her close.

"As you can see, Jean-Michel sketched your face and also different features so he could focus on them," I told her quietly, flipping the page over to show her the next image. "On each sketch, he's written instructions and suggested products and shades."

I flipped the next page, looking at her to see she was looking down with rapt attention at the images.

"Once your grounding is over, if your father will allow it, we'll journey to the mall and I'll purchase some of these products for you," I offered.

When I did, she tore her gaze from Jean-Michel's sketch of her eye, shaded beautifully in a matte palette of browns and greens, and she looked at me in wonder.

And I wished I'd had a camera so I could show her how much more attractive she looked with marvel lighting her features rather than petulance.

"Seriously?" she asked (this word, I thought, but did not share at that juncture, being overused by the Spear family).

"Yes," I confirmed.

"But," she looked down at the sketch then back to me, "I know those products and they don't come cheap."

"A birthday present," I stated.

"But my birthday was months ago," she replied.

"A belated one," I amended.

"I would so love that," she whispered and her pretty face said this was very true.

"Excellent," I returned. "However, I'll tell you now that offer has a caveat and that is that you continue to speak distinctly, no muttering, and you utilize these products as Jean-Michel suggests, not fall back to your flair for the dramatic."

I had considered getting into her attire with this offer and that was to say requesting that she cease dressing like a budding rather inexpensive escort but I didn't want to push too hard too soon.

Alas, at my words, her face turned guarded and she asked, "Are you bribing me with makeup?"

"Absolutely," I confirmed.

She stared at me and did this for some time.

I waited patiently, holding her stare.

Suddenly, she burst out laughing.

I relaxed but did so noting that laughing, she was even prettier.

Her eyes moved to her father and she declared, "You know, Dad, I'd probably be less of a pain in your ass if you bribed me with expensive kickass makeup."

I looked to Jake, who had a warm expression on his face and his eyes on his daughter.

His lips were turned up when he said, "Noted."

Although I very much liked the warm look on Jake's face, I still took that moment to lament that I hadn't included curtailing the use of swear words in my bribe.

"So, can I go shopping with Josie?" Amber asked her father.

Jake moved our way. "After you're done being grounded, knock yourselves out."

I smiled delightedly.

Jake turned his warm look to me.

I kept my smile pinned to my face even as I fought another shiver.

Jake moved and stopped close to me, very close, a familiar, intimate close I liked very much, before he stated, "Need the keys to the Buick, Slick."

"On the counter by the phone," I told him.

He didn't move there. He stayed close, held my gaze and at the look in his eyes, the look I'd seen the first time I had dinner with his family, I fought yet another shiver.

"Got 'em, Dad," Conner called.

"Right," Jake murmured, not tearing his eyes from me.

I began to struggle with my breathing.

This struggle intensified when he leaned in and whispered in my ear, "You're the shit, Slick."

These words meant nothing to me except for the way he said them, which I found in that moment meant everything.

"I'm assuming that's good?" I asked and he pulled back but in a way that his face stayed close.

"You'd assume right."

At his closeness and what it was doing to my breathing pattern, I had to force my smile, but I managed it.

He smiled back but, alas, he turned and moved away.

"Let's go," he said to Conner.

"Can we make the sauce now, Josie?" Ethan asked me. "I'm freaking *starved*."

"Of course," I replied, looked to Amber to see her attention back to the sketches, turning the pages (there were many, Jean-Michel had been very generous with his time and talent), studying them intently. "As you can see," I started quietly and she turned her eyes to me. "You are very pretty, Amber. *Very*." I stressed and that marvel again suffused her face as I carried on in a whisper. "Don't hide that, lovely girl. Give us a treat and show it to the world."

Her lips parted and I reached out a hand to touch the back of hers before I decided to leave her be and move to Ethan.

<hr/>

"STOP RIGHT THERE!" I demanded.

It was after dinner and we'd retired to the family room to watch TV.

At dinner, Conner had attempted to eat his asparagus but it was evident by the look on his face whenever he took a bite that he did this to be polite (which I thought was quite nice and said good things about him). However, as he wasn't enjoying it, I informed him he didn't have to force it down at the same time making a mental note to try broccoli on him when they were again dining at Lavender House.

Now, Ethan was on the floor at the coffee table doing homework. Amber was sitting in an armchair, having told us (what I thought was suspiciously) that her homework was already done. And Conner was somewhere else in the house having taken a call from one of his "babes" (this, strangely, got him a pointed look from his father to which Conner mouthed, "I know," before disappearing from the room).

I was sitting next to Jake on the couch, a place he had put me by seating himself and grabbing my hips when I got close in order to use them to plant me beside him.

Although I obviously preferred to select my own seat, there was something about his actions (not to mention my location) that I liked more.

A great deal more.

Amber was in control of the remote and she'd just happened upon a show I much liked.

At my command, she paused it at the same exact time Jake rumbled, "Babe, we are *not* watchin' Project Runway."

"No way!" Ethan put in his vote.

But I'd turned my head to Jake. "But we *must*. This show is *excellent*. I've seen it several times before and it's marvelous."

Jake held my eyes as he replied, "Josie, no reality show is marvelous."

I felt my brows draw together as I informed him with authority, "It's not reality. It's fashion."

"I *so* am seeing how Josie being around is gonna be *way* cool," Amber stated at this juncture and I looked to her. "Another chick in the mix means reruns of Project Runway and no Monday Night Football."

Amber's comment pleased me greatly thus I turned my head back to Jake and smiled, whereupon he declared, "We were gonna miss the beginning so we're tapin' the game at home. My boys and me can watch it later. But now, we should watch something we all wanna watch."

"Yeah," Ethan agreed.

I had a feeling that the divide between what Amber and I would wish to watch and what Jake and Ethan (and Conner, when he returned from his discourse with his "babe") would want to watch was such that it would be impossible to traverse.

But, I wasn't dwelling on this.

I simply wanted to watch Project Runway.

To make this happen, I leaned into Jake and spoke cajolingly.

"Jake, you don't understand. What they do on this show is remarkable. An artist is inspired by many things but they're normally free to be inspired by whatever moves them. On this show, they're *given* the inspiration they must utilize and it's most difficult to create under those kinds of conditions. *And* they have an impossibly short time to come up with a vision and the period in which they have to create the actual garments is, well…nearly *criminal*."

Jakes brows lifted as his full lips quirked and he asked, "Criminal?"

"Indeed," I answered with the utmost seriousness. "And Tim Gunn is exceptionally talented. He has an eye the likes I've never seen and I've worked in fashion for twenty-three years. Not to mention, his manner is most appealing and his ability to communicate with emotion, candor *and* diplomacy is a marvel. He in and of himself is worth watching that show. However, the judges are quite savvy as well and their commentary is most illuminating."

Jake was losing the fight with his smile and I was hoping losing the will to deprive Amber and me of our program so I leaned closer to him to continue beseeching.

But as I did so, Amber spoke.

"Oh my *God*," she breathed and I looked to her. "It just hit me. Do you know Heidi or Zac?"

My head tipped to the side in confusion. "Zac?"

"Zac Posen," she replied. "He took over for Michael Kors."

"My goodness," I whispered with delight. "Zac Posen is on the show now?"

"Yeah. And he rocks," Amber told me.

This I just *had* to see.

Therefore, I whipped my head around to Jake and shared, "Zac Posen is immensely talented. This is *most* intriguing. The loss of Michael Kors is a blow but I'm *very* interested to see what Posen contributes to the show."

And in order to fully communicate my point, I leaned in on my "*very*" and added putting my hand to his chest in entreaty.

When I was done speaking, I saw his eyes had warmed and I sensed I was going to get my way so I felt a variety of places warm on me, including my heart.

He proved me right when he murmured, "We'll watch your show, baby."

I smiled big.

Jake's eyes dropped to my mouth.

Ethan exclaimed in outrage, "Dad!"

Jake looked to his son. "It's an hour, Eath. You'll live."

"It's an hour and a half," Amber contradicted.

"Jesus," Jake muttered, the dread in that one word unmasked and I curiously found this most amusing.

Thus, I smiled at him again.

His eyes dropped to my mouth again, another area of my body warmed and it wasn't my heart.

"Right on!" Amber cried. I forced my eyes from Jake and looked to her. "So," she pressed. "Do you know Zac or Heidi?"

"Alas, no," I replied and her face fell. "Henry has, of course, taken photos of Heidi so I have spoken to her people but he did the shoot while I was at another location, preparing for him to film a video. Though, I was once at a party with Nina Garcia. But I got a headache and had to leave before I was able to meet her."

"Bummer," Amber mumbled.

It was. I'd quite looked forward to meeting Ms. Garcia.

I let Amber's mumble go and settled in, turning my gaze to the TV, ordering, "Let's begin, Amber."

"Cool," she said and hit the button on the remote.

I was watching carefully as they were showing scenes from the episode before since I wanted to catch up as best I could. That said, it was far from lost on me that Jake's arm went along the couch behind me and directly curled around my shoulders so he could pull me into his side.

He was warm, the position was comfortable and in order to make it warmer and more comfortable, I leaned into him and lifted my legs to the couch at my side to curl even closer.

At this point, Conner joined us and when he did, he murmured, "What the hell? Seriously? Project Runway?"

"Shush!" Amber hissed (before I could).

I lifted my eyes to Conner to see he was not looking at the TV in disgust but at his father and I curled on the couch together and he was again doing this with speculation. His eyes moved to Amber but I was missing the show so I moved my gaze back to the TV.

Jake slouched into the couch, lifting his booted feet to the coffee table and pulling me closer.

I settled in, placing my cheek to his chest with a sigh.

And I watched Project Runway with Jake's family, liberally conversing with Amber through it, doing this to share our opinions and commentary and surprisingly (and gratifyingly) always agreeing.

In the end, when the designer we wanted to win won, and the one who (alas) produced an unusual outfit that didn't quite hit the mark that Amber and I both agreed should be dismissed was dismissed, she and I shared a harmonious smile.

And that warmed me too.

"GIVE US A second," Jake ordered, grabbing my hand and moving us away from the car salesman.

It was afternoon the next day and I'd decided on a car.

A car, I could tell as I studied his profile while he was moving us away from the salesman, that Jake didn't agree on.

He stopped us out of hearing distance and kept hold of my hand as he turned his body to face me.

"Babe, you're not buyin' that car."

I blinked up at him. "But Jake, it's a nice color."

He stared down at me and if I was reading him correctly, it was with disbelief.

"And it's inexpensive," I continued, even though the cost was not really a concern.

This I'd shared with Jake earlier, which meant we'd already been to the Porsche, Lexus and Cadillac dealerships before we stopped by this used dealership on my whim. That whim being me seeing the car we just test drove in the lot and crying out, "Let's stop here!"

Jake, being Jake, had swung into the lot.

"It's cheap because it's a year old and has sixty thousand miles on it," he stated.

"Is that a lot?"

He stared at me another moment before he shook his head, looked at his boots then looked back at me. "Yeah. It's a lot," he told me. "That kind of mileage means its first owner drove the fuck outta it. Which, before you ask, is not good."

"Oh," I murmured.

"Since you can afford it, you're gettin' the Cayenne," he declared.

I had to admit, the Cayenne was very luxurious and the ride was exceptionally smooth.

Even so, I noted, "It's my understanding that purchasing a new car means that when you drive it off the lot, it loses a good deal of value."

"You wanna sell it in a month or a year, that's a problem," he replied. "You buy a Porsche, though, it's a high-performance vehicle, any problem you have will be down the road and I mean *way* down the road and it'll likely be about wear and tear and nothin' else. It'll be solid. It won't cause you any headaches. And you can probably own it for twenty years and not have to deal with shit except regular maintenance."

I had no idea what my future held, I just knew it held Lavender House and Magdalene. And thus, when there, I would need reliable transport. And it was highly unlikely I'd wish to engage in the onerous activity of car shopping again in six months, a year or even ten of them.

"And it's black," he went on and I focused again on him. "Black is hot. That Cayenne in black is hotter. You in anything, even a mini-van, would be hot. That's just you. You in that Cayenne..." he paused and grinned big, "*Smokin'.*"

"I'll get the Cayenne," I agreed immediately.

"Good call, Slick," he approved, grinning bigger.

I grinned back.

He then moved us toward his truck, his hand still in mine, as he turned his head and called to the salesman, "Thanks for your time."

The salesman's face fell.

Jake bleeped the locks on his truck, took me directly to the passenger side door and opened it for me. He also helped me up. He got behind the wheel and we started the twenty-mile drive back to the Porsche dealership.

As with everything Jake gave me, his time that afternoon had been generous.

Therefore, I remarked into the cab, "For your assistance this afternoon, I think I owe you and your family another dinner."

"Babe, after last night's salmon and sautéed potatoes and that un-fucking-believably good hollandaise sauce followed by homemade tiramisu, I'm not gonna say no. But just sayin', I like bein' with you so I got a shot at that, I'm gonna take it even if it means drivin' all over the county, lookin' at cars and dealing with car salesmen. So you don't owe me shit."

I had ceased breathing when he said he liked being with me.

It must be said, I also liked being with him. A great deal. And every time I was with him, I liked it more.

Alas, I liked it in a way he *didn't* like it.

Regardless, I had liked being with Henry for years in a way Henry didn't like and I'd lived.

I could do it again.

It wouldn't be easy and the more I got to know Jake (and his family), the less easy it became.

But my only alternative was not having Jake (and his family) and I already knew in the short time that I knew all of them that would be worse.

So I would do it, no matter how not easy it was.

For as long as I could do it.

"Though, pointing out, my boys and I could do without Project Runway. Watchin' that shit meant Ethan paid attention to his homework and not the TV but I think it nearly killed Conner."

I grinned at the windshield at his quip and offered, "Next time, Amber and I'll watch it on a set in another room."

"Strike that, you watch it on a set in another room, you aren't on the couch with me so I'll put up with Project Runway."

My grin got wider.

Yes, he liked being with me.

And I liked that.

A great deal.

We drove to the Porsche dealership in Jake's truck.

I drove back to Lavender House in a new black Cayenne with Jake trailing after Jake drove a hard bargain.

For me.

THE NEXT AFTERNOON, to turn my mind from Eliza Weaver and the alarmingly quick devastation her disease was causing, I left their house when Mr. Weaver came back from the office.

I got in my new Cayenne and backed out of their driveway with my phone in my hand.

When I was on my way, my next destination was the mall. This was not because I was running out of clothes (I flew first class and thus could have more than the normal allotted luggage, but even so, I knew how to pack and was *always* prepared for *anything*) but because I needed a different kind of clothing.

I also needed to make my daily call to Henry.

The ones for the last several days had been rushed and short, mostly because he had little time to give to me. That said, I'd made them and he seemed to be mollified.

So I made today's call on the go and multi-tasking.

"Josephine," he greeted with a smile in his voice.

"Hello, Henry," I replied with one in mine as well since I was smiling.

"How are you, sweetheart?" he asked.

"Fine," I answered. "Busy. There's much to do. As I said I would do, I did manage to buy a new car yesterday, which is good. That said, the search for it and paperwork, which is most time-consuming, not to mention annoying, ate up the afternoon and I need to get some clothes as there's more work to do in the garden and to see to that, I shouldn't be wearing Versace."

"Work in the garden?" Henry queried.

"Yes," I stated, hitting the turn signal and slowing for an upcoming stop sign, thinking while feeling the smooth deceleration, Jake was very right about this vehicle. It was sublime. "And I need to get to the mall and home and do it quickly because Jake phoned," I carried on. "He has a lock on someone who's interested in buying Gran's Buick so I need to be back at Lavender House to meet Jake there so we can be there when the buyer arrives."

"Has a lock?" Henry murmured strangely then went on with, "We?"

"Indeed," I confirmed, making my turn. "Obviously, I have no idea how to sell a car so Jake's going to negotiate the sale for me. And tomorrow, the cable people are scheduled to come to the house to set up Internet and, of course, Amber's grounding is done so back to the mall we go, as I need to buy her some makeup. I'm also helping out by starting to look after Ethan for Jake after school, but this time, Amber will be with him seeing as we're going to the mall."

"Amber and Ethan?"

"Jake's children," I explained then went on to share, "There's also Conner. He's the oldest. I don't see him as often since he works in town at Wayfarer's and has a variety of babes who take up his time." I drew in breath and asked, "So, how are you?"

Before he answered, my phone beeped.

"One second, Henry," I murmured, looked at my phone quickly then put it back to my ear. "So sorry," I went on. "That's Jake. I need to take the call. It might be about the Buick."

"Jose—"

"I'll phone tomorrow," I said swiftly so I didn't miss Jake's call. "But I hope you're doing well. Take care, Henry."

Before he could say a word, I accepted Jake's call and put the phone to my ear, greeting, "Hello, Jake."

"Hey, Slick. You good?"

"I am," I answered then shared, "Eliza isn't."

There was a moment's silence then, "Fuck. She gettin' bad?"

"Her deterioration day to day is distressing."

"Baby," he said softly and that one two-syllable word didn't heal the concern I had for Eliza Weaver but that didn't mean it wasn't a balm for it. "Worried about you doin' that," he continued. "She's goin' downhill that fast, you've got a lot on your plate and that might be too much."

"I'm fine, Jake," I said quietly. "It's Eliza who isn't."

"I get that and that sucks for her in a big way. I feel for her, for Weaver, but I don't know them. I know and care about *you*."

He cared about *me*.

He was *so* lovely.

"Really, Jake, it doesn't feel good to watch her decline but it does make me feel good to be there for people Gran cared about and do my bit to help."

There was a pause before he replied, "All right, honey."

I took us away from that unhappy topic and asked, "Are you calling about the Buick?"

"Yeah," he answered. "Conner's been spreadin' it around at the store that the Buick is on offer and we got another bite. I asked the other buyer to come about half an hour after the first. If he's interested, he'll know someone else is interested and hopefully that'll help us get you a good deal."

"Excellent," I replied.

"Yeah. So see you at your place at four?"

"Yes, Jake, see you there," I confirmed.

"Right, Slick. Later, babe."

"Later, Jake."

For some reason, he rang off chuckling.

As for me, for reasons I knew very well, just having spoken to Jake no matter what it was we were talking about, I rang off smiling.

⸺ ◆·◆·◆ ⸺

FOUR HOURS LATER, I stood in the lane at Lavender House with Jake watching the Buick drive away, two cars following it. One, the man who bought the Buick for his wife, the woman currently behind the wheel of Gran's car. The other, the disgruntled loser of the negotiation that Jake made a passing attempt to moderate but it got so heated they upped their own offers, haggling amongst themselves without any input from Jake or me.

Indeed, it got to the point where it was ridiculous. Not knowing one thing about cars, I still knew this as the wife grew openly alarmed when the discussion carried forward to become not about two elderly gentlemen wishing to own a ten-year-old Buick but two elderly gentlemen wishing to best one another.

Regardless, in the end it would seem this served me quite well.

Therefore, when we lost sight of the last car, I looked up at Jake and noted, "I think that went well."

He burst out laughing but did it turning to me and pulling me in his arms for a tight hug.

That felt so lovely, I wrapped my arms around him and hugged him back.

When he was done laughing, he looked down at me and remarked, "You crack me right the fuck up, babe."

I took that as confirmation the negotiation on the Buick went well but more, I liked that I amused him so I smiled at him and replied, "Good."

His arms gave me a squeeze and his face changed to what could be nothing but disappointment (and it must be said, I looked hard to read something else in his features and saw only that) before he announced, "Need to get home, get the kids dinner, make sure they're not killin' each other."

I was suddenly disappointed too, but had no choice but to agree.

"All right."

He gave me a squeeze.

I forced another smile.

Then he bent his head and my breath caught when, this time, he brushed his lips just half an inch from the side of my mouth *and then*, before moving away, *he brushed his nose against the side of mine.*

I fought to get my breath back. Winning that fight, I then had to fight to modulate it as he pulled away and whispered, "Talk to you later, Josie."

Unable to speak, I nodded.

He gave me another squeeze, then let me go and moved to his truck.

I waved as he pulled away and saw through the back window as he lifted his hand and flicked it out, indicating he saw my wave.

I watched Jake's truck out of sight and moved back to the house thinking that for the first time in days, there was nothing scheduled, imminent or otherwise that would mean I would see or even hear from Jake again.

And this made me feel unusual—distraught and downhearted.

But I knew from experience of caring for Henry in a way he didn't return, with my relationship with Jake, it was a feeling I would need to get used to.

Thus, I sighed deeply as I closed the door to Lavender House behind me thinking a word these days I thought frequently and knew I would continue to think with regularity when it came to Jake Spear.

And that was...*alas*.

Ten

SHOWING ME HOW IT'S DONE

I felt something tickle my nose and, mostly asleep, I brushed it away.
It went away but came back and I felt my brows draw together as I kept my eyes closed and batted at whatever was disturbing me.

It went away again but then came back so I lifted my hand again to stop the sensation and sleepily caught the offender.

It wasn't such as an insect.

It was a hand.

A hand!

My eyes flew open and slid sideways to see Jake was sitting on the side of my bed, leaned into me, one arm on the other side of me, hand in the bed, one hand in my face holding a lock of my hair with which he obviously had been tickling my nose.

I shot up in surprise, did this fast and thus slammed my head into Jake's jaw. Luckily, through this, he released my hair. Unfortunately, the crack to my head (and his jaw) was hard and caused a sharp pain but it was thus and it went away almost immediately.

So I scooted so that my back was to the scrolled iron headboard and stared at Jake who had not moved except to lean back a few inches.

"I-I'm sorry," I stammered. "Is your jaw okay?"

"It's fine, babe. Serves me right for freakin' you out."

I said nothing.

Then it occurred to me I was the one apologizing but *he* was in my bedroom for reasons unknown first thing in the morning.

Therefore, I asked, "Um…what are you doing here?"

He didn't answer. He was busy and what he was busy with was that he seemed rather taken with examining the entirety of the vicinity of my head.

"Jake?" I called when this lasted some time, and his eyes came to mine.

"Hair looks good down, honey," he said softly and his tone was not one I'd ever heard from him before. It was quite low and very rumbly. Indeed, it was so much of both it had a physical effect on me that was not good when Jake was sitting on the side of my bed in all of his big man beautifulness. "*Real* good," he went on and that sounded like an actual *growl*.

Oh my.

"Well…thank you," I whispered.

We stared at each other, me finding it difficult to breathe. I didn't know what Jake was experiencing.

Finally, I forced myself to speak but the only thing I could get out was, "Uh…"

"Right," he stated, his voice now sounding hoarse. He cleared his throat and went on, "Before you're off to the Weavers, I'm takin' you to the gym to work out."

I blinked at him.

Then I asked, "Work out?"

"Yep," he answered.

"I…well…" I stopped talking because I didn't know what to say.

Jake didn't have the same problem.

"First, we gotta get food in you so we're gonna do that and then you're comin' with me to my gym to work out."

I belatedly saw that he was wearing a pair of navy track pants with one wide white stripe down the side and a white long-sleeved shirt made of breathable material that fit snug to his shoulders, chest, arms and abdominals.

At this vision, my mouth went dry.

"You got something to wear to work out?" he asked.

Although there was much I would do with Jake Spear just to be with Jake Spear, for instance, watch football while partaking of a dip that was made from Velveeta and, say walking to the ends of the earth and jumping off hand in hand, working out was not something I wished to do with Jake or...*ever.*

Therefore, I latched onto the excuse given to me quickly.

"No, Jake," I replied. "I don't have workout clothes."

"Then how do you keep that body?"

"Well, I walk," I informed him and usually I did. Quite often. Most specifically after an evening meal. I hadn't been doing that lately because I was out of my normal schedule but I did it because I enjoyed it but also because it helped me to stay active and increased my daily energy levels.

"Today, you're gonna do more than walk," he returned.

"I'm afraid I don't have the attire to do this, Jake."

He grinned, bent to the floor at the side of the bed and I heard rustling. The rustling continued as he straightened and dumped a plastic grocery bag filled with clothes on my lap.

"Amber got a wild hair last summer that she wanted to get fit. Mostly, she wanted another reason to buy clothes. So she did. Figure what's in that bag'll fit you and doubt any a' that has even been worn."

I stared down at the offending bag in my lap and this was a mistake.

It was a mistake because my hand was seized as was the bag and, not paying attention, this came as a surprise. The bag was dumped by Jake on the bed beside me and my hand was tugged by Jake, so I had no choice but to come to my feet at the side of the bed.

When I was standing, I looked up at him to see he was looking down at me and that would be *down*...to my nightie.

I looked down too, taking in the midnight blue silk with its simple bodice and deep hem of delicate smoke-gray lace.

"Fuckin' hell, Slick," Jake muttered, his voice holding a nuance of how it sounded earlier and I looked up at him to see an unusual look on his face that could be displeasure or possibly, and strangely, acute pain.

"You don't like it?" I asked stupidly because it didn't matter if Jake liked my nighties or not. I'd never have the opportunity to wear one for him in one of the particular ways nighties were designed.

At my words, his eyes sliced to mine and he replied, "Babe, a man tells you he doesn't like that nightie, he's either gay or lying."

I had no earthly idea what to do with that other than to feel relief (and other things) that he liked my nightie.

He let my hand go and ordered, "Suit up," as he began to walk to the door.

I searched for any excuse not to go work out with him and if not that, at least delay so I could find an excuse not to go work out with him. This was difficult seeing as I was enthralled with watching his shoulders move in that tight white shirt as he sauntered away.

I finally found an excuse and called, "I need coffee before I do anything in the morning, Jake."

"Then it's good there's a cup of it on your nightstand," he returned as he disappeared out the door.

I looked down to my nightstand and saw a cup of coffee, its color black, like I took it at The Shack.

I would need milk and sweetener.

I moved my eyes to the plastic grocery bag, finding myself oddly intrigued with the idea of discovering what kind of athletic apparel Amber had chosen.

Therefore, I decided to peruse what was in the bag before I went to prepare my coffee.

Ten minutes later, I found myself in said apparel (skintight black capri leggings with a thin piping of lavender down the side, a skintight tank top in lavender that had a built in bra and a racerback, a rather attractive zip up jacket with gathers at the bottom side seams and at the bottoms of the long sleeves as well as Vs made of netting along the shoulders and coming up from the back hem, and I'd added my walking shoes).

I also found myself carrying my coffee downstairs to prepare it.

But when I did, I did this in a travel mug.

"WHAT D'YOU WANT, Slick?"

I tore my eyes from the wall of donuts on display and looked up at Jake standing at my side.

"You eat donuts before you work out?" I queried.

"Not every time, but do it occasionally to remind myself why I'm workin' out," he responded.

This was absurd but I had to admit, it also made an absurd kind of sense.

"Josie, need to get to the gym to open it," he told me and prompted, "What d'you want?"

I looked back to the wall. There was a large variety and donuts were donuts. It was impossible to make a split-second decision when donuts were on offer.

"Um…" I mumbled.

"Fuck it," Jake mumbled back, then louder and to the counter assistant. "Two Boston creams. Two glazed. Two cinnamon twists. Two maple glazed. Two chocolate glazed. Two buttermilk."

"You got it," the counter assistant assured and moved to the back, grabbing a box.

"Is it necessary for us to have that amount of donuts?" I asked and Jake looked back down at me.

"It's necessary for me to open my gym which means it's necessary for me to get you to get a move on, so yeah. You got choice. And what we don't eat, the boys will."

"Oh."

He tipped his head to the travel mug I was still carrying with me, holding it like it was a lifeline, even though we'd entered an establishment that served coffee and he asked, "You need that warmed up?"

I absolutely did.

I nodded.

His lips quirked and he looked back to the counter assistant. "And my girl here needs a warm up."

His girl.

Oh *my*.

"No problemo," the clerk assured again and dropped the box of donuts on the counter in front of us.

I got a warm up.

Jake just got a coffee.

I ate a Boston cream in his truck on the way to the gym.

"RIGHT, NOW, SKIP rope," Jake ordered and I stared at him.

Donut consumed, travel mug sitting on a ledge beside where we were standing in his gym, I stared at him.

Suffice it to say, my perusal of his gym from my car through a dreary day was not thorough. I knew this when we entered it from the back ten minutes ago and I looked around, taking off my jacket, while Jake walked around, turning on lights and unlocking the front door.

It was much larger and that was to mean *cavernous*.

There were not two boxing rings but three.

There was also a good deal of equipment. Further, there was an office at the back that was several steps up from the main floor and was made mostly of windows so you could see the gym from there. Beyond the office were doors that had words on them that I assumed described what was behind them, one declaring it was the Locker Room, another declaring it was Equipment and the last that it was Utility.

And finally, on the walls in the gym proper in very big script quotes were painted, including:

"Life is like a boxing match. Defeat is declared not when you fall but when you refuse to stand again."

And *"Champions aren't made in gyms. Champions are made of something they have deep inside them—a desire, a dream a vision. They have to have the skill, and the will. But the will must be stronger than the skill. – Muhammad Ali"*

And *"I can show you how to box. I can teach you every technique and trick I know, but I can never make you a fighter. That comes from inside, and it's something no one else can ever give you. – Joe Louis"*

And my favorite *"Impossible is just a big word thrown around by small men who find it easier to live in the world they've been given than to explore the power they have to change it. Impossible is not a fact. It's an opinion. Impossible is not a declaration. It's a dare. Impossible is potential. Impossible is temporary. Impossible is nothing. – Muhammad Ali"*

I had no time to share with Jake that I thought his inclusion of these quotes was quite clever. He took my coffee, set it aside and gave me a jump rope. I noted he had another one in his hands.

This was when he ordered me to use it.

"You wish for me to skip rope?" I asked.

"You gotta warm up," he informed me. "You also gotta work off that donut."

I stared at him some more then asked, "By skipping rope?"

"Babe, not much you can do that'll burn more calories than jumping rope. Also gets the heart beating, increases stamina, challenges agility and works the entire body."

"Skipping rope?" I asked incredulously.

He grinned at me and commanded, "Josie, just do it."

I studied him a moment before I prepared my rope and started skipping and I did this by literally skipping over the rope, one foot and then the next, like I learned decades ago on the playground at school.

Jake watched my feet and he did this smiling big then he looked at my face and he was still smiling big.

And his voice was shaking with humor when he ordered, "Stop."

I stopped.

He kept ordering by saying, "Now watch."

I watched.

Jake started skipping rope but not like me. I was pretty certain my lips had parted in wonder as the rope went so fast it whistled through the air and he jumped on the balls of his feet, sometimes lifting one but an inch to jump on one foot, then moving to the other, then using both of them.

He ceased doing this and asked, "Can you do that?"

"Absolutely not," I answered truthfully because I...could...*not*. I might kill myself and this was not an exaggeration. Me, rope, speed and jumping was not a good mix. I knew this about myself completely.

He was smiling again when he noted, "Slick, it isn't hard."

"Jake, I think it isn't lost on you that I'm not the most graceful of females," I pointed out.

Or males. Or any being with legs.

I didn't go on to include these options.

"Yeah, in heels," he replied.

"Also not in heels," I shared.

"And when aren't you in heels?" he asked.

"This morning, when I slammed my head into your jaw."

"I surprised you."

This was true.

"Try it," he encouraged.

It was then I found myself wondering how I was wearing Amber's workout clothes, had a donut in my stomach, far less caffeine than was required for me to face the day and was in Jake's gym at the ungodly hour of seven fifteen in the morning contemplating the idea of taking my life in my hands to skip rope for Jake Spear.

My eyes wandered to his body-hugging t-shirt and I had my answer.

Thus, I arranged my rope and started.

First pass was good, second pass I caught the rope on my ankle and tripped.

"Shake it off, try again," Jake murmured then began jumping rope.

I took in a deep breath and tried again.

Three jumps into it, I failed again.

"Again," Jake said, still jumping.

I gave him a look and tried again.

Ten seconds later, I failed again.

"Don't give up, babe," Jake urged.

I sighed and tried again, failed again, tried again and failed again.

Jake stopped jumping and I looked to him.

"Right," he said, his voice again trembling with humor. "Do that schoolyard skipping thing instead. It's not as fast but it's something and we need you warmed up."

"I feel like a fool," I murmured, looking down and preparing to start again, the girlie schoolyard way with Jake beside me doing it the manly boxing gym way, but my hand was stayed by Jake's fingers wrapping around my wrist.

I looked up when the fingers of Jake's other hand curved around my jaw and I saw he'd gotten close.

Very close.

"You are not a fool," he whispered. "You can never be a fool. You're total class from top to toe. You're also a klutz. Own that, baby, because it's cute and because it's you. If you learn to accept yourself just as you are, learn to laugh at your quirks instead of hating them, show the world all that's you without tryin' to hide things that are not even a little unattractive, that makes you *more* attractive. What you got is a fuckuva lot. You own all of it and let it all hang out, you'll go off-the-charts."

My heart was racing and not from exercise when I blurted, "You're very sweet."

"And you're very cute," he returned immediately then grinned. "Even cuter standin' in a fighter's gym skippin' rope the way you do it. So own that, Josie."

That was so nice, his words made me feel so lovely, I could do nothing but nod.

So I did.

After years of Gran saying much the same thing and me not taking it in, for Jake, I'd own it.

For Jake, alas, I had a feeling I'd do anything.

He unfortunately let me go and stepped away.

He started jumping rope and I began skipping it. I continued to do this for some time without catching my rope on my ankles or any other mistakes and suddenly found it was kind of fun.

On this thought, the phone in the office rang.

Jake stopped jumping rope and said to me, "Keep doin' that, Slick. Only stop if you get too winded."

I nodded.

He moved to the office just as the door behind me opened.

Still skipping and doing it concentrating so I wouldn't falter, I turned to it and saw a brawny man walking in wearing workout clothes and carrying a workout bag over his shoulder. He was, perhaps, two or three inches shorter than Jake (which, I should note, still put him at tall) and he had his dark brown hair clipped close to his skull in an attractive cut. He was quite muscled, and although his muscle was bulky, it was not as pronounced as Jake's.

He also had his eyes on me as he moved into the gym and he further had his lips turned up into a grin.

I kept skipping rope, doing it *owning* it as Jake said I should and I saw as the man approached that he did not seem to think I looked a fool. Not if I read the look in his eyes correctly.

"Hey," he greeted, stopping close (though not too close, my rope was still swinging).

He had lovely blue eyes.

"Good morning," I replied, still leaping over my rope.

He looked me up and down before he again caught my eyes. "You new to the female league?"

"As I don't know what that is, the answer would be no," I answered and his grin got bigger.

"Female fighters," he explained.

"Yes, my answer is no," I confirmed.

"Good to know, seein' as no one should put a glove to that face," he remarked.

Since I agreed I wanted no boxing glove hitting my face, and since I thought this was an unusual but quite nice compliment, I said nothing.

His grin turned into a smile. "Name's Mickey," he informed me.

"Josephine."

"Nice t'meet you, Josephine."

"Likewise," I replied.

"Please tell me that Jake's opening the gym to aerobics classes and you're the instructor," he begged good-naturedly.

"Alas, I must dash this dream," I told him.

He burst out laughing and I found the sound of it most attractive.

When he stopped, he asked, "So, seein' as this gym is fighters only, you wanna share what you're doin' here skippin' rope?"

"She's with me."

This came from behind me and it came from Jake.

Mickey's eyes moved to Jake and I looked over my shoulder at him (yes, still skipping rope).

"You can quit, Slick," he said to me.

I stopped skipping.

"We got a new gym policy?" Mickey asked Jake as Jake came to a stop close to my side.

"Yeah, the policy is, seein' as I own the joint, I can let anyone I want in," Jake answered.

"Well, in case you want feedback, I approve of your choice," Mickey returned and I looked to him and smiled.

When I did, I felt Jake get closer to me.

Mickey looked at me. "You comin' to the Saturday night match?"

"The what?" I inquired.

"Adult league," Mickey stated and it was clear he felt he answered my question but he didn't.

So I queried, "Pardon?"

"Adult league," Jake repeated Mickey's words and I looked up at him. "Mick and me belong to an adult league. We box in Saturday night league matches."

Intriguing.

"Every weekend?" I asked.

"Can't fight that much, Slick," Jake answered. "One match every month, short matches, three rounds."

"You wanna come, I'll leave tickets for you at the office," Mickey invited at this juncture and I looked to him.

Before I could answer, Jake put in, "She wants to come, I got her covered."

I looked to him.

"You got three kids and DeeDee to cover. I got her," Mickey returned and I felt my insides squeeze.

DeeDee?

Who was DeeDee?

"Dee's gone, Mick," Jake said in a quiet voice that strangely also sounded quite lethal. "You know that," he finished and that sounded even more lethal.

My insides relaxed.

"You been on and off for two years, Jake," Mickey remarked.

My insides seized again.

"We've been off for five months, Mick," Jake returned, his voice still quiet, but now tight and also terse.

"Right," Mick murmured but it was the odd mixture of both taunting and disbelieving.

I wasn't entirely certain what was happening. I just knew it was danger-ous and I also knew I was the only one there who could do anything about it.

Therefore, I did and I did this by turning to Jake and noting, "I think I'm warmed up, Jake. Can I punch a punching bag now?"

Jake looked down at me and I saw his face was also tight, most specifically his strong, square jaw.

Oh dear.

It relaxed but only slightly when he replied, "Yeah, babe. I'll show you how to work the bag then we'll finish you up on the speed bag."

I had no idea what was what but I still said, "Excellent."

He jerked up his chin and stated, "Let's move." But he was the one who moved me, doing this by putting a hand in the small of my back and giving me a gentle shove.

I got moving.

Jake said over his shoulder, "Later, Mick."

"Later, Jake," Mickey replied and then, clearly to me, "If you come to the match, I'll have a ticket waiting for you, Josephine."

Jake made an annoyed noise low in his throat that was, like all things Jake, attractive. Intensely so.

Even thinking this, I called noncommittally, "Thank you, Mickey, and nice to meet you."

"Likewise." I heard him say as Jake stopped me at a long, cylindrical bag.

I decided my best course of action was to leave my discourse with Mickey at that and turn my full attention to Jake.

He still looked annoyed. Vastly so. He was also looking at the punching bag like he wanted to rip it from its chains and throw it out the window.

To stop him from doing this, I said, "All right. What do I do now?"

Jake looked down at me and it took a moment for his expression to clear, but finally it did and he gave me a small grin.

"You ready to kick the shit outta that bag?"

"Kicking is involved?" I inquired, somewhat surprised.

It wasn't that I didn't know that bags such as that were used in that manner. It was just other types of fighters, not boxers, used it thus.

"It will be the way you're gonna use it."

I looked at the bag thinking this might be fun.

So I looked back up at Jake, smiled and said, "Splendid."

Finally, Jake's face totally cleared and he smiled back.

Then he said, "Right, Slick. I'll show you how it's done and then it's your turn."

At that point, Jake pushed me slightly back and commenced "showing me how it's done."

And thus, at that point, watching Jake, I knew without any doubts why I'd allowed myself to be pulled from my bed and dragged to a boxer's gym at an ungodly hour of the morning.

I also knew I would allow the same to happen tomorrow.

And the next day.

And the next.

Just as long as I got to watch Jake "showing me how it's done."

———◆◆◆———

ALTHOUGH IT WAS unnecessary, after our workout, when Jake took me home, he walked me to the front door of Lavender House as well as through it.

I felt quite strange seeing as I was sweaty and I was never sweaty. My body also felt fatigued and my body never felt fatigued unless the day was a rather long one or the evening included dancing. And I was not in my usual attire which put me off-balance. Amber's choices were lovely but they weren't me.

So when Jake closed the door against the chill of the morning and turned to me, feeling off-balance and having a morning that started with Jake waking me up by tickling my nose with a lock of my hair and ended with him and I both getting sweaty (alas, not in a way I would chose but it was far from bad, especially watching Jake do it), I had a near overwhelming desire to move into him. To curl my arms around his neck. To press my damp body to his then press my lips to his.

Fortunately, before I gave into this urge, Jake spoke.

"Amber's done bein' grounded today. You still good to look after Eath this afternoon?"

I stared at him a moment in surprise.

Had a week passed since we discussed this?

It had.

"Of course," I replied.

"He gets off school at two forty-five," he told me. "I'll text Amber and let her know she's off-duty."

I nodded.

"Got shit to do at the gym, got shit to do at the club," Jake carried on. "And the kid's league is startin' up again so I got shit to do for that. You good to keep him for dinner?" he asked.

Sharing dinner with Ethan.

I would very much enjoy that.

"Certainly," I answered.

"It'll help a lot, Slick," he shared.

"Ethan's very good company therefore this is hardly a bother, Jake," I assured him with complete honesty.

He grinned then said, "I'll pick him up around seven thirty."

Hmm.

Another early dinner.

Oh well.

"All right," I replied.

"Tomorrow night, we're goin' to the football game."

I blinked before I asked, "Pardon?"

"Friday night high school football. You, me and Ethan are goin'."

My heart made a flutter and not at the prospect of going to a high school football game. "That sounds fun," I partly lied because football would likely bore me silly.

Being with Jake was another story.

And knowing I'd be spending even more time with him was yet another story.

He grinned again and moved closer.

My heart fluttered again.

"You pick up Eath after school. I'll pick you both up later. We'll grab some food and go."

I forced myself to speak normally when I asked, "Amber and Conner aren't going with us?"

"Amber's goin' with her friends. Conner is either goin' with one of his girls or he's goin' with his buds. They're in high school. They don't hang with their old man. But their old man goes to games to keep an eye on them, specifically Amber, who'd probably be under the bleachers doin' shit that even thinkin' about it for a nanosecond makes my gut twist and my mouth taste like acid so I try not to think about it. I also fail."

"Is she…well," I started carefully and finished with, "promiscuous?"

"I hope not," he replied immediately, sounding like he very much meant those three words. "That said, she wants to be popular, she wants to be liked, she wants boys to notice her and this Noah kid is a senior and he shares the title of the big man at school with Con. He's a hotshot basketball player so he doesn't play football but he goes to the games. With the way she wants all of that shit and the fact she got her hooks in Noah, who she's had her sights set on since she was a freshman, it means anything can happen."

I was not surprised that Conner was the high school "big man." However, it was my experience when I was in school, and my understanding it was still true, that the athletes were the ones who earned that honor.

"Does Conner play sport?" I asked.

"He boxes like his dad," Jake answered.

"Is he good at it?" I went on.

"In his current league he's undefeated three years running," Jake stated without even attempting to hide the pride.

And there was the reason he was the high school "big man."

I grinned at Jake. "Good for him."

Jake grinned back but said, "Not good. He works at it. You see those quotes on the walls of the gym?"

"Indeed." I nodded. "I meant to mention that they were all very inspirational and I thought it was very clever that you had them painted on your walls."

He was grinning bigger when he replied, "Glad you think so, Slick, but those quotes, Con lives them. He's hungry for the learning but he's got the soul of a fighter. I started the junior league for him hopin' that would be the way. When I started it, he was too young to be in it. He got old enough, he took to it better than I'd hoped. And if he's not with one of his girls or at work, he's at the gym."

I watched with some fascination as his face changed and listened with even more fascination as his voice roughened when he finished.

"Makes what Lydie did for me and my family even better, knowing she made it so I could give my boy a place to train. A place that's mine to give him. A place that'll be his one day if he wants it."

"Yes, Jake," I said softly, at his words, his look and his tone, again having an overwhelming urge. But this one was to touch him, take his hand or lay mine on his chest or his jaw. It didn't matter how, I just wanted that connection. Any connection. Or all of them.

I couldn't have it so I didn't take it.

But I wanted it.

"Right, so I'll see you tonight at seven-thirty," Jake declared. "You wanna hit the gym tomorrow, let me know and I'll pick you up at seven. Tomorrow night, I'll pick you and Eath up at five-thirty. And Saturday, the matches are at the arena in Blakeley. Got a lot of matches to get through so they start at nine in the morning with the flyweights. I fight heavyweight, which'll be one of the last, so my match'll be around eight at night. You can come and watch as much as you want. I'll have a ticket waitin' for you at the office."

As much as I wanted was not very much. I didn't even know if I wanted to watch Jake box, I certainly didn't want to watch anyone else. I knew by then that I'd watch Jake do practically anything, but I wasn't eager to watch someone hitting him.

But it seemed he wanted me to go.

So I would go.

Thus I again nodded.

"We've got a plan," Jake murmured and got even closer. "And you gotta get to the Weavers."

I sighed and nodded. My sigh was not only about the fact that Jake was soon to leave, it was also about seeing Eliza Weaver and knowing she would be worse than yesterday, and worse still tomorrow.

Jake read my sigh and I knew this when he said gently, "You can give up any time."

"I'm there until Mr. Weaver no longer needs me," I replied.

He held my eyes a moment before his warmed in a way that warmed me all the way through and then it was his turn to nod.

After he did that, he lifted a hand and I braced, waiting for it, delighted he was going to give it to me and he didn't disappoint.

He cupped my jaw and bent in, brushing his lips against the skin that was mere centimeters away from the corner of my mouth.

He drew back only mere centimeters as well so I could feel his breath on my lips. Thus, my breath stopped altogether.

"See you later, Slick," he whispered.

"Later, Jake," I pushed out.

I watched his eyes smile.

Seeing the smile in the stormy gray of his eyes in my dimly lit foyer, my belly dipped.

Then he bent in *again* and gave me *another* brush of his lips against the corner of my mouth before he added something new. He moved his hand from my jaw and tugged gently and playfully at my ponytail before he moved away and I watched him walk out my front door.

IT WAS AFTER school and Ethan and I were at Wayfarer's.

I had picked him up from school, or, more accurately, he'd seen me in my Cayenne and nearly given me a heart attack by dashing across the road with extreme excitement (and not checking the street before he did so), throwing open the passenger door and shouting, "I can't wait to get a ride in this totally awesome ride!"

He did not delay in achieving his purpose, climbed up and buckled in. I set us on the road while I allowed him time to get his "ride in this totally awesome ride" before I used measured words to explain he should always scan the street before crossing it.

"Whoops," was his reply.

I decided to take that as him having heard me then I shared our afternoon endeavors were that we were going to make cream puffs from scratch.

To that, a yelled, "*Awesome!*" was his reply.

And to that, I'd smiled at the windshield.

Ethan chattered to me while we moved through the aisles at Wayfarer's, picking up what we needed. But when we approached the checkout counter, Conner came in the front doors.

"Con!" Ethan cried and Conner's head turned our way.

He spied us and moved in our direction while smiling.

"What's up?" he asked when he arrived.

"Cream puffs, dude," was Ethan's answer.

"Awesome, little dude," was Conner's response, still smiling at his younger brother.

"Hello, Conner," I greeted.

"Yo, Josie," he replied, turning his smile to me. "You doin' good?"

"I am, indeed," I answered. "And you?"

"Nothin' gets me down," he stated breezily and I couldn't help but smile at his words and tone. "Love to rap but gotta clock in," he told us.

"Later, bro," Ethan said.

"Good-bye, Conner," I said.

He jerked up his chin, so very much like his father, gave us a low wave (also like his father) and moved away.

"Amber's a pain in the butt but Con is the bomb," Ethan told me and I looked down at him.

"Amber is a teenaged girl who's trying to understand her place in this world and is erroneously assuming that that place is dependent on how many boys find her attractive and how popular she is at school. Your brother has a good deal of confidence due to his good looks and, likely, his prowess in the boxing ring. When Amber finds what she excels at, she'll cease being a pain in the behind."

"I hope she finds what she excels at soon," Ethan muttered.

"I do too," I murmured back.

"What's erroneous?" he asked and I grinned down at him.

"Mistaken," I explained.

"Right." He grinned up at me then went on, "So what's prowess?"

"Ability. Skill," I told him.

"Right," he repeated, still grinning.

At this point, the cashier told me my total.

I paid for the groceries and Ethan insisted on getting two of the three handled brown paper bags (also, it would appear, like his father). I took the remaining one and we left the store.

Cross Street had been (and still was) rather busy when we arrived at Wayfarer's and thus we'd needed to park well down from the store. We set off on our journey, carrying our bags, Ethan again chattering.

"They got cream puffs at the bakery but I bet yours will be better," he noted.

"As Americans often put sweetened whipped cream or vanilla pudding between the choux pastry, and we'll be making crème patisserie, this is indeed a fact."

"What's crème patisserie?" Ethan asked.

"Proof there is a God," I answered.

He burst out laughing and I liked the sound so much, not to mention liking that it was me who gave it to him, I smiled down at him just as I heard, "Yo! Josephine!"

I stopped and saw that we were standing in front of one of the two large opened bays of the Firehouse. I peered into the shadows beyond the shiny red fire truck and out came Mickey from the gym.

And I saw that this time, Mickey from the gym was not in workout clothes, which suited him greatly, but instead in dark blue trousers and a lighter blue t-shirt with an insignia over his heart. As these were the apparel of a firefighter not actually fighting a fire, but still being a firefighter, they suited him even better.

"Mickey!" Ethan exclaimed, clearly knowing the man.

"Yo, Eath," Mickey replied on a grin at Ethan and his grin, like it had been that morning, was also quite nice.

"You know Josie?" Ethan asked and Mickey moved his grin to me.

"We met at the gym this morning," Mickey explained.

I felt Ethan's eyes and looked down at him just as he was inquiring, "You were at the gym this morning?"

"Your dad and I worked out together," I shared and Ethan smiled big.

"Cool," he said in approval.

"Wanna check out the firehouse, little man?" Mickey surprisingly asked at this juncture and my eyes shot to him.

"Seriously?" Ethan breathed.

Before I could get a word in, Mickey gave him a head jerk toward the firehouse and replied, "Absolutely. I'll look after your bags. You go in."

Without delay, Ethan dropped his grocery bags by Mickey's feet and raced into the firehouse.

He did this so quickly, I lost sight of him immediately.

I looked to Mickey. "Um…Mickey, Ethan's my charge and I'm uncomfortable with him being out of sight."

To that, Mickey twisted his torso and bellowed, "Yo! Jimbo! My boy Eath is in there. Keep an eye on him, will you?"

And then I heard shouted back, "Got it!"

Mickey turned back to me and opened his mouth to speak but I spoke before he could say a word.

"I appreciate Jimbo's assistance but as I don't know Jimbo, I still would prefer it if I was aware of Ethan's activities and by that I mean that I could actually *see* him."

Mickey's (not unattractive, to say the least) lips were spread in a wide smile by the time I was finished speaking and when I was done, he assured me, "Ethan'll be good."

"But—"

"Listen," he interrupted me. "You got plans tomorrow night?"

I closed my mouth.

Oh my.

Was yet another man in Magdalene going to ask me out?

I'd been there but a week and a half, having attended Gran's funeral on a Monday, and if Mickey was indeed asking me out, that made him the second man to do so in that short period of time.

It was not lost on me that I was attractive. I was no beauty, I'd spent my life around raving beauties so I knew beauty and I did not have that. But that didn't mean I was unattractive. I also received my fair share of attention and partook of that attention when the spirit moved me.

But this was ridiculous.

And what made it worse was the fact that the one man I wanted to give me more than a fair share of attention was, indeed, giving me more than my fair share, just not the way I would wish.

"I—" I started.

He interrupted again before I could reply. "'Cause I'd like to take you to Breeze Point for dinner."

Yes, he was asking me out.

And doing it to take me to Breeze Point, which said a good deal about how he wished this date to go.

And this felt nice.

Even so.

"I'm sorry, Mickey," I said quietly. "Jake and I have plans tomorrow night."

Mickey's face went strange and for some reason he looked over his shoulder into the firehouse before he turned back to me and inquired, "You and Jake an item?"

Even though I knew what an item meant, the question threw me mostly because the idea of me and Jake being one was both infinitely desired and completely impossible, thus I asked stupidly, "An item?"

"You seein' him, darlin'," he explained.

Oh, how I wished.

"No, we're just friends," I shared, successfully keeping the note of disappointment out of my voice.

His face cleared and he gave me another smile. "Then are your plans with him solid on Friday?"

Any plan that included Jake was solid.

"Yes," I answered.

"Right. Then I'm boxin' on Saturday. How 'bout we do dinner Sunday night?"

I opened my mouth to decline then I closed it.

Quickly studying him so I didn't delay in giving him an answer, I noted yet again he was very attractive. He was taller than me and I was, as usual, in heels. He had a very nice body. And he was not in the least like Boston Stone. Mickey's smiles were frequent and genuine. His manner easygoing. He had confidence, not arrogance. Further, he had an obvious rapport with Ethan.

And last, he liked me and he did it in a way that felt nice.

"I'd enjoy that, Mickey," I accepted.

"Excellent," he said softly and I gave him a small smile. He dug his phone out of his back pocket and, still using his soft voice, requested, "What's your number, honey?"

Another man who called me honey.

And another time I liked it.

I gave my number to him while he programmed it into his phone.

"I'll call you later," he told me, shoving his phone back in his pocket. "When're you done lookin' after Ethan?"

"Jake's collecting him at seven thirty."

"I'll call you after that."

"I'll look forward to that," I replied, and I found that I meant it.

He smiled at me again.

I smiled back.

Yes, he was very easy to look at and his smiles were genuine and I liked all that.

Alas, I had cream puffs to make.

"I better go," I said, sounding disappointed because I actually was. "Ethan and I are making cream puffs."

When I uttered the words "cream puffs," something else changed on his face and this was not difficult to read.

It also changed the way my legs were able to support me and that was to say, it made them feel shaky mostly because they were trembling in a way that felt too lovely when I was standing on a street in front of a firehouse.

"Save one for me," he requested, his voice having lowered, and at his tone and the vision of him biting into a cream puff that suddenly filled my head, I forced myself not only to remain standing but also nod.

Then he turned and bellowed, "Eath! You got cream puffs to make!"

Seconds later, Ethan sprinted out of the firehouse. A second after that, Mickey approached me and took the bag from my hand, moved to Ethan's bags, took one of his and he walked us to my Cayenne.

"Sweet ride, babe," he stated after he'd stowed the groceries in the back.

"Thanks," I replied, idiotically feeling pleased he liked it.

Ethan climbed in the front and Mickey walked me to my door, opening it for me and saying before he closed it, "See you Saturday night...and Sunday."

"Yes, see you then," I returned.

He gave me another smile and closed the door.

I found my breathing mildly affected as I turned on the car, pulled out of the spot and headed the Cayenne toward home.

"You goin' to Dad and Mickey's fights Saturday, Josie?" Ethan asked.

"Yes," I answered.

"Awesome," he decreed. "I usually go but *Combat Raptor* comes out tomorrow and I'm goin' over to Josh's on Saturday, we're goin' to the movie then I'm sleepin' over and I can't…freaking…*wait*."

"*Combat Raptor?*" I queried.

"Yeah. The…*coolest*…movie *of all time*," he declared.

"And you can make that assessment prior to viewing it?"

"Uh…Josie…it's *Combat Raptor*," he stressed the title to the movie in a way which couldn't be mistaken. However, I still didn't understand but I was also not an eight-year-old boy.

"It's good you have such exciting plans for the weekend," I told him.

"Yeah. It is. Totally. Josh and me have been waitin' for this movie for-eh-*ver*."

"And now it's finally here," I noted.

"Yep," he agreed.

"Will Amber or Conner be going to your dad's fight?" I asked.

"Amber, no way. She's not grounded anymore so she'll totally be on a date if Noah asks her out or she'll be doin' stuff with her friends as well as sulking if he doesn't. Conner normally always goes but he's scrapin' off all his girlfriends so he'll probably be breaking some chick's heart Saturday night."

I looked to Ethan in surprise then back to the road. "Conner's breaking up with his girlfriends?"

"All but one," he answered. "Dad laid down the law. Said he'd had his fun and it was time to pick one. I heard Con talkin' to his bud on the phone. He hasn't picked one but he already got rid of Shantay. Three more to go then we'll know who made the cut."

I heard his words and they weren't great words as pertains to discussing the hearts of young women but I couldn't get into that because Ethan said that Jake had "laid down the law."

"Do you know when your father discussed this with Conner?" I asked quietly.

"No clue. But Shantay bit it over the phone on Sunday."

And Jake and I had discussed Conner and his girlfriends Saturday night. Which meant Jake had discussed Conner and his girlfriends with Conner very quickly afterward.

I felt something strange, strange and miraculous and beautiful and strong budding inside me. Something I liked in a way I knew I could love. Not even love but adore. Worship.

Need.

"Anyway," Ethan continued, breaking into my thoughts and, perhaps fortunately, taking my focus off that feeling, "I hope he picks Ellie. She's not only the prettiest one, she's the sweetest. She's all shy and stuff and she never acts like she doesn't want me around when she's over like the other ones do. And it's cool how she's so pretty and so shy at the same time. No one that pretty should be shy but she is. I like her best."

Just from his description, I liked her too.

"Well," I started as I turned off Cross Road to take us toward the cliffs and Lavender House, "I just hope Conner chooses well and is sensitive as he goes about ending things with the others."

"Conner is totally into his babes. He'll be cool with them," Ethan assured me.

That was a relief.

"Good," I said softly.

"I hope you have a killer after school snack because I'm freaking *starved,*" Ethan proclaimed and I smiled.

He was frequently starved.

And I had a variety of killer after school snacks.

I also liked having a full refrigerator because I often had company over and people dining at one of my two tables.

In fact, I liked simply having a refrigerator.

And tables.

I further liked knowing that Ethan would be sharing Lavender House with me that afternoon and evening, and the next, like he did with Gran.

And last, I was looking forward to introducing him to crème patisserie. He was going to love it.

And I was going to love giving it to him.

"Whatever I have is yours," I told him.

"Awesome," he replied.

I smiled and turned into the lane that led us to Lavender House thinking he was right.

Giving whatever I had to Ethan was, indeed, *awesome.*

⋯⋯⋯

"NO SHIT? YOU know Dee-Amond?" Mickey asked in my ear.

I grinned to the window of the light room where I was reclining on the window seat, drinking tea and chatting to Mickey who'd called five minutes after Jake had come to collect Ethan.

Jake had done this in his normal friendly, lovely Jake way, including partaking of a cream puff and after doing so, reacting to his enjoyment of it by catching me in his arms and giving me a tight hug while declaring I was the best cook he knew and not even my Gran had given him better.

I liked this in a way where I wished I could keep him thinking this way by cooking for him every night. After thinking that, I'd instantly buried the distress I felt that I knew I never would.

They'd left with some swiftness due to the fact that Conner was at work and Amber was supposed to be home shortly after "hanging with her buds" after school and Jake wanted to make sure she got home when she was due and also got her schoolwork done.

He was a very good father.

Actually, he was simply a very good everything.

"Yes, I know Amond," I told Mickey. "I've known him for years."

"Guy's a genius," Mickey told me.

I was fond of hip-hop, I felt it was an underappreciated form of expression, and thus I agreed.

"He is, indeed."

This was met with silence then I received a soft, "Dig the way you talk, darlin'."

How lovely.

"I'm glad," I replied just as softly.

We'd been talking for nearly an hour. The conversation was interesting and easy. It was also entirely led by Mickey who made it this way.

And this made me look forward to our dinner Sunday night even more.

During our conversation, he'd learned a good deal about me, not just that I knew Amond.

I had learned he was divorced and had two children who he shared custody with his ex-wife. He was a volunteer firefighter, his day job was construction and roofing and he'd been boxing on and off since he was twenty, which meant he'd been doing it some time since now he was forty-seven.

Taller than me. Very good-looking. Older than me. And easy to talk to.

Definitely lovely.

"Sucks 'cause it was cool talkin' with you," he started. "But I gotta be at the gym early and then I gotta be on the job so I gotta get goin'."

This did "suck."

Even so, I said, "All right, Mickey."

"See you ringside Saturday."

Oh dear.

Ringside?

That was close. I didn't know if I wanted to be that close to a fight.

I didn't share this with Mickey.

I said, "Yes. See you Saturday."

"Lookin' forward to it."

"Me as well."

There was humor in his tone when he said, "Later, babe."

"Later, Mickey."

I rang off, tossed my phone to the seat, took a sip of tea and stared at the inky night lit with bright moonlight on the sea and twinkling stars in the sky.

I did this thinking that I'd made the right decision to take a break and spend time in Magdalene, being where I felt safest, at Lavender House, getting to know Jake and his family, now meeting Mickey. I didn't remember when I'd last stayed in one place as long as this without being constantly busy with work and dinners and parties and phone calls and emails and keeping schedules and making arrangements and running errands.

And I sat there hoping that Henry would agree to let me run his life from the computer that was now connected to the internet that was but feet away from me at Gran's desk.

But I worried he wouldn't. Although quite a bit of what I had to do was over the phone and on the computer, there was much of it that required me to be at Henry's side.

I just found that for the first time since I started with Henry, I had little desire to be the very many *theres* that was working for Henry.

I'd had a beautiful life, seen many amazing things, been many wonderful places, met many vibrant and interesting people.

And I didn't want that to end, not forever.

That said, this felt good, sipping tea and chatting on the phone with a handsome man who wanted to take me to dinner. Knowing the next day meant more time with Ethan and also more time with Jake. Knowing my life was full and I was busy but there was a steadiness to it that I'd never had but enjoyed greatly.

On this thought, my phone rang.

I looked down, saw the display and what was on it made me snatch it right up, take the call and put it to my ear.

"Hello, Jake," I greeted.

"Slick," he replied. "Forgot to ask before I left, am I pickin' you up for a workout tomorrow?"

There was a nagging ache all throughout my body that was not terrible but it didn't feel brilliant either.

Even so, I queried in return, "Does Amber have another outfit I can borrow?"

And there was humor in Jake's tone when he answered, "She has about seven of 'em."

"Then the answer is yes. But I'll meet you at the gym and use your locker room to change there," I told him.

"Can't make you an energy shake before we go, you meet me at the gym," was his reply.

This didn't sound appealing.

"Uh…" I mumbled.

"Be there at six thirty. Be up. I'll bring your gear."

Six thirty?

Earlier, he'd said seven.

And seven was already an hour (or two) too early.

"Uh…" I repeated.

"You're in charge of coffee."

"Um…Jake—" I started.

"Shit," he muttered in a distracted way before I could say more. "Con just walked in. The look on his face, he's got somethin' on his mind. Gotta go."

I had a feeling this had to do with Conner perhaps making another "cut" of one of his "babes." And if he was sensitive to them and cared about them, regardless of how many there were, this would be unpleasant.

He'd need his dad.

And Jake, being Jake, would be there for him.

My heart swelled, my belly dipped and my head revolted.

It was my head that knew how to react but this had happened with Henry too. When the pain of not having what I so very much wanted escalated before I settled into the knowledge that what I had was better than not having anything at all.

"All right, Jake. See you tomorrow," I said.

"Yeah, baby. See you," he replied softly. "Sleep tight."

"You too."

"Later."

"Later, Jake."

He rang off.

I stared at my phone.

Then I sighed, tossed my phone to the seat, took another sip of my tea and turned my eyes to the sea.

I had a luxurious vehicle. I had a beautiful home with a beautiful view that held beautiful memories. I was becoming part of a beautiful family. I was building a friendship with a beautiful man. And I could take solace in the knowledge that my beautiful grandmother had given all of this to me because she loved me very, very deeply. It was mine. And it was far more than I'd ever had in my life.

Thus, I told myself, I had nothing to complain about and much to relish. And taking another sip of tea, I decided to do that.

I also decided that after school activities with Ethan tomorrow would include going to the mall in order that I could buy my own workout clothes.

And maybe we could take Amber with us so I could purchase her makeup for her.

I grinned at the thought, for Ethan may not like a trip to the mall, but Amber would love it.

Yes, much to relish.

Starting the next morning with being in charge of coffee.

Eleven

PRETENDING

I was pretending.

Indeed, I'd been pretending all day.

I'd started my pretending by not setting the alarm. This meant Jake woke me up again that morning. But this time he didn't sit on the bed and tickle my nose with a lock of my hair.

Instead, he'd bent over me, shifted the hair off my neck and trailed a finger down my jaw, murmuring, "Wake up, sleepyhead."

His touch and his voice warmed me even more than the downy covers over me and I'd opened my eyes, this making Jake the first thing I saw for two mornings in a row.

This being something I knew with ridiculous certainty at that point in our acquaintance I wanted every single day for the rest of my life.

"You hit snooze or forget to set your alarm?" he asked softly.

"I forgot," I lied.

He grinned.

Then, alas, he straightened and said, "Clothes in the bag. I'll do coffee." He'd tipped his head to the armchair in the corner telling me where the clothes where. Then, without delay, he left my room.

It was regrettable he was leaving. Still, I got to take in his electric blue workout shirt spread across his broad shoulders as he did so, therefore the view was outstanding.

Mickey showed that morning at the gym as he told me he would do the night before.

But even though Mickey made it clear he wished to approach, Jake stuck by my side like glue during our workout. He did this acting like a drill sergeant while I punched and kicked the bag as he instructed (this time with my hands taped which made me feel oddly less of an impostor, not to mention Jake taping my hands expertly was quite a sight to see *and* feeling to feel).

Thus, Jake gave neither Mickey nor I an opening other than to smile at each other, me to wave and Mickey to lift his chin to me.

When we were done, Jake whisked me out of the gym saying I had to get to the Weavers and he had "shit to do." He did this while Mickey had his back to us, working a punching bag, so he didn't even see us go.

After that, Jake took me home. He again took me inside, I got another kiss on the cheek (close to my lips) and a ponytail tug as Jake reminded me of our plans and the timing of them for the evening.

Before he left, I also got Amber's mobile number and I'd texted her to see if she'd like to join Ethan and me at the mall after school.

It took her an hour to reply but she'd politely excused the tardiness of it by saying she was in class, which I found gratifying, as politeness wasn't Amber's strong suit, not to mention, she shouldn't be texting while in class. She went on to take me up on my offer and she did this exuberantly (yes, even via text).

Thus, I was able to continue pretending that my life included Jake Spear *and* his family.

I did this by taking Amber and Ethan to the mall directly after school, Amber meeting us at Lavender House in her car before we went.

I learned during this experience that Ethan might enjoy cooking but he did not enjoy shopping. As we had a list of specific cosmetics to buy and I knew what suited me even before I tried it on (I still tried them on), our forays in the women's athletics store as well as at the cosmetics counter were short. Even so, Ethan still vociferously shared that he was not enjoying himself.

The only time he seemed placated was when he declared he was *starving* and I'd purchased an enormous soda for him along with a big bag of soft pretzel bites that included a tub of liquid cheese that was an alarming orange color. Nevertheless, Ethan found it delicious and I knew this because the entirety of this rather large snack was gone within five minutes.

We got him home and Amber and I sat at the kitchen table with a hand mirror as she tried out one of the looks Jean-Michel suggested. Watching her do it, I found she was quite adept with the brushes I bought her and, in the end, we were both pleased with the results.

Me specifically.

She was lovely normally.

Made up like that, she was beautiful and I didn't hesitate to tell her this. Then I made a note never to hesitate to share things such as that with her because the look on her face was very much worth the energy it took to utter the words.

However, during this, I learned that Ethan was not a fan of "girl stuff" on the whole. I learned this as he shared it in disgust, staring at the cosmetics and brushes on the kitchen table. This he did before he took himself off to watch TV.

This he did with me smiling at him, for even when he was disgusted, he was endearing.

Shortly after, Jake arrived to take us to dinner and then the game.

And I kept pretending when he took one look at his daughter made up in a soft, subdued, romantic palette of colors.

And what I was pretending was that he was mine and in doing so, I daydreamed a variety of ways I would reward him for what he did with Amber when he saw her.

This was catch her chin with his fingers and let his eyes roam over her face.

They finally caught hers and he said quietly, "Jesus, honey. Knew you were beautiful. Didn't know how much of that beauty you were hidin' until just now."

It was then I watched Amber's face change, turn radiant with a hint of hopeful and I felt a lovely feeling gather tight around my heart as she smiled at her father.

He bent in and kissed her cheek and that feeling around my heart tightened brilliantly.

When Jake let her go, she turned her smile to me and said, "Thanks, Josie."

"It was my pleasure, lovely girl," I replied.

She kept smiling when she declared to both her dad and me, "Gotta get to the Taylors. Later."

"Later, babe," Jake returned.

"Have fun tonight, Amber," I said.

She grinned at me then turned her head toward the family room and yelled, "Later, runt!" to her brother.

"Don't call me runt!" Ethan yelled back.

I smiled at Jake when he did.

Jake returned my smile but his wasn't about the engaging way his children teased each other. His smile was different, deeper, filled with gratitude and something else I didn't completely understand but knew was meaningful in a way that was gravely important and also *very* good.

It said he liked the way his daughter looked. Very much so.

And he liked that I gave her that.

Very much so.

And I liked that.

Very much so.

Not only for Jake, but for Amber.

Feeling the lovely feeling Jake's smile gave to me, I kept pretending when he took us to Weatherby's Diner in Magdalene for dinner. I pretended I belonged to him and Ethan as we walked in, Jake's hand holding mine. I pretended that the looks we got were looks I deserved, the women's eyes going to Jake then going to his hand clasping mine and turning despondent.

I continued pretending when Jake slid in the booth beside me.

I kept at it when he slid his arm across the back of the booth, fantasizing this was done in an act of not only affection but also possession when it was more likely that he was a big man and it was simply more comfortable for him to spread out in this manner.

Even knowing this, I didn't let go the fantasy. I was enjoying it too much.

And it was the only thing I'd ever get.

Therefore, I carried on pretending when we left the diner and Jake drove us to the high school football field as Ethan chattered animatedly (something he also did during dinner making Jake and my participation in our dinner conversation mostly responding to Ethan or smiling at him because we couldn't get a word in edgewise).

Combat Raptor was the main topic, his enthusiasm that his wait was *finally* over as well as an in-depth description of the characters and actors who played them and how he felt about all of that.

I continued to pretend when Jake again took my hand at his truck and we walked through the parking lot and into the stadium.

I persisted in doing it as we made our way to our seats and more glances came our way. Some from people I didn't know but Jake did and he lifted his chin to them. Some from people I'd made the acquaintance of and I smiled at them or gave them a brief wave. And then there were the others, from men who looked at me then to Jake and their faces closed down. The women who did the opposite but with the same final reaction.

I enjoyed doing it so much I got lost in it when Jake choose our seats and I stood in the bleachers watching him spread a thick woolen blanket across the metal bench. But before he did this, he shook something from the blanket. And once the blanket was arranged, before we sat on it, he turned to me.

I held my breath as he wrapped a long maroon wool knit scarf around my neck and tied it at my throat, doing this murmuring, "Gotta keep my girl warm."

His girl.

Oh, how I *wished*.

The night was chill and overcast and Jake had remembered my scarf that morning we had breakfast at The Shack.

Oh yes.

How I wished.

Even though the scarf didn't quite match my outfit.

I was forcing myself to breathe when he lifted his eyes to mine as he lifted a hand to my jaw and informed me, "Lydie knitted that for me three Christmases ago."

Gran had made it for him.

The soft wool at my neck got warmer and instantly I felt my eyes get wet.

I said nothing mostly because I couldn't.

Jake didn't miss it and I knew it when he bent slightly toward me and stated, "Looks good on you, baby. But it bein' from Lydie, I'll want to keep it close."

I nodded and forced out, "Of course."

His smile was slight—it simply tipped up his lips and softened his eyes.

But it was beautiful.

So beautiful, I leaned into him. When I did, his eyes changed completely. They went from soft and warm to intense and something else.

Something that looked darker.

Heated.

Even *more* beautiful.

I was trying to understand that reaction when Ethan broke the moment, crying loudly, "Dad! There's Josh and Bryant! Can I hang with them?"

For a moment, Jake's gaze held mine captive even as the pads of his fingers dug into my jaw.

Then he unfortunately dropped his hand and turned to his son.

"Not out of my sight, bud," he ordered.

"Got it," Ethan confirmed, jumped on the empty bench in front of us and dashed along it to the steps. He raced down the steps to two boys who were standing by the fence by the field.

"Sit, Slick," Jake invited.

I looked from Ethan to him and I sat.

He sat next to me, curved an arm around my waist and pulled me the mere inches that separated us so that we were hip to hip, thigh to thigh.

Oh.

My.

I took in a trembling breath and looked about the space.

The field was bare as were the player's benches. The away crowd bleachers were filling up fast but not as fast as the home crowd's section around us. There was a lot of yellow and blue, which I knew were the school colors.

I saw the cheerleaders milling about behind the team bench, preparing for their work that evening. The air was very chilly and the spectators were suited up to battle the chill in hats, scarves, heavy parkas and jackets and even gloves. And there were many children and young adults about, the young adults not nearly as prepared to face the cold evening, as it was clear they preferred their peers to see their fashion selections and not to cover them with heavy coats that would keep them warm.

It was then it occurred to me that the last sporting event I attended was a football game at my own high school decades ago.

And it also occurred to me that back then for a brief period of time, I'd loved football.

My clandestine boyfriend Andy played thus I never missed a game. I never even missed a play. I was enthralled by watching him on the field. And I looked forward every Friday night to going to the game with my girlfriends, watching my boyfriend play football then sneaking in a date with him after, and after that, sneaking in kissing him for as long as we could do it before it became too dangerous to continue and we'd have to stop so I could get home.

I'd been happy then.

I'd been normal then.

I didn't have to pretend.

I had it all.

And then my father took it all away.

"You good?"

Jake's voice pulled me from my maudlin thoughts and I looked to hm.

"Yes," I answered.

"Warm enough?" he went on.

"Indeed, Jake." I quieted my voice when I said with feeling, "Thank you for the scarf."

I got the slight smile with soft eyes before he carried on, "Can you see okay?"

He was so very kind, considerate...*amazing.*

I nodded.

"Good," he murmured, looking to the field and giving me a squeeze, which pressed me even deeper to his side.

I wanted to keep pretending. I really did. And how I wanted to do that was to press even closer. Put my head on his shoulder. Wrap my arm around his back and hold him to me too. Even wrap both my arms around him, stomach and back, keeping him close.

But I couldn't keep pretending.

And further, I had to find a restroom.

"Before things start, I need to use the facilities," I told his profile and got his eyes, which were now not softly smiling but openly doing it, as was his mouth.

"Right, Slick. The *facilities* are behind the concession stand, south end of the field," he informed me, tipping his head to the left.

"Thanks, Jake," I murmured. "I'll be back."

"You got time. Game doesn't start for fifteen minutes," he told me as I stood but he carried on. "Sayin' that, hurry."

I looked down at him to see him looking in the vicinity of my behind in my jeans exposed by my gray suede jacket before his eyes drifted up and caught mine and they were still smiling.

"I'll hurry," I assured him then I did just that.

I hurried.

Or, at least I started out hurrying.

After I washed my hands and left the restrooms, I mentally shook myself from the fantasy world I'd allowed myself to live in all day.

It was pleasant being there and it was lovely giving myself that but I couldn't stay there for long. I had to remember how things were. If I stayed in that world too long, I knew I'd eventually get a reminder that it wasn't mine and the pain that would cause would be harder to overcome the longer I allowed myself to pretend.

On this thought, I saw movement out of the corner of my eye and looked right to see Conner standing under a light pole some distance away from the bleachers but also not close to the concession stand.

He was standing with a flaxen-haired girl who was quite curvy, quite tall and very attractive. I also liked the way that it didn't seem she cared what people thought of her attire. She was trussed up warm but she'd managed to do it fashionably with a thick loosely woven oyster-colored scarf around her neck and a dusky pink corduroy jacket. She was even wearing a cute pair of mittens.

She was also standing close to Conner, looking up at him and smiling in an appealing way that was genuine if a little timid.

She must be Ellie and just seeing her made me agree further with Ethan that I hoped Conner chose her in the end.

Jake's eldest must have sensed my eyes for his came to me; he grinned and jerked up his chin. Ellie looked my way and as she did so, slid slightly closer to Conner who took that opportunity to curve his arm around her shoulders.

Yes, they looked lovely together.

I gave them a wave and a smile and decided not to approach. This was a high school football game and he was with his girl (or one of them). He didn't need an adult intruding.

But as I moved away, I took in the lines standing in front of the concession stand. I also noted that the game had not started although the players had taken the field and were warming up. And finally, it occurred to me that hot drinks might warm Jake and me from the inside.

Therefore, I moved to the back of the somewhat long line, pulled my phone out of my purse and called him.

He answered with, "You get lost?"

I laughed softly and replied, "No, Jake. But I'm in line at the concession stand. I thought we could use a hot beverage. Would you like a coffee or cocoa?"

"I'll meet you there."

So.

Very.

Amazing.

"Jake, I can handle a few drinks. What do you want?"

"I'll be there in a minute and I'll get it."

"Jake," I said softly. "You bought dinner at The Eaves, and our omelets, and dinner tonight. In return, the least I can do is purchase two beverages and carry them back to the bleachers. Further, if you leave our seats, we might lose them."

"The blanket's here," was his reply and at hearing it, I burst out laughing.

Yes.

So.

Very.

Amazing.

When I stopped laughing, I asked, "You're quite determined to take care of me, aren't you?"

His voice was low in a way my stomach dipped when he returned, "Glad you noticed."

I couldn't *not* notice, and with the way he behaved, I was finding it hard not to pretend.

My voice was just above a whisper when I requested, "Please let me buy you a drink."

"Hot chocolate," he finally ordered and I smiled into the phone.

"For Ethan?" I asked.

"Ethan's got ten bucks. He wants something, he'll get it. But it won't be hot chocolate. It'll be a load of crap."

I was still smiling when I replied, "All right," then moved the two centimeters forward that the line had moved. "I'll be back in a few minutes."

"Later, Slick."

"Later, Jake."

I rang off at the same time I became aware that the young man in front of me was staring at me openly, his lips parted.

As I became aware of this, I noted that he was somewhat short, very slim, obviously effeminate and he was wearing a daring pair of houndstooth trousers. He'd accompanied these with a rather stylish pair of black suede loafers and a black turtleneck sweater.

The ensemble could use a fedora as a finishing touch but regardless of that assessment, I was taken with his flair for fashion.

"Hello," I said when he continued to stare at me in apparent astonishment.

"You're Josie," he informed me of a truth that was nevertheless surprising that he knew.

"Indeed I am," I confirmed. "And you are?"

He stuck his hand out. "Taylor. I'm Amber's bestest bestie. Or one of them."

Ah.

The Jean-Michel devotee.

This explained the trousers and the loafers.

I took his hand and gave it a squeeze. "Delighted to meet you, Taylor. Amber's spoken of you."

He squeezed my hand back and let it go, saying, "She's spoken of you too, like *lots*. She thinks you're the bomb."

I had learned this was good and I knew it felt good so I smiled.

Then I shared, "Your ensemble is very fashion forward and you carry it off with aplomb. However, it needs a fedora."

His face lit up, he leaned in and exclaimed, "I know! Right?" He leaned back and smiled, finishing, "But not sure I could pull off a fedora at a Magdalene High game. I'll be lucky I don't get tripped, pushed or run down before the night is through just wearing these trousers."

He waved a hand to his lower body but I felt my brows draw together.

"And why would you get tripped, pushed or run down?" I asked.

"Uh…I'm a seventeen year old gay guy wearing houndstooth at a high school football game?" he asked back as an answer.

Ah.

That certainly answered that.

"I see," I murmured. "Well, I wish I had some sage advice for you, young Taylor, but alas, I don't. Small-minded fools are everywhere and those with the courage to be who they are often have to suffer them. It's your lot, I'm afraid. But at least you can rest in the knowledge that you are true to yourself knowing they live in a narrow world, a narrow world is a barren world while yours is vibrant, and that's *their* lot."

When I finished speaking, he was staring up at me again with his lips parted, astonishment awash in his features and I was just about to say something (such as that he should move forward the seven centimeters the line had moved) when I felt others joining the line at my back.

They were talking. They were also boys.

And what they were discussing gained the entirety of my attention.

"You totally looked through Amber like she wasn't even there," a boy said.

I blinked as I watched Taylor's eyes get very wide.

"She looks good tonight. Real good. Somethin' different about her face," another boy mumbled.

"You done with her?" a further one asked.

"Bitch has got to toe the line," a fourth one with a very deep voice declared. "Don't dig teases. Amber Spear is a total tease. All that hair. Short skirts. But I got my hands on her and she won't let me get one up that skirt? Fuck that."

My back went straight and I watched Taylor's face pale.

"And her dad's a pain in my ass," the fourth one with the deep voice concluded.

"You're just shit scared of him 'cause Spear could *kick* your ass, even if he's an old guy," one of the other voices said.

Excuse me?

Jake was *not* old.

Actually, I had no idea of his age but I knew he wasn't old. I knew this because I'd seen him work out.

"Whatever," the deepest voice went on. "He won't let her go to Boston to see Bounce with us. I mean seriously? What's up with that? That's fucked up. Chelsea and Brooke are goin' and their parents don't give a fuck."

The concert Amber wanted to see was Bounce.

At that point, I wished she'd informed me of that.

And two second later, after the one with the deep voice said what he said next, I made a split-second decision and, rather foolishly, sallied forth acting on it.

"Thought I'd get in there, pop that. She's hot but if Amber likes her cherry that much, she can keep it."

I saw Taylor snap his mouth closed and his jaw get tight but that was all I saw before I whirled.

Behind me, there were four boys. All tall. All relatively good-looking. The tallest and far best looking one was an African-American young man.

I knew instinctively he was Noah.

I could see Amber wanting him.

But she wasn't going to get him.

Or, more aptly, *he* was not going to get *her.*

"Are you Noah?" I asked.

He smiled slowly; an appealing white smile and I knew he thought I'd heard of him as he was a high school big man basketball player.

Upon his smile, he replied, "Yeah. I'm Noah Young."

I nodded. "Well, Noah Young, you should know that Amber is not going to the concert with you because she and the Taylors are going with me. Lavon doesn't like an extortionate amount of people backstage and Amber preferred to give the backstage passes I could acquire for her to her bestest besties. And apparently, you aren't one of them," I lied.

Or, more aptly, I lied right then.

I'd need to speak with Lavon's people to make it a truth.

Lavon Burkett was the front man for Bounce. Henry had directed four videos for the band. Lavon thought the world of Henry and, by extension, me. He'd give me as many backstage passes as I wanted, even if it was true that he didn't like to socialize with a vast amount of people after a show. He liked me enough to do whatever I asked as he was very generous with his friends. I knew this when he sent me a fabulous flower arrangement after I'd set up the arrangements of his first video, a magnum of champagne after the second, the original sheet framed of lyrics he's jotted down to my favorite Bounce song the third and a pair of diamond stud earrings the last.

Noah Young was blinking at me but I was far from done.

"As for your assertion that Amber is a tease, she isn't. She just isn't that into you."

This was, of course, an outright lie and I heard a gurgling noise come from Taylor behind me perhaps exposing my perfidy.

Nevertheless, I persevered.

"Although she recognizes you're quite good-looking, she also doesn't feel you respect her very much and is having issues with that, wondering if *you* will eventually toe the line. But alas, from your comments tonight, it seems you won't."

I held his eyes and lowered my voice.

"You see, a woman who knows herself and her worth knows that her time is valuable and her heart is precious. She doesn't give either to a man who can't respect the gifts he's being offered."

Noah kept blinking and I raised my voice slightly as I finished.

"And anyway, she's been Skypeing Julian. I introduced them online. He's French Canadian and I believe he's doing a fashion shoot in Fiji at the moment but he'll be back in New York next week. He's quite the outdoors type, even if he's a model, and he's keen to come and meet Amber as well as see Maine. I'm sure Amber will enjoy showing her home state to him when he arrives."

This was all a lie too, of course, but that didn't stop me from lowering the boom as a finale.

"He's nineteen and her father quite likes him even though Julian's a bit older than her. This is because Julian spends a fair amount of time around very beautiful women and thus he knows how to treat them but more, he knows a quality individual when he meets one. Even if only online. So please do totally look through Amber," I invited. "It will only save you frustration and perhaps heartbreak when she eventually understands how shallow you are, finds you tedious and cuts you loose."

"Holy shit," one of his compatriots muttered and that reminded me I wasn't done.

"Just one final thing," I began. "There are men who can carry off foul language. But they are *men*. When you use it, you sound absurd, like you're desperately trying to be something you're not. Furthermore, badmouthing a young woman when all and sundry can hear is just bad manners. *Extremely* bad manners. It says nothing about the young woman you're referring to and everything about your own character. And just to say, none of that everything is good."

On that, I turned my back to him and looked to Taylor.

"You may wish to move forward, young Taylor," I stated. "The line has advanced."

He tore his incredulous eyes from me and shuffled forward the twelve centimeters the line had moved.

"C'mon, let's get out of here." I heard mumbled from behind me and I felt the boys' presence leave as the line behind them closed in and Taylor again caught my eye.

"That...was...*epic*," he breathed.

Although I found "epic" an overdramatized word, I was still pleased he thought so. But now that the deed was done, I was beginning to get anxious.

For Taylor might think so but I had grave concerns Amber would *not*.

"Do you have your phone?" I asked.

"Yeah," he answered.

"Hurry and text Amber. Tell her to come here straight away. We need to warn her that event just occurred."

"You got it," he muttered and dug his phone out of his back pocket.

I continued, "After you get in touch with her, you may wish to get in touch with your parents and ask them if you can attend the Bounce concert with me. Please assure them I'll provide transport and accommodation and act as your chaperone."

His thumbs stopped flying over the screen of his phone and he looked up at me like I was an angel fallen to earth.

He went back to his phone as I tried to breathe normally, becoming more and more worried that my intervention in Amber's romantic life would not be well received. I continued worrying even as the line shuffled forward.

Amber finally joined us as Taylor stood beside me and I took the two hot cocoas in one hand that were in a brown cardboard holder.

Amber also had a young woman with her and I momentarily forgot my fears as I took her in.

She was very tall, at least two inches taller than Amber and I, putting her to my expert eye at five ten. She was also very slender. Her hair was a shining black sheath. Her clothing, like Taylor's, was not suited to Magdalene High but instead suited to waltzing along the sidewalk in Manhattan on her way to meet friends for a salad even if she was in a pair of jeans, boots and an extremely well-cut leather jacket.

Her features were mixed race, Caucasian and more than likely Korean with high, rounded cheekbones, elegantly formed dark brown eyes and absolutely flawless porcelain skin.

She was stunning.

"Hey, Josie," Amber greeted. "What's up?"

At Amber's voice, my fears returned and I tore my eyes away from the girl at her side and looked to her.

"We need to find some privacy, lovely girl. I need a word," I told her.

Her face went guarded but Taylor came to my rescue.

"Totally, Amber. You gotta hear what just happened."

Amber looked to her friend, her expression even more wary and we moved away from the concession stand to the open grassy area between it and the bleachers. We found a large patch of grass where no one was standing close and we huddled together.

"What's going on?" Amber asked immediately.

I opened my mouth to answer but her friend spoke before me.

"By the way, I'm Taylor or, uh…the *other* Taylor. Amber and Taylor's bestest bestie," she introduced herself.

"Lovely to meet you, Taylor. I'm Josephine."

"I know." She smiled, her features rearranging subtly into another extraordinary view. "Amber's makeup tonight is *sick*. Everyone is checking her out. It's *awesome*."

I was pleased she thought so and I smiled but I said no more as I had more pressing things on my mind.

Before I could share these, boy Taylor stated, "Girl, Noah got behind us in line at the concession stand and I don't think he saw me because he and his posse trash talked you *extreme*."

Amber's face lost all its color as she stared at her friend.

"Don't worry though. Josie totally *laid him out*," boy Taylor went on to assure her.

Her pale face turned my way and it was clear from the look on it she was not assured.

I got closer, feeling my heart beating harder. "I'm so sorry, my lovely girl," I said gently. "He was saying some awful things and I simply couldn't help myself."

"What'd he say?" she whispered.

Boy Taylor (and girl Taylor) huddled closer and boy Taylor shared quietly, "He called you a tease and said if you like your cherry so much, you can keep it."

Pink tinged her cheeks at that even as she winced.

"What a dick," girl Taylor decreed at this point and I looked to her to see her looking at Amber. "I so totally told you, Amber. He's completely up his own ass."

"He is, girlfriend," boy Taylor agreed. "He thinks he's all that when *you're* all that and tonight with your face like it is you're even *more* all that. And anyway no guy should trash talk a girl for anyone to hear or…freaking…*ever*. But he did and he's *so* not worth putting up with this. Even if he was, he still wouldn't be."

"I believe this is true," I told her, still going gently and she looked to me. "And I'm afraid I shared this with him and, perhaps, fibbed a bit," I finished on an admission.

"You fibbed?" she asked, her voice weak as she accepted these rather vicious-to-a-teenaged-girl blows.

"Yes."

"About what?"

I took a deep breath and on the exhale explained, "Well, I told him I was taking you and the Taylors to Bounce, which I didn't know that was the concert you wanted to see in Boston. Since I know Lavon, I'll be happy to do that if we can talk your father into letting you go."

Her mouth dropped open and I looked to the girl Taylor.

"You may wish to share this with your parents. Lavon will gladly give me backstage passes should I ask, something I'll be doing first thing tomorrow. Please assure your parents all travel arrangements and accommodation will be covered by me and I'll be with you at all times."

Her striking eyes were big and she asked, "You know Lavon Burkett?"

"Of course," I murmured, but felt it imperative we return to the matter at hand.

To do so, I looked back to Amber.

"I must share that I also fibbed about the fact that you're talking with Julian online. Julian is a model that Henry often works with. Of course, I can introduce you to Julian and make that fib true too, but I'm uncertain how your father will react to that so let's get the concert issue dealt with first and then we'll move on to Julian."

Amber was now blinking up at me, clearly unable to process all that was coming her way, but before I could even attempt to reassure her, boy Taylor exclaimed, "Oh my *gawd!*"

"What?" girl Taylor asked.

We all looked to him to see he had his phone screen turned our way. On it was a picture of Julian emerging from the surf, fully wet, his well-defined body alluringly bronzed, wearing rather skimpy black bathing trunks, water dripping from a dark lock dangling from his forehead, an arresting yet mischievous smile on his face.

"Please tell me he's really gay," boy Taylor breathed.

"Alas, I can't tell you that young Taylor, for he very much is not," I replied.

"I'm in love," girl Taylor whispered.

"You can introduce me to *him?*" Amber asked breathily.

My eyes moved to her and I saw my mistake so I moved instantly to control the situation.

THE WILL

"Let's stay focused," I urged. "First, your friends need to get permission to go to the concert and I need to discuss that with your father to make certain you can go. Second, you need to handle yourself tonight very carefully. I've no idea how Noah will react to my set down but he might take that out on you."

I got closer and spoke quieter.

"You, my lovely girl, must act like you don't care. You can take him or leave him. If he ignores you, bury any reaction you may have to it. You can talk to your friends about it or even…" I hesitated before offering, "*me,* if you would trust me enough to share your feelings. If he doesn't ignore you, give him your time but not much of it. His words and behavior tonight proved he's not worth it."

Amber proved she had a one-track mind—that being the boy track— when to this she repeated with a jerk of her head in the direction of boy Taylor's phone, "You can introduce me to *him?*"

"Amber, did you hear what I said?" I asked.

I watched her swallow, her eyes get bright and her words were trembling when she asked back, "He called me a tease?"

At the look on her face and the sound of her words, I felt my heart get heavy.

My poor girl.

I leaned into her and lifted a hand to her jaw.

Stroking her soft cheek with my thumb, I whispered, "Yes, my lovely girl. He was most ungentlemanly."

"He acted like he liked me," she whispered back.

"He likely does," I told her. "He also has to show a certain face to his friends and feels he has to play his role as big man in a way that he can keep that role but has the mistaken and rather juvenile impression that doing that means gathering conquests and behaving very badly."

She was still whispering when she told me, "But Josie, I've liked him since…*forever.*"

I pulled in another deep breath, long since gone from my high school years but remembering quite acutely what it was like to crush on a boy and have him show me the attention I so craved.

Thus, I stroked her cheek again and replied, "I think now you're experiencing a lot of things, my lovely. And one of them is simply the fact that he

225

does not live up to what you thought he would be. But he doesn't. It may take some time for you to come to terms with this but the fact of the matter is it's true. And perhaps my words tonight will penetrate in some way and he'll look at you with different eyes. But if he does and his attention returns to you, you *must* not accept anything but that which is grounded not only in attraction but also respect, kindness and affection."

"He's the cutest guy in school," she informed me.

"This may be true but I assure you, if you heard his words tonight, he would appear *far* less attractive to you, even if those words hadn't been spoken about you," I shared.

"That's totally true, Amber," boy Taylor put in at this juncture and I dropped my hand as we both looked to him. "He was totally a douche."

"He's always been a douche," girl Taylor murmured.

"It's extremely improper for me to call a young teenaged boy a douche," I stated and everyone looked at me. "That said, Taylor is right. He was definitely a douche."

I saw Amber's eyes widen to extremes as both Taylors burst out laughing.

Then to my relief, I saw Amber's eyes light as she joined them but grabbed my hand, held it and forced through her amusement, "Josie, you saying the word *douche* is the funniest thing I think I've heard *in my life*."

I liked it that she was holding my hand. I liked it that she didn't dissolve into tears at hearing what had occurred with Noah Young. I liked it that she didn't get angry with me and cause a scene by throwing a tantrum that it was arguable, but having been a teenaged girl at one point in my life, I would weigh in that it was deserved.

Last and most important, I liked it that now she was laughing.

I stopped liking it or thinking anything when we heard a shrieked, "*Seriously Conner! You think you can scrape me off?*"

"Uh-oh," Amber mumbled, her hand squeezing mine as our eyes darted to where I'd seen Conner with his girlfriend before.

He was still there, as was she. They were still standing close. But now Conner had moved the blonde girl behind him in a protective manner as a rather voluptuous (for a high school girl), relatively petite and definitely angry girl faced off against them.

"*You, yeah you!*" she kept shrieking and now was pointing at who I assumed was Ellie. "*You think I can't take you?*"

Conner's face was a frozen mask of anger and he took a step toward the brunette even as he shoved the blonde further behind him and it was at this that I found my feet moving without my brain telling them to do so.

They did this, taking me straight to Conner.

I felt Amber and the Taylors trailing me.

I stopped wide to the side (and Amber and the Taylors stopped with me) and looked to Conner who was looking at me.

He started, "Josie—"

"I think you need privacy with this young lady," I said quietly and pointedly. I then turned my eyes to the blonde as well as reached a hand out to her. "Come," I encouraged.

"Ellie," Amber whispered close to my back.

So I was correct.

I nodded and pushed my hand further toward Ellie. "Come, Ellie. Let's go sit, watch the game and await Conner."

Ellie looked to Conner who was looking over his shoulder at her.

"Go," he said gently. "Josie'll take care of you."

She pressed her lips together, hesitated but a moment and finally moved toward me.

"Watch your back," the brunette hissed as she got close to me.

Ellie scuttled closer and I took her hand. Hers clasped mine surprisingly tight even though she had to have no idea who I was (outside of the fact that I was with her boyfriend's sister).

I took her hand and moved her away, my gaze going back to Conner.

His eyes were on me. "I've got this, Josie."

"Yeah, you *think* you do," the brunette was still hissing. "But you *don't.*"

Oh dear.

It appeared Conner had his hands full.

I moved Ellie clear of the burgeoning fray and did it quickly, Amber and the Taylors trailing.

We got well away, moved in close to the side of the bleachers, and I found us another pocket of privacy. I could tell the game had started but I could also see Ellie's face was pale and stricken and her hand had not loosened even a smidgeon in mine.

I turned to her when we stopped and Amber and the Taylors huddled close.

"I'm Josephine," I introduced myself.

"Yeah," she said quietly, her voice timid, her eyes not exactly meeting mine. "Con told me about you. His dad's new girlfriend."

At her words, I felt shafts of fire burn through me like spears were drilling from top to toe. This feeling was painful because this feeling was hope in the face of hopelessness. It took everything I had not to focus on that feeling and instead focus on this frightened shy girl.

"I think Conner would like it if you would sit with myself and Conner's dad. He'll find us when he's done with that young lady," I told her.

She shook her head. "It won't matter. She'll get to me. She's been saying at school for days she's going to take me out."

"Then you shouldn't be alone," boy Taylor stated, getting close.

"We'll stick by you, Ellie," Amber assured, also getting close.

"Mia's just ticked she knows she's not going to make the cut and you are. She'll burn out," girl Taylor told her, also getting close.

When she did, I sighed.

Make the cut, indeed.

Conner had weaved this tangled web. I certainly hoped he had it in him to unravel it without too much heartache.

"I think I need to sit down," Ellie said softly.

"Let's get her to the bleachers," I urged and immediately moved my charges to do just that.

I found the set of stairs that were closest to our seats. I also saw Jake sitting amongst the crowd, a seat open on either side of him on the blanket, one for the absent Ethan, one for the absent me.

I let Ellie go but curled my fingers around Amber's arm and dipped down to say in her ear, "Can you take Ellie up and ask your father to come down?"

When I pulled away, she caught my eyes and nodded.

Boy Taylor grabbed the forgotten cocoas from my other hand and they all scrambled up. They then pushed in front of the four spectators to get to

Jake. I saw Amber bend down and talk to him then I saw his eyes come to me. He stood, his eyes never leaving me as he and the children shuffled around. He eased in front of the spectators then I watched as he jogged down the stairs to me.

When he got to me, I took his hand without a word and tugged him to the spot the youngsters and I had vacated earlier.

I stopped us and got close.

Thereupon, I got up on my toes to get closer and launched in.

"I have much to say and not much time," I announced.

His brows shot up.

I sallied forth.

"I'll explain later so you can get angry without an audience as to what prompted me to make a number of rash decisions but right now I'll break it down. With your permission, I'll be taking Amber and the Taylors to see Bounce in Boston whenever it is they're playing there. I know the band and am relatively close to the front man so I can get backstage passes. I'll chaperone them. But I want very much for Amber and her friends to have this as I've met Noah Young, it was not a pleasant meeting, I dislike him greatly and I wish for Amber and the Taylors to be able to rub his nose in their not only attending the concert but meeting the performers."

Jake blinked.

I carried on.

"Conner is currently calming down a rather irate young lady who has threatened bodily harm to Ellie. Amber, the Taylors and I forged to the rescue and thus Ellie is with us awaiting Conner's return. I would think that he may need you to intervene at some point as, for reasons unknown to me, it would seem the girls may start turning on each other rather than aiming their ire at Conner, who I imagine could take it and who arguably deserves it. It isn't my place to say but he may need a mature guiding hand as he maneuvers the minefield toward monogamy."

Jake said nothing. He simply stared at me.

"And, just to say," I continued. "Amber and Noah, if they were ever officially together, have broken up. I played an, um…rather substantial hand in that, alas. It's likely there will be some teenaged girl moods in your house for the foreseeable future. Or, uh…*more* of them. I'd like to apologize for that in advance."

I stopped speaking and Jake continued to stare at me for a moment before he asked, "Jesus, Slick, how long were you gone?"

It seemed like a year.

I didn't share this. In fact, I decided not to speak at all.

"Does Con need me now?" Jake asked into my silence.

"He says he has it," I shared.

"Then he has it," he muttered, looking down to his boots.

I got closer and realized I was still holding his hand. I drew back on mine but couldn't release his because when I did this, his fingers tightened.

"I'm sorry, Jake. I may have made a bit of a mess."

His eyes cut to mine. "What went down with Noah?"

Oh dear.

"Perhaps I can tell you later," I suggested.

"What went down with Noah, Josie?"

I stared into his eyes and noted he was not going to back down.

So it was me who held his hand tighter and I again got closer before I shared, "Obviously, he has no idea who I am and thus I overheard him—as boy Taylor put it—*trash talking* Amber."

Jake's mouth got tight in a way I found vaguely frightening but I persevered.

"I'm afraid I lost my temper and gave him a talking to," I admitted.

"You gave him a talking to," he repeated.

"Indeed," I confirmed.

He said nothing to that and asked, "I need to have a word with Noah's parents?"

I shook my head quickly.

Jake studied me.

Then he asked quietly, "He was trash talking Amber?"

I nodded my head slowly.

His big man energy started expanding all around.

"What'd he say?"

It was then I got even closer, lifted my free hand and put it on his chest, trying to find the words I needed.

I found them from memory of what boy Taylor had said and stated, "It doesn't matter, Jake. I laid him out."

He again studied me before asking, "Amber know what he said?"

"Some of it, yes. But I think the Taylors have that in hand. They're quite supportive in a way it's most gratifying. Further, neither of them likes Noah very much."

"Was she there?"

I shook my head.

He took in a big breath and exhaled.

Then he shocked me by grinning, turning into me so he could sling his arm around my shoulders and tuck me into his side as he moved us toward the bleachers, stating, "Then I guess we're goin' to a concert in a couple weeks, Slick."

We?

I didn't ask this.

And I didn't because I was noting that it was awkward walking with him with his arm around my shoulders and mine hanging down at my sides, so I slid one of mine around his waist.

Jake kept us connected until we hit the steps that led to our seats in the bleachers. He bid me to go before him and did this by putting a hand in the small of my back and gently pushing me toward the stairs.

I ascended, noting that the children had appropriated more seating for us and Ethan had returned.

Though there was no sign of Conner and Ellie didn't look any less anxious.

Jake maneuvered the seating arrangements so he was sitting between me and his daughter. Although extra seating had been procured, it was close and my side was plastered to Jake's, including hip and thigh.

But he didn't curve an arm around me again.

Instead, he curved one around his daughter and pulled her close to his other side, bending to kiss the top of her head.

When he lifted away, she tipped her face back to gaze at him, her eyes soft and partly lost, partly loving, and seeing that I thought she never looked lovelier.

And seeing Jake silently give his daughter his loving care, I thought he'd never been more wonderful.

And he was normally *quite* wonderful.

Clearly father/daughter affection was acceptable only for short periods of time at high school events for Jake released Amber a short time later and turned his attention to me, again curling an arm around my back and pulling me even tighter to his side.

It was then it occurred to me why Conner would think I was his father's new girlfriend. Jake's easy, and frequent, affection could undoubtedly be misconstrued in this manner.

I wondered if I should talk to him about this for I felt it might be confusing to the children and if he should (regrettably, but very probably) find another woman, they might not understand.

I was thinking this when Conner returned and Jake didn't budge from my side even as his sharp eyes locked on his son.

But Conner saw no one but Ellie. He went directly to her and claimed her from boy Taylor who was sticking close.

Upon witnessing this, it became clear that Ellie was the one who was going to make "the cut." Watching them after he returned, I noted that Conner seemed very attentive of her, also very protective and, as they said these days, very "into" her.

Our seating became even tighter when Conner joined us but the other spectators were involved in the game so they didn't appear to notice.

Needless to say, our cocoas were lost in the shuffle and eventually got kicked under the bleachers without even being sipped. This was done by an excited Ethan, who did it when the Magdalene Tritons made one of their many touchdowns. This situation was rectified at halftime when Jake sent Ethan (who was accompanied on this errand by Conner and Ellie) to procure all of us warming beverages.

Except for the fact that it was a rather exciting game and even though I had not watched one in some time, I saw the Tritons were very talented, it seemed our drama for the evening was thankfully at an end.

The only thing earth shattering that happened (and this was only my perception) was that when we were seated (in other words, when Jake wasn't clapping or cupping his hands around his mouth and shouting encouragement at the team I was relatively certain they couldn't hear or jumping to his feet like all of those around us, applauding and shouting), Jake held me to him the whole time. And some of that time, I even felt the tips of his fingers stroking my hip (yes! stroking my hip!) through my jeans.

It was a lovely feeling (*very* lovely) but it was another display that more than likely, if caught by his children, could be confusing.

When the Tritons emerged victorious, after the raucous applause ended, Jake commanded to our brood to, "Roll out."

We all moved.

Once on the graveled lane in front of the bleachers, Ethan leading the way followed by Amber and the Taylors, their heads together, looking like they were plotting, followed by Conner and Ellie with their arms around each other, heads also together, looking like they were doing something vastly different, Jake again claimed me. He did this like his son claimed his girlfriend except without our heads together.

No, when I slid my arm around his waist, I looked up and saw his head was held high and regardless of the drama that began our foray into high school athletic spectatorship, his expression seemed most content.

Perhaps his most handsome look.

Then again, that would be hard to judge as they all were.

I started to look to my feet in order to best negotiate the gravel in my high-heeled boots but my eyes caught on Ellie's thumb hooked in the belt loop of Conner's jeans.

When it did, I had another overwhelming urge—an urge so overwhelming, it was a yearning to do the same to Jake.

More accurately, to be to Jake the person in his life who could stake that kind of claim of his jeans (an inappropriately heated thought).

But more, his person.

I sighed as I realized my pretending needed to be well and truly done for even if Jake was holding me close, I knew it was simply Jake doing with me what he would do with his daughter if she would allow him to do so in front of her peers.

On this thought, I spied Noah standing with his companions to the side of the end of the bleachers. In spying him, I saw he was studying Amber and doing it closely.

His friends were as well, and if I was not mistaken, a couple of them were doing it not with speculation or indignation but admiration.

I looked to Amber and saw her resolutely avoiding eye contact with Noah and I knew, as a woman but also someone who was once a teenaged girl, she knew he was there.

Her slight of Noah didn't go unnoticed. I saw his jaw get hard and then I saw his gaze turn to me.

I held his eyes momentarily before I looked away, fought back my grin but didn't fight back my murmur of, "That's my girl."

I knew Jake heard this when his arm around me got tighter. I also knew Jake saw it when Amber looked over her shoulder and leaned to the side to catch my eyes.

I winked at her. She grinned at me. My entire frame warmed delightfully and it warmed even more when Jake pulled me so tight to his side, I had to twist slightly into him to accommodate the embrace.

"You take care of my girl," he said softly.

I looked up at him. "Yes, Jake. But I believe I get more out of it than she does."

His gentle gaze held mine captive when he replied, "Then you believe wrong, Slick."

I pressed my lips together and looked away for the warmth I was feeling was so acute, so lovely, even precious, I needed to concentrate on walking so I didn't get overcome by the feeling and fall flat on my face.

It was within five more feet of our advance when it happened.

And what happened was that a remarkably attractive, tall, buxom red-head approached our parade, crying out, "My babies!"

"Fuck," Jake muttered.

I quickly glanced up at him as he stopped us.

He no longer looked content.

And I saw when I looked in the direction his eyes were aimed that he stopped us because the advance of our party was halted by the woman bearing down on Amber to give her a tight hug that Amber markedly didn't return.

The woman didn't seem to notice as she let Amber go and moved promptly to wrest Conner away from Ellie and do the same.

Unlike his sister, Conner hugged the woman, though it appeared to me that he did this more out of consideration than fondness, and I knew in that instant the woman was Donna, Conner and Amber's mother.

It was then my study of her heightened and I noted she looked very like her daughter except for the fact she was far more curvaceous. And this last wasn't lost on me in any way that Donna, Jake's ex-wife, had big hair and big...*other stuff*.

Precisely the reason that Donna was Jake's ex-wife and I would never be Jake's anything.

She turned to Amber, pouting disingenuously, "You never call."

Before Amber could reply, her eyes went to her son.

"And if I didn't see you at Wayfarer's, I'd never see you."

"Mom—" Conner started but it was then, two things happened.

One, I noticed a man hovering a bit away, watching these proceedings.

He was very good-looking. He was also quite young. I would place Donna at around my age, no younger, perhaps older. The man hovering in a way that made me think he belonged to her couldn't be older than thirty, but he could be younger.

And even good-looking, at a glance I knew he wished to be just like Jake. He wanted to have that big man commanding presence, the self-confidence, the manner, but this would always be nothing but a desire. To have what Jake had you had to be born the man he became. You couldn't want it. You simply were going to *be* it until you *were* it.

The other thing that happened was that Donna's eyes came to Jake and I, took us in quickly with back and forth flicks of her gaze (most specifically our arms around each other), and finally settled on Jake.

"Jake," she greeted.

"Donna," he returned.

Her gaze came to me just as I noticed out of the corner of my eye that Ethan was sidling close to Jake.

"This is Josie," Jake introduced me, unnecessarily indicating I was the Josie he was speaking of by giving me a slight shake.

"Yeah, Lydia Malone's granddaughter," Donna stated, her gaze moving the length of me.

"Yes," I confirmed. "And you're Conner and Amber's mother. Lovely to meet you."

The last was a lie.

It was this because she had once had Jake in the way I wanted him and I had to admit I was envious. I wasn't proud of that emotion but I couldn't deny I had it.

It was also a lie because she threw Jake away and I read between the lines of what he told me about their end that this had hurt him and I very much didn't like that.

It was also a lie because neither of her children had mentioned her once and it was clear at the very least that Amber needed her mother and her mother was not available to her.

It was further a lie because neither Conner nor Amber seemed comfortable in her presence and this spoke volumes.

And last, it was a lie because she had procured a trophy boyfriend who she treated precisely thus. This was likely one of the reasons her children were uncomfortable.

Her having her young man mattered not to me. I had the philosophy to each their own.

However, I didn't have children but if I did, I would care very much what they thought about the people I spent my time with and if those people were important, I would do what I could to communicate that to my children and make them feel at ease in their presence.

This man didn't say hello. He barely even approached. And she didn't introduce him to anyone.

He was on display.

He didn't matter.

And although Donna was very attractive, I didn't understand why he would allow her to treat him this way.

She nodded to me and murmured, "Yeah. You too." Her eyes went to Jake. "Heard you two were an item."

I braced in order to withstand the blow of Jake correcting her and was more than mildly surprised when he didn't and remained silent.

She looked back to her kids. "Any chance I'll see you this weekend?"

"Busy, Mom," Conner said softly.

She accepted this without comment or apparent rancor and looked to Amber, raising her brows in affectionate inquiry.

"Seriously?" Amber asked with some sarcasm and also incredulity.

The Taylors closed in on Amber and I again stiffened at what I read in this action.

"Well, yeah," Donna, not seeming to read her daughter's tone or demeanor, replied. "We can do a girls night in tomorrow." She grinned. "A slumber party."

Amber's eyes narrowed angrily before she repeated, "Seriously?"

Donna's face melted to confusion and she also repeated, "Well, yeah."

"I haven't seen you in over a month," Amber informed her.

That was a long time.

I felt my own eyes narrowing.

"Well—" Donna started.

Amber threw her hand out and declared, "We lost Lydie."

"Honey—" Jake began quietly, his arm around me loosening and I was certain this was because he intended to go to his girl.

Donna's expression softened and she said gently, "I know, baby girl. I phoned."

"You phoned," Amber spat out. "Once."

"I—" Donna started again.

But Amber kept spitting. "Save it. We lost Lydie but we got Josie. When we had Lydie, we didn't need you. Now we have Josie and we *still* don't need you."

Donna looked stricken.

"Amber—" Conner said quietly, warningly but also soothingly.

But it was then Jake moved.

As for me, my mind was at war. I found I absolutely adored what she said at the same time I detested it.

"No!" Amber cried as I felt Ethan get close to me after losing his father who was approaching Amber. Amber lifted up her hand to her dad at the same time I curled my fingers around Ethan's shoulder. "No," she repeated, dropping her hand when Jake stopped moving. "I'm good. I'm fine. Everything is just fine. It's always fine because it has to be."

She then proved it absolutely was not when her face crumbled and she belatedly attempted to hide this by turning and rushing away.

The Taylors rushed after her.

Ellie gave Conner a look, Conner gave Ellie a nod, and Ellie rushed after her too.

Jake turned to Donna then took four strides to the side, getting out of the lane of traffic of exiting spectators that we had, I hadn't noticed until just then, been forestalling due to our scene.

As he moved, he caught Donna's forearm and tugged her along with him.

I didn't know what to do outside of taking the drama out of the main thoroughfare so I shuffled with them, shuffling Ethan with me.

The silent man that belonged to Donna didn't make a peep as he moved two feet to the side. He also didn't even look askance at Jake's hand on Donna's arm.

And last, Conner moved with us, his eyes sharp on his mother and father.

With one look at Jake's face, I had the feeling that an emotional situation was about to worsen significantly.

"Not now," I heard Jake growl, "but when we don't have an audience, you and me gotta talk."

"Jake—" she started, looking up at him still appearing stricken but also bemused and I could not imagine how the latter could be.

She had to know that not seeing her daughter for a month was wrong.

"Shut it," he clipped and looked to Conner. "Take Josie and your brother and find Amber."

"I got things to say to her too," Conner replied.

Oh dear.

I put pressure on Ethan's shoulder in preparation to exit this scenario when Jake demanded, "Get your brother and Josie outta here."

Conner ignored his father and looked to his mother. "She needs you."

"Honey—" Donna again began but got nothing out.

Conner interrupted her. "You need to pull your finger outta your ass and soon, Mom, or you're gonna lose her forever."

On that, her mouth dropped open but Conner was done. He turned to me and Ethan but his eyes only sliced through me before he looked down at his brother.

"Come on, Eath," he said, holding out a hand.

Ethan ran to him.

Conner then looked to me. "Stay with Dad," he ordered rather bossily and then he took his brother's hand and they were away.

I looked to Jake.

Jake was scowling at Donna.

"I hope he does it for you," he said in a deadly quiet tone, his head jerking to the man who still had nothing to say. "I really hope he does. 'Cause what he gives you has got to be worth what you're losin' if you don't fuckin' clue in and soon."

She opened her mouth to say something but this time she didn't even get a word out before Jake prowled to me, claimed me with an arm around my shoulders again and guided me firmly to the now light traffic exiting the stadium.

I gave it some time for Jake's mood was encasing us in its heated grip and I felt I needed to give him that time to sort through his thoughts.

When his mood didn't dissipate (in the slightest), I ventured, "Are you all right?"

"She's a good woman," he strangely replied. "No joke, Josie. She's a good woman who loves her kids. I know this. So I don't get this kick she's on."

Cautiously (*very* cautiously), I reminded him, "You also didn't get the kick she was on that ended your marriage."

His arm gave me a squeeze. "Yeah. That's the God's honest truth. Fuck, but that woman needs to learn how to communicate. And Con's right. She also needs to get her finger out of her ass."

Although I knew very little, from what I'd seen it appeared he and Conner were right.

Therefore, I whispered, "Indeed."

"My girl's had a tough night," he murmured, his voice lower and deeper with feeling.

I looked up at him to see his eyes aimed at something so I looked that way and saw Amber at Jake's truck surrounded by her brothers and friends.

I was still whispering when I agreed, "She has."

Jake stopped us some distance away and looked down at me. "Was gonna drop Eath at home seein' as Amber and the Taylors were gonna hang there tonight after the game. Then I was gonna go hang with you at your place. But I need to be home for my girl."

I liked that he had intended to hang with me and I had many ideas of what we could do while hanging. Ideas of things we'd never do.

Even so, it would be lovely simply to share a drink and a quiet conversation in the light room again.

But he was right. He needed to be there for his girl.

I nodded.

Then I found myself blurting, "I still have cream puffs."

Jake's brows drew together. "Come again?"

"Well," I began to explain. "You have some experience with women so it's probably has not been lost on you that often when women face difficulties, food has a calming influence. Food and friends. The Taylors, Conner and his girl, Ethan, you...all of you can come to Lavender House because I have plenty of cream puffs and they're still delicious."

At that, Jake's face gentled, and he stated, "And that way, you can also see to my girl."

Yes.

And that way, I could also see to Amber.

I said nothing.

He started us moving again, murmuring, "Cream puffs it is, Slick."

Cream puffs it was.

And as it was, I felt better.

I just hoped cream puffs, friends and family would make Amber feel the same.

Twelve

COMING OUT OF MY SKIN

The next morning, I wandered through the kitchen in my robe and nightie, going straight to the coffeepot. I hit the button to turn it on and heard it immediately start gurgling. I then pulled down a mug, grabbed a packet of sweetener and went to the refrigerator to get the milk.

I set the milk on the counter by the waiting mug, turned my back to the counter and leaned against it, aiming my eyes out to the gray day and stormy sea.

All of this, I did smiling.

I did it smiling because the cream puffs last night had worked.

I found the Taylors had been to Lavender House with Amber (repeatedly) and were glad they had the chance to come back. I'd also found that Ellie had never been and she'd always wanted to see the house (and *loved* it—her words, her emphasis).

By the end of the evening, with all of us gathered close around Gran's kitchen table, we'd consumed cream puffs and hot cocoa and everyone, including Amber and Ellie, had ended up laughing, tickled by the absurd conversation led by Ethan, who seemed determined to entertain us. And he did.

I also studied the view smiling because when the night had finally come to an end and I'd walked them all to the door, Jake was the last to leave.

When he hit the door, he'd stopped and dipped his head to me, his smiling lips not brushing my cheek, his rising hand not going to my hair to give my ponytail a tug (as I didn't have a ponytail, I had my hair up in a chignon at the nape of my neck).

No, instead, his smiling lips had brushed *my* lips and his hand had risen to cup my jaw when he did so.

Of course, it was just an affectionate brush but it was so lovely, it left my lips tingling in a way that was more pleasant than any kiss I'd ever received. Even far more ardent ones (and it must be said, Dee-Amond was a fabulous kisser and that brush even beat Amond's kisses).

I'd liked it enough to allow myself one more moment to pretend. Just that one. And I gave myself that moment.

Just that one.

But it was a very, *very* good one.

When he'd lifted his head, he'd whispered, "Way you took care of my crew tonight, owe you another dinner at The Eaves."

I'd eat a picnic in Hades with him.

I didn't share that.

I'd replied, "That's not necessary, Jake."

"Oh yeah it is," he'd returned, giving me a gentle squeeze at my jaw before he released me, murmured, "Later, Slick," and he was gone.

I'd stood in the open doorway and waved as all the cars drove away.

And I'd gone to bed with hot cocoa and cream puff in my belly, the whisper of Jake's lips on mine, and I'd slept like a baby.

Now, I had to figure out my day.

The plants in the greenhouse needed tending. I needed to research hiring an accountant, as there were likely inheritance taxes to see to. I also needed to get to a grocery store that was not Wayfarer's as Ethan's appetite was such he'd eat me out of house and home and he didn't really care if his sustenance was gourmet or not.

But before all that, I needed to call Lavon Burkett's people and procure backstage passes.

And that night, I needed to go watch Jake fight so I needed to find out where the arena was in order to journey there.

On this thought, my phone in my purse on the butcher block rang. I moved to it, dug my phone out of my bag and saw the display heralding the fact that Henry was calling.

I took the call, put the phone to my ear and greeted, "Hello, Henry."

"Hey, sweetheart," he replied softly. "How're you doing?"

"Splendid," I told him, moving back to the coffee, preparing a cup and resuming my position, back to the counter, eyes to the window, sipping and sharing the events of the day before (*sans* kiss on the lips from Jake and the way I'd pretended all day).

When I was done, there was a moment of silence before Henry noted, "Seems you're getting close to this Jake and his kids."

"They're all lovely," I told him as my affirmative.

There was another moment of silence before, cautiously, he asked, "You sure that's a good idea, honey? Kids can become dependent on someone, especially someone like you and especially if they get someone like you and their mother is absent. When that happens, they don't need another woman eventually absenting herself, especially a good woman. "

At Henry's words, it occurred to me that I hadn't yet explained the fact that I wanted to slow down and work as often as I could from the light room and thus Jake's children would have me around more often than not.

But Henry would have me around far less often than usual.

This was not something in my currently content state of mind that I wished to deal with.

So I decided not to.

"Well, it isn't like communication in a variety of ways is difficult in this day and age, Henry," I pointed out somewhat misleadingly at the same time leadingly, as in, leading *him* to understand I could do much for him even if not with him (paving the way for when I decided to broach that subject, that was).

"True," he murmured.

I changed the subject. "And you? You're well?"

"You know me," he replied and I did. This meant he was working a great deal, socializing a great deal and I didn't ask but it was likely his latest lover had at some point joined him in Italy and thus he was doing other things a great deal.

"You journey to Paris soon," I noted.

"Yes," he confirmed.

"And Daniel's working out?" I asked.

"He's not you," Henry answered without really answering although what he said was quite true.

"Indeed," I agreed just as the house phone rang.

I studied it as I set down my coffee mug, walked to it and asked, "Can you hang on for a moment? Gran's phone is ringing."

"Of course, sweetheart," he answered.

"It'll probably just be a second," I assured him. "I'll be back."

"I'll be here," he said with a strange mixture of gentleness, depth and rigidity that I'd never heard before.

However, my mind was not on Henry but on the ringing phone so I gave it no thought, took my mobile from my ear and grabbed the phone from its cradle on the wall. "Lavender House."

"Josephine?"

It was Arnold Weaver.

I felt my heart seize for a call from Mr. Weaver could mean anything, and part of that anything could be very bad, and I forced out, "Mr. Weaver. How are you?"

"Arnie, Josephine, I keep telling you, please call me Arnie."

"Of course," I murmured.

"Listen, I've called the kids and they're all coming this weekend so Eliza will have quite a bit of company."

I did not take this as good news.

I also understood what he was saying.

"All right," I said softly. "I'll let you and Eliza enjoy your children being home."

"Thank you, Josephine. I'll give you a call should..." He paused and it was a long one before he carried on. "I'll call you later. It's likely I won't be going into the office for some time so I can free up your mornings."

I understood that too.

"Of course. I'll await your call. Please give Eliza my love."

"I'll do that. Enjoy your weekend, Josephine," he told me and I could hear in his voice that even though his children were arriving, he would not be doing the same.

Still, I wished him, "You do the same, Arnie."

"Take care, Josephine and"—another weighty pause—"thank you. Eliza looks forward to your visits. It's just with the kids and grandkids…" he trailed off.

I rushed to assure him, "I understand. I'll see you soon."

"See you soon. 'Bye, Josephine."

"Take care, Arnie."

He disconnected and I put the phone back in its cradle thinking I needed to talk to Jake.

Immediately.

I needed this because I knew Eliza was slipping away and doing it rapidly. I knew that Arnie had called his children to attend her because time was short and thus precious. I knew he was preparing. And I knew that I needed to prepare, and as mad as it sounded, I understood in a way that was absolute that the best way to do that was to hear Jake's voice.

Alas, I could not beleaguer him with this information. I knew very little of what a boxer had to do to prepare for a fight but I didn't think it would be good for him to have the knowledge a dying woman was closing in on her passing on his mind, even if he didn't know her.

I heard Henry calling from my mobile and my head gave a slight jerk.

I'd completely forgotten he was on the line.

I put the phone to my ear. "Henry."

"Is everything okay?" he asked.

I didn't want to tell him about Eliza. I didn't want his reassurances, his compassion, his thoughtfulness, his concern, all of which I knew he'd give to me.

I wanted Jake's.

"Uh…yes," I lied. "Just a friend of Gran's calling." Luckily, that wasn't a lie. "Listen, I have to go. I'm still in my nightie and I have some errands to run today."

"All right, honey," he replied then asked somewhat strangely, "You're going to be at Lavender House all weekend?"

"Of course, Henry. Where else would I be?" I responded.

That was, I'd be there (mostly) when I wasn't at the arena watching Jake (and Mickey) fighting.

I didn't share that, however.

"Just checking," he murmured then, louder, "I'll talk to you later."

"All right, Henry. Speak with you tomorrow."

"You will. 'Bye, honey."

"Good-bye, Henry."

Without listening to his disconnect, I accomplished my own and immediately scrolled down my phone and hit Jake's number.

It rang twice before he answered with, "Slick."

I took in a breath and greeted, "Hello, Jake."

"How's your mornin'?" he asked.

"Delightful," I lied. "How are Amber and Conner?"

"Con's not up yet," he told me. "He dropped off Ellie and then they talked probably until two in the morning on the phone. Amber seems fine and this might have to do with the fact that I okayed a sleepover tonight at Taylor's."

"Boy Taylor or girl Taylor?" I asked.

"Boy Taylor and the big deal about that is that he's got a better makeup collection for them to screw around with. Girl Taylor has a better closet of clothes but she's not Amber's size so that's not as fun."

"Ah," I murmured with a smile in my voice as one was on my lips.

"That why you called?" he asked.

"Um...no," I answered.

His voice dropped lower and sweeter when he queried, "Why'd you call, baby?"

"Well, I just wished to tell you to...I don't know. What do you say to someone prior to a fight? It's probably not telling them to break a leg."

I heard his chuckle before, "No. That's not what you say."

"Well, whatever you say, I wanted to say that."

"Kick his ass, mess him up, knock him out, floor him...those are the usuals," he educated me.

"Well, do all that," I encouraged.

I got another chuckle before he said, "Good luck also works."

"Then good luck too," I stated.

"Can't not have good luck, you sittin' ringside watchin' me fight."

I blinked at the phone on the wall as warmth swept through me at his words.

And as this warmth spread through me, I realized that as much as I loved how wonderful he was, I was beginning to wish he was a little *less* wonderful. Jake being so wonderful was making it hard not to pretend I was living in a world where I could experience just how wonderful I actually wanted him to be.

He seemed not to mind my non-response for he went on to inquire, "You headin' to the Weavers this morning?"

"Well, um…" Drat! Why was I finding it difficult to prevaricate? "Arnie called this morning and asked me not to come. His children are visiting this weekend and therefore Eliza already has a good deal of company and it's doubtful Arnie will want to go to the office," I found myself announcing.

This was met with silence.

Then I heard, "Fuck."

He understood the reason for the Weaver children's visit.

"I'm sorry, Jake," I said quietly. "I didn't wish to tell you. I didn't want to take your focus off your fight tonight with that kind of news. I know you don't know them but you worry about me and—"

He interrupted me. "No matter what, babe, it's on your mind, you need to let it go, you tell me. I don't give a fuck if I'm set to fight Holyfield, I wanna know."

Yes, it would be a lot easier if he was less wonderful.

"You doin' okay with this news?" Jake asked.

"No," I whispered, again honestly.

"You need company?" he went on.

I didn't need it. I'd be all right.

That didn't mean I didn't want it.

But Jake had a fight so I shouldn't ask for it.

"No, Jake. I have quite a bit to do today. Once I get started, it'll take my mind off things. Then I have your event tonight to look forward to. I'm fine."

"Sure?" he pressed.

"I'm sure," I told him.

He didn't respond for a moment then he said, "Okay, baby. You get unsure, you call. Right?"

Oh yes.

It would be *much* easier if he was less wonderful.

"Right, Jake," I agreed.

"Shit," he muttered suddenly then he told me, "Sounds like Con's up. I wanna have a word with him before he has to get to work. I gotta let you go."

"That's fine. I'll, well…see you tonight."

"You will, Slick. See you then."

"Yes, Jake. Good luck and, um…mess him up."

That got me another chuckle before, "My promise to you, I will, Josie. Later, honey."

"Later, Jake."

Unlike Henry, I waited to hear his disconnect before I put down my phone.

I went back to my mug, took a sip of coffee and resolutely turned my eyes to the plants and herbs in Gran's greenhouse.

I needed to get in there. And I needed to because they did need attention. But I also needed to so I could take my mind off Eliza Weaver, Arnie Weaver and the reason their children were visiting.

But mostly I needed to because I needed to get my mind off just how wonderful Jake Spear was and just how much I needed him to be a little less wonderful.

I WAS WORKING in the greenhouse when the house phone rang again.

As I'd suspected, I'd managed to procure backstage passes to the Bounce concert in Boston that was to occur two weeks hence. I did this by calling Bounce's manager and he hadn't even talked to the band before he said, "No probs, Josephine. We'll have the Malone party on the list and they'll be instructed to give you as many passes as you need."

I'd texted this information to Jake who'd texted back, "Gotcha, Slick."

I'd also texted this information to Amber, telling her to share it with the

Taylors so they could confirm with their parents. Her reply was oddly, "SQUEEEEE!!!"

I'd hit the greenhouse and started work but it was no surprise it was not easy to take my mind off Jake. Though I did manage to focus on the less difficult things, such as going to his fight that night and primary to that, what I'd wear.

I'd never been to a fight. I had no idea what attire was appropriate.

It was this that I was thinking when the phone started ringing.

I put down my clippers and headed to the phone, brushing small dead leaves of thyme from my fingers. I grabbed it and put it to my ear.

"Lavender House," I greeted.

"Josephine?"

"Yes?"

"It's Reverend Fletcher."

Slightly surprised, I settled a hip to the counter and said, "Hello, Reverend Fletcher. How are you today?"

"I'm well, Josephine, thank you for asking," he replied. "I don't want to take up much of your time but it's come to my attention you're looking after Eliza Weaver as well as collecting Ethan Spear from school."

It was not a surprise that he knew this. Magdalene was a small town but news traveled fast even when one was not in a small town.

What was a surprise was that he phoned and referred to it.

"Yes, Reverend, I am," I confirmed.

"Does this mean you're planning to stay in Magdalene for a while?" he went on to query.

"Indeed it does," I told him.

"That's lovely news. Ruth and I would enjoy seeing you at services and perhaps you'll join us for dinner one evening."

Services would not likely be on my agenda. Although I quite liked the Fletchers and obviously, being Gran's granddaughter, I believed in God and honored Him (mostly), services tended to occur early. I'd wake up early to work out with Jake but I wouldn't relish doing it to get dressed up to listen to a sermon.

Dinner would be nice, though.

"That would be lovely," I said.

"I'm also calling for another reason," he shared.

"And that would be?" I prompted when he said no more.

"I believe you know Pearl Milshorn?"

"Of course," I told him. "She's one of Gran's closest friends."

"Yes, well, you also probably know her son is in Portland, her daughter in Bar Harbor and her grandkids are scattered everywhere. She has folks who come in a few times a week to help her with groceries and cleaning and Ruth or one of my parishioners picks her up for church on Sunday mornings but she doesn't get many visitors. And she walks with that frame so can't get around easily. I know Lydia visited her once a week if she could, or Pearl came to Lavender House. I'm worried with your grandmother gone she's getting quite lonely and—"

I interrupted him, feeling terrible I hadn't thought of this myself. Since I'd been in Magdalene, Pearl had phoned and she'd been one of the few who'd given me a hug at Gran's funeral. I hadn't thought of her again since but it was rare when I came to visit Gran that I didn't see Pearl, even in passing.

I should have thought of her.

Therefore, I interrupted him to say, "I'll pop by. Look in on her. See if she needs anything and if she's up for regular visitors."

I said this but I thought that Ethan seemed rather fond of senior citizens (and pretty much anybody). He might enjoy visiting Pearl and getting to know her and I knew she'd enjoy the same. In fact, being Gran's dearest friend, he might already know her.

"That would be wonderful, Josephine. Thank you," Reverend Fletcher said.

"It would be my pleasure. I've had many things on my mind, I should have popped by before," I told him.

"You're doing it now," he reminded me.

I was indeed.

"I'll see you at services tomorrow?" he went on to ask.

This would be doubtful.

Still, I said, "I'll do my best."

"Perhaps you can bring Spear and his children," he suggested.

It seemed he was not only intent on looking after the soul of Pearl Milshorn but perhaps saving one (or several).

"I'll discuss it with Jake," I replied, and since I didn't wish to lie to a pastor, I decided at least to mention it to Jake. If Jake said no, he'd say no but I wouldn't have committed a sin by lying straight to a man of God.

"Excellent," he said. "I'll get Ruth to call you about that dinner. Take care, Josephine."

"And you, Reverend."

We rang off and when I put the phone back in the cradle, my mind on finding Pearl's number and giving her a ring, it jumped straight to Dee-Amond.

And it jumped to Amond for Amond would have the answer to my earlier dilemma.

Therefore, I found Pearl's number and felt even guiltier at hearing her delight when I greeted her and arranged for a meeting on Tuesday afternoon.

After that, I put the phone in the cradle, moved to my mobile and called Amond.

"Beautiful," was his greeting.

"Hello, Amond. You're well?"

"Lagged, girl. Just got to Paris yesterday and that ride kicked my ass," he answered.

"Sorry," I murmured, feeling his pain. I'd been jet-lagged so many times it was impossible to count and it was never enjoyable.

"Why're you callin'?" he asked when I said no more.

"I wanted some advice," I told him.

There was a moment of silence then, strangely cautiously, he asked, "Advice on what?"

"Well, you see, I'm going to a boxing match tonight," I shared. This was met with utter silence so I carried on, "And I don't know what to wear. I've heard you mention that you've been to the fights and I thought you might be able to advise me on what attire would be appropriate."

More silence before, "You're going to a fight?"

"Not one, several. They've a league here and the bouts go all day. But I'm hoping to time it so I only have to attend two."

"You're going to a fight," he repeated, not in a question this time.

"Well, yes," I replied.

This brought more silence before, "And why you goin' to a fight, beautiful? That's not exactly your style."

"I've been asked by the fighters," I shared.

"Fighters…plural?" he asked.

"Yes."

"Both opponents?"

Oh dear.

Neither Jake nor Mickey told me who their opponents would be and they both fought in the heavyweight class.

I hoped they weren't fighting each other.

Obviously, I'd want Jake to win if this were true. Unfortunately, I wouldn't want Mickey to lose either. Mostly, I didn't want to watch them hitting each other.

Yes, I hoped they weren't fighting together.

"No," I gave him my hope rather than the true answer, as I didn't know the true answer. "Just two different fighters."

To that he murmured, sounding amused, "That's my Josephine girl, been there a coupla weeks, she's setting Maine on fire with her ice."

I felt my brows draw together. "Pardon?"

He didn't repeat himself or explain, he said curiously, "This is gonna be good."

"What's going to be good?" I asked.

"Nothin', beautiful. Just suddenly got an urge to haul my ass to Maine to see shit play out."

It was then I smiled, though I still didn't entirely understand him. However, the thought of him visiting was more than lovely.

"I would love that, Amond. You can stay at Lavender House with me, I've plenty of room. And I know you're fond of boxing and it appears the local community embraces it wholeheartedly. Even the youngsters do it. You could go to a bout with me."

I didn't actually wish to attend more fights (at all) but I liked spending time with Amond and I'd wish to do things he enjoyed so I would, if pressed.

"I'm thinkin' things are gonna be pretty crowded for you, girl," he informed me, again strangely. "But I'll think on that, let you know. I got a video to shoot before I can show my face in Maine, though."

How could I have forgotten that?

"Of course," I replied.

"As for what to wear, won't matter. You smoke everything you put on," he continued and did so very kindly. "But trick yourself out. A fighter asks a woman to come to his fight, he sees her ringside, she's lookin' ice-cold and shit-hot, it'll be ammunition for him to kick some serious ass seein' as he'll wanna impress her."

I didn't think this would motivate Jake but I had a feeling it would Mickey.

"Tricked out it is," I agreed.

I heard his low, attractive chuckle before he said, "Have fun, Josephine."

"I will, Amond," I assured him though I wasn't assured myself. Still, dressing up would be fun as it always was.

"You doin' okay otherwise?" he asked, his voice lower and sweeter.

"I have moments," I shared quietly. "But Gran has good friends and they're looking after me."

"Good to hear," he said. "I'll talk to Ginny. See if she can loosen things up for me to get to Maine. Let you know."

"Okay, Amond. I hope so and I hope to see you then."

"Me, too, girl. Later."

"Later, Amond."

We rang off and I went back to the greenhouse to finish with the plants, my mind inventorying my wardrobe.

I hit on the perfect outfit at the same time I thought I might need to call my friend Dakota in LA. Ask her to go to the pool house, pack a few boxes of shoes, clothes, accessories.

I was going to need them.

I put that on my mental agenda of things to do that day, picked up the clippers and got down to doing the things I needed to do that day.

Eventually, I accomplished it all.

Unfortunately, although I did this, I failed to accomplish not thinking too much about Jake.

I knew I'd someday beat that urge.

But that urge was so strong I also knew it would take time.

Lots of it.

And it didn't help I saw him so often.

With Henry, I saw him every day, sometimes all day every day and therefore that wasn't easy.

But somehow, I knew with Jake it would take longer.

And it would be far more difficult.

———◆••◆———

I WALKED INTO the arena finding that Amond was right about the attire. Nearly every woman there was tricked out (except for some who were rather slovenly who I figured were not there to catch the eye of a fighter but instead watch them fight).

Although it was an amateur league and all of the men were dressed in jeans and mostly t-shirts, there were quite a number of women who were very dolled up. Of course, their hair and makeup were brasher than mine, their clothes more baring and not as high quality. But seeing as my dress was couture, given to me by a designer who had wanted to sleep with me (I took the dress, I didn't take the invitation), I had an unfair advantage.

Although I was not alone in being tricked out, when I took off my coat in the outer area of the arena by the ticket counter, many eyes came my way, male and female. It would seem they were between fights so the area was packed with spectators getting refreshments and using the facilities, therefore my audience was somewhat vast.

I was surprised by the number of people there and slightly nervous. It would be difficult to perform in front of a huge audience and I worried for Jake.

Of course, if he had pay-per-view fights, his audiences in the past could have conceivably been millions but they weren't all in the same room with him.

Shirking off this thought as absurd, seeing as Jake was quite confident and probably rarely (if ever) suffered nerves, I gave out small smiles to a few people whose eyes I caught as I waited in line at the ticket counter and folded my coat over my arm.

I also smoothed the silk over my hip.

I was wearing a dress in a striking print of jewel colors, mostly sapphire and emerald with some ruby and pearl. The bodice was blousy but it exposed skin, indeed, the entirety of my arms, shoulders and shoulder blades were bare, with the neckline having cut-in shoulders and being mock-turtleneck. The waistline was a delicate row of gathers that went to my upper hip. The skirt was skintight and allowed movement due to a daring slit up the back.

I paired this with a pair of red stiletto-heeled sandals with a delicate slim crossover strap and peek-a-boo toe that even I thought were racy. In fact, the first time Henry saw me wearing them, his expression had changed to one he wore on occasion which I found gratifying (even if it was never in all our years acted upon)…sheer male admiration.

And now I saw the shoes had not gone unnoticed for some of the males were looking at my behind, but most at my shoes.

I finalized my look with a side ponytail that was a mass of teased out curls and a slim, stylish red handbag with a short strap.

And I waited in line patiently, not wishing to enter the arena too soon. But unfortunately, I made the front of the line in no time.

When I did, I opened my mouth but before I could get a word out, the man behind the window said, "Josephine Malone."

"Why, yes," I replied, surprised he knew me.

"Jake and Mickey both described you," he explained then went on in a highly flattering manner. "Though they didn't do you justice."

"Well, thank you," I said softly.

He gave me a crooked grin and looked to the side. He then slid out two envelopes and pushed them through the opening at the bottom of the window.

"Mick's ticket and Jake's," he shared. "Mick's up next so you better get a move on. But I'd use Jake's ticket. He set up the league yonks ago so his seats are freakin' fly."

I looked down to the envelopes, both being identical, and then turned my eyes back to the man. "And which is Jake's?"

"Turn 'em over, darlin'. Jake's says 'Slick,' Mick's says 'Josephine,'" he answered.

I turned them over and saw this was true

"Thank you," I again said to the man.

"My pleasure, darlin'," he replied.

I smiled and moved out of the way. I then opened the envelope from Jake and pulled out the ticket. It was a real one with a section, row and seat number printed on it, which I thought was quite impressive. And the good news was that I only had to traverse a short area of the outer corridor to find the stenciled notification above a doorway that would lead to my seat.

I walked down the aisle to see the arena was rather large and rather full. Yes, this community embraced boxing.

I couldn't be surprised at how good my seat was as the ticket said "row 1, seat 2." I figured that had to mean it was a very good seat.

I found this to be true when I made my way to row one and saw the two seats next to the aisle were empty. When I smiled at the lady (also tricked out as I was), who was in seat 3, she gave me a head to toe and smiled back in camaraderie, which I thought was rather pleasant. I sat down in my chair and realized why I was in seat two.

Seat 1 was too close to the corner of the ring and could be obstructed on occasion.

Seat 2 had a wide open view.

Oh dear.

The woman next to me leaned in and I looked to her to see she had her hand (with its black with white polka-dotted talons) extended my way.

I took it and she declared, "I'm Alyssa, Junior's woman."

"Hello, Alyssa," I greeted. "I'm Josephine."

She squeezed my hand and let it go, saying, "I know. Jake's woman."

I blinked.

She carried on before I could correct her, mistaken in my reaction. "Word gets around."

"Uh…" I mumbled but said no more before she continued.

"Junior's up next. Fightin' Mickey. Don't worry when Mickey messes him up. No one beats Mick but Jake. Then again, Jake fucks *everyone* up."

This was good news on two fronts, one being Mickey was not fighting Jake and two being that it was likely Jake would win which was something I'd much prefer watching.

It was bad news for Alyssa though as it would be unpleasant to watch your "man" messed up.

"I'm sorry," I said.

She grinned and shrugged, her long blonde locks brushing her shoulders. Seeing this, I bit back my advice that she use a roller brush and not hot rollers as her hair was quite lovely, but it was now arranged in a coiffure that made her head twice the size as it normally was, taking attention away from her very attractive face.

Then again, with the amount of cleavage she was displaying in her tight black dress, it was doubtful anyone but females would be looking at her hair.

"Junior doesn't care. Trust me. He's used to losin', bein' in a league with Jake and Mick," she shared.

"That's good," I remarked, her grin got bigger and she leaned in again.

"He gets to celebrate after, win or lose. You get me?"

I had a feeling I did so I nodded.

This made her grin become a bright, appealing smile and she leaned in even further. "Nothin' better," she said quietly, her eyes dancing. "A fighter after a fight, all that aggression, all that adrenaline still flowing. I *love* fight night."

Oh yes, I "got her."

"Indeed," I replied.

She moved in a way that she bumped my shoulder with hers in another show of camaraderie as I felt a change in the air.

She twisted and looked behind us.

"Here they come," she announced.

I looked behind us as well and saw she was correct. Down the aisle, wearing a green satin robe with white lapels, came Mickey. As he did, I noted that only men like him could carry off a robe like that.

And carry it off he did.

I had to admit to feeling a tingle when he made it close to the ring, caught me sitting there, his head tipped to the side in what appeared to be confusion before it cleared. He gave me a highly attractive smile then he entered the ring.

The back of his robe proclaimed him "The Irishman."

That wasn't as good of a nickname as "The Truck" but it wasn't terrible either.

He promptly took off his robe and I saw what I saw at the gym but more of it seeing as he was only wearing boxing shoes and a pair of green satin boxing trunks with a white waistband and little white shamrocks at the outer side hems.

I saw the man who had to be Junior in the other corner wearing white trunks with a red waistband and stripes down the side.

However, he didn't look like a Junior. He looked like a Bruiser. He was completely bald and seemed bigger and scarier than Mickey.

At once, I was alarmed.

I became more alarmed when Alyssa cupped her hands around her mouth and shouted, *"Fuck him up, baby!"*

This was tremendously vulgar, though I thought it was kind of sweet when Junior turned his eyes to Alyssa, lifted a gloved hand to his heart then to his lips then punched it out at her.

"Love you, tiger!" she shrieked in reply.

I couldn't help but grin since I felt this was all very cute.

The boxers danced around their corner talking to men outside the ring and I crossed my legs, tossed my coat in the empty seat beside me and tucked my bag in my lap.

"He's a southpaw." I heard Alyssa say as the man in black pants and a gray shirt—also incongruously wearing a ridiculous black bow tie—motioned the boxers to the center of the ring.

I turned to her and asked, "Pardon?"

"Mickey," she replied. "He's a southpaw. Left-handed. His power's on the wrong side for Junior. My man has trained all year with left-handed sparring partners to move up in the league which means beating Mickey seein' as Mickey's always number two, Jake's always number one and Junior's smart enough to know he's never gonna best Jake. But I'm not thinkin' good thoughts. Mick has *killed* everyone all season. He's in top-notch shape."

"If this is the case, isn't it difficult for you to watch your partner fighting?" I inquired, truly curious and she grinned again.

"This your first fight?" she asked.

I nodded.

"You'll get me, honey," she stated. "Trust me. You watch Jake out there, I swear, your panties'll be *drenched* within *seconds*. I'll be home bangin' my man's brains out by that time but if I wasn't, on my way back to Magdalene, if I saw

Jake's truck was on the side of the road with the windows steamed up, that would not be a surprise."

This was rather alarming (and crude) news. Therefore I couldn't stop myself from biting my lip.

She looked at my lip and burst out laughing before she leaned in and advised, "Get ready for the ride of your life, girlfriend."

Now, I was beginning to fret for a different reason.

Jake simply breathing I found alluring. Panties drenched for a man who didn't find you attractive was not something I looked forward to.

Luckily, my attention was turned to the ring when I heard a very loud and excited voice come over the audio system. Through this, I found out that Mickey's last name was Donovan (The Irishman, indeed). They didn't waste much time after talking up the fighters and the referee having a brief word with them. They went to their corners and nearly directly back to the center of the ring where they touched gloves top to bottom and again.

Then the bell rang and it began.

The good news was, watching Mickey (who Alyssa was correct, even not knowing a thing about boxing, it was not hard to miss he was quite a bit better at it than Junior), my panties didn't get drenched. It also wasn't nearly as horrifying as I thought it would be.

It was actually, I found, quite interesting, in a somewhat sweaty, grunting, gruesome way.

Nevertheless, I was glad it only went three rounds and, although I quite liked Alyssa, regardless that she was very loud and seemingly bloodthirsty (not to mention foul-mouthed) as she shouted encouragement to her lover, I was happy to see Mickey's hand lifted when the judgment came down. Though, in deference to the woman at my side, I only politely clapped when he won.

After spending some time accepting his accolades from the spectators, Mickey didn't delay in leaving the ring and he also caught my eyes doing it, grinning and winking.

That was lovely so I smiled back.

"What gives with that?" Alyssa asked as Mickey jogged back up the aisle.

"Mickey goes to Jake's gym," I answered without telling her the full story but it seemed she understood me (though obviously not fully) when she lifted her chin and said, "Ah."

She then grabbed her purse and dug out her phone, beeping buttons and saying, "I gotta dash…get my post-fight drilling from my man, so quick, give me your number. We'll do lunch. Or drinks. Or somethin'. You can even come in and I'll give you a freebie mani-pedi. I live in Magdalene and got a shop there." She stopped beeping buttons, looked to me and smiled impishly. "You can tell me how much fun Jake is after a fight."

"I, well…"

"Hurry," she urged.

I liked her very much regardless of her loudness and crudeness. Further, I was going to be in Magdalene for some time and didn't know anyone of my age who wasn't the wife of the pastor of the local church. Therefore, I quickly gave her my number. I was about to go on and share that she had the wrong idea about Jake and I before she shot out of her seat and looked down at me.

"Jake's up next. Have fun and don't leave a wet spot," she declared, still smiling madly before she bent in, touched her cheek to mine, did the same on the other side then she tottered swiftly away on platform sandals that looked a great deal like the ones Jake's dancers wore.

I watched her go then I turned my attention to the ring.

Jake was up next, the last fight of the night. Although from their haggard appearance, it seemed a number of the spectators had been there since the very beginning, the air was humming and electric. Like the headline act was about to take the stage at the end of a festival that had been going on for days.

It was not hard to read they liked Jake and this would be proven positive when a chant of "Truck" started low and quiet but gained in momentum until the crowd burst out in applause.

He was coming.

Unexpectedly, I found my stomach was in knots, my legs were shaking even though I was sitting down, my hands the same.

I clenched them together, leaned to the side and looked over my shoulder to peer down the aisle.

Not everyone but a goodly number of folks were standing, chanting, shouting, clapping and through this, I saw Jake.

Midnight blue robe, dark gray lapel, dark gray stripes down the inside seams. He was being followed by a man that was older than him and appeared to have had much the same frame as him, but perhaps fifteen years ago.

Mickey wore a boxing robe well.

Jake in one made Alyssa's prediction start to come true and I knew this because my legs and hands weren't the only things trembling.

Something was fluttering in a very private place. A very good private place.

Slowly, even on unsteady legs, I found myself rising to my feet even though I didn't tell my body to do it. The entire time my eyes were glued on Jake.

Nearly to the end of the aisle, his focus, which seemed to be on the floor in front of him, started shifting to me.

Yes, he wore that robe well and that pre-fight intensity on his face was breathtaking.

That flutter grew.

He caught my eyes and I began to smile.

But my smile froze on my face when his expression changed instantly upon locking on my gaze.

And it was then I felt it.

The heat. The pressure. The stifling, smoldering sensation of Jake Spear's fury.

His eyes were also heated and I'd never seen them like that. His anger, certainly. But this wasn't anger. This was extreme.

This was rage.

And I knew instinctively it was not directed at the opponent he would soon be facing.

For some reason, it was directed at me.

He tore his eyes from mine and I stood frozen for long moments, caught in the residual beam of his furious gaze. My body only woodenly moved in a pivot as he walked by me and I watched him enter the ring.

Throughout the pre-fight activities, he didn't look at me again. And I was so struck by the burning look of wrath he'd directed at me I only had it in me to sit and tuck my purse in my lap.

I vaguely noticed that his skintight workout shirts only hinted at the exceptional, defined, perfect male beauty of his body as he took off his robe to expose midnight blue trunks with dark gray stripes and waistband.

I became more aware of all this as he danced in his corner. Shook out his arms. Jerked up his shoulders. Tipped his head sharply side to side. Punched lightly into the air. His muscles flexing and bulging with each movement.

The vision of all that was him cutting through the haze of his earlier look, I became aware that the flutter was back and growing stronger than ever.

They did the introduction bit and Jake got a loud, boisterous round of applause (even I clapped heartily, though I didn't shout any encouragement).

Jake and his opponent went back to their corners, did some listening and nodding to the men outside the ring then they dance-jogged back to the center, listened to the gray shirted man, more nodding, gloves tapping…

And then it happened.

The bell rang and I watched Jake Spear do what Jake Spear was clearly born to do.

And in doing so, my world combusted.

Everything I was.

Everything I knew.

Everything I'd worked so long and so hard to make real.

I watched the primal beauty of Jake fighting and did it coming out of my skin. It split and shredded and fell away. It did it fast and suddenly it was gone and I was there, sitting, legs crossed, stylish handbag tucked in my lap, feeling raw, bare, vulnerable, electrified, old and new.

The area between my legs was pulsing.

My focus was riveted.

I was gone.

I wasn't me.

And I was.

For the first time in years, I was *me*.

And that time was watching the beauty of Jake beating the absolute *shit* out of the man in the ring with him.

He did this in five minutes.

Five.

I noticed it dazedly on the big clock with the red numbers that was beside the ring in front of the judges.

And he did it after hitting his already struggling challenger twice in the body then his powerfully muscled, sleek with wet right arm went out wide and he landed a blow to the man's head that would have normally made me swallow with sick. The man's head jerked brutally, sweat flew, his eyes closed and he hit the mat with a loud thud, not even lifting a hand to break his fall, his big body shuddering from top to toe on impact.

The crowd went wild.

I sat frozen in my chair staring at Jake dancing close to the body on the mat as the referee crouched beside him, counting to ten, his arm striking out to the side with each beat, his mouth moving with the numbers, his words swallowed up on the roar.

He finally stood, lifted Jake's arm and the crowd got even louder. So loud it was deafening.

Jake, however, did not bask in the glory.

He moved to his corner and left it with no ado whatsoever. He didn't put his robe on. He didn't gesture to the crowd.

He didn't look at me.

I slowly stood and turned as he prowled down the aisle and disappeared at the back of the arena.

Not thinking, not me, or not the me I'd made myself be, I bent and snatched up my coat.

I then moved.

Swiftly, I walked up the aisle. At the top, I looked right, then left and saw a burly man wearing a bright yellow polo shirt with the black word "security" printed boldly over his heart.

I moved quickly to him.

I was unable to get a word in when, his eyes going top to toe, he asked, "Who d'you belong to, gorgeous?"

His eyes came to mine and I stated, "Jake."

He grinned and stepped aside. When he did, I saw a door behind him. I pushed the bar and went through, hearing him continue to speak as I did.

"Left at the hall, first door to the right."

The door closed behind me as I practically ran down the hall, turned left and went immediately through the first door on the right.

I saw lockers. A trash bin. A table that looked like a medical table in the middle. A big, workout bag on it, gaping open, Jake's boxing gloves resting on top. The man that accompanied Jake to the ring.

And Jake, sitting on the table, the man before him, but his eyes cut immediately to me.

I opened my mouth but again was able to say nothing when Jake commanded, his one word like a whiplash, "Out."

Somehow, I knew he wasn't talking to me.

I was right. I vaguely noticed the man look to me and back to Jake before he dropped his head, grinned at his shoes and did as ordered.

Jake jumped off the table and moved with him instantly. With both of them coming in my direction, automatically I shifted out of their way, moving further into the room.

I turned back to Jake to see him lock the door.

I knew why I was there and I didn't. I was scared and I wasn't. I didn't feel right and I did. I didn't know what to do but I still knew what I had to do.

I wasn't me.

Yet I was.

I opened my mouth to speak, not knowing what I was going to say but knowing I was going to say it.

I again didn't get the chance.

"You goin' out with Mick tomorrow night?" Jake growled, his eyes burning into me, his fury saturating the room.

"Not anymore," I whispered immediately.

"Good fuckin' answer, Slick," he rapped out, each word hitting me like a blow at the same time they felt like a caress.

I stood unmoving, locked in place by his scowl, my heart beating hard, my breath coming funny, my sex drenched and pulsing.

Then he moved.

Right to me.

I didn't. Not a muscle.

So when he hit me, taped hands to my hips, I staggered back on a thin heel and dropped my purse and coat.

But Jake was not going to let me fall. I knew this when he kept going, I kept staggering back, and his fingers clenched into my skirt.

My back hit wall and my skirt hit my waist a half a second before Jake's body hit mine.

"Panties off, Josie," he ordered, his voice rough and commanding, and it was good I was against the wall for the quiver his words sent through my legs was so powerful, if I wasn't, I wouldn't have been able to remain standing.

I licked my lips, my sex throbbing so deeply I felt it shudder down my inner thighs and straight up to my throat as I carried out his command. I avoided his hands still clenched in my skirt to hook my thumbs into my panties and I tugged them down.

They slid over my shoes when Jake's hands came to my bottom and hefted me up.

I wrapped my legs around his hips, my arms around his shoulders and tipped my head back just as Jake's came down, his mouth slamming into mine.

I opened my lips, which was good because Jake's tongue was already thrusting in.

When I finally tasted him, that deep need I'd had for what seemed ages finally assuaged, his taste so beautiful, so *Jake*, I whimpered down his throat. My limbs clenching around him, he kissed me brutally and pressed his hips between my legs.

Feeling him hard, the satin of his trunks soft and me so sensitive, I lifted a hand and clutched it in his short hair as best I could and pressed into him as hard as I was able.

His hand left my behind and it was between us. I felt it move then it was back at my bottom, tipping my hips and suddenly he was in. *Deep* in. Slamming inside me, filling me repeatedly, violently, splendidly, *magnificently* as he grunted into my mouth and I held on tight for the ride, moaning into his.

Suddenly, I was pulled away from the wall and Jake stayed inside me as he moved us to the table and bent us over it. My back hit the table and Jake continued thrusting, *drilling*, taking me rough and hard in a locker room at an arena.

And I welcomed every stroke, gasping, whimpering, moaning, clutching with my arms and legs and fingers and sex, any way I could hold him to me, take him inside me, urge him to give me *more*.

He did. One hand going between us, his thumb moved hard over my aching, wet, sensitized clit and I cried out, at first in his mouth then I yanked my lips free, turned my head to the side and kept doing it while I came, fast, hard, long, the orgasm ripping through me and if I hadn't already shed my skin, that would have shredded me and I would have been born anew.

Jake's hand moved from between us and both of them slid up my inner thighs, the tape wrapping his hands coarse against my soft skin. He caught me behind the knees and yanked my legs high as he lifted his torso away and captured my gaze, his blazing, his eyes a remarkable midnight blue, his handsome face nearly savage with passion.

He was the most beautiful thing I'd ever seen *in my life*.

And he kept taking me, pounding between my legs and it was arguable but this might have felt better than the time before and even during orgasm. Being in the moment, not lost to it, feeling every stroke, every inch, the power of his body, his fingers clamped tight around the delicate skin behind my knees, his grunts filling the room.

Then it happened. He drove in one last time, the entire table moved several inches and his head snapped back, the corded column of his throat exposed to me, veins standing out in his neck, his groan of release was loud and so unbelievably gratifying, it felt like I'd moved not a mountain but an entire range.

The Rockies.

The Himalayas.

The Andes.

All three.

His head dropped, his neck bent deep so I had a view to the back of it and his fingers clutched the backs of my knees as his hips powered out and in for one last glorious thrust that felt *divine*.

Finally, he stayed embedded.

He didn't move.

I didn't either.

Moments passed.

Suddenly, the effect of the last twenty minutes started reversing. Something was coating my skin. Covering me. Smothering me.

"Jake," I whispered as he stayed in position, neck bent, apparently studying our connection.

The instant I said his name, his head shot back, his hands released my legs but they did this curling them around his back and he dropped his torso to mine.

"Don't," he whispered.

I opened my mouth but didn't say anything when his hand came up, cupped my cheek and his thumb pressed against my lips.

"Don't," he repeated. "Don't say anything, baby. Don't think anything. Don't *be* anything but with me. Not until I get you safe. Not until we can talk this out where I know you're good. Promise me that."

"I don't—" I started, my lips moving under his thumb, but I stopped when he pressed in with his entire body.

"Promise me that, honey." He was again whispering.

He held my eyes with his now beautiful blue ones and I let him do this for long moments.

Then I nodded.

I barely got that movement in before he pulled out. I felt my lips part at the unwelcome but still lovely sensation but I didn't get to process it.

Jake reached beyond me to his bag. He came back with a towel and his eyes held mine as he gently pressed it between my legs, cleaning him from me.

I knew my face got soft because that felt rather nice and I knew this because his face reciprocated the gesture.

I couldn't see me but I still would argue his look was better.

He tossed the towel somewhere I couldn't see. I felt his hands working at his shorts before his fingers were at my hips. He yanked me roughly off the table but he didn't let me teeter. One arm slid around me tight and held me to him as his fingers worked my skirt, yanking it back down. Then both hands were to my waist and I was up and my bottom was planted on the table.

Once he got me there, I watched him move quickly. His back to me, he went through the room, first picking up my purse and coat then moving to the wall to snatch up my panties.

I bit my lip when he did this and not in embarrassment. It was highly titillating watching Jake in boxing trunks seize my panties from the floor by the cinderblock wall where he'd first taken me.

It was not romantic in any sense.

But having been the one who experienced it, I knew it was the most romantic thing that had ever happened to me. In fact, I knew if any other woman had had it, she'd feel the same.

Yet, I was uncertain.

There was something wrong.

Something that needed to be made right.

This thought made my lips move and they moved to call a quiet, trembling, "Jake."

He was on his way back to me and at his name, he did this swiftly. He dumped my purse and coat on the table beside me, wrapped a taped hand around my jaw and dipped his face close as he shoved my panties in his workout bag.

When my eyes went from his bag to his, he instantly started speaking.

"Stick with me," he urged.

My voice was still trembling when I agreed, "All right."

"All right, baby," he said gently before he dipped his head and touched his mouth to mine.

And this time, having had him, having given him me, that touch was even *sweeter.*

After that, he wasted no time. He turned to his bag, dug out a workout jacket in navy blue and shrugged it on. Hands still taped, he tugged out a matching pair of pants and yanked them on over his trunks.

He zipped up the jacket before he pulled me from the table and grabbed my coat. He held it up for me and I turned in a circle, gliding my arms into the sleeves as he settled it on my shoulders.

Once my coat was on, he grabbed the strap on his bag, dropped it on his shoulder and dug into a side pouch, pulling out his keys. He then snatched up my purse and handed it to me.

I took it.

He took my hand and dragged me to the door. He unlocked it and dragged me out.

Immediately, he hauled me close, his hand dropping mine to clasp me around my shoulders and pull me so tight to his side I had to turn slightly, pressing my front to him to accommodate the demands of his arm.

Not only for comfort but for connection, I was sliding my arm around his waist when it happened.

I knew they were there but I was so affected by what just happened, in a fog, I didn't really notice all the people milling about the hall until the clapping started, the hooting began and then someone close by shouted, "Fuck yeah! Class plowed by The Truck!"

We stopped so abruptly I swayed and I dazedly watched Jake's hand slice up, long finger pointed at something.

I looked to where he was pointing and I saw a man in an unbecoming tracksuit (Jake's was much better), his face paling as Jake clipped out supremely irately, "Shut your fuckin' mouth."

His mouth was partly open when Jake made this command but it clamped shut and his lips thinned, such was his intent to clamp it *very* shut.

Jake moved us again and it was when we were about to hit the door to the outside that it penetrated that the applause, hooting and that comment were not about congratulating Jake on winning his fight.

It was congratulating Jake on doing what it was clear many had heard us doing in the locker room.

Good God.

"Jake," I whispered yet again and it was trembling even more this time.

He pushed out the door and ordered quietly, "Josie, stick with me."

I said nothing but I stuck with him mostly because he was holding me so close and he was so determined to get us where we were going I had no choice.

We made it to his truck. He beeped the locks and had me in before I could blink.

With shaking hands, I buckled in as he tossed his bag in the back and pulled himself behind the wheel.

"My car is here," I told him something he had to know.

He looked to me even as he turned the key in the ignition. "We'll come get it tomorrow, honey."

Tomorrow?

I didn't ask. He was engaged in backing out of his parking spot and with that behemoth of a vehicle, I thought his attention should be focused on this endeavor.

I looked back out the windshield when we started moving forward.

It wasn't until we were on our way, headed back to Magdalene when I noticed he had his mobile in his hand. And I noticed this only when I heard Jake talking into it and I looked to him to see he had it to his ear.

"Con?" A pause then, "Yeah, son." Another pause then, "Yeah, I won. I'll tell you about it tomorrow. Listen, I'm not gonna be home tonight."

I drew in a sharp breath and saw Jake's eyes flash to me then back to the road and he kept speaking.

"Curfew's still solid, bud. You're on the honor system tonight. Don't disappoint me." He was silent a moment and then, "Okay, Con. See you tomorrow."

I heard him disconnect and the instant he did, I stated, "Jake, we need to talk."

"We'll talk when we get you home, Josie."

"I think we should talk now."

His mobile hit the console; he grabbed my hand and pulled it so it was resting on his hard thigh.

He then repeated, but did it changing one word and doing it in a tender voice, "We'll talk when we get you home, baby."

I said nothing.

He held my hand tighter.

I blanked my mind.

We'd talk when I was home.

Home.

In silence, he drove us to Lavender House.

Jake collected his bag and then he collected me, even though I had my belt off, the door open and was nearly out of his truck by the time he made it to my side. He still lifted me down right before I was about to jump.

He walked us to the house, opened the door with his key and then he walked us in.

As in *in*.

After locking the door behind us, he walked us straight to my bedroom.

It was then a strange, wondrous, frightening, confusing night got more of all of that.

But mostly the wondrous part.

This was because after he turned on the bedside light, he dropped his bag, took my purse and let it fall to the floor and slid my coat off my arms to join them. He then hooked me about the waist and walked backwards to my bed, taking me with him. He fell and landed on his back, I landed on him and he immediately rolled so he was on top.

Only when he had us arranged did he declare, "Now you're in a safe place, we'll talk."

I was in a safe place.

I was in the only safe place I had.

And Jake brought me here.

"We had sex," I told him something he could not have forgotten.

"Yeah, we did," he agreed, his eyes holding mine, his assessing, warm, but also guarded.

"In a locker room," I went on.

"Yeah," he again agreed.

All right, there wasn't much more to explore with that except, well… *everything* and I didn't have it in me to explore that everything just yet.

"You were angry with me before the fight," I stated, though it was a question.

"No, babe, I was pissed," he answered.

Oddly, I completely understood this distinction.

"Are you angry now?" I inquired.

He stared at me.

Then he inquired in return, "Do I look angry?"

"No," I answered.

"Fuckin' my woman who's wearin' the sexiest fuckin' dress that's ever been in that arena, doin' that for the first time in the arena's locker room, it bein' hot as fuck, all that shit tends to make a man get over bein' seriously fuckin' pissed and it does it fast."

I let most of that slide in order to get to the meat of the matter.

"What did I do?" I asked.

He blinked before he repeated, "What did you do?"

"Yes, Jake, what did I do?"

He stared at me a moment before he answered, "Slick, you're mine and you made a date with another guy."

"Yes, I'm yours, Jake, but not that way."

He kept staring at me then he looked around the room, most specifically at the bed we were on, before he looked back at me.

"You're not mine in that way?" he queried.

I saw his point.

Yet at the same time, I did not.

It was my turn to stare at him for a moment before the words came out of my mouth. And when they did, they came out soft, timid, hopeful and scared.

"Am I yours in that way?"

Understanding, sweet and beautiful, washed through his features. He dipped his face closer and lifted a hand to frame the side of mine.

"You are," he whispered.

I closed my eyes to fully feel his words moving through me then opened them and pointed out (still timid, still hopeful), "I thought you liked big hair and big...other stuff."

His head cocked slightly to the side. "What?"

"You said—"

He interrupted me.

"I know what I said, honey. I also know you didn't like hearin' it and I further know since you called me after you walked in Lydie's bedroom, the way you *were* mine stopped bein' the way and the way you *are* mine started."

"I think I might have missed something," I admitted.

He grinned a small, sweet grin, his finger beginning to stroke me at my temple as he said, "I was goin' gentle, baby, but I also thought I was being obvious."

"You weren't," I shared and his brows went up.

"You hold hands with many guys?"

I didn't. Not with any.

"No."

"Sit tight close to them at a football game?"

"Um...no."

"Lounge on the couch with 'em, your head on their chest?"

I was again seeing his point.

"Oh," I whispered and his grin came back, bigger this time.

"Yeah," he said quietly. "Oh."

This was all lovely, marvelous, the fact that Jake was telling me that when I had been pretending, it had been real.

I was still uncertain.

"But I don't have big hair or big—"

I stopped talking when his face got very close and his finger stopped stroking so all of them could press in.

"Baby, you got everything."

I stared into his eyes, not needing to close mine to fully feel the beauty of that washing through me, and whispered again my, "Oh."

He studied my face, spending particular time at my mouth and I began to hold my breath in hopeful anticipation before his eyes came back to mine.

"You burn hot like that all the time?" he asked softly.

I knew precisely what he was referring to.

"Never," I answered softly.

That got me another grin, this one lighting his eyes in a way I felt acutely and pleasantly in one particular part of my body.

His grin died and his lips commanded, "You gotta call Mick."

My eyes slid to the side as I replied, "It would appear I do."

"Babe," he called.

My eyes slid back.

"You gotta call Mick," he repeated.

"Okay, Jake," I agreed.

"First, we're takin' a shower," he announced.

Oh my.

He wasn't quite finished.

"No, first you're cuttin' this tape off my hands. I got you naked in a shower, I want more than my fingertips. Then, I'm eatin' you. Been hungry for you since our dinner at The Eaves. Got my shot, not waitin' any longer."

At that, a pulse beat through my entire body.

He still wasn't finished.

"Then we're crashin'. Tomorrow you can call Mick."

"Okay, Jake," I agreed again, this time breathily.

"You sleep in one of your nighties. I pick the blue one unless you got something better."

I said nothing.

However, the blue one was dirty.

But I had something better.

"No panties," he finished.

I squirmed under him.

His eyes dropped to my mouth.

I held my breath again.

His eyes came to mine.

"Time to shower."

I said nothing mostly because I didn't have a chance.

I was off the bed and following Jake out the door because his hand was clamped around mine and he was dragging me there.

Though, dragging was perhaps an incorrect word since at that point I would have gladly followed him anywhere.

But especially the shower.

<hr />

JAKE CLOSED HIS mouth over my clit and sucked deep. I felt the pressure release just as his tongue lashed hard.

It was then I came.

Still coming, I felt him cover me and surge inside.

Dazedly, my orgasm still burning through me, I wrapped both legs around his thighs and my arms around his back. He planted a hand in the bed, arm bent so he stayed close, his mouth working my neck, his cock thrusting deep.

I took him for a long time, glorying in the feel, the smell of his clean skin, the power in his movements, the bigness of his body, the noises he made that rumbled into my flesh.

Suddenly, I felt his teeth sink gently into the skin around my jaw, scrape softly down to my chin, the sensation odd yet captivating even as it was titillating and intimate.

I loved it.

Then he again buried his face in my neck, surged inside one last time and groaned into my skin.

I'd touched him throughout, my hands coasting across his hard muscles and sleek skin. But when he climaxed inside me, I wrapped him tight and held him close.

I gave him time, waited for his body to relax into mine, listened to his breathing even and only then did I turn my head and say to him words the likes of which I hadn't said to any man for twenty-three years.

"I like you very much, Jake Spear."

He lifted his head and looked down at me and I saw I was wrong earlier.

His face sated and relaxed, his eyes warm, his cock still inside me, that was the most beautiful thing I'd seen in my life.

He didn't return my sentiment.

He did something better.

He dropped his lips to mine and kissed me, deep, sweet and long.

I held him close and kissed him back.

He broke the kiss in a gentle way, brushing his lips against mine before he murmured, "Gotta see to business. Be back."

I nodded.

He gently pulled out, sliding his nose along my jaw as he did so in a way that made my belly drop and tingles slide over my skin and not just the skin at my jaw. Then he was out of bed. He tossed the covers over me and I watched him walk naked out of the room.

I curled to my side and kept my eyes glued to the door, my mind blank and languorous, my body just the latter and I kept staring at the door until he returned.

Then I stared at him.

He had an amazing body.

Unbelievable.

Exquisite.

That body joined mine in bed. He turned out the light then turned me into his arms.

"You good?" he asked into the top of my hair.

I stared at the shadowed wall of his chest.

"Josie?" he called when I didn't answer

"I'm afraid," I admitted softly.

His arms pulled me closer and I felt his lips on my hair when he answered, "Beat that back, honey. No reason to be scared. Not with me."

I kept staring at his chest as I continued with my admissions.

"There are things to know about me."

"And you got time to share them with me."

I took in a halting breath and put pressure on to pull away but Jake's arms went very tight, one hand sifting up into my still-wet-from-our-shower hair and he held my face pressed to his chest.

Not able to look at him, I didn't give up.

"They're difficult to take."

There was a heavy pause I didn't like very much before he remarked, "You get Lydie talked about you."

I closed my eyes.

I knew.

Now I *knew.*

He gave me a squeeze and his voice lowered, when, still talking in my hair, he said, "She talked about you."

Good God.

God.

Feeling the burning sensation in my chest, I decided I needed to let that go. For now.

Now, I'd move on to something else.

"Something happened to me tonight, Jake," I whispered.

"Tell me," he whispered back.

"I can't. I don't know what it was."

"When did it happen?"

"When you started to fight."

His arms convulsed before he asked, "What did it feel like?"

"Like I was coming out of my skin."

"Coming out of your skin?"

"Yes."

"In a good way or a bad way?"

"Good," I told him. "Very good," I went on.

He said nothing for long moments before he inquired, "Why'd you come to the locker room?"

"I…" I started, about to tell him it was to find out why he was mad at me but that wasn't it.

I just didn't know why I did it.

"Was in there maybe two minutes before you showed," he stated when I said no more.

"I…" I began again but stopped again.

One of his arms left me, his hand came to my chin and he tipped my head back.

His eyes caught mine in the moonlight. "Babe, I was pissed at you but lookin' back at it, not pissed and havin' seen that look now more than once, you walked into that room lookin' turned way the fuck on."

Oh dear.

"I was," I whispered.

"So you came in there to get yourself some."

Did I?

Oh God.

I did.

"I—" I started again but stopped this time because his body was shaking and in doing so, it was shaking me *and* the bed.

This was because he was laughing.

"Jake?" I called. "Are you laughing?"

"Oh yeah," he rumbled, his voice filled with humor and even though I heard him, he confirmed, "Fuck yeah."

"I'm uncertain what's amusing."

His arm went back around me and he used both to slide me up his chest so we were eye to eye.

He still had a smile in his voice when he asked, "You think that instead of you comin' outta your skin tonight, maybe it wasn't that and instead you dropped the disguise?"

"What disguise?"

There was no smile in his voice at all when he said gently, "The one you been wearin' for a long fuckin' time, baby."

Yes, Gran had talked about me.

I said nothing but I did something.

I slid down the bed and hid, doing this by pressing my face back into his chest.

"How 'bout we talk about that later," he suggested, still speaking gently.

I again said nothing but I indicated agreement by nodding.

He gathered me close in his arms again and stated, "Glad you get off on me fightin'."

I took in a deep breath and gratefully accepted his subject change. "I met a woman prior to your bout. Her name is Alyssa and she warned me that would happen."

"Alyssa. Surprised I didn't hear her moanin' through the walls before I came out for my fight. More times than I could count over the years, before the door closes on her ass, me and a bunch of boys have seen her drop to her knees and start to blow Junior just freein' his dick from his trunks enough for her to latch on."

It would seem that fighters and their partners were very blunt when discussing sex.

However, that wasn't what concerned me.

What concerned me was that I might have become the new Alyssa of the adult boxing league that night.

Therefore, I mumbled, "At least you locked the door."

There was a moment of silence before he called, "Babe."

I didn't reply. I quite enjoyed Jake fighting and although I would never have guessed it, I much wanted to see him do it again.

Alas, I couldn't. I couldn't show my face again.

It would be mortifying.

"Josie," he called again.

"I'm tired," I told him which wasn't completely a lie.

"Baby, look at me."

I took in another deep breath before I tipped my head back and looked at him.

He was already looking at me and he didn't delay in speaking when he caught my eyes.

"I get that was probably not your thing but outside of that assclown bein' an assclown and mouthin' off, I'll tell you how that felt for me. You're beautiful. You're classy. You're sweet. You dress fuckin' cool and unbelievably hot. I KO'd the third seed in our league in five minutes and I was prouder of walkin' out of that room with you, knowin' everyone knew you were mine and just how you were mine, what I could do to you and what you could give to me, than I was at watching him hit the mat."

"That's absurd and beautiful, both at the same time," I blurted.

I saw his white teeth in the shadows and knew he was smiling when he advised, "Grasp on to the beautiful part, Slick."

"I'll make an effort to do that, Jake."

I watched his face get closer then I felt his mouth on mine. He kissed me, it was again deep and sweet but it wasn't long before he broke contact with my mouth and lifted his lips to touch them to my forehead.

He then dropped to his back but took me with him, holding me close to his side.

I wrapped my arm around his flat stomach and rested my cheek against his chest.

"You get on with Alyssa?" he asked when we'd settled.

"She was lovely, albeit loud and foul-mouthed."

"She's the shit. Good woman. Good mom. Good to Junior."

"She asked me for my number," I shared and his arm around my back gave me a squeeze.

"I'll talk to Junior. Get hers. She doesn't call you, you call her. You got me, the kids, but women need women at their backs and she'd be a good one."

I didn't have very many women at mine, but the ones I had, I knew this was true.

"I'll call her if she doesn't call me."

That got me another squeeze before he murmured, "Good."

He fell silent.

I stared at the shadowed angles of his chest.

I did this for some time before I whispered, "Jake?"

"Baby, we're good," he whispered back, answering the question I hadn't yet asked. The question that had me most afraid. The question that might lead to what we'd done being a foolhardy act which would mean we'd lose all we'd built. And even in the short time we'd had, we'd built something beautiful I never wanted to lose.

I just wanted to build it higher, stronger and keep it forever.

"What's next?" I queried.

"Don't know, Josie. Just know whatever it is I want you to be a part of it and I hope like fuck you want the same."

I closed my eyes tight and pressed my cheek hard to his chest.

I wanted the same.

I very much wanted the same.

But I didn't expect Jake to want it.

Clearly, he did.

And I didn't know how to feel the feeling I was feeling. I'd been content for so long I forgot how to feel happy.

I turned my head and my lips moved against his skin when I noted, "You like me too."

His hand slid up my spine to curl around the back of my neck when he replied, "Oh yeah, honey. I like you too."

I swallowed the emotion that was clogging my throat and dipped my chin into my neck so I could press my forehead into his skin.

His hand tightened on my neck and he urged, "Go to sleep, Josie."

At his command, I opened my eyes, turned my head and settled in. "Okay, Jake."

He moved his other arm to wrap both around me and I settled deeper into him. With effort, I relaxed against him and it didn't take long before one of his arms slid away, the other one loosened, his hand resting lightly at my waist, and I knew he was asleep.

I wasn't asleep.

The last time I got what I wanted, what I *really, really* wanted was when Andy came to sit by me in lunch at high school.

And that didn't work out very well.

Somehow, it had happened again.

I'd been happy then.

I felt happy now.

Right alongside utterly terrified.

This thought seized me and I rolled away from Jake to turn my eyes to the window.

I couldn't see the sea from where I was in the bed, but I could see the inky sky and bright shaft of moonlight.

I was barely away from him but for seconds before Jake rolled into me and I felt his arm curl around my belly.

He did nothing more. He said nothing. His breath was even. His hold was again loose.

"Jake?" I whispered.

He didn't reply.

He'd rolled into me in his sleep.

I stared at the view and seeing that view, lying in that bed, Jake holding me in his sleep, it came to me that Gran gave this to me.

Gran gave it to me.

All of it.

She knew what she was doing from the very beginning.

So it was safe.

And it was mine.

On that thought, I felt the tension slide out of my shoulders and away from spine, my lips curved up, my body pressed back into the warm hardness of Jake's and my eyelids dropped.

Thus on that thought, I fell asleep for the first time in over two decades doing it carefree.

And doing it happy.

Thirteen

SHE'D LIKE IT A FUCKUVA LOT

Jake opened his eyes and saw white ceiling and white cornices.
But he felt Josie's hair all over his chest and shoulder, her cheek on his pec, her arm around his gut, the warmth of her soft body pressed to his side and the silk of her short nightie on his arm but his hand that was resting on her hip felt nothing but skin.

This was why he smiled.

His eyes caught on the pink of the walls and his mind brought up an image of that room which was almost all flowers, the armchair by the window, the cover on the bed, the toss pillows that were everywhere. The prints didn't match but it worked in a girlie way that was definitely not him, it wasn't even Josie, but it was Lydie. There were even faded pictures of flowers in frames on the walls.

With all that pink and all those flowers, it was a wonder his testosterone levels didn't take a nosedive the instant he entered the room.

Then again, he could get it up for Josie anytime, anyplace. He knew that because he had to fight against getting hard at a fucking high school football game with just her pressed to his side.

He could definitely do it in a room filled with flowers.

He'd proved that last night.

And now.

He wanted her. He was ready for her. His mind was no longer on flowers but on the red silk nightie she was wearing.

His favorite color was blue but that red nightie was the absolute shit. Josie in it, her long hair down and even wet, her in that nightie was the hottest thing he'd ever seen.

But he'd only had one condom in his wallet. He'd taken her without one in the locker room but until they had the conversation, that was all he was going to take.

Which sucked.

This meant he couldn't have her again and with the day ahead, he wouldn't be able to have her until that night.

So they had to have the conversation.

They just wouldn't be having it now.

Last night, they'd taken a giant leap forward, a fucking awesome one. Even with that, he wasn't going to start pushing her now.

To calm his shit down, he was trying not to think of her in that sexy as fuck dress she wore last night, sitting ringside for him, following him to the locker room, that look on her face, that heat in her pretty blue eyes, when she moved her head slightly on his chest.

He knew by the way it felt she wasn't moving in her sleep but instead moving in a way she was trying not to wake him so he knew she was awake.

Therefore he tightened his arm around her and rolled them so he was resting partly on her front, partly down her side. He hitched a knee to spread her legs and rested it almost at the heat of her as he lifted his head and looked down at her face.

Fuck.

So fucking pretty.

Jake slid his hand up her side, over her chest, up her neck and gently spread her hair out, arranging it on the pillow, his eyes watching, and when he got what he wanted, he caught her gaze and whispered, "Mornin', Slick."

Her lips tipped up and she whispered back, "Good morning, Jake."

At the sound of her voice, the feel of her under him, it hit him.

Christ, she was there. Under him. In a nightie. Her hair spread on the pillow. Her hands resting light on his lower back. He'd tasted her sweet pussy. He'd fucked it twice. He'd watched her come in the shower, giving it to her with his fingers. He'd swallowed her whimpers and moans. He'd felt her tighten around him every-fucking-where.

Ethan's mom, Sloane had been the best he'd ever had.

Until Josie.

He'd never, not once, not even knowing how good Sloane could give it to him, lost his control like he had in the locker room last night.

And she'd delivered, along for the ride, clutching tight, pressing close, giving in and taking it.

In her bed later wasn't better, but it was slower, sweeter and he liked the way she took him after he gave it to her.

Clutching tight.

Pressing close.

Holding on.

On this thought, he dipped his head and ran the side of his nose along hers. He felt her body soften further beneath him when he did and he knew in feeling it that he needed to get her ass out of bed, feed her, get her in clothes and get her to his house. If he didn't, they'd be having the conversation he didn't want to have yet.

She seemed good but he knew he had to slow shit down. Go gentle. Give her steady. This was a massive shift for her, seeing as she'd missed him going gently but taking them where they were now.

She wanted it, that was obvious. And they were there.

But that didn't mean he still didn't have to take it slow.

When he lifted his head, her hands started moving, gliding lightly up his sides then in over his chest, up his neck and at the feel of her touch he knew he seriously needed to get her out of that bed.

Then they slid up his neck and both cupped his jaw but one moved and she ran her thumb gently across the scar on his cheekbone.

"How did you get this?" she asked quietly.

"Bar fight," he answered also quietly.

She blinked. "Not a fight fight?"

He shook his head.

"You were in a bar fight?" she asked.

He didn't want to get into this with her, not now. Shit like this was for when she was eating an omelet with him or her ass was in his truck and he was taking her to dinner.

But he'd kept enough from her, the rest he had to give her honestly.

"Donna liked attention," he told her. "When we started, we'd go out, she had me but she still went for it. A guy gave it to her. I didn't like that. I made that clear. He was an asshole. Shit degenerated, both of us spent the night in the tank and I got that scar."

She didn't look surprised anymore.

She looked pissed.

It was cute.

And sweet.

"She sought male attention even in your company?" she asked, her melodic voice going hard.

"Yep," he answered.

Her eyes grew unfocused as she murmured, "I'm beginning to understand Donna."

"You get to that understanding, babe, you tell me. She's been confusing my ass for years."

Her head tipped on the pillow and her hands slid down to his neck, but her face changed and he didn't like the way it did it.

He understood why when she asked softly, "You still care?"

"Nope, not for me," he replied. "But two of my kids are her kids and if I get her, I might be able to help them do it. And Ethan isn't hers but she freaks him out. He knows he's missin' somethin', he just doesn't know what he's missin'. He'll clue in eventually that he doesn't have a mother and that he doesn't like the mother his brother and sister have. He's tight with them and to him, Donna is a wildcard. He might not get it in any real way but that doesn't mean he doesn't get that she has the power to hurt them and if she suddenly pushed gettin' the custody she's supposed to have, he'd lose them every other week. So in a way, I got three kids that are mired in her shit. And because of that, I care."

"This is why he sidled close to you and me at the game," she noted.

"That's why."

"I believe you and Conner are correct," she declared. "Donna needs to get her finger out of her ass."

At those words coming from Josie's lips, Jake's body started shaking with the laughter he was fighting against making vocal but he didn't win the fight against stopping his words from vibrating with it when he agreed, "Yep. Con and me are correct."

Her face went unfocused again, her eyes drifting over his shoulder and he had a feeling, since she was Lydie's granddaughter and had demonstrated repeatedly she had no problems wading into a variety of shit, she was thinking about how to force Donna to pull her finger out.

So he stated, "Baby, it's up to her to do it. It's up to me to cover my kids as she does it or if she doesn't."

She focused on him and murmured a noncommittal, "Indeed."

Jake stared at her and wondered how a Josie vs. Donna would go.

What he knew in his gut was that Josie would rather bleed herself dry than hurt Amber or Conner so he figured if she found her time to get up in Donna's face, it would be Donna's problem and not blow back on his kids.

Still, he said, "Let her work it out."

"Hmm," she replied.

His body started shaking again.

She felt it and her eyes narrowed on him. "What's amusing?"

"You're cute when you go momma bear."

Her face arrested but there was a light in her eyes he liked a fuckuva lot and a tone in her voice he liked even more when she asked breathily, "Momma bear?"

"Yeah, Slick. You layin' Noah out for Amber. Havin' Con's back with his situation. Keepin' Eath close when Donna's bein' her usual clueless. Momma bear."

She covered quickly but he saw her doing it.

Seeing it he knew it sucked for her in a way he felt deep in his gut, but it didn't suck for him or his kids, what she was trying to hide.

Way back in the day, she'd wanted kids and had given up that dream. Now, at her age, it wouldn't be impossible, but it would be difficult and possibly dangerous.

"Well," she huffed haughtily through her cover. "Someone has to do it."

She was way fucking right about that.

"Okay, Slick, lots of things I'd wanna lay on you talkin' about the morning after I've had you for the first time…twice, but Donna isn't one of them."

Her face cleared and softened again, as did her voice when she asked, "What do you want to talk about?"

"Talk, not so much," he stated. He watched her eyes flash, read that too, wished he could give it to her and went on, "Tell you I'm makin' you breakfast, puttin' your ass in my truck, gettin' your car, gettin' it home and then takin' you to my place so we can spend the day there with my kids watchin' football, definitely."

She didn't hide her disappointment when she mumbled, "Oh."

He dipped his face closer and shared, "Had only one condom in my wallet, honey."

"Oh," she repeated, still not hiding her disappointment.

"We'll have that discussion later," he told her.

"Okay," she whispered.

"Now, breakfast," he stated.

"Okay," she repeated.

"You got a spare toothbrush?" he asked.

"I don't know. Gran might have one somewhere. I'll look."

"Good. You got the coffee ready to switch on?"

"I was, well…*occupied* with other things last night when I got home."

He grinned at her and muttered, "Right." He dipped his head closer again, slid his nose from the curve of her nostril to the tip and, staying close, he said, "You find a toothbrush. I'll start coffee."

"All right, Jake. The coffee's in the fridge."

"Gotcha."

He made a move to leave her and was about to touch his mouth to her jaw before doing that when she called, "Jake?"

He lifted his head and caught her gaze. Then he tensed when he caught the look in her eyes.

Shyly, she asked, "This is real, right?"

Fuck him.

Last night, she told him she liked him.

He knew that before she said it.

Right then he knew she *really* fucking liked him.

"You think you're dreamin', baby?" he asked back.

"Yes," she whispered.

Fuck.

Him.

"It's real, Josie," he promised.

She nodded before she lifted her head and slid her lips from the corner of his mouth across his stubble and pressed them to his jaw, the entire trip he felt in his gut, his dick and burning through his chest.

Not that he had to be reminded but her doing this did the trick.

And yeah.

Fuck yeah.

He really fucking liked her too.

She dropped her head back to the pillow, her hair again everywhere, and said, "Toothbrush."

"Yeah," he muttered, bent and kissed her jaw then moved from the bed thinking that if she wasn't cool with taking him ungloved, he was buying a fucking case of condoms and stashing them everywhere so they'd never run out. Her house. Her Cayenne. His truck. His wallet. Her wallet. His workout bag. His office. The club. Her nightstand. His bedroom at home.

Every-fucking-where.

Dozens of those fuckers.

He yanked on his training pants and didn't look back when he exited the room. This was because he'd managed to control his erection and if he saw her in that nightie in her bed with her long blonde hair down, that effort would be wasted.

He was winding his way down the stairs when he stopped dead.

And he stopped dead because he heard someone at the front door and they weren't knocking or ringing the bell.

As far as he knew, Lydie had given keys to him, Conner, Amber and Ethan. The nursing company that came in and looked after her also had a key. And a couple of her younger friends who could still get around and came to visit her often had them.

None of those people, outside of maybe his kids, would open the door on a Sunday morning before ringing the bell.

And he'd locked it last night. His mind was on Josie but he'd never forget to lock the door to keep her safe and he knew he did.

Slowly, he moved around the landing and had his eyes glued to the door, his steps cautious as he watched a man entering.

That man was not one of his kids, anyone from the nursing company or any of Lydie's friends.

He had a big black leather bag in his hand like he was staying a while and he was looking into the foyer sneakily.

Jake again stopped on the stairs, crossed his arms on his chest and demanded, "You wanna tell me who the fuck you are?"

The man's head jerked around and up. Jake watched his face go slack in shock then his eyes moved over Jake from head to toe and his expression hardened with anger.

"Jake, I presume," he said, his voice tight.

Jesus.

Was this guy…?

"You know me, I still don't know you," Jake stated.

"Henry Gagnon," the man answered.

Yep. This guy was Josephine's shit for brains boss.

It was not good the guy was good-looking. It was also not good he was well-dressed. It was further not good that he was clearly fit.

But mostly it was not good that he was *there*.

"Josie's boss," Jake said.

"Yes," Gagnon replied, his voice still tight. "*Josie's* boss and also more."

"More?" Jake asked.

"Much more," Gagnon answered and that was when Jake's body got tight.

Did Lydie not know some of Josie's history with this guy?

He opened his mouth to say something when Gagnon's eyes went beyond him and Jake heard Josie cry happily, "Goodness! Henry!"

He twisted to look at her and saw she was still in her nightie, a black silk robe covering it, the robe not tied, and she was racing down the stairs, her face lit up, her eyes shining, her lips smiling.

She skirted him and the only thing that made him feel even minutely better at witnessing her excited reaction to seeing her boss was that she did this in a familiar and intimate way. This meaning she did it putting her hands to his back and stomach to steady herself as she moved by (because he sure didn't move a fucking inch to let her pass).

Then she flew the rest of the way down to Gagnon and he watched, his body so tight it felt his tendons would snap, as she lifted her hands to rest them on Gagnon's chest and got up on her toes, tipping her head back.

Even though it looked like she was moving in for a kiss, or inviting one, Gagnon instantly dropped his bag, put his hands to her waist and shoved her back a foot. He didn't delay in dropping his hands and moving away from her too, but he took three steps.

Jake descended the rest of the stairs as the air in the room changed and Josie asked with confusion, "What on—?"

But Gagnon cut her off. "This is a fucking joke."

Jake moved around her so he could see both of them. He positioned himself not close but not far and again crossed his arms on his chest as Josie asked, "What are you talking about?"

"This," Gagnon replied, throwing an arm out. "You," he went on, his arm going her way. "This guy." He tossed his arm Jake's way.

Jake said nothing as Josie followed the movements of his arm, her eyes not coming to Jake but to his chest when Gagnon gestured his way, something Jake didn't like all that much. Then her full attention shot right back to Gagnon.

"I don't understand," she said softly and she sounded like she really fucking didn't.

"Jesus, Josephine, how could you not understand?" Gagnon bit out. His eyes flicked to Jake then cut back to Josie. "You failed to mention in all your talk about *Jake* just how close you were getting with *Jake*." And after that, he jerked a hand up, indicating Josie in her nightie.

That also made him feel better and not minutely.

She'd talked about him to this guy.

A lot.

"All right, Henry, this is awkward to be certain," Josie replied, taking another step back from him like she didn't like to be that close to his anger at the same time thankfully closing her robe around her front and keeping her arms crossed there. "But I must note at this juncture that I didn't expect you to be here. We spoke only yesterday and you didn't inform me you were coming. This is a surprise."

"I have to admit, sweetheart, having a second to think on it, this *isn't* a surprise to me," Gagnon told her before he looked to Jake. "Don't get comfortable. I know she's good but she rarely goes back for seconds."

Jake felt his muscles expand, his gut twist and his neck get tight as he heard Josie gasp.

He knew she was good?

"Henry!" she snapped and he looked back to her.

"You can't think in twenty-three years, Josephine, that the men you've fucked haven't talked. Half of them thought I'd already had you. Then again, if that was the case, they wondered why I didn't keep you."

She'd taken another step back, her face pale, and Jake saw that even in profile her eyes were wide.

"Why are you speaking to me this way?"

Suddenly, Gagnon leaned toward her and it was then Jake took a step forward. But he only leaned in and Jake stayed alert but stopped.

"Because, Josephine, I'm fucking sick to death of this bullshit, watching you make your selections and waiting for you to be done with that shit so I can get my turn."

Another gasp came from Josie but Gagnon wasn't done.

"And now you're fucking a man who owns a fucking strip club?"

Her back shot straight and her hands dropped but she was stuck at something he said earlier, "Get your turn?"

"Josephine, for fuck's sake, I've been in love with you since you walked in to interview with me two fucking decades ago."

Josie went still. Jake went still. The air went still.

Fuck, decades. He'd had her decades.

Jake had her for just weeks, he'd *had* her only twice, and now this asshole was finally letting this shit hang out?

"You've been in love with me?" she whispered.

"Since the beginning," he returned.

"I…I…how can that be?"

"How couldn't it be?" he shot back. "You're everywhere with me. You're almost always at my side. I've taken more pictures of you than anyone else and the only photo I carry with me in a goddamned frame and set up in every fucking hotel room I enter is one of you and me."

"I'm your assistant," she reminded him.

"You know a lot of your colleagues. Any of their employers have a picture of them together in a silver frame that goes everywhere with them?"

She shook her head. "You…you had other women."

"You had other men," he clipped.

Her voice was rising when she fired back, "You've found lovers *right in front of me.*"

"And it's clear you didn't give a fuck, you don't give a fuck and you'll never give a fuck."

"That makes no sense," she told him.

But he didn't hear her, he kept on target.

"And now *I* don't give a fuck."

After Gagnon got that out, he moved to pick up his bag and went to the door.

Hand on the handle, he turned to Jake.

"Advice. Be careful. Her thing is give them enough to make them need it but leave them wanting. She gets off on that. Lays devastation in her wake and she doesn't feel it, just keeps sipping her tea and her Chambord and looking for the next fool to leave gagging for it."

Before Jake could say a word or Josie could do it, Gagnon was out the door, slamming the heavy wood behind him.

Jake didn't move. His eyes trained to Josie who had her head turned away from him to stare at the door, he stayed completely still. Tense and still.

He knew she'd been in love with her boss for years. Lydie told him. The same that Gagnon had been in love with her. Lydie told him that too. So Jake had no idea which way this would go.

Seeing as Gagnon was everything she wanted in a man and she'd wanted him for decades, if he was to guess, she'd pull open that door and go running after him, leaving Jake behind.

So that was why he stayed still. Tense and still. Waiting for her to gut him.

Therefore he was shocked as shit when she didn't throw open the door. He watched as her head slowly turned to him and her dazed eyes in her pained face moved over his body before they caught his.

Her voice was also pained and dazed when she asked, "Why are you all the way over there?"

He wasn't all the way over anywhere. He was four feet away.

But he got what she was saying, he fucking liked what she was saying, he felt his neck relax, his gut stopped twisting, and he dropped his arms to go to her.

She beat him to it. Turning and rushing him, she slammed into him full force, wrapping her arms around him and bursting into tears.

No.

Fuck no.

If he would have guessed, this was not the way he thought it would go.

But he wasn't Henry Gagnon. No way he was going to waste the opportunity of what she was giving him.

So he bent and picked her up in his arms. When he had her there she shoved her face in his neck, wrapped her arms tight around his shoulders and he felt her body shudder repeatedly with her sobs.

He carried her to the family room, sat on the couch, putting her in his lap. He twisted them and took them down so they were stretched out and he had her trapped against the back, his body mostly on hers.

He knew she didn't feel trapped. She wanted more. And he knew this because she burrowed into him and held on tight.

Jake stroked her hair as he whispered, "Shh, baby."

Her body bucked and she hiccupped, pressing deeper.

"Shh, Josie. Get a handle on it. Man who talks that way to you is not worth this."

She pulled her face out of his neck, trained her wet eyes on him and cried, "But he's my friend!"

He shook his head. "He's a shit for brains dick who didn't have the balls to work for what he wanted but does have the balls to be pissed at you for not giving it to him. He's not your friend. He's an asshole."

She didn't agree or disagree. She was in her own head and probably not listening to a thing he said. He knew this when she went on and did it loudly.

"It's ridiculous for him to say he loved me. He hit on women right in front of me." She paused before she said, nearly in a shout. "Successfully! At least *I* was discreet!"

He did not want to discuss her being discreet. He actually didn't want to be doing this at all.

But she was lying on her couch pressed to him and not running after that asshole.

And she needed him.

So he was going to do it.

Jake slid a hand to her jaw and dipped his face close. "You seriously didn't know he was into you?" he asked gently.

"Absolutely not," she snapped.

"Lydie did."

She stopped crying abruptly as well as nearly shouting and blinked. "She did?"

"Didn't want him for you."

Her eyes got wide. "She didn't?"

"No, baby. A man whose play for over twenty years was to try to make you jealous enough to make your own play?" He shook his head. "Fuck no. Lydie liked him as a person, as your boss, but she did not want him for you. She knew the guy who got in there with you had to give a shit enough to do the work because she knew you're worth the effort."

Her lips had parted, her eyes got big again and she stared.

Then, thank fuck, it dawned.

He saw it on her face and he knew it when she repeated quietly, "Give a shit enough to do the work."

"Yeah," he confirmed, wrapping both arms around her and sliding under her so she was mostly on top. "'Cause you're worth it," he finished.

She stared down at him for a long time before he felt her body relax, saw her eyes warm and her face get soft.

Then she declared, "I need a Kleenex."

He grinned up at her, giving her that move, allowing her to change the subject because he knew she needed it. Then he asked, "Where are they?"

She looked to the side, murmuring, "Coffee table."

He looked that way, spotting the box. Then he knifed up, taking her with him, arranging her on his lap. He leaned forward and reached out an arm. He pulled more than one out, leaned back and handed them to her.

Delicately, like she was wiping her face and blowing her nose in front of the Queen of England, she took care of business. When she was done, she looked around self-consciously, obviously not sure what to do with her used tissues, this reminding him that pretty much all the time she was totally fucking cute.

He took them from her and she bit her lip as she watched him throw them on the coffee table.

She stopped biting her lip when he lifted both hands to frame her face and her eyes came to his.

"You good?" he asked.

"That was unpleasant," she said by way of answer.

"It was, Slick. But you good?"

"I've no idea what my future will bring, primarily employment, and it will be quite devastating to lose Henry, which after that scene it seems I will. But regardless, he means something to me," she stated.

After that bullshit in the foyer, Jake didn't agree. Then again, maybe if given time, she'd see it for the bullshit it was and come around to his way of thinking.

"So you're saying you're not good," he guessed.

"No, Jake, I'm not good," she confirmed then took a deep breath before going on. "What I am is in dire need of coffee and I've found a toothbrush still in its packaging. I'm not looking forward to football but I am looking forward to seeing your home and spending the day with you and your children so I'll think about Henry tomorrow."

He smiled at her, sliding his hands from her head so he could wrap his arms around her. "Good plan."

"Since I'm down here, I'll make coffee," she offered.

"I'll accept that," he replied and tightened his arms around her, bringing her closer, his eyes dropping to her mouth. "After you kiss me."

He saw her lips part before he watched them coming his way. He felt her hands glide up his arms and around his neck as he dropped his head to give her better access.

She took it, her mouth opening under his and she gave him her tongue.

The second he got it, he sucked it deeper.

When he did, she pressed closer.

Feeling that, he took over.

To do that best, he dropped her back to the couch and covered her.

This meant coffee was further delayed seeing as he liked her mouth, he'd waited a while to have it and he was in the mood to take his fill.

Josie was in a similar mood.

So they made out on her couch in her house, the couch that used to be Lydie's in the house that Lydie had given her granddaughter.

It was a long time after they were done, when they'd had coffee, he'd made her eggs and toast and he was waiting not very patiently in the kitchen for Josie to get ready to take on the day, when he thought that Lydie would like that.

All of it.

And she'd like it a fuckuva lot.

Fourteen

I'D GIVE HIM THE WORLD

I stood in Jake's kitchen, my hips to the counter, Jake standing very close in front of me, his eyes holding mine, his hand wrapped around the side of my neck, my hand wrapped around my mobile which he'd slapped into my palm five seconds earlier and said one word, "Mick."

I did realize that I had to call Mickey, of course. I hadn't forgotten.

However, Jake behaved very patiently and his usual kind and wonderful after that horrible debacle with Henry (about which I *refused* to think for my first reaction might have been tears but after he said the crass things he'd said and the way he spoke to me, so far my second, third, fourth and fifth reactions were wanting to throw something—my sixth was wanting to throw something *at Henry*).

Jake had then been more of his usual kind and wonderful, acting like we had all day to embrace (in other words *snog*, and *very* pleasantly) on the couch and after, making me a delicious breakfast of poached eggs on toast.

Jake's patience clearly ran out after that and I knew this when I was swiping mascara on my eyelashes upstairs and I heard him bellow from downstairs, "How much longer, Slick?"

Yes.

Bellow.

Up the stairs!

It wasn't like he was a stranger to my bedroom. He'd been in there even before we were lovers.

At his bellow, I took my mascara wand and tube with me and walked all the way to the landing, which was half a flight down.

There, I saw him at the bottom of the stairs.

"You ready?" he asked the instant he saw me.

"If you'd like to ask me a question, Jake, you are more than welcome to come to my room and ask it rather than shouting it up the stairs."

His lips twitched and he stated, "I take it that means you're not ready, you're feelin' in the mood to be uppity and tell me off and do it wastin' time you could be using to finish getting ready."

"Yes, indeed, I'm *not* ready but what I'm attempting to do right now is educate you about the fact I do not like to be bellowed at," I informed him.

His lips twitched again before he replied, "Babe, got a voice, one I can turn up the volume on so there's no reason for me to haul my ass up the stairs when I can shout up them."

He seemed not to be listening to me, which I found mildly irritating.

Unfortunately, he was also rather handsome standing at the bottom of the stairs looking amused and I knew teasing me so that irritation was only mild.

He lowered his voice and his face got serious when he said, "Slick, gotta pick up Ethan at eleven and we gotta go to the arena to get your Cayenne before we do that. You need to get a move on."

That was also mildly irritating, the fact that he was justified in his impatience.

"I'll get a move on," I assured him, turning to do just that but stopping when he called, "Babe."

I looked down at him again.

"It will seriously not go unappreciated if you leave your hair down."

For years, I'd arranged my hair in chignons, twists or ponytails. And for years, I had not been the kind of woman who did anything that a man asked me to do (unless that man was Henry but he was my employer).

However, when I returned upstairs to finish preparing for the day, outside of finger combing a fabulous elixir through my locks, I left my hair down.

And I was glad I did when I got the look Jake gave me as I descended the stairs.

I was even more glad when I got the kiss Jake gave me when I reached the bottom.

We got my Cayenne, Jake followed me home and I left it there and climbed in his truck. We then picked up Ethan and as we rode to Jake's house Ethan informed us at length and in great detail about how "awesome" and "epic" and "unreal" *Combat Raptor* was.

While Ethan was rattling adorably on, I found that it was rather a surprise that the morning after Jake and my relationship changed so enormously, I was just as comfortable in his presence...and then some.

This was because gone was the yearning. Gone was the pretending.

This was not a dream.

It was real.

So, although I would have chosen not to have a surprise altercation with Henry in the foyer of Lavender House where he shared he'd been in love with me for twenty-three years yet did not one thing about it (it was at this juncture I decided I wanted to throw something at him), Jake was mine before it, during it and after it.

Thus, I could throw myself in his arms and cry into his neck and feel his hand stroking my hair and listen to his words attempting to soothe me.

And I did.

And I was delighted I could.

Because it felt beautiful to have someone close in a time of need who gave you precisely what you needed. Outside of Gran, I'd never had that.

Thinking on it, since the day after Gran's funeral when I met Jake, I had it.

And now I knew he was marvelous in bed. I knew he was generous there. I knew he cared that he gave me pleasure before taking his own. I knew every inch of his body was beautiful for I'd seen them all and touched most of them. And I knew I very much enjoyed sleeping beside him and (maybe more) waking up there.

But this was the only change.

The rest of it was Jake and me.

In preparing for the day, I took that time to go over Jake's behavior since practically the moment we met and I felt slightly foolish that I had not grasped that Jake and I had been dating thus there *was* a Jake and me.

But that didn't change the fact that there *was* indeed a Jake and me. He liked it. I liked it.

Even so, it was not lost on me that there were some anxieties curling under the surface of my happiness.

The last man I'd chosen, the last one I'd let in, the one and only relationship I had outside of my high school boyfriend…

It didn't bear thinking about.

But Jake was not him.

Nor was he my father.

Jake was gallant, protective, generous, selfless and tenderhearted.

And none of those were my father or…*him*.

So although I'd never attempted to have a relationship with a man, not for twenty-three years, and it was clear I was embarking on a relationship with Jake, and Jake was all things Jake (thus I didn't want to lose any of them), those anxieties were curling under the surface.

Even so, I knew I had only to discuss them with Jake and from what he'd already given me, I had the strong suspicion he'd help me set those anxieties away.

And that felt beautiful too.

We went to his home and I was delighted to discover it was rather an old one, but one in very good condition, standing tall (three stories) and proud. Through some dense trees it even had a view of the sea.

I also discovered during the tour Ethan gave me that Jake had a good eye for decorating, which was rather shocking but not unwelcome. Of course this eye came with a mind to comfort but the colors and pieces he chose were excellent (albeit manly—so manly I feared Amber felt cast adrift in that masculine sanctum), the furniture very high quality and the fixtures and fittings handsome.

He could use some toss pillows to add a splash of color and his wall décor seemed rather slapdash but these were minor issues.

During the tour, I decided I had three favorite rooms in the house.

The kitchen, which was obviously built as an extension, with its exposed beams in a beautiful blonde wood that jutted under skylights so prevalent they appeared to be the entire ceiling, stark red cabinets, stainless steel appliances and black granite countertops.

Jake's bedroom on the top floor, which had a masculine but extraordinary sleigh bed that was so enormous, at first glance it seemed to take up the entire room, and regardless of the fact that it was unmade, it was also extremely inviting. Not to mention its master bath which also had skylights, a very large shower with smooth stone flooring and three shower heads and an oval bath that had steps up so it was sunken and would be a giving-yourself-a-facial, pumicing-your-feet, soaking-your-cares-away woman's dream.

And, last, his office, next to his bedroom, which was what had the view to the sea. It also had a fabulous antique desk and a seating area by the window consisting of comfortable chair with a table and lamp which I took one look at, longed to find a book and curl up there to read and, should my mind wander, gaze at the sea.

On the way back downstairs, Ethan announced, "Dad totally did all this stuff. With Tom and Bert and Coert and sometimes Mickey."

I stared at the back of his head while we were descending.

"Pardon?"

He looked back at me grinning. "Place was a dump. *Totally.* Dad gutted it and fixed it up before we moved in. We got pictures. Wanna see?"

I absolutely did, so I nodded.

We got to the bottom of the stairs and Ethan ran off, presumably to get the photo albums.

This was when Jake claimed me, pulled me to the kitchen, pushed me into the counter, slapped my mobile into my hand and said, "Mick."

I glared at him.

Then I remarked, "Ethan said Mickey helped you renovate your home."

"Yep," Jake replied. "Now call him," Jake ordered.

I glared at him again before I announced, "I am quite capable of telephoning Mickey to cancel our date and doing it without you standing nary an inch away with your hand on my neck."

"I know that, Slick," he stated, his lips again quirking with amusement (although I found nothing humorous in our current scenario). "I also know

Mick's a good guy. He's a bud. Known him a long time and my guess would be he'll be cool with you because he's that good of a guy. But another thing I know is that he was in the hall last night when I finished my fight, had showered and was probably on his way to the empty seat beside yours. So I figure he either saw you go into my locker room or he's heard of it. So he feels like bein' a dick, and gotta say, can't blame him, then I'm here to tell him to go fuck himself because even if I can't blame him, that shit is not going to happen."

It was too mortifying to think that Mickey knew what had happened between Jake and me last night so I decided instead to focus on breaking this down.

"So you're standing very close with your hand on me, demanding I phone Mickey while in your presence in order to be readily available should Mickey be unpleasant."

"Hit the nail on the head," he confirmed.

"You *are* aware I'm a grown woman," I asked.

"Yep. I'm *very* aware of that," he answered on a roguish grin that, even during our mildly irritating conversation, I found highly attractive. "I'm also aware that officially as of last night against a wall in a locker room, you became *my* woman and no man is a dick to my woman."

As ludicrously protective and preposterously overbearing as I knew this was, I couldn't help but like it.

I also found it more than mildly irritating, not only him doing it but me liking it.

Thus, I continued to glare at Jake but Jake continued to stand very close to me with his hand on my neck, holding my eyes.

He lost our staring contest and I was learning I should not be surprised he lost it by demanding with a preposterously overbearing jerk of his head to my phone, "Babe. *Mick.*"

It was then I realized he was not going to move and I knew with no doubts I couldn't forcibly move him so I gave him one final glare, beginning to think Jake and I had more than a few things to talk about as I officially became "his woman."

Then I turned my eyes to my phone and called Mickey.

It rang three times before he answered strangely with, "She finally calls to give me the crash and burn."

"I…uh, Mickey?" I stammered after receiving his greeting.

"Let me guess, Jake's standing right in front of you."

I felt the strong desire to laugh bubble up inside of me at the same time I still felt very badly about what I needed to do, more so if he'd heard what happened between Jake and I last night, either firsthand or through another party.

"Indeed," I agreed, deciding to stare at Jake's throat, but finding it altogether too attractive so moving my eyes to his now t-shirted (he'd clearly changed from his training gear while Ethan gave me my tour) shoulder.

"That's where I'd be," Mickey muttered.

"I'm assuming you know why I'm calling," I said quietly.

"Babe, way you looked at Jake, way he looked at you, I knew I had nothin' but a sliver of a chance to slide in there. I told Jake last night we had a date, a cocky move and cocky's always stupid. He wasted no time and moved to stake his claim. I'da done the same."

I wasn't fond of the terminology "stake his claim" nor was I certain that's what actually happened (though it must be said, Jake rushed me in the locker room, pushing me into the wall; I just didn't stop him). But as Mickey was being very kind about an uncomfortable situation, I decided not to debate that with him.

"You're being very nice about this," I told Mickey as well as Jake's shoulder and I felt his hand squeeze my neck so I looked to his eyes.

He looked relieved and it occurred to me right then that they were friends and this could have been more than uncomfortable in a very bad way.

"Jake and I are tight. Way he looked at you and you him, it was actually me bein' the dick. He staked his claim, I'll stand down. Anyway, a man's smart, he doesn't ever burn bridges with a pretty woman. Shit can go down with you and Jake and I'll still be in position to slide in."

I was uncertain if he was being amusing or serious, although I figured it was a bit of both. Thus, I decided not to make any comment to that. Jake might read it and that relief in his face might disappear.

So I just mumbled, "Mm."

"So I'll see you at league dinners, Jake's barbeques and the gym."

Jake barbequed?

"Yeah?" Mickey prompted when I said nothing, my mind filled with Jake standing on the back deck I'd seen from the big windows in the family room, grilling steaks, and wondering if they tasted good.

"Yes," I replied and looked to Jake's chest. "I'll see you at league dinners and, well, the gym."

I felt Jake lean in and kiss the top of my head before he let me go and moved away.

I felt this as I heard Mickey say, "Right, Josephine. Later, babe."

"Later, Mickey." I lowered my voice. "And I'm sorry."

His voice was lower too, sweet, and there was a smile in it when he replied, "Don't be. I didn't get a catch but you got one. Don't read shit into his history. Jake's a good guy. The best. He's just had shit taste in women. Until now."

Very sweet.

And obviously a good friend.

"Thank you, Mickey."

"You bet, honey. Later."

"Later."

I disconnected to see Jake had his head in his very large, high quality fridge (Sub-Zero! Lavender House needed one of those) and he was now on his phone.

"Amber, babe, haven't heard a word from you in a while. Check in with your old man so he doesn't have to start calling hospitals. And just in case this is incentive, I'm makin' tacos, nuking some Ro-Tel dip and Josie's over here for the day. You haul your ass back here, bring the Taylors."

He disconnected, shoved the phone in his back pocket, came out of the refrigerator with a box and a package of ground beef and before the fridge closed on him, he tipped his head back and shouted at the ceiling, "Con! Kitchen! Don't give a shit who you're talkin' to, come say hi to Josie!"

"I could go to his room, knock and say hello to him," I noted. "Ethan showed me his closed door."

"We got company, my kids come and say hello," Jake replied and I couldn't argue that because not greeting visitors was rude. I didn't say anything, however, because I saw the rectangular yellow box he got out of the fridge had the large words "Velveeta" written across it.

I pressed my lips together.

Ethan came flying into the room, shouting, "Ro-Tel dip!"

"You're on dip duty, bud," Jake told him and without hesitation, Ethan dashed to the pantry, throwing open the door and disappearing inside.

"Can I do something?" I asked.

"Relax, tuck in when it's done and be amazed," Jake answered and I smiled at him, amused at his quip.

He smiled back.

When he did, I decided that that smile, his humor, being in his attractive kitchen that he'd renovated himself and being in it with an exuberant Ethan who came out of the pantry with a tin of something was worth tolerating ludicrously protective and preposterously overbearing.

Most definitely.

On this thought, Conner walked in.

"Hey, Josie," he greeted with a distracted smile at me and in much the same way (with obvious differences) as his father, with casual affection he came right up to me, touched my arm and dipped down to kiss my cheek.

He then turned to his dad.

"Yo, Dad."

Jake was dumping ground beef into a skillet at the stove (it was a Wolf, not an Aga—still, most assuredly not something to sneeze at) but he turned to Conner and replied, "Con."

Then his eyes narrowed on his son.

Conner moved to the pantry asking, "Do we need refried beans?"

"Yeah, and you can get 'em lettin' me in on why you got that look on your face," Jake replied.

Apparently undisturbed that I was in attendance, Conner readily shared, "Called Ellie twice today. Left two messages. She hasn't called back."

"Uh-oh," Ethan muttered, cutting what appeared to be a rather gooey brick of cheese that was much the color of the alarming tub filled with the substance in which he'd dipped his pretzel bites into at the mall.

Jake now had a wooden spoon in hand, but both hands on his hips and he was perhaps the only male in the universe who could look commanding and charismatic standing at a stove holding a wooden spoon.

He also had his eyes to his son.

"You end things with Kaylee last night?" he asked quietly.

"Yeah," Conner answered, his voice telling the tale that this was not an enjoyable event.

It was undoubted that Jake heard his son's tone and this was likely why he let it go and instead queried, "Ellie know she's the one?"

"Told her a week ago, Dad," Conner stated, using a can opener on a can of refried beans.

At this, Ethan muttered, "Righteous."

Jake ignored his youngest son and inquired of his eldest, "You think Mia's still givin' her shit?"

Conner gave his dad a look, a look that said Mia was indeed still giving poor Ellie shit.

Not good news.

"She goes to church Sunday mornings, Con," Jake reminded his boy.

"At nine. It's nearly noon. She's been home for almost two hours," Conner replied.

Jake had no response to that.

"Is Zoey gone?" Ethan entered the conversation.

"Just got off the phone with her," Conner murmured.

I bit my lip.

Jake looked at me.

I stopped biting my lip and stretched my lower one out to communicate my nonsensical "eek!" which, albeit nonsensical, I still felt said a great many things.

At seeing my gesture, Jake dropped his head and grinned at his stocking feet.

He understood the great many things I'd said.

"Josie?" Conner called and I quickly rearranged my face and looked to him. "You're a chick," he declared when I did.

I knew intuitively this wasn't starting very well.

"I am, indeed, Conner," I confirmed unnecessarily.

"What's her gig?" he asked.

Yes, this was not going in a comfortable direction.

All three Spear men turned their eyes to me.

"I'm afraid I don't know her well enough to answer that, sweetheart," I said gently.

"She always picks up when I call or calls back when she can after she gets my message," he told me.

And it kept trundling down that prickly path.

It was then a question that Jake had asked me over a week ago came back and I asked it of Conner.

"How real can you take it?"

"I dig her, a lot," Conner answered, unlike me, obviously understanding the question straight away. "She's sweet. She's really freaking pretty. She's cool. Eath likes her. Dad likes her. Even Amber likes her when Amber's not being a pain in the ass. And I like the way she looks at me and how I feel when I'm with her."

That was quite forthcoming.

And very sweet.

"In other words, you don't want to lose her," I deduced.

"In other words, yeah. I don't," Conner affirmed.

I moved to the island where both Jake's sons were and laid a hand on it, my eyes to Conner the whole time. When I got there, still going gently, I gave him real.

"At the game, you were lovely with her. Very attentive. Protective," I told him.

I liked the way his expression changed, showing satisfaction not only that I noted he was this way but that he gave those things to Ellie.

Unfortunately, I had more to say.

"However, it does not feel good to be one in many. Although she's made the cut, which I will share now with your best interests at heart, that is not the terminology to use when referring to whether or not you wish to carry on a relationship, she could still be smarting about that. But I believe it's likely Mia. She's afraid of her and girls can be quite unpleasant. She'll find her times to be this way to Ellie when you're not around. Ellie knows this. So I advise you give it a bit of time and if she doesn't call you back, you call her again. If she still doesn't answer, seek her out."

"I'll do that," Conner muttered. Then louder, he asked, "Should I lay shit out with Mia?"

"Have you not already done that?" I asked back.

"I told her to lay off and I'd be pissed if she didn't."

"And if you get pissed that she doesn't, what do you intend to do?"

Conner said nothing and I knew why.

He was too much of his father's son to hurt her in any real way so his getting pissed was no threat and Mia knew this.

"As that's the case, if she still intends to harm Ellie, since she's not frightened of your anger, she'll do something to harm Ellie."

Conner immediately looked concerned. "Shit, should I go over to her house now?"

"Give her the chance to call you back," Jake put in at this juncture. "A coupla hours. Then call her and, like Josie said, go over there if she doesn't answer."

Conner didn't look like he liked doing it but he nodded to his father.

My phone still in my hand rang.

I looked down at it and saw it said "Unknown Caller," but the area code on the number was local.

This concerned me, as it was a possibility Henry was staying somewhere close and could be using the hotel phone to call me, though I didn't know why he wouldn't use his mobile if he rang.

Even concerned it might be Henry, I took the call and put the phone to my ear.

"This is Josephine."

"Josie, girl, you…are…*legend!*" a female voice shrieked in my ear.

I narrowed my eyes at the black granite of Jake's island. "Pardon?"

"Babelicious, I heard about last night," the woman stated.

It came to me it was Alyssa right before she kept speaking.

"You rock. You roll. You got it good and from what I hear, gave it better. Girl, I wanna be you when I grow up, walkin' into the arena, pure class, your shit *so* doesn't stink, and then you give Jake the business *in the locker room* and walk out with head held high on your fancy-assed heels. You're so the fucking bomb, you'd level Hiroshima again if you visited."

"Um…" I mumbled but got nothing else out. Not that I knew what to say to her highly unusual compliments delivered with extreme enthusiasm.

"*Ohmigod!*" she shrieked. "I so hope Donna hears about this. That bitch is a stupid bitch. I mean, *hello!* Wake up and look at the near-to teen wolf you got in your bed. He may look a little like Jake Spear of twenty years ago but he is *not* Jake Spear of twenty years ago. You let Jake go, bitch, you're never gettin' him back no matter how many boy-men you bang."

This was extremely insightful.

Before I could share that or, perhaps, walk out of the room, as it was likely, with the direction the mostly one-sided conversation was moving, I should take this call privately, she kept going.

"And who wants a twenty-something? Is she high? Every woman knows they gotta get a man who's sowed his wild oats and, she's lucky, he'll have sowed his wild oats *with her*. She let that shit go and now she's grasping at it to get it back 'cause she knows no way Jake's gonna go there with her because Jake suffers no fool and that bitch, lettin' him go, is *all* kinds a fool."

She took in a breath so deep, I heard her inhaling it over the phone and I thought I'd get a word in edgewise but I wasn't fast enough.

"And don't *get* me started on the way she is with her kids. My head might explode."

This, too, I agreed with her on.

"Indeed," I got in.

"You bet your ass, indeed," she replied, sounding like she was doing it through laughter. "Now, babe, my shop isn't open on Mondays but I'm opening the joint and givin' you a mani-pedi tomorrow just because you're the shit and already so legend that if I tell all my girls that the class-act who's banging The Truck is a client, everyone will want to go there."

Oh dear.

"But trust me, these lips aren't loose," she continued, again before I could utter a noise. "Don't *even* think they are. Junior likes his BJs tight so I don't *ever* go there. Come in at three. It's called Maude's House of Beauty. It was my mom's before me. She's Maude. Obviously, I'm not. We'll go for a drink after I sort you out and that way I can be home in time to feed Junior and the hooligans I pushed out for him and you can get to Jake and rock his world."

"I'm afraid I can't," I told her and I was actually quite disappointed I couldn't. "I'll have Ethan."

"That's cool. We'll drop Eath with my Bryant. They're buds. My girl Sofie will look after them."

"I think I need to clear this with Jake and, well… Ethan," I said.

"You with the big man now?" she asked.

I kept my eyes resolutely to the island and answered, "Yes."

"Course you are," she hooted. "So ask. I'll wait."

I drew in a breath then said, "Please hold on."

"I'll be here," she replied.

I looked up to see Jake had eyes to me but a spoon to the browning hamburger meat.

"This is Alyssa. She says that her girl Sofie can watch after Ethan while I—"

"Yes!" Ethan broke in. "Can I go to Bryant's after school tomorrow, Dad? Can I? Hunh?"

"Yep," Jake answered, grinning at his son.

He then turned his grin to me and winked.

When he did, I felt my belly dip and it was an even better sensation knowing some of the other ways Jake could make my belly dip.

Then I went back to Alyssa. "Jake and Ethan are fine with that."

"Right on!" she shouted. "Okay, see you at three. Maude's. I'm on Cross Street, about two and a half blocks north of Wayfarer's. Later!"

After her farewell, not waiting for mine, she was gone.

I put my phone to the counter.

"Take it you're hookin' up with Alyssa tomorrow," Jake noted unnecessarily and I looked to him.

"Yes," I confirmed.

He grinned and his voice was soft when he said, "Good."

I already liked Alyssa but I had a feeling I was going to like her more because clearly Jake liked her and he liked her for me.

I grinned back just as I heard a commotion at the door to the garage. Mere moments later, the door was thrown open and Amber and boy Taylor surged in. Following them, girl Taylor strolled in like she was arriving at the end of a runway and about to stop to strike a pose.

Amber went to Jake, threw her arms around him (regardless of the cooking meat that was close and the wooden spoon in his hand), got up on tiptoe and kissed his cheek.

She did this quickly and just as quickly greeted, "Hey, Dad. I'm alive."

"I see," he replied, smiling down at his daughter.

That caused another belly dip.

I didn't get to fully appreciate this one as, without delay, Amber rushed to me, grabbed my hand and started tugging, announcing loudly and with great liveliness, "Josie! I'm so glad you're here! I *soooooo* have to talk to you."

She must have very much *soooooo* had to talk to me for she dragged me out of the kitchen, to the stairs and up them. It was clear boy Taylor agreed with her urgent need for communication for he put his hands on my back just above my bottom and gratuitously shoved me up the stairs Amber was yanking me up.

We hit the door to her room. One that I'd noted earlier had a white board on it with little pink and blue flowers drawn in at the edges. But contradictory to the cheerful flowers, the words "Enter and Die!" were printed on it in hot pink in the middle and under that, smaller but in all capital letters, "THAT MEANS YOU RUNT!"

It should be noted that under that, in much smaller letters and in black marker was written in a different hand, "Don't call me runt!!!!!!!!"

This amused me when I saw it earlier and it amused me seeing it again. However, at that moment my amusement was intermingled with confusion as to what was currently happening as Amber threw open her door and yanked me in.

I had not seen any of the children's rooms but Ethan's (entirely decked out in some sporting team's paraphernalia, even the sheets) as Conner and Amber's doors were closed.

Now I saw how Amber could exist in this intensely masculine abode.

There was not one inch of her pink and blue room that didn't scream *"Teenaged Girl!"* from stylish but bright bedclothes to pages cut out of style magazines tacked to the walls to band posters to jumbles of clothes and shoes on the floor and accessories and cosmetics on every surface.

I had little time to take all this in for Amber was standing before me. The Taylors having moved to form a loose huddle around us, the door having been closed, Amber was visibly deep breathing while pressing the air down in front of her with her hands in a way I found alarming, repeatedly, chanting, "Okay, okay, okay."

She sucked in a huge breath.

Then I winced when she smiled an enormous smile and screeched, "*You'll never guess what happened!*"

Although I feared my eardrums were bleeding, her excitement was infectious so I smiled back and asked, "What happened, my lovely?"

"Alexi Prokorov said hey to me!" she cried.

I blinked. "Who?"

"Only *the…coolest guy…in the entire school!*" boy Taylor informed me.

"He is," girl Taylor confirmed. "He's the absolute bomb."

I looked from girl Taylor back to Amber as she again began chanting, "Okay, okay, okay. *Soooo*…we were at the diner last night and he walked *right up to me* and said *hey!*"

"I'd done her face up in romantic palette number two," boy Taylor leaned into me to share.

This was a good choice.

I didn't get a chance to say that, girl Taylor was talking, imparting the unusual news that, "Alexi doesn't date girls from Magdalene High."

"He never has," boy Taylor put in. "He usually goes out with the hottest of the hot from other schools."

"He has a motorcycle," Amber added and when she did, my heart skipped a beat.

Uh-oh.

"And he plays guitar," she went on.

Oh dear.

"*And* he's in a band," she continued.

Oh no.

Her face changed, it went soft and wistful as she whispered, "He's dreamy."

"This is huge," boy Taylor announced. "Huger than huge. The one guy who beats out Noah is Alexi. I mean, girls from Magdalene don't even set their sights on him because they know they have no shot." He smiled big. "This is *awesome*."

"He writes his own songs," girl Taylor added. "I saw his band play in the underage club that's used to be an old garage down by the cove. It was amazing."

"Look," boy Taylor demanded and I looked his way to see he had his phone screen facing me. "I got this pic as he was leaving the diner. It isn't very good but it tells the tale."

I stared at his phone thinking the photo on it did, indeed, tell the tale.

The picture was of an exceptionally good-looking young man. He was rather fit and although he was sitting astride a motorcycle, captured on the phone arrested in lifting up a shiny black motorcycle helmet in front of him, it also appeared he was quite tall. He had very messy but attractive dark blond hair. He had excellent bone structure. He was wearing faded jeans, the knee torn and ragged, black motorcycle boots, a black t-shirt and a black leather jacket.

I stared at the photo thinking the young man in it was every high school girl's dream.

I also stared at it thinking that if this young man came over to take Amber out on a date, Jake was going to lose his mind.

"Um…" I mumbled, fear constricting my lungs as I tore my eyes away from the photo and looked at a beaming Amber.

I got no further as she declared, "And Noah's called me. *Twice*."

"She didn't pick up," girl Taylor shared.

"He left a message. She's leaving him hanging," boy Taylor finished.

Although I was proud of Amber for doing this, her doing it shed even more light on Ellie doing the same to Conner which raised my current anxiety levels significantly, something which was notable seeing as they were already significantly high.

"I think that's very wise, Amber," I told her and she smiled a bright smile. "Now as for this boy—" I began but said no more when she jumped straight to me, grabbed my hands and held them tight.

"Josie, he came *right up* to our table and said *hey* right to *me*. It was the best moment *of my life*."

Oh my.

In the face of her happiness, entirely unable to do anything but, I pulled one of my hands from hers, lifted it to cup her cheek, leaned into her and whispered, "Then I hope he likes you, my lovely. But I expect he does because you're beautiful, you're smart and you're a good friend and he likely knows all of that."

Hope washed through her features making her even more beautiful as she asked, "You think?"

"I think and hope, my lovely girl," I replied.

Her smile got bigger.

Before anyone could say more, we heard bellowed from below, "Dip's up!"

Jake.

Amber let me go, jumped back and cried, "Ro-Tel dip! Yee-ha! I'm starved."

Then she dashed by me and out of the room.

Boy Taylor followed her.

Girl Taylor and I were left behind, staring out the now open door.

I turned to her.

"Is this Alexi a decent young man?" I asked quietly.

"He's more decent than Noah," she answered.

This would not be difficult to achieve and thus didn't make me feel better.

"But if Alexi goes for it, Mr. Spear is gonna freak way the heck out," she stated the obvious.

"Indeed," I agreed to the obvious, looking back to the door.

Girl Taylor got closer to me so I turned my eyes to her.

"He gets straight A's, his music really is super cool and word is he's a one woman man. I also know he's between girlfriends right now. But I've seen him a couple of times with his chicks and he's with them like Con is with his chicks. So she could do worse, that being Noah. But Alexi is definitely better."

I found the news Alexi was a "one woman man" somewhat soothing. The information he treated his girlfriends like Conner did (except having only one at a time) was even more so.

So I smiled at her as I reached out and gave her hand a brief squeeze.

Then I motioned to the door with my head.

She preceded me and I followed her down the stairs.

She said, "Hey, Mr. Spear," as she walked past Jake at the bottom of the stairs, moving toward the living room.

"Hey, honey," he muttered to her as she did, but his eyes were on me.

Then his large body was blocking mine as I reached the bottom of the stairs and thus I had to stop and look up at him.

"Everything cool?" he asked quietly, studying me closely and I knew I was not hiding my unease.

"For Amber, yes. For you, if things play out as she wishes…" I hesitated then finished, "No."

"Come again?" he asked, his brows knitting.

"A young man said hi to her last night at the diner. Boy Taylor showed me his picture and he's very attractive. He was also sitting on a motorcycle."

Jake's brows unknit and his jaw got hard.

I went on.

"I'm informed he plays guitar."

His eyes flashed and a muscle jumped in his cheek.

I continued speaking.

"He also writes his own music and plays in a band."

Jake looked beyond me, grumbling, "Fuckin' fuck me."

"I'm further informed he gets straight A's and he's a one woman man."

Jake's eyes came back to me and I could see immediately he did not share my minor relief at these revelations.

"Who woulda thought I'd miss Noah," Jake remarked.

I pressed my lips together wanting to laugh but knowing I absolutely should not.

"A motorcycle?" he asked.

I tipped my head to the side and gave him a little wince.

He tipped his head back and said to the ceiling, "Why couldn't you have given me all boys?"

I found this obvious conversation with God intriguing and thus asked, "Do you believe in God?"

He looked back to me and his brows were again knit. "Uh…yeah."

"If this is so, I'll inform you that Reverend Fletcher has invited me to attend services and he expressly asked that I bring you and the children along."

"I bet he did," Jake murmured, moving to my side and slinging an arm around my shoulders.

"I'll tell you now, I'm not fond of waking up early but they do have an evening service."

He looked down at me as he moved us toward the family room and I slid my arm around his waist.

"You're not fond of gettin' up early?"

"No."

"You get up early to work out with me."

I just looked at him.

He grinned and did it slowly. He also pulled me closer. Last, he looked in the direction he was taking us.

"Evening services it is, Slick. But not tonight. Next week. Happy to get closer to God to ask Him in His house to look after my girl when basketball stars and guitar players with motorcycles are in the mix."

"Indeed," I agreed but the word was weighty which earned me a squeeze of his arm and him tipping his head down to give me another grin.

He moved us into the living room where there was a football game playing on Jake's extortionately large television and children all around consuming orange dip with red and green bits in it, doing this utilizing corn chips.

Jake, in Jake fashion, seated me himself. He did this in an overlarge club chair with matching ottoman that was really meant only to seat one but he made it seat two, albeit snugly.

He then commanded, "Eath, get Josie and me another bowl a' that and bring in a fresh bag of chips."

Ethan jumped off the couch and raced to do as his father bid. Therefore, in no time at all, I was confronted with a bowl of dip held in Jake's big hand, the bag of chips resting in his lap.

It was time to make my judgment.

And I was much surprised to find the dip tangy, spicy and of a very smooth consistency that was quite nice and the chip was fresh, crispy and salty.

An excellent combination.

"It pass inspection?" Jake asked as I went for another chip.

I looked to him to see him studying me, lips again quirking.

"It's not camembert," I shared. "But it's tasty."

His lips stopped quirking and he yet again grinned as he went for his own chip.

Football game watching commenced and I found I liked sitting very snugly in Jake's chair with Jake watching it with our lively company around. Ethan very into the game, thus shouting a lot. Conner and Jake often commenting about players, plays or calls. Myself engaging in conversation that had very little to do with football and much to do with fashion, makeup, skincare, and accessorizing as well as commentary on the good-looking players on the field with Amber and the Taylors.

After the first game ended, Jake ordered us all to the kitchen where we prepared our tacos (the meat, Jake explained to me, had to simmer awhile "for it to be real good, honey").

Although I saw the envelope from which he'd poured the spices, and thus suspected the fare would be mediocre, he was not wrong. The tacos were delicious. Ethan and Conner microwaved the rather spare remains of the dip and spooned it into their tacos and I decided to try that should I have another taco afternoon at Jake's for I thought it might be rather appetizing.

We ate in front of the TV and Amber and the Taylors had taken our used plates and cutlery back to the kitchen and refreshed our drinks when it happened.

The doorbell rang.

"Amber," was all Jake said and she surprisingly dutifully got up and went to the door.

The front door was not close (there was an informal living room that looked more like a romper room for teenagers with a large sectional in it that had two laptops and a tablet scattered on it, as well as exploding backpacks on the floor, and also a dining room at the front of the house).

Not being close, we only heard murmurings and no one seemed overly bothered they had company.

Until Amber came back and my head snapped her way when I heard the trembling tone of her voice.

"Um…Dad, Con…uh, Mr. Earhart and Mia are here to talk to you guys."

Mia?

The young woman who confronted Conner and Ellie at the football game?

I felt Jake's body get tight next to mine, heard Con mutter, "What the hell?" but my eyes were riveted to Amber's face.

She looked afraid.

Suddenly, I was out of the chair because Jake put his hands to my waist and shoved me to my feet.

Then I was moving toward the front of the house because Jake was also out of the chair, had grabbed my hand and was dragging me there.

He did this rumbling, "Con, with me and Josie. Amber, keep everyone in here."

But Jake did not need to issue this order to his eldest. Conner was at our heels. I felt him there.

I just didn't know why I, too, was attending this impromptu and clearly not welcome meeting.

I thought little of this the minute I hit the foyer and saw the man standing there.

He was not as big or fit as Jake but then again, not many men were. They were much the same age, I guessed. But even not as large or conditioned as Jake, this man was no pushover.

The other thing he was was enraged.

Utterly.

And his incensed eyes were glued to Conner in a way that I genuinely feared he might cause him bodily harm.

Without thinking, I pulled my hand from Jake's and took a step back. My shoulder hit Conner and I stopped, forcing him to stop with me.

Then my eyes moved to Mia and my skin started prickling.

She was up to something. I could tell by the light in her eyes and the smirk on her lips. In the face of her father's extreme fury, she should not be smirking.

Something was wrong and whatever it was, she was behind it.

"Neal, what's up?" Jake asked casually but cautiously and I looked to him to see he, too, was positioned between the man and his son.

The man named Neal tore his gaze from Conner and looked to Jake.

"We gotta talk," he bit out. "Private."

Jake studied him only a moment but did it closely. He then nodded and held out a hand to the living room, which was a room that had a door, unlike the others on the bottom floor.

We trundled in, me holding back which meant Conner had to hold back and this meant I maneuvered it so that Conner and I were the last to enter the room.

I kept him well removed from Mia and her father and twisted to ask him quietly, "Please close the door, sweetheart."

I could see by his face he was confused, perhaps a bit angry, and also very wary.

He closed the door.

When he turned back to the room, so did I.

"What's this about?" Jake asked.

Neal didn't delay in laying it out.

"Mia's pregnant."

Oh my.

He wasn't done.

"*Your* boy got *my* girl *pregnant.*"

The room became stifling. I felt it coming from all directions as I watched Jake's face turn to marble.

But I heard Conner clip, "That's complete bullshit."

"Mind your boy, Jake," Neal instantly demanded in an irate rumble.

Jake turned to Conner but said nothing when Conner repeated, "It's total bullshit, Dad."

"I can't believe you," Mia hissed at this point and I looked to her.

And it was then I knew that if she was going to instigate this kind of drama in order to salvage her wounded pride and inflict pain on the one who wounded it, she should be a much better actress.

"And I can't believe you," Conner shot back. "You know that's totally whacked."

"It is not!" she snapped.

"If you're pregnant, whose is it? 'Cause it sure isn't mine," Conner returned and the air in the room grew even heavier.

"Con," Jake said in a warning tone.

"You need to be *real* careful, son," Neal just warned.

"May I ask how you know you're pregnant, Mia?" I queried at this juncture and I saw her eyes come to me but felt her father's do it.

"Can I ask who you *are?*" her father inquired.

I looked to him but Jake answered. "Neal, this is Josie Malone. She's close to the family."

"I wish it was better circumstances, Neal," I said quickly but softly. "But really, it's rather important to know the basics of what's happening here so we can have a constructive discussion."

"I took a pregnancy test," Mia stated before her father could reply.

I looked to her.

"A drugstore one?" I asked quietly.

"Yes," she answered.

"Do you have the results with you?"

Her face got hard but I noted it did this to hide the shifty. "I freaked when I got a positive and threw it away."

"I bet you did," Conner muttered and the air shifted again so I turned to him.

"Please, sweetheart," was all I said.

He held my eyes and shut his mouth, his jaw going hard.

I turned back to the room and looked at Mia's father. "I'm very sorry, Neal. I know this is extremely upsetting for everyone but I hope you can understand that if this news is indeed true, much needs to be discussed as much may change. Indeed, entire courses of the lives of very young people. We'll have to ask for Mia to take another test so we know what we're dealing with."

"She says she's pregnant," Neal returned.

"She's also recently sustained a break up with our Conner and I myself witnessed her behavior at the game so I know that she was understandably upset about that," I told him and his eyes narrowed.

"Are you sayin' my girl would make shit like this up?"

I shook my head but held his eyes.

"I'm saying that this is a volatile situation but in the end what may come of it affects all parties and thus all parties should be involved in every step of the process." I looked to Mia. "I'm happy to go get a test right now. I'm of the understanding it takes little time to take them. You can do it here and then we can resume this discussion."

Her face got harder but I saw her mouth move in a telling way before she stated, "I'm not takin' another test. Taking the first one was bad enough."

"Alas, young Mia," I said, forcing my tone to be gentle. "With pregnancy, much will be unpleasant in the coming months. But Conner deserves to see the results."

She tossed her hair and crossed her arms on her chest. "He doesn't deserve anything. Playing me, knocking me up and then dumping me. He doesn't deserve crap."

Conner had done well with being silent and not escalating matters, but with that, he was just done.

"Not sure how I could knock you up since we haven't had sex, Mia."

I found this interesting and a huge relief.

Because I believed him.

Completely.

"Neal," Jake quickly put in at this juncture. "Unfortunately we got a he said, she said situation goin' on here and there may be an easy, quick fix. I'll go get the test. Josie can stay here with you and Mia. Conner can go in the other room. To get to town and back, Mia takes the test, we'll know what we're dealing with in less than twenty minutes."

Jake said this but Neal was staring at Conner and he wasn't exactly furious anymore (or at least, not entirely). However, I knew him not at all. Therefore, I didn't know what he was.

Then he looked to his daughter and his face gentled. "Just take the test, honey."

It was then I knew what he was. He was a man who was simply a man therefore was once a teenaged boy so he knew how he'd feel if a girl's father showed up at his doorstep with this news.

Her back shot straight as her face started to pale and she snapped, "I'm not takin' another test."

"It'll take no time at all and—" Neal began.

She leaned into her father, her face twisting. "I'm not takin' another test, Dad."

"Mia—"

Her eyes shifted around the room and she interrupted her father to announce, "I'll take it at home."

"I must insist you take it here," I stated.

"Don't know how *you* can insist on anything. It's my pee. It's my body. And you aren't even family," Mia fired back.

I held her eyes and, unperturbed, replied quietly, "You know why I can insist."

"Respect, Josie, but I'm not real big on you standin' there callin' my daughter a liar," Neal said with forced calm.

Before I could say anything, Conner did.

"She's pregnant, she shouldn't have any problem takin' a test. Why do you have a problem with it, Mia?"

"Because you're a dick and I can barely stand bein' in the same room with you. I'm not gonna hang around for twenty minutes doin' it," she retorted.

"Now, Neal, I'm gonna have to ask you to ask your daughter to be careful," Jake said in his quiet, angry voice.

Neal turned to his daughter. "This isn't easy for any of us, honey. Don't make it harder."

"It's hardest *for me*." She leaned toward her father and jerked her thumb to herself at her last two words.

"Actually, it's hardest for me," Conner stated firmly and angrily and I looked to him to see his eyes slice to Mia's father. "Mr. Earhart, I have not had sex with your daughter. I broke things off with her and she wasn't happy about it. Josie saw her make a scene at the game and so did my sister and her friends and probably a bunch of other people. Pretty much anyone will tell you she's made threats to the girl I'm seein' and made more scenes than just the one at the game. But bottom line, no lie, if she's pregnant, it's absolutely not mine."

After this rather well delivered speech (I thought), I turned back to Neal and saw him again studying Conner.

He did this but moments before he looked down at his daughter.

"You're takin' the test, Mia. Here."

"Am not," she spat.

His tone was deadly when he decreed, "You absolutely are."

And when he did, Mia's face went ashen.

Her father didn't miss it and I knew this when he whispered, "Please tell me you did not lie to me about Conner Spear gettin' you pregnant."

She said nothing but visibly swallowed and her body language changed from extremely cross to exceptionally nervous.

Her father didn't miss that either.

"You lied to me," Neal stated, still in a whisper.

She rubbed her lips together as she rubbed her palms on her jeans.

"You're not pregnant?" her father asked, his voice now sounding choked.

She stared into his eyes for some time before she finally jerked her head in a negative.

"What were you gonna do when that shit was found out?" her father asked incredulously, a question he probably didn't want the answer to, but asked it anyway.

She shifted on her feet.

"Mia," he started, his voice awful and I didn't know him, but I felt for him. "What were you gonna do?"

"Get pregnant in the meantime, but pin it on Conner," she whispered, voice trembling, eyes glued to her dad.

"Jesus," Neal bit out, staring at her like he'd never seen before.

Her face screwed up and she threw out a hand Conner's way. "We dated for three months and he just *blew me off.*"

Good goodness.

All of this for *three months?*

I was aghast.

"Go to the car." Neal was again whispering.

She looked to Conner. "You can't be with a girl and just *blow her off.*"

"Mia, *go to the car,*" Neal demanded, a lot louder this time.

She looked to her father. "He *humiliated* me. I was the second one cut!"

"Swear to Christ, Mia, you don't go to the car right now..." Neal trailed off.

She looked to Conner and hissed, "You're still a dick and you'll *always* be a dick."

That was when Jake was done.

"Not sure your girl is welcome in my home, Neal," Jake said low.

"Mia—" Neal started but her bravado disintegrated as her face crumbled.

I felt no pity for her.

Lying about a pregnancy and conniving to become that way?

Unacceptable.

"You hurt me," she whispered to Conner.

Conner said nothing.

"Car, Mia," her father ordered but his voice was gentler, thus giving some understanding of why Mia was as Mia was. What she'd done was not suitable by any stretch of the imagination, but she showed some emotion, and her father gentled to it.

She stared at Conner with wet eyes then looked to her father and without a word or another look at anyone, she rushed by Jake, by me, by Conner and out the door.

Neal lifted a hand and ran it through his hair before he looked to Jake.

"Jake, don't know what to say," he murmured.

"Nothin' to say," Jake replied. "Kids do crazy shit. It's done." Jake paused as he held the man's eyes before he finished, "Though, would appreciate it you have a word with your girl about shit she's pullin' with Conner's girl, Ellie. She's pissed at Conner, I get. Her doin' this, I don't get, but we're past that. Her messin' with Ellie, that shit isn't right."

Neal stared at him a moment before doing the only thing he could do at that juncture, nodding and moving. He gave a curt jerk of the chin to me and looked to Conner.

"Conner, son. Sorry."

Conner said nothing.

Even without a response, Neal nodded to him too and walked out the door.

Conner delayed not a moment before shutting it behind him and cutting his eyes to his father.

"She told Ellie that shit. Or got someone to do it."

She did indeed, I thought.

"Yep," Jake said.

"That's why Ellie's not calling me," Conner went on.

It certainly was, I thought.

"Yep," Jake said.

"I gotta go to her," Conner announced.

He absolutely did, I thought.

"Yep," Jake said.

Conner put a hand to the door.

"Son," Jake called.

Conner looked to his father.

"Lesson," Jake said gently. "Man's got the power to break a woman's heart. Women have their own power. Learn this and in future, choose better."

Conner's jaw got hard then he jerked up his own chin, threw open the door and exited the room.

Jake walked to the door, closed it again and turned to me.

"How'd you know?"

"She's an immensely unpleasant young woman and a terrible actress."

He tipped his head to the side. "She gonna cause more problems for my boy?"

I drew in a deep breath and lowered my voice when I replied, "Unless her father successfully imparts wisdom through appropriate punishment, it's highly likely she'll do that every chance she gets."

"Conner shares, not everything but we're tight and he gives a lot to his old man," Jake told me. "He made no promises of exclusivity to any of them, not until he told Ellie she's the one. I'm a man so I'm gonna think this kinda punishment doesn't fit the crime 'cause I'm not sure he committed one."

I said nothing.

"You got a take on that?" he prompted.

"It wasn't like he was dating five women in a large cosmopolitan city, Jake. He was dating five girls in a small high school. This was a recipe for disaster. But, in essence, you're correct. If he made no promises, the punishment doesn't fit the crime. He simply chose poorly." I paused and finished. "*Very* poorly."

"And how does he deal with this girl, she keeps fuckin' with him?"

"He gives her what she deserves," I told him.

His brows went up as he asked, "And what's that?"

"He ruins her."

"Come again?" he asked, brows still high.

"I am not a man, or a teenaged boy becoming a man, and I've never been either. But I would guess if I was, if it was known a girl would go to these extremes simply because her non-exclusive boyfriend of three months broke up with her, she would not be high on my list of girls I'd wish to spend time with."

"So he spreads this," Jake said.

"No. That would make him look tactless and it would be obvious. But the Taylors could do it. However, in all honesty, in high school with his station in it, I don't believe it would be untoward for him to do it himself. That was an extreme, completely uncalled for and utterly overdramatized reaction to a breakup. Young Mia has a lesson to learn too."

Jake shook his head. "Unless he asks, I think I'll let him come up with that. Even if he asks, not sure I'll give him that option."

"Pity," I replied. "Although he was quite angry and it's unlikely he'll keep this to himself, she came to his home with her father demanding to see his father, dragging you both into something exceptionally unpleasant and she did something that is utterly inexcusable. I, for one, hope she gets what she deserves."

At that, Jake grinned and moved to me.

He had his arms around me and had drawn me close to his front before he muttered, "Momma bear."

"I do not like that young woman," I declared, my body stiff even being held in his arms.

He kept muttering and grinning. "Total momma bear."

I stared up at him and noted, "This must be excruciatingly difficult for you, to be close, for matters to mean so much, but to be mostly powerless as your son and daughter learn how to make decisions in their lives and sometimes are forced to face the consequences."

"It ain't a walk in the park," he agreed.

"Hmm," I mumbled, looking at his shoulder just above where I'd placed my hands on his biceps.

"Babe."

I looked up at him.

"You're the shit."

I stopped thinking about Conner and Ellie and Mia and Amber and boys with motorcycles and smiled.

"Wish like fuck I could strip you bare and fuck you on my couch right about now."

I stopped smiling and experienced a rather intense and exceptionally pleasant tingle.

His mouth dropped to mine and I felt as well as heard his next words. "Sucks the kids are in the next room."

It most certainly did.

"Yes," I breathed.

His lips brushed mine and then slid along my cheek to my ear where he whispered, "Take you again in your bed when I take you home tonight."

My fingers clenched into his biceps when I whispered back, "Yes."

"Really lookin' forward to that, Slick." He kept whispering.

"Me as well, Jake."

"You gonna give me somethin' to go on until then?" he asked.

I absolutely was.

I didn't tell him that.

I gave it to him. Turning my head, he felt it, turned his, and our mouths collided.

In the end, it wasn't entirely correct that I gave it to him. It was more that he took it from me.

But pressed tight to Jake Spear in his living room with his kids' laptops and tablets and backpacks all around, being kissed dizzy, I didn't mind him taking anything he wanted.

No.

I didn't mind at all.

Because I'd give him anything.

I'd give him everything.

If I had the power, I'd give him the world.

"UM...THAT SWEATER...no," boy Taylor decreed.

It was over an hour after the day's latest debacle had finished and we were watching an interview with a quarterback who was wearing a cream lapelled cardigan that did him no favors.

Conner had not yet returned.

Jake nor I had shared what had occurred in the living room with the kids in the family room, although we did receive speculative glances.

I'd turned attention away from this curiosity by asking to see the photos of the Spear house prior to renovation and Ethan had run to get the envelopes of pictures. I'd then seen that Ethan was indeed correct. The house *had* been a "dump," completely ramshackle. I shouldn't have been surprised, yet I still was, that Jake had wrought miracles.

Now we were carrying on with football Sunday but without the food fest. Though Jake did say he was going to order pizza in about an hour.

"Indeed," I agreed with boy Taylor. "He's very pretty. Too pretty and he knows it. An African-American football player could pull off that sweater by sheer force of will. A rougher man, with, say, no neck and a crew cut, absolutely. A pretty man who knows he's pretty, he simply looks ridiculous."

"Totally," girl Taylor agreed.

"I'm psyched Josie thinks he's a pretty-boy. Everyone thinks he's so hot. He does nothing for me and never has," Amber put in just as I felt Jake move and then felt his lips at my ear.

"Uh...babe, just sayin', that's my team's quarterback."

I turned my head to look at him, uncertain why my assessment of the man's looks and attire would mean anything regardless if he played for Jake's team.

"And Ethan's," he finished when I caught his eyes.

It was then I looked to Ethan who was sitting on the couch, legs out, arms crossed, lips pressed tight, eyes glued to the television, looking fit to be tied.

I found this interesting.

Apparently my assessment of a man's looks and attire *did* mean something if that man played for a beloved team.

"Taylors and Amber," I called out. "We should cease insulting this man's sweater. It's upsetting Ethan."

They all looked to Ethan.

"Sorry, Ethan," girl Taylor said.

"Sorry, Eath," boy Taylor said.

"Sorry, runt," Amber said.

Ethan screwed up his face and glared at Amber.

"Don't call me runt!" he snapped at his sister, uncharacteristically indignantly.

"Eath—" she started but Ethan looked to his father.

"Is Conner okay?" he demanded to know.

My insides melted.

He was possibly upset about our insulting his quarterback's knitwear but he was more worried about his brother.

He was *such* a good child.

"He'll be okay, bud," Jake replied.

"That's not okay now," Ethan pointed out rather astutely.

And he was *so* very bright.

"You're right, Eath," Jake said gently. "But he will be."

Ethan glared at his father for a long moment then demanded, "Promise?"

"Promise, son," Jake promised.

Ethan kept glaring at his father before he turned his glare to the television and declared, "I'm never dating *ever*."

Jake made a grunt that sounded like a swallowed chuckle and the Taylors and Amber grinned at each other.

"I'd like to rewind our afternoon and go over that safety business again," I announced to change the subject and perhaps lighten the mood. "I know your father explained it to me when it happened but I fear it still makes little sense. Ethan, please expound on that explanation."

"It's super easy, Josie," Ethan told me. "It's when the offense gets downed in their own end zone."

"And what's an end zone?" I inquired.

Ethan blinked.

Jake emitted another grunt.

"That big part at the end of the field," Ethan explained. "Where you go to get a touchdown."

"Ah," I murmured. "I thought so."

Ethan studied me narrowly and asked, "Are you bein' full of it?"

"Entirely," I answered.

At my admission, his face cracked in a grin, which pleased me greatly.

Alas, with very bad timing, at that very moment we heard the garage door going up and Ethan's smile froze as his eyes went to the entryway to the family room.

In no time, Conner appeared in the entryway with eyes only for his father, his expression making my stomach clench, and I knew Jake's assertion that he would be okay in the future was in jeopardy.

"Dad," was all he said before he disappeared from the entryway.

That was all he had to say. Giving me a quick squeeze of the knee before he pushed out of the chair, Jake followed his eldest son.

"Uh-oh," boy Taylor murmured.

But Amber got up and walked to her little brother, sat next to him on the couch and bumped him with her shoulder. "Want a hot fudge sundae?"

"Not hungry," Ethan muttered, the first time he had been thus since I'd met him.

Very worried about his brother.

"Wanna help me make some for the Taylors and me?"

He looked up at his sister. Then he nodded.

They got off the couch and went to the kitchen but not before I caught her hand as they passed me and gave it a squeeze.

She gave me a worried look but squeezed my hand back.

She was *such* a good sister.

The Taylors and Amber were consuming their sundaes (and Ethan must have given in because he was consuming one too), when Jake appeared in the entryway.

"Josie," was all he said but he didn't then disappear.

He waited until I made it to him before he turned to the side to let me precede him but did this in a way that I knew we were heading to the kitchen.

I went there. Jake followed.

I moved to the far side of the island, stopped and rested a hip against it. Jake got close and did the same.

"Is Conner all right?" I asked quietly.

"Not by a long shot," he answered.

Oh dear.

I waited and Jake gave it to me.

"Seems Mia Earhart is a real piece of work."

I said it out loud this time.

"Oh dear."

"Oh yeah," Jake agreed. "Orchestrated one helluva maneuver. Got one of her friends who's mom is friends with Ellie's mom to tell that mom that Conner got Mia pregnant. That mom didn't hesitate to tell Ellie's mom. Seein' as Conner's been seein' a lot of Ellie, this did not go down real good. Ellie's mom and dad told Ellie that she had to break it off with Conner at school tomorrow and was not to have anything to do with him before or after that shit went down. Seein' as Conner showed at their house, this sped that up and got Conner not only a face to face with a very irate father who wants him to have nothin' to do with his daughter, it got him a face to face with a girl he likes a whole fuckin' lot who thinks he's a dick."

"But Mia isn't pregnant," I reminded him.

"I know. They weren't so easy to convince."

I pressed my lips together before I got closer and noted even more quietly, "The truth obviously will out."

"Not sure my boy's real hip on waitin'. Liked her, didn't know just how much until he lost her. He's gutted."

I looked to the door and whispered, "Poor Conner."

I looked back to Jake when I felt his hand curl around my neck and when I did I saw his face was closer.

"Puts a hitch in my plans for us tonight. He's probably not gonna come outta his room but that doesn't mean I shouldn't be here for him just in case that happens. And I gotta get to the club later but wanna do that when all the kids are asleep. So after pizza, when you're ready, I'll drop you home but I can't stay."

That was highly regrettable, but also understandable, so I replied, "Okay." Then I suggested, "Perhaps you could phone Ellie's parents and explain this situation."

"I offered, Con said no. He's hurt and for a guy, hurt equals pissed. He can't believe Ellie doesn't believe him because he, thank Christ, hasn't done the deed with either of them. Don't know if my boy's a virgin. Hope to God he never shares that with me just as I hope to God he's bein' smart about that, somethin' I've shared repeatedly that he should be. Just know he hasn't gone there with either of those two. Possibly outta self-preservation with Mia, definitely outta respect for Ellie. So he says it's her loss, she didn't go to bat for him with her parents because she believed Mia's lies, and he doesn't want me to get involved."

"I can't say he's wrong, Jake," I told him.

"She's a good kid," he told me. "But yeah. He's always been way more into her than the others and she's shy, he's all about that, likes that about her, likes lookin' after her and at their first hurtle bein' exclusive, she fell. I get him bein' pissed. He's hurt he lost her and he's hurt she didn't believe in him and stand by him in an extreme situation. That's a lotta hurt so it's a lotta pissed and both are justified. "

"Agreed," I stated then repeated. "Poor Conner."

"Yeah," Jake murmured and studied me a moment before he asked, "Do you think your shit for brains boss is gonna fuck with you?"

I felt my brows draw together at this swift change in topic. "Pardon?"

"He gonna show again at your place," he explained.

I couldn't have any idea what Henry would do for that morning he had shocked me with his behavior not to mention even being at Lavender House at all.

"I've no idea," I told Jake.

His eyes went over my head as his fingers pressed into my skin.

"Jake?" I called, uncertain what was on his mind outside of what obviously was with his son, and he looked back at me.

"I think the kids get what's happenin' between us but it's way too soon for you to be spending the night."

"Of course," I agreed readily.

"But I'm not real big on you bein' there alone, him havin' a key and maybe showin' his face to fuck with you."

It was at that, I understood.

And I liked what I understood.

So I slid my arms around him and pressed close, tipping my head way back to keep his eyes and dipping my voice low to assure him, "I'll be all right."

"I get you got a long history with him and he means somethin' to you but I don't think you get what he did this mornin' was fucked. I don't want him messing with your head."

"If he comes around, I'll ask for him to return the key and then ask him to leave and tell him we'll speak later when things aren't as fresh and I'm not as angry."

His head tipped to the side. "You're angry?"

I nodded. "His behavior this morning was uncalled for. You were correct, if he had feelings for as long as he said he did, he should have done something about them long ago. He should not have communicated them well later when too much had happened and it was way too late."

I took a breath and held his eyes before I cautiously continued sharing and did it candidly.

"I cared about him, Jake, deeply, in just that way some time ago. It was painful to do that thinking he didn't return those feelings. I don't understand why he, as you say, played it the way he did. I've been very forthcoming about the way things have progressed, coming to know you and the children. I didn't share how they are now as you know I wasn't even aware of where things were heading. But I suspect he was reading between the lines and, as Mickey would say, came to stake his claim. I daresay he was about twenty years late doing that. How he could not know that, I can't fathom. That he would put our business relationship and more, our personal relationship at jeopardy to do this, I can't fathom either. It hurts. How he did it was extremely inappropriate. So yes, I'm angry."

As I was speaking, he started to stroke my jaw with his thumb and his eyes warmed. As I continued speaking, they warmed more.

When I was done, they were so warm, they warmed *me*.

"Just to make things clear in case you aren't gettin' it, baby, I'm hopin' things with you and me and my kids keep progressing."

At his words, I melted deeper into him and whispered, "I hope they do too."

He dropped his head closer and touched his mouth to mine, lifting away nary an inch before he went on, "I'd like other things to progress too, a lot faster than they are, the part that just you and me can do, but we'll have to find time tomorrow."

I understood precisely what he was saying so I melted even deeper into him and replied, "Okay."

"A lot of time," he stated.

I bit my lip, let it go and repeated, "Okay."

His mouth came to mine and he whispered, "Fuckin' *hours*."

I trembled against his frame.

He slanted his head, slid his hand back into my hair and kissed me.

I pressed even *deeper* and kissed him back.

Fabulous.

"Gross!" Ethan shouted from close and we broke the kiss but Jake didn't let me move too far away even as we both looked to the door.

Ethan's head was turned so he could shout over his shoulder, "Amber! Get this! Josie and Dad are makin' out in the kitchen!"

"Good God," I breathed.

Jake emitted another swallowed chuckle grunt.

"Get in here, runt, and leave them alone!" Amber shouted back.

Well, there it was. It appeared the kids did, indeed, get how things were with Jake and me.

It was only me who missed it.

Fortunately, I wasn't missing it at all now.

"Don't call me runt!" Ethan yelled, looked at us and demanded to know, "Are you two getting married?"

My entire body seized.

"You think maybe you might not wanna freak out my girl, bud?" Jake asked.

"All girls wanna get married," Ethan told his father authoritatively.

My breath started coming in pants.

"I'll try something else," Jake said. "You think your old man might want a little privacy?"

Ethan looked to me and announced, "I'm not wearing one of those monkey suits."

"So noted," I forced out.

That seemed to assuage him for he turned and strolled out of view.

When he did, Jake's hand that had been resting on the counter beside us (even through our kiss) came to me so he could wrap his arm around me and his hand that had not left my hair glided through it.

I looked back at him.

"Your home is not boring," I remarked.

"Nope," he agreed.

"It's been a very interesting day," I noted.

"Yep," he agreed, lips twitching.

"And oddly, I'm hungry," I shared and his lips curved up.

"Time to feed my woman."

"Mm," I mumbled.

"No delivery. We'll pick up the pizzas, leavin' right after we order so we can make out in my truck waitin' for them."

"Mm," I repeated but the noise had a different meaning this time.

Jake didn't miss the meaning and I knew this when his mouth came back to mine even as he held my gaze. "Let's do that now."

"Okay," I breathed and got another smile from Jake, this one I saw only in his eyes but felt against my lips.

It was extraordinary.

Then he slanted his head and kissed me again.

In other words, we didn't order pizza right then. We ordered pizza five minutes later when Jake stopped kissing me.

And we left two seconds after he disconnected.

Fifteen

SAY HER NAME WITH HIS LAST BREATH

I felt the bed move before I felt my hair slide off my neck.

I opened my eyes, turned my head and saw Jake. He was sitting on the side of my bed, his weight in his hand in the bed on the other side of me, his eyes on me.

"Is it time to work out?" I asked sleepily.

"Oh yeah," he answered, his voice strange, deeper and rumbly, the sound, especially first thing in the morning, utterly lovely.

I decided against telling him that and instead turned to my back and shared, "I have new workout clothes so I don't have to borrow Amber's anymore."

He dipped closer to me and his voice was even deeper and more rumbly when he told me, "Way we're gonna work out, Slick, clothes are unnecessary."

I felt my entire body melt into the mattress.

Oh my.

Jake kept talking.

"Opened the gym, got boys there, they'll keep an eye on it." He got even closer. "We got hours."

"Hours?" I breathed.

His mouth hit mine but his eyes didn't close so I was staring into their deep blue depths when he whispered with emphasis, "*Hours.*"

"Oh my," I replied and watched his eyes smile.

Then I closed my own for I'd seen his head slant and I knew he was going to kiss me.

He did and I melted deeper into the mattress. But only for a moment. When my mouth opened and his tongue slid inside, his arms closed around me and he pulled me out of bed and across his lap.

Still kissing me, he fell back on a twist taking me with him so he was properly in the bed and at once, he rolled so he was on top.

I liked him waking me. I liked that he was the first thing I saw in the morning. I liked his voice all deep and rumbly. I liked him in bed with me. I liked that we had hours.

And I *very* much liked his kiss.

So much, I wanted more of it and of *him*. Therefore, I slid my hands into his shirt and pulled up by dragging them up the warm skin of his back.

Alas, when I did this, he detached his lips from mine. Fortunately, he did this only to arch away so I could drag the shirt up further and when my arms could reach no more, he assisted and yanked it off, tossing it aside.

I caught a glimpse of his wide, defined chest before he settled on me again and took my mouth. My mind lost in Jake's deep kiss, my body knew what it wanted. Thus, I bent a knee, planted my foot in the bed and bucked.

Jake, being Jake, gave it to me by giving in and allowing me to roll him. I rolled with him, broke our kiss and lifted up to look down at him.

His dark hair on my pillow. His eyes heated but languorous. His jaw stubbled. His corded throat and muscular chest right there.

All of it amazing.

And all of it right there.

For me.

I decided to take it and dipped my head to slide my lips against his rough jaw, liking the sharp, bristly feel against my soft skin. Liking it so much, I went for more, trailing them down his neck.

This brought in sight his throat and I'd always liked that so I moved to take that in with my lips. My hand was encountering warm skin over hard muscle, which brought to mind his chest so I leisurely made my way there.

Since that expanse was so vast, I really needed to be in the proper position to do it justice so I moved over Jake, straddling his hips.

Trailing my lips everywhere, I engaged my tongue on a little mew when I felt Jake's hands slide up into my nightie then down into my panties to cup my behind.

The pads of his fingers were not smooth. He was a man who renovated his own home, owned a gym, boxed. Thus, his fingers were calloused and abrasive.

And, like his voice earlier, utterly *lovely*.

I encountered his nipple and brushed my lips across it. Back. Again. And again. On the next pass, I grazed it with the tip of my tongue.

I heard Jake emit a noise that sounded like it came from deep in his chest. A noise that reverberated pleasingly between my legs, just as his fingers dug into my bottom, something I liked. Very much.

I lifted my head to see his on the pillow, his chin tipped down, his eyes on me.

Another pleasant sensation pulsed between my legs at the increased heat in his gaze. I liked the look of it. I also liked that it was me who put it there.

I held his eyes as I dipped my head and lapped at his nipple.

His gaze heated further and his fingers clenched again at my behind.

I kept lapping as I kept the connection of our gazes then finally I closed my eyes, turned my attention fully to his nipple and suckled it.

One of his hands stayed in my panties while the other one slid swiftly up my spine, into my hair to cup the back of my head as he groaned, "Fuck, baby."

At this indication he much liked what I was doing, I kept pulling at his nipple with my mouth as I slid my hand down his chest to his stomach and lightly explored the ridges there.

These ridges were fascinating.

Utterly.

His hand fisted in my hair.

He liked that too.

I switched nipples and hands, now my right hand was engaged and I trailed it lower, sweeping it across the edge of the waistband of his workout pants.

He slightly lifted his hips.

I knew what that meant and he'd rolled to give me access to all of him, it wouldn't be right if I didn't give him what he wanted when he wanted it like he did for me.

So I directly slid my hand into his pants and curved my fingers tight around his thick, rigid cock.

"*Fuck, baby,*" he groaned again, deeper this time, his hand in my panties going out so he could wrap his arm tight around me.

I lifted my head to look at him and said softly, "I like exploring your body, Jake."

His voice was gruff when he replied, "I like you exploring my body, Josie."

This made me extremely happy.

"It pleases me that I please you," I whispered.

"Honey, this hair all over me,"—his hand twisted gently in my hair— "that soft nightie, your pretty face, your fantastic fuckin' mouth, your hand, no way you couldn't please me."

That meant so much, I kissed his nipple, slid up and kissed his chest, up and I kissed the base of his throat and up where I kissed his jaw before I moved my lips to his.

That was when I stroked with my right hand.

"Jesus," he grunted, his eyes closing, his hips bucking under my hand.

"I want to give you everything," I told him quietly on another stroke.

His eyes opened and captured mine.

"You're doin' a pretty good job of that, Slick," he told me, his hand in my hair sliding out, down my neck, in over my chest and then down where it cupped my breast.

My lips against his parted and I stroked him again.

"You gonna let me give you everything too?" he asked.

I was.

Absolutely.

"Yes," I breathed.

His thumb slid across my nipple over the silk of my nightie. I stroked him again and pressed my hips into my hand working between us.

His hand moved down, in my nightie and up and I had it back at my breast, cupping it, his thumb abrading my nipple.

Oh *yes*.

I stroked again and rubbed against him.

"How hot are you from workin' me?" he asked, his lips moving against mine.

I stroked again, my breathing escalated, and didn't answer.

"How hot are you, baby?" he pressed.

"Very," I breathed.

"Very?" he queried.

"Yes."

As I stroked him again, his arm that was around me moved down so his hand could delve back into my panties were it cupped my bottom just as his hand slid away from my breast, down, in the front of my panties and straight in. His rough finger glided tight over my clit then slid right inside me.

My breath hitched then I bit my lip, biting his as it was right there and he made another low noise that rumbled up his chest as his finger started moving in and out.

"You're right," he said, his voice now hoarse. "You're very hot."

My hand started stroking faster, my fist tighter, the only pauses being when I reached the top and circled his silken head with my thumb before pumping him again. I slid my nose down his and panted as I rocked my hips into his hand.

"You gonna kiss me or just tease me with that mouth?" Jake asked.

"I don't..." I stroked faster as my hips rocked harder when his thumb hit my clit. "I don't think I can kiss you, darling."

His hand moved, his finger going out, two fingers going in and his thumb pressed in and circled.

A sharp noise escaped my lips and I stroked harder as his hand at my behind gripped tight.

"Much as I like it, you're gonna have to quit, Josie. What you're doin' is magic but this is gonna be over way fuckin' soon if you don't."

I most assuredly didn't want it to be over so I slid my hand up and rolled the head with my thumb as he kept at me with his fingers and I rocked into it.

I loved what he was giving me, I loved having him right there with me, but suddenly I needed more.

"I want you inside me."

Jake moved his hand out of the back of my panties, up my spine and curled his fingers around my neck, trapping my hair under them, his thumb firm at my jaw before he said, "Gonna take you there with my fingers."

All right, well…that sounded good too.

"Okay," I panted.

"Then gonna eat you and take you there again."

Oh my.

That sounded better.

"Okay," I repeated on a shallow breath.

"Then you're gonna suck me."

Oh my.

Oh *yes*.

Oh *God*.

That sounded *the best*.

"Okay," I gasped, rocking fast as his thumb pressed deeper and circled harder.

"*Then* I'm gonna fuck you."

"Jake." I was still gasping because I was close. Oh so close. So tremendously, astounding, amazingly *close*.

"That okay?" he asked.

"Yes," I managed to breathe out and then my head would have shot back if his hand wasn't at my neck, keeping me where he could see me as I cried out, grinding into his hand, tightening mine around his cock. Everything ceased to exist but my body straddling Jake's big one, his hand between my legs, his lips brushing mine, his fingers curled around my neck, and the sensations he gave me washing through me.

When it left me, he let me rest my forehead in his neck as he kept his hand at jaw, took the pressure off my clit and his fingers glided gently through the wet folds between my legs.

"You good?" he asked softly.

"Oh yes," I answered quietly, remembering what my hand was curled around and again circling the head with my thumb.

He slid his hand from between my legs, over my hip so it could again cup my behind.

"You want some coffee before I go down on you?"

He knew I needed coffee.

So thoughtful.

So *wonderful.*

However.

"If you leave this bed, I'll be very put out."

His body shook under mine and I heard the humor in his voice when he said, "Unlatch, baby, and roll. Woke up with a taste for my woman's pussy, now it's ready for me, I'm hungry."

I shivered at his words and "unlatched," sliding my hand away from his shaft and lifting my head to look down at him.

I wanted to say something, I knew not what. *Thank you for being all that's you. Or you mean a great deal to me. Or you make me happy and I haven't been happy in decades. Or I'm delighted this is real.*

I didn't get a chance to say any of that. He put pressure on my neck, which meant he could get my mouth to his.

Then he took it as he rolled us.

After that, he set about proving that he did indeed wake up for a taste of me, but more, he was hungry.

Very.

In the end, however, it was me who was slaked.

———•◦•———

I WAS NAKED, sated, on my belly and alone in the bed.

This was because Jake was down the hall in the bathroom dealing with the condom.

I didn't like him that far away from me.

But I'd just climaxed three times, all of them extraordinary, the one when Jake's mouth was between my legs being mind-altering, I didn't have it in me to lament this. Especially since he was coming back shortly.

I sensed movement at the door and turned my eyes there to watch him walk naked down the hall, right past my door.

I blinked.

Where was he going?

Or a more pressing question, where was he going naked?

With some effort, my body much preferring to be fully reclining, I lifted up on my forearm in the bed, about to call out to Jake when something caught at the corner of my eye.

I looked to the nightstand and saw the bent, ripped foil wrapper of the condom Jake had just used.

I also saw his wallet opened and resting there.

And last, spilling out of his wallet, I saw a streamer of condoms.

I reached out and tugged at it. It came loose and I counted.

The streamer consisted of five condoms.

The used one made it six.

I grinned and stayed where I was, hoping whatever he was doing wouldn't take long (at the same time hoping it had something to do with a caffeinated hot beverage) and was pleased when Jake's large frame appeared in the doorway.

When it did, I lifted up the streamer of condoms.

His eyes dropped to it, his lips twitched and he made it to me. Tugging the condoms from between my fingers, he tossed them back to the nightstand then did something wondrous.

He entered the bed but he accomplished this at the same time he gathered me close to his big, strong body and pulled the covers over us. Only when he had us cozy, warm and settled, him on his back, me on him but also partly down his side, did I speak.

"How many hours do we have?"

He grinned at me. "Sucks but not that many. Leavin' that stash in your nightstand."

"Ah," I murmured then pressed closer and shared, "I do take birth control, Jake, and I'm healthy."

His face got soft and he replied, "Good to know, baby. But I haven't had a checkup in seven months and I haven't abstained. Except for you in the locker room, I'm all about protection and never go ungloved. Since it's gonna be just you and me, you're down with ungloved, okay. But you want me to move up my annual physical, I'm okay with that too."

Just you and me.

I *loved* that.

I lifted a hand to his jaw and told him, "You're really very wonderful."

That was when his eyes got warm and he rolled into me so we were both on our sides, Jake's thigh between my legs and he said, "You're pretty fuckin' wonderful too."

"You thinking that makes me happy," I shared.

"You bein' happy makes me happy," he returned and I pressed even deeper.

Yes, he was so…very…*wonderful.*

Jake took the cue and bent his head so he could kiss me. It was light and short but it was still sweet.

He lifted away an inch and said, "Coffee's on."

"Excellent," I murmured then noted, "That's what you did when you walked by the room."

"Yep."

"So you walked through Gran's house naked."

He grinned and his arms got tight. "Yeah. I also walked through *your* house naked."

He did indeed.

My house. Jake naked.

I licked my lips.

His arms got tighter but his face got more serious.

"I take it your shit for brains boss didn't fuck with you last night."

I shook my head. "I've heard nothing from him. And I'm not contacting him until I know what I intend to say."

"Which way you leaning?" he asked.

"I quit?" I asked back as answer.

He grinned but the grin died and he queried, "You in the position to do that?"

I nodded. "I have to meet an accountant but Gran's estate was somewhat substantial. I also have a goodly amount in savings and investments. I'll need to pay taxes on the inheritance but I believe I'll still be comfortable after that." My eyes drifted to his throat when I finished, "It's just that I don't fancy not being employed. I like to be busy. "

"And on the go," Jake stated and I lifted my gaze back to him.

"Pardon?"

"And on the go," he repeated. "Out and about. Flyin' everywhere. Rome. Paris."

"That, not so much," I murmured.

His brows drew together. "Come again?"

I held his gaze and shared, "This feels good, being at Lavender House. Being in Magdalene. There's a break, like a holiday, where you enjoy not being in your routine and you relax into another one. But in the end, you nearly always want to go back to your life. Your home. Your normal schedule. I've been here some time now, Jake, and even before Henry's ignoble visit yesterday, I knew I was going to ask him if I could do much of my job from here because it occurred to me I *am* home and want to stay."

"So you were gonna slow down anyway," he replied.

"Yes," I confirmed.

His arms got even tighter, his face softer and his eyes warmer. "Good news, Slick."

I smiled at his apparent deep satisfaction at this news and repeated, "Yes."

"You'll find something to do," he assured me.

"Yes," I said yet again.

"Now, what the fuck does ignoble mean?"

I giggled, leaned up to kiss him in the middle of it and settled back to see him smiling.

"Not honorable. Shameful," I explained.

"A lotta good things about you, honey. One of them is that Ethan's pickin' up your vocabulary. Swear to Christ, before Conner took him to school today, he said he was vexed about something and if I got it right, he used it right seein' as he was annoyed."

"He used it correctly," I confirmed, but his words troubled me. "Conner takes Ethan to school?"

"Sometimes, yeah," Jake replied. "I open the gym early so guys can get their workouts in before goin' to work. If I can't get back, Conner or Amber take him to school seein' as they both have cars."

It was then it occurred to me that he *did* have to open the gym. He also said last night he had to get to the club and he was going to do it when the kids were asleep.

"Do you often go to the club when the children are asleep?" I asked.

"Nearly every night," he answered. "Gym's runnin' in the black but barely. Wouldn't if I had to have an employee on the books so it's gotta be me who opens and closes. Con helps out with that when he has time, but he doesn't have much of it since he's got another job, I lean on him a lot already at the house and with his brother and any time he's got in between, he needs to be at his books, training or able to have some fun. Got a guy who helps me with the club but shit can go down there. It's a decent place but you gotta work at that. Can't help but attract a sleazy element no matter what you do. Shit can't happen if they know I'm comin' in and don't know when. I could be there all night if the kids are cool to be home with Eath. I can show when the night's done. They never know except for the fact that they know I'll show so if anyone wants to get up to shit, they think again."

"So, essentially, you have the same life you had before you owned the strip club, except you make more money and don't have a wife to look after your kids," I noted.

"Yeah, babe, but I got kids old enough to look after themselves and their little brother. We do all right."

"When did you go to the club last night?" I asked.

"Just after eleven."

"And when did you get home?"

"Around two."

"And then up to open the gym by seven?"

He rolled further into me so I was on my back and he was on me but also partly down my side and he dipped his face very close.

"We're cool," he told me.

"I can tell you're cool," I replied. "Outside of normal teenage stuff, your children are happy. They're healthy. They have a nice house. Rooms they like. They're fed. They clearly love you very deeply. You make certain to be available to them and spend time with them often. They know you care. You're a strict dad when you have to be but still approachable. All that is lovely. Beautiful, actually. And you don't act it, which is nice for them so they won't feel it, but it has to run you ragged."

"So what're you sayin'?" he asked, his head tipping to the side. "That I should dump the gym? 'Cause I can't dump the club. That keeps my kids in rooms they like."

"No, I'm saying that you should sleep in or feel free to get Ethan to school and I can open up the gym and sit in the office until you get in just in case someone needs something. All you have to do is show me around."

Jake said nothing.

So I did.

"It can't be hard. While I'm there, if you don't have a bookkeeper, I can do your books. I did Henry's for him. I don't have a degree or anything but I took some classes early on when I was with Henry so I could handle that for him and have answers at the ready to any questions he might have about his finances."

Jake remained silent.

Alas, I did not.

"Or I could go to the club in the evenings. I'm not a commanding presence like you but if it's known that you and I are together, they'd know I can easily report to you if something is awry or causes me concern and it might deter them from doing it. At the very least, you'd know about it and you could deter them. I'm a night owl anyway. I'd have no problem spending time in the club to keep an eye on things."

Jake continued his silence and when he did, I became concerned.

The reason why I became concerned was that he was definitely a man. A commanding man. He was confident in everything he did, including being a father.

With that, it occurred to me all I was saying might communicate that I questioned his ability to handle his enterprises, his home and his children.

So I rushed on.

"I'm not saying that you can't—"

He interrupted me with, "Quiet, Slick."

I shut my mouth.

Jake stared down at me.

He did this for some time. So much of it, I was about to squirm. Instead of squirming, I opened my mouth.

"I'm sorry. I didn't mean to insult you. That wasn't my inten—"

His hand came to my jaw, his thumb sliding out over my lips, effectively silencing me. When his thumb had made its pass, his head dropped and he brushed his mouth against mine.

That wasn't an angry reaction, thank goodness.

When he lifted away, he whispered, "Momma bear lookin' after my kids. Good woman lookin' after her man."

"Pardon?" I whispered back but I knew what he was saying and I liked it a great deal. And I knew he did too from his soft kiss.

Jake didn't answer my question.

He told me a story.

"Three, four years ago, Junior got laid off. Had trouble findin' work because the economy was in the tank and there was no work to find. Alyssa was havin' trouble too. Easy not to get your hair or nails done when disposable income has dried up. Still, she kept her shop open later and opened on days it was normally closed to give clients more opportunities to come in and see her. She didn't make a big deal about workin' that hard. She still kept their house. Cooked for them seein' as Junior was on odd jobs that had odd hours, takin' whatever work he could get to do his bit. Or he was out for interviews all over the fuckin' state. She never complained. She never rode his ass. He was outta work for nearly three years and you saw them together, you would think they were flyin' high. Sun rises in him for her. It sets in him for her too. Every morning. Every night. And she shows him that every day. He loves her for it. He'd take a bullet for her. Say her name with his last breath. 'Cause she's a good woman lookin' after her man."

When he was done talking, I had tears in my eyes.

I also decided I really, *really* liked Alyssa.

But he was not quite finished.

"Been married three times. Never had that. Not one of the women who wore my ring gave me that shit. Didn't tell me I was wonderful. Didn't offer to pitch in when shit got tight or things went south. Now, things are good, steady, it works, I've known you a coupla weeks, and you're still offering to help out even when I don't need it."

"You can't go to bed at two in the morning and get up at six thirty, Jake. Not regularly. That's not healthy," I said softly.

"Been doin' that shit for years, Josie, it's my life. I'm used to it. Doesn't bother me. I find times to get my sleep in," he replied softly. "What I like a whole fuckuva lot is that you give a shit."

I curled my arms around his back and told him, "I'm glad you like that, Jake. Very much so. But I still believe you should give me keys to the gym or introduce me around the club or both."

Before I was done, his body was shaking. When I finished, the bed was shaking. He was also smiling.

"I'm not joking," I told him.

His deep voice was shaking as well when he replied, "I know you aren't."

"So are you going to give me the keys to the gym and show me around the club?"

He was still smiling when he asked, "Are you gonna shut up about it unless I do?"

"That's unlikely."

"Then I guess I am," he said, *still* smiling.

"That would make me feel better," I told him.

"That's my job, to make you feel better," he stated but it sounded like he was teasing.

I decided to ignore that and declared, "You can pay for my assistance in orgasms."

That got no smiles.

Oh no.

He burst out laughing. He did this so hard he collapsed on me, his face in my neck and I took most of his weight.

He was very hard. Very solid. Very warm. And *very* heavy.

"Jake," I wheezed, squeezing him with my arms.

He lifted up, but did so still laughing quite boisterously.

"I was also not joking about that," I told him through his laughter, which made him drop his forehead to mine and laugh *more* boisterously.

I slapped his back lightly. He lifted up his head and his humor quieted but it didn't go away.

"You *do* give very good orgasms," I informed him.

"Heard that, felt it, watched it, babe," he said through his now-chuckling. "But I'd give you those for free."

Yes, of course he would.

I amended my negotiation. "Then you can pay me in tacos."

He held my eyes as he shook his head and his body again started shaking.

I felt my eyes narrow. "Again, I wasn't being amusing."

Suddenly, his laughter died and he replaced his hand at my jaw. Just as suddenly it seemed not only was his body on mine but his commanding presence was shrouding me, warm and snug, and last and most importantly with what was to come, safe.

"You know Lydie talked about you."

I said nothing. My heart had started beating very hard and my arms had convulsed around him without me telling them to do so.

That was still an answer and Jake heard it.

"I know about your dad. I know about what your dad did to your mom. How he did it often. I know you saw it. I know he'd call you down just to watch. I know that's fucked and I know that fucked with you."

He paused.

I braced.

He went on, "I know about Andy."

I closed my eyes and turned my head away. Even braced I was unprepared for this, but when I moved, Jake's mouth came to my ear.

"And I know about that guy."

I closed my eyes tighter.

"I'm not tellin' you this to freak you out. To hurt you. Lydie told me I figure 'cause she had to let that shit go too. She liked me, she trusted me with that and with that part of you she was givin' to me and that's an honor, baby. From her and to have that about you."

He stopped speaking and stroked my jaw with his thumb.

When I said nothing, he continued.

"I'm tellin' you this now, when you're mine, when you're *with* me, naked, close, safe, we both know we care about each other and want to build somethin' so you know I know that was it for you. You're not a practiced hand at this. You've never really had a man and I get why. I fuckin' do. Down to my gut I do, baby. And we can go there when you're ready. Right now, all you have to know is, I'll make you tacos until you can't stand lookin' at them anymore, if that's what you want and I'll do it just because you want them. The bottom line is, you look out for me, I'll look out for you. I'll make you come as often as you want. I'll make you dinner, take you to dinner, take you to New York to see your friends, fly you to Paris 'cause you wanna eat snails, I don't give a fuck. But I won't do that in return for shit you do for me. That's what you give me. The only time it'll go bad is if you don't feel you get what you need from me and get it just because."

He stopped speaking.

I remained silent.

"Do you understand that, Josie?" he asked.

I took in a breath through my nostrils, opened my eyes and turned to look at him.

All he said was lovely. Truly lovely.

Wonderful.

But what I asked was, "You know about Andy?"

"Yeah, baby," he answered gently.

"Do you know what happened after dad found—"

Jake cut me off. "That he put you in the hospital. Yeah."

I pressed my lips together and rolled them.

"Know Lydie reported her son to CPS and got custody of you when that happened too," he said.

Gran *did* tell him about me.

All about me.

I could do nothing but nod.

He kept speaking.

"Know you spent your senior year at St. Michael's. A good school. Private. Just girls. Safe for you. Close so you could be with Lydie."

I nodded again.

He continued.

"Know you went to college and met a supreme asshole."

My heart jumped.

"Can we not talk about that part now?" I asked in a feeble voice.

His thumb swept my jaw again. "Yeah, honey."

"You're right. I've never been in a relationship. Not, well…since then," I confirmed.

He instantly replied, "And you know I don't have a good track record so we'll both be findin' our way."

I held his eyes, liking that, liking how he didn't make me feel strange or weak for the decisions I'd made or the life I'd led.

And I most assuredly wanted to find the way with Jake.

My gaze drifted to his shoulder and I went back on what I asked earlier.

"I found my dad in him," I shared.

"I know," he replied quietly.

"Not Andy," I stated to make certain he understood. "He was lovely before. He was lovely after. He called. He even wrote. But I couldn't go back."

"I know."

"The other one," I said even though I knew he knew who I was talking about.

"Yeah," he whispered.

"I was worried that was all I'd ever find."

"I get that."

It was then, what he'd said the night we became lovers made sense to me.

"So I put on a disguise so I'd be hidden, in a way, and never find anything."

He kept stroking my jaw and whispering, "Yeah. That's what you did. And you know what I love?"

What he loved?

Loved?

My heart skipped another beat for a very different reason as my eyes shifted to his.

"What do you love, Jake?"

"I love that you shed that disguise watchin' me fight. That whatever broke through for you broke through then. Bein' there for me, watchin' me do somethin' I've always loved to do. I know you didn't wanna go but you went for me. After, you still walk the walk and talk the talk, baby, but since you pulled your panties down for me and took my cock against that wall, all I got is you. All the kids got is you. We had you before but I feel the difference and it's not about havin' you here with me, naked in your bed. It's just havin' *you.* Laughin' and gettin' up in Mia's face in your way and bein' there for Amber when she's excited about a boy and bein' happy and showin' that

I give that to you. You're willin' to take a chance on this. Work on it with me. Takin' that shot for the first time in years. With me. That's what I love."

When he was done speaking, my eyes were again wet so his hand moved and his thumb swept my cheekbone as if preparing to catch the tears should they fall.

"Don't be pissed at Lydie for sharing," he ordered gently.

I shook my head, unable to come to terms with that part of this conversation with Jake warm and close and being more than his usual wonderful.

"I suppose her doing it means I don't have to relive it," I noted.

And I didn't want to relive it.

Gran had managed to give me that too.

But it was me who took a lot of me away and my eyes drifted back to his shoulder when I noted, "I've lost a lot of life to that disguise, Jake."

The pads of his fingers put pressure on my face and when he got my gaze back, he replied, "You're livin' it now, Josie. But can you seriously look back and say you didn't have a full life before, with all you've done, the people you know, the places you've been?"

I shook my head again.

"No," he agreed then smiled. "It's just that now you got more."

Now I had more.

So much more.

"Is this what Gran wanted for us, do you think?" I asked.

I watched something shift in Jake's eyes before his hand slid down to my neck, his thumb started stroking my throat and he answered firmly, "Yes."

"So you think wherever she is, she's happy?"

Another firm, "Yes."

I thought so too, I liked that thought, actually loved it, so I relaxed underneath him. "Good."

It seemed like he was going to say something but then he didn't. He bent in and touched his mouth to mine. Then he did it again. And again. Then he touched his mouth to mine but didn't pull it away because he was kissing me.

As he did, he rolled me so I was on top.

At that point, I kissed him.

After a while, we rolled again so I was on bottom.

And at that point, Jake again took over the kiss.

He ended it by trailing his lips down to my neck where he murmured, "Thank fuck I brought a bunch of condoms."

I was okay with him going "ungloved."

I had a feeling the way he looked out for me though, he wasn't.

But two seconds later, when I felt his hardness pressed against my thigh, his hand closed over my breast and his mouth came to mine, I wasn't thinking about condoms.

I wasn't thinking at all.

Not about anything (not even coffee).

Nothing.

Except Jake.

I WAS IN the garden and I didn't have a lot of time.

September was moving swiftly toward October and I needed the dead plants out, the soil fertilized and turned in order to put it to rest for winter.

I was thinking I'd plant tomatoes in the coming spring. Corn. Potatoes. Pumpkins.

Yes, definitely pumpkins. Ethan might like having a pumpkin from my garden to carve for Halloween.

Jake had left after I made us sandwiches for lunch. He'd been gone half an hour. It was nearing on one. Time was running out.

The garden had seemed a great deal smaller when I'd helped Gran work it years ago. Now it seemed rather large. There was no way I was going to get what I needed to get done that day.

I'd have to do what I didn't get done tomorrow.

This was because I had to be at Alyssa's for my freebie mani-pedi at three, before that I had to pick Ethan up from school. Then drinks afterward. Which meant I needed to look presentable.

I definitely needed to look presentable later. When I picked Ethan up from Alyssa's, Jake said I should stay for dinner at his place since I was going with him to the club after. This was so he could show me the lay of the land "should you hang there and keep an eye on it for me" (this last said with lips quirking like this would never happen and he was humoring me).

But I *was* going to hang there and keep an eye on it for him. He had way too many responsibilities. He didn't think it was true, but he needed my assistance.

I'd show him how much better it was when "his woman" looked after him.

On this thought, I yanked out a dead corn stalk but did it smiling.

My smile froze when I heard, "Josephine."

My head snapped up and I saw Henry standing outside the white fence that surrounded the garden.

Unlike yesterday, when I didn't have the time to make the comparison, today I did.

And I saw what I'd been seeing for decades. That Henry Gagnon was tall, dark and handsome. He had lovely thick hair that seemed immune to gray (and I knew he didn't dye it) and strong facial features that were most striking.

But not like Jake. Henry's looks were smoother, more refined.

It must be said that of the men of our acquaintance, Henry had an edge.

But that edge was nowhere near as sharp as Jake's.

He looked me from top to toe and his blank face turned into a blank mask. The difference was a nuance but I knew him well enough to see it. I also knew what it meant.

He got that look when the person he was addressing annoyed him and he wanted them to know they mattered little to him, if anything at all.

However, that look had never, not once, been aimed at me.

"Henry," I said, traversing the rough ground in Gran's wellies to get closer to him. Once I did, I stopped on my side of the fence and held his eyes, my look for him doubtfully a mask. I didn't care that he knew I was annoyed at him. "I'm uncertain I'm ready to speak with you."

"I leave in the morning to get to Paris," he replied. "Amond allowed a day's delay in the shoot so I could come and spend some time with you. I don't have more. We have to do this now or over the phone and I'd rather do it now."

This explained Amond's strange statements during our phone call. He knew Henry was coming.

He also knew I was going to watch men fighting and had guessed this was because those men were interested in me.

Thus, I was more than mildly annoyed that he didn't warn me Henry was intending to pay a surprise visit.

However, I couldn't think on that.

I could only think on the limited possibilities of what had to be said between Henry and me face to face.

"If you have something to say, Henry, then please say it. I have work to finish in the garden and then I need to get to the school and pick up Ethan. I've plans with a friend after that and I'm spending the evening with Jake and the kids. So I don't have a great deal of time either."

The mask slipped, only slightly but it did it before he said curtly, "Spending the evening with Jake and his kids."

"Yes," I confirmed.

"Do you think perhaps that the local strip club owner knows your grandmother was a millionaire?" he asked and that wasn't curt. It was borderline snide.

My back went up and my skin prickled.

"If you're insinuating Jake's interested in me only for Gran's money, that's both erroneous and insulting. And your spiteful tone in regards to Jake's business concerns is offensive. He runs a very respectable club. Now, is that what you came here to say to me face to face?"

He ignored my question and asked, "Are there respectable strip clubs?"

"Jake's is," I returned. "Now, if this is what you wish to discuss, you made the journey to Lavender House in vain. I've no desire to talk about this."

"That isn't why I'm here."

I said not a word but held his eyes.

His jaw clenched before he released it to announce, "I've spoken with Daniel. He's phoned a company in LA who will be packing all your belongings in the pool house. These will be shipped to you express. You'll have them by the end of the week at the latest. Daniel's also agreed to come on board as my assistant officially. I'll give you six month's severance. This will be transferred into your account within two days. Your paperwork will arrive at Lavender House within that timeframe. You'll need to sign it and return it at your earliest convenience."

I felt not a small amount of pressure building in my head.

"So you're sacking me because I've met a man," I stated.

"I'm severing our professional relationship because it's no longer constructive."

"And it's no longer constructive because you're in love with me, never had the courage to do anything about it, I found a man I care about and you're having a tantrum. And as you hold some power over me, the tantrum you're having is negating my employment."

His expression didn't change. Not even a hint.

"You're a millionaire, Josephine, and the severance package is fair."

"I believe a severance package of a month's wages for every year I've worked for you is more fair, Henry," I returned, simply to be vexing mostly because he was vexing *me*.

"Then I'll ask Daniel to change the amount and the wording in the paperwork," Henry replied instantly.

That was when I felt the shot to the heart. The pierce of the arrow so excruciating it was a wonder I didn't stagger back.

Wounded pride. Again.

But this time, the return arrow was directed at me.

"And this is it?" I asked.

"This is it," he confirmed.

"Twenty-three years at your side and you hand me as much money as I ask for and walk away."

He didn't delay even a moment with his response.

"Yes."

For the third time that day, tears stung my eyes but they weren't good tears, overwhelmed by emotion of hearing a lovely story about a lovely woman or the gentle words from a man I was growing to feel very deeply about.

These were bad tears, overwhelmed by the emotions of loss and betrayal.

"Tears are hardly necessary, Josephine," Henry said dismissively. "We were simply photographer and assistant."

"Outside of Gran, for twenty-three years, you were the only real thing I had."

The mask again slipped but he got it back in place swiftly.

But he said nothing.

I did.

"I've hurt you and done that simply by realizing the possibility I might find happiness and reaching for it and you strike back like this?"

"I'm uncertain what kind of happiness you can find with a small town strip club owner in the middle of nowhere in Maine but if that's what you want, Josephine, you now have a clear shot."

He was giving me a clear shot.

A clear shot by taking himself away.

"My first living memory is my father slamming my mother's head against the kitchen floor."

It came out as blunt and ugly as it was. And when it hit him, the mask disintegrated and Henry flinched so severely, his head jerked back with it.

"Some time later, she left us, never to return. Some time after that, when he discovered I was dating a boy without his permission, he beat me so badly I was in the hospital for a week."

Another wince and, "Josephine—"

"Gran saved me from that. I managed to become normal again. I went to college. Fell in love. He was controlling, this was true, but he was handsome and he cared about me. I thought. Until the first time he beat me. I fell down a flight of stairs and broke my shoulder. I came back to Gran after that too."

His hand came out but I took a step away.

"Did you ever wonder why I was so remote, Henry?"

"Honey—"

"Did you ever think to ask?"

"Jo—"

"No. You didn't. I was so in love with you when we first started working together, every day held pain. But it was put up with the pain or lose one of only two people in my life I cared about and respected. So I put up with the pain."

His face had blanched. "You were in love with me?"

"Head over heels."

His voice was aching when he whispered, "Sweetheart—"

"To find you were the same and you didn't even *ask* why I was protecting myself. Why I was aloof. Why I was disconnected. Didn't even *attempt* to find a way in. I never thought for one moment you returned those feelings because…because…I don't know why you did it but you never, not once, gave me any indication that you felt that way for me. You gave many other women that indication, right in front of me, but never me."

"I showed you all the time, Josephine," he said gently.

"No." I shook my head. "Jake did. He knew all that about me and he knew he had to proceed with caution but the point is he realized he liked me, he was attracted to me and he *proceeded*."

"I'm afraid he had an unfair advantage, honey, because I didn't know any of this shit," Henry pointed out.

"You…didn't"—I leaned in— "*ask*," I hissed and I leaned back. "Two decades and you didn't ask, Henry?"

"How was I to know there was something to ask about, Josephine?"

"If you love someone, you want to know everything. You want to heal all hurts. You want to be there for them when they need you. You just want to be with them all the time."

"Are you saying you're in love with a man you've known two weeks?"

"No, Henry. I'm saying that's what I gave you for twenty-three years."

I watched him flinch again. He knew it was true. Every word of it.

He recovered and inquired, "How do you press something like that with someone you employ? Someone that matters. Someone that, if you don't get it right, you could lose and you know you can't lose."

"I don't know. Maybe you do it because it's worth the risk of whatever might become of it."

"I'll remind you, sweetheart, you felt the same way and you didn't take that risk either," he said softly.

He was right.

Absolutely right.

"I was afraid," I told him.

"I understand that now. I could have no idea then."

He was right about that too.

I looked to the dirt at my feet.

"Josephine," Henry called and my eyes went back to him.

"It wasn't meant to be," I stated.

"How can we know that if we haven't tried?" he asked.

"Because I'm falling in love with a man I've only known two weeks but even falling, I already know I can't imagine what a day would be like without him. No," I shook my head as Henry's face started getting hard again. "I can imagine it. I just don't want to."

"I'm not certain he's right for you," he told me.

"And I'm not certain you would be, saying something like that when you don't know him in the slightest."

"I know we had our words yesterday, Josephine, they were unpleasant, he was there throughout, and he didn't intervene for you once," he pointed out.

"You're right. He didn't. But then again, you were my employer, had been for years, I'm a forty-five year old woman and it really wasn't his place to intervene. However, when I was overcome by emotion after that scene *that* was when Jake intervened, holding me in his arms, stroking my hair and talking to me to soothe me."

"So this guy is perfect," Henry stated disbelievingly and perhaps a little sarcastically.

"Not at all," I told him. "He's ludicrously protective and preposterously overbearing. He's also got this thing where he selects my seat for me, usually next to him, and does this by planting me in it. He can be very dictatorial and it isn't infrequent when he is. He laughs when I'm being serious and bellows from wherever he is in the house at wherever the person he's talking to is. He also uses curse words frequently, even in front of his children, and allows them to do the same, especially his eldest son, this latter I intend to have words with him about very soon. I'm certain he has other bad habits that I'll discover, given the chance. The thing that makes me happy is that I have that chance."

"So it's you giving up on us," Henry noted.

"No, it's me saying that we had our time, that time passed. We both made that mistake. And now it's me moving on. I didn't drive here to fire me, Henry. You did."

"Knowing how I feel about you, can you work alongside me? And if you care about me, can you honestly wish to do that while making me watch you fall in love with another man?"

"No, I intended to resign," I told him honestly. "However, I had hoped to do it and salvage a relationship with someone I love very deeply who means a great deal to me. I just hadn't come up with how to do that yet."

He said nothing but held my gaze.

I did the same.

Henry was the first one to break the silence.

"Fuck, I should have come to Lydia's funeral with you," he clipped tersely.

He should have.

He really should have.

But he didn't.

And if he did, I would not have Jake.

Or Amber.

Or Ethan.

Or Conner.

So I said nothing.

"I fucked us up," he whispered and the way he did made my anger fade but my pain increase.

"We both did," I said quietly.

"You had no choice with your past the way it was. I did."

I couldn't argue that.

"I fucked us up," he repeated and I moved to him and put my hand on his chest.

"Stop it, Henry."

"Twenty-three years, I'd look forward to you walking into my hotel room every morning with a coffee, sweetheart. Daniel's nowhere near as attractive as you and completely the wrong gender. He sends it up through room service."

I closed my eyes and dropped my head to rest it on my hand on his chest.

Oh, how I loved walking into Henry's hotel room with a coffee every morning. The smile he'd give me. We'd sit down and chat, about the work to be done that day, where we were going, what was next, or nothing at all.

And he'd always make me laugh.

Now, looking back, knowing what I knew, I realized he worked for it, worked to give that to me.

Every morning.

His hand lifted and wrapped around the back of my neck and that felt nice and warm in the crisp autumn air. Strong. Sweet. Lovely.

With his lips at my hair, he said, "You find your way to salvage our relationship, you tell me. Then we'll do it."

I moved closer and wished the fence wasn't between us as I turned my head so I could press my cheek to his chest.

His hand gave my neck a squeeze and his lips were still at my hair when he said, "This is killing me, honey, so I must go."

I nodded, my cheek sliding against his shirt and I started to move back because I didn't want to hurt Henry. Not ever.

And I had.

Unintentionally but I'd still done it.

So I had to stop doing that.

But I stopped when Henry's hand at my neck put pressure on.

I tipped my head back to see Henry's descending.

And then he kissed me. Not a chaste brush on the lips. His mouth opened over mine and for some reason, mine opened under his and his tongue slid inside.

He tasted very nice. He kissed very well. I was not surprised at either. He was Henry and almost everything about him was good, but as for the latter, he'd had a lot of practice.

But it didn't fire me the way it should have. The way it could have. The way I knew it would have, even only three weeks ago.

Because I'd had Jake that morning, his mouth, his hands, his body, and he gave so much even while taking, nothing could compare.

Nothing.

Not even Henry.

He lifted his lips from mine and looked in my eyes.

He saw it because I didn't hide it.

His voice was again an ache when he murmured, "Fuck, I fucked us up."

My throat closed and I could do nothing but step away.

His hand dropped away when I did.

My eyes again filled with tears when it did.

How could it be that I felt with Jake like I was getting everything and at that moment knowing Henry was walking away, knowing Gran was gone, it felt like I'd lost everything?

"I wish for you to be happy," he said gently and I swallowed, the tears now stinging my eyes. "I truly do."

"I hope you're happy too."

My throat started aching as Henry tipped his head to the side and said, "Good-bye, my Josephine."

"Good-bye, Henry," I forced out.

He smiled. It was sad. It was adrift.

It gutted me.

Then he walked away.

───

I SUNK MY feet into the tub filled with warm water and bubbles.

The instant I did, Alyssa said, "Okay, honey, tell momma all about it."

My surprised eyes went to her.

It was obviously after Henry left. After I gave up on the garden, went inside and saw I had a flurry of very verbose texts from Alyssa explaining how things would go with Ethan, Bryant and Sofie.

It was after I dropped Ethan off, he raced away with Bryant, I met Sofie (learning that Sofie was the oldest, Bryant the youngest and there were *three* in between). It was further after I saw that Sofie was a younger, shier, quieter Alyssa and noted in the five minutes I was with her she was very sweet.

And it was after Alyssa swept us out to her car. After she'd driven us into town and parked behind her shop. After she let us in, turned on lights and got the pedicure chair prepared. After I'd taken in her shop, which looked not one thing like a Maude's House of Beauty, but instead like a rather posh spa you could find in New York, Los Angeles or even Paris. It was decorated in gold, silver and cream with modern lights hanging from the ceiling with a multitude of crystal lightshades that cast prisms that were very attractive.

It was after all that I looked to her, saw her looking at me with warm concern in her brown eyes and she stated, "I'm drowning in bitches all day, been doin' that shit for years. I know a face like that when I see one. So tell me."

It was then I lifted my hands, covered my face and burst into tears.

I did this for some time before a large bunch of tissues was pressed into the hand she'd pulled away from my face and I turned teary eyes to her.

"Tell me," she urged.

I didn't know why, maybe it was her tone, the kindly look in her eyes, the things Jake told me about her.

But I did.

I wiped my face, blew my nose and told her.

Everything.

I told her how my grandfather treated my grandmother. How my father and uncle did the same as they grew up, in their way, doing precisely what they learned to do from their father. Disrespecting her. Verbally abusing her. Getting into trouble. Carousing. Making her life that was already a living hell much worse. And not giving a damn. Never giving a damn.

I told her of my first living memory with my mother and father and a few more besides.

I told her about Andy. How wonderful he was. How he was the best first boyfriend in the world. How he seemed to understand my father was awful and how he tried in many marvelous ways to make up for that. How he was so gentle with me. How he was so careful in keeping our relationship a secret. How I heard from my friend Alicia that after my father had hurt me, he'd gone quite mad and the police had to come and get him after he broke into my father's house and was shouting at him and destroying things.

I told her how that ended and how my relationship with my father ended.

I told her about how I left Andy behind.

I told her about Gran. How she saved me, took care of me, made me whole again.

I told her about going to university, being carefree and happy and meeting a charismatic, handsome fellow student, falling in love and moving in with him after we graduated.

I told her how he then cowed me, scared me with his temper, and finally beat me.

I told her about how I escaped again to Gran, found Henry, put on my disguise and lived my lie.

I told her about Gran dying, the will, Gran giving me to Jake, and Jake taking me.

And last, I told her all that had happened since then, with Jake, with Jake and Mickey, with Jake and Henry, finishing with my heartbreaking meeting with Henry just hours before.

Through this, she worked on my feet, she worked on my nails and she listened. A woman, who in our limited communications would barely let me get a word in edgewise, said nothing but a few "okays," "mm-hmms," "shits," "holy craps," and the like.

But when I was done, she looked me right in the eye and stated, "Sister, that is one helluva crazy fucked up story."

And strangely, her saying that, her seeing it that way, her confirming what I knew to be true in my heart seemed profound. So profound it opened something inside me that felt like it shone out, starting to burn away the last vestiges of my disguise.

"And hearing that makes you more legend than you were before," she went on.

What she said before felt nice.

That, however, confused me.

"Pardon?" I asked.

"Girl, your dad bein' that big a dick, your mom takin' off on you, your first man fucking you over that huge?" she asked, shook her head and kept speaking. "That'd break a lot of women. Especially that shit happening since freaking birth. Even before, you knowin' your grandmother lived that same life. Fuckin' crazy. But you?" More shaking of the head. "Didn't break you. You got yourself a fancy-assed job trotting around the globe hobnobbing with the coolest of the cool, soaking in all that style and turning it back on the world. You freakin' rock."

"But…um…" I stammered. "Don't you think it's rather weak that I hid and didn't—?"

"Babelicious, we all do what we gotta do to survive. You survived on designer dresses, first class plane tickets, champagne and caviar." She grinned at me. "I think you did all right."

I hadn't thought of it like that.

And thinking about it like that, it occurred to me that I actually did.

"Mrs. Malone, totally the shit," she stated. "Giving you to Jake in her will?" She shook her head, her lips curved up. "Always knew that old broad had it goin' on. Didn't know she *totally* had it going on."

"This is true," I said on a grin.

Alyssa winked at me then looked back at my nails.

"Sucks what happened with that Henry guy, though," she continued. "I mean, I'm sad for both of you, all that unrequited love for *years*. It's like one of those messed up art house movies that you think is going to be this epic love story but ends with no one getting what they wanted and makes you want to go straight to the bar after the movie and down a dozen shots of vodka to forget you saw that shit."

"That *is* what it makes me feel like doing," I confirmed and smiled at her when she looked up from polishing my nails. "But a mani-pedi from a kind woman who's a good listener might be better," I finished quietly.

She gave me a soft look that made her prettiness even prettier before she noted, "What's even better is that I'm gettin' that vodka in you after this shit dries."

"Yes, that's even better," I agreed.

She again focused on painting my nails.

So I said to the back of her head, "Although I'm much looking forward to that, I don't relish telling Jake what happened with Henry today."

When I did, her head snapped back and I saw her eyes were huge and definitely her voice was shrill when she cried, "*Say what?*"

"I…uh…well, don't relish telling Jake what happened with Henry this afternoon."

She shook her head in short shakes like she was trying to clear it even as she shoved the varnish brush back into the bottle. Then her gaze locked on mine.

"Sister, you cannot tell Jake any of that shit."

I felt my brows draw together. "Why not?"

"Why not?" she asked back incredulously.

I nodded.

"Because, girl, he's Jake Spear."

This didn't explain her words or reaction for I knew he was Jake Spear and I was still confused.

"Alyssa—" I began but she cut me off, rolling her little stool even closer to my side.

"Listen to me, Josie. You haven't had a man in a while and the ones you had before were first class asswipes so you don't get this. But when you got a man, that man bein' Jake Spear, you do not inform him that the hot guy who's been in love with you for decades came to your home and lowered the boom when he was not around to look after you. You *definitely* do not tell him that hot guy laid one on you. Not when it's fresh. Not five years down the line. Not *ever*."

I didn't think this was good advice, not with Jake. He was very open and candid and in being so, I would assume, would appreciate the same.

So I said, "I'm uncertain Jake would like me keeping that from him."

She shook her head. "Babelicious, I'm gonna tell you a story 'cause Junior's cut from the same cloth as Jake. Now, it happens we go out for a drink and I might have a guy look at me. And it happens that one will approach, not givin' a shit I got a kickass rock my man gave me on my finger. This happens when Junior isn't close by because if he is, that shit *never* happens. But if he's around, say, comin' back from the john, and he sees it, I get that guy gone and I do it quick and when Junior asks me what's up, I say the guy was askin' for the time. Or if I knew the score of the game. Or whatever. I do *not* tell him the guy was comin' onto me. If I did, Junior would stalk his ass, whip his ass and then I'd be scrapin' together money to pay for his bail."

This news was alarming on a variety of fronts.

"You lie to your husband?" I asked.

"Abso-freakin'-lutely."

How odd.

"Do you think Jake would seek Henry out?" I inquired.

"Abso-freakin'-lutely."

Good God.

"But Henry's flying to Paris tomorrow," I told her.

"He'd have to go to the fuckin' moon to get away from a pissed off Jake Spear who learned that guy paid you surprise visit number two, was an asshole again and that conversation ended in a kiss. Won't matter to him that kiss went nowhere because you're all about Jake. Right or wrong, a man like that takes a woman as his woman, she…is…*his* and *no one* goes there. I don't care if you and that Henry guy were unrequited lovers since you were fifteen and learned what sex was by sneakin' a watch of *Blue Lagoon*. They *definitely* don't blindside her with a nasty confrontation. He might have let shit play out between you and this guy once, allowing you to handle it. That guy instigates a part two,"—another shake of the head—"unh-unh."

"He *has* asked quite frequently if Henry's been in touch since that first time," I confided.

367

"I bet," she replied.

"And when he ordered me to break my date with Mickey, he stood right in front of me with his hand on my neck when I did it."

"I bet he did that too."

I bit my lip for these things gave credence to her advice.

Alyssa didn't bit her lip. She spoke.

"He asks you if that guy's been in touch, you say no. Later, you tell him Henry phoned and it's over between you two. You *never* tell him about that kiss. *Ever.* You hearin' me?"

I nodded my head.

I was hearing her.

Her face softened and she kept speaking.

"Honey, I'll tell you this straight, a woman's got it in her to handle a guy like Jake, like Junior, the reward…*shoo-ee.*" Yet another shake of her head. "Nothin' better. They don't give as good as they get. They get what they get and give better. Knock themselves out doin' it. Work themselves in the ground doin' it. You give it good, he'll rock your world and do it again and again."

That sounded marvelous and I knew it to be true since Jake was already doing that.

However, Alyssa wasn't finished.

"But as that's happening, you gotta learn to *handle* him. The way you look, the way you dress, the way you are…sister, Jake's all that and I'm pretty sure he knows he's got the full package, that don't mean he isn't gonna know he's got it good with you. And he won't want anyone turnin' their eye to you and he'll make sure that doesn't happen. He dealt with Mickey"—she lifted a hand and gave a sharp snap of her fingers—"*gone.* They're friends, he saw he had competition and he swiped you right out from under him and did it *fast.* Now, what would he do to keep you from a famous hotshot photographer? And what would he do if he thought this guy was harming you in any way or makin' a play?"

"Hmm," I mumbled.

"Hmm is right," she agreed.

"I'll think on this," I told her.

"You think on it hard. You still got feelings for this Henry guy and he has the same for you and he doesn't like Jake for you for more than just that he wants you for himself. Jake finds him and rips him a new asshole. What's this Henry guy gonna do?"

I saw her point.

She leaned into me and her voice lowered when she repeated, "Learn to *handle* him. Do your part to keep it good. Yeah?"

"Uh…yes," I haltingly agreed because although I saw her point, and it was a good point, I was still uncertain.

However, seeing as she was very certain, I decided agreement was my best option for now.

"Jesus, now *I* need a drink. And bad," she announced, pulling the brush back out of the bottle of varnish. "Let's get you finished up and get our asses to some vodka."

"Alyssa," I called as she stroked a perfect brush of a very attractive wine color on my forefinger.

She looked up at me. "Yeah?"

"Thank you for listening."

Her eyes lit and her lips smiled. "Anytime, honey."

"If you…well, anytime for you too, I hope you know."

"Oh," she started, tipping her attention back to my nail, "I'll take you up on that. Junior does my head in. My hooligans do my head in. And I got a lot of good friends and a lot of good clients but most of them got big mouths." She finished with my forefinger and looked back to me. "I'm guessin' you know how to keep a secret."

"I do," I assured her.

"Then I just slotted you right up high on my Gotta Find a Sister to Bitch at List."

I liked the idea of being high on that list, so I smiled.

She turned her attention to my thumb. "Anyway, finally got someone to sit with at the matches. And that's *awesome*."

It was.

It was indeed.

All of it.

Especially Alyssa.

"BUT DO NOT, under any circumstances, get the Brazilian blowout. They use formaldehyde. You must get the keratin treatment," I said to Paulette, the blonde dancer at Jake's club, sitting next to her at a dressing table in the dressing room during her break. "Alyssa at Maude's House of Beauty has informed me she does keratin treatments. They're more expensive but they'll leave your hair shiny, very soft and actually treat the hair to make it stronger."

"And this will make it sleek?" Paulette asked.

"Perhaps too sleek," I told her. "It'll be a risk. If you prefer more body, discuss that with Alyssa. But yes. It will leave it quite straight and very sleek. And you'll find your preparation time cut by half, at least."

"It takes me for-freaking-ever to blow out my hair," she murmured.

"Then perhaps you should try it. And anyway, when you do that move with your head and your hair swings out, imagine how it will catch the light with some shine and settle down your back. I would guess it would be quite magnificent."

She grinned at me. "Yeah, that would look awesome."

It would indeed.

I smiled back.

A sharp knock sounded on the door and then Jake's voice could be heard calling, "Man entering the room!"

"Okay!" Paulette called back then leaned into me, pulling her robe closer around her so it was no longer gaping, exposing her rather abundant and totally nude cleavage. "He's the only guy here who does that. "

I felt my brows draw together. "But he's already seen your charms."

"Yeah, he's seen my *charms*, like, a million times," she agreed on a giggle. "Still, he does it. It's cool. And sweet. The other guys just walk in like it's all the same to them, even though Jake's always up in their shit not to do it. If he isn't around, forget it."

I found this didn't surprise me. Jake *was* cool.

And sweet.

And further, Jake should know his employees weren't following orders.

"Yo," Jake greeted as I had this thought and I turned from Paulette to see him moving through the rather cluttered dressing room, his eyes going between us.

Obviously, I was at the club. And I was in the dressing room because after Jake showed me around, introduced me to the bouncers, waitresses and bartenders, one of the bouncers told him he had a call and he left me at the bar with a martini to go to his office and take it.

I watched the show for a bit but saw Paulette duck to the back and thus I decided that since I would be around and often, I'd take my chance, introduce myself to her and share about the benefits of a keratin treatment.

Therefore, I followed her to the dressing room.

And now here we were.

"Take it you met Paulette," Jake said to me as he stopped close to us.

"Yes," I replied.

"Your babe is awesome, Jake," Paulette put in and that felt nice so I smiled at her again.

"As are you," I told her.

She gave me a huge grin. Then she stood, shirked off her robe, exposing her fabulous, toned, tanning bed tanned, oiled body and strutted to the door, saying, "Time to shake it. Later."

"Later, Paulette, lovely to meet you," I called after her.

"Back at cha, babe," she replied on a wink before she went out the door.

I looked up at Jake.

"You tell her to straighten her hair?" he asked.

"I did extend that advice," I answered.

He grinned and shook his head before he bent, grabbed my hand and pulled me out of the chair, murmuring, "Your martini's warm. Gotta get you another one."

I said nothing as I followed him for I had nothing to say. Another martini sounded lovely and I definitely did not like warm vodka.

Jake held my hand as we moved through the club and he seated me at the side of the bar. Only then did he let me go before he slid between the stools to stand close and jerked up his chin to the bartender (the same one from the last time I was there, his name was Adam). In very little time, a fresh martini was placed in front of me as was a fresh bottle of beer for Jake.

He picked it up and took a tug.

I did the same but took a sip.

When I put my glass down, Jake got closer and I looked up to him as he leaned into the bar on a forearm and his hand came to the small of my back, slid under the hem of my sweater and up so he could trail his fingers in a lazy pattern on the skin there.

I touched my tongue to my bottom lip in reaction to how nice that felt.

Through the dim light, I saw Jake's eyes drop to my mouth and he leaned in closer, his fingers ceasing their trailing and pressing into the waistband of my trousers.

His head dipped close and I knew he was going to say something, something that I'd like, something that might make the tingles I was experiencing in a variety of places get stronger.

But for some reason, I spoke before him.

"Dinner was lovely, thank you."

He grinned. "It was just cheeseburgers, babe."

It was. With Velveeta slices. I was finding Velveeta was a staple at the Spear house. I was also finding I didn't mind this. They melted rather well on a thick, hot hamburger and quite enhanced the taste.

"Seems like Conner's in good spirits," I noted for it did. He'd arrived after his shift at Wayfarer's and behaved like the dramas of the day before hadn't occurred.

"He's suckin' it up and beatin' it down," Jake replied. "He's not over it. He's just not gonna let that show."

My brows drew together. "Why on earth not?"

"Because he's a guy, he's his father's son and he's got no choice."

"He's safe to feel the way he feels around his family, certainly," I remarked.

"He is," Jake agreed. "But no purpose in draggin' everybody down, especially Ethan. He needs me, he knows I'm there. But only choice he's got is to keep on keepin' on. He knows that. He'll get over it. He knows that too. We just gotta cut him some slack and let him handle it the way he sees fit."

This seemed a sound strategy so I nodded.

Then I informed him, "The men in your employ walk into the dancers' dressing room without knocking."

He stared at me only a second before he shook his head and murmured, "Little shits."

"I'm uncertain from Paulette's recounting of this that she really cares. However, she does feel it's sweet you show that respect."

"I'll have a word with the boys"—he paused— "*again*. But it'll be a stronger word this time."

I leaned into him and repeated, "I daresay she doesn't care, Jake. But—"

Jake interrupted me. "They got a job, they do it. Onstage. That doesn't make them free-for-alls. Back there is their space. They feel safe in it. They decide who they show themselves to, not my boys. She might not give a shit but I do. If my boys who work with them can't show respect, how do I communicate the customers should?"

"An excellent point," I stated.

Jake grinned.

I inquired, "Can I ask you a question?"

"You can ask me anything, Slick."

I nodded again.

Then I wondered if I should do what I was going to do.

I looked into Jake's eyes that were looking right into mine and thought of all he'd shared with me in a very short period of time. He didn't hold back. He didn't hide. He didn't prevaricate. He wanted me to know him and he set about doing that from the start.

Thus I felt safe in feeling there was nothing between us except what we hadn't yet gotten around to sharing.

And I was relatively certain (*relatively*) that he wanted nothing between us.

That said, in making it so nothing was between us, I would have to "handle" it.

And do it wisely.

"Okay, then, as a hypothetical," I started carefully, held his eyes but licked my lips for a different reason this time, then went on. "Say something happened that I knew you would not like. If that should occur, is it better not to tell you, since I know you wouldn't like it? Or should I tell you because you're quite candid and wish for that to be returned?"

When I finished speaking, his bearing had not changed but it had.

Tremendously.

And not in a good way.

Apparently, I wasn't doing very well in "handling" this.

"What happened?" he asked, his voice terse.

"I'm talking hypothetical," I reminded him and I was.

I also wasn't.

"What happened?" he repeated.

"Jake—" I started but got nothing more out.

His fingers disappeared from my waistband and wrapped around my hand. Then I was off the barstool and being dragged though the club.

The door to his office was at the side of the club and he took me directly there. There was a keypad that unlocked the door and when we arrived, without delay, he lifted his finger so he could jab in the numbers.

The keypad screen went green and Jake pushed open the door.

We'd been in there earlier and I'd noted his office was rather roomy and also quite nice. There was a thick rug on the floor with an attractive pattern on it in blues, blacks and beiges but mostly reds. A plush black leather couch against one wall. Midnight blue leather chairs in front of his large but not too large wooden desk.

There weren't a lot of accoutrements, it was clear he didn't spend a great deal of time there, and when he did, it was for business only, and thus he didn't bother with the décor. But he had still made it a nice space.

It was also four steps up so that the large one-way window that faced the club had an elevated view so it would not be obstructed by patrons.

It was further mostly soundproofed. Not entirely, the music could be heard, but once the door closed, it was significantly muted.

This was what happened right then. The door latched behind us, the music was drowned out, and Jake pulled me up the stairs and across the rug to the front of his desk. He positioned me there facing it, and dropped my hand so he could stand in front of me, back to his desk, and cross his arms on his chest.

When he'd done that, he repeated, "What happened?"

"You left our drinks at the bar, Jake," I told him and I had to admit it was to buy time. He was making me somewhat anxious.

"What...*happened?*" he again repeated.

I studied him a long moment (buying more time, it must be said) then began, "First, can I just say that Alyssa told me that I shouldn't—"

Jake interrupted me. "Babe, what works for Alyssa, and I'm guessin' the way this is goin', Alyssa and how things are with her and Junior, is not us. We are not Alyssa and Junior. You *really* fuckin' aren't Alyssa. And how I am with you is not what Junior gives Alyssa."

"But they seem to have a very strong, healthy relationship," I noted.

"They do. But Alyssa's got a good family who's all living, love her like crazy, have her back and always did. Then she got Junior and got a lot more of that. You had Lydie. That's all you had. Until you got me. But you got me when you lost her. So shit goes down for Alyssa, she's had a lifetime of having a solid foundation and she can take it. Or she's got a lot of folks she can go to to give it to if she can't. You only got me."

As Alyssa had her points, Jake had his too.

"So, Josie." He leaned toward me. "*What happened?*"

"Henry came to Lavender House today and fired me," I blurted.

Jake blinked.

Then he leaned back, far back, resting his behind against the edge of the desk, clipping out, "That fuckin' dick."

"I was going to resign anyway, Jake," I reminded him.

"That doesn't make him any less of a dick," Jake returned and continued, "Fuck him. Sue him. You were gonna resign or not, you gave him no reason to terminate you. No way around it, it's wrongful dismissal. Take his ass to the cleaners."

"He's giving me nearly two years of wages as a severance package," I explained.

"Go for double that," Jake shot back.

"It needn't be any more unpleasant than it already is, darling," I said gently. "We talked further and although it started hostile, it didn't end that way. Instead, it was distressing. He cares for me a great deal—"

"If he did, he wouldn't fire you."

"Please listen," I whispered.

Jake clamped his mouth shut.

"We…well, we shared quite a bit and with our history, I assume you can understand that we both missed an opportunity and wasted a good deal of time and obviously coming to that understanding is going to be painful for us both. And now, for Henry, with me moving on, being happy, it's difficult to take. He's simply losing me. I'm losing him too, which hurts, but I'm also gaining something else, which makes it easier. He doesn't have that."

Jake had nothing to say to that and I decided to take that as agreement he understood.

"So, although the conversation started on a difficult note, it ended on a sorrowful one. I do believe that given some time, we can resurrect a bit of what we had. However, we've agreed we won't be doing that with me in his employ. That would be too hard on both of us."

"Good," Jake grunted.

I pressed my lips together and rolled them.

Jake's eyes narrowed on my mouth then cut to my eyes. "Is there more?"

"Well…" I said and trailed off.

"Fuck me," Jake muttered then asked sharply, "What?"

"Well, I would…I mean, I think…um, truthfully, I don't know—"

"Josie, babe, *what?*" Jake bit out.

"I think he just wanted to see, to try, one last shot but…" I pulled in a deep breath and announced, "He kissed me."

Jake's anger filled the room and I watched with some concern as his body, from top to toe, even resting against the desk, went completely still in a very disquieting way.

"What?" he whispered.

"It was really a good-bye kiss," I shared quickly.

"If it was, you wouldn't feel the need to tell me," he retorted then asked, "He get inside?"

I pressed my lips together.

Jake's brows shot together.

"You let him inside?" he pushed on a sinister whisper.

Perhaps Alyssa was right. At least about this part.

"It was a good-bye, Jake."

He stared at me.

I stood there and let him.

I didn't like the look on his face. It frightened me and not because it was frightening. Because it was angry and Jake had told me just the day before that when a man gets hurt, that comes out as angry.

"Jake—"

"Never do that again," he said quietly.

I swallowed.

"That mouth's mine," he went on just as quietly.

I nodded.

"Never again, Josie. Don't give a shit who it is, what history you got, how intense the situation, how bad you feel for the guy. That mouth is mine."

I didn't think it would be sensible to point out that Henry was the only man who I would allow to do that and only in that time, that situation, and never again.

I also thought it sensible to agree.

"Okay, darling," I whispered.

"Come here," he ordered.

I felt it prudent to go there and do it immediately.

So I did.

When I did, he separated his legs and leaned in, yanking me between them so my body collided with his and his arms clamped around me.

I tipped my head back to look at him.

"Never keep anything from me, I don't give a shit how you think I'm gonna react. I'll react how I react. I will *never* harm you doin' it. But I got enough experience with what doesn't work between a man and a woman to know that keepin' shit from each other is a big fuckin' part of that."

"Okay," I agreed.

"So, that guy contacts you again, you tell me."

"Okay," I repeated.

"Anyone fucks with you, upsets you, whatever, you tell me that too. I don't give a shit if you think it's nothing, like someone givin' you a dirty look at the grocery store that gives you the willies. You fuckin' tell me."

"Okay, Jake."

His arms tightened and he dipped his face close. "Every inch of you, outside and any way you can get inside, baby, physically or emotionally, is mine. You don't share that. Ever."

I'd already agreed to that (essentially, he'd added new things) but it was clear he needed further assurances so I again said, "Okay, darling."

"Alyssa's a good woman and I know she had your best interests at heart when she advised you, honey. But we gotta find our own way and no way to do that but together. We start drifting apart to figure that shit out, we're fucked. You with me?"

"I'm with you, Jake."

When these words came out of my mouth, his arms convulsed and he whispered, "You're with me."

I had a feeling his words were profound in more ways than him knowing I understood what he was saying. A significant kind of profound. A kind of profound that changed lives and mended hearts and rocked worlds. And I liked that profound so I melted into him, sliding my hands up his chest.

"Are you angry with me?" I asked.

"No, because you shared that shit. You didn't and I found out, I would be pissed."

I nodded, sliding my hands up to his neck, at the same time sliding my body up his and tipping my head back further.

One of his hands slid down to cup my bottom and his eyes dropped to my mouth.

"You gonna take my mind off this shit by kissing me or are you gonna take my mind off this shit by kissing me then letting me fuck you on my desk?" he asked.

I melted further into him because his words made my legs tremble so deeply they no longer were holding me up as I replied breathily, "I'm going to kiss you then let you fuck me on your desk."

His mouth touched mine and he muttered, "Good answer, Slick."

I smiled against his lips.

Then I kissed him.

After that, Jake fucked me on his desk.

And much later, when I was back on the stool at the bar, Jake close, only half-listening as he talked to one of his bouncers, I smiled into the fresh martini Adam had made me thinking in the end, Alyssa was right.

I had to learn to handle Jake.

It was just that the way she handled Junior was different than the way I needed to handle Jake.

And she might argue, though I couldn't imagine how she could, the way I needed to handle Jake was better.

By far.

Sixteen

DELIGHTED

My thumb at Jake's nipple rubbing, my other hand wrapped around the side of his neck, my forehead to his, our heavy breaths mingling, his hand at my breast, thumb rubbing, other hand at my hip gripping, his back up against his headboard, knees cocked behind me, I was riding him and doing it fast.

"Jake," I whispered urgently because it was building.

"Hurry, baby," he whispered back.

"Jake," I breathed.

"Faster, Josie," he grunted.

I went faster.

Harder.

Oh yes.

That was better.

He rolled my nipple with his thumb and forefinger, tugging it gently at the same time.

I gasped as that shot straight from my breast to between my legs and moved faster.

Harder.

Oh yes.

It was building.

"Darling," I panted.

"Fuck me," he groaned. "Give me that pussy."

I did, grinding down and his hand at my breast squeezed as my head shot back, my hand clenched his neck and my climax powered through me.

Jake wrapped an arm around my waist, holding me down and his hand at my breast slid up my chest, around my neck and into my hair. He forced my face in his neck as he buried his in mine just before I heard his deep groan.

I breathed against his skin, feeling his breaths whisper against mine, the sensation tingling along my skin, down my spine, over my bottom and between my legs. I liked the feel so much I squeezed him with my sex.

Jake emitted another soft groan as his arm around me tightened.

"Love that pussy," he whispered against my neck.

I was so glad he did.

We stayed close, connected for long moments as our breaths quieted. Then I kissed his neck.

Jake wrapped both arms around me and slid me off, lifting me and turning me so I had my back to the bed, head to the pillows. He stayed leaned in deep, kissing me above the hair between my legs, then my belly, up between my breasts, up and again at my throat, under my chin then he brushed his mouth against mine before he whispered, "Be back."

"All right."

I watched his sated eyes smile before he touched his mouth to mine again and rolled away, tossing the covers over me when he did and then I watched him walk to the bathroom.

I was in his bed.

It was the morning after he showed me around the club.

We were at his house because I'd set my alarm criminally early but I did it so I could be waiting outside the back door at the gym when he arrived.

I'd watched his truck pull in and marveled how he parked, doing it with his eyes on me the entire time.

He got out and when he was walking to me, I called haughtily, "See? I can get up early and open the gym."

He didn't reply. He didn't even say hello.

He swept me in his arms and I saw his huge, white smile before he took my mouth in a deep, long, wet kiss.

Then he took us into the gym, opened up, turned on the lights (all of this I watched closely for when it was my turn) and when the first man walked through the doors, he stated, "On your own, John. You need anything, call," and we were out the door, in his truck and headed to his house.

The kids were still there when we arrived.

Ethan was ecstatic to see us return. It was then I learned the alarming news that the high school started at eight o'clock, Ethan's school at eight thirty so he had to "hang" with this teacher who was "lame" and some other kids who were "losers" for a half an hour when Conner or Amber had to take him to school. He was delighted he didn't have to do that.

He didn't. Jake and I took him to school.

But when I learned this news, I turned to Jake and raised my brows.

He burst out laughing.

Ethan, Amber and Conner looked between us, all their expressions confused.

Jake didn't explain.

Neither did I.

After dropping Ethan, Jake took me back to his house whereupon he pulled me up two flights of stairs, right to his bed, and started the festivities.

Culminating just now.

I watched him saunter back into the room, lift up the covers and then he was sliding in beside me. Half a second later, he was sliding my body on top of his and gliding one hand down to cup the cheek of my behind while he wrapped the other arm around me.

"Right," he began, "I dig the demonstration you can meet me at the gym but only so I can drag your ass back here, take my kid to school then drag your ass up here and fuck you in my bed."

"Hmm," I mumbled, finding my demonstration important for other reasons he should get.

"So how about we plan on doin' that every day?" he suggested.

"That would negate you being able to sleep in, Jake," I pointed out.

"Babe, you give me the choice of sleepin' or fuckin' you, I'm gonna pick fuckin' you."

Although I liked his choice, I still glared at him.

"You don't like that plan?" he asked.

"I'm trying to be helpful."

His arm around me slid up until his hand was in my hair. He used it to bring my face closer to his and said, "You are, baby. We're gonna take a nap right about now and after comin' hard with you ridin' me hard and fast, I'm gonna sleep fuckin' great."

I perked up.

"We're going to take a nap?"

"Yep."

I could use a nap. We'd left the club after one in the morning and I was up at five thirty to shower, dress and get to the gym.

"I could nap," I told him and he smiled.

Then he rolled me, kissing my throat before he lifted his head. "Right. Nap. Up. Shower. Lunch. Then I gotta get to the gym to make sure no one came in and cleaned me out."

Again, I was alarmed. "Is that a worry?"

He chuckled and said, "No, babe."

"Oh," I replied. Then I told him, "I've already taken a shower."

"You're gonna take another one."

"I don't need another one."

He pressed into me, his face got close and his voice got low. "You're gonna take another one."

"Oh," I repeated. "Okay."

"Okay," he replied, then commanded audaciously, "Now shut up and sleep."

My eyes narrowed. "Telling someone to shut up is rude."

"Babe," he returned.

"And ordering an adult to sleep is preposterous," I went on.

"Babe."

"Babe?"

"Babe."

"Is that your response?" I asked.

"No, my response is, babe, shut up and sleep but I already said that so I condensed it to just babe 'cause that's easier to say and might not piss you off."

"I can't read all that in *babe,* Jake."

"You'll learn to read my babes."

Annoyingly, I was looking forward to doing that.

I didn't share that with Jake.

I kept glaring at him.

His eyes were smiling when he bent in and kissed me, not a mouth brush this time, it was deeper, sweeter and much, much longer.

Jake ended it having turned us to our sides. We were pressed close with legs tangled in a delicious way. And after he ended it, he pulled me down and pressed my face into his throat.

"Now, babe, sleep," he ordered.

"All right," I gave in.

He kissed the top of my head.

I cuddled closer, held on tighter and within moments, I slept.

———⬦———

I WAS SITTING on the counter watching Jake warm up a can of soup when my phone in my purse rang.

Jake twisted, grabbed my purse off the counter of the island, twisted back and plopped it in my lap.

I dug out my phone on a murmured, "Thank you, darling," and saw the call was from Amber.

My eyes went to his.

"Amber," I told him, taking the call, looking at my purse in my lap and putting the phone to my ear. "Hello, sweetheart," I greeted.

Instantly, I yanked the phone from my ear when she shrieked, "*You'll never guess what just happened!*"

When I felt it was safe, I put my phone back to my ear and asked, "What?"

But I heard nothing but strange muffled noises and my eyes shot to Jake. His brows drew together.

"Amber?" I called.

"Hey, Josie," boy Taylor said. "Amber's busy hyperventilating and we don't have a lot of time since lunch is over and we have to be in class, but she wants you to know that Alexi sat with us at lunch today."

My heart skipped a beat.

It had been a long time but I remembered how that felt.

And how it felt was *wonderful.*

"He did?" I whispered.

"The entire time," boy Taylor told me.

"Really?" I asked.

"Totally," he answered. "And you should know she was totally cool. Sweet and nice to him, a little shy, but she waited to screech and hyperventilate until after he was long gone."

I smiled at a Jake who still had brows drawn. "Tell her I'm proud of her."

"Will do," he replied. "Gotta go, though. We have to get to class."

"Okay, sweetheart. Have a good day," I said.

"You too. Later."

"Later."

He disconnected.

Jake asked, "What?" the instant I took the phone from my ear.

My heart skipped another beat for an entirely different reason.

Uh-oh.

"Well…" I began and trailed off.

"What?" he repeated.

"Um…"

He leaned toward me and said a warning, "Josie."

"Alexi sat with Amber at lunch today."

Instantly, he tipped his head back and muttered, "Christ almighty."

"She's quite excited," I told him.

He tipped his head forward and scowled at me.

I lifted a hand and curled it around his neck, leaning close and sharing, "She's happy."

"He asks her out and comes on that bike to pick her up, I'm shooting him."

I dropped my hand and leaned back, my brows lifting. "You own a firearm?"

"No," he answered, turning his focus back to our soup. "But today, I'm buyin' one."

I let out a little giggle that I swallowed before it could bloom when Jake's eyes cut to me.

"I'm not joking."

"Okay, darling," I said soothingly.

He looked back at the soup, muttering, "Fuck me."

I jumped off the counter and put my purse back on the island, stating, "I'll get drinks. What do you want?"

"Coke," he answered.

I didn't get him a Coke.

I moved to him, fit my front to his back, wrapped my arms around his stomach and put my chin to his shoulder blade, whereupon I whispered, "You're a good dad."

I gave him a squeeze, kissed his shoulder blade through his shirt, let him go and got him his Coke.

But when I turned away from the fridge, I saw he didn't look quite so aggravated anymore.

And thus, I figured I'd appropriately handled my man.

So I smiled.

—•◦•—

"AND HE WAS all, *Combat Raptor* is lame. So I was all, and *Zombie Mayhem* wasn't? And he was all, *Zombie Mayhem* was the bomb. And I was all, there's no such thing as zombies. And he was all, like men can turn into jets? And I was all, *duh, Transformers…?* And he was all, *Transformers* are robots."

This was coming from Ethan who was, for some unknown reason, lying upside down on Gran's couch, his feet over the back, his head dangling over the seat.

Amber was painting her nails in Gran's armchair.

We'd just had dinner (and dessert) that I'd prepared, but for some reason, Conner was in the other armchair eating the chips and salsa Ethan told me I *had* to buy when we took Pearl on the excruciatingly long (I reminded myself she *did* walk with a walker) trip to the grocery store that afternoon.

And by the by, I was right. Ethan knew Pearl. They liked each other a great deal and our afternoon was quite enjoyable (*sans* the excruciatingly long trip at the grocery store, of course).

Conner not only had chips and salsa but also a textbook opened on his thigh to which he was paying scant attention.

As for me, I'd been planted in the couch between the upside down Ethan and the right side up Jake.

The pre-game show for *Monday Night Football* was on the television. This was because Jake had programmed my DVR (I didn't even know I had one or, indeed, what one was) to "Tape *Project Runway* anytime it shows, even the reruns, so you can watch it whenever you want and Amber can come over and watch that shit with you."

As this was acceptable to Amber and me, *Monday Night Football* it was.

Ethan kept rattling on as Jake slid an arm around me and tucked me close to his side.

I rested my head against his chest, pulled my legs up, tucked them into the seat beside me and studied the commentators.

When Ethan took a breath, I noted, "That tie the bald fellow is wearing is extremely unbecoming."

"I know, right?" Amber agreed.

Jake's arm gave me a squeeze as a soft chuckle escaped his mouth but I heard it come from there *and* from his chest *and* I felt it.

All three were very nice.

"Jesus," Conner muttered.

Without disconnecting from Jake, quietly and cautiously I said to Conner, "You really shouldn't take the Lord's name in vain, honey."

Conner grinned at me and replied, "You really shouldn't talk trash about a Football Hall of Famer's tie."

"Is this a rule?" I queried.

"Absolutely, "Conner replied.

I rolled my eyes and when I rolled them back, he was still grinning at me.

"Whatever," I muttered.

Then I burrowed closer, wrapped an arm around Jake's stomach, he lifted his stocking feet to Gran's coffee table, crossed his ankles and we watched *Monday Night Football.*

———•••••———

ON MY WAY to the gym the next morning, I approached The Shack which I was highly surprised was open at that early hour. But I'd seen the cover gone from the window as I drove by the wharf and remembered the excellent coffee there so I'd stopped.

The window was open, however beyond it was dark and cavernous, so I called a tentative, "Hello?"

"Josie, watcha need?" was called back.

I blinked at the empty window.

"Tom?" I called.

"Right here. You want coffee or coffee and omelets for you and Jake?"

Word most definitely got around.

"Just coffee, Tom," I answered. "Two."

"Comin' right up," the disembodied voice said just as my phone in my purse rang.

I took it out, looked at the display, took the call turning my back to the window and announced, "I'm uncertain I'm talking to you."

"Josephine," Amond said quietly.

"You knew he was coming," I said huffily.

"Had no idea he'd can your ass," Amond replied.

I said nothing.

"Henry's in a bad way, girl," he told me and I closed my eyes against the pain. I opened them and shared, "I've met someone, Amond."

It was his turn to say nothing.

So I did.

"I'm also quite angry with you. You could have no idea, of course, how things would play out. But I'll tell you, it was unpleasant for all of us and perhaps wouldn't have been that way if I'd known he was coming."

"He wanted it to be a surprise," Amond replied.

"Well it was that," I returned.

I heard a sigh before, "I'll talk to him. His new boy, Daniel, is okay but he's not you and everyone's freaking about Henry losing his muse. They think, without you, he'll lose his touch."

His muse?

Oh God, was I Henry's muse?

My mind harked back and noted that he took an inordinate amount of pictures of me. In fact, on every shoot, he'd aim the camera at me at some point, even if I was simply sitting and talking on the phone.

I always thought he was being playful.

But now I knew he was not.

As beautiful as this was, as much of an honor as it was, all of this coming to me at a time when it was gone was too much to bear.

Therefore, I shook it off and said to Amond, "Don't talk with him. A great deal has changed and I was going to speak with Henry and ask if I could slow down anyway. I like being here, in Gran's house, life being less hectic, and as I mentioned, I met someone."

To this he declared, "I'm there the minute this shoot is over."

My hand tightened on the phone for I had the feeling that this meant Amond was coming to check Jake out. And there were very few people who could be a threat to Jake but Amond was one of them. He not only was also quite tall, large and fit, he was not someone you messed with. He further spoke his mind at all times. If he didn't like Jake for me, he'd let me know it.

And Jake.

And Jake might not like this.

"Amond, that isn't necessary," I said quickly.

"Two weeks and you're givin' up Henry and your life for Maine and this guy, it absolutely is."

"Amond—"

"Me showin' up won't be a surprise. I'll let you know when to expect me and you got room in that house of yours, I'm in it."

"Amond—" I said louder.

"Later, Josephine," he said and I heard the disconnect.

I took my phone from my ear and snapped, "God!"

"Coffee's up," Tom declared from behind me.

I whirled and again saw a dark window as well as two white paper coffee cups sitting on its ledge.

But no Tom.

"How much do I owe you?" I asked into the vacant window.

"Come for another omelet, bring Jake, those're free," Tom's voice replied.

He hardly had to bribe me to come eat another of his omelets. They were superb. In fact, I'd no idea why I hadn't returned to get one already.

I peered into the shadows and eerily still saw nothing but, well, *shadows* and some little red lights that undoubtedly indicated cooking implements were on.

Very curious.

I would, of course, come for another omelet. But I couldn't take freebie coffees.

"Tom, really, I'd like to pay," I said into the shadows.

"Not takin' your money so get that coffee to Jake while it's hot."

I stared at the window.

Then, clearly with no other choice, I grabbed the cups and said, "Thank you. I'll see you later for an omelet."

"Tell Jake I said hey," Tom replied.

"Will do," I told him.

I took the coffees, left mine black, poured a frightening amount of sugar and two powdered cream packets into Jake's and called another farewell to Tom as I started to move to my Cayenne.

I was again waiting for Jake outside the back door to the gym but was only there approximately two minutes before Jake's big truck pulled up.

He parked, got out and walked to me, doing all this smiling.

"Two days in a row. I would say I've proved my point," I announced as he made his way to me. "Now, are you going to give me a key?"

He didn't answer me at first.

No, even with two cups of coffee in my hands, his arms closed around me and I was forced to hold my arms out at the sides to save the mysterious Tom's rather delicious coffee. This was made a more difficult endeavor when Jake bent his head and kissed me dizzy.

He answered only when he lifted his head and he did this with a, "Yeah."

Alas, I forgot my question.

"Pardon?"

"I'm giving you a key."

"Oh," I mumbled.

He smiled again.

Then he let me go, tipped his head to my hands and asked, "One of those for me?"

I didn't answer his question.

I blurted, "Amond is coming to check you out."

His brows went up. "Come again?"

"Dee-Amond, a friend of mine and an award-winning hip-hop artist who you may have heard of has learned that Henry sacked me. I've informed him I'm staying in Maine and met someone. He's protective of me. After he shoots his video with Henry, he's coming to check you out."

"And?" Jake queried when I stopped speaking.

I stared at him a moment before inquiring, "This doesn't upset you?"

"What would upset me is if you lived a life where no one gave a shit about you and didn't get worried when you made a major life change and lost your job. This guy worrying about you says he's a good guy who cares about you. He comes, he'll see we're cool. So no. I'm not upset some famous rap star is comin' to check me out."

I didn't know what to say but I did know what to think and that was that Jake Spear was…the…*bomb*.

"What also would upset me is if you keep starin' at me instead of givin' me my cup 'a joe that I know's from The Shack so I know it's gonna be good but not so good if it's stone cold."

I belatedly handed him his cup.

He took it, hooked an arm around my waist and yanked me into his body, dipping his head so his face was close to mine.

"Every singer, designer, model you know showed up here to check me out, the kids out, I wouldn't give a fuck," he told me quietly. "In fact, I want that. They're the only family you had so actually, I *want* to know that part of your life. So bring it on."

Good *God*.

"You keep getting more wonderful," I whispered.

"Baby, it's not yet seven, got my girl who hates to get up early in my arm, a coffee from The Shack she got for me, and I'm gonna get me some in about two hours. I'm thinkin' you keep gettin' more wonderful too."

"Good answer," I replied.

He grinned.

Then he dipped his head to touch his mouth to mine.

After that, he let us in, opened the doors while I turned on the lights, and then he gave me a key.

About two hours later, after Jake took Ethan to school while I stayed at his house and did the breakfast dishes, he returned, dragged me up the stairs and "got him some."

In doing so, he gave me some too.

And it was wonderful.

TWO DAYS LATER, I'd just paid for Alyssa and my lunch of rather delicious cobb salads at Weatherby's Diner when my phone rang.

Again.

"Jesus, you're popular," Alyssa noted as I ignored my phone (again).

"Word has gotten around that Henry fired me," I explained, tucking my still-ringing phone in my bag. "And also that Gran has died. I'm getting dozens of calls a day."

And I was. Some sharing condolences. Most sharing shock that Henry and I were not "together" anymore.

I'd learned from these calls that it seemed quite a few people thought Henry and I had an open relationship but in the end, it was me for Henry and Henry for me.

This also meant that, again, others were clued in far faster than I was about what was happening around me.

There were also job offers, one from a rather talented up-and-coming designer based out of New York who would "die" if I'd offer my services, even if I worked from Lavender House and only went to the City once every month or so.

"With your connections, darling, you'd have me where I wanted to be five years ago and do it in six months," he'd said.

Of course, I thought this was rather sweet, if perhaps incorrect. But I was thinking about it and Jake was prompting me to do it.

"Gives you to us most of the time, but you still stay connected to who you are. Best of both worlds, babe," he'd said.

I was thinking he was right.

I was also thinking that I had a great many acquaintances who I was finding, with their kind concern, were really friends and I wanted to stay connected to them because that kind concern was heartwarming.

It was also overwhelming, but I didn't want to be on the phone all day, and certainly not while at lunch with Alyssa (this was rude) so I'd begun not to take some calls and called them back later.

"Cool your peeps are rallying around you, babe," Alyssa said as we slid out of the booth.

"It is indeed cool," I agreed.

She grinned at me as she got close and slid an arm around my waist.

I reciprocated the gesture and we walked through the diner in this fashion, Alyssa stating, "I'm gonna hang at The Circus with you tomorrow night. Check out the dancers, get me some new moves to rock Junior's world."

We separated to walk out the door as I looked at her with delight.

"I would love that," I shared.

"Then you're on. Meet you there at ten," she replied as we stopped outside in the chill air.

"Excellent. Ten," I agreed.

"Now, you need help goin' through your boxes, you call me. I'd kill to dig through your wardrobe and if you let me try a few pieces on, I'll put you in my will."

The boxes from Henry's pool house had arrived and this was how I told Alyssa I was going to spend my afternoon, sorting through them, officially moving into Lavender House.

Bittersweet.

But it would be less so with Alyssa helping me do it. Therefore, I decided to delay my afternoon's activities until a time she could help me.

"I'll take you up on that," I said. "We'll plan tomorrow night."

"Right on," she agreed.

We did double cheek kisses and she took off with a low wave saying, "Later, babelicious."

"Later, honey," I called to her as I turned in the other direction to head down the sidewalk toward my Cayenne.

I was nearly there when my phone in my purse rang and as it was so soon after the last call, I wondered if it was the same caller and they actually needed to speak to me.

So I pulled it out but stopped dead on the sidewalk when I saw the caller's name on the display.

Quickly, I took the call and put the phone to my ear.

"Arnie, how are you?" I greeted cautiously.

There was a long pause before he replied in a voice that broke my heart, "Been better, Josephine."

I stepped to the side, tilted my head down to stare at my high-heeled boots and gave him my full attention.

"Can I help you with something?" I asked.

"No, my dear. I'm just phoning to let you know we're putting Eliza in hospice today."

Hospice.

Damn.

My heart clenched and I whispered, "So soon?"

His broken heart was in his voice when he replied, "Yes, Josephine."

I felt my hand shaking so I tightened it around the phone when I queried, "May I come and see her?"

"Of course," he answered. "She'll want to see you."

"I…where will she be?"

He gave me the name of the hospice as I took deep breaths to control the tears stinging my eyes.

"I'll come tomorrow," I told him.

"Do it today, Josephine," he said quietly and my eyes immediately got wet.

"Okay." I paused. "I'll, well…I'll let you go."

"I'll see you later."

"You will, Arnie," I assured. "Thank you for taking the time to phone. Until then."

"Good-bye, my dear," he said and rang off.

When he did, I stood on the sidewalk and stared at my boots, tears gliding down my face.

Jake was right. He was very right.

I shouldn't have taken that on.

I couldn't handle it.

On this thought, I heard my name called.

"Josephine?"

I looked up and saw Mickey standing before me. His face was watery but I noted vaguely that he was smiling. However, the instant he caught my tear-stained cheeks, his expression shifted to concern.

"Jesus," he murmured, "Honey, what's happening?"

"Eliza Weaver is going into hospice today."

He said nothing but then again, I didn't give him a chance. I tilted my head down and covered my face with my hands even with my phone still in one of them.

Then I was in Mickey's arms. Feeling their strength close around me, his warmth enveloping me, his kindness melting into my skin, my body bucked and I made one of those awful hiccupping noises through my tears.

One of his arms left me and moments later, as he turned us and started us walking, still holding me close, I heard him say, "Jake, buddy, you gotta get to the station. I got Josephine with me and she's not good. Says some friend of hers is going to hospice today. Think she just found out on the street but I know she lost it."

I lifted wet eyes to him even as he kept moving us toward the station and said, "I-I'll be all right."

Mickey looked down at me but otherwise ignored me and said into the phone at his ear, "Right. Good. See you then. We'll be in the break room. Later."

"Jake's busy," I told him as he shoved the phone in his back pocket.

"Thinkin' Jake's never too busy for you," he replied.

I was thinking this was very true and more, even in my distress, I was very much liking that thought.

Mickey got me to the fire station, upstairs and on a beaten up leather couch in a room that had a full kitchen, a big table and was surprisingly clean as a pin.

I'd managed to get control of my tears and he'd pulled a chair in front of me and was leaned in with his elbows to his knees, his hands holding mine, listening to me telling him who Eliza and Arnie were (he knew of them, but not them) when Jake got there.

I looked up and watched him walk to me.

So tall. His shoulders so very broad. His bearing so strong.

His eyes locked to me.

Mickey let my hands go and leaned back as I stood, my eyes glued to Jake.

Then I was in his arms and I burst back into tears.

"You…you were…were right," I stammered into his chest, folding my arms around him and holding on tight.

"Shh, baby, no I wasn't."

"It-it's…all too much."

"You can handle it," he declared

The instant he said them, his words drove through me in a profound way. Also in that instant, I knew he was right and he was wrong.

When I got the call from the nursing company to tell me that Gran had died, I was on the beach in Malibu. Henry was shooting a model wearing a ten thousand dollar couture gown that was wet at the hem from standing near the surf.

He would have wanted me to interrupt him when I got the news. In fact, when I told him later, he was cross with me that I didn't interrupt him but he tried to hide it due to the circumstances.

Now I knew just how much he would have wanted that.

But I didn't interrupt him.

I moved quietly to the tent set up for hair and makeup, which was thankfully empty, and I spent my emotion alone.

And I'd felt that.

Precisely that.

Alone.

Acutely alone.

With Gran gone, I felt utterly alone.

And lost.

And further, I felt afraid, thinking I'd never really have Henry and with Gran gone, I'd never really have anything again.

Eliza Weaver was not Gran but she was a sweet woman who would make the world poorer for her loss.

I knew it was not just Eliza I was grieving but also the loss that was still fresh that was Gran and the even fresher, albeit different loss of Henry.

But in losing all that, I was no longer alone.

Mickey had found me on the street and he'd taken care of me.

And Jake was right there, tall, broad, strong, holding me close, his big body absorbing my tremors, the physical ones as well as the emotional.

Something I'd never had from anyone, not even really Henry.

No one but Gran.

And now Jake.

So he was wrong, I couldn't handle it. On my own, I could not do that.

But I was not on my own.

I had him.

So he was also right.

I could handle it.

And I loved that.

But mostly, I knew in that distressing instant that normally would have been a sorrowful memory, that I loved *him*.

So I would remember standing in Jake Spear's arms in a fire station, crying for a dying friend, for the loss of my Gran, for the end of what was with Henry.

I'd remember it for the rest the rest of my life.

And I'd treasure it.

"HEY!" I HEARD called.

I stopped pushing my cart through Wayfarer's with some urgency and turned to look down the aisle.

What I saw made my back go straight.

It was Sunday morning and I was heading to Jake's for food, football and family time. The Taylors were coming over. Conner didn't have to work. And I'd talked Jake into letting me cook.

I was in a hurry because I couldn't wait to get there.

But I had to pick up food first.

On Friday, Jake had taken me to see Eliza.

Since then, I had not bothered Arnie, but instead phoned Reverend Fletcher on Saturday to discover if the dire event had come to pass.

"Not yet, Josephine, but I would expect sad news very soon," he'd informed me gently.

I left it at that but asked Reverend Fletcher to let me know if he heard any news.

Thus far, nothing.

Taking my mind off this, Alyssa (who I had called to give her this news after Jake dropped Ethan and me off at Lavender House for we had to go straight to the school from the hospice to pick him up) and I had a marvelous time at Jake's club the night before.

She talked Sofie into watching her kids and Junior came with her.

With Jake (mostly, sometimes he had business to see to), we all sat at the bar, drank and talked.

In doing this, I found that I very much liked Junior. He was surprisingly soft-spoken, though his language was just as coarse as his wife's. Oddly, however, it was rather attractive coming from a large, frightening-looking man with a soft voice

I liked him more watching him with his wife in a gentleman's club and noting that not even once did his eyes stray to the dancers.

He wasn't being good in order not to get into trouble.

He was all about Alyssa.

And when I noticed that, I noticed that Jake did the exact same thing with me. Although he'd had occasion to see the dancers far more often than Junior, a beautiful near-naked woman was a beautiful near-naked woman.

Jake was not interested in them.

But he made it clear he was *very* interested in me.

The night was rather late and unfortunately ended with some incident Jake had to see to so Junior and Alyssa took me home.

Even losing Jake to work, the evening on the whole was highly enjoyable.

However, I didn't care how late the night was before. I'd get up whenever needed to get to the grocery store to buy the ingredients for my truffle risotto, what I intended to make for food, football and the Spear family.

It wasn't tacos and Ro-Tel dip but it was *fabulous* and the way the children and Jake tucked into my food, I knew they'd agree.

What wasn't welcome was the fact that Donna, Jake's ex and Conner and Amber's wayward mother, was hurrying my way.

I drew in breath.

She stopped on a sway and a tentative smile.

"Uh…Josie, right?"

"Yes," I replied, deciding not to correct her that to *her* I was most assuredly Josephine. "How are you, Donna?" I asked although I really didn't care. However, it was rude not to.

"I'm all right," she stated then changed her mind and said "Good. I'm good. And…um, you? Are you good?"

"Yes, I'm excellent. Thank you for asking."

She moved her weight from foot to foot and looked to the shelves beyond me. Alas, what she did not do was bid me to have a good day and move away.

"Is there something you need?" I asked and her eyes came to me. "I don't wish to be rude but Jake and the children are expecting me," I prompted.

"I just…" she started, trailed off and began again. "I'm just wondering about Con and Amber. I heard some things about Con and I'm concerned."

"Have you phoned Conner?" I inquired.

"Well, yes. He said everything's cool," she told me.

I said nothing.

She spoke again.

"But, what I heard was that some girl told folks she was pregnant with his kid, she wasn't, she's getting massive shit from everyone for pulling that, but his girl still broke up with him."

This was true, as with some delight boy Taylor shared with me just days before that young Mia *was* getting "massive shit" from everyone.

Conner was well-liked and had done as I expected, not kept matters to himself.

As per boy Taylor, Mia was now a pariah, not only in the boy department but also in the girl.

Fair punishment, according to me.

I told Donna none of this.

Instead, I simply confirmed, "This did happen."

"I, well…thought he liked that girl who broke it off with him. Um…Ellie."

"He did."

She stared at me a moment before asking, "So is he really okay?"

"No," I answered.

"Shit," she whispered, becoming unfocused for several seconds before she again focused on me. "Is Amber good?"

"Amber's fine," I told her.

"She isn't, well…this is strange, talking to you about this, but she isn't picking up my calls."

I couldn't have agreed more that this was strange and decided to tell her as much.

"It is indeed strange you talking to me about this for I barely know you and we're discussing something colossally important, that being your daughter," I declared. "I can't imagine why you wouldn't be making some attempt to communicate directly to her, even if she isn't picking up her phone. I would assume you know where she attends school as well as lives so these are not mysteries you need to cipher before you make a connection with her."

Her mouth had dropped open making her look rather comically dull but I was far from done.

"Further, if Amber isn't answering your calls, you know her father and you can discuss the daughter you share directly with him. Why you would approach me in a gourmet food store aisle I cannot fathom and I'll tell you now, it makes me uncomfortable."

I stopped talking and she had no reply for long moments before she stated, "Boy, you don't beat around the bush."

"Not normally, no. But when it comes to Jake, Conner and Amber, I never will."

Something changed in her face and her voice was quite strange when she remarked, "It's cool they have that from you."

"It would be cooler if they had something, *anything* from you," I retorted.

Her expression again changed. She flinched.

But she said not a word.

So I did.

"Listen, I've explained to you that I'm quite busy but I'll take this moment to say more. It appears you care that you've lost your connection with your children and I find that quite gratifying but only with the hope you'll do some-thing about it. However, you've been disconnected for so long, it has affected not only your two children but Jake's youngest. Ethan loves his brother and sis-ter very much, circumstances force that family to be quite dependent on each other and as Ethan is still quite young, he's obviously more dependent on his father and siblings than the rest. If you were to suddenly make some overtures, for Ethan's sake, you may wish to be thoughtful in how you do it."

I stopped talking and she remained silent so I went on.

"Also, as I never really had one, I can only assume that a son and daugh-ter would welcome their mother in their life. But as you've blundered quite horribly with your two children, although I urge you to rectify that and do it very soon, I would also urge you to speak with Jake about it so as you do it you don't cause undo upheaval that will be difficult for him and those kids to handle."

"You *want* me talking to Jake?" she asked, sounding incredulous, and I felt my brows draw together.

"You're the mother of two of his children," I answered.

"But I'm also his ex. I mean, we were married and we have history," she told me.

"Indeed. Though your last word is quite crucial. *History*," I replied.

She again flinched.

I studied her closely.

Surely this woman wasn't that oblivious. Years had passed.

"Donna, as I've been blunt, I will continue to be so. If you hold a candle for Jake, I'd extinguish it. He's quite forthcoming and what once was between you is very gone."

Another flinch.

Good God.

She *was* that oblivious.

"Okay, this is weirding me out," she declared. "I'm sorry. I shouldn't have talked to you about this."

"Indeed, you shouldn't have. But you did. And I'd encourage you to take on board what I said." I hesitated to underline my final point. "*All* of it."

She held my eyes and replied, "I don't mean to be funny. Truly I don't. Mrs. Malone was really cool and folks who know you say you're like her. But you should know, Jake and I are complicated and the kind of history we have is never really gone."

She was absolutely that oblivious.

I couldn't believe it, but as it was right there in front of me, I found it very sad.

Therefore, I gentled my tone when I told her, "If you believe that, I'm very sorry. Jake and you are not complicated because there *is* no Jake and you. It appears you've been working under the misconception that that's the case, but I advise you to cease doing so for your own sake."

"Again, not to be funny, but he's come back to me before," she pointed out.

"He also left you, and since then married two other women and then met me," I volleyed.

She shook her head, clearly my words weren't penetrating and this was proved when she started, "I don't mean to be mean but you should—"

"You aren't being mean, Donna," I interrupted her and went on firmly in an effort to end this enlightening but nevertheless wretched discussion. "But you are taking quite a bit of my time. Please, phone Jake. Discuss all this with him. I think it will be difficult for you but in the end beneficial and hopefully beneficial for Amber and Conner too."

"God," she whispered, her eyes widening. "You totally don't have any problems with me talking to Jake."

"Not a one," I replied. "Now, again, not to be rude but I really must be getting on."

"I…" Another shake of her head. "Okay."

"Phone Jake," I urged.

"I…" She shook her head yet again but said, "I will."

"Good day to you, Donna."

"Um…good day to you too, Josie."

I wanted to roll my eyes at her calling me Josie again. It was true that I was getting that from practically everyone these days but from her I didn't like it all that much.

However, I found our conversation more than mildly exasperating and I wanted it to end so I didn't say a word. Nodding my head to her once, I turned back to my cart and my attention back to my list.

It was much later, indeed well after the children and the Taylors gave their exuberant stamp of approval not only to my truffle risotto but to the variety of bruschettas that I'd made as an appetizer, that I was alone with Jake in the kitchen making hot fudge sundaes.

It was then I told him of my conversation with Donna.

As he was stronger, he was scooping out the hard frozen ice cream. With curiosity, I was "nuking" the jars of hot fudge (three of them), a phenomenon I had not yet tasted but was very much looking forward to as Jake also had cans of whipped cream, nuts, sprinkles and cherries.

Even from jars and cans, none of this could be bad.

Involved in our activities, I didn't feel the air until I head Jake's sinister whisper of, "Come again?"

I looked from the revolving jars of hot fudge in the microwave to Jake and saw he didn't find my conversation with Donna simply odd and perhaps a little sad.

No, that was not how he found it at all.

"I—" I began, my mind flying through varying options of how to handle him when he dropped the scoop in the tub of ice cream and prowled to and out the door to the garage.

I fretted over the ice cream sitting on the counter for a brief moment, thinking I should put it back in the freezer. However, as Jake was clearly angry and just as clearly intent to do something about it, I decided to leave it where it lay and followed him.

The large garage was lit, Jake was standing beside his truck parked in it, his phone to his ear and when I arrived, I saw I was too late to stop him when I heard him say, "You have got to be fucking *shitting* me."

Oh dear.

I got close and Jake cut furious eyes to me (now, under the fluorescent lights in the garage, a rather attractive shade of silver I had not seen before and, alas, couldn't fully enjoy considering the circumstances).

"No," he clipped into his phone. "First, you do not *ever* talk to Josie. We do what's the impossible right now and sort this out eventually, you two gotta have a discussion for some reason, I might allow it. After this shit and the shit you've been pullin' with Con and Amber, no. Josie is off-limits to you. I don't care if you're sittin' next to each other gettin' a pedicure at Alyssa's, she doesn't exist. You get that?"

There was a pause and I bit my lip before he powered on.

"And get it outta your head that we're reconciling. That shit is never gonna happen, Donna. How the fuck you can think that, I have no fuckin' clue. It's been fuckin' years since I shared a bed with you and, straight up, when I left it the last time, I haven't even thought of goin' back. Now, forced to think of it through this shit, woman, you cannot believe after you've taken so much twenty-somethin' cock I'd ever go there. The thought turns my goddamned stomach. Get this and get it now, that shit is not gonna happen. Not ever. Now do you get that?"

He was being quite brutal, therefore I wrapped my fingers around his bicep and whispered, "Jake—"

He ignored me and kept speaking.

"You have fucked up royal with your kids. You want me to help you sort that, you get your head outta your goddamned ass. Until you've proved to me you aren't livin' in a fuckin' fantasy world, totally fuckin' clueless to pretty much everything, you got no help from me. They're not slippin' through your fingers, Donna. They're gone. Con tries to be cool with you because he's a good kid. Amber, you've lost. You pull your shit together and find a way back in that works for her and for me, I'll back that play. But not until you pull your shit together. You hear me?"

He stopped speaking and I decided to say nothing and get closer. He didn't move away but I knew he was concentrating on whatever she was saying because, even though he was still looking at me, his eyes had gone unfocused.

Finally, he spoke again.

"This shit, these tears, they mean nothing to me, Donna. We've been done so long, I don't even think about you unless I look at my girl when I know she needs a woman for whatever shit that's fuckin' with her head and I do it pissed way the fuck off that her mother is not there for her. She's got Josie now and you need to wake up. A girl, I would expect, can't have enough good women in her life. But it blows my goddamned mind you'd walk up to Josie at Wayfarer's feelin' funny for her that she's got somethin' good you think she's gonna lose when she's got everything and she takes care of it in a way she's never gonna lose it. Everything you lost because you *didn't* take care of it, you *aren't* takin' care of it, and if you don't sort yourself out, you're never gonna get it back."

He paused to take a breath but kept right on going.

"Now, we're done. Think on this shit, Donna, and please, God, fuckin' wake the fuck up."

He was indeed done for he disconnected and shoved his phone in his pocket.

His eyes were still on me and before I could say a word, he did.

"You got any understanding of that bitch now?" he bit out.

"Would you, perhaps, like a hot fudge sundae to calm you down before we discuss this matter further?" I offered.

"We walk back into that house, babe, this shit is behind us and we eat hot fudge sundaes enjoying them, not thinkin' about Donna's ridiculous bullshit."

As this was what he wanted, and I wanted Jake to have everything, I gave it to him.

"I would assume that most of her lovers look like you or, perchance, behave like you," I stated.

He jerked up his chin in an affirmative even as his jaw clenched but said only, "Least the ones I've seen."

I nodded.

"Then she's attempting to live the glory days with these men who matter very little to her, thinking inaccurately that those glory days will return when the real thing does."

"That's whacked," Jake declared.

"Yes, it is," I agreed.

"She's whacked," Jake went on.

"Yes, she is," I again agreed.

He studied me a moment before asking, "She get in there with you?"

"Pardon?" I asked back, confused.

"She fuck with your head with this shit?"

My brows drew together as I informed him, "Certainly not."

"She and I are done," he announced.

"I know that, Jake," I assured him.

He studied me another moment before his expression cleared and his voice gentled to say, "Sorry that shit happened to you."

"I'm not," I returned immediately. "If this is the precursor to her getting her finger out of her ass, then I'm delighted it happened. Those children need their mother. Perhaps she'll deal with her shit and finally give them one."

I got another moment of study before a slow, attractive grin spread on Jake's face and he moved so he could wrap his arms around me.

"Deal with her shit?" he asked.

"Indeed," I answered.

His grin got bigger and his arms got tighter. "As much as this pisses me off, wish like fuck I was at Wayfarer's watchin' you give her the honesty."

"I can't imagine why," I replied. "It was most irksome."

"Irksome," he murmured, still grinning but now doing it looking at my lips.

My belly fluttered, but my lips said, "Yes. Irksome."

His arms got tighter as his face got closer. "Irksome," he repeated in a whisper, his word sounding on my lips since his were that close.

"Yes," I breathed right before he kissed me.

Delightfully, he did this thoroughly and I melted into him as he did it, wrapping my arms around his neck, gliding my fingers over his hair to hold him to me and kissing him back.

We did this for some time before we were forced to break the kiss when a loud knock sounded at the door right before Ethan shouted through it, "Jeez! What's the deal? Hello? Hot fudge sundaes?"

I smiled up into Jake's smiling eyes just as Ethan went on, still shouting (albeit no longer through the door), and he did it sounding like he was telling on us.

"Con! Dad and Josie are makin' out in the garage!"

I didn't hear Conner's reply but did hear Ethan's shouted one.

"I *don't* care! But I want a sundae!" He knocked on the door again and his next comment was directed through it. "Hurry up!"

"Gotta get a sundae in my kid," Jake said softly.

"You do," I replied.

"Soften him up before I let him know his ass is in church in about an hour and a half," he went on.

"Good plan," I approved.

His eyes warmed, his neck bent, he touched his forehead to mine then lifted his lips to kiss it.

After that, he let me go but grabbed my hand and we went in to finish the sundaes. Ethan was not in the kitchen but he was the first one I went to where he was sitting on the couch in the family room and I handed him a bowl.

He tucked in immediately and was lifting the spoon to his mouth but doing it with his mouth moving in order to declare, "When I get a girlfriend, we're just holding hands. None of that kissing stuff."

I pressed my lips together in an effort not to laugh.

The Taylors and Amber didn't bother.

It was Conner who spoke. "You are so full of it."

Ethan swallowed an enormous bite of sundae and turned his eyes to his brother, "I'm not."

Conner's eyes were twinkling when he replied, "Bud, trust me. You so are."

"Am not," Ethan returned.

Conner grinned at his brother, turned his attention to me and winked, then looked back to the game.

I gave the other bowl I had to girl Taylor before I went back into the kitchen to get more bowls that Jake was assembling.

I did it smiling.

I also did it feeling sad for Donna.

She was very much missing out.

But even sad for her, I was delighted for me.

For I was absolutely not.

"AT THIS VERY minute, the Colts are playing," Ethan, sitting in the pew on the other side of his dad, groused.

"Shut it, bud," Jake, sitting in the pew next to me, muttered.

Ethan didn't "shut it."

He declared, "We're missing it."

"Eath, it's taping," Conner, on the other side of Ethan, pointed out.

"I better not find out the score before we get home," Ethan warned.

"Ohmigod," boy Taylor, sitting next to Amber who was sitting on my other side, whispered excitedly. "There's Kieran Wentworth."

"Where?" girl Taylor's fabulous sheath of shining black hair flew this way and that as she looked around.

"Four pews back, on the other side," boy Taylor told her and went on to note, "He must be home from school for the weekend or something."

I leaned into Amber and murmured, "Who's Kieran Wentworth?"

She leaned into me and murmured in reply, "He was a junior when we were freshman. He's so hot, he's a legend. He's at Boston College now. Taylor has been in love with him since *forever*."

I looked over my shoulder and four pews back on the other side I spied a highly attractive young man with short-clipped dark sandy blond hair, an exceptionally square jaw and cheekbones that would be immensely photogenic.

He also had very broad shoulders.

Further, he was wearing a rather stylish dark blue tailored shirt and wearing it quite well.

I turned back and leaned back into Amber. "He's most attractive."

"Yep," she agreed.

"I cannot imagine he hasn't noted Taylor's charms," I remarked.

"Uh…Josie, he's nineteen and in college. She's sixteen. That's not gonna happen."

Hmm.

"Give it two years," I stated.

"He'll be snapped up in two years," Amber returned.

"Not if he has something to wait for," I told her and felt her eyes turn to me so I turned mine to her.

She was smiling.

I winked.

Her smile got bigger.

I felt Jake lean into me and I turned my attention to him when he said, "I know Taylor's father. Don't go there."

I looked into his eyes then looked away and murmured, 'Hmm."

"Babe, the kid's nineteen," Jake stated something Amber had just told me.

"And?" I asked.

"He's also in college."

"Yes?"

He stared at me.

The choir started singing so I grinned to myself and stood with the rest of the congregation.

I did not miss it when, several minutes later, Reverend Fletcher came out, looked amongst his flock, saw me with the Spear family in our pew and he smiled at me.

Further, I absolutely did not miss it when, some time after that, Reverend Fletcher asked us all to pray for Arnold Weaver and his family as they had, just hours earlier, lost their beloved Elizabeth.

And I completely did not miss it when this was announced and Jake's arm, already extended behind me to rest on the back of the pew, curled around me to pull me tight to his side at the same time Amber reached out and grabbed my hand.

I was devastated for Arnie and his family.

Even so, I couldn't help but be happy for me as I'd finally found one.

Last, not too long after that, I made certain one Kieran Wentworth did not miss it when we were exiting the church and I maneuvered myself, Amber, Jake, Ethan, Conner and most especially the Taylors close to him. He was standing somewhat removed from a woman and man who must have been his parents. I then faked tripping, and as I'd done it so often in my life, I was good at faking it.

Of course, I wouldn't have wanted to fall to the floor so I had to grab something. The something I grabbed was girl Taylor, thus swinging her with me and directly into one Kieran Wentworth.

Jake caught me.

Kieran Wentworth caught Taylor.

He blinked when he looked into the exotically beautiful face of the girl curled in his arm.

I grinned as he did it.

Jake's arm tightened around my belly as he did it and his lips went to my ear.

"Seriously?" he asked and his tone sounded both amused and perturbed.

I had no answer to this question for I didn't understand it as I often didn't understand it when Jake, his children or others around us used this same word frequently. So I decided to ignore it and moved forward, pulling Jake with me.

"I'm so sorry. I'm quite clumsy," I shared, grinning innocently (I hoped) in Kieran Wentworth's face.

With obvious effort, he tore his gaze from girl Taylor and looked to me.

"Uh...not a problem," he replied.

I noted he still had a hand on girl Taylor's waist.

I nodded to him, smiled at him, pried Jake's arm from around my belly but did it taking hold of his hand and then I dragged him away in order to let nature take its course.

"That was *epic*," boy Taylor, trailing us, decreed.

"It's Josie who's epic," Amber, also trailing us, contradicted.

At her words, so much warmth washed through me, I couldn't handle it all and I tripped, genuinely this time.

Jake hauled me close and clamped an arm around me.

He said nothing but when I looked up at him, he was grinning.

We waited at the cars for a full ten minutes before girl Taylor finally joined us.

And I was delighted to see when she did, she looked dreamy.

———

IN THE AFTERNOON two days later, I leaned into Arnie, my hand on his arm and touched my cheek to his.

When I had it there, I whispered, "She will be missed."

"She will, my dear," he replied. I leaned back and he said, "I'll see you at the house."

I nodded, gave his arm a squeeze and moved away. Jake moved in, shook Arnie's hand and murmured his condolences. He did not take a great deal of time doing this and shifted away quickly to allow others to approach.

He got close to me, slid an arm around me and commandeered the umbrella I was holding, pulling me even closer and holding the big black umbrella over our heads as he moved us to his truck.

I walked through the sodden grass of the cemetery trying not to let the spike heels of my black boots sink into the turf, and failing.

They would need to be cleaned, air dried and shined and hopefully, in the end, they would not be ruined.

Jake performed somewhat of a miracle both holding the umbrella over me even as he helped me climb up in the truck, a difficult task in my black pencil skirt.

Once I was in, he closed my door, folded the umbrella, tossed it in the backseat and moved around the hood of the truck with the drizzle falling on his unguarded head and fantastic Hugo Boss suit.

Once he'd climbed in beside me, I noted, "That suit becomes you, Jake."

"Thanks, baby," he muttered as he turned the ignition.

He glided us out onto the lane and as we were approaching the exit to the graveyard, he said, "We don't have to go to the open house if it's too much for you, babe."

"Gran would go," I replied.

"You're not Lydie," he stated.

I turned my head to look at him as he stopped before taking the turn on the main road.

Even with the mist of rain in his hair and on the shoulders of his suit, he was most handsome.

"Yes I am, Jake," I whispered.

He looked to me, studied me, his eyes warm, his face soft, then he nodded.

He looked back to the road and turned onto it. Once on our way, he reached out and took my hand, pulling it his way and holding it against his thigh.

And he continued to hold it all the way to the Weaver's.

<hr />

IT WAS AFTERNOON the day after Eliza's funeral when I looked out the window of Jake's office at the gym and saw him standing with one of the many boys who were there for junior boxing league.

The boy was staring up at Jake with a rapt expression on his face, like I would assume one would stare at Superman if he was real.

"Seriously?" Alyssa's voice asked. "How does he find anything in here? I mean, his membership isn't even computerized. It's all on paper."

I said nothing.

My eyes moved through the gym to Mickey, who was standing ringside, calling out to the two boys in it. They then moved to Junior, who had three boys working punching bags. Finally, I shifted my eyes back to Jake, who had his hands up in front of his face. They were curled into fists and he quickly dropped one, punching it in the air, then the other one dropped and he punched the air then he brought his right one up and jabbed it, also into the air, directly bringing his fists back up to mostly cover his face.

Then he dropped his hands and jerked his chin up to the boy.

The boy lifted his hands in front of his face, changed his stance and mimicked what Jake did.

When he finished, Jake smiled down at him and clapped him on the shoulder.

The boy beamed.

Already lost in that man, seeing all this, all he'd wrought for these kids who clearly loved it, I sent a prayer to God that He'd never let me be found.

"You need to sort his shit out, Josie. How he gets anything done is anyone's guess. This place is a disaster zone," Alyssa announced and I turned my eyes to her, taking in Jake's office as I did.

It was, indeed, a disaster zone.

And the day before, when I informed Jake of this (however, I didn't use the words "disaster zone" but instead "colossal mess") after fully taking it in for the first time when we opened, I also informed him that I could organize it for him if he wished.

His reply was, "I am not a desk jockey, honey. You sort that shit, I'll feed you so many tacos and give you so many orgasms, you won't be able to move."

Although both options (primarily the latter) sounded very good to me, I'd returned, "It'll be difficult to sort your office if I can't move."

This got me a very long, very ardent kiss that was only interrupted when a member came in and shouted jovially, "Yo! Get a room!"

Thus, now I was in Jake's office, sorting it with Alyssa who was there not only because Junior was but also because two of her sons were in the league.

"Josie?" she called when I said nothing.

"Do you think it's possible to fall in love with a man knowing him only a few weeks?" I asked.

Her expression went from questioning to soft when she answered, "Yes."

"I'm in love with Jake," I announced.

"No shit?" she strangely replied.

"No shit," I decided to answer.

Her lips curved up and she shifted so she was leaning against the desk close to where I was sitting in Jake's rather tattered office chair.

She bent to me and shared, "Do you know how long it took me to fall in love with Junior?"

I shook my head.

"Thirty minutes," she declared.

"Thirty minutes?" I asked, surprised for that was no time at all. In fact, that made my falling in love with Jake seem like it took years.

"He picked me up for our date, took me to The Eaves, sat across from me, and after I ordered, I looked at him and he said, straight out, that I was the most beautiful thing he'd ever seen. That did it for me. He put that right out there. He took me to a great place. He didn't piss around with letting me know he was happy to be there with me. I looked into his eyes, saw how he was looking at me and knew right then that that was just the beginning. We've been together for nineteen fan-fucking-tastic years. So I wasn't wrong."

"That's beautiful, Alyssa," I told her.

"It totally is, Josie," she agreed.

"I'm happy you have that," I went on.

"And babelicious,"—she lifted a hand and cupped my cheek, bending even closer—"after your totally fucked up life, I'm freaking *thrilled* you finally have it too."

So was I.

I was delighted.

Over the moon.

Walking on air.

My eyes got watery but my lips tipped up and even with my eyes watery, I saw hers were the same.

Suddenly, she dropped her hand and pulled away, announcing, "If we lose it like big goofball girls, we'll probably be ejected."

She was wrong. Jake would never eject me. Even for crying in a boxing gym. And he took boxing very seriously.

I didn't share this.

I advised, "We should deep breathe."

"Yeah, let's do that."

We deep breathed, making very loud noises doing it.

Then we burst out giggling.

"Woman!" Junior shouted. "There's no giggling in boxing!"

We both looked out the window to Alyssa's man and saw him smiling at us.

He didn't mind the giggling.

In fact, he loved it and he also didn't mind letting that show.

Yes, I very much liked Junior.

My eyes moved to Jake and I saw he wasn't smiling, but he was looking into the office at me and his expression was warm and sweet.

I sent a smile his way.

He smiled back.

"Right, so giggling also could get us ejected. Nothing but serious from now on," Alyssa said, taking my attention off Jake.

I looked to her and pulled a serious face. "Nothing but serious."

She looked at my face and burst out laughing again.

I joined her.

Junior shouted, "What'd I say?"

I didn't know him well but I could tell his heart wasn't in it.

And anyway, for some reason, his shout made Alyssa laugh harder.

So I laughed with her.

TWO DAYS LATER, I lay on my side in Amber's bed watching boy Taylor, with not a small amount of skill and a great deal talent, sweep her face with a brush.

The door flew open and girl Taylor strode in.

"He's pulling up the lane," she announced.

"Oh boy, oh crap, oh God," Amber started chanting.

But my heart skipped a beat and I looked to girl Taylor.

"Please tell me he didn't arrive on a motorcycle," I begged.

"Nope." She shook her head. "A vintage Mustang."

"*Epic,*" boy Taylor breathed.

"His dad restores classic cars for a living," girl Taylor added. "Alexi works with him on the weekends. He's always in some kick-butt car."

"Totally epic," boy Taylor semi-repeated.

Although I found it gratifying Alexi had employment, especially honoring his father by working in the family business, I couldn't think of Alexi.

My thoughts were on Amber.

I looked to her.

She looked terrified.

After nearly two weeks of sitting together at lunch, just yesterday, Alexi Prokorov asked Amber out on a date.

We were away to Boston the next morning for the Bounce concert but we weren't leaving early enough for her to say no to an engagement that night.

She wouldn't have done that anyway.

She was beside herself with glee just as she was nearly shaking with nerves.

Thus, I had two situations to handle and a very short period of time to do that in. So I pushed myself off Amber's bed, got close to her and curled my hand under her jaw, bending to get even closer.

"Listen to me and do not forget this," I said softly. "It is not you who is the lucky one tonight, going out with Alexi Prokorov. It is he who is the lucky one that you said yes. Are you with me?"

Her eyes were big but she nodded.

"You look beautiful," I whispered, leaned up, kissed her forehead and straightened, looking down at her. "Have a wonderful time, sweetheart."

She smiled. It trembled a bit but it was gorgeous, filled with excitement and hope, both of which I hoped Alexi Prokorov fulfilled.

I gave a grin to the Taylors and then walked out of the room.

Once out, I hurried down the stairs and reached the bottom to see Jake opening the door for Alexi.

Luckily, I was right on time.

I noted that Alexi was much better looking in person and I was right, he was also quite tall. Not as tall as Jake but not shorter by very much.

"Mr. Spear," he said, extending his hand to Jake after Jake closed the door behind him.

Jake looked at Alexi's hand.

I moved close.

Jake looked to Alexi.

I slid my hand in the back pocket of Jake's jeans and pressed my body to his side.

Jake heard my silent communication and took Alexi's hand.

He let it go almost instantly and declared, "Her curfew is midnight."

"I'll have her home on time," Alexi replied.

"I hear you got a bike," Jake noted.

"Yeah," Alexi confirmed.

"My daughter's not on it," Jake announced.

Alexi nodded and looked to me. "You're Josie, right?"

"Ms. Malone," Jake corrected.

Alexi's eyes moved to him then back to me and he murmured, "Sorry. Ms. Malone."

I smiled at him, extending my hand, saying, "Yes, Alexi. I'm Josie. Ms. Malone."

"Amber talks about you all the time," he said, taking my hand, gripping it firmly but briefly before letting it go.

"That's nice to hear," I replied but barely got it out before he looked beyond me.

It must be said, I liked how his expression changed for I knew what I'd see when I turned.

And I saw it. Leaving the Taylors behind (it wouldn't do to let Alexi to know they were there for makeup and moral support), Amber was walking down the stairs.

No short skirt. No lady of the evening makeup. She had on a flatter-ing pair of jeans, my blush colored cashmere sweater, her own pair of fun platform sandals that had a muted collage of pink and brown rope adorning the wedge and she had a chocolate brown suede jacket slung over her arm.

She reached the bottom of the stairs, got close to Alexi, looked up to him and smiled a very pretty, somewhat shy smile

Perfection.

"Hey," she greeted.

"Hey," Alexi replied. "You look awesome."

She dipped her chin a bit, tucked some of her beautiful hair behind her ear and murmured, "Thanks."

Sheer perfection.

I was *so* proud of her.

"Someone kill me," Jake muttered, luckily so low that neither Amber nor Alexi heard him.

Or perhaps they were too into each other to hear Jake.

But I made a noise seeing as I'd swallowed my giggle but in doing so, it was a difficult endeavor.

"Midnight, Amber," Jake said and Amber looked to him.

"Okay, Dad," she replied, coming close and moving into his arms.

She kissed his cheek.

He wrapped his arms around her and gave her a tight but brief hug. "Be safe, honey. Yeah?" he asked gently when they'd separated half a foot.

"Yeah, Dad," she replied sweetly.

He grinned at her and let her go.

Alexi leaned in and took her hand.

The instant his fingers closed around hers, her eyes shot to me and they were alight.

"Have a wonderful time," I called.

"Thanks," Amber called back as Alexi moved her out the door.

"Nice to meet you," Alexi said, pulling her down the walk.

"You too," I replied, moving with Jake to the door.

Jake did not share my sentiment and I stifled another giggle.

When they made it to the Mustang, Jake closed the door and turned to me.

I looked up at him and noted, "He seems nice."

"I die a little every time that shit happens."

I blinked at his words before they poured through me, an elixir so warm, so healing, I knew nothing could ever ail me again. Not if he was in my life. Thus, I moved quickly to him and pressed close, wrapping my arms around him.

He returned the gesture and added putting his lips to my hair.

"You're *such* a good dad, Jake Spear," I whispered into his chest.

He gave me a squeeze but said nothing.

"Was it *awesome?*" boy Taylor intruded into the moment by asking.

Jake's arms loosened but he shifted one to wrap around my shoulders as I turned to the stairs to see the Taylors standing at the bottom of them.

"It was awesome," I confirmed.

Boy Taylor smiled huge, jumped, clapped and high-fived girl Taylor.

Ethan walked through, pushing past them on the stairs, ascending them and mumbling, "You all are whacked."

I grinned.

The Taylors laughed.

Jake gave my shoulders a squeeze and muttered, "Thank God I got at least six whole years before I gotta go through this shit again with Ethan."

That was when I looked up at my man and finally let myself giggle.

———— ◆·◆·◆ ————

"JAKE," I MOANED.

"Quiet, baby," he whispered.

"Jake!" I gasped.

"Fuck," he muttered before he drove his hand in my hair, fisted it, pulled it back and slammed his mouth on mine.

And when he did all this, I cried my orgasm down his throat.

He took it, kissed me after it then broke the connection of our mouths to order, "Lean back."

I did as best I could, wrapping my fingers around the faucet and planting my hand in the counter on the other side.

Jake yanked my hips that were on the bathroom counter of my hotel room in Boston deeper into his as he kept powering into me.

I lifted my already lifted knees higher.

Jake's eyes drifted over me and down to our connection.

"Fuck, I love watchin' you take me," he grunted.

I loved watching him watch himself take me. So much, I shivered.

"Beautiful," he whispered.

I clutched him tight with my sex.

His eyes came to mine.

"Beautiful," he repeated, his voice deeper, rougher and looking into his eyes, I decided he was so…very…*right.*

Beautiful.

His hips powered into mine harder. "Fuckin' beautiful."

"Yes," I breathed.

"Come here," he ordered.

I pushed up and wrapped my arms around him.

Jake wrapped an arm around my waist, again drove a hand in my hair, shoved my face in his throat just as it arched back, he thrust in and groaned.

I held him tight to me and traced the ridges of his throat with my tongue.

I loved the feel, the taste, but lost it when he bent his head to bury his face in my neck.

"Sucks, I gotta put you in bed and go," he said there, his voice gruff through his still uneven breathing.

He was right

It sucked.

But it was after the concert. The Taylors and Amber were sharing one room, Conner and Ethan sharing a room with Jake, I was alone in my room at Jake's decree for the very purpose of what we were doing in the bathroom.

A plethora of photos of the kids and Lavon as well as the rest of Bounce were all over Twitter, Instagram and Facebook. They'd had the time of their lives, been fabulously star struck, Lavon had been unbelievably lovely, we'd come back to the hotel and they were so wound up, I thought they'd never get to sleep.

They all crashed within half an hour.

That was when Jake came to me.

And now he had to leave me.

Which very much sucked.

He lifted his head and I bent mine back to catch his eyes.

"Think the kids are used to you?" he asked.

"Um…" I mumbled as an answer because I didn't really know what he was asking.

"Babe, we find our times but I want you in my bed, as in going to sleep with you in it and wakin' up to you in it. Heads up, tomorrow after you leave our house, I'm sittin' the kids down and having the discussion."

"What discussion?" I inquired, stuck on him declaring he wanted to go to sleep and wake up with me in his bed thus not following.

"The Josie's Gonna Be Spending the Night on A Very Regular Basis Discussion."

"Oh," I breathed and did it wondering if I looked as delighted as I was.

His lips quirked and he noted, "See you're down with that."

I looked as delighted as I was and didn't care he knew it.

"I am indeed down with that, darling," I confirmed.

His lips stopped quirking and he smiled. Then he dipped his head to kiss me. He did this for some time, I enjoyed it immensely through this time, and he kept doing it even as he pulled out.

Then he bent deep to kiss my chest before he moved to deal with the condom.

After he was done with that, he pulled me off the counter, took my hand, tugged me into the bedroom and right to the bed. He bent beyond me to pull back the covers before he gently pressed me into it.

I had on my nightie and no undies.

I didn't mind this.

Not at all.

I had my hands in prayer position under my cheek, watching him dress, when I asked a question I knew the answer to, "Do you think the kids enjoyed tonight?"

His head turned and his eyes caught mine. "Seriously?"

I bit my lip.

He pulled his shirt on, moved to the bed and sat on the side. Once there, he shifted my hair off my neck then leaned into his hand in the bed behind me so his face was close.

"They loved tonight, Josie," he said quietly.

I nodded my head on the pillow.

"The whole thing. The trip down. Lobster at a fancy-assed restaurant. Cush hotel the likes none of them have ever seen and girl Taylor's dad is pretty loaded," he went on. "Definitely the concert and meetin' the band."

"I'm glad," I whispered.

Jake's hand moved from the bed so he could use it to cup my jaw.

When he did, I turned into it, pressing my jaw deeper into his hand.

"You mean the world to them, baby," he whispered. "All of them. Even the Taylors."

"They mean the world to me," I replied.

"And you mean the world to me," he stated.

I blinked.

Then I stared.

Then my heart stopped beating.

"Babe?" he called when I said nothing.

"You mean the world to me too," I pushed out and when I did, it sounded husky.

"Thank fuck," he whispered and he meant both words, he meant them a great deal, and that meant a great deal to me. "Kiss me before I do something that does not say good dad and leave my sons alone in a hotel room in Boston all night."

All our rooms were adjoining. Obviously, the door from my room to his room with the boys was closed, as was the door between their room and Amber and the Taylor's, but still.

He didn't want to leave them alone.

Such a good father.

I pushed up and put my lips to his. Then I slid my tongue in his mouth. After mere moments of me enjoying drinking from him, his arms closed around me and he drank from me.

He did it better.

Alas, some time after but still too soon, he ended the kiss, lifted his lips to kiss my nose and put me back in bed.

"See you in the mornin', Slick."

"See you in the morning, darling."

Jake grinned.

I grinned back.

He bent in and kissed my jaw.

Then I watched him move to the adjoining door and through it.

I stared at the closed door long after Jake was gone thinking that I meant the world to Jake Spear.

I meant the world to him.

He told me so.

Thus, mere minutes later, I fell asleep smiling.

IT WAS SUNDAY.

It was dark.

We were back from Boston. The Taylors had headed home. I'd hung out with Jake and the kids at his house. But now it was time to go home.

Jake was standing outside with me by my Cayenne.

I was in his arms and we were standing close.

"I'll call you later and tell you how the talk went," he said.

"Okay," I replied.

"I don't get bad vibes, you're in my bed tomorrow night," he declared.

This made me slightly nervous but mostly happy so I pressed closer and repeated, "Okay."

"Okay," he muttered then dipped his head and touched his mouth to mine. He lifted it and said quietly, "Need to get that shit done."

"Okay, darling. I'll talk to you later."

He touched his mouth to mine, lifted his head again and said, "Yeah."

I gave him a squeeze and a smile.

Jake returned the gesture.

He then opened my door for me, closed it after I climbed in and stood in the lane that led up to his house while I backed out, turned into the street and drove away.

I didn't envy him the impending likely uncomfortable discussion with his kids. It was pretty clear they knew what was going on with their dad and I, but bringing it up, discussing it, moving it forward for them in a way that at the very least Conner and Amber would understand, would not be easy.

But I hoped it was relatively painless.

This was on my mind as I drove home.

This was still on my mind when I drove into the curve in front of Lavender House.

It was not on my mind when I saw the shiny black Mercedes parked in front of my house.

"What on earth?" I asked irately into the cab.

I saw Boston Stone move from the shadowed entry of Lavender House as I parked.

I kept my eyes glued to him as I turned off my car, threw open the door, got out, slammed the door, beeped the locks and started to stalk toward him in order to tell him precisely how I felt, not only about a visit late in a Sunday evening, but about any visit from him at all.

However, before I could say a word, I tripped over my feet, righted myself and stopped dead.

Then I went completely still.

And I did this staring at the man who followed Boston Stone from the shadows of the front door of Lavender House.

Staring unthinking but not unfeeling.

And none of the feelings I was having were even remotely good.

For the man who followed Boston Stone was the second to last man I'd ever want to see again in my life.

It was my uncle.

Seventeen

GONE. DEEP.

After Jake watched Josie drive away, he moved to his house, in it and closed the door behind him. He then moved to the stairs, up them and straight to his daughter's door.

He knocked, waited and opened it, swinging only his torso in when he heard her call, "Yeah?"

She was on her bed on the phone. From the dreamy expression on her face, Jake knew she was talking to Alexi.

"Wrap that up, honey. Family meeting in the kitchen. You can call him back when we're done," he ordered.

"Okay, Dad," she replied easily.

Jake studied her a second before jerking up his chin, swinging back out and closing the door.

He didn't know if it was Josie's influence, Alexi or both, but he liked how she was with this kid.

With Noah, she was anxious, unsure of herself, grouchy and a pain in the ass.

With Alexi, she seemed more relaxed, more certain, timidly excited and not at all a pain in the ass.

It might be the kid, but Jake decided to give Josie the credit.

Alexi got her home on time and she was clearly riding the high of the date in a good way throughout the drive to Boston the next day.

But Jake was exercising a father's prerogative and reserving judgment on Alexi and would keep doing that shit until they broke up or, God forbid, had their first kid in at least ten but hopefully more like twenty years.

On this thought, he turned to the landing and heard the doorbell ring. He was halfway down the stairs when he saw Con walking through the entryway toward the front door.

His son looked up at him as he moved and said, "Got it, Dad."

"Right," Jake replied.

When he made it down the stairs, he turned his head and stopped when he saw who was at the door.

At the same time, he heard his son say, "What the hell?"

And he said this because Ellie was standing outside looking up at Conner, her face hesitant, earnest, scared and shy.

"Con, can I talk to you a sec?" she asked cautiously.

Jake waited to see if Conner needed him and as he did, he heard Con reply, his voice clipped, "Living room."

This was not welcoming but still, Ellie nodded. Conner moved aside to let her in, caught his dad's eyes and Jake saw he had this. Then again, he usually had it. Unlike Amber, his boy was confident with just about everything.

Jake still gave him a look. Conner returned a shake of his head, closed the front door and moved toward the living room where Ellie had disappeared.

Jake got closer to his son and said low, "Don't know what that is but we gotta have a family meeting. Sorry, bud, but gotta ask you to do what you can to make it short."

Conner held his eyes a second before he nodded and moved into the living room, closing the door behind him.

Jake sighed as he walked into the kitchen, taking his phone out of his back pocket. He put it on the charger and went to the fridge, hoping like all fuck Conner dealt with whatever Ellie had going on and quick. He was looking forward to burying Josie deeper into the family fold. He was not looking forward to discussing how he wanted to do that, especially with two teenagers who knew exactly what it meant that he was going to have a woman in his bed.

Luckily, Ethan didn't get it and probably would just be excited to have Josie around more.

He just hoped Conner and Amber were the same.

They gave no indication they wouldn't be.

Still, he had far from abstained since he got shot of Ethan's mom but none of those women had slept in his bed. He'd had them there when the kids weren't around, but his kids never woke up to his women.

So this conversation was not going to be easy.

He pulled out a beer, twisted off the top, tossed the cap in the trash and took a pull as he started to the family room where he could hear a game playing. He was going to tell Ethan they were having a meeting but he didn't get that far.

The doorbell went again.

He felt his brows draw together as he looked in that direction then moved in that direction.

He heard nothing from the living room, which he hoped was a good sign.

But he saw through the windows at the top of the door who was standing outside.

"*Fuck,*" he hissed, not wanting to do it but doing it all the same mostly because he had no choice.

He set his beer on the table beside the door and opened it.

Donna stood outside.

And, someone kill him, she had Ellie's exact expression of hesitant, earnest, scared and shy. Except it was on the face of a woman thirty years older, it was about something she couldn't possibly think was going to happen so it was entirely jacked.

He did not let her in. He forced her to take two steps back as he went out and closed the door behind him.

"Now is not a good time," he growled.

"Jake, we gotta talk," she said quietly.

"Yeah," he agreed. "But now's not a good time. You call before you do this shit, Donna. You don't blindside me."

She took in a deep breath, lifted a hand and placed it on his chest.

Instantly, he moved to the side, clearing her hand and putting another two feet of distance between them.

Her eyes widened in shock as she dropped her hand.

Fucking hell.

Seriously?

She lifted both hands to her sides, eyes glued to his, and stated, "I fucked up."

"We're not doing this," he returned immediately.

"Jake—"

"You talkin' about fuckin' up with our boy and girl?" he asked.

She nodded. "Yes. The kids and, well…us."

"We'll talk about the kids later. Not now. We're not talkin' about us ever seein' as there is no us to talk about."

Her expression turned pleading. "Jake, there's always been an us."

Jesus.

Whacked.

"Donna, since you kicked my ass out the first time, the us there was was gone."

"I know I hurt you," she whispered.

"Woman, that was fourteen years ago."

"We were happy," she told him.

"No, Donna. I was happy. You were never happy. You were always searchin' for something, wanting something, pissed about not finding it or getting it and up in my shit. Those times I was *not* happy and lookin' back, havin' something good now that actually does make me happy, I see it. But none of this shit matters because it's so over it's barely a memory."

She flinched from his blow but he didn't give a fuck.

His boy was inside talking to the girl who broke his heart two weeks ago and he had to monitor that situation. And he had a conversation to have with his children. What he did not have was time to deal with his ex.

Before he could tell her to get gone, however, she spoke again.

"So Josie makes you happy?" she asked.

"Yeah," he answered, "Now, listen—"

But it was then Donna cut him off in order to make a very bad mistake.

And this was saying, "She's pretty, Jake, but she's super weird."

Oh no.

Fuck no.

"She's weird?" Jake whispered.

"She talks funny and, well...*acts* funny. Is that really what you—?"

"It's funny to you that she listens to your daughter, takes her shopping, buys her makeup, is interested in what Amber's interested in and shows Amber she can trust her with pretty much everything she does so Amber actually trusts her?"

"I—"

"And it's funny to you that when Conner had a pissed off dad in his face, Josie stood between him and that man, calmed the situation down, sorted it out and didn't waste any time gettin' Con off the hook for somethin' he didn't do in the first place?"

She shut her mouth and stared at him.

"Newsflash, Donna, that shit is not weird. What's so weird it's god-damned whacked is a woman who gives more of a shit about gettin' off, pretending the men in her bed are the husband she had nearly two decades ago, so that woman has no time to be a mother to her children."

That got him another flinch and he didn't care about that one either.

He kept at her.

"Josie's been more mother to them in the last month than you have in the last five years."

Donna had something to say to that.

"That's a terrible thing to say," she whispered.

"It is. And the fuck of it is, every word is true," Jake returned. "Proof of that is that your kids are inside this goddamned house and you're not here to see them, you're here to talk to me. You haven't even asked about them. And before you think you can backtrack, I'll give you the heads up, now's not your time to have with them. Not with you comin' over without them on your mind. Until you start thinkin' of them, you got no access to them."

Pain suffused her face and Jake didn't care about that either.

He was done.

So he moved to get this scene done.

"I see you haven't thought about shit in the last week. Or, if you have, you've been thinkin' the wrong things. So I'll give you more time to do that.

In fact, take all the time you want. But don't come back here. I don't wanna talk to you. I don't wanna see you. I can't stop you from talkin' to your kids so the only thing I can do is ask, please, God, if you try to sort shit out with them, do it smart, thinkin' about them and not yourself. I don't figure you got that in you so it'll be me and Josie pickin' up whatever pieces you leave behind. But still, I'm beggin' you, try to find it in you to be a decent mom for once. For them. Now, that's all I got to say. Get gone and don't come back. Yeah?"

Her eyes welled up with tears and she whispered, "I don't believe this is happening. I can't believe you're talking to me this way. Even if we're over, Jake, this isn't exactly nice."

Christ.

What was the matter with her?

"It is and I am. Believe it. You do, finally, you'll manage to extract your head out of your ass," Jake returned, moved to the door, opened it, stepped through and closed it without looking back.

When he did, Ethan called out, "Dad! Your phone's been ringin'!"

Jake moved to the doorway to the family room and replied, "Thanks, bud."

His son didn't even look away from the game as he said, "No probs."

"Eath, we're gonna have a family meeting in a minute so find a good place to pause," Jake told him.

Ethan looked to him then and asked, "About what?"

"About Josie," Jake answered

His son tipped his head to the side. "You marryin' her?"

His son's words put the shit he just endured from Donna out of his head, so he grinned but shook his head. "Not yet."

Ethan's face changed before he asked, "She okay?"

"Yeah, buddy," Jake replied quietly.

His expression cleared and he kept up the interrogation. "She movin' in?"

Jake stifled his laughter and said, "Not exactly. But I want her around more and gotta make sure you guys are cool with that."

Ethan looked back to the game and announced, "I'm cool with it, just as long as she and Amber don't gang up on us and make us watch *Project Runway* and crap like *The Voice*." Ethan looked back to him. "So, seein' as I'm cool with it, I don't have to pause the game to go to the meeting. Right?"

Jake opened his mouth to reply but said nothing when he heard his phone ringing at the same time he heard the door to the living room open behind him.

"Find a place to pause, son," he murmured distractedly, turned and looked down the hall to see a sobbing Ellie rushing through it, opening the front door and throwing herself out, slamming it behind her.

Conner then sauntered out of the room and stopped, his eyes to the front door.

Jake moved into the entryway.

Conner felt his presence and looked to his dad. His face didn't say much except whatever that was was unpleasant but Jake was surprised that whatever set Ellie to running from the house crying, obviously it didn't bother Con all that much.

"Everything okay?" he asked.

"Not for her," Conner answered.

"You wanna tell me?" Jake went on.

Conner shrugged. "She wanted to get back together. Feels shit for not goin' to bat for me. Talked to her folks. Talked 'em into lettin' her give me another chance. Another freaking chance." He shook his head, looked to the door then back at his dad and finished, "It's too late. She had her chance and blew it."

Jake held his eyes, knowing this was Conner's decision and not disagreeing that it was the right one, so he let it lie.

Then he said quietly, "She was in bad shape when she left."

Conner's eyes went to the door as he murmured, "Yeah."

"Get in your car, Con," Jake told him. "Follow her. Make sure she gets home okay. Then come back. We got shit to talk about."

Conner looked back to his dad and guessed accurately, "Josie?"

Jake shook his head, again fighting a grin. "Car. Ellie. Home safe. We'll talk when you get back."

Conner nodded and headed to the kitchen but he did it speaking.

"If you're movin' things up a notch with her, just so you know, I'm down with that. She cooks great, even if she always serves vegetables she tries to get me to eat. And if she's here in the morning, I don't have to take Eath to school."

Jake followed his son, stopping in the kitchen doorway and leaning a shoulder against the jamb as Con moved to the door to the garage.

Conner stopped and looked back at him, "So that's my vote. You can have the meeting without me."

"We'll talk when you get back," Jake replied, jerking his head to the door. "Go."

Conner's lips twitched then he was out the door.

"Is Josie moving in?"

This came from behind him. It came from Amber. It sounded hopeful. And when Jake turned, he saw his daughter's face looked hopeful too.

He heard his phone ring again but he focused on his girl. "No, honey. But she's gonna be around a lot more."

"*Awesome*," Amber breathed. "More girls in the house. This means maybe we'll get some toss pillows and I'll get to watch *Say Yes to the Dress* on the big TV."

His plans for a family meeting clearly in the toilet, he made a decision and held his daughter's eyes.

"What I mean is, she's gonna be spendin' the night," he said gently.

When he did, Amber's head tipped to the side and she replied, "Yeah, Dad. Uh…duh."

Jake stared at her thinking this was a fuckuva lot easier than he expected it to be.

She righted her head and noted, "Does this mean I don't have to be at the meeting and I can call Alexi back?"

He had all around approvals and didn't think it was a good idea to make a big deal of something the kids obviously didn't think was a big deal, so he nodded and said, "Sure, honey."

She gave him a huge smile, took a hop to him, leaned up and kissed his cheek.

She did this fast, then raced away and up the stairs just as fast.

He watched her go, thinking of her kiss, her smile, how she was a month ago which was absolutely not like that, and again giving Josie the credit.

His mind on Josie, he moved to his phone to call her to tell her tomorrow night (and the night after, and the one after that), her ass was in his bed.

But when he picked up his phone, he saw he had three missed calls.

All from Josie.

His gut clenched as he moved his thumb over his screen.

He hit go on her number and put the phone to his ear.

She answered in one ring and when she did, her voice was trembling.

It was then his gut twisted.

"Jake."

"Baby, what's up?"

"Boston Stone is here," she told him and a burn started in his chest.

"What the fuck?" he clipped.

Her voice got weak when she added, "He's with Uncle Davis."

Uncle Davis.

Davis Malone.

Lydie's firstborn boy and a supreme asshole.

At this news, Jake yanked the charger out of his phone and moved quickly toward the stairs.

Unfortunately, Josie wasn't done.

"And Terry Baginski just arrived."

"What the *fuck?*" he bit out, hitting the stairs and taking them two at a time.

"They're explaining Uncle Davis is contesting the will," she whispered.

God damn it.

"Hang tight, Slick, I'll be there soon's I can," he told her as he rapped sharply on Amber's door.

"Okay, Jake," she replied just as his daughter called, "Yeah?"

"Be there soon, baby. Yeah?" he said gently.

"Yes, Jake."

"All right. See you in a few minutes," he told her.

"Okay."

"Later, honey."

"Later, Jake," she said.

He didn't want to let her go but he had to let her go so he could get to her.

So he disconnected, opened his girl's door and swung in.

She was in the same position as earlier, on the bed, her phone to her ear.

"Gotta get to Josie," he stated. "Look after Ethan while I'm gone."

She sat up, her eyes not leaving him and he knew she'd read him when she asked, "Is Josie okay?"

"Don't know, honey," he replied. "Gotta go. You're here with Ethan, yeah?"

She nodded, her eyes still glued to him, "Yeah, Dad. Go."

He swung out of her room, not closing the door. He jogged down the steps and when he got to the bottom, called out to his son, "Gotta go do somethin', bud. You're here with Amber."

Lost in the game, Ethan called back, "Okay, Dad."

Delaying no further, he went to his truck, backed it out of the garage and engaged his phone to call Conner.

It rang twice before Con answered with, "Ellie's home okay, Dad."

"You're closer than me so I need you to get to Lavender House right now," he ordered.

Conner's voice was alert when he asked, "Why?"

"Josie's there and so's her uncle."

Josie had been a part of their lives for a lot longer than she'd physically been part of their lives. This was because Lydie had shared liberally with not only Jake but his kids and not only about Josie but also in her frank but gentle way about herself. His kids didn't get it all but they got the jist.

And Jake knew Conner got the jist when he said, "On my way."

"Stick to her like glue until I get there. I'm on my way."

"Got it."

"Later."

"Bye, Dad."

He disconnected, kept his phone in his hand in case Josie called and drove fast.

There were four cars in the curve of the lane in front of Lavender House when he arrived. After Jake parked and got out he noted a wicked wind had blown up. It bit into him the instant he opened his door.

He didn't feel it.

Instead, he saw the shadowy figures standing outside the front door to the house. Five of them. When he got closer, he saw it was Conner facing off against Stone, Lydie's son and Terry Baginski. He was pleased to see that Con had Josie behind him.

Jake made a mental note to put in fucking motion sensor lights the next fucking day as he prowled to the group.

"The cavalry arrives." He heard Terry say sarcastically as he moved to his woman and his son.

"What's goin' on here?" he asked, his eyes scanning Josie's pale face as best he could in the light and not liking what he saw.

"They want in," Conner answered him. "Josie doesn't want them in so they aren't goin' in."

Jake took his place beside his son and turned his eyes to Stone, the old man standing next to him and Terry.

To control his temper, he couldn't look at Stone or Lydie's son. So he focused on Terry.

"Josie doesn't want you in, time for you to leave," he stated.

"We have things to discuss," Terry replied.

"If that's the case, call Josie, make a meeting," Jake returned.

"That's hardly necessary when we're all right here," she shot back.

"It's Sunday night, Terry," Jake reminded her. "Whatever this is, it can happen at a decent hour on a workday."

"What this is is that Lydia Malone made a highly unusual bequest in her will that unfortunately demonstrated she was not of her right mind when she wrote it. This would be proved true as she also didn't include her son in any of her rather substantial behests," Stone announced.

Jake didn't even look at him.

He narrowed his eyes on Terry. "You share the terms of the will and Lydie's assets with Boston Stone?"

"Davis Malone, as the only *direct* living descendent of Lydia Malone, is entitled to know the particulars of his mother's situation and last requests," she answered.

"I didn't ask that," Jake ground out. "I asked if you shared the terms of Lydie's will and her assets with Boston Stone who is *not* a relative."

She didn't reply.

That meant she did.

"At the reading of the will, you mentioned Stone," Jake went on. "Now, you're colluding with him."

"I'm hardly colluding with him," she snapped. "There's nothing to collude about."

"So this isn't a play to get Lavender House sold so Malone can pocket the profits and Stone can doze it or make it into a hotel or whatever the hell he wants to do with it?" Jake pressed.

"I obviously can't know what Mr. Malone will do should he inherit Lavender House," she lied through her teeth.

Jake scowled at her. "Don't know shit about this but it seems a conflict of interest. You got a stake in Stone Incorporated?"

She didn't get the chance to answer. Lydie's fuckwad son decided to enter the conversation.

"This is bullshit, barred from my childhood home."

Even as he felt Josie press close to his back, Jake turned his attention to the man and saw he was old, he was weak, he'd clearly lived a rough life that Jake knew was of his own making and he looked mean as a snake.

"You never lived here," Jake returned.

"Right, then, barred from *my mother's* childhood home," Davis amended.

"Yeah, and if Lydie was here, she'd be right next to Josie doin' that and you know it," Jake told him something he absolutely fucking knew.

"Unfortunately, my mother died before we could make amends," Davis spewed his bullshit.

"Seein' as you had about sixty years to do that and you didn't, I'm guessin' amends couldn't be made," Jake fired back.

"This is ridiculous," Terry snapped. "It's freezing out here. We can discuss this inside."

Jake turned his attention to her. "We're not discussing this inside. Josie'll discuss this with you at the meeting you're gonna arrange. Now, you're gonna leave or I'm gonna call Coert and he'll ask you to leave."

"It's hardly necessary calling the sheriff, Spear," Stone noted and Jake finally looked at him.

And his voice changed significantly when he addressed him.

"You got your panties in a bunch when Josie leveled you, you teamed up with Terry and you found this guy in order to fuck with her because you're so goddamned small, you weren't man enough to take that direct hit and move on. You think you got a stake in this, but you don't. All you did was set yourself up to take another direct hit."

"It's hardly the behavior of a lucid woman to settle a human being on another human being in her will," Stone returned.

"'Fraid I'm gonna have to disagree with you seein' as for Josie and me, that worked out all right, so Lydie knew exactly what she was doin' and that's all kinds of lucid."

"That's absurd," Stone clipped.

"You can think that if you want, but it's still true."

"Fuck me, all this yammering," Davis Malone snapped and Jake looked at him to see his eyes aimed at Josie. "Girl, just open the goddamned door."

Jake didn't let Josie speak and instead ordered, "Go, all of you."

"An arrangement can be made," Terry put in. "Mr. Malone is willing to be reasonable and negotiate a fair division of assets once Lavender House is sold."

At this, Jake felt Josie press closer to his back.

Jake turned narrowed eyes to Terry. "Explain to me how you can act on behalf of Davis Malone," Jake demanded. "You're Josie's attorney."

"Arnie's Josie's attorney. I'm not," she returned.

"You're at the same firm and *that's* not a conflict of interest?" Jake asked. She said nothing.

It was absolutely a conflict of interest, the bitch.

Jake was done.

"You wanna be asked to leave by the sheriff, have at it," he muttered, turning and herding his son into Josie. His eyes found hers through the dark. "Keys out, baby," he whispered. "Let us in."

She stared up at him with wide eyes a moment before she nodded, turned jerkily, teetered on her heel and Jake put a hand out to steady her.

Without Jake telling him to do so, Conner crowded his dad and Josie at the door and he and his son kept crowding her until they got her in, followed her and Jake closed and locked the door behind them.

"Lights, Con," Jake ordered as he looked down to his phone to find Coert's number.

"Jake," Josie whispered and he turned his attention to her, put his phone to his ear and lifted his other hand to her neck where he curled his fingers around the side and gave her a squeeze.

"Just a second, baby."

She pressed her lips together.

Coert answered the phone. "Yo, Jake. You good?"

"I'm at Lavender House with Josie Malone and there are trespassers on the property who won't leave even after we've asked repeatedly for them to do so."

"Fuck," Coert groaned, probably settled in for the night in front of a game.

Jake kept a hand on Josie as he leaned back to look through the window at the side of the door. He saw the cars still there, as were the shadowed bodies.

"I'd owe you one, you roust these assholes," Jake said into the phone.

"You will and big. The Broncs are playing."

Coert gave a shit about the Broncos because he was a transplant from Denver. Jake also knew why Coert got the fuck out of the Mile High City. There were only two reasons a man with a good job he liked in a town he loved would move across an entire country. He fucked up or a woman fucked him up.

In Coert's situation, it was the last.

"Gotta warn you, Boston Stone is one of the assholes I'm talkin' about," Jake told him.

"That got me motivated," Coert surprisingly replied then explained, "Guy's a dick."

"Agreed."

"On my way," Coert stated.

"Thanks, man," Jake murmured.

"Later."

"Later."

He disconnected, looked to Josie who was staring up at him and noticed instantly she was freaked way the fuck out.

That was why his eyes moved to his son as Con got back from going through the house and turning on lights.

"On the phone with your sister. Get her to pack a bag for you, Ethan and her, get your books and haul her and Eath over here. We're stayin' the night with Josie."

"Jake," Josie whispered.

"Gotcha," Conner said and moved toward the kitchen.

Jake looked down to his woman. "Fuck them. You're stayin' in *your* house tonight and you're not doin' it alone," he declared.

She pressed her lips together before she fell forward and face planted in his chest.

He wrapped his arms around her, put his lips to the top of her hair and told her, "It's gonna be okay, Slick."

"He wants Lavender House," she said into his chest.

"He's not gonna get it," Jake returned.

"He's standing out there right now."

"Coert's gonna be here and he'll be gone in fifteen minutes, baby."

Her arms slid around him but the hold was loose, like she didn't have it in her to hold tight.

Fucking Stone.

He orchestrated this, the asshole.

Jake gave her a squeeze and repeated, "It's gonna be okay."

Her head tipped back and she was still freaked but now fear had moved into her eyes.

He'd know why when she asked, "Do you think maybe Dad will come too?"

Fuck.

Luckily, Conner walked in just then and Jake looked to him. "Get Josie a glass of that shit in Lydie's liquor cabinet. Fancy bottle, looks like cough syrup, smells like it. Yeah?"

"No problem," Conner replied and walked right back to the kitchen.

"Jake?" Josie called and he looked back down to her.

"Let's sit down," he suggested then made this so by moving her into the family room and sitting her on the couch.

He wanted her in his lap. Better, he wanted to lie down with her, hold her close and give her what he had to give her when he had her safe in his arms.

He didn't do that because his son might not be comfortable with it, nor Josie.

So he got her as close as he could, wrapping an arm around her shoulders and nabbing her hand.

"Right, a while back, Lydie asked me to look into things," he stated.

She held his gaze and nodded.

"I did," he went on.

She didn't nod, just continued to look into his eyes.

"Your dad's dead, baby."

She stared at him a second, not one thing washing through her features, before she fell forward and did a face plant in his chest again.

Jake wrapped both arms around her.

Conner walked in with a snifter of purple liquid and Jake watched, his boy's eyes locked on Josie, as his son walked directly to the coffee table, sat his ass on it, set the glass aside and reached out to curl his fingers around Josie's knee.

Christ, he was a good kid.

"Kids on their way?" he asked his son.

"Yep," Conner answered. "Amber's all over it."

"Thanks, bud," he whispered.

Conner said nothing, just jerked up his chin.

Josie leaned away, gave Conner a small smile she totally didn't commit to and looked to Jake.

"I need to make up beds for the kids."

"We'll see to that when Amber and Eath get here," he replied.

"But—"

"Take a drink, Slick, relax. We got this covered."

Something shifted in her eyes before her lips formed the words, "You got this covered."

"Yeah," he confirmed.

She stared at him.

Conner let her go to grab her glass and he offered it to her.

Jake unwrapped one arm so she could turn and take it.

"Stuff smells crap," Conner muttered as she lifted it to her mouth and took a sip.

It was at that, finally, when Josie smiled and it was genuine this time.

There it was.

He was right.

They had this covered.

———•◦•◦•———

"MICKEY SAID AND word was you got in there, but Jesus Christ," Coert stated, his eyes to the front door of Lavender House.

Coert and Jake had just left Josie after Coert and one of his deputies moved the stubbornly lingering group of assholes off Josie's property. He'd reported to the owner that he'd dealt with the situation and he'd done this with two things on his agenda. Reporting to the owner that he'd dealt with it and getting a look at Josie.

"Pure class, even rattled," Coert noted, looked to Jake and grinned, something Jake could see since he turned on the outside lights when Coert arrived in his cruiser. "How'd you get in there?"

"She thinks I'm the shit," Jake told him, grinning back.

Coert kept handing him crap. "So you've brainwashed her."

Jake kept grinning but his grin died when he asked, "You know I like taking your shit, Coert, but gotta know. Until shit gets sorted with the will, she got a genuine threat from her uncle?"

Coert's face also got serious. "Judge'll have to make that decision, Jake. Until that time, assets will probably be frozen. If you mean can the old guy make her let him in or even make her let him stay, again, judge'll have to handle that. But until the will is assessed and judgment made, if things are acrimonious, Josie's already here so she'll likely be ordered not to sell anything, they'll let her stay and he might be allowed to get in and look around but other than that, he'll be ordered to steer clear."

"So she's good," Jake said.

"If she's got her own assets to live on, yeah," Coert confirmed.

She did. She'd told him. So that was at least one thing they didn't have to worry about.

They still had two more.

"You know if Terry Baginski is invested in Stone Incorporated?" Jake asked.

"Lotta local folks are investors in Stone Incorporated," Coert answered.

"I'm takin' your non-answer as a no, you don't know."

"Yeah. I don't know for certain but I wouldn't be surprised," Coert replied and his voice got lower when he went on, "Be less surprised she's in on this just to piss you off."

Jake shook his head. "Banged her between number two and number three which was a long time ago," he pointed out. "She was the worst lay I'd ever had, bar none. Been years. I'm not her favorite person but actively tryin' to piss me off…" he trailed off disbelievingly.

"Women do a lot of crazy shit, they get it in their minds to do it," Coert noted and Jake thought he was not wrong, his earlier conversation with Donna being proof of that. Then Coert changed the subject to ask, "Stone after Lavender House?"

"He was," Jake answered. "Then he got a look at Josie and decided he preferred her. She wasn't interested, tried to be cool about lettin' him know that, but she heard him talkin' smack about her. She leveled him and clearly he didn't like that much."

Coert's brows shot up. "No shit? This is retaliation for a crash and burn?"

"More like a detonation, but yeah. Guy's dick is microscopic."

At this, Coert got closer and warned, "He's your threat, Jake. If he's bankrolling that old asshole for a shot at Lavender House, this could get ugly. Lotta folks in this town will stand up for Lydia Malone and say it straight she was all there until the day she died. But Stone's got the money to drag it out if that option's to be had."

This was not good news.

"She gave Josie to me in her will," Jake confided and he saw Coert's brows draw together.

"Say again?"

"Lydie," Jake explained. "She gave Josie to me in her will."

"Josie…the person?" Coert asked, his brows now shooting up.

"Yep," Jake answered.

Coert stared at him a beat before he burst out laughing.

Jake let him but crossed his arms on his chest while he did it.

When Coert got it under control, he stated, "That does it. Clearly Lydia had lost it before she passed, leavin' her girl to you."

"Bite me," Jake muttered good-naturedly but tensed when he saw Coert suddenly get serious.

"Thought the world of you," he said quietly. "Your kids. Everyone knew it. You were the son she never had. The son she always wanted. Your kids the grandkids she never got outside your girl in there. Straight up, man, after you scraped off Sloane, lots of talk in this town, wondering why Lydia didn't fix you up with her girl when she was around, seein' as she was around often enough. Anyone who knows her would not be surprised Lydia wanted that as her final wish. You could get a hundred folks in a courtroom to say that same thing and do it under oath. I am not kidding."

Jake could say nothing. Coert's words about him being the son Lydie never had were stuck in his throat, making it prickle.

When Jake was silent, Coert kept speaking.

"And I only moved here fifteen years ago but think it says a fuckuva lot that I only got a decade and a half under my belt in Magdalene and the specter of Davis and Chester Malone still haunts this burg and those two little motherfuckers didn't even live here. Just caused mayhem whenever they visited their grandparents, the kind it was hard for a lot of people to forget. Including how they took treatin' their mom to new and unprecedented piss-poor levels." He took in a breath and concluded, "What I'm sayin' is, you guys hunker down, it's all gonna work out. You need me in the meantime, call. I figure you got some pains in the ass to deal with for a while but in the end, this will go away."

Jake nodded and murmured, "Thanks, man."

"You still owe me," Coert noted.

"You didn't tape the game?" Jake asked.

"You know it sucks not seein' live," Coert returned.

"Hardly. You get to go home and fast forward through the commercials. Figure we livened up your night and you owe me."

"You'd figure wrong," Coert replied. "I want one of Tom's omelets and I wanna eat it with you buyin' it and bringin' your woman along with you."

At that, Jake grinned. "No way you got a shot. Ask Mick. She's into me."

"Man can still look."

Jake shook his head.

Coert extended his hand.

Jake uncrossed his arms to shake it. "Appreciate it, Coert."

"My job, not a problem," Coert murmured, let Jake go and gave a low wave as he moved to his cruiser.

His deputy was already gone.

Jake didn't wait to watch him pull out. He went into the house, locked the door behind him and went to the family room where he'd left Josie with his kids, Ethan trying to pretend he wasn't freaked for Josie but doing this sitting close to his woman, Amber shocking the shit out of him and hustling around the house to get beds made without anyone asking.

But when he got to the family room, only his kids were there.

"Josie got a call, Dad," Conner informed him immediately. "She went to the light room to take it."

Jake nodded once, turned on his boot to retrace his steps and hit the light room.

A call could be anything. The last two weeks, after Gagnon fired her, her phone rang all the time.

And it could be something bad if Stone, Terry or Josie's uncle had her number.

But when he made it up to the light room, he saw from the single light she'd turned on that she was in the window seat, her gaze to the sea and she was not on the phone.

Her eyes came to him and he saw her face still blank.

He didn't like that. Not only because it was not Josie but because he couldn't read it and he needed to know where her head was at.

He moved to her, sat behind her and arranged them so he had her between his legs up on the window seat, arm around her chest, the other around her ribs, her back to his torso.

He felt better when she rested her head on his shoulder and her arms over his.

"Amond called. He's going to be here Tuesday," she shared once she'd relaxed into him.

Fucking fantastic. Just what they needed. A protective, internationally known hip-hop artist showing up to pass judgment on Jake.

He did not share these thoughts.

He said, "Good you got that visit to look forward to."

She said nothing, just looked out at the sea.

He let her do this for a while and then he was done letting her do it so he gave her a squeeze and said gently, "Baby, you're freakin' me out. Lots to think about, I know your head's gotta be full of it but you're givin' me nothing."

That was when she gave him something.

"How did Dad die?" she asked but she did it like she'd ask what was for dinner.

That was bizarre, but not for Josie. She'd needed to build that wall since the moment she was born. But in the end, her father did it for her.

Still, he drew in breath and pulled her closer before he suggested, "Maybe we can talk about that tomorrow."

She twisted in his arms and he dipped his chin to see she was looking up at him.

"How did Dad die, Jake?"

Fuck.

"A lot hit you tonight. You ready for real?" he asked softly.

"Yes," she answered immediately.

It was the immediately that convinced him. He nodded and gathered her closer, pulling her up his chest so they were near to eye to eye.

Only then did he give her real.

"After Lydie got custody of you, he got himself another woman. He also knocked that other woman around. Unfortunately for him but fortunately for the universe, she had a family that didn't like that much. They got her out of that shit and got her to press charges. It stuck. He went down. Short-term sentence but he clearly was not the kind of man who made friends easily. He got shivved but not bad, guards didn't see it or didn't like him much and didn't report it. For whatever reason, he hid the injury. It got infected and by the time he got treatment, that shit was in his bloodstream and they couldn't fight it. Six month sentence for assault turned into life."

"He died in prison?" she asked.

"Yeah," Jake answered.

"From an infection from a knife wound?" she went on.

"That's what's in his file."

"Because he was too much of a badass to get it stitched up and get a course of antibiotics," she kept on.

Jake said nothing, though he did it fighting back a smile seeing as she used the word "badass."

"That's whacked, Jake," she declared.

At that, he grinned.

"Not sure your father's insanity was ever in question, Slick."

She shook her head like she couldn't believe all she'd heard but did it turning and nestling into him, putting her head on his chest and training her eyes to the sea.

Jake's arms went tighter.

"He's not getting Lavender House," she whispered.

"No, he isn't, baby," he whispered back.

"I don't care if it takes every penny I have, he's not getting anything that was Gran's." She was still whispering but her tone was fierce. And hearing it, he finally felt relief.

"It won't take every penny, Josie. But this will go away," he promised.

She nodded, her cheek moving against his chest, before she declared, "Boston Stone is not a toad. He's an asshole."

Jake grinned again and pulled her closer.

"Got that right, Slick," he agreed.

"And that Baginski woman is odious," she kept at it.

He said nothing.

"What's her problem anyway?" she asked with mild curiosity and in a way she didn't expect an answer. Then again, she couldn't know Jake actually had one.

Shit.

So she had it all, something at this point she needed to have, he had to give it to her.

So he did.

"I regrettably fucked her about ten years ago and didn't go back for seconds," Jake shared cautiously and she jerked in his arms so she could look up at him again.

But he was relieved when she asked, "That's it?"

"Don't know if that's it. Just know you gotta know that history."

Her brows drew together. "What did you see in her?"

"Ten years ago she wasn't in a perpetually bad mood, nor did she wear that shit on her face."

She studied him a moment before she announced the God's honest truth, "Women are very strange."

He decided not to agree verbally.

Her eyes held his and she declared, "So, at least with her, I have the best revenge I can have. I have you."

He stared at her as his body locked.

Fuck him, but he fucking loved her.

"Yeah," he whispered, his voice rough.

"Good," she stated haughtily and settled in again, curving her arms around him this time. "Alas, she'll never learn that I have you for precisely the reasons she doesn't, that she's odious and ridiculous and I'm not. It's my experience that the men worth having dislike odious *and* ridiculous."

Her words forced his body to release since he was fighting back laughter when he confirmed, "Nope, men don't like either of those."

"So she's sad really," she concluded.

"Yep," he agreed.

She fell silent.

He stared at the top of her head, her cheek against his chest, felt her weight bearing into him, her arms around him and having all that, it was whacked, but he knew he wanted to sit there with her forever.

But that shit couldn't happen and he told her why.

"Kids are worried about you, honey. If you're good, you gotta get down there and show them that."

Not surprisingly, instantly she moved.

Pulling out of his arms then grabbing his hand and pulling them both to their feet, she said, "Of course. I should have thought of that."

She started to pull him to the stairs but he stopped her, calling, "Babe?"

She looked up at him.

"You good?" he asked.

Her answer was, "I have you."

He liked that answer but he had to be sure and he communicated this by saying, "Babe."

She got him and he knew this when she reiterated with emphasis, "Yes, Jake, of course I'm good. *I have you.*"

Oh yes.

Fuck yes.

He liked that answer.

Enough to use her hand in his to pull her to him, wrap his free arm around her and bend his head to give her a kiss.

She took it. She liked it. He knew it when she slid her hands around his shoulders and pressed deep.

When he lifted his head, she looked into his eyes and said quietly, "Thank you for taking care of me, darling."

"My job, baby," he replied.

"I'm glad you're good at it," she returned.

Oh yes.

Fuck yes.

He was in love with her.

Gone.

Deep.

He'd lost his heart. He knew she had it in a way he hoped like fuck she never wanted to give it back.

He didn't tell her that. That would be for a time she'd want to remember it, he'd want to remember it, not a night that turned a fantastic weekend to shit.

So instead, he bent in and brushed his mouth to hers then took her to his kids.

———————

FUCK.

Jake held Josie's eyes, ones she'd just cut to him, and they were narrowed.

It was the next morning.

Conner was shoving books in his backpack at the butcher block table.

Amber was running around like a teenaged girl in the throes of a drama. Seeing as she had Josie's entire wardrobe and makeup collection to pick from that morning, she took too long doing it and she was running late.

Ethan was sitting at the table, swinging his legs, shoving Josie's scrambled eggs, bacon and toast into his mouth.

Jake was resting his hips against the counter, his hand wrapped around a fresh mug of coffee.

And Josie was at the sink, doing Conner and Amber's breakfast dishes.

Until a moment ago, all had been well at Lavender House.

Last night, Josie had rallied. The kids saw it and relaxed. And not a one of them said anything or gave a bad vibe after a night where they slept under the same roof that their dad slept under, doing it in a bed with Josie.

He'd gone to open the gym while Josie stayed to make breakfast and control the mayhem that was the Spear kids getting ready for school.

Jake had returned ten minutes ago.

However, Conner had just dropped the bomb that Ellie had visited last night, something Jake had not shared with his woman.

It wasn't the only thing he hadn't shared, the rest of it she still didn't know.

And it was clear from her look she didn't like that he'd delayed in doing this. So he was not looking forward to giving it all to her.

Still aiming her glare at Jake, she asked his son, "Are you okay, sweetheart?"

"Sure. Her loss," Conner muttered.

"Con," Josie called, finally moving her eyes to his son and Jake watched Conner look to her. "Are you okay?" she asked quietly, and so fucking sweet, he tasted that sweetness in his mouth.

"I'm good, Josie," Conner replied, also quietly.

She studied him closely then, obviously approving of what she saw, she nodded her head.

When she did, Conner tipped his head back and yelled at the ceiling, "Amber! Get a move on!"

This got Jake another cut of Josie's eyes and he knew why. She didn't like shouting and obviously held Jake accountable for Conner doing it.

He was already fighting a grin but it became harder when her brows lifted when Amber was heard shouting back, "It's not like I don't have my own car! Go without me!"

She tipped her head to the side and crossed her arms on her chest when Conner continued the shouted conversation with, "You're gonna be late!"

"Conner," Josie called, again with her eyes to Jake.

"Yeah?" Conner asked and she looked to his boy.

"It's sweet you're looking after your sister's attendance record and don't wish for her to be tardy. But if you would do that not shouting the house down, I won't attempt to get you to eat green beans tonight."

Conner grinned big and said, "Deal."

At this, Jake swallowed down laughter.

Unfortunately, he made a noise doing it and regained Josie's glare.

"Later, Eath," Conner said as he slung his backpack over his shoulder and headed out.

"Later, Con," Ethan said with mouth full.

"'Bye, guys," he said to Jake and Josie.

"Have a good day, Conner," Josie called to his departing back.

"Later, son." Jake did the same.

Amber rushed in the second he was gone, crying, "I can't find my geometry book!"

"You've been in five rooms in this house since you got here, honey. Have you checked them all?" Jake asked.

But before his daughter could answer—or from the look on her face lose it—Josie moved, stating, "I'll help you look, Amber."

She disappeared on the heels of his daughter.

Ethan jumped off his chair to take his empty plate to the sink, declaring, "Josie's eggs are the freakin' bomb."

Jake took a sip of coffee and didn't reply because he didn't need to. His son spoke truth.

Ethan put his plate in the sink and turned to his old man. "So, instead of Josie bein' around our place more, we should come here more. She doesn't have as big a TV but her couch is all squishy."

"You'd give up our TV for a squishy couch?" Jake asked.

"It's like it hugs you," Ethan answered and Jake grinned at his son.

"Got it!" Amber cried, waving around her geometry book as she ran back into the kitchen, Josie following her when she did.

Amber shoved it into her bag, dashed to her dad and gave him a kiss on the cheek. She then dashed to Josie and did the same.

As she did this, Jake again gave Josie credit for his daughter's return to sweet.

But it was all Amber when she said to Ethan, "Later, runt."

"Ugh!" Ethan grunted. "You suck!"

Amber halted in her dash out the door, gave her little brother a cute smile and teased, "But you still love me."

"Hardly," Ethan shot back.

"You totally do," she returned.

"I can't love someone who sucks," he told her.

She grinned at him, unperturbed by this, and took off.

"Eath," Jake called and his son turned annoyed eyes to his dad. "Teeth brushed. Get your shit together, bag by the door. Yeah?"

"Yeah," he grunted and stalked out.

"Babe?" he called to Josie who was wetting a cloth at the sink.

She turned eyes to him, looked to the door Ethan just used, looked back to Jake and said one word.

"Ellie?"

He grinned and replied, "Babe."

She tossed the cloth into the sink and put her hands to her hips. Hips she'd put jeans on that morning and it sucked he didn't have her in a nightie but it was the right way for her to walk downstairs to his kids.

"Is Con all right?" she asked.

"He said he was," he answered.

"Is Con all right?" she repeated.

He lowered his voice and replied, "Babe, if he says he's fine, he's fine."

This was clearly not enough for her and he knew it when she asked, "What did Ellie say?"

"She wants him back."

"And he said no and that's it?"

"Pretty much."

"He was gutted two weeks ago," she reminded him.

"Two weeks in high school is two years in real life," he returned and watched his woman snap her mouth shut because it had been a long time for both of them but they both knew that to be true.

"Gettin' it all out there, more happened last night while your shit started to go down here," he shared even though he didn't want to.

But he had to.

Donna lived in that town and Donna had a mouth. Josie could see her or it could get to her.

So his woman had to know.

"What?" she asked

"Donna came around."

Her eyes got wide.

Quick, before Ethan got back, he gave it to her, ending with, "She's whacked but I'm pretty sure this time she got my point."

"She isn't whacked, Jake," she replied. "When you're young you can have everything you want and not realize you have it."

He shook his head. "I was thirty when Con was born, Donna twenty-nine. She wasn't young. She's just whacked."

She also shook her head. "At any age, you can still not realize you have your heart's desire, lose it, and spend years in denial, searching for its replacement at the same time hoping it comes back."

Jake froze.

Your heart's desire.

Those words pounded in his brain so hard he didn't have it in him to reply, to move, to do dick. All he could do was stare at his woman.

Your heart's desire, she'd said and she was fucking talking about *him.*

Fuck, she was gone for him too.

Deep.

He had her heart, he knew it in that instant and he also knew one other thing.

He sure as fuck was never giving it back.

"Jake?" she called when he said nothing.

"Right here," he pushed out.

"Are you all right?" she asked.

Fuck yeah, he was.

"Yep," he answered.

Her head tipped to the side and she opened her mouth but Ethan took that moment to walk in.

"So, who's takin' me to school?" he asked but didn't wait for an answer, he kept jabbering. "I cannot freakin' *wait* to tell everyone I met Lavon freaking Burkett! They're gonna *spaz!*"

Jake pushed away from his spot at the counter, putting down his mug, saying, "I'm takin' you, bud. You're ready, grab your bag and out to the truck."

"Right," Ethan muttered and looked to Josie. "Later, Josie."

"Have a good day at school, honey," she replied.

He took off.

Jake went to her, got close and put both hands to either side of her neck.

"Come nine o'clock, babe, you call the firm and find out what gives with Terry and who they got to represent you."

She put her hands to his waist and nodded.

He kept at her.

"You get a call to arrange a meeting, don't agree to anything until you ask me. I'm coming with."

She nodded again.

"Now, kiss me," he ordered.

Without delay, she rolled up on her toes and gave him her mouth.

He took it and drank deep, but not long before he broke their connection, shifted to give her nose a kiss and he did this giving her neck a squeeze.

When he caught her eyes, he said, "Tonight we're here again. Until I get a lock on what your uncle is up to, we're staking claim to Lavender House."

She pressed closer and said, "Agreed."

"Kids dealt with last night no problems and we didn't have a meeting but I got the chance to talk to each of them and they're good with all of us having more of you."

At that, she melted into him and whispered, "Good."

"I get the good parts," he told her.

And at that, she smiled at him.

Getting that from her, knowing he was leaving her good, Jake bent again and brushed his mouth against hers.

"Later, Slick," he said when he lifted his head.

"Later, darling," she replied.

He gave her neck another squeeze, let her go and walked out so he could take his son to school.

***

JAKE WAS UP on a stepladder at the side of the front door to Lavender House that afternoon when Josie drove up in her Cayenne, Ethan in the passenger seat.

Ethan got out, dashed into the house and did this saying, "Yo, Dad!"

He didn't miss a step or slow. He had a fridge to raid.

Josie got out and walked slowly up to the front door on her high heels, her hips in her jeans swaying in a way he liked a fuckuva lot.

She stopped, looked at the lamp he was installing then down to the boxes of lamps piled on the ground.

"Motion sensors. Every outside light. You got about a million of them," he explained and regained her eyes.

Soft eyes. Sweet eyes. Eyes that said a fuckuva lot.

Then she smiled a soft smile. A sweet smile. A smile that said a fuckuva lot.

After that, she said quietly, "Be careful, darling," and walked into the house.

That was when Jake smiled.

***

JOSIE SLID IN bed beside him after going to the bathroom and cleaning up.

When she did, Jake curled an arm around her, rolled to his back taking her with him and stretched out an arm to turn out the light.

When he settled them in, her mostly on him, partly on his side but still pressed deep, their legs tangled, she said into the dark, "I like ungloved."

He'd had his checkup and the results were in. They were good to give up the condoms, thank Christ.

"I like it too, baby," he replied, knowing he liked it a whole lot more than she did.

She was silent as she cuddled closer and he thought she was sorting herself to go to sleep when she called hesitantly, "Jake?"

"Right here," he said on a squeeze of his arm around her.

"I, well...have something to tell you."

Shit, the way she said that didn't sound good.

Even so, he encouraged, "Tell me."

"Um...well, you know, Amond is coming tomorrow."

"Yeah."

"And you know he's a friend of mine," she went on.

"Yeah, Slick."

She took in a deep breath and gave it to him.

"What you don't know is that we had a night together some time ago."

Shit.

Jake said nothing.

She lifted her head and he felt her eyes through the dark.

"You said not to keep anything from you," she reminded him, her voice soft and cautious.

He did say that, fuck him.

"I said that, Josie," he confirmed.

She didn't go on nor did she move and he felt her vibe, her body beginning to get stiff. No longer cautious, she was getting scared. So he lifted his hand and wrapped it around her jaw, using his thumb to stroke her cheek.

"He's gonna be here with you, I gotta know this. I can tell you know I don't like having that history but I gotta have it. You gave it to me. I appreciate that. But more, baby, I know you didn't live in a nunnery the last twenty years and you know I was no monk. It's gonna come out because it has to, like me havin' to share about Terry. So don't be afraid of letting it out. It's life and we share our lives, yeah?"

"Yes, Jake."

"Now settle in and sleep."

"Okay, darling," she said right before she settled back in.

He gave her another squeeze when she did.

"Thanks for the honesty," he whispered.

"You're welcome," she whispered back and he felt her relax against him.

She fell asleep before him.

But in her bed, in her house with his kids close and Josie tucked tight, he wasn't far behind.

———◆•••◆———

"OHMIGOD, HOLY CRAP, ohmigod, this is gonna be *epic*," boy Taylor breathed and he did this because Ethan just ran into the room and announced loudly that, "About fifty thousand Escalades are pulling up the drive!"

This meant rap star Dee-Amond had arrived.

It was the next afternoon and not surprisingly, after hearing the news he was coming, Amber showed up after school with both Taylors in tow and Conner had switched his shift with a bud so he could be there.

As for Jake, no way in fuck he wasn't going to be around when Josie's friend who also was her ex-lover showed. Mostly because he was male, rich, famous, good-looking and an ex-lover.

Actually, totally because of that.

At Ethan's shout, Josie shot from her chair at the kitchen table and walked quickly on her heels out of the room.

The kids followed her, Jake coming up the rear.

When he got outside, he saw his son was exaggerating but that didn't mean there wasn't a cavalcade of flash Escalades in the drive.

Five of them.

The middle one closest to the house had its back door opening and Josie was rushing to it.

Jake stopped, crossed his arms on his chest and watched as Dee-Amond hefted his bulk out of the SUV, flashed a smile at Jake's woman and folded her in his arms when she threw hers around him.

Shit.

"So…totally…*epic*," boy Taylor declared.

"I can't believe this," girl Taylor whispered.

"I thought I was freaking out with Lavon Burkett but *now* I'm *really* freaking out," his daughter announced in a breathy voice. "I mean, he's right here, in *Magdalene* at *Josie's house*."

"Come." Jake heard Josie order and his eyes went from his girl to his woman to see she was thankfully no longer in Amond's arms but had her hand in his and was guiding him their way.

His eyes were lifted to take in Lavender House and his mouth was moving, "Jesus, beautiful, I'm gettin' it now why you'd wanna stay. This crib is *tight*."

She grinned at him before she stopped him in front of his audience and threw out her hand.

"This is my posse," she stated, words that, if anything else was happening at that moment, would make Jake smile.

He didn't smile.

"Conner, Jake's oldest." She pointed to him and Conner stuck a hand out that Amond took and shook. "Amber, Jake's daughter." She motioned to Amber and his daughter clapped once before she stuck her hand out and Amond grinned at her and took it. "The Taylors, Amber's personal posse, boy Taylor and girl Taylor," Josie went on and Amond was obviously holding back laughter as he shook their hands in turn. "Ethan, Jake's youngest," she continued.

Amond spoke to Eath, saying, "Yo, little man," as he stuck out his hand.

Ethan grabbed it and whispered, "*Awesome*."

"And last, Jake," Josie finished, her smiling eyes coming to him.

Jake looked from her to Amond to see the man had his gaze on Jake.

"Holy shit," Amond said when Jake caught his eyes.

Even with this bizarre remark, Jake moved through the Taylors and extended a hand, muttering, "Pleasure."

Amond took his hand and told him something he knew but was shocked as shit the rap star knew it.

"You're The Truck."

"Whoa! Dad! He knows you!" Ethan cried.

"Yep," Jake answered Amond.

Amond let his hand go and turned to Josie. "Josephine, girl, you didn't tell me your fighter was The Truck." Before she could say anything, he looked back at Jake. "Caught your fight in Vegas against De Matteo. You fucked him up. Judges were jacked. He could barely stand and you were still dancing."

Jake remembered that but he didn't share with Amond that he was moving so he wouldn't pass out.

"Fight fan?" Jake asked.

"Fu…hell yeah," he answered.

"We're even then seein' as your music's the shit," Jake replied.

Amond grinned, the diamonds in his ears twinkling in the sun, his teeth so white, Jake was almost blinded.

"Everyone inside," Josie ordered and he looked to her to see her grinning big, pleased Jake had passed preliminary inspection or pleased her friend was there. Or both.

It was Jake who was pleased when she moved to him, clasped hold of his arm in one hand, pressing to his side, and she turned back to Amond to extend a hand, noting, "I'm sorry, Amond. Circumstances have changed. We have a full house. But it's a big house so we have your room covered. Though, I'm not sure where your crew is going to stay."

"They got rooms in town," Amond noted and Jake looked to the lane to see that his "crew" was already rolling out, leaving an Escalade behind for the boss. Jake looked back at the man when he went on, "I can stay there if you're full."

But Amond was watching her closely, probably wondering why the house was full.

"The kids would be disappointed if they didn't get to brag at school that Dee-Amond was hanging with them tonight," Josie told him the truth.

Amond looked from her to Jake, back to her and murmured, "Can't disappoint the kids."

"Absolutely not," Josie agreed, dragging Jake in after latching on to Amond's hand and doing the same with him.

Jake detached to close the door but Josie kept dragging Amond toward the kitchen, saying, "Let's get you a drink before I start dinner."

Before she disappeared into the kitchen, she threw a smile over her shoulder at Jake.

This meant Amond threw a look over his shoulder at Jake.

He was not smiling.

Then they disappeared.

Jake sighed, locked the door and followed them.

HIS CELL ON his desk at the club rang. Jake looked from the booze inventory to the phone and took the call.

"Yo," he greeted.

"You are not gonna believe this shit, but fuckin' Dee-Amond just walked in the door and asked to see you," one of his bouncers said in his ear.

Not unexpected.

But still unwanted.

Earlier, drinks had gone well.

Dinner had gone well.

After the kids went to bed and they were sitting around talking, Jake eventually saying he had to get to the club had gone okay, but only okay because he wasn't big on leaving Josie with Amond.

This was because it was clear Josie thought the world of Amond in a way he could accept but Amond thought the world of Josie in a way he didn't like all that much.

He had no idea how what was about to go down would go.

Since the man got there, conversation had been surface. Josie led it, Jake followed. He thought at first it was because the kids were around, excited and what was hanging over her head was not something she wanted to get into when they were there.

But even after the Taylors took off and the kids had called it a night, Josie kept it surface. She wasn't nervous. She didn't give the vibe she was trying to hide something. And in the end, Jake took it as her wanting to enjoy her time with her friend and not have that shit fuck it up.

However, he'd not shared the particulars about anything but his gym. Jake had no clue how Amond would react to his club being a strip club. The man had an interesting past so he might be cool. He also might not like what Jake had being linked to Josie.

"Bring him to my door," Jake said into the phone. "I'll meet you there."

"Gotcha," was the reply.

He dropped his phone to the desk, got up and moved to the door.

He had it opened when Amond, not surprisingly garnering a shitload of attention, was ten feet away.

But Amond's attention was centered on Jake.

"Totally cool to meet you," his bouncer said when they stopped at the door, extending his hand to Amond.

"Yeah, brother," Amond muttered over the music, taking his hand, gripping it, letting it go and turning right back to Jake.

Jake gave his boy a chin lift then turned to the side to let Amond in. Amond took the invitation and Jake followed him up the stairs, the door drowning out the music as it closed behind him.

Jake let Amond set the scene. The only thing he took was moving to the front of his desk, sitting his ass on the edge of it and crossing his arms.

Amond stood in the center of the room, leveled his eyes on Jake and opened with, "Got yourself a titty bar."

Not starting great.

"Yep," was Jake's one-syllable reply.

Amond studied him.

Then he quit doing that and stated, "We'll get this out there seein' as I'm gettin' the feeling it's not lost on you. I've had Josephine."

And not getting any better.

"She told me," Jake shared.

Amond nodded and went on. "Wanted to keep her, she was not hip on that, so I kept her the only way she'd let me do it. I'm unattached but this is not about that. This is just about her bein' a good woman that means somethin' to me."

Jake did nothing but nod.

Amond kept going.

"That's outta the way, she's dancin' around shit and I'm guessin' that you and your kids got a place seein' as you live here but you're in her house. And her house is a fuckin' nice house. What I wanna know is, what is she dancin' around and why the fuck you got you and your kids in my girl's house?"

"I want her safe," Jake replied.

"From what?" Amond fired his question back instantly.

"Her uncle is contesting the will. Since this news came down on her, we've not heard anything. The firm her grandmother has used for years for counsel is not returning her calls. Her uncle is old but he's got a history of bein' a supreme asshole. That house means a lot to her, I'm not lettin' her alone in it or takin' her away from it to keep her at my place when he's out there and I don't know what he's up to. But more, she doesn't know what he's up to and I know she feels safe there so that's where she's stayin'. Since she is, to keep her feelin' that way, so am I. And I come with my kids."

Amond moved to one of the chairs in front of his desk and leaned his weight into a hand at the back of it before asking, "What's the story on this uncle?"

"I was close to her grandmother and she told me she's not talked to her son for twenty-eight years, this bein' when she got custody of Josie when her other son beat the shit outta her, put her in the hospital and she was not down with that. Her older boy was not big on her gettin' involved. Bad blood turned acid and that was the last she ever heard from her boys. Seein' as they were hanging tight after Josie's dad knocked the crap outta her, I see where Lydie was comin' from, cuttin' those ties. Now, he's in it for the money and maybe to jack Josie. I'm gonna see that doesn't happen."

He kept talking even when Amond's eyes narrowed and his pissed off energy filled the room. When he was done talking, the man's demeanor didn't change even a little bit.

"Put her in the hospital?" he whispered.

"Yep. But he's dead. His brother unfortunately isn't. They were bad seeds from the beginning and grew that way, taught by a dad who by Lydie's account was even fuckin' worse."

"Jesus, fuck." Amond was still whispering.

"That's about it," Jake agreed.

"I didn't know any of this shit," Amond told him.

"If Lydie didn't share, I'd still be trying to crack that nut. Josie didn't give it to anyone. Not even Gagnon, until recently," Jake replied.

"This guy have a name?" Amond asked.

Now, thank fuck, their conversation was getting better.

"You wading in?" Jake asked back.

"Fuck yeah," Amond said.

"Davis Malone, the uncle," Jake shared immediately. "Think he's bank-rolled by Boston Stone, a local big man who has a small dick, Josie wasn't interested in it, made that clear and he wants to make her pay by gettin' Lavender House. They got counsel by the name of Terry Baginski whose ass I unfortunately tapped a long time ago, didn't enjoy it, didn't call, and I don't know if she's just a bitch or a bitch with a grudge. But she's waded in too."

"How dirty you want it?" Amond asked and Jake didn't exactly understand the question but he also didn't care.

"I'm in love with her so I want her breathing easy and doin' that quick. That house is all she's got left of her grandmother. I got her in a good place where she feels safe with me, my kids, but I figure it's still the only place she truly feels safe. She doesn't wanna let it go. They'll never get that house but even the threat of it is gonna fuck with her head and I'm not good with that. Stone has the power and money to drag this out and I'm not good with Josie dealing with that either. They're also bringing up bad shit she should not ever have to face. So I don't know what you're asking but you feel like getting dirty, however that comes about, I'm not gonna stand in your way."

"I can get very dirty," Amond told him.

"I'll repeat, I'm not gonna stand in your way."

"Where are you with dirty?" Amond asked.

"My hands gotta stay clean seein' as I got a woman and kids I need to see to after this is done."

Amond didn't miss a beat before he asked, "You're in love with her?"

And Jake didn't miss a beat before he answered, "Absolutely."

"She loves you," Amond informed him.

"I know," Jake replied.

Amond held his eyes.

Then he whispered, "Fuck, that kills."

Fortunately, Jake was not, nor would ever be, in the position to feel his pain.

Still, he got him, but he said nothing.

"I'm gettin' Henry's fucked up vibe right about now," Amond shared.

"She's in good hands," Jake told him.

"She been to your titty bar?" he asked.

"Prefer strip club, man, and yeah. She advises the girls on how to do their hair to get maximum tips."

At that, Amond burst out in deep, loud laughter.

Jake let himself smile as he did.

When he was done, Amond gave him the stamp of approval by saying, "We're good."

"No offense," Jake replied. "But I wouldn't care if we weren't. She's mine and that's not ever gonna change. But for her, I'm obliged. She's essentially had one woman as her entire family her whole life. That one woman was a really fuckin' good one but Josie deserves more. I'm givin' her that. You keep things good with all of us that gives her more. And I want her to have everything."

"Point made, brother," Amond replied quietly, his eyes never leaving Jake's.

"Excellent," Jake returned.

Amond grinned. "Now I'm in the mood to check out your talent. Gotta get my crew out here, bring a roll of fifties 'cause I snuck a peek, man, and gotta say, bumfuck Maine has got some seriously fine tail."

And that was when Jake grinned.

HOLDING HER DOWN with his hands at her wrists in the pillow over her head, Jake rode his woman.

The only thing she could use to latch on with were her legs and her pussy so she had her legs wrapped tight around the backs of his thighs and her pussy was pulsing around his cock.

Jesus.

Heaven.

Just like Josie, she was getting there fast.

"Hold on, baby," he whispered against her mouth as she panted against his.

"Jake," she breathed, squirming under him.

He rolled his hips, thrust in and he knew he hit the spot when her pussy clutched him tight.

Jesus.

Heaven.

"Hold on, Josie."

"*God.*"

He kept taking her.

She kept squirming, panting, her legs tightening.

"Let me have my hands, darling," she begged.

"Let me ride you, honey," he returned, rolling his hips back, powering in, and getting a soft, sexy gasp.

Beautiful.

He kissed her, driving his tongue inside as he drove his dick into her.

Her head tilted at the same time it came off the bed so she could press her mouth against his to get more.

He drove in harder.

She tore her mouth from his, turning her head to the side, whimpering, "I can't hold on."

"Then let go."

She let go, he heard it and felt it. Gliding his hands up, he threaded his fingers in hers and she clasped tight as she moaned low and used his thighs as leverage to lift her hips into his thrusting ones.

He took her harder.

She kept whimpering, moaning, panting and clutching him with everything she had, her fingers releasing and gripping each time she took his cock.

Gorgeous.

So fucking gorgeous, it moved over him. He slammed deep, shoved his face in her neck and let it happen.

She slid her heels up his thighs so she could wrap her legs around his hips and she did this tight, holding onto his hands, clenching her pussy around his cock.

His hips bucked twice as he poured himself inside her.

When it left him, he tasted the skin of her neck, smelled the remnants of her perfume, the scent of her hair, liking all that but not as much as her pussy undulating against his cock in her own aftermath.

Fuck yeah, he liked to have her ungloved.

Finally, he felt her lips at his ear where she asked quietly, "Can I have my hands now?"

He pressed his forearms deeper into the pillow, pressing her hands deeper into it, as he lifted slightly up to look down at her, her hair now dark in the shadows, spread all over. He couldn't see her distinctly but he still knew she was the prettiest thing he'd ever seen, the best lay he'd ever had, the best thing that had ever happened to him.

So he gripped her hands harder with his fingers and dropped his head to give her a slow, deep, long kiss and he kept giving it to her until her legs grew taut around his ass and her fingers clenched his.

Only then did he let her mouth and hands go.

She immediately moved her arms to wrap them around him and she used them as well to hold on tight.

"I think I like you waking me up when you get back from the club," she noted and his body started moving on hers, doing it to shake with laughter.

She would.

He'd woken her with a kiss then he kissed her other places and did it for a long time. Only after that did he fuck her.

She liked his mouth.

She liked his cock better.

"I'll make a note of that," he replied.

She started moving her hands light on his skin and Jake had never had a woman whose touch was so light. So sweet. How it could be delicate and give so much, he had no fucking clue.

He just knew it did.

"You wanna clean up?" he asked.

"Yes," she answered but she sounded like she preferred the opposite and he knew it was because she would be losing him and she didn't like that.

But he liked that she didn't.

He kissed her again before he lifted up to kiss her forehead, down to kiss her nose, down to kiss her throat, down to her chest and he slid out, kissing her ribs. He rolled off and kissed her stomach.

Only then did he plant a forearm in the bed beside her, lift up to look at her and order, "Hurry."

"All right," she replied, moving into him to take his jaw in both her hands, touch her mouth to his and slide off the bed.

He watched through the shadows as she pulled on her nightie, her panties then she grabbed her robe off the end of the bed and swung it on before she padded barefoot to the door. She was careful not to make a noise leaving the room and he knew she was careful once she left the room because he didn't hear shit until she was back.

He had a light on and was out of bed by then. Having rooted through his bag to get his pajama bottoms, he had them on and was tying the string.

She came right to him, shrugging off the robe and tossing it aside to land on the bed before she slid her arms around him and pressed close, tipping her head back to catch his eyes.

"Things go all right with Amond at the club?" she asked as he curved his arms around her.

"He had six boys in his crew, his manager, his other manager, two bodyguards, his music director and some guy he introduced as a 'consultant.' He told me they left his publicist and stylist behind because they're chicks. But they didn't leave the rolls of fifties and hundreds behind. My girls freaked and right now, by my count, four of 'em are gettin' laid and the other manager, both bodyguards and the consultant are gettin' lucky but only because they primed that luck by handin' out cash. And by handin' out cash, I mean I counted but quit after I got over three grand and they were far from done. My girls had a good night and it was clear they were ready to show their gratitude."

"So I take it that it went well," she noted.

"They all drank top shelf and by that I mean the *top* top shelf. The shit we gotta get outta the safe when someone's either so drunk they don't give a shit they're maxin' out their credit card on hundred fifty-dollar snifters of cognac or they're celebrating something huge. Even I haven't tasted that shit until tonight."

When he finished talking, she was smiling when she repeated, "So I take it that it went well."

He grinned into her smiling face. "Yeah, it went well."

She pressed closer, saying, "I knew he'd like you."

He gave her a squeeze. "Baby, he likes *you* and he'd like whatever made you happy, he wouldn't give a fuck what that was."

Her face got soft and he thought it was for Amond but what she said next proved him wrong.

"Yes, he'd like whatever made me happy."

Fuck, but he liked to see that look on her face, that shine in her eyes, all of it directed at him, giving it to him. And what she gave him was the knowledge that he gave it to her.

He never expected this, but there it was.

And it took everything he had not to kick his own ass that he didn't go for it before.

But he didn't.

Now he had it.

That was where he was, that was where he had her.

So he had to focus on moving forward.

"We gonna stand here huggin' all night or are you gonna let me get some shuteye?"

She let out a quiet giggle before she gave him a squeeze, rolled up on her toes, tipping her head way back and he accepted the invitation, dropping his to brush his lips against hers.

When he was done, she said, "I'm going to let you get some shuteye."

Her arms loosened, his did too and they moved to the bed. He was turning out the light even as she was cuddling into him so by the time he was settled, she was tucked tight, tangled up and relaxed deep.

"'Night, Slick," he muttered.

"Goodnight, darling," she whispered into his skin giving his stomach a squeeze.

He reciprocated the squeeze and after a few minutes, felt her weight settle into him.

A few minutes after that, his weight settled into the bed as he fell asleep.

Eighteen

AT LEAST TWICE

The next morning, I opened the door to Maude's House of Beauty and only had one foot inside when I heard Alyssa command, "Get over here, get those fancy-assed pumps off and sink your feet in the drink, babelicious, 'cause I…got…*news.*"

I looked into her excited eyes, then moved my gaze and saw she had the pedicure chair ready and even had a glass bowl filled with foamy water sitting on the ledge by the arm of the chair.

She was ready.

With a look back at her face, I wasn't sure I was.

But I nevertheless hurried to the chair, took off my jacket, plopped it and my bag in the chair beside it and pulled myself up.

I barely got my bare feet into the warm sudsy water before Alyssa reached out a hand, grabbed my wrist, plonked my fingers in the bowl and announced, "Got bitch dirt, and by that I mean Donna Spear *and* Terry Baginski bitch dirt."

I felt my back go straight and my eyes go wide as I asked, "Really?"

"Really. Big dirt. A freakin' avalanche of full-on mud."

Oh dear.

"Is it good?" I queried.

"Uh…sister," she started, yanking one of my feet out of the tub, setting it on the pad, dabbing it with a towel then reaching straight to her cart of implements to grab some cotton wool, doing all of this talking. "Would I be nearly creaming my pants to tell you if this shit was bad?"

"Um…no," I replied.

"Right, no. Now, listen up," she ordered and sucked in a huge breath.

I braced, furtively looking around and seeing two of her hairdressing chairs were taken, stylists working on clients, but they were all the way across the salon so we had a least a little privacy.

My gaze went back to Alyssa when she launched in.

"*Soooo,* Donna's got a best friend, they been tight for freakin' *yonks.* Her name is Rita. She's a good gal. Really like her. She's been a client for a long time, got a couple kids who are the same ages as a couple of my kids. We did the carpool thing back in the day and—"

"Not to be rude, sweetheart," I cut in gently. "But do I need this Rita history prior to you telling me about Jake's ex and the woman who seems to have it out for me?"

"Right," Alyssa mumbled and switched my feet, doing this talking. "Just to say, she's cool. And the way she's cool is that, first, she stood by her girl for a long time and a lotta that time was hard time. And second, you know this 'cause you two are scary open in a way that gives me the heebie-jeebies"—her eyes came to me—"but you told me that Jake laid Donna out this weekend."

I grinned at her "heebie-jeebies" comment, especially when it was caused by honesty between partners, and confirmed, "Yes, I know it."

She nodded and looked back to my feet. "Okay, so Donna was cut up about this, like, in a big way. Called her girl over to moan about Jake and do it inhaling rum. Now, Rita's been listenin' to this sad song for a long fuckin' time and that night, she got over it. *Way* over it."

"Oh my," I whispered.

"Yup," Alyssa agreed then carried on with my pedicure right along with her story. "So Rita decided to perform a one-woman intervention right there, though with bad timing seein' as Donna was drunk off her ass. But that didn't stop her from laying it out for Donna, telling her everyone in town knew Jake was a no-go for her and was never gonna be a go for her again. She also shared that most people in town thought it was sad, and by that she meant pathetic, that Donna fell into her cougar ways. Not done, she told Donna that everyone in town also thought she was a shit mom. Thought mega-less about her because of it. Thought Jake was the bomb 'cause he stepped up so huge in takin' care of his kids without her help. And new talk in town was that everyone was super excited that Jake found you 'cause folks have always wanted him to get himself a good woman, and he did. But more, they wanted his kids to have a good woman in their lives and they got that too."

This felt very nice, that I had the townspeople of Magdalene's seal of approval as Jake's woman, but I was still concerned about this Rita woman laying it out for Donna.

"And how did Donna take this?" I asked.

"Not real great 'cause Donna is not about honesty. Donna's about denial. Gettin' it straight from Jake and her best friend all in the same night?" She shook her head. "Had a piss fit. A big one. Kicked Rita out then called around to the rest of her crew to start moaning about Rita. Problem with that was, she did this, they all agreed with Rita and walked right through the door Rita opened to tell her that shit."

"Oh goodness," I murmured.

"Mm-hmm," Alyssa replied, grabbing some cuticle clippers. "So, I'm sure it won't surprise you that Donna didn't nurse her hangover thinkin' things through and deciding to get her shit together. *Nooo.* Instead, she nursed her hangover, walked into work yesterday morning and gave notice. Word is, she's moving to Boston."

I felt my entire body get tight.

"Pardon?" I breathed.

Alyssa looked at me. "She's chucking it in. Another client of mine said that a friend of hers said that she talked with Donna in the grocery store and Donna told her she can't live in the same town with a Jake Spear who has another woman, so she's gone. That woman didn't ask Donna but she did ask my client how Donna managed to miss the fact that Jake had two other wives and a few others besides but apparently her dream world was a fortress until Jake blew it to smithereens and she missed this shit."

I was barely listening.

I had only one thing on my mind.

"She isn't thinking of trying to take Conner and Amber with her, is she?" I asked urgently and Alyssa stopped working on my toes, wrapped a hand around my foot and squeezed reassuringly as she looked up at me.

"Honey, no," she said gently. "Has that woman ever considered her children when she's made a decision?"

I had only known her a very short time but what I knew of her, the answer to this was no.

But I answered, "I don't think so."

"No. She hasn't. Donna thinks of one thing: Donna. Strike that. She thinks of three things: Donna and Jake or gettin' laid by someone who looks like him."

I bit my lip.

Alyssa studied me before she noted, "You don't look happy."

"Boston is two and a half hours away," I reminded her.

"Yeah, and Junior's got no exes that had his ring on their finger but if he did, I'd be a lot happier they were two and a half hours away."

"I *would* be happy, if that didn't mean she wasn't also two and a half hours away from her children."

Her face got soft and she muttered, "See your point."

"Do you think she'll follow through with this?" I asked.

"No clue. She could have had a wild hair and now think better of it. Or she could be gone. She's got a good position as a manager at Anderson's dealership. Be stupid of her to give that up."

"I need to tell Jake this," I pointed out the obvious.

"Well, hang tight, babelicious, because I'm not done."

Marvelous.

I "hung tight," Alyssa refocused on my toes and kept talking.

"This is the big shit and I saved the best for last."

I hoped so.

She kept her eyes to my toes as she said, "Okay, well, I got a client, she's a paralegal at Weaver, Schuller and Associates. She came in right before you and she told me this on the hush-hush so I'm gonna work on your feet and act like I'm just gabbin'. Think she doesn't know I'm tight with you but she lets shit spill all the time. I don't say crap but seein' as all that's goin' down with you is goin' down, you gotta know. But she's a good gal so you just let this play out and don't get her in trouble, 'kay?"

"Okay," I said quietly.

I had, of course, told Alyssa all that was happening since we talked daily. Something she started and something I kept up because she was funny, kind and becoming a very good friend.

"So, the thing is," she carried on. "Boston Stone and Stone Incorporated are clients of Weaver, Schuller and Associates."

"Oh no," I whispered.

"Hang on, babe," she replied. "Now, see, Terry Baginski is an associate part of that 'associates,' not a partner. And Davis Malone's got nothin' to do with Stone Incorporated. So, when he 'approached'—and I can't use my hands to put that in air quotes, honey, but you get me—no matter he did it through Stone, she shoulda told him that it was a conflict of interest seein' as Mrs. Malone, and by extension *you*, were long time clients. Instead, she made the decision to make Stone happy by takin' on that case. Or at least that's what she told Schuller when Schuller got wind of it. She advised they take on your uncle and leave you hanging out to dry. Problem is, she didn't have the authority to do this seein' as she's an associate. Only a partner can make the decision on which client they want to represent."

I took in a deep anticipatory breath.

Alyssa kept talking.

"Thing is, that firm actually drew up your granny's will so they can't exactly not defend it when it gets contested. And Arnold Weaver may be on a leave of absence due to the sad fact that his wife just passed but he didn't die with her and Schuller and him have been partners a long time. They're best buds. And they don't do shit without there bein' a consensus between them so when Schuller took this to Weaver, apparently, Weaver lost his ever-lovin' mind."

Suddenly, I felt better.

Alyssa continued.

"Weaver went into the offices and he and Schuller dragged Terry in and told her to pack up her desk, she was out. Flies came outta the woodwork then, assistants and paralegals tellin' the partners that Baginski did to other clients what she did with you, that bein' pushing a variety of Stone Incorporated crap on them including advising sales of properties and investment of assets and this was because she'd invested and heavily. Now, don't have any legal knowledge but this didn't make Weaver or Schuller all that happy so I'm thinkin' this isn't a good thing."

I didn't have any legal knowledge either so I couldn't confirm or negate.

"Anyway," she went on. "Stone got wind of this and walked into the office without an appointment, demanded to see the partners, told them they had to reinstate Terry and take on your uncle's business or they'd lose his. They asked him where he'd like his files sent."

"Good God," I breathed.

"I know," she agreed. "But, way my client tells it, Stone might be loaded but Weaver and Schuller have pretty much cornered the market on legal counsel in this county. There are a couple ambulance chasers here and there but if you want someone who knows their shit, you go to them."

I started smiling.

She looked up at me.

I finished smiling and did it big.

"So they called his bluff," I noted. "What did he do?"

"Blustered, sayin' he'd inform them who he was goin' with and took off. He's only got one real choice. Terry." The light in her eyes dimmed when she concluded, "And now she needs the work and he's a big client even if he's only one so I don't think this is over for you."

"But hopefully it means my attorney will phone me," I replied.

She grinned before looking back to my toes, saying, "Hopefully."

"Thank you for telling me this, honey," I said. "And I'll be discreet about what you shared from your client."

"Wouldn't have told you if I didn't believe that to be true."

"I'd give you a hug if I wasn't pretty certain that I'd fall out of the pedicure tub trying to do it."

She looked up at me and grinned.

I looked into her warm brown eyes and swallowed.

Then I told her, "The best decision I ever made in my life was to give up the life I had and stay in Magdalene."

Those warm brown eyes got bright and she ordered, her voice husky, "Now, sister, don't go makin' me cry. Cuttin' cuticles and swiping polish may look easy. But it isn't."

"Okay, I won't make you cry."

"Instead, let me know which outfit of yours I get to borrow for when we go out with you and Dee-Amond to The Eaves tonight."

These were our plans for the evening. Jake, me and the kids, Alyssa, Junior and their kids and Dee-Amond and his posse at The Eaves. His manager had sorted it. They were setting up a function room for us.

I couldn't wait.

I smiled and invited, "Come over whenever you can and you can have your pick."

"I just decided to cancel my last client."

My smile got bigger. She returned it and then turned her attention to my toes.

I took in a deep breath and let it go.

An hour and a half later, I gave my friend a big tip.

She tried to refuse.

But I refused to let her.

And after that, I finally got to give her my hug.

———————

I TRIPPED ON my fabulous Christian Louboutin pump the instant I walked into Jake's gym.

This was because Jake was in the middle ring wearing loose gray workout pants, boxing shoes, boxing gloves, one of those padded things on his head and nothing else.

And he was slick with wet and sparring with a gentleman I didn't even look at.

I didn't look at his sparring partner because I felt a spasm in a nice place and had to concentrate on walking as I moved further into the gym, noting distractedly that it was quite full.

This was something I found a minor marvel, as it was quite full frequently, even now, mid-day, when most people should be working.

It was fuller today because Amond's entire crew was working punching bags or weights. All except Amond, who had on a very flattering tracksuit but was standing close to the corner of Jake's ring.

Jake being focused, it was Amond who turned to me and called, "Hey, beautiful."

I got looks and greetings from the men I knew as I made my way across the gym but I was still concentrating on Jake even as I called, "Hello, Amond."

I heard Jake grunt a garbled, "Hold," this being garbled because he had a mouth guard in his mouth.

His partner moved away and Jake turned my way, lifting a glove and spitting the guard into it, his eyes on me, his lips lifting in a smile.

"Yo, Slick," he called.

"Hello, darling," I replied.

He met me at the ropes.

Then he did something lovely, bending his big body over the ropes so he could get his face close to mine.

I took his invitation, tipped my head back and lifted a hand to cup the padding of his headgear at his jaw. He touched his mouth to mine and moved back an inch.

It was then I said quietly, "I have news."

His eyes roamed my face before they locked on mine and he asked, "Yeah?" right when my phone in my purse rang.

"Hang on, honey," I murmured. "I'm hoping for a call."

I looked to Amond and gave him a smile before I dug my phone out of my purse, saw a number displayed on it I didn't know but took the call anyway because that number was local.

"This is Josephine Malone," I said in greeting.

"Josephine, my dear, this is Arnie."

I looked to Jake, my lips still curved. "Hello, Arnie."

Jake's brows shot up.

"Listen," Arnie started. "I'd like to begin by apologizing that we haven't responded to your calls until now. We've had some internal issues that needed my attention. But we've sorted those out and I just wanted to inform you that I'm aware that Lydia's will is being contested and I'll be dealing with this issue personally."

"Arnie," I said softly, shifting my eyes to Jake's chest, deciding that was too distracting a view so I moved them to his feet. "That's not necessary. In this time—"

"It is, Josephine," he interrupted me to say. "I drafted that will. It's sound. I've known Lydia for thirty years and know her mind was sound. This is a nuisance lawsuit and I'll be handling it as a priority."

I lifted my eyes to Jake's when I replied, "That gives me much relief, Arnie."

"If I should need you, my dear, I'll call. But first allow me to see what I can do when Mr. Malone has found new counsel."

Faking confusion and hoping I pulled it off, I asked, "New counsel?"

"He was erroneously taken on at Weaver and Schuller. We've dealt with that matter and it's been explained to him he needs to find alternate representation. I'll let you know when he has and how things will proceed."

"I'd appreciate that," I told him.

"And don't worry, Josephine," he assured me, his voice low but firm. "As I said, this is a nuisance suit, it's my top priority and everything will be just as it should be in the end. That being you having what Lydia wished for you to have, Lavender House, her monies and her possessions."

"Thank you, Arnie," I said softly.

"My pleasure," he replied.

"Until we speak again," I said as my farewell.

"Until then, my dear. Take care."

"You too."

He rang off and I looked up at Jake, smiling big and declaring, "As I mentioned, darling. I have news."

He grinned at me, straightened and turned to the man in the ring. "We're done, Troy. But meet my woman," he invited and the man moved our way. "Troy, Josie. Josie, Troy," Jake finished.

"Lovely to meet you, Troy," I said.

"Same," he replied in a garbled way on a black grin since he hadn't taken out his mouth guard. He spit it into his glove and looked to Jake. "You're dropping your left."

"Noticed that," Jake replied.

"Bring it up," Troy returned, jerked up his chin, punched Jake affably in the shoulder and then moved to the ropes and through them.

I took a step back so Jake could do the same and Amond was at my side when Jake jumped down.

"Gear, gloves, babe," Jake ordered between his teeth seeing as he had the laces of one of his gloves between them.

He tugged.

I watched and felt another spasm.

He tugged at his other one.

I again watched and felt a spasm.

Then he shoved his hands my way.

That must have been what he meant by "gear, gloves, babe" so I pulled his gloves off.

Amond demanded to know, "What's the news?"

I looked to him to see him looking intently at me.

I looked back to Jake to see him yanking off his headgear as he explained, "Filled him in at the club last night, Slick."

My eyes went back to Amond. "It's really not a big deal."

"What's the news?" Amond repeated.

I sighed and looked to Jake.

Jake held my eyes but reached behind him, grabbing a sweatshirt from the side of the ring and saying, "Let's go into the office."

We moved there and once there, Jake dumped the headgear on his couch, took his gloves from me, they joined the headgear and then he yanked on his sweatshirt.

Once he had it down his stomach, I started, "I—"

"Didn't want to bother your friend with your shit," Jake finished for me. "I get that you want to have a good visit, babe. But you gotta get that you got a problem, you throw every resource you got at solving it."

Now I was confused.

"Pardon?"

"Don't matter," Amond entered the conversation. "What's the news?"

I looked to him then to Jake and said, "Obviously, I now have counsel."

"Give us more," Jake immediately replied.

I sighed and told them everything Alyssa had told me including asking them to keep it on the hush-hush. Although Amond would have no one to tell, Jake could.

"Good. That bitch got canned," was Jake's reply.

Once he said this, he looked to Amond and so did I.

Amond was looking at Jake. He lifted his brows.

I looked to Jake and saw Jake shake his head.

I looked back to Amond who had his mouth tight and he looked to his feet.

This was when I announced, "I am aware that I have a uterus but I've not known that ever to interfere with a woman's ability to speak English or deal with a variety of situations, including stressful ones."

At that, I got two highly attractive grins.

However, I got no words.

"Well?" I prompted.

Jake's grin died and he said, "Stone and your uncle still need to be taken out."

"Indeed," I agreed.

"So we're not out of the woods yet," Jake went on.

"I haven't opened a bottle of champagne, Jake," I pointed out and got another grin.

I also got, "Keep bein' a smartass, Slick, and your man here is gonna get an eyeful of just how much I like your mouth, even when you're usin' it to be a smartass."

At that, I closed my mouth.

Jake's grin got bigger.

"Thinkin' I need to give you two the room," Amond noted and I looked to him.

"Sorry, Amond. But actually you do. I have other news for Jake that's private."

"Not a problem, beautiful. Came here to get my sweat on and been jackin' around. I'm gonna go do that."

On those words he left with a low wave and closed the door behind him.

"What's the private news?" Jake asked the minute the door clicked.

I turned to him then I got closer to him and when I did, I shared what I learned about Donna.

This news was clearly not welcome and I knew it when Jake's eyes heated with anger and the room heated right along with them.

"The bitch is gonna take off?"

"We don't know that for certain, darling. This is beauty salon news. We probably shouldn't jump to conclusions."

It was like he didn't hear me.

"My boy Ethan's bitch of a mom took off. Calls him whenever somethin' reminds her to feel guilty she left his ass, which isn't often. Sends birthday cards with a shitload of money in them, expensive presents for Christmas, neither replacing him not havin' a fuckin' mom. Makes plans she doesn't intend to keep for me to send him down there in the summer and on spring break and then breaks them. Now my other kids' bitch of a mom is gonna hightail her ass outta town?"

I said nothing.

"I don't believe this shit," he clipped.

It was on that I went to him and put both hands on his chest. "Jake, we don't know she's leaving for certain."

"She'll leave. She's finally clued into the fact that everyone in town thinks she's a joke, she'll clue in she's dug a hole she's gonna find it hard to dig out of. And unfortunately, she's not the kind of woman who understands that it's worth scratchin' and clawin' your way out of the pits of hell if it means takin' care of your kids."

I pressed my lips together even if I liked very much that that was how he felt about his children.

"She's a bitch," he bit out.

I pressed in at his chest and moved closer. "Would you like me to contact her?"

"No," he clipped. "I'll get a hold of her ass."

"Uh…just to note, darling, that the last time you got *a hold of her ass* led to this reaction. Perhaps I can be more diplomatic."

He clenched his jaw.

"Let's think on this," I suggested gently. "Give it some time and see what she does. There's no reason to react, spending that emotion and maybe creating more bad blood if she eventually changes her mind."

Jake moved his hands to curl his fingers around my hips as he agreed curtly, "Right, Slick. We'll do that."

I slid my hands up to curl them around the sides of his neck, pressing closer as I said, "I'm sorry that I upset you."

"You didn't pick her, I did," he replied. "Fuck," he ground out. "Thank fuck I finally fuckin' picked right the last time."

My stomach dipped, my body melted into his and my hands clenched into the muscles at his neck.

When the latter two happened, he focused on me.

"I'm glad you think that," I said softly.

"Don't think it. Know it," he said firmly and that got another stomach dip, bigger than the last and much better.

However, even feeling it, I advised, "Please stop being hard on yourself. You were in love, and the man I know, I trust there were reasons for that. What these women are doing is their choice, their responsibility and in the end, Jake, they're missing out on great beauty and that's their consequence. You're not. You sacrificed for your children and you give them everything you can. They're going to understand that one day and feel deep gratitude for it, if they don't already."

"Love your words, baby, but hard not to kick myself in the ass for the choices I made."

"Well…" I rolled up on my toes and finished firmly on a squeeze of his neck, "Try."

He looked into my eyes for some time and finally his lips quirked as his hands moved so he could wrap his arms around me.

"Smartass and bossy, what got into you today?" he asked.

"I'm just handling my man," I answered.

His lip quirk turned into a full-blown laugh as his arms convulsed around me and he roared with his amusement.

I watched, nestling in and enjoying it.

I enjoyed it more when he noticed me doing it, dipped his head and kept doing it but with his mouth on mine.

Oh yes.

I enjoyed that more.

A great deal more.

And I showed him how much by sliding my arms around his neck.

At that, Jake got serious and I let him.

I enjoyed that even more.

So in the end, not only Amond but his crew and several of the members of Jake's club got a good view through Jake's office windows of just how much he liked my mouth.

And I didn't care.

Not one bit.

———•••———

"OKAY, BEAUTIFUL, THIS is what I see and what I see I'm gonna tell you and you gotta work some freakin' magic or I'd say in about a week, a month or, from the way of Jake's boy, a day, you're gonna face Armageddon."

This was whispered to me from Amond who'd leaned into me from his place at my side at the big rectangular table we were all sitting around in the function room at The Eaves.

I looked to him and raised my brows. "Pardon?"

"Right, you got a lot goin' on so I'll break this down. See your girl's girl, she shows at your place, all tricked out and I mean *tricked out*, lookin' good like she wants someone's attention. But your man's boy treats her probably like he's treated her since they were kids seein' as he's probably grown up with her."

My eyes drifted around the table, slightly confused at his words, until I put it together that "my girl's girl" was Sofie and "my man's boy" was Conner.

Then my eyes darted to Conner.

"Now, sweet Sofie, she didn't like that seein' as she tricked herself out for Conner," Amond continued. "And after he was all friendly but nothin' else, when he wasn't lookin', her face looked like the world was about to end."

Oh dear.

"Then," Amond went on, "we get to the restaurant and we're walkin' through and he just happens to be walkin' behind her. He also just happens to see that there was not one but a fuckin' *slew* of males, old and young, who got off on watchin' the eye candy parade walk by. You. Your girl. Your man's girl. And your girl's girl."

I looked from Conner, who was cutting his steak, to Sofie who let out a giggle at something her father said at her side. Then I swiftly looked back to Conner who was now very much looking at Sofie.

"Oh dear," I said out loud this time.

"Yeah," Amond agreed. "Your boy caught that girl gettin' attention and suddenly the blindfold was yanked off. And she ain't stupid. She's noticed it.

She just doesn't know what to do with it. But what she does know is how to be goofy, cute and sweet and your boy Con is clearly all about that because he went from mildly interested to all over that shit in about ten minutes."

"Damn," I whispered.

"Now, I got three kids and all three of them are girls and I'll tell you this, your boy even looked at them, I'd lose my mind. That Junior guy loves his wife. He loves his family. He's all good. But he'll stop bein' all good when he cottons on to this shit. And the ones who talk soft are the ones to look out for 'cause you don't know what's hit you when he explodes."

I looked to Amond and declared, "Conner is a fine young man."

To which Amond smiled a big white smile and replied, "You can say that, not bein' a sixteen year old girl whose ass he wants to tap."

I felt my eyes get wide, leaned in, and hissed, "I'll have you know, Conner has abstained from sexual intercourse with at least two of his girlfriends."

His brows shot up and his grin turned wicked when he asked, "A whole two?"

I harrumphed and settled my behind more firmly in my seat as I turned deeper to him and stated, "And one of them was quite shy and very lovely, just like Sofie."

His head cocked to the side. "Jesus, you that tight with him?"

I took in a breath and shared, "Circumstances were such with one of his ex-girlfriends that this news came to light."

"I bet," he muttered, still smiling.

"He's quite protective and thoughtful with his girlfriends," I informed him.

"I bet," he repeated, *still* smiling.

I started to get a niggle of anxiety and murmured, "Though he's completely unattached now."

"Won't be for long," Amond murmured in return.

I took in another breath and looked to Conner. Alas, when I did this I saw him smile. It was directed at Sofie so my eyes moved to her. I knew she caught it because her cheeks were becomingly pink and she was staring at her lap even as she reached for her water glass. This was a doomed endeavor, I knew too well, and I was right. She knocked it over and thus shot out of her chair, her father doing the same, both of them tossing their napkins to the spill.

My gaze went back to Conner to see him grinning rather knowingly and somewhat alarmingly handsomely at his plate.

Blast.

Amond chuckled.

I turned to glare at him.

At that point, I felt Jake lean into me on my other side and, lips to my ear, he said, "We're fucked. Con's on the prowl. Target: Sofie. Junior gets wind of that, he's gonna lose his mind."

I turned my head to him, lifted my brows with fake innocence, and murmured, "Hmm?"

Jake took in my expression, shook his head and declared, "You are so full of shit."

"All right, so I noticed," I admitted. "But only because Amond just pointed it out."

"Yeah," Jake said. "Noticed that's been his entertainment all night but he doesn't have to deal with a kid he wants to have everything he wants and a friend who wants to rip his kid's head off."

Although the situation was possibly dire, Jake's words made me stifle a giggle and I repeated my advice of much earlier that day, "Why don't we see how things play out?"

"I know how they're gonna play out, Slick," he returned. "See, I got klutzy and cute sleepin' beside me at night so I know it's sweet. And I got a boy who's just like me. So I know what he's gonna go for and now I gotta make certain he doesn't *go for it* in the backseat of his car. I like my son. I want him on this earth awhile. And I like Junior. I don't want to have to beat him to death in an alley for takin' my son out."

"You're being very dramatic, Jake," I pointed out. "I think should something happen, they'll be quite sweet together."

"You got the mind of a once sixteen year old girl. I got the mind of a once seventeen year old boy. And newsflash, Slick, so does Junior."

I bit my lip.

Jake watched me do it then his eyes came back to mine and he said, "Right."

I turned my attention back to the halibut on my plate but felt something strange and looked across the table.

Alyssa was sitting there between Amond's bodyguard and his "other manager" and her eyes on me were huge as was the smile on her face. I watched as they darted comically and quickly to her side then she jutted her chin out and they darted across the table and back. She repeated this four times before she lifted a hand in a thumb's up gesture then curled it in a fist and pumped it up and down three times before she turned her attention back to her plate.

I stared at her, nonplussed, until Jake again put his lips to his ear.

"Well, we got that goin' for us. Alyssa's fired up about her girl landing the high school big man. My son makes his move, you play that angle. I'll keep an eye on Junior."

Ah.

So that was what that was all about with Alyssa.

I turned to Jake. "Deal."

He grinned at me, leaned in and touched his mouth to mine.

"Gross!" Ethan shouted and both Jake and I looked at him in time to watch him announce to the whole table. "They do that all the time."

"Just you wait until you get your turn, little man," Amond advised.

"I'm not kissin' Josie," Ethan returned, looking a little sick.

"No, boy," Amond replied. "When you get a woman of your own."

"She's gonna cook like Josie. She's gonna dress like Josie. She's gonna talk like Josie. But we're just holding hands," Ethan informed Amond superiorly and my heart jumped as my belly melted.

"At least you got good taste, even though I'm makin' a pact with you that I'm callin' you in fifteen years and we'll see about that holdin' hands business," Amond replied.

Ethan grinned, likely only hearing that Amond was calling him in fifteen years, and agreed, "You're on."

Amond threw him a smile.

I reached out for my glass of champagne.

Jake reached for his beer and as he did so, slid an arm around the back of my chair, leaned behind me and said something to Amond.

But I wasn't listening.

I was looking.

And I was feeling.

A table of friends from two different worlds, talking, eating, laughing and making a beautiful memory with me smack in the middle, able to drink it all in even as I felt my man close, his arm on my chair, claiming me.

And it was then I knew.

It wasn't Jake Gran wanted me to have.

It wasn't Jake and his kids.

It was this.

It was a good life. A happy life. Safe with people I cared about and trusted.

And in giving me Jake, this was what she gave me.

I felt my eyes sting, put my champagne back and focused again on my halibut.

After I took a bite, chewed and swallowed, I took up my champagne again and looked to the ceiling that was painted an attractive wine color that had a lovely wash to it that made it look like undulating satin.

I didn't see the lovely paint job.

I wasn't seeing.

I was speaking.

Silently.

Thank you, Gran, I said, lifted my glass minutely then took a sip.

I put it back to the table and turned my attention to the halibut.

———•◦•◦•———

THE NEXT AFTERNOON, I watched Amond and his posse hand out hugs and handshakes around the Escalades making note that when Jake and Amond clasped each other's forearms, they kept hold and leaned into each other, talking in ears.

I decided to ignore this. They were bonding and it wasn't lost on me they were bonding over my troubles with my uncle and Boston Stone. But they were bonding, that was what was important.

I gave out my own hugs to Amond's crew and he was the last for me.

He pulled me in his arms; he did this close, his arms going tight.

And he shocked me, honored me and wounded me when he whispered in my ear, "This is precisely what I wanted to give you, beautiful."

I said nothing, just held on.

"Even not givin' it to you, sure as fuck am glad you got it."

I closed my eyes and held on tighter.

"Love you, Josephine," he finished.

I opened my eyes and turned my head so my lips were right at his ear.

"And I love you, too, honey."

He gave me a squeeze, pulled back an inch, looked deep in my eyes and smiled.

I took in a breath through my nose and smiled back.

He let me go and got in the back seat of one of the Escalades. As he was doing this, Jake got close and claimed me with an arm around my shoulders. The kids then claimed me just by huddling close.

Thus Jake, Conner, Amber, Ethan and I stood and waved Amond and his crew away.

And when we lost sight of them, we all walked together back into Lavender House.

THE NEXT MORNING, I followed Jake and Ethan out of the kitchen, pad of paper and pen in hand, scribbling.

"Babe, just give it to me and text me if you forget anything," Jake ordered impatiently.

"Just a second," I murmured, hurrying after them and still scribbling.

"It's a grocery list, not the Magna Carta, Slick," Jake noted. "Just give it to me. I gotta get my boy to school and then I got a session at the gym."

I looked up and narrowed my eyes, reminding him, "I don't understand why you're going to the grocery store when I've got nearly all day to do it."

He stopped at the door. "'Cause I'm gonna be in Blakely to meet my liquor distributors and no reason for you to go over there when I'm already over there. And anyway, you got a boatload of laundry the kids dumped on you last night."

"I can do laundry, grocery shop and, FYI, also drop Ethan."

"I'm already out on the road to get to the gym. No reason for you to be too."

"Okay then, I—"

He cut me off to ask, "Babe, you ever done five people's laundry?"

"No," I gave him the answer he already knew.

"I haven't either. But I've done four. Trust me. It seems the machines do all the work but that shit sucks your time. You got dishes in the sink and Pearl to take to Alyssa's and it isn't me who fired your cleaning service because they missed polishing the fuckin' door."

Ethan giggled.

I glared at Jake and I did this mostly because I hated it that he was right.

"That wood is over one hundred years old, Jake. It needs constant care," I informed him haughtily.

Jake sighed before he replied, "Are you gonna give me the list or what?"

I tugged off the sheet on top of the pad and jerked it his way.

He took it, shoved it in his back pocket then asked, "Now you gonna give me a kiss or what?"

"I'm going out to the truck," Ethan announced at this point.

But I was considering my options of kissing Jake or what.

Ethan went out the door.

"Baby, get your ass over here," Jake ordered.

"I'm supposed to be helping," I told him.

"Tonight, I get home, you get the fifty loads of laundry you're facin' done, I sit my ass down with my kids and eat the dinner you cooked, we'll talk about how you aren't helping."

Hmm.

Well, the way he said that seemed helpful.

"Babe. Kiss," he growled impatiently.

I moved to him. He swept his arms around me, dropped his mouth to mine and I didn't give him a kiss, he took one.

And it was a lovely one.

When he was done, he ran his nose alongside mine and whispered, "Later, Slick."

"Later, darling."

I watched his eyes grin then I watched him go.

When the door closed behind him, I turned and tripped, nearly going down on my hands and knees. I caught myself just in time and looked at the floor to see what caught at my foot.

It was a tennis shoe.

I also saw its mate to the side and another pair of shoes. High-heeled boots.

Not mine. Amber's.

I looked up and on the sturdy, handsome coat tree by the door I saw jackets and scarves thrown over it, only two of them mine.

I turned and wandered down the hall and took in an iPad, Ethan's, sitting on the table in the hall, plugged in to charge under it.

I kept wandering and hit the family room. A laptop on the couch, Amber's. Some discarded papers on the table by the armchair. I didn't know what they were but I knew they were put there by Conner who did his homework there last night.

I moved to the kitchen and stopped, taking in the skillet on the Aga, the dishes in the sink, the juice glasses and coffee mugs beside it.

I wandered to the kitchen table and looked out the window at the gray blustery day, taking in a stormy sea, the fenced garden put to rest for the winter, the wisteria around the arbor cut back and ready to grow in and bloom come spring.

Next year, I'd plant pumpkins in that garden for Ethan and tomatoes in hopes I could get Conner to eat them.

I knew this.

I loved this.

This was the life I'd wanted since I could remember, the dream I thought had died that night my boyfriend sent me crashing down the stairs. The beautiful bubble of that dream had popped the instant I heard my shoulder crack and the pain radiated out, obliterating the dream to the point I didn't even remember I had it.

But I remembered it right then.

That was why I stood looking out a window I'd looked out hundreds of times in my life. Perhaps thousands.

But this was the first time I did it at the same time I started laughing. Which was the same time I began to cry.

———•••••———

JUST AFTER NOON the next day, I stood in the pharmacy by the Redbox, jabbing my finger on the screen to make my selection. Or, more accurately, Ethan's selection since his friends Bryant and Joshua were coming over that night for a sleepover and a video orgy (Jake's words) was on the agenda.

I managed to get one DVD to spit out just as my phone rang.

I dug it out of my purse, saw the name on the display and took the call.

"Young Taylor, how are you?" I greeted boy Taylor.

"Update, Josie," was his greeting to me.

I had learned since he got my number that boy Taylor was a bit of a gossip. A *fair* bit of one.

This was not unwelcome. In fact, it was always interesting and quite often amusing.

"Fill me in," I ordered, jabbing the screen on the Redbox to make my next selection.

"Con's having a time of it," he shared readily. "Sofie is not shy. The girl is uber freaking *shy*. Every day this week he tried to execute an approach at lunch but she sees this and takes off running, even leaving her lunch tray on the table to do it."

"Oh dear," I murmured as the box spit out my second DVD.

I kept jabbing the screen as boy Taylor kept speaking.

"Today it was worse."

"Oh dear," I repeated.

"Yeah. She tripped when she took off. Took a header right in the cafeteria. *Splat!*"

I winced.

Poor Sofie.

Boy Taylor went on.

"Then, swear to God, it was like a teenaged Nicolas Sparks movie. Con moved in, picked her up, asked her if she was okay and she burst into tears right on the spot and took off. The whole school is yammering about it."

This might not be good news.

"Good talk or bad talk?" I queried.

"Uh...Josie, Con's hot, he got screwed over by Mia *and* Ellie so everyone's thinkin' he's the misunderstood hero with a wounded heart. And Sofie's pretty, sweet and far's I know, never been kissed. Every girl who keeps a diary is going to be chronicling this story in pink ink with *loads* of hearts drawn around it."

"I'll take that as good," I stated as the last DVD regurgitated itself from the tall red box.

"Yeah," he replied and I could hear his laughter. Then he went on, "Oh, and Amber's waving and yapping at me. She wants you to tell Mr. Spear she's gonna be late tonight. She and Alexi are going to a movie after school then he's taking her out to dinner."

This was a smooth maneuver a la Amber, giving me this information to give her father who was resigned to his daughter dating but that didn't mean he liked it.

"Tell her I'll handle that," I said.

"Cool," he replied.

"Now, you have a good afternoon, young Taylor. Stay alert in class."

"Will do. You have a good afternoon too, Josie," he replied.

"I will. Take care and say hello to Amber and girl Taylor for me."

"Consider it done. Later," he bid his farewell.

"Good-bye, Taylor," I bid mine, added the last DVD to my pile, turned and stopped dead.

Then I took a step back and ran into the Redbox.

"Stupid little *bitch*," Uncle Davis hissed, leaning into me threateningly.

I stared at him, my body frozen, but my heart was slamming in my chest.

I'd taken him in that night he'd made his surprise and unwelcome visit but that night was dark.

Now, it was a shock to see what the years had done to him.

When I was young, he seemed so powerful, so threatening, so fearsome. He terrified me, even more than my father. I knew my father had violence in him, I'd witnessed it and experienced it from the moment I had memories.

But Uncle Davis somehow was worse.

Now he was a shell of his former self. A fragile, chipped one that appeared easily crushed should you trod on it.

I had these thoughts in a blink of an eye.

And in that same blink, Uncle Davis got close.

"Asshole who found me and told me about the wad Ma laid on you had that attorney's firm on retainer. Now, seein' as he has to pay for that shit outta pocket, he don't feel like ponying up. Especially when that stupid bitch who told him she had it all covered and…fuckin'…*didn't* then told him it wasn't gonna go easy. She also laid that shit on *my* door when the first judge she was tryin' to get to fast track me to my rightful inheritance refused the case since he said me and Chess played some fuckin' prank on him a half a fuckin' century ago and he's not over it so he can't be impartial."

I blinked as all this information, and there was a good deal of it, processed through me.

Uncle Davis seemed not to know, or possibly care, how much he was giving because he kept giving it.

"Now, that asshole Stone says it's up to me. I got me a lawyer who'd take the case for a percentage of what he gets me and then *your*"—he jabbed a finger at me so close to my face, I made a futile attempt to press further into the Redbox—"lawyer buried him under so much shit, now *he's* sayin' *he* needs a retainer from *me* to stay on the case."

I swallowed.

Uncle Davis's eyes narrowed and he got closer, his mouth opening to say more but he didn't get it out.

This was because someone close ordered, "Step away from Ms. Malone."

I looked to my left to see Magdalene's tall, handsome sheriff there, wearing a sheriff-style shirt but with jeans and although tall and handsome (something I noticed when I met him several days ago, seeing as he was *that* tall and *that* handsome, it was hard to miss—something I noticed even more now for that sheriff shirt was quite something on a man like him). However, tall and handsome he was, he was not happy.

"What's goin' on here?" I heard at that point and looked to my right to see Mickey bearing down on us.

But, alas, Uncle Davis was focused.

On me.

Thus I had no choice but to focus on him.

"I'm not payin' for this shit, shit I shoulda got straight from Ma," he announced.

"Sir, I asked…step away from Ms. Malone," the sheriff repeated.

Uncle Davis again ignored him.

"That house and that money are mine, bitch, and the half I was willin' to give you outta the goodness of my heart is really Chess's and since I didn't fuck Chess over like you did, I figure that's mine too."

The sheriff and Mickey were much closer when the sheriff reiterated, "Sir, I will not ask again. Step away from Ms. Malone."

He didn't get the opportunity to comply. Mickey wrapped his hand around my bicep and slid me out from in front of Uncle Davis then he pressed me behind him as he stepped between me and my uncle.

Uncle Davis glared at Mickey. "I wasn't done talkin' to my niece."

"Oh yeah you were," Mickey replied quietly.

Uncle Davis's brows shot up. "You takin' on an old man?"

"Just tellin' you whatever else you gotta say to Josephine, you're not gonna say it," Mickey returned then shifted slightly my way and ordered, "Get to your car, honey."

"Don't you move a fuckin' muscle," Uncle Davis commanded, again lifting a hand and jabbing a finger my way.

Mickey stepped to the side, between me and my uncle's finger, at the same time shielding me from view.

"Sir, calm down and move away from Mr. Donovan and Ms. Malone," the sheriff demanded.

Uncle Davis leaned to the side to catch my eyes. "This is not done, bitch. I'm gonna get what's mine, however I gotta do it."

"Now I gotta ask you to stop threatening Ms. Malone and remind you that not only are you doin' that in front of witnesses but an officer of the law."

Uncle Davis turned to the sheriff. "You think I give a shit?"

"I think you aren't very smart if you don't," the sheriff returned.

Uncle Davis opened his mouth to speak but I did it before him.

"Bring it on."

I felt all attention come to me and stepped from behind Mickey so Uncle Davis could see me clearly. Mickey wrapped his fingers around my wrist but that was all he did before I started talking again.

"Do you honestly think I'm still frightened of you?" I asked.

"I think you never learned that lesson from your father like you should," he answered.

Highly inappropriate.

So Uncle Davis.

"Yes, I did, Uncle Davis," I told him. "I absolutely did that last time when he put me in the hospital."

I felt Mickey and the sheriff go alert but I wasn't done.

"But I'm older now. Wiser. And you're older too. Weak. And not very smart. And all this is just what you do. Making people's lives miserable because you're a sociopath and you enjoy it. I think it's only fair to warn you that you can put a good deal of effort into trying to make me miserable but you won't succeed. It will end being quite frustrating so I'd advise you to cut your losses now."

"I got a hankerin' to put a fair amount of effort into it, Josephine," Uncle Davis replied and I shrugged when he did.

"My invitation still stands. Have at it. It'll be your time and money that you lose."

His eyes narrowed on me, something shifting in them before they did, and he offered, "Make things easier for you. You give me a check, I'll get outta town."

And I knew precisely what that meant. I remembered the way I grew up. I remembered the way he and my father were. How they lived. How my father living that way meant I lived. Even as I kid, I knew it because, especially as a kid, you couldn't miss it.

"What you're saying is, Boston Stone paid for your trip here and now he's washed his hands of you, you don't have the money to get wherever home is."

He glared at me but shifted on his feet.

This meant I was correct.

"You won't get a penny from me," I told him.

"Then I'll get it all from you by takin' that house and Ma's money," he fired back.

"If you honestly think you can win that fight, bring that on too," I retorted. "It's not me who's seventy-two years old and out of money in a place without a friend."

"We'll see," he returned.

"We most certainly will," I agreed. Then I dismissed him and looked to the sheriff. "Lovely to see you again, sheriff."

"Coert," he corrected, grinning at me.

Another unusual name. I wasn't sure how I felt about it but it was better than Boston.

"Coert." I smiled at him then looked up at Mickey. "Thank you, Mickey."

"No problem, babe," he replied.

"Maybe you'll come to dinner soon?" I asked.

"Yeah," he answered.

"Good," I murmured then looked between the two men, ignoring my uncle, and decided to get on with my day. "Later, gentleman," I said as I started toward the door.

"Later, Josie," Coert called.

"Later, darlin'," Mickey said.

I lifted a hand in a wave and walked out the door.

I was halfway back to Lavender House when my phone rang. I took the chance to glance at the screen as it was sitting face up on my passenger seat. When I saw who was calling, I broke a rule I normally always kept, grabbed my mobile and put it to my ear.

"Hello, darling," I greeted.

"Seriously?" Jake replied.

Again, I thought this word was overused, and further, particularly in this instance, I didn't understand it.

So I asked, "Seriously what?"

"Just got off the phone with Mick."

"Oh," I said.

"Oh?" he asked. "That asshole pins you against a Redbox, you don't call me? Then I call you and all you say is 'oh?'"

"Jake, darling," I started soothingly. "He's quite elderly. Boston Stone has withdrawn his assistance. I'm relatively certain he's destitute. Although that encounter was unpleasant, he's hardly a threat and anyway, Mickey and Sheriff Coert were there."

"Yeah, but *I* wasn't and that shit happened to *my* woman. And I gotta know when shit like that goes down."

"You can hardly beam yourself to me on a whim should you get a sense I'm in danger," I pointed out.

He said nothing so I went on.

"And furthermore, it's over. I'm fine. And he did impart on me a good deal of news that was not good for him but is very good for me, that being that Boston Stone has washed his hands of Uncle Davis and Arnie is on the case so he's finding it difficult to hire alternate representation."

"Babe," he said low and not soothingly. "Hear me. Shit goes down with you that's unpleasant, I don't care how unimportant you think that unpleasant is, *you tell me.*"

"I dislike speaking on the phone while driving," I shared. "But just so you know, I did plan on sharing this with you over dinner."

"Dinner is five hours away."

I said nothing for there was nothing to say. This was true.

Jake, however, said something.

"Remember what I said about you even feelin' funny about a look you get in the grocery store?"

Oh dear.

I did remember that.

"Yes," I answered quietly.

"So, next time something unpleasant happens to you, what are you gonna do?"

Apparently, I was going to share this with Jake without delay.

"Contact you," I replied.

"Good answer, Slick."

I gave it a moment, kept driving and when he said nothing more, I shared, "I was able to acquire all Ethan's viewing selections for him and his friends this evening."

His voice was a strange combination of exasperated and amused when he replied, "Excellent news."

"I was worried at least one would be checked out but that's not the case," I informed him.

"I'll bring the champagne."

I grinned at his quip.

Since he was quipping, I decided to share news he would like much less than me getting all the videos his son wanted for that evening.

"Amber has a date with Alexi that starts after school. She'll be home late."

"Great," he muttered unhappily.

"And reportedly Conner behaved like the hero from a romance film when Sofie dashed away from him, took a tumble and he picked her up off the floor."

There was a moment of silence before, "Jesus, boy Taylor's got a big mouth."

"He keeps me informed."

"He fuckin' does," Jake agreed before querying, "Con get in there with Sofie?"

"Alas, she burst into tears and ran away."

"Good for him to have a challenge," Jake murmured as if to himself. "Don't appreciate it unless they make you work for it. You win it, you know what you got, you know to take care of it."

This was when I was silent but I was this way with my belly feeling very warm.

Jake broke into my silence to say, "Right, see you later."

"Okay, darling. See you later."

"Bye, Slick."

"Good-bye, Jake."

He rang off.

I tossed my phone to the passenger seat when he did and finished driving home.

THE MATTRESS MOVED and I felt a blast of cold as I lost Jake's body because he was exiting the bed.

I turned and called out sleepily, "Jake?"

"Do not turn on the lights. Get your phone. Listen. You call 911, you hear something you don't like."

My heart shot to my throat so I had to push through it, "Pardon?"

"Motion sensor light, baby. Back door. Phone. Now," he said into the dark then he was gone.

I lay on the bed frozen for a moment before my body became a flurry of movement. I threw back the covers, grabbed my robe from the end of the bed and tugged it on. After that, I reached out and grabbed the phone and, fumbling but succeeding, I tied the belt on my robe once I got the phone in my hand.

My eyes went to the alarm clock, which told me it was 4:12 in the morning then they moved to the window. I could see dim illumination coming up from the light at the back door and I stared out the window wondering how on earth Jake sensed that when he had to be dead asleep.

That was when I heard the faraway crash of a window breaking.

My heart seized but my thumb flew over the keypad of the phone which fortunately lit up the instant I pressed a button.

I hit the three numbers as I dashed to the table by the window where I knew an antique bank made of iron and shaped like the Empire State Building sat. I grabbed it and ran to the door as the 911 operator answered.

I hit the hall and said, "This is Josephine Malone at Lavender House in Magdalene. Ten Lavender Lane." I stopped dead in the hall, tucked the phone between my ear and shoulder and lifted a hand sharply when I saw the shadow of Conner coming out of his room and kept talking. "We're experiencing a break in and my boyfriend is downstairs."

Conner heard me, moved swiftly my way, which meant toward the stairs, and the 911 operator spoke to me but I hissed to Conner.

"Con, no!"

He ignored me but grabbed the iron bank out of my hand before he moved past me and disappeared down the stairs.

I followed him and interrupted the operator to say, "Now Jake's seventeen year old son is going down there."

"I've dispatched a unit. Please get to a safe place and lock yourself in if you can."

I hesitated at the top of the stairs and looked down the hall.

"We have three eight year old boys in this house and a sixteen year old girl," I told her.

"Assemble them and lock yourself someplace safe. A unit is on the way."

I dashed down the hall to Amber's door, asking, "What about Jake and Conner?"

"Ma'am, take care of the children."

Blast!

Of course!

I threw open Amber's door, raced to the bed and put a hand to her, shaking.

She turned, murmuring, "Wha?"

"Up, honey, hurry. We need to get to Ethan." She didn't move for a moment so I ordered urgently, "Up, Amber."

She threw the covers off and had her feet on the floor when we both shrieked as the lights went on.

Conner in a pair of sweats with a bare chest stood in the door.

Vaguely I noted I was correct upon seeing him some time ago at Gran's funeral. He'd inherited much from his father, including his physique.

"Josie, Dad's got your uncle in the kitchen. He says to call 911 and get Coert out here to take him away," Conner announced.

"Ma'am, what's happening?" the operator asked in my ear.

But I wasn't listening.

I was fuming.

And thus I stomped to Conner and handed him the phone, ordering, "The 911 operator is on the line. Inform her of this news."

I then stomped around him, down the hall, the stairs and into the fully lit kitchen.

There I saw Jake in pajama bottoms and nothing else towering over my uncle who was sitting at the kitchen table.

I watched as my uncle tried to stand and Jake put a hand on him and shoved him back in the chair.

"Sit. Stay. Do not try to get up again, old man. I don't give a fuck I could break you in half. Give me a reason to do it and I'll take it," Jake growled.

"Jake," I called, advancing into the room.

Jake sliced angry eyes to me and asked immediately, "You call 911?"

"Yes. Conner's on with them now," I answered, my eyes going to my uncle who was glaring up at Jake.

My words were proved true when Conner came in behind me still on the phone. "Yeah. It's okay. The guy who tried to break in is about seven hundred years old. He's not a threat. He's sitting at the kitchen table. Okay. Thanks." He beeped off the phone and looked to his father. "Police are on their way."

"God damn it," Uncle Davis muttered.

And that was when it happened. That was when it came right out of me. I couldn't stop it.

And I totally understood it.

I looked to my uncle, brows raised, hands lifted up at my sides, and I asked, "Seriously?"

"Josie—" Jake started but I cut him off.

Still addressing my uncle, I asked, "Are you whacked?"

"Girl—" he began but I cut him off too.

"What did you think you were going to accomplish?"

He didn't answer my question.

He groused, "Stupid motion sensor lights. Dark day they were invented."

"Uncle Davis!" I snapped loudly. "What did you think you were going to accomplish?"

He glared at me but said not a word.

"God, you're an idiot," I shared.

"Respect your uncle, girl," he bit out.

"I would, if you'd ever given me one, single, itty, bitty, miniscule reason to do so," I fired back, then huffed, "Yeesh."

He glared at me again.

I rolled my eyes and looked to Jake. "Are you all right?"

"I am but the window to the greenhouse door isn't," he answered.

I cut my eyes to my uncle. "You're going to pay for that."

"How?" he asked back. "Givin' blood? Girl, I broke in so I could get some shit to pawn 'cause I can't even afford the gas money to get home."

"Well, a better solution to your problem was to give blood to get your gas money because you're not getting a *thing* from this house or a *dime* from me," I told him then kept at him, "The good news is, at least you have a free place to sleep tonight because I'm *so totally* pressing charges."

He glared at me again.

I decided I was finished with him so I moved to the coffeepot and announced, "I'm making coffee. Jake? Coffee?"

"Yeah, babe," he replied but his voice was trembling with something I knew very well.

Humor.

I hit the button to start the brewing process and looked to him.

"Are you amused?" I asked.

Even through his very large grin, he lied, "No."

I narrowed my eyes on him. "That's the right answer even if it's a false one."

His voice was still filled with his amusement when he replied, "It's still the answer I'm givin' when you're this pissed and this cute."

"Angry is not cute, Jake," I educated him.

"It is the way you do it, Slick," he returned.

I shot him a look but rearranged my face when I looked to Conner. "I woke your sister and possibly frightened her. Perhaps you could tell her all is well and she can go back to sleep."

"You got it, Josie," Conner murmured, grinned at his dad and took off.

"And put on a sweatshirt!" I yelled at his back. "You'll catch a chill!"

That was when Jake burst out laughing.

I again cut my eyes to him and asked an exasperated, "What's amusing now?"

He didn't answer me.

Instead he declared, "If it wasn't sick, I'd totally make out with you right now in front of your shit for brains uncle."

Alas, that *was* sick and perhaps one of only a handful of times I could conjure in my head where making out with Jake would be unwelcome.

"We'll make out later," I told him.

"You bet your ass we will," he muttered.

"Someone get me a bucket," Uncle Davis begged.

"That's enough out of you," I snapped.

Jake burst out laughing again.

I rolled my eyes and went to the cupboard to get mugs for I needed to prepare. I had a feeling it was going to be a long morning

THE CRUISER WITH Uncle Davis in the backseat had pulled away and I was standing in the foyer with Jake, Conner and Sheriff Coert.

"Thank you, Sheriff Coert," I said, extending my hand.

He took it, gave it a light squeeze and replied, "Just Coert."

"All right. Just Coert." I grinned, and gave him a squeeze back.

He let my hand go and looked to Jake.

"Bring Josie to the department in a couple of hours. The old coot can get used to his bunk and Josie can press charges at a decent hour."

"Got it," Jake said.

The sheriff looked back to me. "Sorry this happened, Josie."

"I'm not. I sincerely doubt if he should possibly be able to talk anyone into representing him in contesting Gran's will that a judge would smile upon him breaking and entering. I would say he hammered the final nail in his coffin so I'm quite all right with it."

"Good to look on the bright side," Coert noted.

"Indeed," I agreed.

"Love to shoot the shit for the rest of the morning, man, but need to get my woman and son to bed," Jake said at this point, sliding his arm around my shoulders.

"Right," Coert murmured then looked to Conner. "Con."

"Later, Coert," Con said.

Coert looked to me. "Josie. Next time I see you, let's make it for a good reason."

"I'll look forward to that."

He jerked up his chin, clapped Jake on the shoulder and Jake let me go to follow him to the door.

Jake closed and locked the door behind him then turned to Conner and me.

"Go on up," he said to Conner and his eyes came to me. "I'll be up in a bit."

A bit? Why in a bit?

"Are you okay?" I asked.

"Got a window to board up," he answered.

Of course.

Jake was going to board the window to the greenhouse in the wee hours of the morning.

My man was *so* wonderful.

"I'll help, Dad," Conner offered.

And Conner was *such* a lovely young man.

"I got it, Con. Hit the sack. It's barely five. You gotta work today and you need your sleep," Jake said to his son.

"I'll help, Dad," Conner repeated and didn't wait for his father again to refuse.

He turned to the steps and took them two at a time, likely going up so he could put some shoes on in order to help his father.

I looked up at Jake. "Your son is lovely."

Jake's eyes got warm and he agreed, "Yeah, babe." Then his warm eyes moved to the stairs in a way that made mine move to the stairs and I saw Amber halfway down them looking like she was sleepwalking.

"Eath's barfing, Dad," she announced.

Oh dear.

I looked up at Jake and said, "I'll get Eath. You get the window."

"Right, babe," he answered, bent into me and touched his mouth to mine.

Jake headed toward the kitchen and I headed to the steps and up them, following an Amber who was meandering so much, I lifted my hands to her hips and guided her back to her bed where she collapsed.

I threw the covers over her, quickly tucked her in then I went to the bathroom where Ethan was indeed barfing.

Five minutes into this unpleasant experience, Bryant wandered in and then he and Ethan took turns barfing.

It was then I made a mental note that perhaps next time I would not purchase so much snack food and allow them to consume it at will while staying up to all hours and watching DVDs.

SOME TIME LATER, I felt the bed move as Jake joined me in it.

I turned to him, cuddling closer, murmuring, "Is all well with the window?"

"Yeah, babe. Eath good?"

"Yes, darling."

"Good," he muttered, pulling me closer.

"Jake?" I called.

"Yeah?" he asked.

"How did you know the light had gone on outside? You had to be dead asleep."

"Sixth sense," he replied. "Man's any man at all, Slick, he's got his family under a roof, he's attuned to what happens around that roof, especially if it might be a threat."

My drowsy eyes fully opened and I stared at the planes of his chest in the weak light of dawn.

"Sleep, babe," Jake ordered preposterously.

"Okay," I lied, still staring at his chest, feeling the power of his body stretched out, mine resting against it, the covers over us creating a warm cocoon.

But the warmth I felt had nothing to do with covers.

It had to do with feeling safe and being part of a family.

I liked that feeling so much, I allowed myself to bask in it. Thus Jake fell asleep before me.

A little after he did, I joined him.

"HEY, JOSIE."

"Hello, Deon," I replied on a smile as he opened the door to The Circus for me and I sauntered in.

I walked through the club, waving at Paulette (whose hair looked *fabulous* after her keratin treatment) and Shoshana (who had reported to me that her tips were mostly the same but her boyfriend *adored* her as a brunette now that she dyed it from the red) as well as nodding to Adam behind the bar.

I hit the door to Jake's office and punched the code into the keypad thinking that pressing charges was a rather lengthy process. Luckily, Ethan, Bryant and Joshua, who were with us until three that day, thought a trip to the police station to press charges against a "lame old loser" (Ethan's words) was the bomb.

Fortunately, Junior and Alyssa felt the same way.

Joshua's parents were rather alarmed his sleepover included a trip to the sheriff's department but Jake had a word and they got over it.

Nevertheless, all the activity meant a delay in Jake and my make out session, especially when girl Taylor showed at the front door about an hour after the boys went home, jumping up and down, squealing.

I was concerned she drove in that excited state but I understood it when I learned that Kieran Wentworth was yet again up from college for the weekend. It would seem he was thus simply to "run into" girl Taylor who had mentioned when she met him at church several weeks before that her younger brother was to participate in some martial arts event that day.

It would seem she was correct about her hopeful deduction that he was up just for her, for Kieran Wentworth had no younger brother in this event. Although he participated in the same martial arts practice and had a black belt so he at least had a slim cover story.

He sat with her throughout the whole event.

She was beside herself with glee.

The evening degenerated when Conner returned from attempting somewhat the same maneuver and therefore after work had gone to some choral performance the school was putting on. A performance in which Sofie had a solo.

Conner approached her after the performance was over to compliment her on her singing. Strides were made when she stood with him long enough to listen to this. More strides were made when she expressed her gratitude for the compliment. Gains were lost when Conner asked for her number. It was reported through Conner from Jake to me that she then told him that he was the cutest and sweetest guy in school and "deserved someone worthy of him, like Ellie and not like me."

At this point, she teared up and made her escape.

Conner spent the rest of evening phoning around to get her number. He succeeded in this endeavor and disappeared into his room. He had not been heard of since and I hoped he at least got Sofie to converse with him over the phone.

I didn't want him to give up. There was a challenge and then there was beating your head against the wall. But I suspected Sofie would be worth it. I just hoped Conner would understand that, keep at it and break through whatever was creating that wall.

It was at this point that Jake needed to go to the club so he left.

Thus all day and no promised make out session.

Therefore, I made certain the kids were taken care of, Ethan in bed and asked Amber to keep an eye on things and make sure all was well at Lavender House while I went to the club. She agreed. I then took myself off to my room to prepare.

Little clingy black dress.

Very high heels.

Evening make up.

Hair down.

I put on a stylish coat that concealed this outfit and it was tied shut as I made my way up the stairs to Jake's office.

He was sitting behind his desk and his eyes were on me as I walked up the stairs.

"Surprised, babe. Didn't know you were coming," he said on a smile.

"I'm here," I replied just as my phone in my purse rang. "Hang on a second, darling," I said, keeping my eyes to him.

I took my phone out of my purse and saw it was Alyssa calling.

I dumped my purse in one of the chairs in front of Jake's desk as I took the call and put it to my ear.

"Hey, honey," I greeted, tugging on the belt to my coat.

"Ohmigod!" she cried in my ear. "You...would not...*believe*," she stated.

She was quite excited but then again I had a feeling I knew what she was talking about since Conner had secured her daughter's number.

"What wouldn't I believe?" I asked, eyes on Jake as I shrugged my coat off one shoulder.

"Is it too late?" she asked back.

"No," I answered, shrugging my coat off the other shoulder and watching Jake's eyes drop to my rather clingy dress.

"Get this," she started. "I just got a call from one of my girls who told me that Pearl Milshorn pulled her money out of the new development that was supposed to be breaking ground in two weeks up by Mills jetty."

I tossed my coat over the back of the chair, eyes to Jake, assessing his reaction and uncertain why this information so excited my friend, thus murmuring, "Hmm?"

"Pearl is pulling her money out of that development, Josie," she mostly repeated as Jake's eyes came back to mine and I held them but his dropped again when I shimmied up my tight skirt. "The one out by Mills jetty. The fancy one with all the shops and stuff they're putting in. Pearl's the biggest investor. She was doing it for her kids. She knew inheritance taxes would eat some of it up so if she did that and turned over the shares before she died, she'd be able to give a gift that keeps on giving without Uncle Sam taking a chunk."

Hand under my skirt, I hooked my fingers in my panties and slid them down my legs until they fell freely to the floor.

I stepped free of them.

Jake's eyes darted back up to my face and a quiver glided along my inner thighs at the look in them.

As this happened, I said to Alyssa, "That's quite interesting."

"Josie," she sounded impatient. "Pearl was investing in that development. And I mean big time. The woman is drowning in money. She's the biggest investor in the project, except for Boston Stone. But her pulling her money means that huge project is dead in the water."

At the mention of Boston Stone, I blinked and looked to the floor.

"Pardon?"

"She heard what Stone was doing to you and she yanked her funding. That's *massive* Josie. She told the other investors the only way she'd go forward is if they found someone to replace Stone. She's squeezing him out and *they're breaking ground in two weeks*. We're talking jobs, material, a lot of people are depending on this and everyone is looking to Stone who screwed the pooch because Pearl made it known she wouldn't do business with a man who behaved the way Stone behaved with you. This project is gonna cost millions but word is it's gonna rake in millions more to the investors. Stone backs out, he's taking a huge hit. Those investors are not gonna let this deal die. They're going to find someone else and he's the mastermind behind that. He'll lose all his time and effort and he won't make a penny."

"Oh my goodness," I breathed just as Jake's body came into my eyesight which was a fraction of a second before my skirt was yanked all the way up to my hips and I started moving backward because Jake was pushing me that way.

I lifted my eyes to him, caught the look on his face and my mouth got dry as I experienced a full body spasm.

"Isn't that *awesome?*" Alyssa fairly shrieked in my ear.

"It is, sweetheart. Very awesome. But I have to go. I'll call you back tomorrow," I told her.

"Everything okay?" she asked when the backs of my legs hit couch and Jake's hands found my behind.

"Yes," I said breathily. "Thanks for calling me and telling me that. I have a feeling it's very good news."

"No probs and I have a feeling it is too," she replied. "Talk to you tomorrow."

"Goodnight, honey."

"'Night, babelicious."

I barely heard her finish her farewell before Jake had my phone out of my hand. He tossed it without looking in the general direction of the chair in front of his desk. I heard the plonk, however, and knew it hit the floor.

I put my hands to his biceps and told him, "I have some news about Boston Stone."

"Right now I do not give one fuck about Boston Stone," he replied.

"Okay," I whispered.

"You got something else you wanna play out here, baby, or is it my turn?" he asked.

I actually had an entire scenario I wished to play out but although I thought Alyssa's call was only making that scenario better, it distracted me.

Now I wanted Jake to have his turn.

"Your turn," I answered.

"Do you know what it does to a man to have a beautiful, classy woman who is looking more than her normal fine—when her normal fine is off-the-fuckin'-charts—walk into his office, show him her fantastic body in a fuckin' amazing dress then take her panties off right in front of him?"

"Um…" I mumbled.

It must be said I knew what I'd *hoped* it would do to him.

But by the look in his eyes and the sound of his voice, it was clear I'd succeeded well beyond my wildest imaginings.

He didn't share this wisdom overtly but he still did.

And he did this by stating, "You got one choice, you either suck me or I eat you. After that, I take over."

This was hard. His mouth between my legs was heaven.

But I very much enjoyed how it felt when I had him in my mouth, the way he tasted, how big and hard he got, the noises I could make him make, the satisfaction it gave me that I could excite him in that way.

"Josie—" he started.

"Um…" I mumbled.

"I eat you," he decided for me. "I want you spread on my couch in that dress and you can't do that blowin' me."

"Uh…all right, darling."

He dipped his head and his mouth came to mine but he didn't kiss me.

He ordered on a whisper I felt *everywhere*. "Down, baby, and spread."

Then he brushed his lips against mine.

After that, I lay down on the couch and spread.

Jake's eyes raked over me before his hands moved to the backs of my knees, shoved them up which slid me up the couch so I was nearly hanging over the arm and then he joined me, well down from me, his mouth closing over me between my legs.

My legs tensed in his grip and my head fell back.

Jake ate me.

And not that he hadn't already taken over, after he made me come with his mouth between my legs, he made me come three more times "taking over."

It was better than making out.

Much better.

In a *big* way.

THE WILL

THE NEXT AFTERNOON, with my uncle incarcerated and unable to come up with bail money, even for a minor breaking and entering (although, since he had a record, minor had turned into somewhat major), we were back at Jake's.

And it was me who had a bag in his bedroom.

I was heading to the living room from the kitchen with a bowl of Ro-Tel dip I'd nuked and another of chips when the doorbell rang.

"Got it!" I called and moved to the door.

However I saw who it was through the windows and stopped dead.

He saw me too. I knew this when his already hard face got harder. But when I didn't move the doorbell rang again.

"Babe? You got it?" Jake yelled from the family room.

I stared at Boston Stone through the window and yelled back, "Darling, I think you need to come here."

I had not moved an inch before I felt Jake's presence and then I heard him growl, "Oh no. This shit is *not* happening."

He then stalked around me, threw open the door and ordered, "You get off my property in five seconds or you get to have another conversation with Coert and slapped with a restraining order."

"It's necessary I speak with Josephine." I heard Boston say but I only heard it. Jake was barring the door and I couldn't see him.

"The fuck it is. Five seconds, Stone," Jake returned.

"I came to apologize," Boston announced.

What on earth?

"Write her a letter," Jake clipped.

"If I apologize, this is done," Boston told him.

"One," Jake started counting and it was then I moved.

I got close to him, put the bowls on the table by the door and my hand to Jake's back.

Through this, Jake didn't move a muscle except the ones around his mouth in order to say, "Two."

"Jake," I said softly.

"Three," Jake said to Boston.

"Jake." I pressed my hand into his back. "Please. If we can get this done, let's do that."

507

"Listen to her, Spear."

Jake stopped counting but still didn't move.

I pressed my hand deeper into his back.

Finally, he shifted to the side.

But barely.

Nevertheless, I had a view to Boston and he looked directly to me.

"Right, Josephine," he bit out. "I apologize. Now call off your dog."

I felt my brows draw together.

My dog?

Was he referring to Jake? For he couldn't be referring to Pearl.

Could he?

"I'm uncertain what you mean, Boston, but if you're referring to Jake or Mrs. Milshorn, that's quite offensive."

Boston straightened his shoulders even as he continued scowling at me. "You know what I'm talking about, Josephine. Now tell your dog I apologized and this is done."

I straightened my shoulders as well and informed him, "I can't control Pearl. And Jake's right here so if it's him you're attempting to appease, I would suggest you do it in a less insulting manner."

"I'm not talking about Pearl or Spear," he ground out. "I'm talking about your other dog. The *black* one."

I shook my head in confusion but this confusion was cleared when Jake murmured, "Amond, babe."

I looked up at him to see he was struggling to keep his composure and that was to say he looked like he wanted badly to smile but was fighting it.

"Amo...?" I started then the light dawned and I stared at Jake.

Then I looked to Boston Stone.

"Are you speaking of my friend, Dee-Amond?" I queried.

"What I'm speaking of is that I was told if I apologized directly to you and made you the promise that I would no longer involve myself in your life in any capacity, some difficulties I've suddenly found myself facing would disappear. So I'm apologizing directly to you. I will no longer involve myself in your life in any capacity. Now, I request that you phone your friend and share this with him."

Suddenly, it was me having difficulty fighting back my smile.

Through this struggle, however, I told him, "There is one small matter that needs addressing."

A muscle jerked in his cheek before he asked, "And that would be?"

"My uncle has no way home and I'd like him to go home and stay there. I'll drop the charges against him if you would see to that issue and that would be, getting him home and giving him plenty of incentive to stay there."

Boston said nothing, just scowled at me.

So I continued.

"And that would be *plenty* of incentive, Boston. Alas, he's a greedy man and he's also an unpleasant one. Unless you're certain to neutralize him, since he knows where to find me and what I have, it is likely he'll continue to bother me until the day he dies."

"Which could be any day, Josephine. He's not exactly young," Boston pointed out.

"He also shouldn't be my problem," I said softly. "And wouldn't be if you had left well enough alone. That's your mess, Boston. Clean it up or I make no calls."

He drew in a deep breath, his neck going red before he said, "I'll deal with your uncle."

"Then I'll be certain to call my friend when I have time," I assured him.

"At your earliest convenience, if you wouldn't mind," he clipped.

"Of course. However, the Ravens are playing and I rather like their uniforms so it'll have to be after the game."

Jake made a strangled noise and Boston's jaw clenched.

Then he forced out, "My gratitude."

"Have a lovely Sunday, Boston," I bid him.

He scowled at me, didn't even look at Jake, turned and stormed down to his Mercedes.

Jake gently shoved me back with a hand in my belly, shut the door and locked it.

I looked up at him and burst into laughter. In the midst of doing this, his arms closed around me so I got to finish it with my arms around his neck and my face in his chest.

It felt so nice laughing in Jake's arms I made a mental note to do it more often.

Perhaps once a day.

When my laughter was dying I looked up into his smiling face.

"Perhaps I should call Amond," I suggested.

"It's only first quarter. You got most of the game to appreciate the Ravens' uniforms," he replied.

"Yo!" Ethan shouted from the living room at this point. "What's taking so long with the dip? I'm starved!"

And that made me burst out laughing again so I shoved my face in Jake's chest and held on tight doing it.

Therefore it was then I amended my mental note do to this more often.

I wouldn't aim for once a day.

I'd aim for at least twice.

"I'll go nuke the dip again," I told Jake.

"I'll take in the chips," he told me.

"All right," I agreed but he didn't let me go.

I would know why when he asked, "You good?"

The look in his eyes and expression on his face changed the instant I answered, "Of course. I have you."

I loved the look in his eyes and expression on his face. I loved it so much, I wanted to give it to him again.

Regularly.

But I wouldn't aim for once a day.

I'd aim for at least twice.

Nineteen

GOOD ANSWER

"*That's it, baby!*" Alyssa shrieked at Junior fighting in the ring. "*Mess him up! You know mama likes it like that!*"

I grinned at my lap before looking back up to the action.

We were at the arena in Blakeley for the adult league matches and Junior's opponent this time was a fair sight less talented than he was.

Bryant and Ethan were sitting in the row with us, both of whom had bags of Halloween candy they'd brought with them for treats. I was monitoring their consumption as I wanted to see Jake fight, not be in the bathroom with Ethan vomiting. That was unpleasant enough the first time for me to take pains not to let it happen again.

This was difficult as Halloween had been just two nights before and Ethan, Bryant and Joshua had pulled in large hauls, putting a fair amount of effort into it by traipsing from house to house in their *Combat Raptor* costumes, followed by Jake and me, Jake carrying a flashlight.

We'd hit four neighborhoods. Four *large* neighborhoods.

Therefore, by the time we were done, I was exhausted. I had just enough in me when we got back to Jake's to tell Ethan to go easy on his consumption, eat a handful of pumpkin seeds (which were, I found, addicting) and go to bed.

We had a vast amount of seeds because, a few days before Halloween, we'd carved five pumpkins, one for each of us, and put them around Jake's front door. I was surprised to see in their teenaged coolness that even Conner and Amber got into the carving process.

Then again, I'd learned it was a family tradition that they never missed and enjoyed greatly. I knew this because I found it was highly enjoyable.

I knew it more when Amber declared, "Even when I'm married and have kids of my own, we're coming to Dad's to carve pumpkins."

The "when I'm married and have kids" comment made Jake's mouth go tight, this making me fight a grin. But in the end, Amber's sentiment was very sweet and after experiencing pumpkin carving at the Spear household, I understood why she felt this way.

By the way, Jake was a master pumpkin carver. I knew this because he helped Ethan freehand carve a *Combat Raptor* pumpkin that, if there were such contests, would win an award. I was sure of it.

Conner, Amber and Alexi stayed behind to hand out candy at Jake's (this Jake arranged, with Conner being a vaguely disguised chaperone) while we took Ethan out.

When we got back, I asked Conner to keep an eye on his brother's candy consumption and went to bed without Jake for the first time since we started sharing one. Which was to say, unless Jake was at the club, Jake and I went to bed together every night since we started sharing a bed.

Jake joined me later, waking me as he pulled me in his arms and I fell right back to sleep hearing him mutter, "Next year, you're gonna stay home and hand out candy so you don't pass out after walkin' twenty miles watchin' Ethan get his haul."

I was just happy there would be a next year.

This was why I fell right back to sleep.

It was not lost on me that I had sat beside the runways of the most lauded designers of our time. I had traveled to five continents and done it repeatedly. I knew the best place to buy croissant in Paris. I'd eaten pizza at the *Antica Pizzeria Port'Alba* in Naples. I'd sunbathed on Bondi Beach in Australia. And I'd slept in an actual igloo in Alaska.

But carving pumpkins and roasting pumpkin seeds in Jake's kitchen were the most fabulous things I'd ever done.

Bar none.

On this thought, with senses attuned from taking care of two eight year old boys who'd evacuated their stomachs due to overindulgence, even over Alyssa's shouting and a rabid fighting crowd, I heard a candy wrapper. I looked down to see Ethan opening up a fun-size Snickers.

I leaned into him and said in his ear, "Honey, I know you like your treats but I suspect you'd prefer to ingest that and not re-experience it later, hanging over a toilet bowl. So let's make that the last one tonight, hmm?"

I pulled slightly away and caught his eyes. They were looking in mine and Eath (such a wonderful child) nodded.

"Thank you, sweetheart," I said.

He chewed, swallowed and grinned a chocolate, peanut, caramel and nougat grin.

I grinned back.

At this point, Alyssa shot out of her chair, jumped up and down on her strappy, high-heeled sandals and started screeching, "*That's right, baby! Get in there. Don't let up! Take him down!*"

I allowed myself to admire her attractive, albeit brief and tight, red dress before I looked to the ring to see Junior had his opponent up against the ropes and was landing a succession of combinations that his competitor was having difficulties defending against.

Alas, the referee pushed them apart and moved in to assess the condition of Junior's challenger. The man shook his head side to side to clear it then looked the referee in the eyes and nodded.

The referee let them loose again.

"Stupid ref," Alyssa groused, plonking herself down in the seat beside me, her eyes never leaving the ring.

The bell rang and since it was only the second round, we had another one to go before Alyssa again shot from her seat, lost her mind, shrieking, clapping and jumping up and down when the referee lifted Junior's hand.

He smiled down at his wife.

She blew him a kiss that was so exaggerated she came off her feet when she swung her arm wide. Then she turned instantly to the seat, snatched up her purse and coat and her eyes came to me.

She leaned into me and said low, "Right, Operation Tag Team commence. You got Bryant. I get home with my man and get laid. You text when Jake's done, drop Eath and Bry at our place so you can get laid. Yeah?"

I nodded, enjoying the happy light in my friend's eyes and trying to ignore the happier feeling between my legs considering what was to come for me.

"Yes," I agreed.

She lifted her fist, knuckles facing me, something Conner had taught me about a week ago was a "fist bump." He did this after he did the same to me and I stared at his hand nonplussed for half a minute before he showed me what to do.

Thus, I knew what to do, bumped my fist against hers, and she breathed, "I love fight night."

I giggled as I encouraged, "Go."

I needed to give her no further encouragement. She dashed to her son, grabbed either side of his face, gave him a loud kiss right on the mouth, which made him shout, "Euw, Mom!"

She then tousled his hair, looked to Ethan and said, "Later, buddy."

"Later, Mrs. Harper," Ethan replied.

Alyssa gave me a finger wave and took off down the aisle.

"Can we get popcorn?" Bryant asked and I looked to him.

"Think hard about your stomach, the fullness of it, the possibility if more was introduced that it may need to purge some to fit the rest and then tell me if you really want popcorn," I stated.

"What's purge mean?" he asked.

"Evacuate," I answered and he grinned.

"What's evacuate mean?" he asked.

At that, I grinned.

"Empty," I answered.

"You talk so freakin' cool," he replied. "Weird. But cool."

"Indeed. And you will find, young Bryant, as you grow older that things that are normal are just normal. Anyone can be normal. Thus it's my experience that most things that are weird are cool."

"So you sayin' we should try to be weird, Josie?" Ethan asked, a teasing glint in his eye.

"I'm saying that you shouldn't try to be anything. You should be you and however you are will be cool unless however that is, is you trying to be like everyone else, which is just normal, which is *not* cool," I answered.

"Well, I've decided to be a con artist turned FBI consultant like that dude in *White Collar*. Is that weird and cool enough for you?" Ethan shared his latest plans for his future, that teasing glint still in his eye.

This was a program that Ethan had recently discovered on Netflix. I knew this because he not only told me but he also talked about it all the time. And watched it all the time. And as I was with him a fair amount of that time, I watched it too.

It was an excellent program.

However, a life goal to be a con artist, even a stylish and intelligent one who had a definite flair with wearing a fedora, such as "the dude on *White Collar*," was not optimal.

"If you skip past the con artist part, and simply aim to be an FBI agent, yes," I answered.

He shook his head but did it grinning.

I looked to Bryant and prompted, "Your popcorn assessment?"

"I'm thinkin' I wanna keep those fifteen Kit Kats in my stomach, Ms. Malone," Bryant replied.

"Good choice," I murmured.

We settled in, me examining the crowd, the boys jabbering to each other. We then watched the next fight, Mickey's, the boys encouraging him rather boisterously to win, and although I didn't shout, I did clap when Mickey's arm was lifted.

It was after that I started to get excited.

Because Mickey's victory heralded the last fight of the night.

Jake's fight.

As the delay between fights began to feel incessant, I started fidgeting. But when the announcer introduced the fighters, like everyone else, I came out of my seat, clapping, but doing it on legs that were trembling.

I felt my mouth go dry when I saw Jake coming down the aisle. I then felt my heart swell when he stopped at our row, put a gloved hand to Bryant's head, then Ethan's.

And I found it took everything to remain standing when his eyes came to me. They heated instantly before they swept me from top to toe. They came back to my face and they were even *more* heated which made it even *more* difficult to remain standing.

I had, of course, tricked myself out.

This being that I had my hair down but curled so there seemed more of it.

Much more.

And I had a midnight blue dress on, high collar and halter, which left my shoulders and back totally bare. The dress was almost blousy at the bust but clung rather alluringly everywhere else. It had a slit up the front and came to just below the knee. And last, the midnight blue had an almost elusive wave of burnished silver through it so I also had on my delicate, very strappy and very high-heeled silver sandals.

It would seem Jake appreciated my efforts.

Very much so.

And I appreciated his appreciation.

Very much so.

Finally, he released my eyes, which he was holding captive, and went to the ring.

I thankfully sank into my seat.

But the fidgeting had not stopped.

No, because shortly after, the fight started.

Jake did not knock his opponent out in the first round this time. It went all three. Which was sheer torture for I was *very* ready for it to be over when it was finally over since watching Jake fight meant I was ready for it to be over about one minute into round one.

But one could not say that watching him box, the brute force, the focus, his muscles moving, his body shifting, his utter command of not only the fight, not only the ring, but the entire arena, was a sight to behold.

Even so, I was beyond thrilled when his hand was lifted at the end. I again rose from my seat, shooting from it this time, clapping fast and hard, smiling wide.

Jake gave the boys a smile and me a wink as he walked back up the aisle and hurriedly I turned to Ethan and Bryant.

"All right, boys. Get your things. Check around to make sure you didn't forget anything. Let's go," I urged.

They did as told. I slid on my coat and grabbed my bag. When we were ready, I herded them up the aisle and to the door to the locker rooms.

The same security man was there and he smiled at me when I approached with the boys.

"Same room, babe," he told me.

I nodded and ushered the boys through the door. We hurried down the hall to Jake's door but this time, I knocked.

"Yo!" we heard from the other side.

Ethan charged in, followed by Bryant, and I came up the rear.

I felt a rush of wet between my legs when I saw Jake in the same position as last time, sitting on the table in his trunks, his friend and trainer, Bert, standing in front of him.

"Dad! You killed it!" Ethan shouted, rushing up to his father to give him a hug.

Jake jumped off the table to get it and hugged him back. When they separated, he looked down to his son. "Like that?"

"Heck yeah!" Ethan yelled.

"You're the master, Mr. Spear," Bryant told him.

"Thanks, Bry," Jake murmured on a grin to Bryant then he came to me.

He got close, slid an arm around my waist and put his mouth to my ear.

"Love my kid, babe, you know it. But get him and his bud in the car, dump them on Alyssa and meet me at your place. Fast."

He had his gloves off but, as I mentioned, he was still only in his trunks. Thus, as he was speaking, I had a view of his shoulder, which, when he leaned back, became a view of his slick chest.

My eyes lifted to his, and suddenly incapable of speech, I nodded.

His eyes dropped to my dress then came back to my face.

"Fast," he ordered, his voice low.

"Okay, darling," I forced out.

He dropped his arm and moved away. I turned my eyes to Bert.

"Hello, Bert," I greeted.

"Good to see you, Josie," he replied.

I felt that did well enough for the niceties so I clapped my hands and said, "Right, boys. Let's go. Time to hit the Cayenne."

Ethan looked to me. "I dig the Cayenne, Josie, but we wanna ride with Dad."

"Got stuff to do here, bud. It's gettin' late. Go with Josie," Jake replied.

"But—" Ethan started.

"Bud. Josie," Jake stated firmly.

Ethan held his eyes then looked to his feet and muttered, "All right."

I put a hand to Ethan's shoulder and started herding him and Bryant again, calling my farewell, "I'll see you at the gym sometime, Bert."

"Yeah, Josie," Bert replied.

I looked to Jake. "Later, darling."

He looked to me and firmly in a way that was not a farewell but a promise, he said, "Later."

That got a thigh quiver that was very strong so I had to force myself to focus on getting the boys to my car.

I texted Alyssa after I started up the Cayenne and then I took the boys to her house.

Alyssa, in a robe with very mussed hair, answered the door and accepted delivery, but she did this with a sated smile and a lascivious wink.

I winked back (mine probably not lascivious), moved quickly back to my car and drove carefully, but swiftly, to Lavender House.

Jake's truck was in the lane and I could see lights coming from the windows at either side of the front door.

I got out of the Cayenne and hurried to door.

It opened before I got there.

Seeing it open, in my excitement, I stumbled, but Jake's arm shot out and caught me around the waist, pulling me forward so I collided with his body. He kept me pressed there as he dragged me into the house, slammed the door and locked it. He then shifted me to the side and pressed me against the wall.

Oh my.

I tilted my head back just in time, for the instant I did, his lips were against mine.

His hands came to my coat and yanked it down my arms.

I dropped my bag and the coat fell to the floor.

"Panties, babe."

A shiver slid through my entire body.

Jake helped, yanking up my skirt.

I pulled down my panties and they dropped to my ankles.

Jake lifted me free from them and pressed me against the wall at the same time his lips against mine opened.

Sliding my arms around his shoulders, curling my legs around his hips, I reciprocated the gesture and his tongue slid inside.

Having waited for what seemed like years since he walked down the aisle of the arena in his boxing robe, I was so ready for the taste of him, when I got it, I whimpered into his mouth.

One of his hands left my behind and slid through the damp between my legs.

When it did, his lips glided to my ear and his fingers slid from between my legs to go to his training pants.

"My woman gets off on watchin' her man fight," he murmured in my ear.

"Yes," I whispered.

I felt the tip of him, caught my breath, and then he was inside.

"*Yes*," I breathed.

"So wet," he groaned.

"Yes."

"Fuck yes."

I held on as Jake pounded inside me, running my nose along his jaw, my lips along his neck, my tongue around his ear.

Jake grunted.

I whimpered.

Jake clenched his fingers into the cheek of my bottom, tilting my hips and he thrust harder.

I moaned.

Jake caught my mouth with his and kissed me rough and deep.

I curled my legs tighter around his hips, slid a hand in his hair and wrapped the other one around the back of his neck, gripping hard.

Jake drove in faster.

It built and I knew it was going to explode so I broke our kiss and whispered against his lips, "Darling."

"Yeah."

"*Jake.*"

"Fuck yeah, baby."

My lips parted, and as the deliciousness of the orgasm he gave me overwhelmed me, I felt his tongue trace my bottom lip, this making it all the more delicious.

Then his tongue was back inside as he slammed into me, pounding me into the wall.

I kept holding him close, clenching him tight with everything I had, feeling everything he gave me, everything he was giving me, loving every sensation, until he broke the kiss, shoved his face in my neck and thrust deep through a long, beautiful groan.

He held me against the wall, keeping me close, stayed inside as he breathed heavily against my neck and I held on.

Finally, I turned my lips to his ear and whispered, "I *love* fight night."

At hearing that, Jake lifted his head, caught my eyes, his still heated, but satiated and happy, his most beautiful look of all, and he smiled.

"SHE WAS BULLIED."

It was the next morning and I was pushing a cart through the grocery store, Amber at my side. We were preparing for the feeding frenzy that was Sunday in front of football.

And we were talking about Conner's still unsuccessful, but thankfully undeterred, pursuit of Sofie.

However, this had gone on so long I was getting concerned.

Sofie liked Conner that was clear. Conner liked Sofie and that was abundantly clear because he was pulling out all the stops to make it that way. Alyssa was all for the duo and she'd been making that clear. Junior was not all for it, but like Jake, he was resigned to the fact his daughter would eventually date.

Further, Alyssa told me Junior was beginning to get concerned that she was sixteen and had never been out with a boy. Although Conner had a reputation, he was Jake's son. Junior knew him to be as a seventeen year-old boy with a girl in his sights, but he also knew Jake and Conner very well. Therefore, unlike the dire predictions when we first became aware that Conner was interested in Junior's daughter, even if he wasn't all for it, he wasn't avidly opposing it.

So, in the end, the only obstacle to Sofie and Conner being a *Sofie and Conner* was Sofie.

And thus, Alyssa was getting concerned. As was I.

I stopped pushing the cart and looked down to Amber. "Pardon?"

"Sof," Amber replied. "Back in Junior High, she was bullied and it was pretty bad."

I stared at her, not believing this.

Sofie was very sweet, very pretty, quite intelligent, had a lovely figure and a sense of style that was cute and girlie and very becoming.

She also, apparently, had great talent as a singer. I was much looking forward to the high school Christmas concert during which she was to have two solos. This was unheard of as Alyssa told me the choir director tried to hand out solos with a fair hand in order to give as many of his students as possible the opportunity to shine.

But Sofie was that good.

What on earth was there to bully her about?

"How was Sofie bullied?" I asked and Amber shrugged.

"It was Mia and her crew," she answered and I felt my mouth get tight at the mention of Mia. "Everyone knows Mia for the bitch she is now, and sorry Josie, but no other way to say it. Mia's a bitch."

As much as it pained me to agree on this fact about a high school girl, I couldn't help but do it. Though I decided to do it silently by not rebuking Amber for her language.

Amber kept speaking.

"But Mia was top dog and had been a long time before what happened with Con. And Sofie is really cute. Back then, all the guys were waking up to girls and they *way* woke up to Sofie. Mia didn't like that."

"Indeed," I said, suspecting this to be very true.

"But it was more,' Amber went on. "Mr. Harper was out of work and money was tight and Mia's dad's got a good job so they have a nice house and she had all the cool clothes and Sofie…" She shook her head. "Well, they didn't have a lot and she wore that fact on her body. Mia made fun of her 'cause she got her clothes at TJ Maxx and stuff. It sounds stupid. TJ Maxx stuff is great and I find a lot of cool things there. But that kind of thing, especially the way Mia and her girls ganged up on her, can really hurt."

It most certainly could.

"Is that when she became shy?" I queried.

Amber screwed her mouth up for a moment, thinking on this, and then said, "She was always quiet but yeah. That's when it got worse."

"Does Conner know this?" I continued.

"He's a grade ahead of her in school and a guy so I'm guessing he didn't pay a lot of attention back then to how Mia targeted her prey and shredded them. If he did, he wouldn't have asked Mia out. Con's not big on that crap."

This was also likely true.

"Anyway," she carried on. "By then, it was ancient history, except for Sofie."

"Hmm," I mumbled, turning my attention back to the cart and moving it along, wondering how this information could be imparted not only on Conner so that he could revise his strategy, but on Alyssa so that she could see to her daughter's state of mind.

Suddenly, something occurred to me and I stopped.

I looked back to Amber and asked quietly, "Did Mia bully you?"

She held my eyes, shook her head and said, "No. Seein' as Con's my brother and she always had her sights set on him like all the girls do. She knew she shouldn't do that because we Spears might fight amongst ourselves but no one outside hands us any crap."

At least this was good.

But…

"Did anyone else bully you?" I pressed gently.

"Kids can suck," she said by way of affirmative.

"Honey," I whispered, now understanding her attitude when we first met.

"It's not like that anymore," she told me, beginning to look uncomfortable.

I didn't want her to be uncomfortable but I couldn't quite leave the topic. Not yet.

I had one more thing to say.

And I got close to say it, reaching out my hand to take hers and hold tight.

"If something like that ever happens again, or you have anything that's preying on your mind that you wish to discuss, I'm here. If it's a danger to you emotionally, I may need to speak with you about sharing it with your father. But if it's girl things and you need to talk with someone who has moved beyond it and survived, please consider talking about it with me."

She was staring into my eyes, hers looking somewhat startled but amidst that there was something profoundly beautiful in the way she was gazing at me. Something I was memorizing, it was just that precious. And as I was memorizing it, a voice we both knew very well came our way.

"Uh, can I talk to my daughter?"

I tensed.

Amber tensed.

And both of us looked to Donna.

Donna was looking at our clasped hands.

Oh dear.

I was deciding to drive the extra half an hour to the grocery store in Wells to avoid running into Donna when Donna shifted her gaze to me and asked, "Do you mind?"

"I don't but it's up to Amber," I replied, my heart beating harder in my chest as I felt Amber's hand curl tighter around mine.

"Nothing to say," Amber put in and Donna looked to her daughter.

"Just two seconds, sweetie, please?" Donna asked.

"No," Amber answered.

Donna sidled closer. "You aren't taking my calls and I have something important to tell you."

"I'm not taking your calls because I don't need to," Amber returned. "See, I figure, I haven't had a mom in a long time, like, you know, she's been dead or something. So, I figure, when Dad marries Josie, she can just adopt me legal-like and then I'll get a real mom. You know, like I never had."

This attack was so brutal, the blow landing full force, I could see the impact on Donna's face.

Thus, I squeezed her hand and whispered, "Amber."

She let me go, pushed in front of me and grabbed the cart, shoving it forward. "We gotta get this done or Eath is gonna have a tizzy. His breakfast probably wore off an hour ago."

This was surely the truth but as much as I didn't enjoy being in Donna's company, or Amber being in it when she didn't like it, I couldn't leave it where it was.

"I think perhaps we should all go get a coffee," I suggested.

Amber stopped and looked back at me, her face set, her eyes flashing. "No freaking way."

"That's okay," Donna's voice was a squeak and when I looked to her I knew this was due to her struggling to hold back her emotion. "I'll, uh...I'll just..." she trailed off, looking around and I knew she was going to flee.

Which meant then she was going to *flee*.

I turned my gaze to Amber. "Sweetheart, take care of the list. I'm going to have a word with your mother. I'll meet you at the checkout."

"Works for me," Amber said readily and sauntered off, pushing the cart like she didn't have a care in the world.

I looked back to Donna and invited, "Perhaps we should go outside."

She stared at me and I knew she wanted to say no. But it was obvious she was so wounded she could do nothing but nod.

We moved outside the store and down the walk in front of it to be away from the doors.

Only then did I speak.

"Are you leaving Magdalene?" I asked.

She blinked.

"It *is* a small town, Donna," I reminded her.

"I...well...Anderson offered me a raise to get me to stay but there's a job in Boston that pays more and—"

I cut her off. "You cannot leave town."

She stared at me.

"Jake doesn't want you to leave," I shared and her mouth dropped open. "He wants the mother of his children to be a mother to his children. Although it probably matters not to you, I don't wish for you to leave either, for the same reason. Your children, alas, likely won't let it show that they care one way or another. But I can assure you, what they let show and what they feel will not be the same things. You have essentially abandoned them. If you do this in an official capacity, it will wound them in a way they will never forget their whole lives and that way will be a way where it will never heal."

"But she hates me," Donna whispered.

"She has a right to that emotion," I told her truthfully. "And you have the capacity to turn that emotion around. She's angry and it will not be an easy fight. But it'll be worth every blow she lands in order to succeed."

She shook her head before she asked, "How do I even start to do that?"

"You start by taking that raise and not leaving town," I answered. "Then you start by just *starting*."

"People think—" she began.

"Your ex-husband runs a gentleman's club to provide for his family," I interrupted her to point out. "Do you think it matters what people think when it comes to your children?"

She shut her mouth.

"Call her and ask her if she'd like to go shopping. If she refuses, ask her to a movie. Call Conner and ask him to dinner and request he brings his sister. If they refuse, keep calling. Text to let them know you're thinking of them. Ask them to spend the night at your house. Buy them things to bribe them into paying at least scant attention to you. It doesn't matter what you do, what tactic you use, you're fighting to win back your children. Do it. Use it. Grovel. Beg. Apologize. Show them every way you can think of that they mean something to you. I cannot guarantee that any of that will break through. The only thing I know is that they're worth the effort."

"Do you have kids of your own?" she asked and I couldn't help but feel the sting of the question even though, from the look on her face, it wasn't meant to bite.

"No."

"Then how do you—?"

"Because my mother left me to a monster," I told her bluntly and watched her eyes grow wide. "She saved herself and never looked back. I haven't heard a word from her in thirty-five years. But I not only needed her to protect me from my father, I just needed *her*."

She pressed her lips together and the way she did, I decided I'd done all I could do.

Therefore, I said, "The decision is yours. But I hope you make the right one. Have a lovely Sunday, Donna."

I turned and started to walk away but I heard her call my name so I turned back.

Donna asked the instant I did, "Is Lucky Brand still her favorite store?"

Relief swept through me and I nodded, adding a, "Yes, Donna. It is. She also finds things she likes at Anthropologie. Further, she often finds things at Buckle."

Donna nodded quickly.

I held her eyes and said with feeling, "Good luck, Donna."

Her voice was hesitant and croaky when she replied, "Thank you, Josie."

She gave me a wave I didn't return for she'd turned and started walking away.

I found Amber standing in the checkout line.

The instant I stopped close, she asked, "Did you tell her to vanish?"

"No, my lovely, I did not," I said gently.

"She doesn't give a crap about us, Josie."

"We shall see."

She turned a set face to the line, doing it murmuring, "Yeah, we will."

I sighed.

Amber was quiet all the way to Jake's and after she helped me get the bags in, she went directly to and up the stairs, undoubtedly seeking the sanctuary of her room.

This meant she was calling one of the Taylors or Alexi, who was, according to boy Taylor, a good listener.

Alas, I also knew from boy Taylor that he was a good kisser.

I was glad to know the first.

I wished I did not know the last.

"What gives with that?" Jake asked from close to my back.

I turned and looked up at him. "Are the boys involved with the game?"

"Oh shit," he said as his reply.

I put a hand to his chest. "Are the boys involved with the game, darling?"

"Yeah," he answered, watching me closely.

"Then I'll share in the kitchen."

This I did while emptying a bag of Ruffles in a bowl and watching with some interest mingled with trepidation as Jake spooned an entire container of sour cream into another bowl before he emptied a packet of instant soup into it and stirred it to blend.

When I was done telling my tale of grocery store woe, he didn't look happy, he didn't look angry.

He just looked concerned.

"We gotta keep our eye on that," he told me.

"Agreed," I replied. Then to take his mind off this, I asked, "What's in that bowl?"

His eyes came to me. "Onion dip."

I pressed my lips together.

He grinned before saying, "You're gonna love it, babe."

"Is there anything you serve your children that isn't mixed from an envelope, unearthed from a box or heated from a jar?"

"Yeah. When you cook."

I rolled my eyes.

By the time I rolled them back, Jake had his fingers wrapped around the side of my neck and the bowl in his other hand.

"Ethan's bitchin', need to feed my boy," he told me.

"Then let's not delay in going to the family room so you can continue your quest to preserve your children's bodies through chemicals."

Jake burst out laughing.

I allowed myself a moment to watch, my lips curved up, then I grabbed the bowl of chips.

JAKE'S ARM AROUND my belly gave me a squeeze as he nuzzled his face into the back of my hair.

I closed my eyes, stretching my arms out in front of me even as I pressed my hips back. In return, Jake shifted his hips upward, gliding his cock deeper inside me.

We'd both just come, Jake making love to me spooning. This was after Monday morning mayhem at his house, Jake going to the gym to open up, me taking Ethan to school, both of us returning in order to enjoy a mid-morning session in Jake's bed.

His hand slid up and cupped my breast, his thumb stroking the side as he asked, "You gonna take a nap?"

"You aren't?" I asked back.

"Got a guy comin' in for training. Unfortunately, gotta hit it."

"Mm," I mumbled, settling further back into him.

"Jesus," he growled, pressing deeper into me as his hand tightened at my breast. "You make leavin' hard."

"I suppose there are things to do," I gave in.

"Yeah. And for me, one of them was my woman. Did that. Gotta get my ass in gear."

I grinned at his words as Jake lifted up, kissed my shoulder and pulled gently out. Then he shifted in a way I knew what he wanted. So as he rolled back, I rolled toward him, lifted my head and looked into his eyes.

Now a deep blue.

Phenomenal.

I loved his eyes.

I loved his hair.

I loved the scar on his cheek.

I loved the power of his body.

I loved his warmth.

I loved the feel of him still between my legs.

I just loved him.

"Fuck," he whispered and my thoughts moved from loving Jake Spear to the actual Jake lying in bed with me.

"What?" I whispered back.

His hand came up to cup my jaw and he answered, "You make leaving hard."

"I wasn't doing anything, Jake."

"You were lookin' at me thinkin' somethin', Slick, and whatever it was you were thinking makes leaving you hard."

I drew in breath.

He lifted up, touched his mouth to mine and left it there, his eyes peering into mine when he said, "Lucky I know I get to come back."

"Yes," I said softly. "That makes me lucky too."

His eyes smiled and it was warmer and deeper than his usual smile, which meant I enjoyed it more than I usually did before he brushed his nose against mine and moved away.

I watched him exit the bed and stroll to the bathroom, pulling up the sheet and informing his back, "I'm going to laze for a bit."

"Have at it," he called.

I had at it and was still where he left me when he came back, dressed in workout clothes. He put his hands in the bed, leaned deep and kissed me.

"I'll see you tonight," he said when he pulled away.

"You certainly will," I replied.

Another smile in his eyes before he lifted up, kissed my temple and I watched him walk out of the room.

It was then I smiled to myself and curled my arms around his pillow.

Five minutes after that, I remembered I had a lunch date with Alyssa and I needed to get back to Lavender House to repack my bag as all the clothes I'd brought were dirty. There was also laundry to do. And I needed to make certain we had what we needed for dinner that night.

Which meant I needed to get a move on.

I pulled myself out of bed, gathered my clothes from the floor and went about getting ready to take on the day (again).

But when I was done and as I was walking to the stairs, something caught my eye.

I turned to look into Jake's office and stopped dead.

On his desk was a framed photo of me.

I shook my head, staring at it.

I knew that photo. Henry had taken it several years ago. We were on the beach in Cannes. The photo shoot had been completed the day before. Henry had decided we were going to stay an extra couple of days to unwind. We'd been walking on the beach and Henry had been making me laugh.

It was a good memory, now a bittersweet one.

Why on earth did Jake have that photo?

I moved into the room, thoughts and questions overtaking my brain.

As Henry gave that photo to Gran, Gran must have given it to Jake.

But why?

And I had not been in Jake's office frequently, but I'd been in it more than once and never saw that picture displayed. In fact, the top right drawer of his desk, which was never open, was now open.

Had the picture come from there?

And if it had, why did he keep it in a drawer?

I was thinking that maybe he forgot he had it for whatever reason Gran gave it to him. One of the many things she did regarding Jake the last seven years that I was unclear about but stopped concerning myself with for the end results could not be argued.

On that thought, I stopped dead as my throat closed when I saw the pile of envelopes bound by a blue ribbon sitting in the drawer.

"Oh my God," I whispered, the words sounding strangled as I stared at those envelopes.

I knew what they were. I'd seen them on Gran's desk often enough over the last twenty years.

And Jake had them in a drawer in his desk with a photo of me.

Why?

Why did he have them?

Gran had to have given them to him but why would she do that?

And why wouldn't he tell me he had them?

Why?

I reached out a hand slowly and curled my fingers around the pile. Something vastly unpleasant washed through me as I encountered the paper and lifted them out of the drawer, thus proving they were real. They were there.

My whole history. My whole life.

In letters.

In Jake's desk.

Gran hadn't told Jake about me and Gran hadn't given me to him in her will.

She'd already given me to him. Completely.

But she didn't *tell me*.

And neither did *he*.

"Babe, forgot my wallet," Jake called from close and I turned woodenly to face the door.

I saw him make the landing and I also saw him turn his head, see me, see what I held in my hand, and stop dead.

And I knew by the look on his face that the picture, those letters, they had not been something he'd forgotten he had and therefore forgot to tell me he had them.

No, they were something he was hiding.

Honest, *real,* lay-it-out Jake Spear who gave me everything had a secret he'd been keeping.

From me.

He started into the room, his eyes locked to mine, and began, "Slick—"

I lifted the letters slightly and cut him off to ask, "Did Gran give these to you?"

He stopped an unusual distance away, which was to say any distance at all, and responded very unsuitably.

"What were you doin' in my desk, baby?"

"Did Gran give these to you?" I repeated.

He didn't answer. He reiterated his question.

"What were you doin' in that desk, Josie?"

"It was open. The picture out." I moved to the side to expose the picture. "It caught my eye, as it would, seeing as it's of me and it's Gran's and I didn't know you had it."

Jake looked from the picture to me. "The picture was out?"

"Jake," I said steadily, although I didn't know how I managed it since everything else about me was trembling. "The picture being out is not the issue. Did Gran give you that photo? These letters?" I lifted the letters up again.

His eyes again locked on mine and he finally answered, "Yes."

My heart squeezed.

"Did you read them?" I asked.

"Baby—"

My voice was sharper when I asked, "Did you read them, Jake?"

"Yes."

I looked down to the letters then up to him. "How many times?"

"Honey, it doesn't matter."

"It does to me," I returned. "How many times?"

"You know Lydie told me about you," he pointed out.

I kept hold of the letters but dropped my hand, agreeing, "I know she told you about me. *Told you*, Jake. I had no idea she shared my *private* letters with you. Why would she do that? And why would you read them?"

"Because she gave them to me."

"But they were"—I leaned toward him—"*private.*"

He stared into my eyes but said nothing.

So I asked, "When did she give them to you?"

"A while ago."

"How long of a while ago?"

He took a step toward me, saying, "Josie—"

But I stepped back.

He stopped and I snapped, "How long of a while ago?"

I saw his jaw clench before he answered, "Five, six years."

I stared at him, my heart squeezing harder.

"Five or six years?" I whispered.

"Yeah, baby. Now—"

I lifted up the bundle again. "You've known this much about me, *everything*, laid bare to you by my own hand, through my grandmother's betrayal for *five or six years?*"

His entire body got still as he said, "Lydie didn't betray you."

That was when it happened.

It broke.

Or *I* broke.

And I did this by throwing the bundle violently against the wall and shouting, "*She fucking did!*" He moved again to me but I retreated then skirted him and when he didn't stop, I warned, "Jake, you get fucking near me, I swear to God, I'll leave and you'll never see me again."

Instantly, he stopped.

In any other frame of mind, I would have found that unbearably sweet.

In my current frame of mind, I found it the same but not in a good way.

"Why didn't Gran introduce you to me?" I asked.

"Josie, we went through this," he told me.

"We did and it didn't make sense. And you know what, Jake? None of it does. None of it ever did. She was tight with you, the kids. She loved you.

She spent a lot of time with you. She opened her home to you. She opened her heart to you. She told you about her and she told you about me. She gave you everything. So how in God's name have I not met you?"

"We can't know why she did it now, honey. She's gone."

"No," I agreed quickly. "We can't. Just as we can't know why she would meet a man and share not only all of *her* deepest darkest secrets but also *mine*."

"Slick, just take a breath and—"

"I'm not going to take a fucking breath, Jake," I bit out. "Do you not find that strange? Utterly bizarre? Why would anyone do that?"

"We can't know—"

"I bet we can," I hissed, leaning back and crossing my arms on my chest. "So, tell me, she gave you those letters, what did she say, Jake? 'Here, take these. Some bedtime reading to put you to sleep.' Is that what she said?"

Jake didn't reply.

He didn't *reply*.

Jake, who laid it all out about everything, didn't reply.

Oh God, he was absolutely hiding something.

"She gave me to you before she *gave me to you*," I told him something he well knew. "You had me in your house." I motioned to the picture and then to the letters. "All of me. Every thought. Every secret. All of me that should be *mine* to give."

"Would you have given it?" he asked gently.

"I would have liked to have had the option," I shot back.

"Would you have given it, Josie?" he pressed, still going gently.

"Maybe not," I conceded sharply. "But even so, if she had some grand scheme, as she had to have had seeing as the evidence is clear." I swiped the room with my arm. "Perhaps you could have shared it with me as she obviously shared it with you. Doing this, I don't know, maybe one of the times I wondered out loud why on earth she did the things she did. Telling me, I don't know, just how much you actually knew about me and that you had everything."

"Babe, it happened and we are where we are now. Why does it matter?"

That was the *wrong* answer.

"Because I'm asking questions I think are important and the only person in this room who has the answers isn't giving them to me," I retorted.

He said nothing.

Nothing.

Just held my eyes and said nothing.

Why?

"Why won't you tell me?" I asked.

"Because it doesn't matter," he answered.

"It does to me."

He again said nothing.

And, again, *why?*

"You're keeping something from me," I whispered.

"Baby, you got all of me."

"No, *you* have all of *me*," I returned. "There's something of you that you're keeping from me."

"Can we please let this go and move on?" he requested.

"Whether you agree or not, Jake, the extent of her sharing meant my grandmother betrayed me," I informed him. "To you. And in the time we've spent together, the things we've shared, you not telling me the extent of it is, by extension, a betrayal too. So, no. We can't move on from this until you explain to me what *precisely* you and Gran had been up to in regards to me for the last *five or six years.*"

"What matters to you is important to me, honey. Straight up, bottom of my heart, it is. Believe that. But I gotta tell you, it's important to me that you let this go."

"How would you feel, someone you didn't know knew every word written on your soul for *years* and then they become important to you and they don't share that with you and won't tell you why? How would that make you feel, Jake?"

"I'll say what you have to know, that both Lydie and I had your best interests at heart."

"Really?" I asked, throwing out my arms. "Because if you did, I would have met you five or six years ago instead of you and your children being kept from me."

At that, he flinched.

Oh God.

Why?

"Jake—"

"Let it go."

"Jake!"

"God damn it!" he suddenly shouted, leaned into me and roared, "*Fuckin'
let it go!*"

I took a step back.

Jake scowled at me.

"You know when my father threw my diary at me and gave me a black
eye," I whispered.

"Let it go, babe," he ground out.

"You know when I got my period."

"Let it go."

"You know when I lost my virginity."

"Jesus, fuckin' let…it…*go*."

"You got to share your life with me in your truck. Over dinner. In bed. I
didn't get that luxury, Jake. Why?"

"Josie, for fuck's sake—"

"*Why?*" I shrieked.

"*Let it go!*" he thundered back.

"No," I whispered and watched him wince even as his jaw got hard. "Tell
me, Jake."

"No," he returned.

We stood there, silent, staring at each other and we did this a long time.

It was me who broke the silence.

"How can this be?"

Jake didn't respond so I kept on.

"How is it that we were as close as two people could get half an hour ago
and now we're done?"

I watched Jake's body jerk. "We're not done."

I didn't reply to that.

I asked, "How could she do this to me?"

"She didn't do anything to you, Josie, except give you your dream."

Oh yes.

He'd know about that too.

He knew *exactly* what he was doing.

"Own her, no," he'd said at the reading of the will. *"Do precisely what Lydie wanted me to do with her, yes."*

Yes, he knew *exactly*.

"I know you'd know that," I said quietly, my voice awful and I knew Jake heard it because his jaw again went hard but his eyes went warm and alarmed. "I know you've read that. You know what I *don't* know?"

He didn't answer.

So I kept speaking.

"What the foundation of my love for a man is based on. And I don't know that because *he won't tell me.*"

His face changed, softened and he said, "You love me."

"Yes," I confirmed.

His face softened more and his voice was utterly beautiful when he went on, "Baby, I love you too."

"Not enough."

His body again jerked.

I walked out of the room.

Jake followed me.

I went directly to my bag and when he put a hand on my arm, I yanked it free and took a step back.

"Don't touch me."

"Josie, dammit—"

"I'll ask that I can speak to the kids at some point to explain why I have to sell Lavender House and leave."

He took a step toward me, his body alert, his eyes back to alarmed. "What the fuck?"

"We're done."

"We are not done."

"We are, Jake."

"We fuckin' aren't, Josie."

I locked eyes with him and declared, "We very much are."

"Jesus, do not do this shit. Trust me, it's not worth it."

"I think it's me who gets to make that determination and as I don't have all the facts, I can't make it. I can only make a decision. And I'm doing that."

"You're throwing away everything for nothing."

"Again, I can't know that."

He leaned back and crossed his arms on his chest. "Fuck, you're stubborn."

I moved to my bag and hefted it up, settling the strap on my shoulder.

I then squared off with him again.

"Do not mistake this for a tiff. This is not a tiff. This isn't something you can bide your time and wear me down to coming around to your way of thinking. This is it."

He shook his head, studying me closely.

"I don't understand if it's gettin' too real for you, you're lookin' for reasons to put your disguise back on so you don't have to live your life and if that's the case, the question would be why. Why, when we got somethin' this good, would you walk away for somethin' that means nothing?"

"If you need to ask that question then you didn't pay very much attention to the letter where I told Gran about my dream," I replied and I walked away.

I did not cry. Not when I grabbed my purse and coat and hurried out to the garage.

I did not cry when I took the opener Jake gave me and put it on the workbench.

I did not cry on the drive back to Lavender House. Nor did I cry when I called the locksmith to have him come and change the locks and do it with urgency.

I only cried once that was all done, I was locked in and up in the light room.

I didn't feel safe there. Not anymore.

I wasn't safe anywhere, since Gran had betrayed me.

But it was as good a place as any.

THAT AFTERNOON, JAKE stopped at the door to Ethan's room and looked in at his son who had a controller in his hand and was playing some video game on his Xbox.

"Yo," Jake called.

"Yo, Dad," Ethan answered, not looking away from the TV.

"Bud, I got a question," Jake told him.

"Yeah?"

Jake took in a deep breath and asked, "You been in my office?"

"What?"

"My office, Eath. You get in my desk?"

That got him a glance from his son that included a proud grin before he looked back to his game and answered, "Yeah. Totally. Picked the lock with one of Amber's bobby pin thingies. It was awesome. Bryant's been tryin' to pick locks for ages and he hasn't got close. I win." He gave his father another brief glance before he stated, "That picture of Josie is cool. You should put it in the living room."

Jake took in another calming breath.

It wasn't his son that fucked up. It was him that fucked up.

Even so.

"Bud, pause the game a sec, yeah?"

Ethan must have registered his tone because he didn't delay in pausing the game and looking to his dad.

"Just need you to know somethin'," Jake said quietly. "We got a lot of people in this house and Amber, Con or me, we might have things that we want to keep private. One day, you might have things like that too. You gotta respect that, Eath, because it's the right thing to do and because you'll want that returned to you."

Ethan's face had changed in a way Jake didn't like and he'd know why when Eath asked, "Did I screw up?"

"No," Jake lied.

Then again, Ethan didn't screw up.

Jake did.

Ethan's face was even worse when he asked, "Is what I did why Josie didn't pick me up from school today?"

"No, bud," Jake said firmly.

Another lie.

Fuck.

"Just want you to be cool about that kind of thing," he went on. "You get me?"

"Yeah, Dad."

"Thanks, Eath," Jake muttered. "You can go back to your game," he told him before turning to walk away.

Ethan caught him by calling his name and Jake turned back.

"Where *is* Josie?" he asked, watching his father closely.

"She's got some shit to do." Probably not a lie. "She'll be back, son." Fuck, he hoped that wasn't a lie.

Ethan studied him a moment before he murmured, "Cool," and turned back to the game.

Jake walked away from his door thinking things were not cool. Not by a long shot.

Fuck, he'd fucked up.

And he had to fix it.

But he figured Josie needed time.

She had the night.

Then, tomorrow, he'd go to his woman and he hoped like fuck he could make things "cool."

—•◦••◦•—

THE NEXT MORNING, Jake heard high-heeled shoes on his wood floors in the gym and his head whipped around just as his heart thumped in his chest.

He straightened away from his desk, clenching his teeth when he saw Alyssa.

No.

Strike that.

He saw Alyssa fit to be tied.

She made a beeline to his office, her eyes never leaving him, his never leaving her and the instant she cleared the door, he stated, "Alyssa, don't got the time."

She slammed the door, crossed her arms on her chest and returned, "Make the time."

"Woman—" he started but she cut him off.

"Josie stood me up for lunch yesterday."

Jake sighed, leaned against his desk and curled his fingers around the edge of it.

But he said nothing.

"Called her all day. Finally got through to her late last night. She said things have changed. She's putting Lavender House on the market. Takin' some job with some designer in New York City and leavin' the first chance she gets."

His heart again thumped in his chest. This time so hard it fucking hurt.

"What happened?" she asked.

He finally spoke. "See you think Josie made this your business. But it isn't."

"You're wrong. She's my friend. She's a good friend. I care. And outside of her grandmother, you're the only good thing she's had in her life and she knows it. Now she's leaving?" she asked then went on before she got an answer. "Why?"

"I'm gonna sort it out," he assured her.

"Well, hurry, Jake," she shot back. "Because she didn't sound right. She sounded all cold and haughty and she's got that uppity thing workin' for her in her way but this wasn't that. She was *cold* as fucking *ice*."

That was not good.

Fuck.

Alyssa was not done.

"You've had three women slip through your fingers, Jake. They were slippery and not worth the effort of holdin' on. Now you got one who is. Since that's the case and you know it, don't know why you're in your goddamned office doin' whatever-the-fuck you're doin'." She threw out an arm. "But I'd get the lead out, babe. You don't, she'll slide away."

"Respect, Alyssa," he said low. "You know you got that from me. But you gotta back off and let me and Josie work this shit out."

She held his eyes a beat before she leaned in and whispered, "*Hurry*."

And with that, she turned, threw open the door and stomped out.

Jake watched her go.

Then he grabbed his keys from the desk, walked into the gym and called out to Troy who was at a speed bag. "Gotta go do something. Text me, you leave and no one's here."

"Got it," Troy replied, his eyes never leaving the bag, his gloves constantly moving.

Jake went straight to his truck.

Then he went straight to Lavender House.

He did this thinking about his kids last night. The questions. The confusion. The unease. Josie had been with them every night for weeks. Now, she was gone.

They didn't like it.

They were freaked by it.

And he had no good reason to give them why she was.

Except he was a fucking moron. But he didn't share that with his kids.

He should have told her, straight up, from the beginning.

And when he didn't, when he saw her with those goddamned letters, he should have come clean.

He didn't.

And he didn't because he was an idiot. He didn't because of pride. He didn't because he didn't ever want to lose that look in her eyes she gave him just half an hour before, her in his bed, her hair down and mussed, his cum still inside her.

Contentment.

Safety.

Happiness.

Love.

When she knew, it would be like when your kid first finds out you can't make miracles.

Like when your daughter's grandmother dies and you can't bring her back and she knows you want to heal every hurt and thinks you can move mountains to do that. And when she figures out you can't, you still have her love, you still have her heart, but you've lost something precious. What you've lost is that understanding that runs deep that you can do everything.

And when you want to give her everything, seeing it in her eyes she knows you can't fucking kills.

He wanted more time to have that from Josie.

He should have just told her.

Now, he was going to tell her.

541

And thank fuck, he could do that, he saw as he drove up the lane to Lavender House and her Cayenne was parked out front.

She had several out buildings, one of them being a garage that looked like it was built the year the Model A rolled out. It needed to be fixed up, a decent door put in so Josie could park in there. Especially since the weather was going to get worse.

Or it needed to be knocked down and something built onto the house so she didn't have to walk outside at all.

He'd discuss that with her and deal with it later.

After he got this shit done.

He got out, went to the door and turned the knob.

He stared down at it when he found it was locked.

He then hit the doorbell as he found the key on his ring.

He stared down at the lock when his key didn't fit.

Jesus.

Was she so far gone she'd change the locks?

He hit the doorbell again and knocked.

No sound came from inside, not that that thick wood door would let any out.

He again tried the key.

No go.

"Jesus," he whispered out loud this time, hitting the doorbell again.

Nothing.

He pulled out his phone and called her.

He got voicemail.

"Fuck," he muttered, disconnecting, his heart again thumping in his chest. He moved around the house, trying the key in each lock and looking in windows.

She'd changed the locks on all the doors and was nowhere to be seen.

At the back, he moved beyond the greenhouse and took in the landscape. The sea. The arbor. The empty garden.

He turned and looked up at the house.

He saw her in the light room.

She was in the window seat staring down at him and he began to lift a hand but went solid when he watched her stand up, turn away and disappear.

"Fuck me, fuck me, fuck me," Jake whispered but moved swiftly to the greenhouse, trying the door he knew was locked and looking through.

She didn't appear in the kitchen.

She didn't appear in the family room when he walked by.

Or the living room.

Or at the front door when he went back to it and hammered.

Jake hit her number on his phone and when he got voicemail, his chest was burning and his jaw was tight.

"Baby, call me. We got shit to talk about. I'm drivin' away now, givin' you time. Tomorrow, we'll meet at The Shack for an omelet. Nine o'clock." He drew in breath and finished, "Kids miss you, Slick, and so do I."

He disconnected, moved into the lane and looked back up at Lydie's house. Josie's house.

Fuck, he should have just told her.

Then he got in his truck, his chest still burning, his jaw clenched, his gut tight, and he drove away.

AT NINE FIFTY-FIVE the next morning, after getting a coffee and standing at the end of the wharf for nearly an hour, Jake Spear walked away from The Shack.

And Tom watched him do it.

Then he slid the steel shutter over the window.

"I'LL LEAVE YOU to it," the bank manager murmured as he took his leave.

"Thank you," I replied, took a deep breath and looked down at Gran's safety deposit box.

Keeping my mind off things I should have my mind on, I opened it.

I'd found the key I'd completely forgotten the day before when I was going through my bag, again keeping my mind off things I should have had them on.

This precisely being the fact that I'd done much the same as what Donna had done.

I'd had a drama, made a silly decision, stuck my feet in and refused to look at the facts.

These being I was in love with Jake, Jake was in love with me, we were happy and whatever it was between him and Gran was between him and Gran.

He wanted to keep it that way and I had to trust he had his reasons. He told me it was important that I let it go and he'd also told me it was not that big of a deal.

These two contradicted each other.

But even as they did that, I knew two other things.

Gran loved me.

As did Jake.

And the first time he told me that, I'd walked away.

I just didn't know how to fix it even though he'd told me how.

Call him.

Meet him at The Shack.

I didn't do either.

The last boyfriend I had I fought with and the results were very unpleasant.

Jake was not him.

I still didn't know how to go about seeking someone out to admit you'd been a fool and apologize.

Jake had not called again.

Jake had not called after I didn't meet him at The Shack.

And now it was past one o'clock, which was a long time since I should have met Jake at The Shack, and I was going from feeling imprudent to being scared.

Thus, on a kind of autopilot, I was carrying on with inconsequential things when I should be finding Alyssa and picking her brain in order to sort out the mess I'd made.

"I'll do that after this," I murmured to myself as I looked through the things in Gran's box.

Stock certificates. A goodly number of them. Jewelry. A great deal of it, all high-quality and expensive. Birth certificates. Hers. Mine. My father's and uncle's. Surprisingly, a deed to a plot of land in Florida.

And, at the bottom, a plain white envelope.

I pulled it out and saw that there was not a letter inside but something else.

And on the outside was written *For my Buttercup* in Gran's hand.

I felt the envelope and noted it felt like one of those small tapes from a dictation machine.

Either Gran had a message for me or this was a tape that exposed such as the identity of Deep Throat from the Watergate scandal.

I was suspecting it was a message from Gran.

Oh God.

Hurriedly, I replaced all the items in the box and shoved the envelope in my bag. I moved to the door, opening it, and caught the bank manager's eyes.

"I'm done."

He nodded, came in, grabbed the box and we went back to the vault where he returned it. He turned his key. I turned mine.

"Thank you," I said.

"Certainly," he replied.

I gave him a small smile and directly left.

With care, I drove home thinking about Gran's desk. I hadn't scoured through the drawers but I didn't recall seeing a tape machine in there.

However, if she'd recorded something for me, she had to have one somewhere.

I just had to find it.

This was on my mind when I drove up the lane, seeing a rather well-kept but nevertheless very old white pickup truck in the drive. Closing in behind it in my Cayenne, I saw a tall, sturdy, somewhat older man step out from the entryway of the front door. The wind was whipping his silver-gray hair and his jacket, his eyes in his (it had to be said) rather weathered face squinting in the sun.

I'd never seen him before in my life and, although he looked kindly, I didn't want visitors.

I needed to find a tape recorder, listen to that tape, call Alyssa, ask her how you admitted to your man that you'd been an idiot and then find Jake and, well...*handle him.*

Nevertheless, since doing the first part of that required access to Lavender House, I had to get out of my car and approach the house.

This I did and I did it calling, "Hello."

"Josie," a somewhat familiar voice replied.

He knew me.

But upon closer study, I again noted I did not know him.

"I'm sorry, have we met?" I asked.

"Tom," he answered.

I blinked.

Tom?

The mysterious Tom from The Shack?

"Jake missed you at The Shack this morning," he went on.

Oh my.

It *was* the no longer mysterious Tom from The Shack.

At my door to tell me Jake had been there and I had not.

Oh dear.

"Um..." I began.

"It was me," he stated.

I blinked at him again.

"Pardon?" I asked.

"Me," he repeated. "Me who told Lydia you should be with Jake."

At this shocking news, I drew in such a deep breath I was forced back on a foot to do it.

"I'm sorry?" I asked, sounding winded.

"Worried about you, she was. Worried about you all the time. Wanted you to be happy. Wanted someone to look out for you. Make you laugh. Give you a good life. Came to The Shack a lot. Liked my coffee. We got to talkin' and she told me. She told me what you needed. Said they had to be tall. Good-lookin'. Smart. Protective. Fierce. Said they had to live local so she could have you but mostly so you could have Magdalene and Lavender House. She told me all that, I told her about Jake."

Oh my God.

He kept talking.

"Jake was married to Sloane back then but I still told her about him. Probably more hope than anything, but I didn't think it would last with Sloane seein' as she was not a good woman. Looked good. Could turn a man's eye, not like you 'a course," he said complimentarily, grinning and tipping his head at me. "But she was pretty enough. All about Jake in the beginning. Then again, they always are. See a man like that, way he looks, way he is, think it's gonna be smooth sailin'. A strong man like that, he'll pound out all the kinks of life and all you gotta do is sit back, enjoy the life he gives you and let him. But, you know, life is life and, pardon my French, but shit happens. Shit even a man like Jake can't make not happen."

When he stopped speaking and it seemed something was required of me, I said, "Of course."

But before I could invite him inside or say more, he kept going.

"So, I still told Lydia about Jake, kind of hopin' that he'd get quit of Sloane. Now,"—he raised his hand—"don't be thinkin' I don't believe in the sanctity of marriage. I do. Just not a marriage that involved Sloane."

At this, I had the hysterical need to giggle and nearly choked when I swallowed it down.

Tom kept going.

"Think Lydia had a gander at Jake, probably caught sight of Sloane and definitely had the same idea as me. Think that because the next thing I know, Jake's over at her house cleaning out the gutters. Kids are over there after school and on the weekends. Jake's in her garden helpin' her out 'cause we all know, Lydia liked fresh veggies from her garden."

Jake.

It was Jake, who had worked the garden for Gran.

Because, no matter how busy he was, no matter all the plates he had spinning in the air, that was what Jake would do because Gran liked fresh veggies from her garden and he loved Gran.

I felt my eyes begin to sting.

"Now, don't know, even though Jake and I know each other real well. I was his father's best friend, best man at his dad's wedding, watched Jake grow up. And Lydia and I could have a good natter over a coffee when she could still get around and when she couldn't, I'd find occasion to bring her a coffee and gab with her here. But even with all that, still don't know, when he got shot of Sloane, why she didn't get him to you," Tom said. "Years, I waited to see if that would happen."

I held my breath.

Tom kept speaking.

"Didn't."

I swallowed.

Tom continued.

"Then I saw you."

"You saw me?" I forced out.

"Pretty thing you are," he told me on another grin. "Pure class."

"I…" I cleared my throat. "Thank you."

"No need to thank me for statin' the truth," he said. "Figure Jake got a good look at you too, what with all those fancy pictures of you in Lydia's house."

My throat closed again.

Tom held my eyes, doing it intently, and went on.

"Man could fall in love with a girl, just like that." He snapped his fingers and I was so engrossed in what he was saying I jumped. "If that girl looked like you do in those pictures."

Oh…my…*God.*

"So pretty, like a movie star," Tom carried on.

Oh my God.

"Tom," I whispered.

"Back that with Lydia talkin' you up the way she did. Folks around town who know you and know what a good heart you have. Way everyone knows how you loved your Gran, always visiting, always talkin' when you're not. Yeah,"—he nodded—"a man could fall in love just like that."

I swallowed to open my throat in order to breathe.

"But see," he continued with his story. "She's ridin' first class on jets and got herself a fancy job workin' for a rich guy and hobnobs with superstars. Wears expensive clothes. She's got no baggage. No ex-husband. No kids. Man who can't give her all that. Man who's got that kind of baggage and then some. A man who makes a good livin' but one off exotic dancers. Man like that could steer clear 'a that woman, hopin', even if he knows he'd kill for a shot at her, she'd find something better.'"

"There's nothing better than Jake," I said softly.

"Good answer," he replied just as softly.

I stared into his eyes as I straightened my shoulders and stated, "I'd ask you in for a drink but I'm afraid it's rather urgent that I find Jake."

He nodded, his lips curving up, his blue eyes twinkling. "I understand."

"I'll, um…perhaps see you tomorrow for an omelet."

"Now, I'll look forward to that, Josie."

"I…well…it was lovely to see you, Tom."

"Same."

I nodded and moved swiftly to my car. I started it up, drove by Tom's truck and did this with my phone to my ear.

I got Jake's voicemail.

"Blast!" I snapped, pulling out of Lavender Lane and onto the road. I listened to Jake saying, "Spear. Leave a message." Then I said, "Jake… darling, I…well, we need to speak. I've been…" Drat! "We need to talk. As soon as possible. I'm in my car and I'll come to you wherever you are. Just phone."

I disconnected but held my phone in my hand as I drove, knowing that Jake could often leave his mobile in the office at the gym if he was working out, sparring or training.

Maybe that was why he didn't pick up my call.

I'd go to the gym.

I hit Cross Street and my phone rang in my hand.

My heart leaped and I looked to it, disappointment sweeping through me when I saw it was Alyssa.

I took the call anyway because I knew she was worried about me. Actually, I couldn't not know this. When I gave her my ridiculous waffle about selling Lavender House and leaving Magdalene, she'd replied, "Babelicious, straight up, this is whacked and I'm *so* worried about you."

I needed to brief her so she'd worry no longer.

And I needed to get to Jake.

So I greeted, "Hey, Alyssa. Now's not—"

"Babe, shit, crap, fuck, *babe*," she cut me off to say, sounding tremendously freaked.

My heart skipped this time and it wasn't a good skip. "Are you okay?"

"No!" she cried. "My Sofie's in the clink."

Another skip of the heart that was far from good.

"She's in jail?" I asked incredulously, for sweet, quiet, shy Sofie in jail was impossible to believe as well as a disaster.

"School jail," Alyssa told me. "The principal's office. I'm headed over there now. You need to get there, babelicious. Conner's in the clink with her."

Another skip of the heart. This one worse.

"*What?*" I nearly yelled, turning off Cross Street to head toward the high school.

"Yep. Sofie called, totally freaking *out*. Barely got a word from her that made sense but since I got so many of them, I managed to put it together. I guess that little piece of work, Mia, was all up in Conner's shit about how he ruined her life. They were in the hall and Sofie saw it happening and, don't know what got into my girl, but she got involved. It started with words but I guess Mia got nasty so Sofie slammed her into a locker and kicked her in the shin. Mia went ballistic and jumped her. Conner waded in to separate them and got himself clocked, unfortunately by Sofie, but he fell into Mia and she's sayin' he attacked her. Which we both know isn't true. No Spear man would take a hand to a woman, she deserved it or not, seein' as Donna needed some sense slapped into her about decade ago and that shit never happened. And I won't even *start* on what should be done with Ethan's mom."

Oh God.

Poor Conner.

Poor Sofie.

And that little fink, Mia.

What a mess!

"I'm on my way," I told her.

"I just got here," she replied.

"Is Jake there?" I asked.

"Shit yeah," she answered. "See his truck but Sofie said he showed when she was on the phone with me."

Well, that answered why he didn't pick up when I called.

I didn't know if I should be relieved or not. I didn't want Conner in the school clink but I wasn't certain how Jake would react after I'd muddled things up so horribly and then showed up at school.

There was nothing for it.

I'd just have to handle it, whatever it might be.

"See you soon," I told Alyssa.

"Later, babe. And just, you know, sayin'…that Mia girl's around and I see her get up in my daughter's shit, I give you permission to tackle me, shove me out of the room, whatever you gotta do. Talked to my girl about that bullying you told me about. Now this. That Mia needs a lesson but I don't need an assault charge."

"I'll be sure to tackle you or…whatever," I assured her hoping I didn't have to do that.

"Right. Later."

"Later, Alyssa."

She disconnected.

I drove and my heart skipped another beat, this one anxious, when I saw Jake's truck in the lot in front of the school.

I parked, got out and hurried into the school.

The administrative offices were at the front and I walked right in.

The receptionist looked up at me. "Can I help you?"

And that was when my heart fluttered and my belly dipped.

This was because I heard Jake say, "She's with me."

I looked to the side to see him standing in an open door, his arm up and extended my way, his eyes locked on me.

Relief sweeping through me so profoundly it nearly brought me to my knees, I struggled past it and, without delay, moved to him, lifting a hand and taking his.

His fingers closed around mine and they did this tight, his eyes never leaving me.

Then he pulled me into the room.

———————

"GO," MIA'S FATHER, Neal ordered.

"But Dad—" she started.

"Not another word, Mia," he warned. "Told you, stay away from Conner Spear. Told you, you act like a decent person, you'd win folks back around. You didn't listen to me. Now, we're gonna find out if I can find other ways to make you listen to me."

We were standing outside the high school and apparently, spoiled Mia had pushed her father too far.

Finally.

Mia had been suspended for three days.

Sofie had been suspended for one.

Conner had been released early seeing as, after the situation finally got sorted out, it was the last period of the day and there was no point in him going back and disturbing class. Especially after the ruckus that many in the school had seen and probably now all of the school had heard about.

The truth had outed, all of it, including the past bullying which Conner had stared intently at Sofie all the while she'd recounted it (in a rather adorable stammer, I might add).

It also included the lie about the pregnancy, something Mia's father shared himself by saying, "First you lie about Con knockin' you up, spreadin' that crap around, and now this? God, what am I gonna do with you?"

Apparently the principal was rather hands on and had seen Mia at work, knew Sofie was an honor roll student and the belle of the choir, and thus understood the situation.

Therefore Sofie got suspended for pushing and kicking Mia but Mia bore the brunt of the punishment for starting the situation, not backing down, getting physical right back with Sofie and hurling rather unladylike profanities at Conner, then Sofie, doing this at the top of her lungs.

We watched Neal march Mia to his car and the minute they were out of earshot, Alyssa turned to her daughter.

"You…so…rock," she stated and pulled Sofie into a tight hug. "So proud of you, not takin' any shit."

I saw Sofie's tentative proud smile as she hugged her mother back. However, this hug was prematurely ended when Conner wrapped his fingers around Sofie's bicep and gently pulled her from her mother's embrace.

Alyssa's arms dropped and her eyes moved to Conner.

"Takin' Sofie home, Mrs. Harper," he declared.

Oh dear.

"But, I—" Sofie began but she snapped her mouth shut when Conner cut his eyes to her.

"Takin' you home," he repeated a lot more firmly this time and considering his earlier declaration was very firm, this was rock-solid.

Oh my.

Sofie looked terrified. But then her eyes drifted to the red mark on Conner's cheekbone, one she put there. Accidentally, of course, but she'd done it.

Then she whispered, "I...okay," though she didn't really have a choice.

Conner continued not to give her one.

He did this by sliding his hand down to hers, grabbing hold and dragging her down the sidewalk.

We all watched until they turned the corner toward the student parking area, Sofie looking back at us with an expression I couldn't make out due to the distance, before they disappeared.

The instant they did, Alyssa turned happy eyes to me.

"Figure, she gets home, my girl's gonna have the taste of Spear on her lips," she announced ecstatically.

I pressed my lips together in order not to smile.

Jake muttered, "Jesus."

Alyssa looked at Jake.

"Jake, babe, you do not get this but I'll let you in the know," she started. "See, a girl never forgets her first kiss. And this may not go anywhere with our two, but that doesn't matter. I figure he's got enough experience to give her a good one. He's smart. Cute. Sweet. And very into her. So all her life she'll look back at that and smile. And for a mom, well, a mom knows her girl got that, she thinks that's a little bit of all right."

"Can we stop talking about this?" Jake asked.

Alyssa smiled big and looked to me. "For a dad, the thought of his daughter's first kiss is when latent murderous tendencies wake up. The thought of his boy kissing a girl, that's when he starts buying stock in Babies 'R' Us."

"I'm seeing we can't stop talking about this," Jake murmured.

"Okay," Alyssa said. "We'll talk about you two and how I'm freakin' *thrilled* you sorted your shit. So this means we're on for a barbeque on Saturday. This bein' because I know my Sofie and if she feels like buildin' a wall back up after Con spends the next hour tearin' it down, she will." She raised a hand and pointed a finger at Jake. "You get your son there. I'll forget to buy somethin' at the grocery store. I'll ask Sofie to go get it. You get your boy to take her." She looked to me. "'Course, I'll already have it 'cause I hope Con'll take a *very* long time gettin' her back home and we don't wanna do without."

"Are you honestly standing here plotting to get my boy alone with your girl?" Jake asked disbelievingly and Alyssa shrugged.

"He's got the goods this afternoon, won't have to bother and they'll be cozy by Saturday anyway," she replied.

"I'll ask again. Can we stop talking about this?" Jake repeated.

Alyssa looked him in the eyes. "Yeah, Jake. But I'm gonna tell you one more thing. I know your never forget your first kiss and, you get a good one, you never forget your first boyfriend." She then turned to me. "And landing a Spear as your man is bound to be unforgettable."

That was sweet.

And so very true.

Jake said nothing.

I didn't either.

"Right, gotta dash," she announced. "I left a client in foils and hope like fuck Lindsey got her sorted out like I asked or she's not going to have any hair left when I get back," She gave us a finger wave and then jogged gracefully on the toes of her high-heeled boots to her car.

I watched her do this until I couldn't watch anymore because Jake's chest was in my vision.

This was it.

Either he was angry or something else.

I held my breath and looked up.

"Got your call when I was in the principal's office, honey. Couldn't take it."

I let out my breath.

He was something else.

That something else being Jake.

"That's okay," I replied.

"You ready to talk?" he asked.

Good God.

I so…*fucking*…loved him.

That was why I said, "No."

His brows knit even as I saw his frame stiffen.

"It's important that you don't share," I stated. "What's important to you is important to me so if you don't wish to share, you don't have to. However, if you're not talking about that but instead want to talk about what I'm making for din—"

I didn't finish.

And I didn't finish because Jake was kissing me.

There were classrooms facing where we were on the sidewalk so it was likely students and teachers could see us.

This was unseemly.

But I didn't care.

I kissed him back with everything I had.

This went on for some time before Jake lifted his head nary an inch and stated, "You know I'd make out with you anywhere, anytime for as long as I can get that mouth. But my son needs to be picked up from school. Now, who's gonna be doin' that, you or me?"

"Me," I answered immediately.

And that was when I got Jake's smile back.

It had only been two days.

But, goodness, how I missed it.

———

AMBER, WHO HAD arrived home ten minutes ago after doing her homework at girl Taylor's, walked into the kitchen and when she did, I looked at her.

When she'd come home, she'd come in from the garage, saw me cooking, gave me a look of surprise, then hope, then something I couldn't read that was not nearly as good as the former two before she'd mumbled, "Gotta dump my bags," and rushed to the stairs.

In the last two days it had not been lost on me that in having my drama and carrying it out to its ridiculous and inappropriate fullest, the consequences were not simply mine and Jake's but also the children's.

Ethan, when I showed up at his school to pick him up, had simply climbed into the Cayenne, looked at me and declared, "Lunch sucked. I need pizza."

So that was good.

And Conner had seen me with his father in the principal's office. He'd shown signs of relief when he did, but he was more interested in what was going on with Sofie than his father and me.

Conner had not returned. Then again, he had a shift at Wayfarer's and wasn't due to return for half an hour.

Now, with one look at her, I knew I had to deal with whatever consequences I'd earned with Amber.

"Dinner's done. And there is no way Ethan can wait for it to be served and your brother isn't going to be home for a bit," I told her quietly. "So could you do me a favor and prepare a plate for him, put foil on it and put it in the oven to keep warm?"

Not looking at me, she muttered, "Sure."

I did not take this as a good sign. She had not been muttering or mumbling since we made our deal weeks ago.

I went to the cupboard to get plates, wondering how to handle this situation.

I stopped wondering when Amber instigated the discussion herself.

She did this by saying, "Don't screw Dad over."

I looked to her to see her standing at the other side of the island, her eyes on me, her pretty face slightly pale. I could also see she was struggling.

I did that to her and my heart took a beating in knowing it.

"Sweetheart—" I started.

"I love you, Josie," she declared and my heart stopped beating altogether when she did. "You're awesome. We all think you're the bomb. Me, Con, Eath. We do. You're cool. You're cool with us. But the most important of all that is you make Dad happy."

I held her gaze, loving what she said but hating the look in her eyes.

She kept speaking.

"The last couple of days, Dad wasn't happy."

"Amber—"

"That stupid skank Mandy took off on him. Ethan's stupid mom Sloane took off on both Dad and Ethan. Crazy. Dad's the best guy there is. But we know. Me and Con, we know the reason they did is because of us."

"That may not be true," I told her gently.

"It's true," she returned swiftly. "They wanted Dad. They didn't want us."

I closed my mouth for I knew from Jake this was not wrong.

It just pained me to know Amber and Conner knew it.

"But we all come together," she stated.

"I know that, my lovely."

She didn't nod. She didn't give any indication she believed me.

She just repeated, "Don't screw Dad over, Josie."

I drew in a breath, pulled up my courage and walked to her.

She didn't draw away so I lifted my hands, framed her face and moved mine close to hers.

"Your father and I had an unpleasant discussion," I shared carefully. "I reacted to this badly. I have not had a good deal of experience with relationships, my lovely girl, but that's no excuse. When I say I reacted to it badly, what I mean is that I overreacted. But I've thought things through since then and I love your father, I love you kids, and I've learned not to do that again."

She didn't touch me, didn't say anything, but she did keep her gaze steady on mine so I felt it safe to continue.

"Things will not be smooth sailing, Amber. Life is life and we'll all have issues crop up out there as well as amongst ourselves. But I'm hoping we're building a foundation where we'll weather all those storms. The last two days, I learned that I need to stand strong and weather those storms. I'm so sorry I went away. It was the wrong thing to do. The only thing I can promise is that I won't do it again."

"Ever?" she asked.

And when she did, I thought about it for I knew my answer was crucial and it also had to be completely honest.

But even as I thought about it, I knew.

I knew Jake would not hit me. Jake would not wound me with words. Jake would not cheat on me. Jake would not lie to me. Jake would not gamble or steal or throw away money or go out and rape and pillage.

So I knew.

"Ever," I promised her.

When I did, she closed her eyes and dropped her head forward so her forehead rested on my mouth, her hands coming up so she could wrap her fingers around my wrists.

"I love you, my sweet girl," I whispered against her skin, pressing in with my hands.

She pulled away, caught my eyes and squeezed my wrists. "Back at cha, Josie."

I smiled.

She smiled back.

Thank goodness.

We let each other go and I went back to the plates. I handed her one and she got down to the business of preparing it for Conner as I went to the drawer to get the cutlery.

I was counting out forks and knives when her phone in her back pocket sounded the alert she had a text.

I looked to her and saw her pull out her phone, look at it, then shove it back into her pocket.

Unusual.

Amber usually responded to texts immediately unless she was at school.

"Everything okay?" I asked.

"Yep," she answered.

"Amber," I called, seeing the stiffness in her frame.

She looked to me.

"Is everything okay?" I repeated.

"Mom keeps bugging me," she told me.

I was uncertain how to proceed so I did it cautiously, "Bugging you how?"

"Wants to go to a movie this weekend."

"Ah," I murmured.

"Said no and it's like she doesn't get it. But she hasn't asked about the movie again. She just texts and asks how it's going. Wants to know if I wanna get a coffee. She even sent me a picture of a sweater at Lucky she thought would look good on me and asked if I'd like to have it."

"You said?" I prompted when she spoke no more.

"I texted back, 'whatever,'" she shared.

"Did you like the sweater?"

She focused on preparing Conner's plate and answered, "It was kind of kick-butt."

I grinned as I moved to the pantry to get napkins.

"She's bugging Con too," she told me while I was on the move.

"Is that so?" I asked from inside the pantry.

It was when I came out that I felt her eyes on me so I looked to her.

"You did this," she stated.

It wasn't an accusation even when it kind of was.

"Yes," I confirmed honestly.

Her face set stubbornly. "I'll take the sweater, Josie, because it was cool. But I'm not goin' to a movie with her or coffee or whatever."

"Your choice, my lovely," I replied, moving back to the island.

"You see her, you can tell her that," she said.

I would do no such thing.

Therefore, I didn't answer.

"Josie?" she called.

I looked to her.

"Love you, but you can be a pain in the butt."

I smiled.

Amber stared at me a moment.

Then she smiled back.

JAKE'S VOICE WAS low and gruff in a way I liked very much when he warned, "You don't want the results of that work in your mouth, baby, you best get up here."

My eyes lifted to him as I slid my mouth up his cock, sucking as I went, then rolling the underside of the rim of the head with the tip of my tongue.

I felt his legs tense at my sides as I saw a muscle jump in his jaw, his heated eyes that were on me firing.

I knew these signs very well, so I released him with my mouth, gliding my fist that was wrapped around it up after I did so. I let him go and then moved. Crawling on all fours over him, I took my time at the ridges of his stomach. I took more time at his nipples. I then moved to take time at his throat, his neck and behind his ears.

By the time I got to the last, I was straddling him so I worked at his ear as I felt him glide the tip of his cock in the wet between my legs.

He rubbed it over my clit and I gasped against his skin just as he wrapped an arm around my waist, slid his cock back and pushed me down, filling me.

My neck arched.

Jake's other hand sifted into my hair at the back of my head and he kept us connected as he rolled.

Then he was on me, thrusting slow and sweet, his mouth to mine, his tongue inside, tasting, drinking, but giving…slower and sweeter.

My hands moved over his skin and I wrapped a leg around his hip, the other one around his thigh as I kissed him back.

His thrusts started to get faster, but no less sweeter, building it beautifully as he broke our kiss but didn't lift away, his lips brushing mine, his breaths mingling with mine, his eyes holding mine.

I held his gaze and I saw it smoldering there, the heat he was creating, what he was building in me, what I was building in him, but there was more. A flame that would never extinguish.

The love he had for me.

Seeing it, I tightened my legs around him, tipped my hips for him and glided a hand into his hair.

"I love you, Jake," I whispered and the instant I did, his thrusts got even faster, much sweeter, our breath coming heavier.

"Fuck, baby," he whispered back.

"I love everything about you."

"Fuck, Josie," he groaned.

It was building higher and my body tensed all around him, my eyes going unfocused as it started to engulf me and I was ready to feel the burn.

"Josie," he called.

I tried to focus but found it hard. I wanted to give in. I wanted what he could give me, every time, some harder, some faster, some slower, some sweeter, some longer, but I always got it because Jake always gave it to me.

And I wanted it now.

"Darling," I whimpered.

"Look at me when I tell you I love you," he ordered.

I focused on the man I loved who loved me in a return for an instant before he said the words.

"I love you, baby."

I heard them in a way so profound, I *felt* them, the feeling taking me there and I cried out, the sound drowned when his mouth took mine in a deep kiss.

Minutes later, he drove deep, planted himself and smothered his groan in the same fashion.

I knew when it left him because he again started kissing me.

And again, I kissed him back.

It was slow. It was lazy. It went on for a long time, even after Jake slid out. Then he branched out, kissing my neck, my collarbone, between my breasts, my ribs, my midriff, my belly.

Showering me with kisses. Spreading his love everywhere.

I closed my eyes and did my best to stay connected, my fingers in his hair, my hand at his neck, as he gave me everything.

Finally, he covered me with his big body and looked into my eyes.

"I gotta tell you something," he said, his voice thick but firm and I knew what he was going to say.

I knew what he was going to give me.

And I knew I didn't need it.

"No you don't," I told him quickly.

"Babe.—"

"You don't, Jake."

"Right now, you under me, your hair spread on my pillow, your clothes on my floor, I've had it time and again and I still can't believe it."

My mouth closed, my throat closed and my eyes stung with tears.

"It was me who refused to meet you," he stated.

Oh God.

"Darling—"

"Lydie asked me…fuck, don't know how many times. Every time you came to visit, for certain. And she'd even make up shit to get you to visit so we could meet. Tried everything she could to make it happen. She gave me your email. She even gave me your Skype account and said she'd introduce us on the fuckin' computer."

"Darling, you don't have to—"

"First time I walked into Lavender House, looked left, saw that photo of you behind the couch…" He shook his head. "I was with Sloane, shit was not good with her, but it still makes me a dick because I took one look at that picture and fell in love with you."

Oh…my…

God.

A tear slid out of the corner of my eye and Jake caught it with his thumb but he didn't quit talking.

"Every word Lydie said about you, it got worse. I fell further. 'Cause of that, I knew, if I saw you, shook your hand, you didn't want what I could offer, it'd gut me. So I couldn't let that happen."

I slid my hands up his back, in and up his chest and further to curl them around his jaw.

"She pushed," he went on. "But she didn't force it. She got me. I knew it. I also knew it bothered her. So she didn't give up. She gave me your picture. Then she gave me your letters."

"Jake—"

"I got you. I knew you. She gave me all of you. And having it, I wanted you to find better."

Oh *God.*

"Please, darling," I begged.

"I wanted you to have what you wanted. Someone gentle, patient, sophisticated, successful. And that was not me."

I closed my eyes and tears escaped both sides, rolling down my temples.

Jake caught them with his thumbs and I opened my eyes.

"I wasted years," he whispered, his voice now hoarse, regret etched in every feature.

"Don't," I whispered back.

"I didn't fuck that up, coulda tried to make a baby with you."

"*Don't,*" I pleaded, pressing into his jaws with my hands.

"Had no clue you'd want me."

"You're everything," I told him.

He shook his head. "I'm not everything. I got three kids by two women, three ex-wives, a gym that struggles to stay in the black, and a fuckin' strip club that makes it so I can breathe easy, my kids can have cars and clothes and shit. I know from experience not a lotta women want to buy into any of that. Me, yeah, they'll take me. The rest of it, they want nothin' to do with. But with you, it was more. I can't put your ass in a first class seat on a plane and take you wherever you wanna go, whenever you wanna go there."

"Why would I need to go anywhere when I can be here with you?"

He blinked.

"I never wanted anything but you, Jake," I told him and he simply stared at me so I went on. "And I wanted you before I even knew you. Someone handsome and strong and protective and fierce. You're everything I ever wanted, darling."

"Baby," he dropped his forehead to mine, lifted it and continued, "Look at your life the way it was. Look at mine the way it is. Can you see how that's where my head would be at?"

"Definitely," I agreed. "But can you see that the person who knew you were right for me was the only person who knew the true me, knew what I wanted, knew what I *needed,* and picked you for me?"

He said nothing so I took that as a yes.

"You did what you had to do," I said quietly. "And it's done. And in the end, I have my dream. And I'm hoping since you love me that you have what you want too. Now can we let it go and move on?"

"I know you wanted kids, Josie."

"And now I have them, Jake."

I felt his body lock on mine so I took that opportunity to use my hands at his jaws and pull him down to me. I lifted my head at the same time and touched my mouth to his before I dropped back to the pillow.

"I thank you for giving that to me, darling. You didn't need to but now I have it, I'll treasure it. *All of it*. But seriously, can we let this go and move on?"

"It's gonna sting, baby, havin' you, havin' what we got, knowin' I coulda had it longer, givin' it to you longer, givin' you even more, all of that if I got my head outta my ass."

I smiled at him and replied, "I'll make it better."

He stared into my eyes and whispered, "Fuck, I love you."

I'd never tire hearing that.

Never.

Even with the expletive.

"And I you," I shared. "And now I'd love it if you'd get off me so I can clean up and we can sleep. Six o'clock rolls around fast and tomorrow, I've got to hire some interior decorators. We're moving into Gran's room upstairs. It has its own bathroom and as it is, it's kind of a pain to tiptoe down the hall so I don't wake up the kids when I have to go clean up after you make love to me."

Finally, his eyes smiled.

"We movin' to Lavender House?" he asked.

"Your house is wonderful, Jake, and you fixed it up. The kids love it here. As do I. But we'd all love it more being with Gran."

His thumb swept my temple and he whispered, "Yeah."

"But only after I redecorate the master suite. All those flowers..." I trailed off as I shook my head on the pillow.

That got me another smile and another, "Yeah."

"Now, are you going to get off me?" I asked.

"Yeah and no."

This confused me so I tipped my head to the side. "Pardon?"

"This is the no part," he stated right before he kissed me, long, deep, wet and sweet. When he lifted his head, he finished, 'Now you get the yeah."

I laughed softly as he rolled off.

Then I rolled into him, bent and kissed his stomach, his midriff, his ribs, between his pectorals, his collarbone, his neck, under his ear.

Showering him with kisses. Spreading my love everywhere.

When I finished and looked into his eyes, I knew he'd felt it.

And he liked it.

So I kissed his lips, rolled off the bed and went to the bathroom.

I cleaned up and tugged on a nightie before sliding into bed beside him.

He reached out to turn out the light and cuddled me close as he settled us in.

I cuddled closer, murmuring, "Definitely need to move to Gran's room just for the master bath."

"Yeah," he replied.

I nestled deeper.

Jake gave me a squeeze.

"Love you, darling," I whispered into his skin.

"Right back at cha, Slick," he did not whisper back.

I smiled.

And mere minutes later, tucked tight to my man, I fell asleep.

——◆•◆•◆——

"YO! JOSIE!" I heard Jake call.

It was early afternoon the next day and I was in the light room looking for a recorder.

"Light room!" I yelled, shuffling through the detritus in Gran's desk and deciding that tomorrow I would tackle it and organize it.

I'd need to do that since I had not only managed to make appointments with the two interior designers that had businesses in the county, I had phoned New York and began negotiations to take the job with the up-and-coming designer. He was considering once every six weeks visits from me for a week so I could take meetings as well as very limited travel for runway shows and the like.

Thus, if my conditions were accepted, I'd need an organized desk.

I was looking forward to working in the light room, being with Gran as I did it.

So I very much was hoping he'd accept my terms.

"Babe." I heard Jake say and looked from the desk to the opening of the spiral staircase where he'd appeared.

"Hey, darling," I replied.

"How'd shit go?" he asked, moving to me at the desk.

"Two appointments with designers, both tomorrow. And I called New York. My conditions are being considered," I answered, having turned my attention back to what I was doing, still rifling through Gran's desk.

I felt him stop by the desk as he replied, "Right," Then he asked, "What are you doing?"

I looked up at him then reached to the desk and took the envelope with the tape in it and gave it to him.

He looked down at the writing before he looked into the envelope I'd opened and his eyes cut to me. "From Lydie?"

"I found it in her safe deposit box," I shared.

"Fuckin' hell," he muttered.

I again focused on the drawer I was going through. "I'm looking for a recorder so I can listen to it."

I found nothing but heard Jake slide open a drawer to help.

Seconds later, he said, "Here."

I looked to him to see he had a dictation machine held up in his hand.

And suddenly, I found I couldn't catch my breath.

"Slick," Jake called and my eyes lifted to his. His roamed to my face and his voice gentled when he noted, "You can give this time."

Slowly, I shook my head.

Jake took that in, assessed my expression for long moments then nodded.

I watched as he loaded the tape into the machine and after that, I had no choice but to follow him to the window seat since he'd grabbed hold of my hand and guided me there.

In Jake fashion, he then arranged us in the seat as he wanted us. Jake behind me, his legs up on the seat surrounding me, my back against his front, his arms wrapped around me, cocooning me in his strength, his protection, his safety.

I drew in a deep breath and rested my arms on his at my middle.

"Ready?" he whispered in my ear.

"Yes," I whispered to the sea.

I heard a click then nothing for long seconds before I heard Gran's voice.

Josie, my buttercup, she said. *If you're listening to this, I'm gone.*

I closed my eyes tight.

And by the time you listen to this, you'll have met Jake.

I opened my eyes and Jake's arms pulled me deeper into his body.

I knew the moment I saw him that he was perfect for you. I also knew from the expression on his face when he saw your picture, he knew you were perfect for him too.

Oh God.

I made a noise in the back of my throat as I swallowed the tears clogging there and turned. I wrapped my arms around Jake and pressed my forehead into his neck as I continued to stare at the sea and listen to the beloved voice of my Granny.

It's likely, by this time, Gran went on, *that Arnie's read my will to you. You're probably confused and perhaps alarmed. I don't wish to pain you with this knowledge, but even after your assertions that you were content with your life, I was troubled. I didn't want you to be content, my buttercup. I wanted you to be happy. So I did what I needed to make you that way. I gave you to Jake and doing it, gave Jake to you.*

I pressed my forehead in Jake's neck.

He'll make you happy, my precious Josie.

A tear slid down my cheek and, as if sensing it, Jake pulled me even closer.

Now, there are some things you need to know, Gran stated, suddenly sounding all business. *Conner, Jake's eldest, has a tendency to collect girls. I think for boys of his age this is not unusual. But for Conner, I feel it's something else. He admires his father but he's very intelligent. I think, watching his father be unlucky in love, he's searching for the right one. But he's going about it the wrong way. You need to handle that.*

It was then a giggle escaped my throat just as a chuckle rumbled in Jake's chest.

And he won't tell you, he prefers filling his body with what he calls proteins and carbs, by that he means meat and rolls, but he needs vegetables and it took me some time but I found that Conner likes peas.

"Peas," I whispered, wondering why I hadn't yet served them and knowing that night, I would.

Amber, Jake's daughter, Gran continued, *is enchanted with an inappropriate young man. She is very sweet but has no idea of her charms. She thinks she's fortunate to have caught his eye and doesn't understand it's the other way around. You need to find a way to communicate that with her and untangle her from that situation. From what she's told me, this Noah person is unworthy of her but I have not been able to get her to understand this is true. Please see to that, for Amber deserves much better.*

A huge smile had spread on my face and I felt Jake's body shaking with laughter.

Finally, Ethan, Jake's youngest, well…what is there to say about that darling boy? Not much except he's a darling boy who needs a mother.

My smile died and Jake stopped laughing.

See to that too, buttercup, Gran ordered. *And in doing so, watch his diet. He's a growing boy and it's understandable that he's hungry nearly constantly. But sometimes he overindulges. Put a stop to that, will you?*

Warmth spread through me for a variety of reasons when Jake rested his jaw on the top of my head and gathered me ever closer.

I have many things to say about Jake, Gran remarked. *But I have a feeling they won't need to be said. This is because I've no doubt Jake will show you all that needs to be said. I just encourage you, my precious girl, to allow him to say them in his way. I promise you…promise you, Josie, you'll wish to hear them.*

I curled my fingers into Jake's sweater.

My girl, know this and never forget. It's never too late to reach for happiness and no matter what life has done to you, it's never too late to find it. Please don't be offended when I share with you that I know you've been hiding. I know why. I understand it, buttercup, but it's time to come into the light. I've found someone special to help guide the way. Please, Josie, take Jake's hand and let him guide you to happiness.

The tears slid down my cheek and Jake pressed his jaw into my hair.

And last, I love you, Josie. I know the things I just told you are true because I had many things happen in my life, things that would lead me to believe I'd never find anything but contentment at best. But when you entered my life, I found happiness.

My body bucked with my sob and Jake pulled me up so I could shove my face in his neck.

Thank you, buttercup, Gran said softly, *for being the light of my life. I treasured you from the moment you were born, to the time I sit here saying these things to you, to the time I take my last breath and I'll treasure you beyond it. This is because you're a treasure, my Josie. You always have been and you always will.*

My breath hitched with my sob as the tears flowed freely down my cheeks and into the skin of Jake's neck.

Tell Jake, Conner, Amber and Ethan they held special places in my heart, will you, buttercup? I know it will be sad to know that when you weren't with me, although I had a full life, I often felt empty. Until I met them and they filled my life with such beauty. Such great beauty.

"Jesus," Jake murmured, his voice rough.

I knew what that meant and gave him a loving squeeze.

And I know they will do the same for you, Josie, if you let them. Please let them, buttercup.

I drew in a deep breath to control my tears.

It didn't work.

Good-bye, my precious girl, Gran said and the tears slid faster down my cheeks. *I'll love you always. Forever and completely.*

I heard the click, then silence which was broken by the sound of my sob as it filled the room.

I knew Jake put the recorder aside when his arms got even tighter and one hand slid up into my hair, his fingers gliding through it, holding me, stroking me, soothing me.

He held me close for some time. It could have been minutes; it could have been hours before my tears abated.

Then he held me for longer.

My eyes scratchy, my heart hurting, my lips moved.

"She gave me everything," I told Jake.

"Yeah, baby," he replied.

"And then she died and she gave it to me again."

I felt his body give a slight jerk before it settled and he said, "Yeah, Slick, she gave me that too."

Gran gave Jake that too.

I closed my eyes.

Then I opened them, pulled slightly away and lifted my head to catch my man's gaze.

"I need to clean up and go pick up Ethan."

Jake looked into my eyes for long moments.

Then finally, I watched fascinated as his eyes—an unusual stormy gray—changed colors to a beautiful light blue.

And this was when they smiled.

FOREVER AND COMPLETELY

"It's done?" Jake asked.

Arnie nodded, smiling, "It's all there."

Jake looked at him and then looked down to the envelope Arnie had just handed him wondering how something so huge could be contained in an envelope.

"Dad!"

He heard Ethan shout and moved his gaze in that direction.

Ethan, in his little man tuxedo, was racing toward him and doing it so fast he wasn't able to control himself so when he arrived, he slammed into Jake.

Jake stood steady, steadying his son by doing it, and put a hand to his boy's shoulder.

Ethan was staring up at him and his voice was excited when he asked, "Is that it?"

Jake looked down at his son, memorizing the expression on his face, hoping like fuck he never forgot it.

"Yeah, bud, that's it," he confirmed.

"*Cool,*" Ethan breathed, jumped away and declared, "I'm gonna go get Con and Amber. Can we do it now? Can we?"

They sure as fuck could.

"Absolutely," he replied and he didn't have the full word out before Ethan sprinted away.

"This is perhaps the most beautiful present there ever was," Arnie stated and Jake turned his eyes to the man. "I'm honored to have played my part," he finished.

Jake smiled at him and replied, "Still plannin' on payin' the bill."

At that, Arnie shook his head, "Oh no, Jake. My present to you. And Josie. And your children on this joyous day."

Before Jake could protest, Arnie clapped him on the arm and quickly walked away.

Jake watched him for a beat then he turned his head and took in the expanse.

There were white tents to either side of the back of Lavender House, these and the tables set out in the sun were decorated with bouquets of sprigs of lavender taken from the bushes around the house, white roses and lilies of the valley.

The sea glinted in the sun.

The garden had been planted but there wasn't much there but rich dark dirt broken up by green shoots.

And the wisteria over the arbor was in full bloom, but many of its purple petals had detached in the slight breeze, drifting confetti across the space. In fact, forty minutes ago, when he kissed Josie there after she was declared his wife, a breeze blew up, scattering petals everywhere.

He hadn't seen it. He was busy kissing his wife. But Alyssa told him about it, showing him and Josie a picture Junior had taken on his phone, declaring it, "Effing *awesome.*"

And from what he saw in the picture, Jake had to agree.

He turned his eyes back and saw that Ethan had found Amber and was pulling her away from Alexi, boy Taylor, girl Taylor and Kieran Wentworth. This meant Ethan had pulled Amber from Alexi's arm, which was wrapped around her waist. He tore his eyes off that and saw Kieran's arm the same around Taylor.

It was then he grinned.

Girl Taylor was a stunning, loyal, sweet young woman any guy would be lucky to have.

But still.

That was all Josie.

He watched his daughter in her lavender bridesmaid's dress and his youngest son move across the grass and he looked in the direction they were going.

There he saw Conner in his tuxedo lounging in a white chair at one of the tables. Sofie was sitting close to him and Con had his arm slung along the back of her chair.

Sofie reminded Jake a lot of Josie so Jake was unsurprised when they finally got their shit together, got tight and kept tight. Conner was happy. Sofie was happy. Alyssa was ecstatic. And Junior had managed to hold his shit. Like Jake when it came to his daughter having a boyfriend, not enjoying it much, but he'd done it.

Conner would be going to Boston University in a few months, which would totally fucking suck.

Luckily, Jake knew without a doubt he'd be coming back a lot. To see his old man, his family and his girl.

Right then, he saw Conner had his arm on Sofie's chair but his eyes were aimed at his brother and sister.

He knew it was time.

They'd planned this.

All of them.

Therefore, before Amber and Ethan made it to him, Jake watched as Conner turned his head to his girl and said something in her ear that made her smile.

Then he kissed her briefly, got up and looked to his dad.

Jake jerked up his chin.

Conner nodded and started to make his way to Jake.

That was when Jake again scanned the space but he knew where she was.

Still, in doing it, he saw Donna sitting with Alyssa. Alyssa, also in a bridesmaid dress, was talking. Donna was smiling.

She'd pulled her head out of her ass and it took her a while but she put in the effort and got results.

Conner and Amber didn't stay at her house but they saw each other and often.

Not done, Josie had then instigated part two of her plan and got it to the point where Donna came over for dinner (rarely, but it happened, mostly on special occasions like birthdays and Easter).

Josie had given his boy and girl their mother. Donna did the work; he had to give her credit for that. She'd sucked it up and made it happen.

But Josie instigated it.

His eyes kept going through the guests talking, drinking and eating the fancy shit from silver trays that waiters were carrying around.

As they did, he saw Bert. Troy. Mickey. Coert. Pearl. Junior. Reverend Fletcher and his wife Ruth. Girl Taylor's parents. Boy Taylor's parents. Nearly every member of his gym. All his bouncers and their women. All his dancers and their men. A bunch of his kids from the junior boxing league and their parents.

He also saw, mingling with the townies, the makeup artist Jean-Michel DuChamp, the supermodel Acadie and the front man for Bounce, Lavon Burkett. Not to mention, some big name designers Amber had freaked when she found out they were coming and more recording artists that all his kids had freaked when they found out they were coming.

And last, he saw Josie standing close to the cliff, the sea her backdrop, her face bright with a huge smile as she stood listening to Amond.

Taking her in yet again, he noted her gown was un-fucking-believable. He thought it right then. And he thought it an hour ago when she walked out of the house on Tom's arm, both of them moving to him, his boys standing at his side, Alyssa and Amber having just made the same journey.

The designer Josie worked for made the gown especially for her.

It was white and hugged her from shoulders to knees. Sleeveless, v-neck, a deep vee in the back exposing a lot of skin, the dress flared out in a wide but elegant puff of netting at her knees.

But the white body of the gown was covered in a deep lavender lace that bled into the netting that had some pieces of the lace stitched into it.

She looked what she was.

Pure class.

Pure style.

Total beauty.

Except her hair was up.

It looked fucking gorgeous but he'd be taking it down the first chance he got.

His attention was taken from his wife when his kids huddled close.

He looked to Conner. "Con, do me a favor, get a pen."

Conner reached into the inside pocket of his tuxedo and pulled one out. "Already got it."

Jake smiled at his boy.

"Dad! Let's do this!" Ethan demanded impatiently.

Jake looked down at his youngest.

Yes.

He was impatient.

And this was for him as well as Josie. It was for Jake, too. And it was for Conner and Amber.

But mostly, it was for Josie.

And Ethan.

And what his boy and his woman wanted, Jake wanted to give to them.

Therefore, Jake looked up and shouted, "Yo! Slick!"

Josie turned her head his way and even from the distance, he saw the fall of her grandmother's diamonds and amethysts sparkle at her ears.

With the help of his daughter, it was his diamonds and amethysts that sparkled at her neck and wrist.

The huge ass diamond he'd planted on her finger Christmas day right in front of his kids was also his. As was the band set with diamonds he'd planted on it that day.

Josie had taken Amber on a girl's trip to New York so Amber had seen her dress. She'd also gone with Jake to pick that shit out. Last, she'd given Jake's necklace and bracelet to Josie during preparations because Amber, Alyssa nor Josie would allow Jake to see his woman prior to her walking down the aisle.

He found this annoying. He liked tradition at Christmas, Thanksgiving, Halloween.

He did not like sleeping without his woman.

But he couldn't fault their strategy. That gown she wore was amazing but it was even more amazing him seeing her in it for the first time as she walked to him in order to become his wife.

He jerked up his chin again to communicate he wanted her ass moving his way.

He couldn't see her roll her eyes but he knew she did it.

Then he watched as she said something to Amond and he swallowed a bark of laughter when she started coming his way, got tangled in the netting around her legs or got the heel of her freaking expensive shoe stuck in the grass and she started to take a dive.

Amond luckily caught her but Jake saw her mouth move and he knew she'd snapped "drat."

Cute.

Klutzy.

His woman.

His wife.

After averting what would be considered a wedding disaster, Amond clearly thought it necessary to escort Josie across the grass because he did this.

"You summoned?" Josie asked when she arrived and Jake grinned at his wife then transferred his grin to Amond.

"Thanks, man," he said.

"Grass stains would not go good with that dress," Amond replied.

This was true and Jake again swallowed laughter but his kids didn't. He had to do it yet again when he saw Josie roll her eyes.

He wrapped his arm around her waist, pulled her close and told her, "Kids wanna give you our wedding present."

She lost her annoyance immediately and smiled bright, looking to Conner, Amber and Ethan.

"How fun," she declared.

She had no idea.

Amber bit her lip.

Conner smiled at his father.

Ethan jumped forward, grabbed Josie's hand and tugged her toward the house, nearly shouting, "*Come on!*"

Josie turned happy, but curious, eyes Jake's way before she let herself be pulled into the house.

Ethan had one of her hands, Jake the other, and he felt Conner and Amber follow them in.

Jake tossed a grin at Amond as they went.

Amond grinned back.

Ethan led them to the family room.

That room looked no different. Neither did the living room, dining room, kitchen, light room, den, greenhouse or the guestrooms.

However, since they moved in after Christmas, Amber's room, Conner's room and Ethan's room had all been changed to be precisely what they wanted. Josie saw to that.

And Jake and Josie's room at the top floor had not one single fucking flower in it. It was decorated in gray, cream and a beige color Josie informed him was taupe. It was stylish. The sheets fucking heaven. It felt every night like he was climbing into bed with his woman in a five star hotel. And with his kids a floor away, the house built sturdy and strong, if they closed the door, they could get as loud as they wanted when he fucked her.

Jake loved it.

Josie did too.

"Okay, let's *do this,*" Ethan demanded when they all stopped, huddled close and Jake didn't move.

Jake looked down to his son, held his eyes and said quietly, "All right, bud." He handed him the envelope and finished, "Do it."

Jake watched as the excitement leached from his boy's face and anxiety replaced it.

Conner saw it too, and being a good kid growing into a good man, but definitely a good brother, he stepped in.

"Okay, Josie, we talked, all of us"—he indicated his sister and brother with a jerk of his head—"about what to get you and Dad for your wedding. It was Amber's idea. She talked to me. We talked to Eath. Eath was all for it in a big way. So then we had to talk to Dad so he knows about it."

Josie, her hand held tight in his, had her eyes glued to Conner through this and when he stopped speaking, she said, "All right, sweetheart."

"Dad had to talk to attorneys," Amber put in and Josie looked to her, her eyes widening. "And, well, someone else." His girl looked down to his son and then back to Josie. "She agreed."

"So here it is," Ethan butted in verbally at the same time jerking the envelope to Josie.

Josie stared down at the envelope before she took it, asking softly, "What is it, sweetheart?"

Jake gave her hand a squeeze before letting it go and encouraging, "Open it."

Her eyes came to his before they slid through his kids and then she turned her attention to the envelope.

He felt his chest get tight as he watched her open it. He felt his children get tense as they watched her do it. And then he saw Josie's entire body go still when she slid the papers out and saw what was written at the top of the first sheet.

"It's me," Ethan whispered, his voice now croaky, and Jake felt his own throat scratch as he looked down at his son. "We're givin' you me for your wedding."

Josie said nothing. She just stared down at Ethan.

When this lasted awhile, Jake put his hand to the small of her back and got close.

"Adoption papers, baby," he said something he knew she knew because it was right there on the papers for her to see. "Sloane agreed. She's signed them. You just have to sign them and Ethan's your boy."

As beautiful as this was, Jake was conflicted about it.

It was truth that in the last nine months Josie had been more mother to Ethan than he'd had in eight years from Sloane.

But it still stuck in his craw remembering his call to Sloane to broach the subject of her giving up all legal claim to her own son. It stuck in his craw the memory of her trying to hide the relief in her voice through the fake uncertainty she used to ask, "Are you sure, Jake?"

In the end, he knew down to his bones it was her loss and he knew precisely how huge that loss was.

And her loss was his wife's gain.

And his son's.

And Amber's and Conner's.

And last, his.

He knew Josie felt this, all of it when Jake saw the pink move into her cheeks, her throat convulse, the wet hit her eyes, eyes she didn't tear away from Ethan.

Finally, her voice husky, she whispered a question, a question that Sloane didn't ask. That being how Ethan felt about it.

"Are you sure, honey?"

Ethan's reply was, "Can I call you Mom?"

It was then Jake knew his son knew what he'd been missing.

And was happy with what he got.

So maybe it wasn't so bad when a kid got put on this earth with a shit mother that he got to choose the one he wanted.

Josie knew Ethan was happy too and Jake knew that when the papers fluttered to the ground as Josie covered her face with her hands and almost went down when her legs went out from under her.

Jake caught her and hauled her into his arms, hers closing around his shoulders as she shoved her face in his neck and her body shook against his with her tears.

He held her close and stroked her back as he heard Ethan ask in confusion and some fear, "Does that mean she likes it?"

Amber's breath hitched so it was Conner who answered.

"Yeah, Eath, bud, she likes it."

Josie jerked out of his arms and turned to Ethan, dropping down to her knees and taking his face in her hands.

She yanked him close and said, "No, I don't like it, sweetheart. I *love* it. Because *I love you*. So it makes me *very* happy. I'm delighted it makes you happy too. And I'd be honored if you'd call me Mom."

Ethan lips quivered then he fell forward, Josie caught him in her arms and Jake had to reach out, claim his daughter and hold her close because she was now sobbing loudly.

Conner let this go on for a while before he asked with fake exasperation, "Crap, are you gonna sign the papers, or what?"

Still holding Ethan close, Josie looked up at Jake.

"Darling, I believe I need your assistance. I don't think I can get up in this dress."

At that, finally, Jake allowed himself to laugh.

Conner did it with him.

Ethan, probably not knowing why he was doing it, still joined in.

Amber sniffled but through it giggled.

But Josie simply stared up at her husband and raised her brows.

Jake let his girl go and helped his woman to her feet.

Conner retrieved the papers from the floor and got out the pen.

The second he did, Josie snatched both from him, strode to a table by the window, and without further delay, she signed them.

When she did, Amber burst into loud tears again and Conner looked to the ceiling but did it pulling his sister in his arms.

Ethan hugged Josie around her middle.

Jake got close to his wife and their son, put his hand to his boy's head and his arm around his woman's waist.

It was then it happened.

He looked to Con, saw his son's gaze on him and he read it in his eyes.

He felt his daughter looking at him and he saw it there too.

He looked down at his youngest to see Eath looking up at him and he saw the same.

And finally, Jake looked into his wife's face and it was shining from her eyes.

Fuck.

Fuck.

It was right there. He was getting it from all of them.

Christ, they'd never quit believing he could make miracles.

Jake felt suddenly raw. Humble. Grateful. Honored.

Loved.

And his family being in the moment, it was lost on all of them that outside, the breeze blew wisteria petals like purple confetti through the air and the lavender bushes swayed in a way that could only mean the very heavens sighed.

———————◆•◆••◆———————

THERE WAS A knock at the door to their suite and Jake, finally shrugging off his fucking suit jacket, thanking fuck this was the last time he was getting married, looked that way.

Josie was in the bathroom. She'd gone there almost the minute she walked in.

She had a shit ton of suitcases.

This was because, the next day, they were driving to Boston and flying first class to take their honeymoon in Paris.

Along with the jewelry, this was his wedding present to his wife.

But the bag Josie took in the bathroom was a lot smaller and separate from her suitcases and Jake looked forward to seeing what she had in it because he figured whatever that was was *his* wedding present.

He also figured Josie would give him a good one.

He tossed his jacket over a chair and moved to the door. Looking through the peephole, he saw what he expected to see.

Room service.

But when he opened the door, he saw what he didn't expect to see.

There were strawberries, a bowl of whipped cream and chocolates, as he'd ordered.

But there was not one bottle of Dom Perignon that he'd also ordered.

Instead, there were two.

He looked to the guy who had his hands to the tray.

"Only ordered one bottle of champagne," he said, not minding having two but he wanted his wife to have good champagne, not get slaughtered on it.

"The other is a gift," the guy replied.

Amond.

He found this acceptable so Jake moved out of the way, the guy wheeled the cart in and Jake gave him a tip.

He put out the do not disturb sign, locked the door behind him and picked up the little card that was resting against one of the champagne buckets.

On the outside, it said *Josephine and Jake*.

He slid his finger through the flap, opened it and pulled out the card.

Then he froze as he read:

Be happy.

Henry

Fuck.

The man had been invited to the wedding. He was not over it so he didn't come. He'd been gentle with Josie telling her this but that didn't mean she wasn't disappointed.

Jake got him. If Josie was marrying another man, he'd be on another continent to get away from that shit.

Which was where Henry was.

But the champagne was a solid gesture that would make Jake's wife happy.

Even so, when he heard the door open behind him and he turned and watched his woman walk out in figure-skimming, all lace ivory nightie through which he could see little ivory panties, her hair down and curling around her shoulders, he tossed the card to the tray.

He'd tell her later.

Now, it was Jake who was going to make her happy.

So he set about doing that and started by walking across the room straight to her.

The instant he moved her way, her pretty blue eyes got soft in that way he knew now from experience was when she was thinking about how much she loved him, and she smiled.

In the end, it was Josie that made him happy.

A while later, he figured, as he licked the last of the champagne from between her breasts and heard the purr glide up her throat, he hadn't done half bad.

———•◦•◦•———

IN WHAT WOULD soon be the demolished garage at Lavender House, Jake moved a box from a shelf.

When he did, he watched a white envelope become dislodged from behind it, fluttering to the ground.

It landed face up and Jake saw the writing.

It was then he froze.

He was in the garage cleaning it out. It had to go because they needed the space. The architect had designed a garage that would fit perfectly with the house, not altering the look too much, not altering the feel of the place at all, and it would allow them to enter through the pantry. It was going to be three cars so Amber, and then Ethan, would not have to walk through the weather to get to the house or scrape their windshields.

This had been Josie's idea. Jake had wanted a two-car garage.

But Josie wanted three so he was going to give her three.

First, the old garage had to go.

So, while Josie was in the garden with Ethan, Jake was in the garage, beginning the clear out, something that Conner would help him with after he got off work.

Jake stared at the envelope on the floor even as he went down in a squat and set the box beside it.

He knew the writing on the outside, writing that said only, *Jake,* and he felt his heart thump as he reached out and nabbed it.

He straightened, turning the envelope so he could open the back.

Then he pulled in a breath as he pulled out the paper inside.

He had to pull in another one, sharper this time, when he opened the paper and started reading.

Jake,

I knew you'd eventually get around to giving Josie a decent garage so she wouldn't have to get wet or trudge through snow.

"Jesus," he muttered, even as he kept reading.

So I put my message to you here because I also knew it would be you that would be dealing with the rubbish.

Other things I knew were that she'd make you happy. And I knew you'd make her happy.

I tried very hard to convince you that you could do that, as you know. But where I failed in life, I knew I'd succeed when I'd gone for when I gave you the most precious gift I had to give, I knew you'd take care of it at the same time you'd make that so.

I knew this because you and your children made me happy. Very happy, my lamb. When I found you, Conner, Amber and Ethan, me, a woman who at one point felt she had nothing, suddenly had it all.

Thank you for giving that to me.

Thank you for making my precious girl happy.

Thank you for being all that's you.

I love you, my Jake, always.

Forever and completely.

Lydie

Jake stared at the words and cleared his throat.

Then he read them again.

And again.

And once more.

Then he put the letter back in the envelope and walked out of the garage.

Through the abundance of lavender, Jake saw his wife and son in the garden across the way.

He didn't go to them.

He went into the house and up to their room. He put the letter on his nightstand to share with Josie later. When they were alone. When he could give her what she needed when she read it, and he could take what he needed from her when he re-experienced it.

He left the room, walked down the stairs, through the house and outside.

The minute the sun hit his face, he heard laughter coming at him from the garden.

He looked that way and saw his daughter had come home. She was there with boy Taylor, girl Taylor, his wife and their son.

And Josie's head was tipped back, the sun shining in her hair, the breeze drifting through it so tendrils floated around her face. Her hips were encased in short-shorts, her long legs golden with tan. One of his old t-shirts hung loose at her top, her grandmother's wellingtons on her feet.

She and the kids were laughing, loud and long. Ethan was even doubled over with it and boy Taylor was repeatedly smacking his leg, on which, for some reason, the kid was wearing pink jeans.

Jake had no idea why they were laughing and he didn't give a fuck.

They were laughing.

They were together.

They were happy.

That was all he cared about.

That was all he ever cared about.

And he had it.

On this thought, it happened.

He watched his wife put a hand to her hip and lift the other to pull her floating hair back. She held it at her crown, but even with this effort, tendrils were flying around her still laughing face.

She was in Maine, in short-shorts, an old tee and Wellingtons, but it was a live-action recreation of the picture he'd had for years.

And that live-action kept going when she caught sight of her husband and her laughing face beamed so bright, Jake could feel its light all the way across the expanse. She took her hand from her hip to lift it to her lips and blow him a kiss.

A dream come true.

His.

Fuck.

Beauty.

He sent a smile her way then, still smiling, Jake Spear turned toward the garage in order to get back to work.

His wife and kids needed something.

Or more to the point, *he* needed to give his wife and kids something, that being keeping them protected from the elements.

So he had to set about doing that.

And, as always, he did.

Printed in Great Britain
by Amazon